# THE WARRIOR MOON

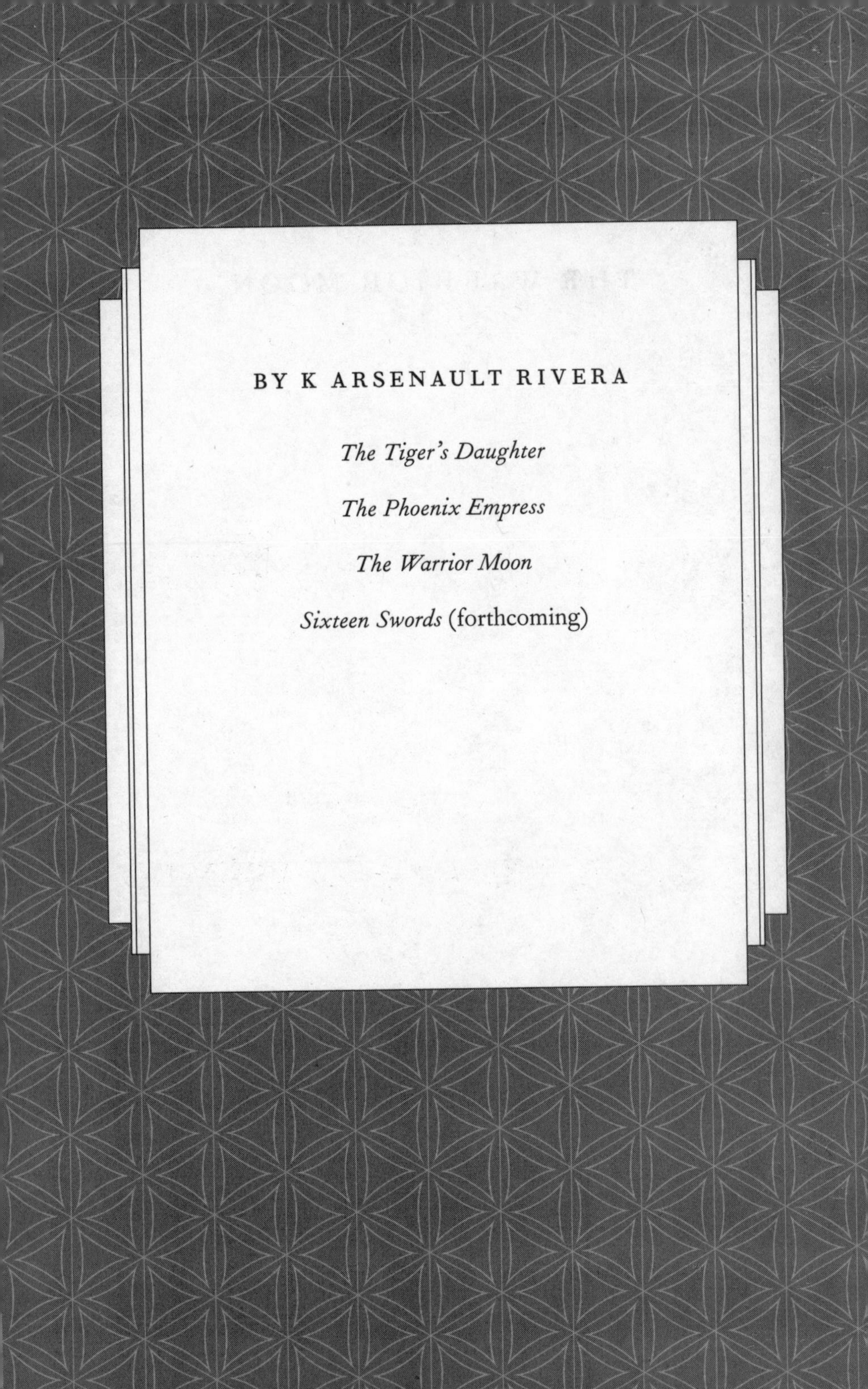

BY K ARSENAULT RIVERA

*The Tiger's Daughter*

*The Phoenix Empress*

*The Warrior Moon*

*Sixteen Swords* (forthcoming)

# THE WARRIOR MOON

K ARSENAULT RIVERA

TOR

A TOM DOHERTY ASSOCIATES BOOK

NEW YORK

This is a work of fiction. All of the characters, organizations, and events portrayed in this novel are either products of the author's imagination or are used fictitiously.

THE WARRIOR MOON



Edited by Miriam Weinberg

A Tor Book
Published by Tom Doherty Associates
120 Broadway
New York, NY 10271

www.tor-forge.com

Tor® is a registered trademark of
Macmillan Publishing Group, LLC.

The Library of Congress Cataloging-in-Publication Data
is available upon request.

ISBN 978-0-7653-9259-6 (trade paperback)
ISBN 978-0-7653-9260-2 (ebook)

Our books may be purchased in bulk for promotional, educational, or business use. Please contact your local bookseller or the Macmillan Corporate and Premium Sales Department at 1-800-221-7945, extension 5442, or by email at MacmillanSpecialMarkets@macmillan.com.

First Edition: September 2019

Printed in the United States of America

0 9 8 7 6 5 4 3 2 1

For Charlie,

who told me they were happy to see me writing again

Wasteland
Hirose
Tokuma Mountains
Imperial Barracks
Kirin River
The Kirin's Horn
SHIRATORI
Azure Promise Road
The Father's Teeth
Shiratori Palace
Nishikomi
Shigeoka
Minami Lands
Nagosu
Father's Seas
Kakize
Ban-diam

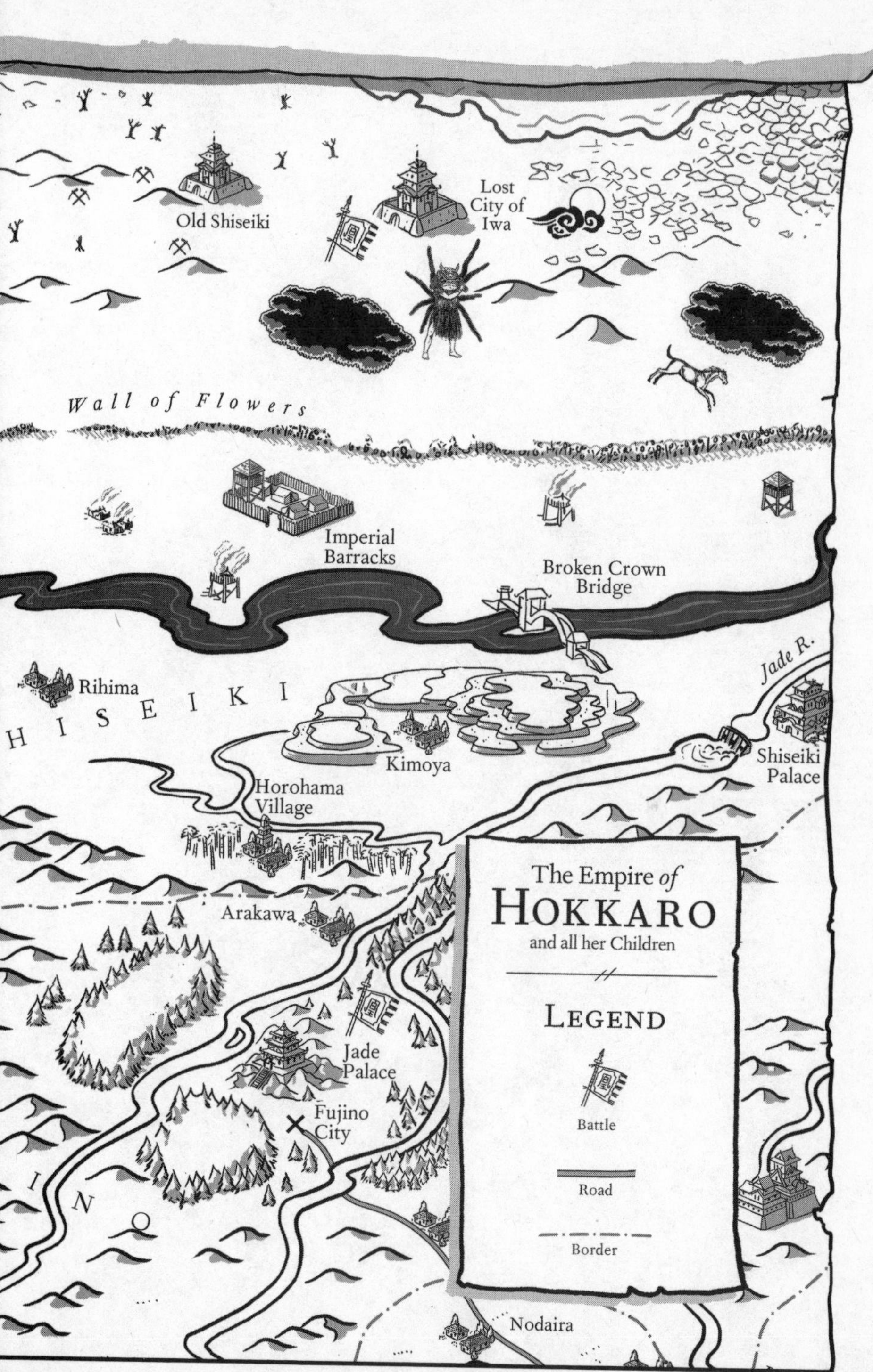

Old Shiseiki
Lost
City of
Iwa
Wall of Flowers
Imperial
Barracks
Broken Crown
Bridge
Jade R.
Rihima
H I S E I K I
Kimoya
Shiseiki
Palace
Horohama
Village
Arakawa
Jade
Palace
Fujino
City
I N O
Nodaira
The Empire of
HOKKARO
and all her Children
LEGEND
Battle
Road
Border

# THE WARRIOR MOON

# BARSALAI SHEFALI

## ONE

Within the Bronze Palace there is a war room, and within that room is a massive table. On that massive table is a painstaking replica of the Hokkaran Empire—the mountains rendered in gleaming porcelain, the forests represented by gathered twigs and grass. All the major roads are marked, with well-armed soldiers representing patrols; all the rivers flow in miniature down to the drains around the edges. That is the trouble with the map—while it leaves the Empire itself looking splendid beyond imagining, it does not include the Father's Sea.

O-Shizuka, seasoned Empress and nascent god, remedied this problem with a simple wooden board she placed along the western side of the table, just over the drains. With her impossible calligraphy, she has labeled all the major port cities of the coast. Her wife, Barsalyya Shefali, says that it won't be as accurate that way, since Shizuka hasn't measured the distances with exactitude, but Shizuka continues all the same. She's in no mood to summon a cartographer.

For boats she's chosen to use the replica siege engines, which will be confusing down the line. Shefali's told her *that*, as well, but Shizuka will insist that there aren't enough model ships, and if she paints the siege engines gold, no one will make any mistakes. Thus there are two dozen catapults now gathered off the shore of Nishikomi, south of shards of broken clay. The Father's Teeth, pulled from Grandfather Earth.

At least the horses are all right, Shefali tells herself, shaking her head. There are near a hundred of them over the Wall. She spends more time staring at their little manes than she does preparing for the meeting. There's no need, as far as she is concerned; Shizuka will do most of the talking, and it isn't as if Burqila Alshara would deny Naisuran's daughter aid. Oh, she'll be gruff, and blunt, and likely insult the whole table—but she will say yes.

It's the meeting with Baozhai that Shefali's worried about.

Baozha the Thorned Blossom Queen, who has overseen Xian-Lai through its recent growth; the woman who, before that, lent her army to Shizuka for the purposes of overthrowing the old Emperor; Kenshiro's wife, Baoyi's mother, Shefali's sister-in-law. To trifle with her was to trifle with a hurricane.

There was, of course, also the fact that Shefali was dying—but in the face of Baozhai's arrival that is hardly a concern at all.

"Perhaps my mother was right," Shizuka says. "I should have been an artist."

Shefali does not have the heart to tell her wife that her contribution to the war map is, at best, unsightly. Shizuka's proud of it, and so it's beautiful. That is how Shefali's world has always worked.

"You can be," says Shefali. "No rules against it."

Shizuka blows air between her lips. "No rules, but no time, either," she says. "I suppose my decrees will have to suffice. What a bore. Have you arranged the Qorin?"

Shefali did not realize she'd been given an assignment. She picks up the horses with ginger hands and moves them over to Fujino. Even that feels too rough. Whoever crafted these little creatures really did do a wonderful job; that one has such a healthy coat—

Shizuka covers her mouth with her sleeve, stifling a laugh. "I should have known you'd get distracted," she says.

It is the happiest she has sounded in days. Happy enough, almost, to erase the memory of why they've come to the war room at all. A smile blossoms on Shefali's face only to die away. They are here to plot an attack on the Traitor. The beginning of Shefali's final journey, one way or another.

*No rules, but no time.*

There were now only weeks left, at best.

Well. If Shefali died a warrior's death and made her wife laugh, three weeks would be plenty.

Shefali's reverie ends as four servants arrive in lockstep. Two women in elaborate hairstyles, their bodices tightly fitted beneath gauzy silk jackets, launch into playing their flutes the moment they cross the threshold. The two men following them wear something closer to a deel and riding pants, and bow at perfect right angles on either side of the door. Xianese, then.

Baozhai has come.

"Announcing the arrival of Her Eternal Majesty, she who shields the nation, the Thorned-Blossom Queen!"

Ah. Not Baozhai at all. Shefali repeats the title under her breath. Names are important things, not to be misused. The Qorin have always known this, and it seems the Xianese do, too. It is only the Hokkarans who fell behind. Even if it is difficult to think of her sweet sister-in-law as such an imposing figure.

That notion is dispelled the moment the Queen walks into the war room. Gone were the soft greens and violets that their sister-in-law so often wears, replaced with verdant emerald and deepest black. Gone her Hokkaran-styled robes: now she wears a gown beneath an oversized coat, her sleeves so long they nearly touch the ground. The embroidery alone must've taken a small village's worth of people years to finish. Sable lines her sleeves and collar, the lush black fur drawing attention to her exposed collarbones.

And that is only the dress! Her hair is piled higher than any Hokkaran woman would dare, tightly bound so that it juts out over the front of her head. In lieu of the hanging ornaments Shizuka often favored, Baozhai wore emerald pins in the shapes of various flowers. Where Shizuka has painted her skin white and her teeth black, Baozhai wears a face full of color. A green-violet flower is painted between her brows, her eyelids shimmering with the same. Even her lips bear a dot of green and violet at the center.

Baozhai always had a regal bearing—but that is comparing a pleasant stream to the raging rapids of the Rokhon. It is that river that stands before them now.

A woman who does not bow when she enters, only inclines her head; a woman who dares to meet the Empress's eyes; a woman as imposing as she is beautiful.

Were it not for the smell of her, Shefali would swear that it wasn't her sister-in-law at all.

But there she is—and to Shefali's surprise, Shizuka is the one who bows first.

"Thorned-Blossom Queen," she says. "We of the Empire thank you for hosting us."

"And we of the South thank you for your invitation," says Baozhai. She dismisses her servants with a wave of her hand; two golden talons gleam on her lowest fingers. "What will be the language of the discussion?"

At first Shefali thinks of it as a strange question—but it occurs to her after a beat that Baozhai speaks all three languages with varying degrees of fluency.

Shizuka and the others speak only two.

Shefali expects such barbs from courtiers; not from Baozhai.

"We suggest Hokkaran," Shizuka says, "the common language for all who will be present today. We've prepared a seat for you, if you will?"

"We doubt there will be need," says Baozhai. How it vexes Shefali to hear them both speak to each other in such a way—all this plural talk. The Kharsa speaks for all Qorin, and you do not hear her saying "we" this or "we" that.

But something in the air changes, just then: a note of salt and metal meets Shefali's sensitive nose. Not from Shizuka—who for all her outward calm smells like a storm—but from Baozhai.

Regret?

"Empress, we will keep this brief out of respect. Xian-Lai will not be lending you any foot soldiers for your campaign," the Thorned-Blossom Queen says. Though she speaks a touch more quickly than usual, her eyes never leave Shizuka's. "We gave you our daughters and sons twice-two years ago; we granted you the Bronze Army to seize your throne. We cannot continue to die for you. We welcome you to use our ships, provided you man them—but we will *not* provide you people."

Shefali winces. It was the right decision for Xian-Lai. The right decision as a Queen. Yet Baozhai is more to them than this. Hadn't she sworn earlier this week that she would help in whatever way she could?

Shizuka has fought to keep her mask in the face of the Thorned-Blossom Queen—but these words are a hammer against porcelain. Already she is shattering; already she grows sharper. Shefali cannot say anything to mend this—but she can abandon setting down the miniature horses; she can stand at Shizuka's side as she says whatever foolhardy thing she is going to say.

"The Traitor himself is marching on Nishikomi," says Shizuka, "and you will not send your army?"

"The Traitor is a problem of the North and East," Baozhai answers. She anticipated this. How talented she is—so little emotion shows in her face, but Shefali can smell how this is paining her. "The South has no cause to join this war."

"How can you say that?" Shizuka snaps. Shefali touches her hand. Shizuka squeezes hers in answer, her temper cooling not at all. "How can you stand here and say that to me, knowing what I've done?"

"Empress," says Baozhai. Level and calm. "This is not a decision we've made lightly. We speak for our nation, as you speak for yours; we guard our people as you guard yours."

For a long while there is silence. Shizuka trembles as she endeavors to contain her wrath. Baozhai is the first to falter, the first to break eye contact.

"We can provide only ships," she says, but it is quieter now, almost an apology.

Shizuka's gaze is a pyre. "Is this the decision of the Queen of Xian-Lai?" she asks.

"It is," says Baozhai. "We regret the pain this causes you—but we must think of our own people."

Shizuka sniffs. "Very well," she says. "We of the Empire accept your ships. Your gracious offer."

"Empress, our offer is as gracious as it can be," Baozhai returns. At last her level tone begins to break; at last she is starting to sound angry. "We will send further word—but our sailors at Chenyi will depart as soon as they can. The nearest port in your territory is—"

"Sejan," finishes Shizuka. "They will be ready." The line across her face seems harsher given the glare in her eyes. "Is that all, Thorned-Blossom Queen?"

"Should we not be asking you that question?" returns Baozhai. "For it was you who summoned us, and not the other way around. We've nothing further to discuss in such a state as this. If you should wish to visit us by the violets, that is another thing entirely."

Shefali is grateful, just then, that she loves both woman and Empress. To love one and not the other would be an agony—and it is agony gnawing at the edges of Shizuka's soul now. Perhaps Baozhai's mention of violets has soothed her somewhat, for when she finally answers, the air around her has cooled.

"We would enjoy that," she says. "In two days, perhaps, after preparations are complete."

Then, for the first time, Baozhai looks right to Shefali. The sudden attention makes Shefali conscious of her size, of how little experience she has with tactics. What could the Queen of Xian-Lai possibly have to say to her?

"And you, Empress Wolf?" she says. "Will you be traveling to Nishikomi with your honored wife?"

So calm, the question, and yet—she *knows*. Shefali's mouth goes dry.

"Yes," she says.

And there—for the first time, the Thorned-Blossom Queen cracks. A shadow passes over her like the clouds over the steppes.

"We wish you well," she says.

What misery—to hear such words and know them to be sincere! "Thank you," Shefali mumbles.

All three of them exchange bows. Baozhai leaves with the same pomp and circumstance as she arrived—the servant women reenter to recite a poem prepared specially for the occasion. Shefali wonders if all that opulence is meant to make Shizuka seem modest by comparison. She wonders what the fashions will look like in ten years, when Xian-Lai has further asserted its independence, and when Shefali will not be around to see them.

"I can't believe she'd say that," Shizuka mutters. Shefali throws an arm around her. "I . . . I've told her about you and me, and him. Every single Hokkaran ruler has had his corrupt blood flowing through their veins. How can she say it isn't her problem?"

"Not the South's problem," Shefali says. A gentle correction, born of love. "She's worried about you. Her people aren't."

Shizuka leans on her shoulder and lets out a long sigh. Shefali knows well enough by now the way crowns change the women who bear them, but that does not mean it does not hurt. Shefali thinks of changing the subject—bringing up Ren, or Sakura perhaps—but Shizuka acts first as always.

"You moved all the horses," she says. "I was worried you'd start naming them."

Shefali did, but this isn't the time to admit that. "They're warhorses," she says. "They have important jobs."

And cute, accurately reproduced saddles.

Shizuka chuckles. For a moment Shefali thinks that perhaps things will be all right, or as all right as war can be. Baozhai has refused them, but Burqila won't. The road to Nishikomi will be a long one—the last one—but Shefali will travel alongside her family, nearly all her loved ones. When they strike down the Traitor, she will be happy to join the stars.

If the Traitor does show himself. The woman, Sayaka, was probably right; it is probably a trap.

But it is one they'd face together.

"Your mother's almost here," Shizuka says.

Shefali can only nod. After all the anxiety of the past few days, the arrival of her family should be a blessing. Instead it has created a particular kind of knot in her stomach. Alshara wrote not long ago—she is proud of her daughter. And the rest of the Qorin must be eager to sniff her cheeks and tell her she smells as if she is dying. Her lips turn up at the corners at the thought. Qorin humor is one of her few remaining comforts.

There is no one better at Qorin humor—and no one Shefali dreads seeing again more—than her cousin Otgar. Otgar, who had been at her side through six years of wandering; Otgar, who knew her better than almost anyone. Otgar, who told her when she left for Hokkaro that she was a disappointment to her clan and her ancestors.

*Barsatoq has not seen you in eight years. Burqila has not seen you in twelve—and you're telling me you're picking your wife over her?*

Shefali squeezes her eyes shut.

"It won't be as bad as you think," says Shizuka. Gone, her earlier fury; gone, her amusement. When the two of them are alone, Shizuka wears her most private expressions—her amber eyes go honey sweet. "She'll be happy to see you."

"I'm dying," Shefali says, for it is the abject truth of the matter.

Shizuka flinches. She takes Shefali's hand in her own and holds it against her cheek. "All the more reason," she says. "Petty squabbles are meaningless now, aren't they? You're her favorite cousin."

"Am I?"

"I'm certain you are," Shizuka says. Shefali squints. She and Otgar share well over a dozen cousins. Many of them are funnier than Shefali, many of them are better wrestlers, almost all of them have spent more time with the clan.

Shefali sighs.

Shizuka—the Empress of Hokkaro, the final scion of the storied Minami line, descendant of a Traitor god—grabs one of the stools and drags it behind her wife. Before Shefali can ask her what she's doing, Shizuka is atop it, her delicate hands on either side of Shefali's shoulders.

"Shizuka—"

"Relax," is the answer, accompanied by a tap on Shefali's head. "You do so much for me, and I know you're in pain."

She is. Pain has become something of a sense to her, at this point—an ever-present sensation she must try to tune out if she is to get anything done at all. Some days she is more successful than others.

Today it is only a little pain. Shizuka's massage, truth be told, doesn't do anything at all to alleviate it.

But they have only a few weeks left, and Shefali will treasure every moment they have together.

# MINAMI SAKURA

## ONE

Minami Sakura is every bit as stubborn as her Imperial Cousin.

Perhaps more.

Sakura had to earn every scrap she'd had, painting or playing the shamisen. She isn't going to take no for an answer.

It's in her bloodline, for one thing. In all the continent there was no bloodline more stubborn—of this there could be no doubt. Minami Shiori claiming an errant sunbeam as her sword was one thing; everyone knew about that. *No one* knew that Shiori's granddaughter Shikei had, when summoned to the palace to kill one of Empress Yukari's many imagined enemies, stayed put in her ancestral lands. What's more—Minami Shikei sent the Empress a fine lacquered box painted with raccoon dogs. Inside? An object about the length of a woman's forearm, and a little smaller around than her wrist. The only surviving record of the incident said it was polished to a mirrored shine.

If Minami Shikei could tell the Empress to go fuck herself, then her granddaughter eighteen generations removed can make demands of the Empress Consort.

Sakura marches down the halls toward the war room. Unlike some other visitors to the Bronze Palace, she knows how to keep her wooden sandals from clacking against the hard flooring. They won't hear her coming. The Empress Consort's got a nose like a perfumer—so Sakura bathed in Peizhi Lake this morning, and had the servants wash her clothes with the Crown Princess's. If this is going to work, she needs to catch them both off guard.

Although—is it possible to catch the Empress Consort by surprise?

Only the people who never get anything done sit around asking questions like that. Sakura's never been one of *those* people.

Eight years ago she had come to the Bronze Palace with an undecipherable letter in her pocket—the only keepsake her birth mother left behind. Her ploy was as bold as her dress: to find a tutor who could teach her how to decipher it. For the most part, it had worked even better than she could have imagined. Scholars in Xian-Lai are reading things she's written with her own two hands.

But it took eight years to find someone who could read that letter—because it took Barsalai Shefali that long to come back home.

And to this day, Barsalai had not divulged its contents to her.

What could *possibly* be worth hiding from Sakura in this way?

Nothing. Whatever secrets lay in that letter were hers by birthright.

SHE COMES TO a corner and leans against it. Here is the trick: she will act as if she is reading until Baozhai walks by with her entourage, which surely will signal that the meeting has adjourned. All Sakura has to do is slip in afterwards, distract her cousin, and drag the Empress Consort out for a little one-on-one. Easiest thing in the world.

One breath, two breaths, twenty—she counts them to pass the time as she idly stares at the scroll she's brought. A gift for her cousin, prepared two months ago. Sakura knows every word. She wrote them all. Of course, this means she doesn't want to *read* any of them ever again, so she isn't actually paying attention. The strokes are nice, she supposes. Just as nice as her cousin's. It's only a distraction, after all. An excuse to pry apart Empress Phoenix and Empress Wolf, if only for a few hours.

It is two hundred breaths before the Thorned-Blossom Queen emerges from the war room. She and her entourage walk right by Sakura, leaving the air behind them thick with the scent of fresh-cut flowers. The girls with the flutes—Meili and Songli—start up one of their more complicated melodies on the way. The two men Sakura doesn't know—but she catches one of them eyeing her and does her best to stare him down.

The Thorned-Blossom Queen sees her, too. Sakura is sure of that much; there is little in the Bronze Palace that escapes Baozhai's notice. Even before the revelation about their ancestral relationship to this place, Sakura had been certain there was some sort of thread. Like a mother always knowing when her son had wandered into the Shrine of Jade Secrets, no matter what lie he'd fed her beforehand.

Six years spent in someone else's company is long enough to learn their tells—even if it's the Thorned-Blossom Queen, who does her absolute damnedest to hide them. That she calls the entourage to a halt is notable enough. On any other day she might have kept on walking without acknowledging Sakura at all. On days when the Queen was in a good mood she might nod in Sakura's direction—that was about the extent of their niceties when she was in that getup.

But today the Lady of the Bronze Palace comes to a full stop, and today she meets Sakura's eyes.

It's the proper thing in this sort of situation to bow. Sakura's never really cared about the proper thing to do, but when the Queen looks at her now, she feels hands on her shoulders, forcing her down. This time, she'll acquiesce. It's one thing to give your cousin's sister-in-law a little lip over dinner—it's another thing entirely to upset an angry sovereign who has never really liked you.

"Court Historian," the Queen says. Kenshiro insisted she be granted a formal title two years ago. A gift, of sorts—if she had a title, then Baozhai could not ignore her at *all* times.

"Your Majesty," Sakura answers. Brevity is the soul of keeping your head attached to your shoulders.

"Do you have business with the Phoenix Empress?" Sakura hasn't known her to be so blunt in years. And there's something else, too, lurking in the corners of her eyes.

"With Empress Consort Wolf," Sakura says. The tension is thin as fraying rope—she does not want to be the one to sever it with a misplaced title.

The flower painted between her eyes wrinkles. "See that you are brief," she says. "Her Highness should not be bothered with trifling concerns."

*Trifling concerns?* Sakura must have misheard her. Maybe it was the Xianese. "I'm sorry; what was that?" Sakura says, this time in Hokkaran.

"The Queen of Xian-Lai is not in the habit of repeating herself," is the answer, a serpent's bite in green and violet. "Our honored Sister-in-Law has chosen to live a short life. I—We—shall not stand idly by while you ruin her remaining days—"

"No," says Sakura. "I'm not going to put up with this. You can talk to your subjects like that, if you want, but I'm not one of them." More tumble out of her before she can stop herself—and in spite of the Queen's lips parting in surprise. "I didn't toil away for six years in your dusty libraries for you to talk about me *ruining* her."

If she waits around for a reply, she might get thrown in prison. Not that Baozhai would ever dream of imprisoning her own family, even if by marriage—but until today Sakura thought their personal distaste extended no further than trading jabs at the dinner table. To be spoken to like that! She turns on her heel and storms toward the war room before the Queen can stop her.

Just who does she think she is? Put a crown on her head and she starts to act like she owns the place. So what if she does? So what if she *is* a Queen? That doesn't give her the right.

Sakura's cheeks go hot.

She hates it—all of it. Gods, how could Baozhai say something like that?

On the doors of the war room are two of the four Xianese gods—one of the men, and one of the women. Sakura knows their names but she is not inclined to give them her attention at the moment. If she does, it might get back to Baozhai somehow. Instead she grabs one of the handles and pulls. Her shoulders whine; her sandals skid along the smooth floor. The fifth king of Xian-Lai commissioned these doors, and he decreed that they be heavy enough that only an army or the gods themselves might rouse him from his plans. A lovely sentiment, to be sure—who beneath the sun and sky doesn't want a little private time?—but in truth it takes only four soldiers to open each one.

Or a single woman, if that woman is the Empress Consort.

Sakura isn't, but she isn't going to let that stop her from trying. She steps out of her sandals. The floor is cool against her bare feet. Part of her thrills at the contact—not because it is pleasant, but because no one walked barefoot in the Bronze Palace. A grin spreads across her face.

*So sorry for tainting your floor,* Sakura thinks to herself.

Yet the added traction does not help. She grabs the signal fan–shaped door handle and pulls. *Heaves,* really; all her weight is focused on this particular endeavor.

Then again—Sakura does not weigh much.

For one minute, two minutes, three, she attempts this. Sweat beads on her brow. She lets out the most indelicate sounds in the world as she pulls and pulls and pulls, though not the most indelicate sounds she's ever made.

All for Barsalai Shefali, Empress Consort, to open the other door with one hand.

Sakura is always a little surprised by Barsalai on the best days. It's difficult not to be. Towering over her by two heads, wearing her tiger-striped deel and laughing fox war mask, Barsalai cuts an intimidating figure. That her face is hidden away does not help terribly much when her steel eye is still perfectly visible. She keeps one hand on the door and the other behind her, as if she knows her talons are off-putting.

And that is the most incredible thing about her cousin's wife: everything about her is intimidating except for her personality. In all her years working at the pleasure house, Sakura never encountered anyone quite so tranquil in the face of adversity. To be near Barsalai—to be really near her, near enough that you can hear her soft-spoken words—is to be reassured. She is unbreakable. Keep close and you might become unbreakable, too.

But Sakura has been unbreakable for thirty years without the help of anyone. That's why she's going to win today.

"Need help?" Barsalai says. Her voice is surprisingly relaxed for a woman so near to dying. Sakura kept expecting her to have an accent in Hokkaran, and maybe there is, but she hasn't been able to catch it the whole time she's been here.

"I'm fine," she says. "Is my cousin in a state for visitors?"

She abandons her efforts, taking a spare moment to smooth over her robes and tuck a stray lock of hair behind her ear.

Barsalai's head turns, like an owl's, toward the inside of the room. Sakura cannot see it with her standing in the threshold.

"You could come in and ask me yourself, you know," comes the answer. "It isn't as if I'm a god." There's no mistaking the particular combination of arrogance and playfulness.

"Your wife is kind of in the way," says Sakura, raising her voice so that it better carries into the war room. "Are you in a state for visitors?"

Barsalai leans against the door, crossing her arms over her chest. There's a sliver of the room now visible. Are those . . . ? Has Shizuka substituted catapults for boats?

"Are you the visitor?"

"I am," says Sakura. "I got you a gift and everything. For Your Most Serene Majesty, the Daughter of Heaven, Empress—"

"Finish that and I'm exiling you," says Shizuka—but unlike Baozhai, there is no venom in her voice. This is the sort of teasing they've always done, the sort of banter that puts Sakura at ease.

Not too at ease. Her eyes flick up to the teeth of Barsalai's mask.

*Don't take no for an answer.*

"Come in, come in," Shizuka says. Barsalai opens the door wider and Sakura does just that. Her Imperial cousin—among the most important people in the world—sits with one leg crossed over the other on a stool near the table. If any of the Hokkaran courtiers were to see her like this, they'd drop dead on the spot; most of her right leg is visible. As Sakura enters, Shizuka smiles. "So you *didn't* bring me an army? Sakura. I'm disappointed."

"Baozhai hates me enough without my marching an army through this place," Sakura says.

Shizuka's smile goes flat. She turns her attention to the catapults, idly pushing one closer to the shards of a shattered pot. "Yes, well," she says. "We can't have that, now, can we?"

Given how short their audience had been, and given the lack of Xianese soldiers on the map, it's easy to hear the real meaning. You learn, when you grow up in a place like the Shrine of Jade Secrets, how to shape a conversation the way a gardener shapes his trees.

Sakura takes the scroll case from her back and sets it in her cousin's lap. "I'll tell you what you *can* have," she says. "Your birthday present."

"Isn't it a little late?" Shizuka says. She crooks a brow—but she sets the case up vertically and starts teasing out its contents.

"Didn't feel right to hand you a gift with everything going on," Sakura says. Her eyes flick over to Barsalai once more, who stands now behind her wife. She is the largest, most brightly attired shadow in creation.

"Everything is still going on," says Shizuka. The scroll now free, she lays the case on the map without care for what it knocks over. It is Barsalai who steps in to save the model horses. "For you, there's only been more trouble since the double eighth."

Is "trouble" the right word for your life's ambition collapsing in on itself? Perhaps. But Sakura doesn't let it bother her. "It's about that, sort of. I wanted to thank you—both of you—for what you did for me," she says. She's careful to catch Barsalai's attention.

Barsalai sniffs. Sakura is acutely aware of a bead of sweat rolling down her neck. She hopes it offers the Empress Consort's nose no answers.

Shizuka glances at the title of the work in her hands. The Empress of Hokkaro has an honest face; outside of court she never bothers to wear her courtier's mask. Except now. She slips into it, her whole face going smooth as polished stone. Only her eyes give away her disappointment.

*Shit,* Sakura thinks.

"Shefali did all the reading, but you've only come with a gift for me," says Shizuka. Her tone stays friendly, if a little strained; she does not hate Sakura for the gift. Only for its contents, it seems. But why? Shizuka loved stories about the Minami clan. "Don't tell me you're holding out on her. My wife is very sensitive, you know."

She is—Barsalai leaves the horses altogether to stand at her wife's side. Shizuka takes her hand.

Sakura is beginning to feel as if she's getting pulled into an undertow. Give Shizuka a nice gift, offer to listen to Shefali tell her histories, confront her about the letter. That is how this was supposed to go. But the look those two are sharing! Something must have happened after Shefali read that letter. There's something in it they're not telling her. Well—a lot of it they aren't telling her, because she still doesn't know a single thing about it. Whatever Spiderlily Sayaka wrote in that foreign alphabet had soured Shizuka on her entire clan.

Their clan.

And yet Shefali still isn't making any moves to share.

Sakura wants to grit her teeth. She can't, given the situation, so she digs her fingernail into her palm. She's going to get to the bottom of this.

"I was going to offer my services," she says. Lightening the mood might give her room to break the surface of this frigid water.

"Oh, please," says Shizuka. "Shefali's never had a fondness for painting."

"That's not true," says Shefali. The whole room goes quiet to hear her; Shizuka is practically holding her breath.

"What do you mean that isn't true?" says Shizuka.

"Ikhthian paintings," answers Shefali. "They're beautiful."

"And *huge*," says Shizuka. "Aren't they as big as that wall, there?"

Shefali nods. "Easy to lose yourself in the details. Like looking in on another world."

Shizuka gives her a quizzical look. It hasn't escaped Sakura's notice that she's set the scroll down near its case. If she were not so determined, she'd feel a little insulted. Instead, she just feels relieved the joke worked. It's easier to breathe now.

"A lot of people talk about the Qorin that way," she says. Now to put her piece on the table. "I was thinking that you didn't have someone to tell your story, and I thought maybe I could be that person. I won't be able to finish it in time, but I might be able to get started."

*Won't be able to finish it in time*. Sakura suppresses an internal wince. She needed Barsalai to buy this, needed her to accept. There were so few things in this existence Barsalai wanted; an opportunity to be remembered is the only one Sakura can offer.

And later, it can be the chip Sakura can exchange for the letter's contents.

Barsalai tilts her head. She doesn't talk very much, but she's expressive. *Why you?* she's asking.

"Ken-lun's closer, you're thinking," she says. Barsalai nods. "He's also busier. All this research he's been doing with me—he hasn't been able to see Baoyi at all. If you want him to write it, then I can take notes and pass them on to him. I get it, I do. You want a Qorin to tell a Qorin story."

Shizuka perches her head atop her hand. "A history would be useful," she says. "If you are right about . . . our legacies."

Sakura knows that she is, and that is the worst part. Reading histories from the time of the First Emperor is an absolute nightmare. All the stories about him and his son blur together; it's near impossible to tell one from the other. And every now and again, you'll catch a glimpse of another figure—someone hidden like a fishmaiden in the mist. Another ruler, one deposed when Emperor Yamai came to power.

There have been other empires than this. Perhaps that's something

Shizuka can tell her about—when this is all over. If her cousin makes it back at all.

It's a stupid thought. Sakura shoves it aside. There are other things to focus on.

Like Barsalai. How is she taking the idea? She's narrowing her eyes not in suspicion, but in thought. Her posture's easing, too; she's set her hand on Shizuka's shoulder.

So she isn't saying anything yet. Sakura knows Barsalai well enough to assume there's some kind of epic being composed in that skull of hers.

But it wouldn't be such a bad idea to nudge her along. "Like I said, if you want him to write it, I'm sure he'd be thrilled. But having my notes would make things much easier, and it'd only take a Bell or two. I write pretty quickly."

Silence. Consideration, really; Barsalai is a woman of many silences.

"We don't have much time before we leave," says Shizuka. "Shefali's setting out the day after next to meet up with the Qorin."

Sakura smiles. "It won't take long," she repeats. "I promise."

Shizuka covers Shefali's hand with her own. The two exchange a look. In that moment, Sakura knows she might as well be in Ikhtar for all the attention they're paying her.

Gods might have an eternity to deal with, but all three of them were still mortal. Some more than others. Not to mention if they waited too long, it'd be time for dinner, and that was more inexorable than even the blackblood's call to go North.

How she wants to clear her throat, to give them some sort of reminder . . . but look at them! How is she meant to interrupt when they're busy writing love poems with their eyes?

Minami Sakura counts to eighty-eight and then clears her throat. It's the politest thing to do. When she reaches again to sixty-five, Barsalai turns toward her.

"All right," she says. "Before I leave, we'll talk."

"Good," says Sakura. *This* smile is genuine. "Do you want to get started now? We've got a Bell and a half before dinner, and, ah . . ." Her eyes fall once more to the table. "Well, it seems like you're finished here."

Barsalai looks to her wife. Sakura braces herself for another ten minutes of them gazing longingly at each other. There's no need; they keep this one brief.

"Yes," she says. "Now will do."

Sakura bows. "Thank you," she says. "I promise I'll return her in good condition, Cousin."

Shizuka scoffs. "You couldn't break her if you tried," she says. But she pulls her wife in for a kiss, all the same.

Sakura takes the opportunity to step back into her sandals—let them have a bit of privacy.

And it gives her time to think. This hasn't gone quite according to plan. She doesn't have her calligraphy set with her, and they are going to have to meet either in the library or her room. The library holds too many awful memories at the moment, and her room is, well . . .

She's found ways to work out her frustrations. Ways that have left the room a wreck, and ways that would plague Barsalai's sensitive nose.

Still. She is going to have to find some way to make this work.

People have tricks, after all. You learn them well enough, and you know how to approach them. Back home it was Sakura's whole livelihood. A man comes in wanting an ingenue, you can't give him the naughty governess. It was her job to figure out which girls to recommend to their clients, and she often had only a couple of moments to do the figuring.

Barsalai's trick is simple: she can smell lies. She likes honesty. Anything you say to her must be said with sincerity.

Which means that Sakura has just talked herself into being her historian.

Well. There are worse fates. Whatever Barsalai has been up to during her wanderings is sure to make a great story, and, truth be told, Sakura *does* like the woman well enough to want to tell it.

And somewhere along the line, she's going to get her answer.

# O-SHIZUKA

## ONE

"General Dog-Ear."

One salutation is all it takes to put Shizuka's mind back in her soldier's boots. For a moment she forgets that she is in the dining room of the Bronze Palace. The storied scrolls on the wall give way to maps hung inside a tent; the faint smell of incense to the pungent odors of men at war; her family gathered around her for her brothers and sisters in arms.

That name—one she used to loathe—was granted to her by her comrades. They were the only ones who called her that, or the only ones that could. Shizuka's cropped ear has made her feel self-conscious for eight years; it was only during the war that it became a secondary worry, at best.

But only because they were trying so hard not to die, and because she was too drunk between battles to duel anyone who thought to weaponize the name.

If she heard it on the mouths of a common courtier, she'd be liable to split their own ear and see how they liked it. But as the person doing the calling is Lai Xianyu—sister to Queen Lai Baozhai and Shizuka's most trusted adviser during the war—she will allow it. In truth, there is some comfort to the title. Shizuka's accumulated so many now that they cling to her like moths: Daughter of Heaven, Four-Petal, Peacock Princess, Phoenix Empress.

At least she came by General Dog-Ear honestly.

"General Lai," Shizuka says. "To what do we owe the pleasure of your attendance tonight?"

In spite of their formal addresses, Xianyu's turned up to dinner in casual clothing. Perhaps that is why Shizuka had such trouble recognizing her when she came in—she can count on one hand the number of times she's seen Xianyu in anything but armor, uniform, or armor over her uniform. The lustrous jacket she wears over her white dress is robin's egg blue; her cloudy attire is at odds with her grave features.

"Your impending death," says Xianyu.

Shizuka cannot tell if that's an attempt at levity or an honest statement. Xianyu's flat delivery makes it difficult indeed to decide between the two.

Thankfully, Baozhai has known her eldest sister all her life, and is a quick judge. As she heaps her daughter's plate full of vegetables, she spares a moment to illuminate matters. "You will, I hope, forgive First Sister for joking about such a thing."

To Shizuka's surprise, it is *then* that Shefali decides to chuckle. She and Sakura—seated to Kenshiro's right, across from them—arrived last. Shizuka has not had a chance to ask her how their little history-recording session went—but that is a question for another time.

Everyone knows better than to trespass at dinner.

No matter how their . . . other personalities might clash. Shizuka spent all her childhood in the Jade Palace, bumbling from one court to another with her father. She knows well the lines drawn between sovereigns and people. Her father found a frequent political ally in Doan Jiro, despite how Jiro-tun despised him. Jiro was the sort who called any clean-shaven man a woman, and thus found much to mock in the pampered Poet Prince.

Yet Jiro was also the sort of man who despised war in all but the most necessary cases, and there were fewer allies more powerful than O-Itsuki in that regard.

As a child, Shizuka always knew she'd one day find herself in a similar position. Well. As a child she assumed she'd solve all her problems with duels. Once Shefali showed her the idiocy of that line of thought—then she'd had her realization. And, sure enough, she hated Shiratori Ryusei almost as much as she needed his support.

But to have a dear friend disappoint you in such a way when you are both wearing your regent's masks . . .

That is a new pain.

"Of course," Shizuka says. "The Qorin often tell such jokes. Don't they, Shefali?"

She squeezes her wife's hand, and Shefali squeezes hers in turn. "Yes," she says. "It's because we spend so much of our lives dying."

Kenshiro winces, but Sakura lets out a black laugh. "People who don't run from the truth," she says. Shefali nods with pride.

Baozhai sighs. She's finished at last with Baoyi's plate—stacked almost as high as the girl herself is tall—and begins on her own. Pinetree eggs, duck, tender steak, a bowl of porridge and a larger bowl of rice—has Shizuka ever seen her eat so much?

"You aren't really going to die, are you, Aunt Zuzu?"

The table goes silent. As it should, given a question like that. Baoyi sits wide eyed on her own chair, with that big plate before her, reaching for a dumpling. She pops it into her mouth and starts chewing before she even gets an answer. Her cheeks swell with food.

Shizuka's heart is a storm, and yet she does not hesitate giving the answer. She can't. "No," she says. "I'm not. There isn't anything in creation that could hope to kill me, Baoyi. Haven't I told you already?"

She smiles, at the end, to make it truer. Baoyi smiles back, and when she breaks into a giggle, a bit of dumpling falls onto her fine dress. Shizuka—seated between Baoyi and Shefali—cleans her niece off with her own storied sleeve.

"As long as the sun rises every morning, you'll know I'm still with you," she says. "And as long as you see the moon, you'll know your aunt Shefa is with me."

"But what about all that time Auntie Shefa was away?" asks Baoyi. How quick she is.

"I carried part of her soul in mine," Shizuka answers. Shefali squeezes her hand again.

The mess now cleaned, Shizuka touches her niece's nose before sinking back into her seat. Baoyi laughs again—though thankfully, this time she's already swallowed her food.

Yet the rest of the table is sitting on broken glass, judging from the looks they're giving her.

Do they think Shizuka is lying? She cannot afford to lie; not about this. She is going to live. She must live. She must crush the Traitor's neck beneath her boot; she must make him answer for this foul bloodline he has unleashed upon the world.

The Eternal Empire.

What nonsense.

She helps herself to a little duck, though Kenshiro is staring at her and Sakura cannot meet her eyes.

If they think she has lied to a child, then they do not know her very well at all.

"Your aunts are going on a long journey north," Baozhai says, by way of breaking the silence. "They're going to fight to keep their empire safe."

*Their empire*. It isn't wrong, it isn't—but Shizuka hates to think of Hokkaro as *hers* anymore. Knowing the seed it came from has poisoned the fruit.

"Oh," says Baoyi. "Can I come?"

"Maybe when you're older," Sakura says. "The stuff they're doing is for grown-ups."

Kenshiro nods. "When you get to be as old as your aunt Zuzu, you can do whatever you like."

Only Xianyu remains silent. Shizuka watches her as she cuts into her steak. When Xianyu catches Shizuka staring, she gives her a look. Suddenly, Shizuka's transported back to a tent just outside a bamboo forest.

*Never lie to your troops, but never break their spirits.*

*I'm not lying*, Shizuka wants to say to her, but the words die too soon.

"Your aunts are as brave as Chen Luoyi. Braver, maybe," says Baozhai. "Tell us what you learned about General Chen today."

It's a simple change of subject, but an elegant one, and Baoyi is happy to play along. She's soon rattling off a story about the Three-Family War, the sort of puffed-up thing that neglects any of the actual bloodshed. Shizuka learned about the battle in question during her own war—and for that reason she chooses to ignore the story.

Shizuka lays her head on Shefali's shoulder. "How did it go?" she asks.

Her wife knows, of course, that Shizuka is trying to avoid her memories. "Well," she says. She keeps her voice low enough that they do not interrupt Baoyi's spirited tale. "Sakura-lun listens."

"Lun?" says Shizuka. A smile tugs at her lips. "Are you so close now?"

Shefali nods, tracing the crescent scar on Shizuka's palm. "She is good at listening."

"You must have been comfortable if you did so much talking," Shizuka says. "I was worried she'd have to pry it all out of you question by question."

"Once I started, it was hard to stop," says Shefali. She looks toward Baoyi, though she, too, is not quite paying attention to the story. "She was right. It's important that someone remembers."

Slogging through the mud and the blood with Xianyu. Walking through the gardens with Baozhai. Listening to Kenshiro drone on and on about a book he had to import all the way from Axiot, which came to him in three crates filled with polished bronze sheets. Setting herself on fire in front of Sakura.

Shizuka looks around the table. "They'll remember us," she says. "Even after we're gone."

"So long as our names are on the wind," Shefali says. She kisses Shizuka on the forehead.

Baoyi's finished her story. Xianyu's cutting in now, having grabbed a spare plate. A rough re-creation of the battle is painted upon its surface in soy sauce. She's asking Baoyi to name all of Chen Luoyi's captains—and sure enough, the girl is already a third of the way through the list. Shizuka supposes she shouldn't have expected anything less from her.

"Shefali-lun," says Kenshiro. Shizuka looks up, though she wasn't called. Kenshiro's shaved off his beard. Seeing him clean shaved now makes him seem even younger than before. "Baozhai tells me you're leaving in the morning?"

Shefali nods.

Kenshiro holds her gaze for a while before looking down to his meal. "I sent out the Royal Messengers to find our mother this morning. With any luck, they'll precede your arrival by a day. Aaj will have warning that you are coming."

Warning? Is that the word he wants to use? The man is a White-Leaf Scholar; he knows plenty of ways to make his meaning plain. Why, then, has he chosen "warning"? As if Shefali and her mother are still at odds! She is already worried enough without her brother saying such things.

Shizuka long ago learned to love Kenshiro in spite of his flaws and gentle lies. She takes a sip of her tea and reminds herself, as she does occasionally, that he means well. Perhaps he meant only that it is good Shefali will not be surprising Alshara.

"You want me to tell her something," Shefali says. It isn't a question.

Now it is Kenshiro who nods. "I'll have a letter ready for you, if that's all right. It's been . . . well, you know how Aaj is. Running a clan occupies so much of her time that she seldom finds occasion to return my writings."

Shizuka has written a letter to Burqila Alshara once a week since she returned from the war. After that first month, she has received a response every week without fail.

"I'll take it," says Shefali.

Kenshiro's relief is as clear as the waters of Peizhi Lake. He lets out a breath. "Thank you," he says. "Truly. And I'm sorry we don't have any good stew for your last dinner here."

"Couldn't taste it anyway," says Shefali. She picks up a cup of dried tea leaves Baozhai prepared for her and shakes it. "This is enough."

"Baozhai picked those leaves herself, you know," Kenshiro says. He's getting started; Shizuka can tell. Kenshiro clings to small talk the way children cling to their parents' legs. "It's a special variety of tea native to the region. Well. All tea's native to Xian-Lai, but this tea in particular is grown near the Grand Temple. It takes five years to grow, and so it's a bit opulent to purchase it in bulk, but all the money goes toward maintaining the temple."

Shizuka glances at the cup. She has never been particularly fond of tea—it's more a necessity to her than a thing she enjoys.

"Did you pick any?" Shefali asks, tipping the cup toward her.

"No," says Shizuka. "But I do remember when harvest rolled around. Half the temple was out in the fields picking tea, and the other half was inside drying it out."

"And you were?" says Sakura.

"Arguing with ghosts," Shizuka says. Her throat feels a little dry, and she wishes she had a bit of rice wine to soothe it, but she knows how that will turn out. It is better if she doesn't. She's made the decision not to be that woman anymore.

"That sounds like you," says Sakura. "Actually, that sounds like the both of you. All my life I'd never met a single person who fought a ghost, and now here the two of you are, making up for the rest of the fucking Empire."

She laughs, but Baozhai shoots her a glare. This only emboldens Sakura. "I'll say what I want, all right?" she says. "My cousin's leaving tomorrow, and I might not—"

It is Kenshiro who stops her this time, with a squeeze of her shoulder.

Shizuka's eyes fall to Sakura's cup. *She's* drinking.

"My love," she whispers to Shefali, for the clear surface of the rice wine is something Shizuka does not wish to go near. "Could you . . . ?"

Shefali needs no explanation. Shizuka falls in love with her all over again at the moment, as she quietly takes Sakura's cup and empties it out over her shoulder. While Kenshiro distracts her, Shefali fills the cup with water and sets it back down.

Kenshiro offers Sakura the swapped cup. Sakura realizes the second it touches her lips what they've done—her eyes go a little wide—but she makes no motion to complain. When she has drained the cup anew, she leaves it on the table.

"Since when do you worry about me so much?" says Shizuka. A little gentle ribbing might set dinner back on a pleasant track.

Sakura's brows come together. She picks up the cup just to gesture with it. "I've always worried about you. Y'know, I'm the closest thing to a big sister you have."

The closest Shizuka ever had to a big sister was Daishi Akiko. She does not correct Sakura. Like her teacher, she means well. "If you were my elder sister, you'd be the Empress," she says.

"Pah," says Sakura. "I would've abdicated. Won't catch me on a throne. Too much going on, too much to take care of. I wasn't built for that sort of thing."

Yet the more Shizuka considers it, the more she likes the idea. Sakura's protests don't mean very much to her—no one who *wanted* a throne deserved one, except Baozhai. And, like Baozhai, Sakura excelled at dealing with people. Even courtiers disgusted with her origins found themselves soon disarmed by her charm, her directness. It was difficult not to like her.

"It's much like raising children," says Baozhai.

Sakura's jovial expression darkens. "Yeah, and I know so much about that."

"I wasn't implying that you did," is Baozhai's reply, delivered with perfect detachment.

Well, everyone liked Sakura except for Baozhai. The air between those two is like a cart full of Dragon's Fire. One day one of them is going to set the whole thing off.

But there must be something in the air today, or else the prospect of this being their final dinner as a family urges Baozhai to take a more sensitive approach to their battle of words. Shizuka can see it happening—the consideration in her eyes, the way the lines of her face smooth as she relaxes.

"You should not be so modest, Sakura-lun," she says. Shizuka's surprised at her choice of honorific. "You've watched Baoyi plenty of times, and she has nothing but wonderful things to say about you."

Baoyi perks up at the mention of her name. Her little head whips toward her mother. Baozhai straightens one of the ornaments in her daughter's hair. "Isn't that right? You love Sakura-lao, don't you?"

Baoyi's nod sends her ornaments into disarray. Baozhai clucks, renewing her dedication to the task at hand.

Sakura looks as if someone has placed a block of jumbled scrolls in Jeon before her and asked her for a translation. "Where's this coming from?" she says, wasting no time with niceties.

Shizuka squeezes her wife's hand again.

"At our last dinner?" she whispers to Shefali.

"Let them talk," is the answer.

Shefali is the most stable woman Shizuka has ever met. If she says to let them talk, then that is exactly what Shizuka will do. Besides, she's had enough of her dinner now that she might turn her attention to dessert, and Baozhai's set out a whole plate of orange-glazed rice dumplings.

"From experience," says Baozhai. "It would be unfair of me to deny that you've been a great help with Baoyi."

Sakura's confusion grows. She leans toward Baozhai. "What are you hiding?" she says. "You've been all over the place today. That nonsense earlier and now this."

"Nonsense?" Kenshiro says. As usual, no one stops to explain to him what is going on. Xianyu at least has resigned herself to this place of ignorance—she, too, is helping herself to dessert.

"I've no idea what you're talking about," Baozhai says coolly. She pulls Baoyi onto her lap.

"Mother's right tit, you don't," snaps Sakura. Xianyu flinches. "You know exactly what I'm talking about. What's with you lately? Five different designs for the handmaiden's dresses; different flower arrangements every day, and never mind what happened to the old ones; snapping at family just because you're in a dark mood, but singing their praises two Bells later; duck at every single dinner right next to the gods-damned fermented natto, of all things. That shit *stinks*, Baozhai, and you're the only one who eats it! I'm sick of it. I'm sick of this whole place bending to your will just because—"

Baozhai scoops Baoyi up in her arms and stands. The whole table holds its breath, Sakura included. Baozhai has never in her life abandoned a dinner.

"First of all," she says, her voice as cutting as it is calm. "I will ask you to remember that *not everyone* was raised in a pleasure house, Sakura-lun. Please watch your language."

"I don't have to—"

Baozhai's glare is enough to kill that retort before it can be born.

"Secondly," she says. "I was going to wait until later in the evening to tell you all, but I suppose now is as fine a time as any. I'm pregnant. The physicians tell me I am due in Tokkar."

Xianyu's brows shoot halfway up her forehead. Within a heartbeat, Kenshiro is on his feet, too, rushing to his wife's side. Sakura sits there catching flies, as Minami Shizuru would have said.

Shizuka, for her part, cannot decide how to feel. Happy, obviously. Baozhai is her closest friend, and Kenshiro is Shefali's brother; her niece is one of Shizuka's favorite things about this forsaken existence. That Baoyi will have the joy of growing up with a sibling is a wonderful thing, and Shizuka's heart swells to imagine it.

But they are beyond the simple stage of things. Baozhai is not simply Baozhai, nor Baoyi simply Baoyi. According to Xianese tradition, it is the youngest child who inherits the largest kingdom—the thinking being that all of the elder children will have been trained to act as steward should anything happen to them.

That means that the child now growing in Baozhai's belly will inherit Xian-Lai, so long as they don't have any more children.

And that means that Baoyi will now inherit Oshiro, a land she has never visited.

"Congratulations," she says. "Daughter or son, I've no doubt they'll be a proud, wise leader for their people."

"Congratulations," Shefali echoes. "May the Sky smile on all of you."

A new heir. All this talk of dying. There is a question burning in Shizuka's throat—but it would be terribly uncouth to ask at a time like this.

The Empress and the woman stand eight paces apart in Shizuka's mind. Sunlight gleams along the edges of their sharp blades. At once, they strike.

It is the Empress who stands alone at the end—and the Empress cannot afford to feel any shame for what she has done.

"Forgive Our bluntness," says Shizuka, "but We've a proposition, if You of the South are willing to hear it."

Baozhai—glowing beneath the ministrations of her husband's affection—looks to Shizuka. It is as if a lantern has been extinguished behind her eyes. "A proposition at dinner?" she says. There is an awful sadness in her tone.

But the Phoenix Empress knows they have so little time remaining to them.

"The circumstances demand the matter be handled with utmost expedience," Shizuka says. She is aware—terribly aware—of Shefali's radiating disappointment, of Xianyu staring at her as if she has grown a second head. She must press on. "The Jade Throne is guarded at present by Lord Oshiro Yuichi. We have yet to name a regent. Lai Baoyi boasts two royal lineages, and a third by marriage. Failing Our return, there is no one alive with a stronger claim."

As soon as the words leave her, she feels she's made a grave mistake. Baozhai's eyes go wide. Even Baoyi is confused—mumbling to her mother, asking why they've switched to such formal Hokkaran. It is a long while before Baozhai speaks—but not long at all before she looks away.

What subtle pain! She cannot tear her eyes away from the other queen, from the child in her arms. They are going to be remembered, they must be remembered—and if the Empire is to survive, then the best thing for it is a queen raised outside of its toxic grasp, her blood free of His corruption.

So what if it's a personally uncomfortable thing to ask? Who she is as a person has never mattered.

"Shizuka," Shefali whispers in her ear—but she is too far gone to let even her wife's soft voice steer her off this path.

"Please," she says. "Little time remains to us. If You of the South agree—"

"We of the South have agreed to nothing," Baozhai says. Without Shefali's gift of scent, Shizuka must navigate only by tone and body language. Baozhai is a careful keeper of both. "What, precisely, are You of the North suggesting?"

Even Baoyi is quiet. She's clinging to her mother's shoulder as if she is afraid something might hurt her. What sort of person has Shizuka become, that she is so insistent they discuss this now?

"Lai Baoyi, should she be willing, becomes the heir to the Phoenix Throne," she says. The words are as impossible as they are necessary. "Oshiro Kenshiro is named her regent until she comes of age. While We war in the North, they travel to Fujino and claim their now rightful places. When We return, We shall formally coronate Lai Baoyi."

"Me?" says Kenshiro. "Shizuka-lun—"

"You are a natural choice, Oshiro-tun," Shizuka says quickly. She hopes the switch in address will key him in. "Your father will hardly argue with his favorite son's gaining control of the Empire; you are well liked by the other lords, and respected enough by the South. Their like of you shall transfer onto Baoyi, and in time they shall see her as more your heir than Ours."

Kenshiro shrinks.

"You can't seriously be bringing all this up now," says Sakura. "If she goes to Hokkaro—Shizuka, you're asking—"

"Minami Shizuka asks for nothing," she says. "We are Empress Yui, Twentieth Empress of Hokkaro, and We are speaking for Our people. Hokkaro has too long endured expansionists and tyrants. Listen to Us! The Empire is a sword so covered in blood that it has gone to rust in its sheath. If We are to survive—if We are ever to regain our brightness, our sharpness—We must scour away the old."

As if she is breathing fire. Her throat aches and she finds herself straining to catch her breath.

Now they are truly staring—but not at her. There is something cool and wet near her fingertips. Has she gotten her fingers in the tea? No—it is worse and better than that. Sprouting up between her thumb and index finger is a cluster of violets, their roots sinking into the table itself.

Well. There are worse flowers to summon than violets.

Shizuka plucks the violet from its unlikely bed. She extends her hand toward Baozhai, toward Baoyi.

The fate of her kingdom resting on the dewy petals of wildflowers.

Baozhai only stares. It is Baoyi who makes the decisive move—she grabs one of the flowers and shoves it right into her mouth.

The Queen of Xian-Lai sighs. Once more she meets Shizuka's gaze. How is it that hers is always the stronger, always the more dignified? In truth, though Shizuka has trained all her life to be a god, she has never mastered being a ruler the way Baozhai has.

"You are asking Us to let Our daughter be raised far away from Us. You are asking Us to send Our husband away for an indefinite length of time—during our own confinement. Have You considered this at all, O Phoenix?"

"We have," Shizuka says. "But so have You."

"She is offering much," says Xianyu. At last, some relief. If Xianyu thinks there is merit in what Shizuka is saying, then there must be. "Going from living under their thumb to ruling them in one generation is appealing."

And yet Baozhai's eyes do not go any softer. She is looking at her sister with a mixture of disbelief and displeasure, with no sign of changing her mind.

Can't she see? Can't she see this is the best thing for all of them?

Perhaps Baozhai thinks this is born of Shizuka's ego. Perhaps she thinks this is simply a spoiled princess asking for another gift—for more toy soldiers, for more favors she cannot hope to repay.

So Shizuka stands. She walks around the corner of the table until she is right in front of Baozhai, until there are only two hands of distance separating them.

And then Empress Yui of Hokkaro gets on her knees to prostrate herself. Her forehead and palms touch the ground and she thinks to herself, *This is terribly uncomfortable*. It is the first time in her life she has ever bowed to anyone.

Her ancestors would be disgusted to see Shizuka like this. Knowing that soothes her.

"Please," she says. Can Baozhai even hear her, with her face so low to the ground? "Please. We are begging You."

She hears the silk of Baozhai's skirts moving, hears Kenshiro's gentle *hup* as Baozhai hands him their daughter. She is kneeling right in front of her.

"Lady," says Baozhai, and with that word, Shizuka is suddenly in the gardens with her again.

*When you were gone to war, every flower made me think of you. I would visit the gardens to talk to you, as if you could hear me if I spoke to the waiting blossoms*, Baozhai had said to her then. *When you are a god, I hope you will listen for me on the spring breeze.*

What a ridiculous thing to say to a person.

But that is Baozhai, isn't it? The woman and the Queen linked together. Impossible to love one without loving the other.

Which is it that speaks to her now, in hushed tones, as the two sovereigns kneel?

"Lady, make me one promise, and I will give you what you've asked."

"Name it," says Shizuka. She does not dare to look up. What if her strength falters? No, she cannot, she cannot; she must be an unerring arrow.

"I would surrender my kingdom and everything I am for my daughter's well-being," Baozhai says. "You know that. And you know, too, that you are sending her into the lion's den—no matter how much they love my husband. You are soon to be a god. Promise me that you will look after her. Promise me that no harm shall come to her. Give me *your* word, Shizuka, and not Yui's."

Could she promise such a thing? Could Shizuka, in good faith, promise to look after her niece when they very well may be marching to her death?

No. She would not allow herself to die; there's too much left to do, too much left to sort out—and she's yet to find a way to save her wife.

And so long as Shizuka did not die, she could make that promise.

Warmth courses through her. She feels the familiar pull of the strings on her soul—of the demands made by her people, who do not know she hears them.

She still has the violets. Shizuka sits up now, staring down at them, her fingertips glowing like a smith's tongs. One by one she pinches the petals of the flowers, willing part of herself into them, until all of them glow the same way. The light creeps down the stems until all eight of the remaining flowers are gold.

"Here," Shizuka says. She is surprised by the sound of her own voice—how much brighter and louder it is. "Four for you, and four for her. So long as you keep these with you, I'll be able to keep an eye on you."

It is the first time she's ever done something like this—but she feels confident in saying it all the same. When Baozhai takes the flowers in hand, there is a part of Shizuka that feels her touch.

Baozhai looks down at the flowers. She bites her knuckle. Shizuka does not need Shefali's nose to know she is trying to keep from crying.

"Then We agree," she says. "Baoyi shall be Your heir."

# BARSALAI SHEFALI

## TWO

Barsalai Shefali leaves Xian-Lai for the last time the next morning, in the middle of a monsoon.

"Stay for a few hours more," says her wife, standing under the roof of the Bronze Palace. "You can't mean to travel in that nonsense. What of your horse?"

*I'll live,* says the gray, but Shizuka cannot hear her.

"She's had worse," Shefali says.

"Then what about you?" says Shizuka. "Aren't you in pain? Won't the humidity make things worse?"

Shefali's kept two of her best wolfskins just in case she gets caught in the rain. A Qorin is prepared for any eventuality—the steppes have so many ways to kill, after all, that it is only sensible. She wears the larger of the two now wrapped around her shoulders. Rain drips from the furs onto her thighs. A wolfskin cap—given to her as a cheeky gift by Otgar—keeps her braids and head safe.

Oh, she is in pain already. Shizuka had to help her onto her horse this morning. The knuckles of her right hand are swollen and stiff; she will be using her hips to urge Alsha in the appropriate direction, she's sure. But even that will take its toll on her! How long will it be before Shefali resorts to telling Alsha, "Turn here" or "Slow down"?

Still. Her wife has no need to know all of that—Shizuka's worried enough as it is.

"I'll be fine," she says.

"You've taken your medicine," says Shizuka.

"I have."

"And you've taken the remaining vials along with you? They're properly packed, and won't shatter?"

"You packed them yourself," says Shefali, a small smile tugging at the corners of her lips. When did her wife become such a worrywart?

Shizuka pouts at her. "Don't make that face," she says. "You're leaving me to go to war. I'm allowed to worry."

"You're leaving *me* for war," Shefali answers. "On boats."

The pout changes into something more serious. Shizuka takes two steps forward. Sheets of rain threaten to swallow her, but she remains where she is, her Imperial Gold robes going dark brown. Even through the scent of the rain—the scent of all that is green yawning to life—Shefali can smell her wife's fear.

The water. Even the rain is too much for her, if it's soaking her like this.

What's Shizuka thinking, stepping out into it like that? Look at how she's shaking; look at how her shoulders tremble! Shefali clucks her and her gray obeys, taking her closer to her wife. Mounted, Shefali must lean almost ninety degrees if she wants to hold her wife's face—but she does so anyway, in spite of the pain that brings. Her arm is on fire as she cups Shizuka's cheek. Let the fire burn—there's enough water coming down from the sky to put it out.

"I don't want you to go," says Shizuka. She covers Shefali's hand with her own.

"It isn't a matter of wanting," Shefali answers.

Quietly, Shizuka nods. She raises herself up on the tips of her sandals. When at last her eyes meet Shefali's, they are bright as cinders. "He is making us do this," she says. Has the water washed away her wife's softness? For this voice is sharp and unyielding. "All of this is because of Him. Going north. Your getting sick. This whole Empire being what it is . . . I'm sick of all of it. I want to end all of it. I want to see him burn."

As the breath in her lungs, as the Sky above, as the moon and stars, Shefali loves her wife. Yet love is not a passive thing—it is an active one. To choose to love someone even when they are being difficult, to try your best to support them and urge them on the path that is best for them—that is love. To know that there will be someone by your side all the days of your life, to know that they will tell you if you've wandered—that, too, is love.

And so it is Shefali's task to soothe the fires burning in her wife's soul. The more Shizuka speaks of this, the brighter she burns. At what cost, that fire? What is it using as fuel? For this is not the first time since that night that Shizuka has gone on such a tear, and each time she seems a little more hollow afterwards.

Barsalai Shefali, about to leave for war, is more concerned with her wife's mental state than she is the encroaching demon hordes.

"The Traitor will burn," says Shefali. "But you can't let his fire capture you."

Shizuka's brows come together, but only for an instant. "What do you mean? He cannot burn a phoenix, Shefali—"

How quick Shizuka is to reach for such audacious statements. It has been like this since they were children, and in some ways it is a comfort to hear her brag. Any glimpse of the fire-hearted girl Shizuka once was is a treasured thing.

"I know," Shefali says. She touches her thumb to Shizuka's nose. "There's no need to tell me."

Shizuka's eyes are melting back into honey again—in spite of the rain plastering her hair to her forehead. "Promise me you'll be at my side when I find him."

Shefali can count on one hand the number of weeks remaining to her. Death is coming, she is sure. Akane's covetous glance in the Womb made that clear.

And yet she has made this promise to Shizuka time and again.

With the saddle horn as her anchor, Shefali leans even farther out. On better days, she can pick a coin up off the ground in the middle of a full gallop. Today, she is worried that her arm will snap off at the shoulder like old twine. The fear isn't unfounded. Limbs falling off would be new but not surprising; she has lost control of herself more than once.

It's a risk she's willing to take.

The muscles of Shefali's shoulder fray. She cannot hold herself here for long—but she needs only a moment.

One moment to bring their lips together, one moment to remind herself why she is collecting her mother's army for a suicidal attack, one moment to stretch into an eternity.

Their hands link; their scars grow warm.

"Together," whispers Shefali, her breath on her wife's lips.

"Like two pine needles," Shizuka answers.

And so it is—they share their last kiss in Xian-Lai. Who can say how long it lasts? For Shefali has no need of breathing, and Shizuka has no breath while Shefali is near her. Together they are in that raucous downpour; together they are in the early light of the morning; together they are, and let the gods try to pry them apart.

But even gods can be slain, and even this moment must pass.

When at last they part, Shizuka holds her wife's gaze for several heartbeats.

"Come back to me," she says.

"Always," Shefali answers.

*It's time,* her horse mutters. *Your mother's liver mare isn't going to stand around all year.*

It is true—that mare is all fidgets.

Shefali kisses her wife once more. As she leaves, she hums to herself an old Qorin song, its words more sound than lyrics. No one remembers what they mean anymore.

But they remember. Still, they remember.

SHEFALI DOES NOT sleep.

She tells herself it is because she does not need to, has not needed to, in four years. This Shefali knows in her bones to be a lie. When she was a child, there was talk of a man in another clan who lost the ability to fall asleep over two years. Like rainfall eroding a fine bow—so the lack of sleep eroded his mind. His temper frayed down to a single strand waiting to be snapped; he lost all track of time and said the strangest things in the middle of the day. When his clan set out along the Burqila trade route to Sur-Shar, he remarked that he had never made the trip before; this, in spite of making it twice in his lifetime.

There was little the sanvaartains could do. Sleep drafts worked at first, until his body became accustomed to them and they lost their potency. Many volunteered to solve things the Qorin way—hit him hard enough and he was sure to get some measure of rest. In his desperation, he allowed this.

Still sleep eluded him. Still he sat in his family's ger, staring at swirls of felt, swearing to anyone who would listen that there were people trapped within. That he could hear them.

After three months with no sleep at all, his clan took him hunting, and that was that. He died atop his horse; he died with bow in hand; his body was laid out beneath the sky. In the end, the crows carried him to Grandmother Sky's arms. What more could a Qorin ask for?

This is only a story she has heard, but all stories are true in their own ways, and it is not the sort of thing the Qorin would lie about.

Besides, she has felt the truth of it herself. In the four years since Barsalai Shefali left the Mother's Womb, she has slept precisely twice. There is, she thinks, one more sleep left in her. Her bones are heavy enough for it; she can see its paw prints in the snow of her mind. One night it will come to her and she shall not fight it.

But until then her days and her nights are as the head and tail of a false-faced serpent. Every morning its fangs sink deeper into her temples, until she has trouble stringing together thoughts. Every evening its hiss crackles over her memories.

She repeats the important things to herself over and over, in soft Qorin syllables: *You are going to meet your mother, and your cousin, and the clan that loves you; you promised your wife you would stay safe; you are going to war; you are dying.*

These things are impossible to forget—but Shefali is worried, all the same.

Twice while she is traveling her body loses its shape. The first happens thankfully—if anyone can be thankful for such a thing—in the middle of the night, when there is no one around to see. The serpent coils itself around her arm in the morning; by nightfall, she can hardly feel her fingertips. It is not until she reaches for the golden flower tucked into her belt that she realizes her right arm has shriveled into a husk. Skin clings to bone like old leather wrapped about knobby twigs.

She looks down on this shriveled hand, and she thinks: *At least my scar is still there.*

For it is—a single line of silver amid the gray of what was once her palm.

Shefali decides this is as good a time as any to let her mare rest for the night. There is no rest for her, of course—there is never any rest for her when she is so far estranged from her wife—but she acts as if there will be. With her shriveled hand and the ache in her joints, she has no hope of assembling her ger; instead, she lays out a roll of felt, and lays herself upon it, and imagines she can hear the voices of her ancestors as she sees them shining overhead.

*We will remember you*, they say. *Here—right here—is the spot we've saved for you. The view is beautiful in the mornings.*

Yet Shefali is in no rush to join them. However beautiful the view from the stars might be—the whole world spread out beneath her like a masterwork of glass, the steppes forever shining in the morning light—it cannot hope to compare to the sight of Shizuka sucking her thumb in her sleep.

Hours pass. When the sun rises, Shefali reaches for the golden flower again, and finds her hand has returned to her.

THE SECOND TIME her body betrays her, she is riding through a small village. She does not know its name, or even whether it is Hokkaran or Jeon. Wide, cuffed sleeves; patterned clothes—these things speak to Hanjeon more than Fujino, but then, she has been away so long that perhaps these are the newest fashions.

Whoever they may be, the people here are not fond of her. Who would be? A lone Qorin riding through a village, along no major road, in a war mask though there are none of the enemy to be seen. Their eyes are needles digging into her shoulders, into her chest, into her sides, and into her thighs.

*Are they jealous of me?* asks her mare.

Beneath her mask, Barsalai Shefali smiles.

It is this that dooms her. Like paper torn across, her lips and mouth; she hisses in pain as the skin peels off. Wet and cool, the skin slaps against her neck, dangling below the lip of her mask.

The villagers have not yet noticed.

She has only moments. A rattling breath, a command in a tongue of swaying grass—her gray mare knows it is time to leave. With every fall of her hooves, the muscles of Shefali's jaw grow thinner and thinner.

Yet what is stranger than a lone Qorin riding through a sleepy Jeon village in the middle of the day?

That same Qorin tearing through the village at a full gallop, letting out quiet gurgles of pain, her hand beneath her mask as she desperately tries to keep her jaw from falling off.

"Blackblood!"

The first to shout is a woman weaving; she leaves her loom, scooping up her child in her arms and running into her house. The cry spreads: "Blackblood! Blackblood!" shouts a man playing at dice with his friend; "Get away!" shouts the friend. In their haste, one of them knocks the board over; dice scatter upon the earth.

It will not be long now.

Fear is thick as fog in the air. Sweet. *Terribly* sweet. Spit drips onto her bloody hand; her top teeth ache in anticipation. Her tongue, thin and rapidly growing longer, wraps around her wrist to better taste it all.

And yet to scent something is not the same as to taste it. Barsalai Shefali has known the taste of fear. It has burst beneath her teeth like fruit; it has filled her mouth and dribbled down her chin.

Lust for it threatens to overcome her. As the village's warriors grab their bows and nock their arrows, she thinks of how easy it would be, how simple, to taste their fear again.

How long she has hungered.

Barsalai Shefali presses her eyes closed, knowing it will do little to help—her sense of smell is vision enough. Behind her there are three archers. She sees them as clearly as if she stood among them, sees their bodies young and old like shadows at midday.

Three whistling sparrows, three arrows in flight.

If she wanted to, she could turn and catch them. If she wanted to, she could throw herself from her gray mare and land as a wolf. If she wanted to, she could devour everyone in this village.

But though her sleepless years have worn her, though her blood runs black as ink, though she lopes closer to death every day, and her stomach rumbles for something succulent—Barsalai Shefali is no monster.

With no way to speak to them, she cannot tell them who she is; she cannot tell them not to worry. If she fights, she will kill them.

Hokkarans do not retreat. To do so is seen as a great weakness: If you do not have the conviction to die for your beliefs, then why are you on the battlefield at all? This practice has won them wars and earned them a reputation for fierceness on the continent.

But they still lost to a nineteen-year-old Qorin who knew that if you retreated—if you allowed your troops to regroup—you could come back stronger the next day.

Shefali, like her mother, knows the value of retreat. Three arrows are a small price to pay, in comparison.

She braces herself for them. One screams over her shoulder, landing with a thud in the earth; one pierces the back of her right arm. The third is the last to launch—and its archer a novice who forgot to account for distance. If Shefali does not do something to stop it, it will hit her mare.

*No*. Shefali would rather swallow molten glass than let her mare come to harm.

Feet still in the stirrups, Shefali throws herself backwards so that she covers as much of her horse's back as possible. Now she opens her eyes, now she sees the arrow plummeting, plummeting—

*Chnk.*

Bone piercing bone.

She coughs. The arrow, lodged in her chest, wobbles with the motion. With her left arm—the arm not ensnared by her own tongue—she holds it in place. It'll be easier to remove it when she can safely shift.

And she cannot safely shift her form here.

As she forces herself back upright, she can feel the arrowhead grind, the awful sensation traveling all the way up to her teeth. What remains of her teeth. Blood drips onto her thighs and she hopes—how she hopes!—that none has landed on the ground.

But there is little time to worry about that now. She sucks in a painful breath and gives her gray mare a kick. There are only three archers and no one here owns a horse—if she can crest the next hill, she will be free.

*You didn't have to do that*, the mare says to her. *Aren't you in enough pain already?*

*What's a little more?* Shefali thinks. In truth, she is more worried about keeping together than she is about the pain. The pain at least gives her something to focus on. Her pierced arm feels very much hers when there is a piece of bone slicing through her triceps.

Cresting the hill makes everything worse—her tongue tightens around her wrist; her stomach is threatening to tear itself apart. Galloping full tilt away from a fine meal, though she dares not think of it that way, is taking its toll on her. How much longer can she stay mounted? How much longer can she cling to the saddle?

Sky. She is a doll stuffed too full of felt. Weeks from now her seams are going to burst—but how it aches to feel them strain!

Over the hill, careening down—her horse knows well enough to slow down, now that they are out of eyesight. She cannot yet dismount, cannot yet truly tend to herself until there are at least two li between them. Breathe. Breathe, and the rest will follow.

*Kumaq*, she thinks. *To help me focus*.

With her free hand she reaches into her saddlebags. There—a full skin, the liquid sloshing as she pulls it free. Shefali flicks it open with her thumb. The acrid scent of fermented milk fills the air. She breathes deep of it—breathes deep of home, of the steppes. Cool air fills her lungs and freezes there. The cold radiates outward—up her shoulders and down her arms, rolling like a stone down into her belly.

Another breath, another.

*I am Barsalai Shefali Alsharyya, and this body is my own.*

Again and again she thinks it, again and again she forms herself from snow and ice and hardship. With both hands she sets her jaw back in place.

Will is the key, isn't it?

She focuses all of hers—all the cold, all the prickling energy it brings with it—onto the tips of her fingers. These she presses against either side of her jaw and—

*There*.

Frozen in place.

It aches, of course, with the numbing ache that only cold can bring, and she likely could not open her mouth if she tried at the moment.

But she has a mouth, and it is not falling onto her neck.

She takes another breath—through her nostrils this time, cool at the back of her throat—and focuses on the shedding skin. As if she is wiping the snow from a tarp, she wipes across the glistening skin beneath her mask. Cold as a fifth winter, cold as a sixth. How strange, to feel the frost forming beneath her hand! As if she is summoning glass from the ether, as if she is . . .

As if she is a god.

By the time Shefali is done, there is a patch of ice the size of her hand covering the bottom of her face. She cannot move it; she can feel nothing but acute, throbbing numbness.

Yet it is whole. And it is her.

She would laugh if she could. Where did she get such an idea? From listening to her wife, no doubt. If Shizuka can hold a branding iron bare handed, then perhaps summoning ice is not so strange at all.

Still. It feels . . . It feels as if she has left part of herself behind with the skin she shed. The Barsalai of a year ago would never have attempted such a thing.

*Don't forget your other wounds.*

Her horse is sensible, as always, but there will be time to deal with the arrows. Compared to losing control of her body, they are a mundane worry at best.

Barsalai Shefali taps her horse's flank twice. Two more li. She hopes the message is clear without her having to say it.

There are few people who know Shefali well. Her wife, her mother. Otgar, perhaps, though they did not part on good terms.

Her gray mare, though not a person, counts among them.

Two more li they travel, Barsalai clutching at the arrow in her chest the whole way. Dismounting is simple enough—all the excitement has granted her the energy to do so with little trouble.

It is the healing that will be the issue.

She slumps against a tree. Her blood drips onto the earth and she curses. Trees may be eternal symbols of everything the Qorin dislike, but that is no reason to poison them. When she is done, she will see if the kumaq can cleanse it.

But there is the matter of the arrows first. She snaps the shafts between her fingers. Shoddy craftsmanship, to start. Fletching with sparrow feathers is always bad luck. That the arrows are bone tipped and not metal should make this a little easier—they're narrower. If she focuses, she can feel its shape.

Another deep breath.

Shefali stares at the arrow in her chest, at the wound around the base of the shaft, and wills the laceration to expand. Shifting her form like this takes focus—but it is easiest when she can stare down at the thing she wants to change. Holding the image in her mind is the integral part, after all.

Widen.

Grinding bone, creaking muscle—the sounds soon reach her ears as her pain spikes. If it were not for her frozen face, she'd be grunting with effort. Slowly, like a potter shaping a bowl, she shapes the hole around the arrow.

When at last she pulls it out—what relief washes over her! She cannot sigh, only puff through her nostrils, but even that feels a little satisfying.

Her arm is shorter work—she's reshaped that more times than she can count. In truth, after all the commotion, she is of half a mind to leave it there. What is it going to do—go sour on her? She isn't going to die for another three weeks; surely it can wait.

A breeze carries the scent of foxes to her. Shefali shudders. Her lack of sleep has taken much from her, but she remembers clearly that day in Salom—the fox woman's teeth at her throat.

*Everything about you is rotten.*

Perhaps she really should leave the arrowhead in. If she got any more rotten, it might serve as fox repellent.

Yet she promised Shizuka she would stay safe. Out it goes.

It takes hardly any time at all; the soft flesh of her arm is far more responsive than the bone and cartilage of her chest. If anything, it is *too* responsive: the hole she makes is wide enough to fit two of her fingers together.

Despite her earlier misgivings, it *does* feel good to be rid of the arrowhead. As if she has expunged the last of the incident, the last of that animal hunger is gone with a spurt of black as the wound closes up.

Something deep in her wants to thank the Sky for this. Knowing what she does—that Tumenbayar is Grandmother Sky, that Grandmother Sky is no single person, that she, too, will take up the name—makes no difference. The Sky has watched over her all her life, no matter what names they both wore. To thank her is only natural.

Shefali glances up to the cloudy sky—and that is when she catches the second scent.

Horses.

Not one, or two, or three—enough of them that she can smell them though they are at least five li away.

And though she has taken an arrow to the chest today, though her mouth is sealed shut—it is this that makes her heart stop, it is this that robs her breath.

No one in the Empire has so many horses except the Qorin.

They're close.

If she tries, can she . . . ? No, she is too far still. Only the scents of the horses are coming to her.

How much longer will it be before she sees them again? Her mother, her cousin. Temurin, Uncle Ganzorig, and all her cousins . . .

Shefali gets to her feet, her chest rattling with a cough she cannot properly air, and reaches for her saddle.

*Are you sure you should keep traveling today?* the gray says.

Shefali narrows her eyes.

Her gray whickers. *I'm only asking. You're so stubborn!*

Shefali relents, but only enough to give her gray a light pat at the withers. Left with no way to communicate save acting, Shefali mimes running in place.

If it were anyone but her horse watching, she'd feel foolish—but her horse has never made her feel that way. They were raised together, after all.

*I could use the rest,* the gray admits.

Shefali's shoulders slump. They're so close! But . . . to meet them in such a state as this, covered in black blood and her mouth frozen shut . . .

Her mother had written to her of heroes. She looks a mess now. Better to come on them tomorrow, better to prepare.

But how?

Shefali reaches into her deel. The arrow, thankfully, did not puncture the bag she keeps her mare's sweets in. She tosses her one. The mare catches it midair, and Shefali sets about undoing her saddle.

In the morning, she will go to meet her mother.

But a Kharsa greets everyone mounted, Alshara always said, and

Shefali means to make sure her horse is in even more splendid condition than usual.

She may not sleep, and she may not know what she will say when she returns to the clan—but she can at least do this.

# MINAMI SAKURA

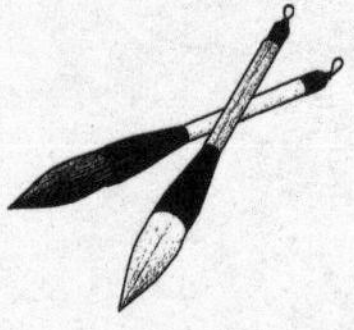

## TWO

If Sakura didn't know her better, she'd be furious. She still is, a little, as she sits down to break her fast with her cousin. Just look at Shizuka's state! Sitting in soaked-through robes, staring at nothing, pinpricks under her eyes from where she's been trying desperately to cry. How is Sakura supposed to see her cousin like that and not feel anything but sympathetic tenderness?

"Good morning," Sakura says. She keeps her voice light and friendly in spite of her own feelings—Shizuka doesn't need any more stress. "I've got our morning rice, and some extras I sweet-talked the kitchens into giving us."

Her cousin barely looks up. Sakura frowns. Last time things were this bad with Shizuka, she'd been drinking. Part of Sakura wants to search the room for any bottles—but she trusts her cousin.

She'll do it later, after Shizuka leaves.

For now she sets the tray of food down on the bed. Shizuka's favorite teapot sits at the center; Sakura quickly sets about pouring them both their morning cups.

"I bet you aren't going to miss the rain when you leave," she says. "Took me forever to get used to the monsoon season. You remember, I ruined my best set of robes in one of them?"

Shizuka glances up at her, but only long enough to sink further into the pit of her depression. "You were chasing after me," she says. "Because I was trying to duel the sun."

"Good thing the sun's so high up in the sky," says Sakura, handing Shizuka her cup. "You would've gotten it otherwise."

Shizuka lets out a long sigh. For a moment, Sakura's worried she's fallen so far in that she won't eat or drink—but she sips from her cup. Even lets out a small little sound of surprise. "Don't think I've ever had this one."

Sakura's plan is coming to fruition. She smiles and sets the bowl of rice in Shizuka's lap. "Got it from Baozhai's personal stash," she says. "Along with—"

Sakura uncovers the rice. Sitting atop the fluffy white are two fillets of fresh salmon, glazed in soy sauce and honey. The smell alone is enough to make Sakura's mouth water.

Shizuka, for her part, covers her mouth. She's surprised enough to laugh—and she gets nervous about people seeing her scar wrinkle up at the edges. "Where did you find *salmon*?"

"You should be asking your friend that," says Sakura. "I don't know if she's importing it from Shiratori or what, but she just got a whole shipment in."

"On the day I'm leaving?" Shizuka says. She sounds a little crestfallen, and Sakura can't blame her—it's Third Bell, and she's due to leave at Fifth. There won't be time for dinner. "But I *love* salmon. . . ." In truth, it is the only fish the Phoenix Empress can still stand to eat.

"That's why I got some for you today," Sakura says. "Enjoy."

She doesn't need to tell her twice. For all Shizuka's despondency, the woman cannot refuse a hearty bowl of rice. Sheepishly, at first, she helps herself—but both her fillets are gone before Sakura's finished even one.

"You eat like an animal, Your Majesty," Sakura teases her.

"Shut up," is Shizuka's answer. "I told you, everyone ate like this at war."

They've had this conversation before, but it's a rhythm that's easy to hold on to—a rope thrown at the lip of Shizuka's pit. She's pulling herself up out of it now, and Sakura feels a little swell of pride.

The Queen isn't the only master of social manipulation.

Although—she doesn't want to think of this as manipulation. She's just helping out. It's half the reason she came here—and most of the reason she's had such trouble leaving. Shizuka is not a woman meant to function on her own. Left alone for more than a quarter of the year, she turns to bad habits and worse decisions.

"Wonder if it's the same for sailors," Sakura says. "Are you sure you're gonna be all right out there?"

It's a risky question—but the prospect of being without Shefali for half a month seems to bother Shizuka more than the prospect of going to war again. Perhaps the reality of the latter hasn't set in for her. Sakura would be more surprised at her insistence on doing things this way were Shizuka not the most bullheaded person she knows.

The Traitor said—in the letter that Sakura cannot *read*—that he'd meet her at Nishikomi. Probably thought he could frighten her.

The joke is on him—if you even imply to Shizuka she can't do something, she'll go and do it. That's just who she is.

Shizuka—the Empress of Hokkaro—tilts her bowl to get more rice into her mouth. Her cheeks are puffy as a squirrel's for long moments before she finishes chewing.

"I'm going to have to be," she says. "I'm going to kill him."

"It's probably a trap," says Sakura. "I mean, I wouldn't know without looking at the calligraphy—the *exact wording* of these things is very important—but in my professional opinion—"

"Shefali has her reasons," Shizuka says. As quick and simple as parrying a blade. "I myself don't know all the details; only what she's given me. If she says he will be there, then . . ."

Sakura's mood sours. She tries to hide it by taking a bite of her salmon, but even its formidable flavor does little to help. "But what if it's not him?" she says. "What if it's one of his lieutenants? He isn't going to come down from over the Wall to fight you in a bay, Cousin."

Shizuka, to her credit, does at least consider this next point before answering. Eight years ago she might not have. Regardless, the answer is the same.

"Then I suppose I'll kill his lieutenant, and march over the mountains to get him," she says. "Whether or not he's there—I promised Shefali we'd go over to rescue the trapped Qorin."

"You never do things the easy way," says Sakura.

"No Minami ever does," says Shizuka. She is not wrong. The Minami family history is rife with twenty-ryo solutions to ten-bu problems.

Something in Shizuka's face changes then, as Sakura is mid-bite. The look that's come over her is dangerously close to the one she had at dinner, when she decided to put the Empire's future in the hands of a girl who thought paper was delicious.

Sakura hardly has time to brace herself.

"You're going with me, aren't you?"

So easily, so casually, she says such a thing! As if she's asking Sakura to sneak her out to a temple and not to accompany her into war. It takes everything in Sakura's power not to choke.

"What?" she says. Grains of rice fly from her lips; her mother would've beaten her for letting something so unattractive happen. "I'm a *painter*, and you want me with you on some battleship bound for who knows where—"

"Bound for Nishikomi," says Shizuka. "Your hometown! We could let you off at the docks while the actual fighting went on—"

"And what if it spills onto the streets?"

Shizuka has never been fond of physical contact. Sakura figures it's her upbringing—she never really learned how to respond to physical affection. She's more likely to buy you something or write you something than she is to embrace you.

But then? At that moment?

Shizuka takes her cousin's hands.

"You'll be safe," she says. "I'll have Captain Munenori watching over you; nothing awful will happen."

Sakura can't believe what she's hearing, can't believe what she's seeing. Why is Shizuka so intent on this all of a sudden? With all the nonsense popping into her head of late, Sakura's wondering whether or not Shizuka's pregnant, too. Can that even happen? They're both gods; they don't have to obey the rules of nature, do they?

"Cousin," she begins. "You don't need to be worrying about me while you're out there fighting."

Like a lantern going out—the look on Shizuka's face. It's painful to see, and even more painful to be the cause. Still, Sakura's mother raised her to take care of herself. A battle between gods is no place for a painter, no place for a singing girl, no place for a scholar. Arrows flying all over the place, blood in the streets, the screams of the dying—Shizuka can't seriously mean for Sakura to endure all of that.

For what, company?

"I . . . You know what you're asking, when you ask me a thing like that," continues Sakura. "I'm not cut out for war. The Sister made me to read books and paint robes; I can't do that when I'm trying my damnedest not to die. Not everyone is . . ."

The words she wants to say are *as brave as you are,* but they do not feel right. To say that would be to imply that she herself is a coward, and that isn't true at all. Sakura just knows what she's good at and what she isn't.

"I wasn't built like you," she says instead.

"Is that so?" says Shizuka. She's gotten to her feet. With one hand she drains the last of her tea; with the other, she begins to work the knots of her outer robe. "I thought you came to Xian-Lai to shoulder my burdens with me, to keep me company. Was I mistaken?"

Her empty cup clatters as she sets it onto the tray. Two steps she takes, and she is by her mirror, furiously shedding her wet clothes.

"It isn't like that," says Sakura. She turns away. Awkward to argue with someone who's half-dressed, though she's done it plenty of times. "I just don't want to—"

"You don't want to what?" snaps Shizuka. Her outer robe crumples to the ground; the inner belt soon following. "I was under the impression, Sakura-lao, that you now wanted to record histories. What better history is there than this? A divine war, for the sake of our people's future—you'd balk at recording a thing like that?"

Sakura pinches her nose. It's hard to stop a wildfire once it's gotten started; it's harder still to stop Shizuka. That girl spent most of her life expecting the world to roll over for her and ask for belly rubs.

"You can't expect everyone to do whatever you say just because you're the Empress," says Sakura. It's better to be direct with her when she's like this. Sometimes it gets her to stop and consider what she's saying—sometimes. "I've got things left I want to do before I go traipsing off to the North to die."

"You *won't* die," Shizuka says sharply. "I won't let you."

"But that's just what this is about," says Sakura. Now she, too, is on her feet, gesturing at the screen she painted for Shizuka five years ago. "You aren't letting me do anything. You aren't making me do anything. I'm more than one of your subjects; you can't just order me around. I've got no military training. I've never seen someone get hurt too badly, let alone die. You think I'm cut out for war?"

Where was all of this coming from? Sakura wishes she had Shefali's nose—from the sound of things, it made it a lot easier to understand where people got ideas like this. Shizuka's whining like a child, for the Sister's sake!

"You lied to me," says Shizuka.

Sakura flinches. "About what? I've been nothing but honest—"

"When you came to meet me," Shizuka answers. "You said you came out of the goodness of your own heart, but that wasn't true, was it? You came because of the letter."

Shit.

How's she supposed to explain that it isn't like that when, on some level, it is? How's she supposed to do that without lying about it? And—why does it hurt so much to hear it put in such a way? What Shizuka's asking for is, objectively, a *terrible* idea.

Sakura saw well enough what happened when her cousin had been to war. How could she ask anyone to go through the same, knowing they aren't even a warrior?

"That was all you wanted, all along," Shizuka continues. "I've got to say, I admire your dedication."

Sakura wants to scream. She isn't sure what words would come out, and she isn't sure it matters.

She turns around. Shizuka's got her long blouse on; she's in the middle of stepping into her pants. To be arguing with her when she's in such a state is the height of ridiculousness. If Sakura had told her mother eight years ago that she'd be screaming at the Empress, in the middle of dressing herself, in her own bedroom—well. Her mother would have slapped her.

"What I wanted," Sakura says, "was to be a good person. To help you out when you needed help. And maybe along the way, I'd be able to ask you for help with something important to me. Sister's tits, why are you so self-centered? Not everything under the sun is about you, Shizuka!"

This, at last, seems to pierce through that thick skull of hers—Shizuka stops mid-motion, staring back at her cousin with anger and confusion alike.

It's too late for Sakura, though; she's done her fair share of enduring her cousin's nonsense for one morning. She loves her, truly—but she does not make herself an easy woman to love. Barsalai Shefali might be the most patient woman on the continent.

Sakura tugs at her hair.

"I'm leaving," she says, because it is all she can trust herself to say. With a bow more courteous than sincere, she departs. Shizuka calls out for her, but she does not turn around, not even when she remembers the perfectly good red bean mochi she left on that plate.

It's not worth it. It's not.

Sister. She's always wanted to travel, she has, but . . .

And so what if Sakura *does* love history? It isn't like she set out to fall in love with it; it isn't like she stayed up all night as a young woman dreaming about paying witness to battles. Kenshiro, maybe, but not her.

Though now Kenshiro's going to be headed straight to Fujino because of Shizuka's nonsense. Regent for the Imperial Niece. He's due to leave tomorrow morning, and Sakura's got no intention of interrupting his last day with his wife for the foreseeable future.

Because she's a good person.

*Ugh*. As she walks past one of Baozhai's flowerpots, she has to suppress the urge to knock it over. What sort of woman would make a demand like that?

The thought comes to her like many thoughts born of anger do: in a whisper.

*In ten years, no one will even remember her.*

She stops. The jovial azalea arrangement next to her sways mockingly in the breeze.

That's just it, isn't it? In ten years, no one will remember Shizuka, and no one will remember Shefali, and all that will remain of them are records that will one day pass into myth. Kenshiro won't even remember his own sister—though he might, with the story Sakura's been recording.

Yet what will remain of Shizuka? Her letters, her edicts? A name is a simple enough thing to fake, and her deeds are already legendary; who will believe that the woman who raised the New Wall once sat the throne?

That look, just before she'd made her ridiculous request—it was fear, wasn't it?

Sakura grits her teeth. She closes her hands into fists.

*Fuck, fuck, fuck.*

Gods, she doesn't want to go back in there. She doesn't. If she does, then she's just going to leave Shizuka feeling justified about that fit she threw, and she *can't* feel justified about it, because expecting people to die for you is *wrong*.

It's like dealing with a child, isn't it? If one washes this set of dirty robes, then the other will never learn to wash them on her own.

Except that Shizuka's leaving for war, and might not come back, and if Sakura doesn't wash the robes, then they very well may still be unwashed when she is eighty years old. Worse, she will look on them and wonder—*Who left these here?*

Sakura throws her hands up and groans.

It is then, of course, that Baozhai decides to show up with her attendants in tow. Baozhai, and not the Queen—she's wearing one of her more casual dresses, and her makeup is far more restrained than usual.

But that does not stop her from looking imperiously down her nose at Sakura. "This palace is a terrible place to be upset," she says. "Is there something I can do to alleviate the issue, Sakura-lao?"

Sakura's dealt with lords and ladies. The Gem Lords of Shiratori are rich enough to . . . Well, on second thought, Baozhai must be richer. But the point is—Sakura's dealt with her kind before. Few things infuriate her more than the way a wealthy person smiles. Baozhai is no exception.

And yet—Sakura's going to need her help, after all.

"What do I have to do," she says, "for you to get me passage to Nishikomi?"

Now it is Baozhai who stops, tilting her head. With a motion, she dismisses her attendants—two girls Sakura does not know, one of whom carries a box nearly her own size on her back. She touches a fingertip to her lips in thought. Sakura feels as if she might implode.

"My, my," says Baozhai. "How unexpected. I thought you'd ask me to move your quarters closer to the libraries."

Sakura frowns. She *would* like that, except that she isn't going to stay anymore, because her cousin is an idiot who deserves to be remembered. "I had a change of heart."

"I see," says Baozhai. "One that you are not bringing up with your cousin."

A detail like that was never going to escape Baozhai's notice. Sakura fights the urge to cross her arms.

When Sakura gives her no more thread to pull on, Baozhai makes a small, amused sound. "I can grant you passage," she says.

"What's the price?" Sakura answers. There's got to be one, and it's better to ask sooner rather than later.

"It's terribly impolite to be so direct," says Baozhai. "In the North, it's custom to refuse a gift three times."

"Is it still a gift if I'm paying you?" Sakura says. Her patience is wearing thin—she does have enough money of her own to charter a ship, but whatever Baozhai gets her will be fast.

"A fair point," Baozhai says. She takes a fan from her belt and opens it. The sight of it sets Sakura's stomach twisting—the whole thing is mother-of-pearl and onyx, with gilt leaf accents. "My price is small, and I'm certain you'll agree it's fair. All I ask from you is that you keep an eye on your cousin."

Sakura's brows nearly meet over her eyes. "That's it?" she says. "That can't be it. And how do you know I'm going to be with her, anyway? I could be leaving all this behind."

Baozhai fans herself. "Oh, it's a simple thing, Sakura-lao. A scholar can recite even their least favorite texts," she says. Sakura bristles, but Baozhai snaps the fan closed to cut her off before she can begin. Her voice goes from her usual haughty tone to something far quieter, far more personal. "I am serious about my request."

"What's it matter to you, anyway?" says Sakura. "If she dies—"

"She won't," says Baozhai firmly. "I shall say this only once to you: I owe you a great debt. The Lady of Ink is my dearest friend. There were days when I, trapped as I am here, could do nothing but watch her dance upon her own funeral pyre. You are the woman who kept her from that end. I do not know why you need this ship, though I have some idea; I do not know why you are not asking her, although I have an idea there, as well. I do not need to know. All that needs be agreed on is this: I will grant you your ship, and the debt between us will be settled. Is that clear?"

Sakura knows all about their friendship. She saw it grow herself, during Shizuka's rare visits to Xian-Lai. Even when Sakura had gone to Hokkaro, she saw stacks of Baozhai's letters kept carefully apart from all the others. There were days that Shizuka was so drunk she could not remember her own name—but she remembered to write Baozhai back.

In some ways, it makes sense. Both women are as immensely likable as they are difficult—and they can talk about flowers for days.

Where Shizuka is a fire, Baozhai is a cooling spring. The two of them together make for a fine summer's night.

Keeping an eye on Shizuka is the whole point of this trip. Sakura can't shake the feeling Baozhai knows this. She doesn't like that. It feels as if she's fallen into the same pit twice—going to war in behalf of two queens.

She's always wanted to travel, hasn't she? And if she makes it back to Barsalai, maybe she can ask her about the letter again.

"Fine," Sakura says. "Fine, I'll keep an eye on her."

# O-SHIZUKA

## TWO

Minami Shizuka stands on the docks of Nagosu, a fishing village half a day's sail south of Nishikomi. Before her, the Father's Sea stretches out like a living eternity, rising and falling, rising and falling. Strange that an ocean should breathe steadier than an Empress. Stranger still that she should choose to face it at all after the things she's seen.

She must remind herself that it is a gift to even face such a thing. So many of her comrades were scattered to the wind four years ago. So long had she stayed before their pyres that she is sure some of their ashes soaked into her skin. Surely, too, those who had drowned beneath the Great Wave had lent something of themselves to her. Why else would she see them so often in her nightmares? Perhaps, then, she is less alone than she thinks.

But with Shefali off to the North and Sakura back at the palace, Shizuka feels more alone than she has in years.

It is the thirty-fifth of Rokai. Summer has trampled over gentle spring now, and pressed her glaive to its throat. Soon it will be Shizuka's birthday.

The head of the Traitor would make a fine gift, or so she tells herself as she forces herself to look on the ocean. Difficult, it is, and yet the simplest thing in the world: her mind scrambles away from the sight like a frightened hunter, but her muscles lock in place like a stag's, and so she continues to stare.

At the endless blue.

At the imagined shapes beneath it.

At the cresting waves, who know well what she did on the shores of the Kirin.

The waters are hungry—she can feel this in the pit of her stomach—but they are not the waters of the Kirin. Bodies do not lurk below. Up ahead there are children sitting at the edge of the pier with makeshift fishing poles. In the time Shizuka's been staring out at the water, not a one of them has caught anything—but that doesn't stop them singing their songs, doesn't stop them waving their sand-covered feet.

Live children. Not dead ones. Listen to them sing—there isn't anything wrong. They aren't afraid, and so why should Shizuka be?

It's a sensible thought, but fear is rarely sensible.

A wave rises up. She tenses, expecting somehow to see Mizuha beneath the glassy surface. When it crashes against the shore, when the spray of it hits her skin, Shizuka flinches.

A sea battle. Why did she think this would be a good idea? She should have hired some navy captain to handle this, she should have manned the infantry and Shefali the cavalry as they'd agreed, but her stubbornness got in the way. What is she going to do if one of those waves knocks her overboard?

*Walk on the water,* she thinks. *I've done it before, haven't I?*

She closes her eyes and imagines that she is on the banks of the Jade River as a child, with her parents, watching her mother try to catch fish barehanded. She pictures the flopping fish, pictures its glittering scales, pictures her mother chasing after her with it.

Water has not always been terrible to her.

Another sensible thought drowned by the memory of the Kirin. Here the water is safe enough, but when they are out to sea, who can say? They're sailing toward the Traitor, after all; what will she do if they pull her under once more?

What will she do when the water is rushing up her nose and down her throat and into her lungs?

What will she do when there is darkness all around her and no light, no light; what will she do when she sees the bodies again, what will she do when Daishi—?

"Your Imperial Majesty—eight pardons, but are you well?"

Captain Munenori. Shizuka forces her eyes open. The sea is there, waiting for her; she summons all her willpower to turn away from it and face the man next to her instead. Captain Munenori Tsurushi spent the better part of his youth stationed just south of Tatsuoka, his parents sailors who ferried merchants to and from the Sands. The leathery look he won then has not quite left him even after years inland. Shizuka's grateful for him, and grateful, too, for the Doanese sea captains who've volunteered for the mission. Now that she has looked away from the sea, she realizes most of her army—her fleet, now—has already boarded.

Only Munenori and the other captains remain on the pier, decked in their armor, awaiting her. Again she is the child among adults, but at least she has grown old enough to be comfortable with the position.

"Yes," she says. "Yes, Munenori-zul, I'll be quite all right. Have we settled on a plan of attack?"

The captain nods. To question the Empress would be beyond impolite—it would trespass into blasphemy. And so he does not, in spite of the disbelief plain on his face. "If Your Majesty would follow me to the others?"

And Shizuka does, every step creaking against the pier, every creak against a backdrop of waves. The sound alone is enough to sour her stomach—and this on solid ground.

She thinks of Shefali vomiting over the side of a ship years ago. She thinks of the things she said to her then, the teasing. She wishes that her wife could have come with her on the ships, instead of staying with the cavalry—but there was no arguing it. Shefali wants to fight alongside the Qorin. It is the best place for her, too; should the worst happen and a demon assault meet them, Shefali alone would know their names.

It is for the good of the Empire that Shefali is not here.

But, oh, how Minami Shizuka suffers without her. How alone she feels!

But the Empress is not alone; the Empress has business to attend to. Four Doanese captains await her. Trin Kiyam is the first of them to speak—youth triumphs over experience when it comes to these things.

"Thread-Cutter Empress!" he calls with a short bow. "It is good to see you have joined us. Are you well?"

Why is it that genuine concern can so often feel like an invasion when it comes from someone you do not know well? Still—etiquette must have its due. "Yes," says Shizuka again. "Trin-tun, Dai-tun, Nuyoru-tun, Nim-tun—the Empire thanks you for your services. Have you eaten rice?"

Nuyoru, the eldest of the Doanese captains, tugs at his beard. "We have," he says. "Have you?" He does not say that it is an honor to serve, which is what any Hokkaran would be compelled to say in such a situation. Shizuka respects them all the more for it. The threads binding Dao Doan to the Empire are stretching thinner and thinner.

"We had a small breakfast with the departing army," Shizuka says.

"Then if we are all well fed, all that is left is to discuss the matter at hand," says Dai Hoyan. Studded rubies decorate her sailor's coat—a tradition relating to the amount of journeys she's made. Dai is the only one who bears rubies—Nuyoru has lapis, reedy Nin has jade, and Trin has pearls. Geometric patterns adorn them all: crisscrossing lines and overlaid triangles nothing like Hokkaran flowers or waves.

Trin claps his hands together, grinning ear to ear. "We've kept it nice and easy, Your Majesty." Has he seen combat before? Shizuka saw that sort of excitement only on the greenest recruits, only on the village bullies who thought their dominance would transfer to the battlefield.

Nin is the one who unfurls the rough-drawn map over their makeshift table. To the northeast, Nishikomi; to the north, the Father's Teeth. Ships are marked here near Nagosu. Arrows travel from Nagosu to Nishikomi, where someone—probably Trin—has drawn old-fashioned demons. Another set of arrows points from the demons to the Teeth, where there are more ships helpfully drawn ramming into the demons, and demons drawn cut in half against the rocks.

"We approach from the south and trap them against the Teeth?" says Shizuka.

"Easy as can be," says Trin. He points to a spot on the map closer to shore, where he attempted to draw horses and instead drew funny-looking dogs with people on them. "The horsetamers are going up to the Tokumas, in case something comes down toward us." He points to the shore itself, where he elected to draw a forest of glaives instead of an army. "Your infantry wait on the shore in case something shows up there."

"We don't know yet how many enemy ships we're facing," says Dai. "This plan is simple enough that it can be adapted to a variety of situations, as needed. Once we're closer, the *White-Winged Crane* will signal more detailed maneuvers."

"Your ship, *Heavenly Ambition*—it's the huge one over there, do you see it?" says Nuyoru. He points to the largest of the ships, and the strangest of them. All the Doanese vessels have simple roofs reinforced with bronze to protect them from projectiles—but for the most part, their decks are open enough that you can see the sailors within.

The *Ambition* yields little of itself to the viewer. Because the ship is covered from top to bottom with only slits here and there, it is difficult to imagine there are people within it at all. More of a floating castle than a ship, really; the *Ambition* is at least three times larger than anything else in the fleet. Shizuka's throat closes at the thought. Of all the places to spend a battle.

"If the Grandfather brought down his hammer on that ship, it would not sink," says Nuyoru. "The safest place you could possibly be. I don't know what the southerners are paying their shipwrights, but it's well earned. Only one problem."

"The cannons," says Nim. It is the first time he has spoken, and Shizuka understands why. The man is more rasp than voice.

"*We* don't have cannons," says Nuyoru. Again he is tugging his beard. "That doesn't sound right to me. We weren't allowed to have them when we sent word to your requisitions officer."

"Seems to me that if we're going up against the Two-Tongued Prince, we should have ourselves the best weapons we can," says Nuyoru.

"Dragon's Fire is volatile. Don't forget what happened to General Hirota when he attacked your people. All *his* cannons ignited at the same time, and to this day, there's a crater where the man once stood," says Munenori. "Good reason to forbid the stuff, if you ask me. Are your people used to working with it?"

"Are yours?" says Nim.

Sailors are much like soldiers—put too many officers in one place, and a fight is inevitable. Shizuka decides to put an end to this one now.

"We've thirty Surian firebreathers," she says. "We can spare ten of them. You've no cannons to speak of, and we've no time to craft them, but they are skillful with many types of weaponry. You may find yourself with something useful."

Nuyoru and Nim nod, Nim smiling a little like a weasel. "A pleasure doing business with you," says Nuyoru, "Thread-Cutter Empress."

Dai sniffs. "Leave the trickery to Nim and Nuyoru," she says. "I've no need for unnecessary risk. Have you any further questions, Your Majesty?"

*How shall I do this? How shall I walk into a ship like that without screaming?*

"No," she says. "We thank you all again, and wish you smooth sailing."

A small smile tugs at Dai's lips. "In Dao Doan, it is bad luck to say a thing like that," she says. "Choppy waters teach you more than still ones ever will."

"We say 'may you be up to the task' instead," offers Trin.

"Then may you all be up to the task," says Shizuka. How little time she has spent in Dao Doan. She wishes she'd traveled more before all of this. "We shall see you on the sea."

They bow to her and she nods to them, and soon Munenori is walking with her to the *Ambition*.

The gangplank is before her now, inviting her up into the darkness. Up in the ship itself, she sees the vague shapes of her sailors. Shadow swallows them, and for a moment, just a moment, it is easy to imagine them floating in the blue.

Munenori has taken his first step onto the gangplank. He is walking now, while Shizuka remains at the foot of it staring, staring.

If she boards this ship, there is no returning. If she boards this ship, she cannot simply tell them to turn around if she gets frightened, if the world starts to close in on her. She cannot let the others see her in such a state. She must be the Empress, resolute and serene; she must be anyone but the girl beneath the waves—

"Your Majesty?" says Munenori. He has stopped midway on the gangplank.

Shizuka's forehead is slick with sweat.

There is still time to join the infantry—but that isn't what her mother would do, is it? That isn't what Alshara would do when faced with her greatest fears, either.

If she hesitates, she is lost.

She takes a step. The wood gives a little beneath her, and her heart sinks into the earth itself.

Captain Munenori Tsurushi walks toward her. There is enough room on the gangplank for the two of them to stand shoulder to shoulder, and that is what Munenori does. He turns his body so that no one can see Shizuka from the shore—and then he offers an arm.

"If you need it," he says.

The sailors waiting at the gates can still see them. Then again, they can already see her trembling. The proper thing to do would be to force herself to walk the whole thing on her own regardless of her fears.

But she thinks of Baozhai's admonitions to be safe, to accept help.

And she takes the captain's arm.

# BARSALAI SHEFALI

## THREE

Plumes of white smoke curl against the ash gray sky. Shefali counts them in the early hours of the morning. Two hundred. Her heart swells at the thought—when last she left her mother, there had been only one hundred twenty gers in the Burqila clan. How many more cousins await her? How many wide faces, how many full cheeks, waiting to be pinched? To see their numbers swell in such a way . . .

Barsalai may have journeyed eight years so that she could return to her wife—but part of her always dreamed she might look out on a sight like this again.

The gers, the dogs running free, the children squatting over a game of anklebones—she sits astride her gray mare and she drinks in the sights, the sounds, the smells. Like warm kumaq, they fill her belly. Her vision goes a little fuzzy around the edges; giddy laughter bubbles up from her throat. Look at them! That boy's chasing after his sister, his miniature deel flapping against his body!

Is there anything more joyous than seeing your people prosper?

Being among them.

Ah, but that—that will take some doing.

Barsalai Shefali once stared a serpent woman in the eyes. She has wrestled with stone men; she has raced a lightning-dog twice around the palace of Ikhtar; she has refused the advances of a fox woman and paid her price in flesh.

But going to see her mother after eight years apart frightens her.

*She will be happy to see you*, says the gray.

"I know," Shefali mumbles. Alshara's letter had said as much and more—things Shefali never imagined her mother might say to her.

Yet still she sits and watches. Watch—that boy's sister has turned on him. Head down, she charges straight toward him, sending him tumbling onto the earth.

*All of them will.*

"Except Otgar," Shefali says.

*Even her*, says the gray. *You should listen to your wife. She has a good head on her shoulders.*

"She lit herself on fire once," Shefali says. Much as she loves Shizuka, sound judgment has never been among her virtues. A twinge of worry comes to her with the memory. Everyone who spoke of the incident did so in passing. What were those days like in the palace, if lighting oneself on fire merited only a little attention?

Shefali lifts her mask enough to palm the lower half of her face. Still cool to the touch from yesterday's incidents, though at least the snow has melted enough that she can speak. Only a thin layer of frost clings to her skin, as if she is a pond in the first days of winter.

The gray mare huffs. Suddenly, she takes a step forward—and then another, and another. Shefali jerks up in the saddle.

"What are you doing?" she says, leaning over so that she can whisper into her horse's ears.

*I told you, you're too stubborn*, says the horse. *If Temurin's still riding that handsome seal bay, then you aren't going to keep me waiting here all day.*

Shefali grits her teeth. She can yank on her gray's reins; she can hop out of the saddle and stop her. Both would keep her right in that spot near the outcropping, where she can safely observe her family.

Until they find her, that is.

A hunter who does not leave his ger is no hunter at all. Shefali steels herself. *They are your family*, she thinks. *They will be happy to see you.*

Closer and closer, her gray carries her. The two children she was watching earlier are now rolling in the mud. The girl is on top, but the boy's limbs are long and whip lean; he will have the upper hand soon.

She tries to keep her eyes on them, and not on the green and violet banners of Kenshiro's messengers.

Her mother will know she is coming. Otgar, too, will know.

Are they waiting for her? Shefali has told her mother of her exploits—but Otgar, too, was there. "Soul" and "story" share a word in Qorin. That is no coincidence. Whatever story Otgar told Alshara of their travels, she has told her aloud, breathing her own soul into it, shaping it into a living thing.

Shefali's tale is only ink on paper. It will not be alive until someone reads it aloud, until the winds carry it to the Sky.

Her Hokkaran side again.

Who among the Qorin would prefer the living to the dead?

*Shizuka likes my writing,* Shefali thinks. It comforts her more than she would like to admit. Her wife, who has been swamped with love letters since the moment of her first bleeding—she liked Shefali's letter. Loved it, even.

So it is only ink and paper. It is alive enough.

A familiar scent jolts her from her thoughts: campfire smoke and polished metal; resignation and dedication.

Temurin.

Shefali's throat closes up. She can see her now, standing at the very edge of the camp. Someone not far away is playing the horsehead fiddle, and she is tapping her feet to the rhythm. Time wisely took one look at Temurin and decided to find easier prey elsewhere—the years have not changed her at all. Gaunt as ever, tall and thin, her sword still hanging at her hip, she is as lean as a hunting hound.

And keen eyed, still. It is she who first sights Shefali approaching on her mare. Surprise cuts through her scent like a blade through felt.

"Barsalai? Is that Alshara's girl?"

The name is rough on her lips—ill used and coated with rust. Hearing it makes Shefali wish she'd said Barsalyya instead. That is who she was when she last visited the camps.

"Can't be Barsalai—look at that mask. That's Hokkaran made," says her partner. Standing next to Temurin makes her look younger than she is, though she *is* young. Pale skinned, her thick hair cropped short—a Hokkaran. Strange. Foreigners often came to join the clan. If they had useful skills, they were welcomed; if not, then they had to pay a bride-price.

But Shefali cannot remember the last time she saw a Hokkaran show up at the edge of the camp. Ren had, yes, but she did not stay with the Burqila clan, and the business of sanvaartains is theirs alone.

This woman's even wearing a deel. No braids in her hair, so she has not done anything of note, but perhaps her standing there at all is notable enough.

"What the fuck are you talking about?" says Temurin. "Look at that mare. Star, strip, and a snip. She's lighter than the last time I saw her, but that is Barsalai's horse."

Ah, so the years have not blunted her, either. Shefali smiles beneath the mask. Temurin's temper is funny when she isn't the one on the receiving end of it.

Perhaps this will not be so hard as she thought.

"How was I supposed to know," says the Hokkaran girl under her breath. Temurin glares at her for only a moment—Barsalai stops in front of her not long after.

Temurin stands tall. Shefali, still mounted, shrinks in her saddle.

"Barsalai Shefali," says Temurin. Her eyes narrow as she crosses her arms. "Burqila gave strict orders. You are not to return to the clan until you have mastered yourself."

Shefali does not want to remember that day at Imakane—but she does. Her aunts and uncles gathered together in her mother's ger. The scent of blood, the taste of it.

She says nothing. Temurin is not yet finished, judging by the set of her shoulders.

"Understand this: She has given you your name, and she has told all of us here to wait until you arrived, and so we have. But I remember that village, and I remember the way you staggered back to camp like a mangy wolf. Prove to me you have mastered yourself, or I won't let you among our people. Burqila's trust is valuable, but our children's lives are worth more."

A painted opera singer slinks onstage with a dagger in hand. The lead, a promising young woman from Fuyutsuki, is in the middle of the most famous song in the work. Listen to her as she laments her fallen lover, listen to her as she asks the Mother to take her, for she cannot bear to imagine life alone. How smooth her voice! How full of emotion! Gently she sways upon the stage, her eyes wide, her face pale even beneath the layers of paint.

Closer creeps the man with the dagger.

The lead staggers. In her sorrow—her character's sorrow—her voice cracks. Somehow, it is more beautiful than awful. She falls to her knees.

The man with the dagger, having raised it to stab her, stops. The lead has fallen flat on her back. She reaches out for him and he can only stare down in horror. He drops the knife, scooping her up in his arms though he is her sworn enemy, and she expires on the spot.

The crowd cheers, not realizing yet that the girl is well and truly dead.

So it is for Shefali.

*Our children's lives are worth more*.

A dead woman astride a horse.

Barsalai reaches for her boot knife. She hands it to Temurin, the point facing in, and waits.

Temurin takes it. There's no need for any more talking. Temurin undoes the clasps on her deel. The chest and shoulders of it hang around her waist, leaving her wiry arms exposed to the rising sun. With her right hand she draws the knife across her left arm. A cut the size of her own severed fingers begins to weep.

Morning light makes blood shine like Ikhthian rubies. Hunger twists at Shefali's stomach again; her jaw tingles beneath the ice.

But the ice holds. She breathes of it now and reminds herself: She is Barsalai Shefali, not Barsalyya. The tiger holds no sway over her.

One hundred heartbeats, two hundred. Barsalai does not move from her saddle.

Temurin's flint-hard face softens. "Oh," she whispers. "Oh, it *is* you."

Shefali nods.

"Get off that horse," Temurin says. Her voice cracks. Has it ever done that before? "You fool girl. Running off for eight years; abandoning us for the northerners . . ."

Luckily for Shefali, she took her medicine less than a Bell ago. It's dulled her pain enough that she can dismount on her own, that she does not flinch as Temurin throws her arms around her and draws her close.

"Take off that mask and let me smell you," says Temurin. She has not bothered to put her deel back on; Shefali can feel the rapid beat of her heart.

But can she take the mask off? For surely once Temurin sees her, she will run, she will run . . .

Shefali swallows. She shakes her head. "I look awful," she says.

Temurin tilts her head. "You won't let me smell you?"

"That means she's a—" begins the Hokkaran girl, but Temurin cuts her off with a glare.

Shefali squeezes Temurin's shoulder. "She isn't wrong."

Peppery anger; sour confusion. Temurin's scent swirls. Now she draws away; now she slips back into the sleeves of her deel. "Your horse has not left you," she says. "Let me smell her mane, at least."

It is a fair compromise. Shefali takes her boot knife back and cuts a small lock of her mare's mane. This she offers to Temurin, who takes a deep whiff of it and hands it to the Hokkaran girl. She, too, takes a breath of it. Shefali feels a little strange, having her soul offered to a stranger in this way—but if she is part of the clan, this unmet young woman is not truly a stranger.

Temurin looks Shefali up and down. For a moment, Shefali worries she will find something to say—that she holds herself like a northerner, or that the tiger-striped deel does not suit her.

Instead, she nods.

"You've grown," she says. "Come. Your mother's waiting. Cheregaal, here, can handle your gray."

Shefali swallows. The fear she'd conquered rises up again—she is so close now. In her mind she composes all the things she will say, as if she is writing a letter.

They walk past the children wrestling. The boy is on top, laughing, and the girl is laughing with him.

"Are you really the Beast of Rassat?" the Hokkaran girl asks. The question is like a lightning bolt from a clear sky. How does she know about that? Otgar is the only one who knows the truth of that story, which would mean . . .

"Could you transform for me?" says the girl. "I don't have any money, but I can make you a bow, if you'd like. Dorbentei says you have a bow nicer than any I could hope to make. But, well, I thought I'd offer."

Otgar is telling stories about her?

Quicker and quicker Shefali's steps. Up ahead is the horsehead banner of her mother's ger. Each step sends another jolt of lightning through her.

"Barsalai?" the girl repeats. "Are you listening?"

"No," says Temurin, who is not wrong.

Three dogs lie in the sun outside Burqila's tent. As one they roll over, tapping their feet against the earth. Tongues loll out of their mouths and they bark in the way they have always barked, low and rumbling. Burqila's hunting dogs run to Shefali's side. Fearless as always, they lap at her hands. None Yesterday threatens to bowl Shefali over; Less Today keeps running between her legs like an overgrown cat.

She is coming home.

The bright red door looms before her. Through it, her mother; through it, her cousin.

Barsalai throws it open. "Catch your dogs," she says. The point is moot but she must say it all the same; the words leave her without her thinking.

And then—then she is among them.

Here is her uncle Ganzorig, sitting by the fire with a knife in one hand and a rack of ribs in the other.

Here is her aunt Zurgaanqar, beating a length of felt.

Here are her cousins, five of them together, playing anklebones near the bookcase.

And sitting to the east is Burqila Alshara.

Hokkarans have found beauty in transience for the better part of two thousand years. The Qorin have their own thoughts on the matter. Is it beautiful to move from one place to another, desperately attempting to keep your family fed? It is *necessary,* but not beautiful. Romance creeps in over the generations, as does poetic dedication to this culture they've chosen, but is that beauty? The songs that spring from horsehead fiddles are beautiful; the stories told in hushed voices around a fire are beautiful; the delicate embroidery that tells their story across every deel is beautiful.

But there is nothing appealing about transience itself. One moment you are enjoying yourself, and the next you are not. This is an ineffable law of creation. The sun rises and sets; the moon takes its place; everything you know and love will one day die. It is a Qorin's place to exist in spite of all this.

And exist Burqila has. This is the woman from Shefali's memories, and this is not. When did her mother grow so much older? For there are crow's-feet at her eyes now, and the pale straw of her hair has begun to go silver. Burqila Alshara took a world that wanted to kill her and broke it over her knee—how is it that time's hunting dogs have finally found her?

Shefali opens her mouth. There is no air to form words, even if she knew the words to say. Pressure mounts behind her eyes and she knows, she knows, that the tears will soon well out.

Burqila once rode half a day away from the clan to weep where no one could see her. A Kharsa must be as unyielding as the lands that birthed her, she'd said. If anyone thought differently, they must be shown otherwise.

What will the clan think if they see her weeping? If this is the thing to bring her to tears—the sight of her mother after so many years?

Twenty years ago they had called her weak for crying from pain.

She finds she does not care what they think anymore.

Barsalai Shefali, twenty-three years of age, runs to her mother's arms with all the grace of a newborn fawn. In the five steps it takes her to close the distance, all her worries fall away, all her self-consciousness, all her doubt.

"Aaj," she says. "Aaj, I'm sorry."

Silence, her answer, but not silence alone. Burqila Alshara squeezes her daughter tight, rocking her back and forth as she does. Shefali's ribs hurt and she feels she cannot breathe but she does not pull away—her mother smells of horses and wind and campfire smoke. How can she pull herself away?

This moment, too, is transient. Let her enjoy it.

It is Burqila who separates them in the end. She holds her daughter at arm's length. She taps her fingers against the muzzle of Barsalai's mask. Though the years have written their tally on her face, Burqila's eyes are as piercing as ever.

Shefali swallows. Can she . . . Can she expose her face to her family? Can she bear it if her mother finds her horrifying?

*Shizuka did not find me terrifying,* she thinks. *Ren didn't either, or Kenshiro, or Baoyi.*

And if a child did not find her frightening, what are the odds that Burqila will?

Shefali lifts her mask. Her heart is beating like thunder drums.

Burqila holds a hand in the air. Her fingers move in quick shapes, and it is then Shefali remembers that her cousin is also in the room. Dorbentei Otgar wears five braids in her hair now—two more than the last time Shefali saw her. She can hazard a guess as to the reasons. One for returning from the Womb, and the other for, well . . .

Shefali braces herself for the arrow. Any moment now, her cousin will berate her for what she's done—for taking so much time to return to her own family, and for letting herself grow roots. How much longer will that smirk stay on Dorbentei's face? She must be preparing something cutting indeed.

"Burqila says that you need to spend more time in the sun. You are too pale; you look like a dying woman," says Otgar. "For my part, I say that you could not pay me enough to return to the desert. Not you, not your wife, not Halaagmod's southern flower. I've had my fill of it forever."

Dorbentei's grin brings out the dimples in her cheeks. Shefali half laughs, half snorts. To her surprise, Burqila mirrors her.

The truth can be the funniest thing in the world.

Soon, she's walking over to slap her cousin on the back. "Welcome home, Needlenose," she says. "If you ever leave us again, I'll throw you off a cliff myself."

One by one, Shefali's aunts and uncles join in, until all of them are bundled up together—laughing, and crying, and squeezing.

"I wouldn't dream of it," says Shefali.

THERE IS NO feast, for there is no time. Qorin cooking is an all-day affair—and if they are to meet Shizuka by the Kirin's horn, then they must leave at moonrise.

Yet the evening is not a complete culinary loss. Barsalai's uncle Ganzorig has been slaving over his stew all day in anticipation of his niece's return. The whole ger is thick with the smell of it; Barsalai is convinced that if she cut a swath of felt from these walls, they would hold that scent for years. Once everyone has been served—and greeted, of course—Shefali's youngest cousin, Soyiketu, puts out the firepit. Aunt Zurgaanqar puts a table down over it.

Burqila Alshara brings her folding seat closer to the table. She looks over it expectantly, signing in deliberate motions. Otgar starts translating only after tipping the bowl up and drinking the remnants of her meal.

"Burqila says," she begins, but a burp interrupts. She beats her chest a little. "Sorry. Burqila says that your wife sent you here to gather us for war. The messengers said as much, anyway, before they turned tail and ran back to the South."

"Their banners?" Shefali says, narrowing her eyes. Her uncle gave her a bowl of stew, too. To refuse it would earn her a heckling—she forces herself to drink it down. The thick texture combines with the taste of ash to clog her throat.

Dorbentei leans over and slaps Shefali on the back. "Don't go getting yourself killed just yet," she says.

"You've spent too much time away," says Ganzorig. He clucks. "If you'd stayed with us, you could eat by now."

Aunt Zurgaanqar slaps him on the shoulder, but he does not seem remorseful. A year ago such a comment would have bothered Shefali—now she is happy she is around to hear it.

"We told them they could leave if they wanted, but that they had to leave their banners," explains Otgar. "You're a hunting dog, Needlenose. I figured you were following their scent."

Shefali narrows her eyes. She looks to her mother and then back to Otgar. There was no signing as Otgar spoke. Is she making decisions for the clan now?

But Dorbentei Otgar has been all her life a canny woman—she catches Shefali's wandering green eye. "No one knows you better than me," she says. "Burqila asked my opinion and I gave it."

Otgar takes a breath.

"To get back to the point—Burqila has a few questions before she sends all of us marching up to the North."

"Ask them," Shefali says. Unlike Shizuka, she takes no offense at the questions. There are precious few Qorin left; if they are to be deployed en masse, then Burqila must be absolutely sure of why.

As algae on the surface of a pond—the scent of fear, the scent of the stew.

What do her aunts and uncles think of her asking them to die?

Burqila gestures as if unrolling a scroll, then points to the table. Shefali reaches into her saddlebags. A single scroll case is tucked beneath the box that holds her medicine. She plucks the paper from within and spreads it out on the table—a now outdated map of Western Hokkaro, with Xian-Lai still marked as one of the provinces.

As Shefali reaches for the models, Burqila signs, and Otgar speaks.

"Burqila thanks you for bringing a map of these confounded lands, for she has in all her travels never encountered a land she hates more than this. Rocks and trees together, hills so high that it dizzies her people. She swears that even the kumaq does not taste the same here. Set up your map however you like—her first question is how many of us you will need."

Shefali does not feel dizzy at all, but perhaps that is because of her condition. Her lips have felt awfully dry—but that is hardly a thing to complain about. And kumaq tastes the same to her wherever she goes.

Still—she arrays the small horses near the Azure Pass, the toy soldiers at Nishikomi, the golden catapults on the sea, just south of the Father's Teeth.

Burqila sniffs; Otgar laughs.

"Don't tell me Barsatoq is taking the siege engines out on the water," she says.

"They're boats," Shefali explains. She sets the last of the horses into place, and then reaches into the bag for the last of the markers. Her wife had not included them during the meeting with Baozhai, for she had not thought their presence would sway her much. Shefali knows they will make all the difference here.

"How many is that, Needlenose?" Otgar asks. She does not care that Shefali has not finished. "Is each horse one tumen?"

"Yes," Shefali says. The first wolf tooth goes down north of the Tokuma Mountains.

Uncle Ganzorig sets down his bowl of stew.

"That's fifteen tumen," says Otgar. "You're asking for all of us."

"Whoever is willing to come," Shefali says. She sets the second tooth down, and the third, leading up to a massive pile to the far east.

Wolves have forty-two teeth. Shefali has hunted enough of them to know. Their pelts have value throughout the Empire and outside it; like their cousins, the Qorin, they wander through the continent in search of food. Killing one without making use of its body would be a tremendous disrespect, and so Shefali has found uses for most of their remains.

Except for their teeth.

For years she simply kept them with her. Throwing them away is the sort of thing her brother would do, after all. Someday there would be a use for them that would not insult their former owners.

That day has finally come. The northern reaches of the map are *covered* in teeth, a jagged yellow forest of them.

Quiet comes over the ger.

Burqila breaks it. The Kharsa-Who-Is-Not leans forward in her seat and picks up one of the teeth, rolling it between her fingers. When she sets it back down, the other teeth jump up. Some fall over, and Shefali feels an involuntary wave of shame.

Burqila's signs are sharp.

"Barsalai, these teeth," says Otgar. "They belonged to wolves, didn't they?"

Shefali nods. The scent in the ger goes sour—realization and anger. As Grandmother Sky had formed the Qorin from wolves, so too had Barsalai Shefali used teeth to represent Qorin.

"How many?" Otgar asks again. Her voice is rough as unhewn iron; Burqila, next to her, is trembling at the shoulders.

The whole room is waiting to be shattered.

Shefali swallows. There is little in the world she hates more than having to be a hammer.

"Thousands," she says. "More of us than there are Hokkarans."

Thousands of Qorin trapped beyond the Wall, where they are subject to the will of an evil god; thousands of Qorin whose bodies will not return to the Sky.

Shefali has seen despair on her mother's face only twice before—and never on Otgar's. It is . . . She could have gone her remaining weeks without the sight. There is something uniquely heart-wrenching about seeing your parents in misery. Parents are near to gods—and Burqila Alshara nearer than most.

But even Burqila covers her mouth in shock, in disgust.

Yet Shefali knows she must keep going. You cannot read the bones of a creature until you've laid it out in the sun. "The blackblood is his way of controlling them," she says. The words leave her coated in rot; she feels his presence tingling at the back of her mind. Only when she takes the flower from her belt and holds it in her hands does it subside. She presses her eyes shut and continues. "When it's in you, he can . . . he can speak to you. Control you. You become a vessel for him."

"Shefali . . . ," starts her aunt, but Shefali shakes her head. She must finish this.

"The Fourth wants an empire. He is willing to build it from us. He is willing to plant us in his foul land and watch us grow roots. He delights in it. *Domesticating* us."

Otgar wipes at her eyes again and again, growing ruddier each time, as if getting angrier will burn away the sorrow.

Burqila's signing is erratic and ill contained.

"Are you going over the Wall?" says Otgar, her voice wavering to match. She points to the largest pile of teeth. "When you repel this attack—will you go over the Wall, to this place?"

Shefali has known the answer since she first heard the story.

"Yes," she says. "I will go to Iwa, I will kill him, and I will free them."

Alshara's viper green eyes are wet now, and Shefali does her best not to stare at her mother as she wells up.

"Just like you, Needlenose," Otgar says. "Making promises like that. I was worried you'd gone and lost your head for a little while."

How does one answer a joke like that? The dark faces of her family have gone ashen with despair and anger, with horror and shame. What can Shefali possibly say to ease their worries? She has said all she could—she is going to Iwa, and she is going to free her people.

All that remains to her is hoping they believe her.

Only when Alshara's hands lie silent does Otgar speak.

"When I was a young woman, my mother told me that I was the unluckiest woman in the world. She said to me: 'When you are my age, you will rule over ash and bone. The Sky has abandoned us in our time of need. I wanted a hero, and she gave me only you.'

"I told my mother what I thought of that. I told her that the Qorin would never die, so long as there was wind through the grass of the steppes; I told her that so long as wolves drew breath, we would one day return. I told her, too, that so long as I lived, that day would remain as distant as the towers of Axiot.

"For my insolence, she put out the tongue of my closest friend. Harming me would have been the easier thing to do, but your grandmother was as cruel as winter, and knew what would truly hurt me. Since that day I have been silent, in memory of my friend.

"But not once in my life, Barsalai, have I changed my mind about our people. You tell me now that there are thousands of us over the Wall. You tell me now that you are going to free them.

"I tell you that I am going with you. I have gone over the Wall before; I know what lies in store for me. They can't frighten me anymore. Killing a god doesn't either. My mother was right—I am not the hero she wanted. But you are, Shefali, and I'll lend you my own sword to end that bastard."

True to her word, her mother takes the sword from her own belt and hands it to Shefali hilt first. This is the sword she carried with her over the Wall; this is the sword that severed a demon lord's head. So, too, is it the weapon that carved a path straight to Oshiro.

Shefali can only stare at it. If she takes it . . . If she takes it, what will her mother use to cut down rabid wolves?

Yet Burqila does not falter. Her eyes bore straight into Shefali's, and her hand now holds steady.

Shefali takes the sword.

Tears fall on her deel.

It hits her then like an arrow to the throat: there will be no time for her to return to the steppes.

Had she known that the last time she was there, she would have lain in the silver grass for a whole day and a whole night; she would have named the constellations and the planets; she would have hunted, she would have raced, she would have wrestled her younger cousins.

She thought she'd have the time.

But she won't.

And her mother is following her, knowing full well it might be her last campaign.

She looks around the ger, a dagger in her throat, only to find her aunts and uncles have quietly all drawn their boot knives.

"You've done too much on your own," says Otgar. "Your family's coming along this time, to keep you out of trouble."

To keep her out of *trouble*?

"You might die," she says to her cousin, to her mother, to the gathered Qorin around her.

"Then you'll make stars of us, won't you?" says Otgar. "Wouldn't be such a terrible thing, to be a star."

Fourteen knives, hilt first, beneath a ger in Hanjeon.

Barsalai collects them all—the weapons of the dying.

# O-SHIZUKA

## THREE

For a day and a half, Minami Shizuka waits for news.

The first day is the hardest of them, for that is the day they reach Nishikomi. She should be above deck, with Munenori and the others, to confront whatever might await them. That is what a leader would do.

But if she does that, she'll have to look out on the water.

It doesn't help, of course, that the *White-Winged Crane* sends news that the bay is empty save for the standard traffic coming into the city. Overlarge Axion ships, with masts so tall they scrape against the clouds; sleek little Ikhthian ships filled to the brim with wares; a few Xianese merchant vessels painted with colors you could see from several li away. The Bay of Splendors is as busy as ever—but there is no sign of the Traitor.

So they spend the first day docked, waiting for him to show. Shizuka is confident he will, just as she is confident she will then muster the courage to go above deck.

One hour passes. Another. The third—an entire Bell. The ship's cook calls that the meals are ready. Everyone aboard the *Ambition* dines standing, in case the Traitor should have the temerity to attack them while they're eating.

But he doesn't.

And he doesn't attack them the Bell after that, or the Bell after that, and soon it is Sixth and people are growing tired. The messengers come to her less frequently then, once every hour as opposed to three times. No need to report often if there was nothing to report.

By the end of the first day the infantry have also arrived. If she looks out the window in her quarters, she will see them on the shore, standing tall, staring out at the ocean that so vexes her.

But she does not look.

She waits instead. She focuses on her breathing, on her heartbeat. Anything but the rocking of the ship, anything but the steady whisper of the waves against the hull.

The first night she does not sleep—only stares at the lantern in her room and wills it to keep burning. Somewhere aboard the *Ambition* someone is playing a flute. The tune is familiar to her, though she cannot place it. Long notes held for beats at a time, piercing and clear and very nearly shrill. It reminds her of a bird's cry—not the sweet songs so often emulated by musicians but the cries themselves. A crane fleeing a hunter might make such a sound.

Hearing it makes the back of her head tingle.

The second day, Munenori comes down to see her. Shizuka puts on her war mask to hide the bags beneath her eyes. They exchange pleasantries with Shizuka gripping her own knee as tight as she can. She won't shake. She can't.

"Your Majesty, are we docking?" Munenori asks her.

"Should we?" Shizuka asks. She knows well enough the value of that question.

"We'd be out of the way of incoming merchant ships, then," says Munenori. "While we await the enemy, it is best we remain as unobtrusive as possible. You know how people in this city are about their trade."

She knows. "All right, but what of the army? We've twenty thousand; they're already intruding."

A shade crosses Munenori's face then, as he considers how to phrase what comes next.

"Her Grace Shiratori Ayako has intervened," he says. "She is providing room and board for the Phoenix Guard within the palace. At present there are three companies near the shore itself. Still an intrusion, yes, but the city can handle them well enough. That's about as many sailors as they see in a day."

"How are the people reacting to our presence?" Shizuka asks.

"It's too soon to say," says Munenori. "The *Fragrant Mist* docked for an hour last night; I'm getting my news from their signals. Do you want me to send a few sailors out in plainclothes?"

She considers it. It'd be good to know what people think of her decisions, but in the end it does not matter. She made the best decision she could.

"Yes," she says, "but not to gossip. See if anyone has noticed anything amiss of late. There must be something we're not seeing."

Munenori bows. He turns to leave, but stops at the threshold.

"Your Majesty?" he says.

"Yes?"

"When we dock, you can return to shore if you would like," he says.

Shizuka flinches; only the war mask saves her courtly dignity. She is beginning to understand why Ikhthians are so fond of wearing them all the time. "No," she says. "When they come for us, I will go above deck. I swear it."

If she steps foot on the pier, she might never get back onto the ship.

"As you say," replies Munenori. He bows again and departs.

Shizuka decides it is best to occupy her time with something other than her own thoughts. There isn't much room in her quarters—strange given how massive the *Ambition* is—but she clears a little space for herself and begins practicing sword forms. In them she finds a small measure of peace. It's easy, after all, to imagine that she is cutting down the Traitor for the final time. The Traitor in her mind is an old man with blackened teeth, a man in clothing outdated even by her grandparents' standards, a man who calls her Shizuka-shan.

She cuts him down, over and over.

By the time Munenori returns to her, she can stand without trembling. A small victory—but kindling on the fire of her heart. She stands straighter now, shoulders back, and sheds her helmet.

"Is there word already?" she asks. It's evening now, she knows that much, but the sailors here aren't particularly stringent about calling Bells out when they pass. With her window covered and the room lit only by lanterns, she can imagine she is somewhere beyond time itself.

"Only a little," says Munenori. "Barely a rumor, but I thought I might bring it to your attention."

"Go on," says Shizuka. He has just come to check in on her, then, but he is doing a good job of masking that.

"There's been music in the bay," he says. "We didn't hear it last night, but from what I'm hearing, it's been heard often. The sailors have already made up a song for it."

"An inappropriate one, no doubt," says Shizuka. She knows plenty from her time with the army.

"Yes," says Munenori. "I didn't bother learning the words."

"Did you learn the melody, then, while you were ignoring the words?" she asks.

Munenori hums. It's clear he was never subjected to a zither tutor, but she can suss out the tune well enough. It is the same as the one she heard last night.

Shizuka clenches her jaw.

"You'll forgive my musical ability, I hope," he says. "The original song is played on a flute in the middle of the night, every night, regardless of which ships are docked. Midway through First Bell, usually. All the sailors we've spoken to have claimed they heard it with perfect clarity."

Sayaka's tormentor played a flute. It was the one who said they'd meet again in Nishikomi. Did she really hear its music last night? Why didn't she realize?

"Munenori-zul," she says, "what time is it?"

"A little past Fifth," he says.

Deep breaths. Steadying breaths. She forces herself to approach the window, to move aside the sheet she has draped over it. Through the slit she sees the sea and the sky.

She chooses to look at the sky. It's her wife's favorite—and it's rapidly going rosy.

Minami Shizuka swallows. She thinks, for a moment, of the sky across the Kirin—of the unnatural violet and the yawning pit that followed. When she sees that the sun still hangs in the sky here, she breathes a sigh of relief.

Relief as short lived as winter frost, for she knows now when the attack will come. The music—of course it is the enemy. Of course it plays only at night, when she never feels her best; it's calling out to her. Letting her know that it is here, and it is watching.

She's heard it once before, after all—nearly eight years ago during Jubilee.

It won't be long before sundown.

She reaches for the war mask again. A woman stares back at her from the polished bronze: bloodshot eyes, wan skin, cheeks sunken in. When she places the helmet atop her head, she imagines flames consuming the woman she saw.

Minami Shizuka stands in her place. Not the Empress, her blood stained black; not the General, her hands still unclean.

Her mother's daughter, and her father's. Shefali's wife. The woman who is afraid of water. The Phoenix.

"We're setting sail," she says.

"What?" says Munenori. "We've got sailors on shore still—"

"Recall them," Shizuka says. She turns from the window and tugs on her gauntlets. "The music is the key. It's my own fault; I should have been above deck."

He follows as she heads up, step by step, until she stands above deck. Above her a canopy of bronze and wood blocks out the sky. The sailors salute as she walks by, as she makes her way to the signal-bearer. A wiry little lad he is, his hair a sooty explosion atop his head.

When he sees her, he snaps to his feet, then reconsiders and kneels back down. Shizuka stops him just as his knee touches the deck.

"Send word to the others that we'll be setting sail shortly," she says. "As soon as they've recalled their people. We must be deeper into the bay by nightfall."

They want to taunt her? They want to make her afraid? She'll show them what she thinks of that.

The boy doesn't question this, picking up the fans he uses for his trade and heading toward the window. Shizuka averts her eyes rather than look out onto the water. It's all around her, but if she focuses on the sailors and the ship, she can pretend they're in a strange-looking palace.

Munenori's gone to speak to some of the others—they hurry off down the gangplanks to recover their companions. As he returns, he calls out for the firebreathers to ready the cannons. The *Ambition* is humming now, as if it has awoken from a long sleep.

"What can I help with?" she asks Munenori. He is so stunned by the question that it takes him a moment to respond. When he does, it's with a joke.

"We've always need of more strong backs to row," he says.

Shizuka nods. "Send for me when the moon rises."

Before he can stop her, she descends the stairs again. If the Daughter herself had joined the rowers, they might've been less surprised. To question her would be suicidal, but to stare at her quizzically—this is allowed.

"Your Majesty?" says the headman.

"Don't mind me," she says. "I'm only here to help."

She takes a seat at one of the benches and grabs hold of the oar.

They won't be moving for a while yet, but it's good to have a spot. The man next to her goes milk white. She gives him a good-natured elbow. The sort of thing Dorbentei would do. Dorbentei seems like the woman to emulate about now, not that Shizuka would ever dream of telling her so.

"What's the matter?" she says. "Never seen an Empress before?"

He guffaws. "Can't say I have," he says. "Let's hope your back is as strong as your sword arm!"

It is easier, here, where there are fewer windows. So long as she does not look out the portholes, she won't have to deal with the open sea.

Well—it is easy until it is hard. When the foreman first beats the drum, when they first begin to row, Shizuka's back ignites. Duelists aren't known for their strength, and she is no exception. Were it not for her seatmate Haruki-tun and the other rowers, she'd be flying off wherever the oar led her. When had it gotten so hard to row? Had it always been this way? No wonder sailors appeared so often as romantic heroes, no wonder she'd never met one who did not have aurochs' shoulders. The oar is moving her, and not the other way around!

Yet even this is comforting in its own way—the beating of the drums drowns out the sound of the waves, and focusing as she is on the motion of the oar, she cannot focus on the ocean itself. When the rower's song starts, she fumbles through the words, and that, too, is comforting, for if she is singing, then she cannot think.

She has almost forgotten that she will have to leave when Munenori appears in the doorway, when he jerks his thumb up toward the deck. From the set of his jaw, the news isn't good.

In her haste to rise, she does not time it well. The oar slams into her stomach. Armor can soften a blow, but it can't negate it, especially when the blow in question is delivered by six men in unison. Winded she doubles over, reaches out to steady herself and—

A child in a bath has paper boats to amuse her. When one displeases her, she brings her fist down on the water. The waves the little god summons threaten to upend the ships, sending them careening this way and that.

The *Ambition* is one such ship. All at once the decks quake, all at once a massive hammer strikes at their hull, all at once the rowers on that side are flung from their seats as the ship itself tilts sideways. What was once the ceiling is now her right-hand wall. Like dolls the sailors fall from their places—the rowers on the left side of the room cling in desperation to their oars to avoid sliding across the ship.

Shizuka isn't ready.

When the blow strikes them, she is already on shaky footing; she can't right herself in time once the ship tilts. Though she windmills her arms to try to find some new balance, it's no use. She falls to the ground, knocks her head against the deck, and slams right into Haruki. Her ears are ringing; Munenori's shouting something at her but she can't hear him, can't hear anything except her own heart. Dust and sweat are getting in her eyes. Just as she pushes herself up, the ship rocks back to normal—this time Haruki dares to catch her by the arm before she can fall.

"Thank you!" she shouts, or she thinks she shouts thank you—she bows a little as she pulls away, as she heads for Munenori still standing in the stairwell. He's telling her something and she still can't hear it. Had a cannon hit them? Had their cannons fired? Perhaps this is why Dragon's Fire was outlawed through the Empire; she'd heard thunderclaps with more subtlety.

It's only the war that keeps her functioning, only the memory of the oncoming shades. When surrounded by the enemy, disorientation is the last thing you can afford.

So she slaps at her own ears in a vain effort to awaken them. In the meanwhile she scans the *Ambition:* sailors now running at full tilt from place to place, shouting, pointing to this window or that. Munenori must realize she can't hear a thing: he takes her to a window where she can see the ships burning outside. Two of them—Doanese ships if the shape of them is any indication. Like prayer tags, they're burning, crumpling up at the edges; even from here she can see the tiny shapes of the sailors jumping into—

She sucks in a breath. The water.

Some of the words are starting to come in now. Munenori's screaming in her ear and she is thankful, for she doesn't know if she'd hear him otherwise.

"The *Fragrant Mist* and the *Morning Fog*!" he says. Nim and Nuyoru's ships. No wonder. Part of her feels guilty for allowing them the use of firebreathers—but she tells herself that sailors so reckless would've found some other way to meet their end. Maybe. She'll worry about it later, when they aren't under fire.

And they are under fire, Shizuka can see that now: flaming arrows arc toward them in the night. None of them can pierce the bronze roof of the *Ambition*, nor the roof of the *Crane*, but impact is impact all the same.

"The *Wing*'s readying their trebuchet," says Munenori. "We can't see them, but she's going to take her best guess. We've orders to follow her lead. Are you confirming?"

Which one is the *Wing*? Ah, she sees it now on the other side of the ship; the massive trebuchet atop it is a little hard to miss. Nothing like the Qorin models Shefali's aunt always seemed so proud of—this is the sort powered by ropes your whole crew pulls on at once. Dreadfully inefficient.

But the *Ambition* has cannons. Those are *far* better.

"I already told you, Munenori-tul," she says. "You and the others manage the sea battle. I'll . . ."

She glances out to the ocean again. Forces herself to. Where are they coming from? The arrows fly in from the northeast, but that can't be right—the Father's Teeth are there. To position yourself so close to them is suicidal at best.

The violet sky beyond the Wall, the false sun.

She swallows.

Munenori's left her to give orders to the rest of the crew. Shizuka stands alone near the window, unable to look away as wave after wave of arrows come toward them. As they scrape against the roof, it almost sounds like hail. She allows herself to remember winter on the steppes for a moment, allows herself to remember going out for a ride with Shefali only to be driven back to the ger once the hail started up. Shefali had torn the deel from her own back just to give Shizuka a bit of cushioning against it.

She'd always known. She'd *always* known.

To the left, the *Wing* readies. A creak of rope, a screech of wood—the stones fly through the air to the northeast, batting away the arrows as they go—and then sink into the water without hitting anything at all.

The flute's back. There is the strange melody, there is the prickling at the back of Shizuka's neck. The *Ambition* turns toward the arrows to allow the cannons to fire.

The deck rumbles beneath her; the air smells of pitch and fire. She plugs her ears just before the explosion.

Just before the arrows at last find their purchase.

Through the signalbearer's window come most of them—five that land in the boy's back and send him crumpling forward. Two come in through the thin windows somehow, one landing in someone's leg. The second sailor takes an arrow to the throat and sinks to the deck clutching at the wound. He's trying to stop the bleeding but it won't work, it won't work.

Shizuka's mouth goes dry.

What horrifies her is not seeing them die, what horrifies her is how little sorrow she feels.

When did this become mundane to her? For her first thought on seeing the boy go facedown is that someone should plug up the window, not that he had his whole life ahead of him.

Not that he is here only because of her.

This person she is becoming—is she a person at all, or just a husk of one? How many times can she wander into war like this before something in her dies?

Two sailors rush to the boy and move his body out of the way.

"Did the cannons hit?" she asks, since no one is keen on telling her.

Munenori answers, his voice steady in spite of his own building worries. "No, Your Majesty. *Wing*'s approaching them, or where we think they are; we're following."

Without the signalbearer, there won't be any way to communicate, will there?

She swallows, holds on to the wall as the ship turns once more. Once they've turned, the arrows are less of a worry—the two that slipped through the slits were an exception. They'll be all right now. She tells herself they'll be all right now.

The man with the arrow in his throat dies as they close distance with the *Wing*. She will think of something to say for him and the boy once this is all over with.

Up ahead the Teeth are jutting out of the ocean. Trin's ship, the *Fragrant Mist*, is as close to them as anyone might dare to get. That is youth for you, she supposes; he is swinging in from the west to try to pincer the enemy against the rocks.

The enemy that they still can't see.

If this keeps up . . .

Her eyes go to the window. Baozhai told her to be safe. Shefali told her to take care of herself. She shouldn't consider what's obviously a foolish option.

But if this keeps up, well. Someone is going to have to cut through the veil the enemy's using, and Shizuka is the only woman on board with a magic sword.

The *Wing* readies again, now that they're closer. Shizuka holds tight to the wall—

Another explosion rocks the ship, and this time it isn't coming from below decks. Again the *Ambition* teeters over; Shizuka dangles for a moment from the wall, her arms and shoulders straining to hold her own weight. She can't see for all the wood flying through the air—but there's nothing to stop her hearing. Wails hit her, wails and screams.

"Get down!"

"He's . . . He's in two pieces!"

She is one of the luckier ones.

For this time, it is clear what caused the explosion.

Were she not seeing it with her own eyes, she wouldn't believe it was there: a sickle wide as twenty men, the body of it a strange gleaming black, the blade a shining silver. The chain at the end of it is the same shade of black—and it is just as wide, wider than any Shizuka has ever seen. Somehow the thing punched through the hull of the *Ambition;* somehow it's cut through ten sailors already. Blood coats the decks as they call out for help.

Unfortunately, the healer is among those wounded. Shizuka sees him over by the man who ate the arrow—the sickle sliced into him the way a hungry soldier cuts into their meat.

The air smells of death and sea salt and she can hardly breathe at all—but she has to think. This isn't the worst she's ever seen. To lose herself to the horror of it is to doom all of them. She is a Minami, she is a god, and the water is the only thing that frightens her here. Not the enemy.

She eyes the sickle as they return to their normal positioning, as she can once more stand on her own two feet.

All around her the sailors are panicking. They need a symbol. She will give them one.

She draws the Daybreak Blade in one fluid movement. In five steps she reaches the sickle, reaches the chain.

To her left the ocean roars—but it is nothing compared to her. This fire within her—she feeds the sword only a little of it, and she makes her cut.

She expects a little resistance. She expects that it will hurt her shoulders to do this. She expects any number of things, except for the sword's failing to cut through the chain.

Yet that is exactly what happens—the Daybreak Blade crashes against the metal and bounces off, creating a sea of sparks but not cutting through, not cutting through.

What?

But that is impossible; the Daybreak Blade cuts through thick layers of armor with no issue, it cuts through solid stone, it cuts through *jade*.

And she hasn't severed the chain?

Is it something she did?

She hardly has time to think about it—whoever is on the other end of the chain yanks it back. Only by dropping chest to the ground does she avoid getting sliced in half as it flies back to its owner, tearing open the hull as it goes. Thankfully it's only the top deck, thankfully water isn't coming in, but they're open to the next wave of arrows now.

Munenori's swearing behind her.

The sword in her hand hums. As the sea rages outside, the sword is the only thing keeping her calm: the warmth of it, the brightness of it. All her life the Daybreak Blade has felt like an extension of herself.

And yet it couldn't . . .

She must have cut wrong.

That's it—she must have used the wrong cut.

She won't make that mistake next time. There isn't any space to. Her next cut has to be perfect.

It's going to have to be her, isn't it? For the *Wing* doesn't know where to shoot, and the *Fog* hasn't rammed into anything at all. If she waits much longer, if the sickle comes again, they may not have many sailors left aboard the *Ambition*.

It's going to have to be her.

At that moment, Minami Shizuka's soul is as weary as it has ever been. She didn't want it to go this way. She had wanted to win this battle with her ships and her soldiers; why did she ever think that was possible? Chen Luoyi's first rule of war is to know your enemy. Shizuka knew the Traitor's forces wouldn't play fair, and so why had she bothered?

It was always going to have to be her.

Guilt is a blade she's swallowed. Will she ever learn?

She sheathes the sword. Climbing up onto the roof will be hard enough without one of her hands full. One step, two. She makes her way to where the window once was, where the signalbearer climbed up and out.

In the dark it is harder to tell where the sea ends and where the sky begins; she chooses to believe that the whole world outside the ship is sky. They are sailing through the river of stars now, fearless explorers confronted with unthinkable evil.

"Your Majesty," says Munenori. "I have absolute faith in you. You know this."

When did he get here? Perhaps he sees where she is going, perhaps he has some idea what she is about to do. Well. If he means to stop her, he isn't going to be successful. Shizuka's already made up her mind.

"I do. That is why I trust you to capitalize on the opportunity I am about to create."

"Well," he says, "if you told me, perhaps, what to expect—"

"They're hiding," says Shizuka. She is at the edge now. One wrong step or one more rock will send her falling into the sea. She's dizzy, but she holds on to what remains of the hull here to pretend otherwise. "I'm going to cut through their disguise, that is all. The combat itself I leave to you and Captain Dai."

"Cut through their disguise . . . ," repeats Munenori. "You're going . . ."

Shizuka nods. She doesn't want to say it either, but if she's on the roof, perhaps the next sickle will head straight for her. Perhaps they can avoid any more unnecessary death.

She is gambling her life on this word, "perhaps," but it is better than gambling with others'.

"Munenori-zul," she says, swallowing. "If I should fall—"

"You won't," he says.

"All the same, if I should—promise you will throw me rope. I . . . I cannot drown twice."

He bows deeply. "If you fall, I'll fish you out myself," he says. "Do you need help getting up there?"

Shizuka sees now the hooks the boy used to pull himself up. What a strong grip he must have had—if she falters, she will slip, and if she slips . . .

Munenori will throw her rope, he said. And she cannot die here in Nishikomi so far from her wife. No matter how stupid this plan is.

"No," she says.

One step toward the window, two. Should she remove her armor? It will be harder to haul herself up if she doesn't, but if the enemy fires at her—she's promised Baozhai she'd be safe, she's promised Shefali she will take care of herself. Armor it is—even if it won't help if the sickle comes for her.

She hopes it doesn't. Shizuka has never believed in the old gods, but she wishes she did now, for she wants to pray and there is no one to hear her. Her parents can't grant her their protection, only their approval, and she knows they wouldn't approve of this.

She doesn't want the sickle to come for her. She doesn't want to fall into the ocean. She doesn't want to *die*. She wants to be with Shefali somewhere the two of them can roam like wild horses, somewhere they can be together as two pine needles. No matter what the old gods have to say, she has always had Shefali.

But that is the thought of the woman, and not the god. Her desires are no longer her own—and there are prayers she cannot leave unanswered.

The window is open before her. So close as Shizuka is, it's impossible to mistake the churning black sea for the shimmering sky. In the foam she sees Daishi, the cousin she slew with her own hands; in the bubbles she sees Mizuha, the creature that compelled her to such foul ends.

If she hesitates, she is lost.

Minami Shizuka hauls herself up through the window. Fortunately, as she clings for her dear life to the hooks the signalbearer used so easily, the sea is beneath her. She can't see it, only hear it, and the sound isn't so bad as the sight. She flails a little, clinging to the hook, and finds there is one near her foot. That small amount of stability transfers to her mood. She holds on and she does not fall, and she thinks to herself that she can do this thing.

Another hook is jammed into the roof two handspans away. Shizuka sucks in a breath and reaches for it. At the same time, she hauls up her leg to the hook her hand had previously occupied.

One step up.

This isn't so bad as she thought it would be. Like climbing a mountain, except that she's never been the sort of woman who does that for fun. She wouldn't need to now. The *Ambition* towers over the water; its summit a sight greater than Grandfather's Crown.

All she must do is continue climbing.

She reaches for the next hook, pulls herself up, replaces her leg—

Treachery! Her boot slips on the sea-slick wood. Only her grip on the new hook keeps her from dropping into the deep—and a single hook is not meant to support a person for long. Already it creaks with the weight of her.

Do not look down. If she looks down, she is lost.

She sucks in a breath and swings her body toward the foot-hook. After an eternal moment, she finds her footing. For a hundred beats of her hummingbird heart, she stays there, clinging to the two hooks.

But she cannot stay there forever.

So she pulls herself up again—careful this time. Precise. There are only two more left. She thinks of them as upstart nobles' sons trying to duel her for her hand.

One stroke is all it takes to fell them. One pull.

At last her fingers meet the roof. Two final hooks and she will be on the roof.

Two final hooks and she will see the ocean.

She pulls herself up—and then almost falls back. Yes, that is the sea before her, endless and all-consuming; the infinite ocean! So massive is it that it fills her vision then, end to end, and suddenly the sky is not the sky, it is only the sea, only the sea—

She's going to fall in. She can feel it already. It's in the air. The salt's going to dry her out from the inside and then the sea will fill her and she will no longer be herself, no longer Minami Shizuka—

The melody starts. A single note, played on flute, pierces through the crashing of the waves. Another follows and pierces through the haze of her fear.

The enemy is here.

And she is on her knees atop the *Ambition,* afraid to face them.

But she was afraid when she faced the tigers, she was afraid when she dueled Leng, afraid when she dueled the suitors. Fear is her second-oldest friend. She knows this heartbeat as she knows her mother's voice; she knows this ragged breathing as she knows the halls of the Jade Palace.

One step, two. Shizuka stands on the rolling ship. Fear's left her dizzy; the world feels like an inkwash painting she's blustered into.

But that is all right, that will be all right; once she's spotted the enemy, she can go back into the ship, where it is safe.

Or safer, at least.

She reaches for her mother's sword. A flash of gold, a torch against the night—warmth creeps up her arm as she holds it. The fire within her is burning now, brighter with every passing second. No ocean can dream of extinguishing it, of extinguishing her, of extinguishing the Phoenix Empress.

Where are they?

She scans the horizon as the melody climbs toward its climax. Only sky meets her, only the sea, only—

There! A single spot where the stars do not shine, a single patch of unadorned black.

How far is it?

Does distance matter to a god?

Four years ago she found perfect peace on the banks of the Kirin. As she closes her eyes now, she sets out to hunt it once more—but peace is a wily hare, running where it will, burrowing into the ground when you come near to it. For twenty breaths she chases after it.

But the hare eludes her.

A wave like rampaging bulls knocks into the ship. Shizuka slides on the roof, scrambling to regain her footing. In this she fails—she falls to the ground. Were it not for her armor, she'd have bruised her thigh. Still, there is no real wound except her pride, no real harm done except that her clothes are wet.

Heavy and cold, they are. Her tunic is slapping against her sides. She's beginning to shiver.

No. Not now. Her mother's sword is in her hand; she wears the Phoenix mask. She cannot fail.

She grits her teeth, closes her eyes once more.

The hare hides in a grove of flowers. She sees its ears poking up through the peonies and she laughs, for it is such a silly sight—what is it doing in there? Why not hide somewhere better? All she has to do is call to the peonies and they answer, their vines closing around the hare like a gentle hand. The hand carries the hare to her and she reaches out, grabs it—

Peonies. Of course. She'd always loved them.

They sink into her flesh and she sinks into their tangle.

And soon she can feel the threads again. So many of them! As the threads of a loom are the prayers of the Empire. There are so many weaving together so quickly that she cannot hear them all. Part of her—the flesh of her, kneeling on the roof—regrets that she doesn't have the time to tend to them all.

But the god knows there will be time later.

And she is a god now. Jade and gold her blood; peony-soft her skin. There is a fire within her that she does not understand and does not need to understand: it is a force as gravity is a force; it is eternal as the stars are eternal; it is bright and unconquerable and proud, so proud—

She has always been this woman. She will always be this woman, this fire.

There. Now that she has shed her eyes, she can see them clearly: the stolen ships of Iwa, cloaked in the Traitor's darkness. Forty of them, if she does not miss her guess (and she is not really guessing), and a mixed fleet at that. There are two floating Axion castles, two dozen Hokkaran ships she has seen only in illustrations, one dozen Doanese ships, and two so strange she cannot imagine whence they've come. The two stranger ones are clad all over in metal.

Aboard one of the floating castles is the demon playing the flute. It sits atop the mast, legs crossed beneath it, swinging its feet as it plays. Sayaka was right—its nose is abnormally long and pitted. Atop its head are two stubby horns, like those of a young goat. White, its beard, so fluffy and massive that it looks as if a cloud has consumed the thing's face.

How clearly she can see it! But she must see it clearer still. In her ethereal form, she holds aloft her phantom sword.

One cut is all it takes her.

She sees the burning arc fly into the sky; she sees it burst and fall like burning snow onto the ships of the enemy. Wherever a mote of conjured light lands, a fire is sure to follow. Already the sailors are scrambling to put out the flames.

But these are no normal flames, birthed by no normal woman. As one the sailors move, throwing water onto the largest flame—and to the water Shizuka simply says, *No, you shall not consume me.*

Hotter she burns and hotter the flames on the ships. Her blood sings at the sight. How tall the flames are! Like pillars to the gods they rise, rise, rise—swirling like blown glass, reaching for the heavens! Within moments the ships are only memories, within moments they are cinder and ash swallowed by the boiling sea, within moments . . .

How has she ever been afraid of the sea? For it bows to her now, as it well should. As the demon well should.

But in the chaos, it leaped to the metal ship; in the chaos, it has traded its flute for the chain, and the chain—

Something's tugging at her throat.

A thread?

No, it cannot be a thread; she hardly feels those, and this is pinching at her skin, this is wrapping tight around her, around not just her throat but her body, too. Soon she cannot raise her hands at all; soon her skin is alight with pain.

A sharp yank sends her reeling backwards, and it is only then she realizes what has happened.

For it is then that her head snaps back and she sees the demon's chain wrapped about her body. Then she sees that it is no normal chain at all, but one cast from gleaming black metal. Steam is coming off her body in thick tendrils.

No.

Nonononono.

"A beginner's mistake, Four-Petal," says the demon. "Never leave yourself unprotected."

It steps on the chain and she sees herself fall into the deep. How quickly she sinks, how quickly beneath—and now, though she has no lungs in this form, they are filling with water and she is screaming, screaming—

The chains tighten around her.

With the last gasps of clarity she has, she calls another pillar of flame. Orange and red and gold consume her; the sea beneath her boils and boils. If she burns hot enough, if she burns bright enough—

The chains aren't burning.

The chains *aren't burning.*

Needles in the back of her neck, needles in her throat.

She said she'd be safe. She said she'd be safe and now her body is somewhere in the middle of the ocean and she's . . .

Why does she feel so cold?

No, she knows this feeling and she hates it, she won't let it triumph over her, she won't—

"The Eternal King would like to have a word with you," says the demon. "Aren't you lucky?"

# MINAMI SAKURA

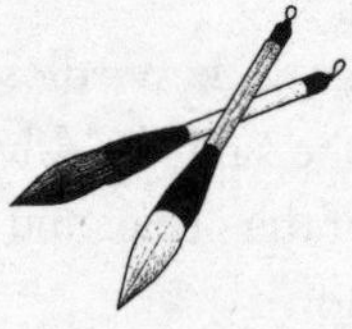

## THREE

Nishikomi is the sort of city you never really leave. Like a dyer's hands are always stained, so is the soul of someone raised in the Queen of Cities.

This is not to say that Nishikomi is as splendid as Fujino. It isn't. The sheer amount of people packed like ants into every crevice and corner of the place sees to that. There are streets you just don't go down—not because they are dangerous, but because that's where everyone leaves their trash.

The dangerous streets are a different business altogether. Any native knows what to look out for—the dripping paint icons of this gang or that, the shift in colors from one neighborhood to the next.

Sakura's known these signs and portents for as long as she can remember. Maneater Matsutake's gang runs the area around the Shrine of Jade Secrets. They came to the shrine three or four times a week, clad in brownish red. Most of the time they didn't cause any trouble—just asked for their cut of the profits, stayed for a couple of drinks, and fucked off. Despite the frightening name, Matsutake knew a happy pleasure house brought in the best customers.

And they thought it was really funny, too, having a kid in a place like that. When Sakura was younger, they'd always have treats for her. They called her Jade-lun. Her real name never mattered much—and maybe it was better, in the long run, if they didn't know it. Most of her memories from childhood involve those people in some way or another—saving her from getting into fights, babysitting when her mother sent her out on errands.

It was one of Matsutake's people who gave Sakura her first set of paints. Nice paints, too. His name was Juzo, and he had a flat look behind his eyes, as if there was something he was desperately trying not to think about. The morning of the Sister's Festival, he stopped by the shrine with a roll of half-decent paper in one hand and a tray of colorful ink blocks in the other.

He called her over, and she hobbled right for him, and when he put the brush in her hand, she was so happy she almost fell over.

"Look," he said. She did. She watched him as he ground the ink and mixed it, as he dipped the brush in the mixture and held it above the paper. Two drops of red fell from the tip of the brush; she watched, wide eyed, as they grew and grew.

Juzo guided her hand, painting a hungry red mouth. Five white teeth—two fangs on the bottom, and three on top—waited to bite at whatever was unfortunate enough to get caught between them.

"As long as you see this," he said, "you're safe."

He probably meant for it to be reassuring—for her to look for that symbol wherever she went in the city. She did.

But whenever she was nervous, she took to drawing it, too. After all, so long as she could see it, she was safe.

Things like that get stuck in the swamp water of your soul. When she first boarded the ship to Xian-Lai, she drew that shape in all her sketchbooks; while she awaited Shefali's reading of the letter, she drew hungry mouths in all her margins.

And she finds herself drawing it now, looking out on five columns of fire in the bay. So bright do they burn that she cannot stand to look at them for long—to do so leaves columns of violet-green in her vision.

She'd promised Baozhai that she'd look after her cousin.

And where is she instead?

On the top floor of her mother's pleasure house.

An awful quiet has seized the place. She does not need to be downstairs to know that the girls have all pressed themselves against the windows. The braver ones, anyway. Those more cautiously inclined will hide behind whatever is available, waiting for the news that it is safe.

Which is Sakura?

She came to Nishikomi, it's true, and she had every intent of going to see her cousin. Of being with her, the way she'd so selfishly asked, back in Xian-Lai. That is a brave enough thing, isn't it? Once all this is over, she can have one of the soldiers downstairs take her to wherever the *Heavenly Ambition* is docking. Shizuka will be surprised to see her, they'll embrace, and she could continue on this insane warpath with a clear conscience.

This is a battle she can safely observe—not one she has to involve herself in.

That was her reasoning.

But—well.

Sakura knows her cousin. This is the first time she's seen a . . . *display* of this caliber, but it is not the first time she's seen one at all. Shizuka's lit herself on fire more times than Sakura cares to count; she's reached into a bonfire to fetch her scalding sake cup. Minor things—but godly all the same. A strange sense of wonder has always filled her watching Shizuka do such things—wonder mingled with worry.

This is different.

There's hardly any wonder at all.

When she glances down at her paper, it is covered in Matsutake's mouths—the white like the marbling on a fine steak. Downstairs she hears someone—probably Momo—trying to soothe everyone's nerves with the biwa. The gentle swell of the music only makes the roaring columns of fire all the more egregious.

Sakura forces herself to look at them—to really look at them. The scholar's part of her mind tries to take in the details. How wide are they? What is their exact color? Is this true fire, or only a facsimile? No, no, it must be true fire—look at how the ocean is steaming.

Five columns. Two distant pyres, too, though those are much smaller and easily explained away as sinking ships. The columns are at least three times as wide, reaching like a desperate hand up, up, up into the night sky. . . .

But why only five?

She taps the end of her brush against the table, sets the brush down, and stands.

It doesn't make sense. It doesn't. And the thought that wanders through her mind is worse than nonsensical—it's outright stupid. She doesn't want to indulge it, doesn't want to leave out any food for it, but as she paces the room, it comes to her again and again, mewling for its supper.

*You promised you'd keep an eye on her.*

And she'll be fine, won't she? She's always fine. Killed-a-demon-at-sixteen-shal, that was O-Shizuka.

Screamed the first time Sakura tried to get her to take a bath when she got back from war, too. That was also O-Shizuka.

And now she's out on the water, and there are five columns of fire, but only five. . . .

Before Sakura knows to stop herself, she's headed downstairs. Just as imagined, there are two groups—those by the windows and those who have upturned the tables to hide behind. The latter group stares at her as she walks by.

"Are you crazy?" calls Tsubaki.

Sakura's not sure how to answer. Maybe she is. If she stops to think about this, she's going to change her mind—though she won't yet admit to herself the decision she's made. Instead of indulging Tsubaki, she keeps headed straight for the door, hopping over dropped instruments and scrolls alike.

Scrolls. Half the girls here can't even read. She idly wonders what secrets those props might hold, and decides that if she lives out the night, she might come back to find out.

Sakura hops up the two steps near the door. Her shoes are waiting for her—absurdly high and absolutely not practical on the best of days. She steps into them anyway.

"You can't be serious," says Kaede, one of the older women who has, by custom, changed her name away from a flower's. "You're going out there? Sa-lun, who knows what's going to happen out there!"

"Didn't I tell you I'm a scholar now?" Sakura answers. "I'm the fucking idiot who's got to write it all down for people."

Kaede puffs, but if she has anything else to say, she's wise enough to keep it to herself. Sakura turns and offers her a quick bow before heading onto the street. Death looming or not, you had to be kind to your elders.

All her life, the streets of Nishikomi have been packed like salmon roe. Tonight is no exception. Orange light paints the faces of awestruck onlookers. She has to push and elbow her way through the crowd. No one can see that she's wearing Imperial Gold in the dark. No one would care even if they could.

"Is that her?"

"Heard about the Wall, thought Toriko was jokin' . . ."

"Who's she fighting?"

"Nice to see she's gotten off her ass for once."

The comments and whispers build up the closer she gets to the bay. The shrine isn't very far to begin with—most of their clientele are sailors. A trip that would take five minutes on any other day is taking fifteen now.

Things get worse when she reaches the docks.

That's where the infantry is waiting, after all—eight companies of the Dragon Guard in their gleaming armor, standing at attention, their spears swaying in the sea breeze. Each company bears a banner with their adopted name and motto. Sakura used to wonder when she was a child what war banners said.

Now she knows they say things like "Duty is a mountain."

The soldiers, of course, are not keen to let her pass. The first step she takes on wood and not dirt is met with a guardsman ramming his spear into the ground before her.

"By order of Her Imperial Majesty, the Most Serene Phoenix Empress—"

All members of the Dragon Guard must stand at least seventeen hands tall. Sakura barely makes it to fifteen. That does not stop her from shoving the fully armored man in front of her.

"Yeah, yeah," she says. "Y'know, she isn't serene at all."

As he takes a stumbling step backwards, she holds up her sleeve, the golden stripe around the hem apparent. With his war mask on, she cannot see his face, but his eyes go from surprise and anger to surprise and resignation. He bows.

"After you, my lady," he says.

Clearly, he has no idea who she is. That's all right with her. She never asked to be recognized, and it's probably better if she isn't.

"What's the situation?" she asks. She does not stop, but she does gesture for this soldier to follow her. She doesn't feel like explaining herself more than once—having a visible escort will make her look more important.

"Two ships down," he says. "Doanese, both of them. The *Ambition* still stands, but . . ."

"But?" Sakura says. She squints. Five columns burning, but there is something else, too. She sees it only when the waves hit the docks, glittering between the drops of sea spray.

A chain?

"But we can't know how long that's going to last," says the soldier. He points to the top of the *Ambition*. She follows his finger, but it isn't until she squints that she sees it: there's someone sitting on the roof of the ship, illuminated by a faint carmine glow; an arc of solid white lies within arm's reach.

Shizuka.

That's her cousin, sitting on top of a ship, channeling the columns of fire.

*Shit.* How is she managing? How is she—? There's open sea around her, how is she not panicking?

"That's her," Sakura says.

The soldier nods. "That's our Empress," he says. The reverence in his tone at a time like this does not escape her; she hopes he is not the sort of man who buys miniature woodcuts of Shizuka's likeness. "We're not sure what she's doing up there, or how long it will take, but when the columns flare, we can see the enemy. There's fewer of them each time. She's doing it—can you believe it?"

"I can," says Sakura. She doesn't want to, but she can.

As they reach the edge of the docks, she takes a deep breath. The salty air of home fills her lungs. She wonders how she went so long without tasting salt every time she breathed, how she ever imagined she might live anywhere but here. In the rush of the waters against the Father's Teeth, against the sand, against the docks, she hears the voice of her childhood: *This is where you have always belonged.*

"Do you think it's hard for her?" the soldier says. "However she does it. If I could control fire like that, I'd make a weapon out of it. Use a spear of flame and you don't have to worry about contamination . . ."

Who hired him, and why? Just because he's tall and broad shouldered; just because he can look intimidating holding a spear? To be mooning over a woman when she's single-handedly saving the Empire—

A wave of pure heat slams into Sakura, passing as quickly as it appeared. The lights flare brighter than dawn; she must avert her eyes if she wants to keep her vision.

"That's the flare I was telling you about," he says. "Always kicked myself for being born too late to meet any of the Heavenly Family, but just look at her go. . . ."

Sakura looks up, all right.

Just in time to watch her cousin tumble from the top of the ship into the water.

She doesn't think of herself as a particularly brave woman.

But that's the thing about bravery—you're never certain whether you've got it until you really need it.

And watching Shizuka fall into the water, knowing full well the fear that will envelop her . . .

Well. Sakura's a Minami, after all. She was bound to do something profoundly stupid at some point.

Shoes off first. She reaches for the soldier to steady herself as the first choruses of dismay rise up from the army. Even this soldier lets out a pained whimper. He reaches out as if he's going to be able to catch her from here.

If you want something done right, you've got to do it yourself—isn't that how the old line goes?

There's no time to waste. Sakura takes the dagger from the soldier's scabbard and cuts through her outer belt. She sheds her outermost robes and, before she can think any better of it, jumps into the water.

The waters of Nishikomi are famously cold. The jolt that meets her is enough to keep her awake for the next five years. Already her heart is hammering to keep her warm, and she has not begun to kick—she is gliding now beneath the surface, her eyes closed.

It occurs to her that there might be creatures nearby. There were creatures in the Kirin, weren't there? Women with needle-teeth, that's what Shizuka said in her drunken rambles. What if they were here, too? What if she were going to die in the bay, some foul creation of evil's evening snack?

What does it matter? She's already made her choice.

Sakura begins to kick. Kelp licks at her ankles, and for a moment she fears the worst, but so long as nothing is reaching out to stop her, she shall not stop. When she breaks the surface, she sucks in the biggest breath she can. The waves crash against her, send her careening to the east.

Against her better judgment, she opens her eyes.

She sees it.

There—floating right in front of the *Ambition*—is the enemy's ship, a stately thing too large for anything but a small army to crew. Shiratori Palace is not so large as this floating monstrosity.

And what is that she hears? A flute? That melody—she knows this song and yet she can attach to it neither name nor lyric. Hearing it is like stepping into a bear trap—she stops moving to better discern the melody. The longer she stays there, bobbing in the wild bay, the heavier grow her limbs. How mournful, this melody; how like the lament of the dying! Her eyes are drooping, drooping; the light of the columns grows dimmer and dimmer. . . .

Why did she come out here again?

All she wants to do is float. All she needs to do is float. Who cares about anything else? The worries of the day cannot reach her here. The cold is refreshing, isn't it? How it numbs her to her pain and her worries. Like Blessing it comes over her, like Blessing.

Her eyelids droop.

*Close your eyes,* the melody sings to her.

But—what is that?

Beneath the surface of the water, glimmering like a carp—what is that? For it is glowing, pulsing, and it looks so familiar—

*Shizuka!*

At once it comes back to her. Sakura has come out here to save her idiot cousin. That music must be one of the enemy's schemes. She can't let herself fall for it!

It is like forcing yourself awake, like forcing yourself to leave the warm paradise of your sheets. What will it takes her, what motivation! Yet this is a woman who left her life behind for the sake of another, a woman who learned to read not only in her own native language but in three others besides, a woman who has proved again and again that she is not so soft as her name might suggest.

Sakura shall not be defeated by a song.

The waters begin to boil around her. If she's going to save her cousin, she doesn't have much time to do it.

"I don't know who or where you are," she shouts, "but you can fuck right off!"

Having said her piece, she takes in a breath and dives. Dark and churning, the waters, though here and there she sees the glimmer she saw ashore. Its shape is easier to discern when there's algae swirling around it—a chain.

Well. She hopes Shizuka can deal with it when she wakes up.

Is it providence that she has not sunk too far, or is it something in her godly nature? Whatever it is, Sakura won't question it. Her lungs are burning enough already. There is her cousin, still clad head to toe in her gods-damned armor, in the grip of an unseen chain.

How long does Sakura have? Seconds, perhaps.

Best to use them.

Yet the moment she reaches for Shizuka, Sakura finds that her Imperial Cousin has started to glow.

And this is not the glow of fireflies on a summer night, not the glow of a lantern boldly lit in the room of a married lover; this is the light of day. These are the rays of the sun crowning the Tokuma mountains. It hurts to look at her, it hurts to be near her—and yet Sakura cannot look away, not even with light and water alike searing her eyes.

The sea itself boils around the nascent god. Sakura throws up her arms out of reflex. Her lungs are burning; she cannot, cannot look away.

For look! There—wrapped about her is the cloak of Heaven itself! A strip of golden flame the width of Sakura's forearm, there is no mistaking what it is and what it signifies.

Her cousin, the god.

And it is not the only thing to suddenly appear: flames consume the armor she wears, leaving bright gold in their wake; a crown of fire boils the water around her head; gold chases the scar across her face, like a streak on mended pottery.

Sakura kicks at the water around her, desperate to stay down here, desperate to watch. Hotter and hotter the chain around her cousin, hotter and hotter, until it too glows a searing white.

*Come on, wake up,* she thinks, but she knows that it's a foregone conclusion: no one wakes an Empress before she is ready, let alone a god. How difficult it is to keep focus. More than anything, she wants to *breathe*—her body is fighting her with every passing heartbeat. To keep from sucking in a lungful of air takes nearly all her attention.

But the chains are about to break now, she is sure of it, and Sakura must be here when Shizuka opens her eyes; she must see the birth of a new god—her cousin!—play out in full. And yet her cousin Shizuka is trapped, still not moving, even as her body undergoes this transformation.

Sakura kicks her way over to Shizuka, every movement a war against her own waning strength. The heat coming off the chains is enough to singe her if she comes too close to touching it—how is she meant to help?

Salt stings at her eyes; her lips are starting to go numb. Nevertheless, Minami Sakura grabs hold of the god by the shoulders and pulls. To her surprise the metal gives instantly, bending like a drunk doubled over in an alley.

*When you wake up,* Sakura thinks, *I'm never going to let you hear the end of it.* Wearing a full suit of armor to a naval battle? What sort of idiot was she? Divine sense is no match for common. How is Sakura going to get her up to the surface like this?

Gods, Shizuka's going to owe her one if they get out of this.

If.

Closer, closer still—kicking is difficult when it feels as if there are iron weights clasped to her ankles. Her lungs burn and it occurs to her in another awful whisper that she could already have surfaced if it weren't for her cargo.

Brushing that thought aside takes too much of her attention.

She opens her mouth to argue and the water rushes in. Fear and panic overwhelm her—she does not think to spit it out, does not think to suppress the urge to breathe. Into her lungs, the water, the water; filling her and suffocating her.

Her vision is starting to blur. Above her is the brilliant light of her cousin.

With whatever power remains to her, Sakura pushes.

Five columns of burning light. Darkness encroaches upon her, yet still those columns burn.

*I swear, if you die . . . ,* Sakura thinks, but it is too much effort to finish the thought.

The water's starting to carry her down. Again, she feels heavy; again, she feels light. All her worries are there, above the surface. If she only sinks, then the sea will carry her far, far—

There—a lance piercing the dark! White as a midnight snow, brighter even than the columns! Its arrival churns the waters. Sakura expects to see the boiling start, but it doesn't—the lance seems to be, somehow, cool to the touch.

She is so far gone by then that it is difficult to think of anything, in the common sense. She does not think to herself that she should grab hold of it—only that it is strange and beautiful, and she should like to know what it feels like.

Her hand closes around the lance.

Like a fish cruelly yanked from the water—Sakura flying up to the surface. Flat on her back, she lands, the air and water alike knocked out of her from the impact alone. Instinct drives her to turn, to cough, to hack out all the rest.

It is then—when she at last forces her eyes open—that she sees the Phoenix.

# O-SHIZUKA

## FOUR

She dreams that she is in a cavern. A true cavern, and not the small caves that dot the seaside here in Nishikomi. This place is more than that. The walls, smooth and slick black, reflect the light of her mother's sword.

In the distance, there is music.

The melody's familiar. Simple, as all the old songs are; a three-note rise and one-note stumble; a two-note recovery and a one-note smirk. The girl who races ahead of the clan atop her gray mare, the girl who can pluck a coin from the ground without dismounting, the girl who can draw a bow no two men can draw together—this is her song.

Her wife's song.

Reaching the source of it is her only thought—surely, her wife will be waiting for her there.

Deeper she wanders. The darkness, too, deepens. Her mother's sword is a beam of sunlight even here—wherever *here* is. The farther in she goes, the brighter the sword burns.

Fifty-five steps in, she stops.

The melody's changing. Faster now, as if whoever is playing the unseen fiddle means for the listener to dance.

Something bruised her shoulders; something crushed her ribs.

She does not want to dance.

The sword heats up in her hands. Faster, the music, faster still, until the stumbling fourth note is quick as a stone skipping across the water. Blood rushes between her ears. She feels it welling up behind her eyes, feels it pressing against her skin from the inside—gold and jade and fire.

Her blood, his blood.

Drawing in a breath is harder than it should be. She is conscious—now that the music is racing so—of something caught in her throat, something that keeps the air from reaching her lungs.

Unseen hands twist a songbird's neck. The music stops.

Of all the silences Shizuka has known in her life, this is surely the worst—there is no air here, after all, and she cannot even hear her own heartbeat. The rush of her blood is all that is there to comfort her.

And what comfort is she meant to find there?

She draws a breath, another, another—all three stop at her throat.

This place—doesn't it smell familiar? Doesn't it look familiar—like somewhere she's been before, with Shefali, somewhere she's forgotten . . .

She closes her eyes.

When she opens them, the woman in the fox mask stands before her. How many years has it been since their last meeting? Shizuka wore an acolyte's robes then, and for a moment she feels their roughness against her skin. The darkness of the cavern does little to hide the horror of the other woman's scarring—the thick seams where flesh meets bronze, her hands dappled with red. White robes replace the armor she wore in Xian-Lai.

But her eyes have not changed. Two suns, encased in amber, burn within the holes of the mask.

"You have a choice to make," she says.

Shizuka's natural inclination is, of course, to argue with her. She is the Phoenix Empress, she is the Daughter of Heaven, she is a trueborn heir of the Minami line—she may go wherever she pleases, and may the dead gods strike her down if they have any feelings on the matter.

But she has the feeling she's speaking to one of them now—or at least someone who knows them well.

This inclination dissolves away like ink in water when the music begins again.

For this melody—this melody is as well known to her as her own name.

A languid rise, a yearning fall.

She is standing outside Fujino, looking toward the palace . . .

*View from Rolling Hills.*

Yes. She knows exactly where she is now. Her mother always warned Shizuka that she'd end up here. How foolish of her not to have realized sooner. If she'd wandered much farther in, she'd break all her promises.

The woman in the fox mask unbelts her sword, which was not there a moment ago. A single sharp note rings as the woman draws it from its home; the blade shines a brilliant gold. She holds it across the palms of both hands as she sinks down to the ground, laying the sword there like an offering.

"If I take it?" says Shizuka. It is her mother's own sword: a pure white sheath chased with gold. When she looks down, it is no longer in her own hands, no longer at her own waist.

"Then this is as far as you go," says the woman. "But you must grasp it by the blade."

There it is once more: her natural inclination to argue. "If I take it by the handle?"

The fox-woman's eyes narrow. Shizuka knows precisely that look—and it is painful to recognize it. "To wield a sword is to be cut by it, one way or another. You must accept that if you are to take it."

She wants to ask. She wants to voice it, this conviction in her heart, this recognition. But if she does—well, this goddess has always hated recognition. "What if I leave it here?"

A pause, pregnant with the unspoken. Yes—she is sure of it, now, when she sees how the fox-woman softens. "Then you keep going."

In the end, it was no true decision. If Shizuka continues into the cavern she will leave Shefali behind, leave her people and duty behind, and that is no existence worth having.

So she kneels.

"You will suffer," says the woman.

"And I will survive," answers Shizuka. The corners of her lips turn up. "I always do, don't I?"

She reaches for the sword.

The woman grabs her by the wrist. Her grip is tight as iron and just as cool. "Are you willing to give your heart? Are you willing to give your soul?"

It hurts: the woman's grip, the desperation in her voice. It hurts, being questioned like this. "I've given both away already. Where Shefali goes, I go. It's always been as simple as that."

Another silence between the two of them. This time, it is Shizuka who slays it. "If you were in my position, you'd say the same thing. You always did."

It is then that the woman drops Shizuka's wrist. She sits up, straighter than before, the mask somehow more of a face now than ever. "You cannot take what the living say seriously," she says. "They do not know."

"I think we know well enough what we're getting ourselves into. I've been to war since I saw you last," Shizuka answers. That they're still arguing, even like this . . . "I am making this decision. I know where it leads. I know it will hurt. I know I will suffer. Still, it is my decision to make."

Once more she reaches for the sword. The fox-woman makes no move to stop her, but does close her eyes. "For the last time," she says. "Please. Please, come home."

Thirteen years of ache and twelve years of an open wound. When the sword cuts into her, Shizuka hardly feels it. "Home is among the living."

Blood slicks her skin. She cannot look at the woman in the mask anymore: she looks at her hand, instead, at the crescent scar on her palm. She expected to see it cloaked in red.

But it is gold, instead: molten gold.

The woman in the fox mask laughs once, twice: a resigned sound, but not one without pride. "The trouble with this bloodline is that we're all too much alike."

Shizuka holds up her hand. "Did you bleed gold, too?"

"One of us did," says the woman in the fox mask. "The memories start to blur, when you're like this."

What would it be like to wear that mask? To have it soldered against her skin? One day, she supposes, she will find out. "What happens next?"

"When you're ready, you leave," says the woman. "Right back the way you came. You go back to your war, and you win it, or else none of this will have mattered."

She wants to stay a little longer. She wants to talk to this woman. There are all sorts of questions she might ask, questions to which the answers will hurt more than the sword, more than her ribs, more than it hurts to breathe.

But she is needed, so she stands. So, too, does the woman.

She takes Shizuka by the shoulder. This time, her grip is looser. Shizuka stiffens, unaccustomed as she is to any sort of contact.

"When you come home," she says, "we can drink together. All of us."

Her throat aches. She shoves the sword into its sheath, and the sheath through her belt. "I don't drink anymore."

Another silence. The woman in the mask softens—before finally pulling her closer. She smells of the sea, smells of Blessing, smells of the forest and the sun.

"Remember," says the woman. "You are—"

"A swamp lily," answers Shizuka. The block in her throat is shrinking, shrinking. Her ribs ache, as if she has been coughing for some time.

The woman in the fox mask nods. "You shall not sink, so long as you allow yourself to float."

"Will I see you again?" Shizuka asks, for by then, she can see from here the black ink at the edge of the woman's wrist, the way she holds her right arm stiff at her side.

She is that woman, and she is not, and Shizuka's heart aches at the thought.

The fox does not answer.

Shizuka's fingers tingle. She doesn't dare to look down, but she can feel what is happening all the same—the threads wrapping themselves around her joints, tugging, tugging.

*You are needed,* they say.

"Please," she says. "Please, before I have to go."

The fox's eyes flare. Shizuka blinks away from the flash of light. In its afterimage, she sees a woman in a soiled bed. Another flare—a woman on her knees before the shores of Nishikomi, a sunbeam piercing through her chest.

The threads wind about her wrist so tightly that she begins to lose feeling in her fingers. Harder, they tug, harder—she takes one stumbling step backwards.

"You have to tell me!" she says. She can hear her own voice echoing off the walls of the cavern. Has she always sounded so young, so afraid?

"You said you'd . . . it would be when I was ready!"

The threads have her by the arm. They pull and pull, strong enough that she wonders if even Shefali would be able to stand against them. No matter how she digs in her heels, she cannot resist them for very long. With her remaining arm, she raises her mother's sword—

Threads wrap about her mouth, about her eyes, about her throat—

*Just one more moment, just one—*

"Listen to your father, when the time comes," says the fox.

Shizuka reaches for her, blind though she may be. The corners of her eyes sting and she feels, for a moment, as if she might be . . . as if in this place, she can . . .

A pike is cruelly yanked from the sea. Air surrounds it, filling its lungs and drying its scales, and it gasps for breath. So terrified is it of this unfathomable world that it does not even realize the hook has already pierced its mouth. It writhes and flaps uselessly, staring at the sea with glassy eyes, yearning, yearning . . .

So, too—Shizuka writhes atop the Father's Sea. Sputtering up water feels like cracking her own ribs open over and over just to empty herself out—but she does. She does. Still, the threads bind her; still they tug at her now-conscious mind.

*Whatever she's doing out there, I hope she wins. My daughter needs to see an Empress triumph.*

*Keep my sailor safe. Please, that's all I ask of you.*

*If I die saving you . . .*

No.

No, all of this is . . .

She can't hear herself think, can't focus. Where is she? Shizuka opens her eyes and wishes she hadn't. Some part of her hoped she'd been brought to shore. The rippling, glass-smooth sea beneath her tells another story.

So, too, does the blazing sword in her hand.

How did she get here? Ah yes—she fell.

Five columns of fire surround her. Their roar makes it even harder to think, harder to remember.

There is *so much,* and she can hear all of it, all of it, and—

Sky, she wants it to stop. She wants to hear herself, she wants to be herself. Her headache will kill her if this demon doesn't.

And there is a demon before her. A whole fleet of them waiting to be dealt with.

Very well—she will deal with them. The Phoenix Empress will deal with them.

But first—there is a thread right beneath her, a thread burning gold amid all the red. Shizuka—no, she has shed that name!—the Empress wills the blade of her sword to lengthen. *Cool yourself,* she tells it, and it is quick to answer.

She drives this lance into the water. The golden thread wraps itself around, and she pulls it back.

Minami Sakura flops like a pike against the water.

"You're . . . ," Sakura stammers. "You're really . . ."

But the Empress cannot afford to divide her attention much further. The Minami woman will need a place to rest, and the water—the confounded water—will not heed the Empress for much longer.

And so she dips her right hand into the murk.

"Grow," she says.

The kelp heeds her. Up and up, higher and higher, weaving itself weft through warp. In her mind she sees the platform—and soon, it floats just beneath her palm.

Shizuka's cousin is swearing up a storm—but she will live, and the kelp has sworn it shall not abandon her.

Which leaves only the ships.

Yes—she sees the creature perfectly well, sitting atop the mast of the largest ship. If she tries—if she forces herself from the constraints of this body—she can see its shock. The flute's quieted. She wonders distantly if that is because the sea has claimed the instrument.

One step forward. Another. The ocean boils beneath her feet; the flaring sun of her blade burns hotter and hotter. Five columns of fire widen and widen. She pulls them in with a thought, as if she is closing the fingers of her right hand.

Like crushing autumn leaves—crushing the ships of the enemy. Fire consumes most of them. The chunks of wood and iron and flesh that fly from her grasp she leaves to the sea.

The demon's ship lies in the center of her palm, untouched by the columns, just as the Empress wanted.

"The Fourth wishes to speak with me," she says in her voice of storms and wonders, in her voice of wildfires and thunder. She notices, in a distant way, that there are flames crowning her—that the light above her comes from a divine shroud.

In desperation, the demon reaches for its chain. Once more it sails through the sky, straight toward the Empress.

Her sword will not cut it.

But her fires might.

With a flick of her wrist, as if she were opening a fan before a suitor, the Empress speaks to her flaming shroud. *Burn,* she tells it, *consume.*

And so it does. Metal turns thick as rice porridge the moment it makes contact with her blue flames.

Still, she walks toward the demon. When she is eight steps away from the towering ship—then she runs a fingertip along the edge of her mother's sword. From orange to blue to painful white, its light.

"Listen to me—I am going to give you my message for your Traitor King."

There is a distant part of her that thinks what she is about to do is preposterous. The girl, most likely; the woman whose body she has worn for so many years; the ashes to which she will soon return. She cannot stay this way forever, she knows; her body is still mortal. It is not yet her time.

Perhaps it is preposterous—but it is necessary, too.

The Phoenix Empress falls into her duelist's stance. Shizuka takes a breath to center herself. It does little, with all the threads straining for her attention, but it is the ritual that is important.

"Tell him I am sick and tired of messengers."

With her next breath, she makes her cut.

As a bamboo cutter's axe splitting a culm—so the brilliant arc of the Empress's sword carves through the floating fortress.

As lightning striking tinder—so the Empress's flames blast the ship's hull.

For a moment, the Empress stays where she is, slightly doubled over with the force of the cut, and admires her handiwork. Truly, it is the finest cut she has ever made—quick and clean, decisive and unerring. Has there ever been a single blow that saved this many lives? For if this ship reached the shore, she shudders to imagine what it might have done to her people. Its belly was empty for a reason.

Yet her celebration does not last long. When she looks up to the mast, the demon is gone.

The Empress narrows her eyes. Is that a glimmer she sees where it once sat? The night sky there is like the wind through a gauzy black curtain; she can see it twisting.

No matter. If the thing had the sense to run, and she'd already crushed the ships, the battle's been won.

She feels no joy. It's difficult to feel anything at all, removed as she is, but she knows she *should* feel proud of herself.

Instead there is only this awful hollowness.

*Please come home,* she thinks, tracing the line of her jaw.

When she returns to her earthly form, she will gasp and tear at her hair, she will rake her nails across her face, she will cry out: *I didn't tell her how much I miss her.*

But the Phoenix Empress will not weep.

She lost that ability long ago.

## BARSALAI SHEFALI

### FOUR

"You've got the map, Soyiketu. Come on. Let's see it," says Otgar. Soyiketu—her half brother—grabs a large tube lying on top of the wardrobe. He unfurls it over the table. Shefali's seen quite a few maps in her time, but this one is more detailed than most. She hadn't known Soyiketu for a cartographer—but then, he was ten the last time Shefali saw him, and now he is a man grown, having paid his bride-price. He's going to get married during the Jubilee. Maybe Shefali will go.

At the sight of the map, Otgar punches her thin cousin so hard on the shoulder that he sways on his feet. "That's it!" she says. "That's my baby brother doing something useful!"

Shefali does not envy him. She turns her attention to his work instead. There they are at the northern edge of the Minami swamps. Half a day's ride away is Nishikomi; two days past that are the Tokuma Mountains. Shizuka and her fleet are represented by a phoenix painted in red out in the bay; the infantry by a caricature at best unkind and at worst . . . Well. She may accidentally spill ink on it later.

She ignores the drawing to focus on the mountains. Shiratori is a craggy province indeed, covered in rocky, treacherous ground; if they are going to ride to the base of the mountain, they will have to take the Azure Promise Road. Qorin horses are fast and hardy—but not so sure-footed as those little Hokkaran ponies.

The Azure Promise Road twists like a serpent in its effort to provide the safest possible journey. Fine enough for travelers, for daredevils intent on climbing the tallest peaks of Hokkaro, but awful for an army. Every bend in the road is another place they might be attacked. Shefali bites at her knuckle without thinking as she studies the map—then quickly bandages herself when she realizes she's broken skin.

Only as she's wrapping her finger does she see her mother gesturing. Otgar speaks soon after.

"Here's the snake we're dealing with," she says. "Since Hokkarans see mountains and rough ground and say, 'Let us live there where the earth hates us,' we find ourselves on this road. It'll be near impossible to defend this position—" She points to the very base of the mountain. "—and so we aren't going to try that. We're going to set up traps instead."

"Engineers setting out tonight, then?" says Auntie Dalaansuv. She's the youngest of Alshara's sisters, only five years older than Otgar. She's also in charge of every single engineer they've adopted into the clan or taught themselves.

"Try after this meal," says Otgar.

Dalaansuv grinds her teeth, shakes her head. "I wanted to do some hunting," she says.

"Why do you need to hunt?" says Ganzorig. "I fed you!"

"It's the feeling of it," says Dalaansuv. "Helps to clear my mind. Barsalai knows what I mean."

Shefali knows exactly what she means, and she also knows that Grandfather Earth has forsaken the swamp. Five days she has hunted here, and in that time, the finest thing she caught was a single deer. One. She's found *plenty* of crocodiles. She has discovered that she *hates* crocodiles, and that they are not overly fond of her.

"Don't bother," Shefali says. "Too moist here. It'll ruin your bow."

Khadiyyar nods. "Already told all my riders to leave their bows in their cases. The air here. Ugh. I'm surprised we could light a fire at all."

"Needlenose is right," says Otgar. "You shouldn't bother. And you should realize when the clan's needs are more important than your own, Auntie. We have to clear the pass of blackbloods if Barstoq's army is going to be joining us."

Dalaansuv glares at her but relents with a sigh. "Suppose you're right, Dorbentei," she says. "What'll we be needing, trapwise? Even you, dear sister, wouldn't send me off to feed the crows on my own."

Alshara smirks. Her fingers form the answer and Otgar voices it. "Would I do that to my own baby sister?"

"To your brothers, maybe," says Khadiyyar, who by all accounts didn't completely hate Shefali's two fallen uncles. She is the only sister who didn't, and at times she and Alshara butt heads over how the situation was handled.

"Our brothers deserved what they got," Otgar translates. "*They* weren't prepared. But we are. Soyiketu, the list?"

Soyiketu quietly fetches another list. He doesn't talk much. Shefali once thought perhaps he'd grow out of it, but he seems just as tight lipped as an adult. She likes him for that, and has spent more than one of these precious nights sharing kumaq with him by the fire.

Dalaansuv studies the list like a Hokkaran studying their family lineage. As she does, all her earlier hesitation melts away. Giddy as a child, she speaks. "Burqila, it says here that we're using cannons."

Alshara returns her sister's grin. Wolfish, she is. "We are," says Otgar.

"You're allowing me to use cannons again."

Alshara nods.

"For the first time since the Wall. Since you let *Khadiyya* use the cannons, and she didn't even like using them."

"They're too loud," says Khadiyya.

"Too loud?!" says Dalaansuv. "They are a wonder of engineering, Khadiyya, you cannot possibly ignore that—"

"You may use the cannons," says Otgar, reading Alshara's gestures. "When I allowed Yuichi to marry me, they made me agree I'd never use them again—but Barsatoq has allowed us, since we're facing the enemy. Fool that he is, he never made me give up the cannons themselves."

"And we've been dragging them through the Empire since," says Ganzorig. "Good we're getting some use out of them."

Even Shefali is giddy. She's seen small cannons during her travels; they are popular in Sur-Shar, where good steel is hard to come by and there isn't enough room to draw a sword. As a child she'd tried to crawl inside the cannons and Otgar had yanked her out every time. To see them in action—well. At least she is fulfilling *most* of her childhood dreams before she dies.

"But don't focus too much on them!" Otgar continues.

"You've already lost her," says Khadiyya, and it is true enough—Dalaansuv's eyes have glazed over with wonder.

"We need trebuchets, as well; we need barbed pits and trip lines. Catapults for flinging tar. Look over the list, Dalaansuv! Actually read it!"

"I will, I will," says Dalaansuv. She manages to calm down enough to turn her attention back to the map, marking off where each particular invention will go. The scent of her joy tingles in Shefali's nose.

"The rest of you," says Otgar. Alshara is signing so quickly that Shefali wonders how her cousin is keeping up. She decides the translation must not be exact. "We're keeping our plan simple, in case we've got to change it while we're out there. This river here, they call it the Kirin's Horn; there's a valley right by it a little off the road. We engage them up by the mountain and beat a retreat down the Azure Promise, turning *here*—" She points to a spot at the source of the Horn. "—where Ganzorig, Zurgaanqar, your people are in charge of digging out that trench. We head straight for the bend and turn at the last moment; they all fall into the valley. Rest of us stand up here on the ridge and fire down."

"That won't kill them," says Zurgaanqar. She says nothing about being paired with a man other than her husband. Uncle Bolodai, to whom she is married, is out hunting at the moment. Aunt Bayaansokh, Ganzorig's wife, isn't here either; she took those who didn't want to fight and brought them back to the steppes. "You remember what happened in the North when Barsalai was a girl. Arrows did nothing."

Alshara meets her daughter's eyes then, and now she is not smiling.

Shefali knows what is coming. She knows what they will ask of her. And what place does she have to refuse? It's safest this way, safest for everyone. Besides—the Mother was specific with regard to the day she'd die, and it isn't yet the first of Qurukai.

"I'll kill them," Barsalai says.

"Needlenose, you've said a lot of dumb things in your time, but that—Sky's end, that's stupid," says Otgar. She's speaking for herself now—Alshara is glaring at her.

Shefali frowns. "You know I can," she says. "More than anyone." That Otgar would doubt her even after their journey into the Womb stings.

"Just because you *can* doesn't mean you should," says Otgar. "What if we send you and some others—?"

"The other people will die," Shefali says. "Send me."

"What's gotten into you?" says Otgar. She's rounding on Shefali now, jabbing a finger in her chest. "If you throw yourself at them, they're going to throw you back at us in pieces."

"They won't," says Shefali. She stands, stares her cousin down. Otgar is speaking out of concern. Shefali knows that.

But she knows, too, that Otgar heard the words of the Mother. The first of Qurukai, and not a day before it.

The rest of the ger watches them in silence. Otgar stares right back at her, steadfast as ever. Neither of them has asked the other about what happened in the city. Otgar called her a coward then. Would she repeat that insult now?

"Burqila," says Otgar. "Tell your daughter she's being a fool."

But the answer that comes makes Otgar ruddier when she sees it. Ruddy enough that she cannot even voice it.

Instead, Khadiyyar does. "She says it's safest that way, Dorbentei. She's not happy about it either—but that's the truth of it."

Otgar, fuming, storms out of the ger. Shefali watches her go with a heavy heart. For a moment she considers going after her. Maybe if they discussed this, the two of them, she could talk some sense into her. But then again, from the look on Otgar's face, she could smoke all the Blessing in the world and still be in a fury.

And so Shefali sits back down in her mother's ger. Her aunts and her uncles are staring at her now, but that's all right.

"I'll go," she says. "The rest of you stay safe."

SHEFALI'S HEARD CANNONS before, but she's never heard them sing. That changes now. Up ahead, as the first ranks of the enemy come spilling down the mountain, Aunt Dalaansuv's cannons go off in time with an old Qorin hunting song. The majority of the Qorin, waiting at the first bend of the Azure Promise Road, cannot help but hum along.

Strange, it is, to mount and fall into formation with her aunts and uncles—but natural, too. When she fought in Ikhtar, she had no idea who was watching her back. Here there can be little doubt. Her aunts and uncles will be happy to save her if something comes at her from behind, and they'll be happy to hold it over her head for the rest of her short life. Yes, seeing Auntie Khadiyyar holding up a massive Surian crossbow is odd, but it is no more odd than seeing your favorite merchant sitting in a teahouse. On some level, Shefali has always known her family is one of warriors. They are hunters, after all, and in the end, what they are doing this night is not so different.

Well.

Maybe a bit.

You don't wear war masks during a hunt.

When she looks around her now, a menagerie is staring back at her. Wolves, mostly, but there are bears and leopards, too; there are plumed eagles and sleek kestrels. Fat Mongke's gone and killed an ibex just to add its horns to his mask. Leave it to the Qorin to decorate everything they can get their hands on.

But Shefali likes it. Each mask is unique that way. Even the wolves are decorated differently: some are painted and some carved; some are howling and some are laughing. Hokkaran war masks are all the same. If you are to face death, then why not tell death about yourself?

She tugs on her laughing fox. It's a full moon night—her favorite kind—and the air's drier up here by the mountains. Good weather for hunting, good weather for war. The bow in her hand—the bow she fashioned so long ago—hums along to the song Dalaansuv is playing them.

Otgar, of course, has started outright singing along. The others join in until the valley near them buzzes with the sound of their combined voices. Even Alshara—wearing a mask of her own angry face—signs along with the words.

Her heart's beating in time with the cannonfire now. Despite the rags she's stuffed into the fox's mouth, she can smell the clan's excitement. She lifts the mask enough to drink in the scent, to let it feed the hungry cold within her. In all the assembled Qorin, there is not a bit of fear. Anger, yes, and hatred for the enemy they will soon face—but not fear.

Good. She isn't afraid either.

They're coming down the mountain now, the blackbloods. Shefali can see them already. Like beetles, they are, the moonlight bejeweling their black carapaces. Great horns rise out from the front of them, not unlike Mongke's ibex. Hundreds of them, if Shefali does not miss her guess (and she is not really guessing). Clouds of dust and gravel follow in their wake as they stampede down the mountain, as they near the first turn. Farther up the path, in the pits the cannonballs made while landing, beetles lie crushed and squirming in pools of inky black.

Why didn't they use cannons before?

The ground is starting to rumble now, as the blackbloods approach.

Alshara holds up a hand and starts to sign.

"Three volleys," says Otgar. "Three volleys and the parting shots. Remember these were people once—aim for the head when you can."

A quiet comes over them.

"Remember you are Qorin!" says Otgar, reading Alshara's signs. "If the Traitor himself comes to face you, chop off his head and use his skull to drink your kumaq!"

The first of the beetles rounds the corner.

"Arrows!" shouts Temurin, and five thousand Qorin reach for their favorite broadheads.

"Draw!" shouts Temurin, and five thousand bows creak in ten thousand hands.

"Fire!" shouts Temurin, and five thousand arrows fly as needles through the velvet night.

There is no time to watch them land. Temurin calls for a second volley before the arrows reach their targets, and third just after that. Aunt Khadiyyar, next to Shefali, gets off only one shot with the Surian crossbow—but it's one she's proud of, for it punches through the thick carapace of a blackblood and pins it to the ground.

"Hah!" she says. "This thing *was* worth it!"

Shefali doesn't have the heart to tell her she pierced through their armor, too, with only her own bow and her arms to draw it. Perhaps because the only reason she can draw at all is Ren's medicine. The pain Shefali feels now is as a cinder to a forge. In truth it's a little intoxicating to be able to move with such ease.

With her knees, for instance, she can urge her horse to turn as the other horses do. Whereas firing a single shot once pained her to no small end she now finds herself reaching for another arrow. Her muscles ache as she draws back her bow for the fourth time, but it is only soreness. In the face of what she used to suffer, soreness is as pleasant as a spring day.

She fires her parting shot, watches it land straight in the screaming mouth of a thing that was once human, watches it writhe and bleed. Not all the arrows have landed, but they've done better than she expected—there are twoscore dead at least as they make for the second turn. As the last of the Qorin clear the turn, Otgar screams for the trebuchets.

The trebuchets don't sing as the cannons do. They creak instead, and the stones they rain down on the enemy whistle before crashing into the rough ground. Hissing and skittering soon follow as the beetles pinned beneath the rocks struggle to free themselves. Given they had time for a single trebuchet volley, only the heaviest rocks they could find were chosen.

"Parting volley!" shouts Temurin. As one, the Qorin turn and draw and fire, and Shefali wonders if this is how it felt to ride in her mother's army so many years ago. Every beetle that falls is a triumph they all share; every arrow that finds purchase belongs to them all. Beneath the laughing fox mask, she is smiling.

The third turn is upon them, the most treacherous before they reach the actual trick turn. The ground here is more gravel than earth, and if your horse isn't as sure-footed as she should be—

Shefali grips the horn as her gray whips past the turn. Otgar and her dun, too, have little trouble. Alshara has already outpaced them on her liver mare.

But Auntie Khadiyya can't get a grip on her horn in time with the crossbow in hand. When her horse skids, she loses her balance for an instant.

An instant is all it takes. She is falling now, tumbling out of her saddle as the beetles draw closer.

The practical thing to do is to leave her. That's what Alshara would do, what Alshara *does* as she continues right on down the twisting road. That it is her own sister lying there near death does not seem to bother her. Why should it? Khadiyya is the only one who did not make the turn. To stop and go back for her would slow the rest of the riders, would risk more lives.

But the heroic thing to do—the thing Shizuka would do—is to go back anyway. That she is choosing to pattern her behavior after the most foolhardy woman she knows is not lost on Shefali, but she won't be dying this day. What is the worst that can happen?

So Shefali pulls hard on her reins and twists her body. Her gray knows what she wants even though she isn't particularly happy about it; they turn from the rear of the riders and bolt straight for the fallen Khadiyya.

Barsalai hears the shouts of her clan, hears Temurin and Otgar telling her she's being an idiot, and ignores them. To do so is a forbidden thrill. At least it is not her mother calling her an idiot—she doesn't know if she could do this if her mother told her to stay.

But she's doing it now, and she understands all of a sudden why Shizuka insists on doing things like this. Facing down hundreds of beetles hungry for her flesh, making hairpin turns, swinging from her saddle and scooping up Khadiyya—she *understands* as her heart hammers in her ears.

This is why Shizuka always said they would be gods one day.

The beetles are less than a horselength away now, with Alsha galloping as fast as she can. Up ahead of them, the Qorin are nearing the fourth and final turn, the turn that is not a turn. Khadiyya settles onto the horse behind her niece. When the beetles crawl over her horse, when she hears it whinny in pain, she turns away from the sight. A pang of sympathy shoots through Shefali, but sympathy won't get them out of this.

The good news is that some of the vanguard beetles stopped to eat the horse, putting a bit of distance between them. The bad news is that there are still several hundred of them bearing down upon Shefali.

It isn't the first time she's been pursued by a mob like this. At least there's sky above her now. She wasn't so lucky with the Rassat, or with the Surians, or in the Womb. The moon hanging high as it is fills her with a hope that stands firm in the face of impossible odds.

Back then, after all, she hadn't had this medicine. Back then she'd had to work around her pain.

Now she doesn't.

She reaches for more arrows. Two at a time she fires them from her stout bow; two at a time the beetles are pierced to the ground. She doesn't need to kill all of them, only enough to create a little distance.

Twenty. Twenty is the right number.

By the fifth shot her shoulders ache; by the sixth they are screaming; by the seventh she is sure she won't be able to lift anything tomorrow. But that is all right. She doesn't need to worry about tomorrow, only today, only now—

Two of the beetles leap toward her just as they rejoin the clan. She didn't know they could do that, but there it is, a beetle the size of a pony attacking, mandibles chittering. Down the middle of it, there is another mouth, this one lined with fangs.

It is good that she has two shots prepared already. Barsalai looses her arrows right at the beetles. Her arrows sink into the softer flesh of the thing's underbelly and out through the other side, dripping black down onto them like shy rain. In midair they let out their death rattles.

But that doesn't stop them falling.

She shoves her bow into Khadiyya's hands and stands in the saddle. The first of the beetles hurtles toward her; she catches it barehanded. A torrent of spit falls on her but she does not let go; her back aches at the weight of it, but she does not let go. As if it were feather light, she flings it at its companion. Both crumble into the ground; both are soon eaten by the oncoming crowd.

When she sinks back into the saddle, she is grinning still, beneath the mask. Even Khadiyya is awestruck.

At least until her horse speaks.

*Never hold something that heavy on me again,* says Alsha.

"Sorry," says Shefali.

*Consider things before you do them, Barsalai.*

Well. What else was she supposed to do? Tear it in half? Oh, she could have, but that would've gotten blood all over Khadiyya, and Shefali didn't know whether her aunt's fall had broken skin. This was the safer thing.

She'd thought about it. She had!

"You done playing Tumenbayar?" Otgar calls out to her.

"Haven't started yet," Shefali says. Which is true enough, for this isn't even the difficult part of the evening.

"Well, you'd better get a move on," Otgar calls back. "We're coming up on the turn!"

And so they are—the final turn, the tricksy slide down into the valley. Uncle Ganzorig makes quick work of it. You won't even see the slope until it's too late. Up ahead, a length of Hokkaran silk tied to a tree signals the drop.

This is going to be close. Closer, even, than the last turn had been. That they've not lost anyone yet is a testament to their own talent and to the Sky's kindness, and perhaps a little to Shefali's foolishness.

There will be people who don't make this turn, people related to her in all likelihood, and she won't be able to save them. She won't have time.

For at the end of that slope is the pit, and in the pit she will fight them. All of them.

How many are left now? She lifts her mask long enough to sniff the air. Still a hundred at least. Minami Shizuru, as fine a warrior as Shefali had ever known, died fighting a tenth that number. Granted, she did not have Shefali's particular talents—but still. No one Shefali has ever heard of had fought so many at once.

Well. It is always Qorin doing things first, isn't it? First to trade with Sur-Shar, first to ride horses, first to discover how to shape their bodies, first to craft bows. This will be no different.

"You're certain of this, Barsalai?" says Temurin.

*I'm always certain, Shizuka would say.*

"Yes," says Shefali.

"If you're torn apart—"

"I won't be," she answers. The turn is coming. She slips out of the saddle, so that only the stirrups are keeping her mounted. "Aunt Khadiyyar, see to my horse?"

Her aunt nods. She pinches Shefali's cheek. "You saw to my life," she says. "I'll see to yours."

Shefali looks out onto the slope. Already the others are getting out their whips to turn. The sea of beetles grows closer and closer.

Three in the lead jump for her.

And so she jumps, too.

For a fight like this, it's time to leave her old shape behind. The wolf, then; she shall wear the wolf's form. So often did she wear it in the first year of her exile that it is as easy to slip into as her deel.

Or it used to be.

Since the Womb . . .

She hasn't truly changed since the Womb. Not all the way. Wearing a different form is like . . . it is like floating atop a lake when the current is trying to drag you under.

Part of her is afraid that shifting will disturb this peace she's won, that her body will disobey her as it so often has. Will she land as the wolf, or will she sink into the water?

Shefali tells herself it will be the wolf, and she pictures it clearly in her head, more clearly than ever, now that the pain isn't distracting her. Four times the size of her mare, with teeth as long as her fingers used to be. For the first time, she imagines herself a coat of shaggy brown fur; for the first time, she imagines her ears.

Grandmother Sky made the Qorin from wolves, and so the wolf she shall be, whole and complete.

When her bones shift, it is a victory; when her muscles tear apart, it is a triumph, when her—

Agony like a knife driven between her vertebrae. Stars explode across her vision even as her eyes have not finished changing; there is a spike being driven up into her skull—

When she lands, it is not on all four legs: she hits the ground like a sack of millet. Her head knocks against the ground. The world spins like an Ikhthian woman's skirts as she tries to steady herself. She's had worse, she's had worse, but the current is pulling her deeper.

*Steel-Eye, do you really think you can hold me off so easily?*

The beetles descend on her as they would a corpse. Soon the pain in her head is the least of her worries: the ravenous mouths of the beetles are upon her. They're gnawing on her now, taking bites of her as she forces herself to stand.

Qorin break horses by tying rocks to their saddle. Two small pebbles at first, hardly anything at all—but each day, you add more and more, until the horse is comfortable carrying the weight of a person.

Though she wears a wolf's form, Shefali feels akin to that horse. The beetles are heavy as mountains. Once, twice, she tries to stand—but how is she to do so when her back is a twig about to break?

And she feels the Traitor Yamai now, his influence spreading to her. She hears it in the chittering mandibles of the beetles, hears it in the beat of her own heart. The image she holds of herself starts to change: the fur falls off, and so, too, does her skin, leaving her skinless once more; her eyes go red and her jaw splits down the middle like some unholy, toothy flower.

*As long as your blood runs black, I will be with you.*

Her muscles are starting to twitch. She knows this feeling, knows it means she's about to lose control of herself again, but—

But who are they to speak to her? And who is *He*?

Does he think that she is afraid of him? Does he think that the daughter of Burqila Alshara, the Wall-Breaker, will allow herself to be leashed?

No.

Not here, not now. She is Barsalai Shefali, the Laughing Fox; she is a hero in Shiseiki and she is a hero now.

She is just as much a god as he is—and this is *her* body. Ren told her she was losing her shape because his will had overpowered hers.

Let him try now.

Larger Shefali pictures herself, larger and larger, until she is taller than the trebuchets Dalaansuv constructed farther up the mountain. The ache of it! For her body was never meant to stretch to sizes like this, never meant to become anything like this at all. For the first time, she feels the weight of her own flesh against her bones; for the first time, she feels her bones bending.

So she imagines them firmer. Unyielding, as everything about her must now be.

A flash of the other image comes to her, but she pushes it away before it can distract her. Will. This is about will.

Teeth dig into her shoulder and she does not waver.

The beetles throw themselves against her; she topples over and she does not waver.

Larger she grows, larger and larger still, and she does not waver even when the chittering speaks to her, even when she hears the call of the undercurrent, even when she feels the caress of the darkness against her skin.

This is a matter of will, and will she has in spades.

The larger she gets, the more it aches, the more she is torn and rebuilt—the more she can bear the weight of the beetles. When at last she rises on all fours, they are so small that she could swallow them, if she wished.

And she does wish to.

For she is hungry in this form, as she always is.

But they will know fear first, as she has known fear. At the bottom of her throat, the howl is building. The buzzing of the beetles, the chittering, threatens to drown out her thought—but she is stronger than this, stronger than them. They are the waves; they are the current.

She has risen above them.

In Nishikomi, they hear the howl that leaves Shefali then, in the Minami lands, in the ruins of Shigeoka.

*My blood is my own,* she says to him. *Try harder next time.*

Only then does she lunge forward; only then does she bite into a dozen beetles at once; only then does she swallow them. The taste of them! How long it's been since she tasted anything at all! Biting into them is like biting into a grape—the carapace pops and their innards fill her mouth with flavor. How it delights her! They fling themselves at her, and it is easy to bat them away, easy to trample them underfoot, easy to send them scattering into the night as the blood trickles down her maw.

With each one of them she eats, the pain fades, until she can no longer feel the current tugging at her, until she is free.

And then, only then—when her belly is full and her hunger is sated—does she sink back down on her haunches.

Only then does she imagine the form of Barsalai Shefali, exhausted and spent, lying at the bottom of the valley.

# BARSALAI SHEFALI

## FIVE

Barsalai Shefali wakes in her mother's ger. The sunlight filtering in through the felt tells her that it must have been hours since their battle, and yet she is hesitant to call this rest "sleep." Especially when it is the pain that wakes her—the throbbing ache in her shoulders a stronger nudge than any her cousins might give her. It is as if someone is driving a stone between her shoulder blades, as if her whole body has been caught between mortar and pestle.

And so she does the most reasonable thing anyone awaking in that much agony might do: she groans.

The gentle clack of her uncle's knife against his cutting board stops. So, too, does the rattling of her younger cousins playing anklebones. Someone much closer—Otgar, it's Otgar—laughs.

"Needlenose, you handsome idiot!" she says. "Six years conning foreigners out of coin, and you never told me you could get that big!"

Shefali groans again. She loves her cousin, she does, but the sound of her voice is like two spikes being driven into her temples. "Medicine," she says.

"Oh, right," Otgar says. "Soyiketu! Get that concoction from her saddlebags."

The boy, seated before the makeshift table with a map spread out before him, gives his half sister a plaintive look. It earns him no favors. Otgar repeats her command and off he goes.

"How long?" mumbles Shefali. Sky, she hurts.

"All through the night," Otgar answers. "It's a bit past Fourth." Her cousin purses her lips. "Your eyes are getting glassy. You all right?"

If she were in a better mood, she might point out that her left eye is steel, not glass, but that is a retort for a woman in better condition. As it stands, Shefali's directing all her attention to not screaming. "Medicine," she repeats.

"It's coming," Otgar says. "Don't you go wasting away on us yet. The babies are too young to know what happened, and they'll never believe me if you're lying in a sickbed when they meet you."

Shefali does not want to think of children. She grunts again. If only she could roll over—but the agony that fills her even at the thought dissuades her.

"Flower," Shefali says.

"Your flower?" says Otgar. She laughs, and Shefali wishes that she wouldn't. "On the way back from Nishikomi now. The morning scouts saw their banners. Shouldn't be long before she's here. If you weren't in so much pain, I'd flick your nose for asking a thing like that."

Shefali closes her eyes. It's about the only movement she can make on her own at the moment.

"My belt," she says.

The sticky-sweet scent of embarrassment meets Shefali's nose as Otgar leans over her. The moment Shefali feels her trying to pluck the flower, she grunts again. Otgar has the sense to stop.

"Put my hand on it," Shefali says.

She half expects her cousin to say something smart. Thankfully, she does not—only picks up Shefali's hand. Even this is difficult, for the stiffness in her joints makes lifting her hand akin to breaking a branch with one's bare hands.

"Brace yourself," Otgar says.

Shefali remembers to breathe.

Otgar's got to throw her back into it. Now she's the one grunting as she lifts Shefali's hand, as she pulls it over to her belt and drops it there without ceremony.

The scream that leaves Shefali then is enough to terrify her family. All at once they leap up out of their seats, staring at her as if she has brought home a rabid wolf and called it their morning meal. Sweat clings to her brow; she's breathing like one of Burqila's hunting dogs in the summer, and each breath only makes things worse.

"Otgar, are you hurting her?" asks Zurgaanqar. The world is spinning—Shefali does not see her aunt coming over, but does smell her. "Get away from her. Poor girl fends off an army on her own, and you're tormenting her like this!"

"I'm not—" Otgar begins, but her mother shoos her away.

"Someone going to get Burqila?" asks Dalaansuv. How anyone tore her away from maintaining the cannons is a mystery to Shefali.

"She's waiting outside for Naisuran's daughter," says Big Tagurmongke, Aunt Khadiyya's husband. This is perhaps the second time Shefali has ever seen him inside the ger during daylight. His deep voice is perfect for stories, and an absolute terror to her now.

"I'll do it," says Otgar. "Soyiketu's coming with her medicine, Aaj. You're going to have to help her drink it."

"Help her drink it?" says Zurgaanqar. "Don't be an idiot, Otgar, she can drink—"

"No," says Shefali. "I need help."

She could go the rest of her life without smelling so much pity in one room. How weak she feels, flat on her back and unable to sit up! How awful! Is she truly the same woman who fought off an army? For now she feels she is a burden; now she can feel their respect for her eroding.

Barsalai swallows.

"Our sister leaves for ten minutes to check for the banners, and you're treating her daughter like this," says Aunt Khadiyya. A weight settles at Shefali's side, and she recognizes the scent of crossbow oil on her aunt's hands. "Come on. Soyiketu's at the door now, let's get you sitting up."

Sure enough, Soyiketu soon shouts for people to catch their dogs, though the dogs are all outside with their master. Shefali hears him hurrying toward them.

Aunt Khadiyya and Aunt Zurgaanqar must coordinate their efforts to get her sitting up—each one slipping their hands beneath Barsalai's shoulders. When Khadiyya says to, they lift as one, pushing her upright. Zurgaanqar has the good sense to sit behind her so that Shefali does not fall backwards.

"Come here," says Khadiyya. Soyiketu does as he is told, placing the bottle in Khadiyya's waiting hand. She uncorks it with her thumb and wrinkles her nose. "This is medicine?"

"Yes," Shefali says. She feels more ashamed now than ever—but her aunt is at least looking at her kindly.

"Well, if it helps," she says. "Open your mouth."

When she swallows, she is aware that the whole clan is watching her, as if the effect should be instantaneous. As if she should jump to her feet and run to her gray, desperate to return to her wife.

She is eager to see Shizuka again—the scent of peonies is faint but present—and yet she knows she will not be moving. Not for an hour, at least. The Empress of Hokkaro is just going to have to be the one doing all the embracing.

Khadiyya sets down the vial. She looks around the ger at her siblings and frowns.

"Will all of you give the girl some room?" she says. "Sky above, you aren't sitting with Tumenbayar."

In some ways, Shefali is lucky she is so stiff this morning—cringing would take too much effort to do. In some ways, her aunt is right. In others . . .

"How are you feeling?" asks Zurgaanqar. "Are you . . . does it hurt?"

"Yes," says Shefali. "But it'll get better."

"What can we do to help?" says Khadiyya.

They aren't calling her weak? And Khadiyya does not smell as if she is lying, does not smell as if there is anything amiss. All Shefali can smell on her is concern and, perhaps, a little guilt.

"Don't let me interrupt," says Shefali. For getting her medicine and getting her upright have brought to a halt all the procedures of the day. She has precious few days remaining to her—she does not intend to spend them as a disturbance.

"That's all?" says Khadiyya.

"You don't want anything to eat? You're getting skinnier every day—"

"She can't eat, Zurgaanqar," says Dalaansuv. Already she is turning her attention to a stack of papers in front of her. How fascinating—only a generation ago, she might have been working in Surian, but now she works in Qorin. "Stop asking her why she's so skinny."

"I worry," is Zurgaanqar's answer. "When Dorbentei was her age, she was wide as two Hokkarans shoulder to shoulder. Barsalai's a strong girl! She should look it!"

Ganzorig drops his finely chopped tubers into the pot. "That's what I keep saying."

"Ganzorig agrees with me," Zurgaanqar says. She brightens immediately, and Shefali cannot help but smile. The two of them are so transparent. Why had they ever married anyone except each other?

"He does whatever you tell him," says Dalaansuv.

"No, I don't," answers Ganzorig. "Wouldn't catch me transforming into a giant wolf to fight off an army."

He winks at Shefali with that last.

Yes—this is home, isn't it? Her family teasing her like this, the conversations that go everywhere and nowhere.

It is easy to forget what has brought her here.

But before she can lose herself too thoroughly in the soothing barbs of her family's banter, there is a knock at the door, followed shortly by the scratching of excited hunting hounds.

"Catch the dogs," says Otgar, who is likely holding them all by their scruffs herself. Soyiketu opens the door for her. Shefali isn't surprised to see her mother standing at Otgar's side, but she is surprised by how quickly Alshara bolts from her. The concern on her face! As if Shefali's been gravely wounded, and not merely overexerted herself.

Alshara's sisters know her well enough to understand her, even without being able to speak. Zurgaanqar gets up—Shefali can thankfully sit up on her own now—and Khadiyya gets a chair. Alshara doesn't bother with it. The first thing she does is kiss her daughter's forehead.

The second thing—and the third, and the fourth—is to check her for any sign of injury.

"Two weeks left," says Shefali, a wry smirk playing across her lips. "Not sooner."

Her mother's eyes have never been more piercing. Burqila looks up from checking Shefali's arm to flick her on the nose. It lasts only a moment—Alshara soon embraces her, and Shefali allows herself to feel some small measure of pride in what she's done.

*We will remember you,* her mother wrote. And they shall—Shefali's sure of it. Stories are to the Qorin as beauty is to Hokkarans; they live in the perpetual pursuit of more.

Last night, she was a hero.

This morning, she is her mother's daughter, niece to seven women and seven men, cousin to more than she can count.

Yes—it's starting to hurt less now.

Otgar hasn't shut the door yet. Sunlight makes her skin glow, and the cocky smile does the rest. Shefali catches sight of her over Alshara's shoulder.

"Hope your heart's not giving you any trouble," says Otgar. "Barsatoq's coming down the road now."

Until that moment, Shefali's heart had given her no trouble at all. The moment Otgar finishes speaking, it flutters. Shizuka. She hasn't thought to ask how the naval battle went, and she isn't sure the Qorin would know to begin with—but to know that her wife is safe . . .

Shefali tries to push herself to stand.

Her mother squeezes her shoulder. Alshara points to Shefali's bed and glares—the message is clear. There will be no leaving bed until she has rested.

Shefali pouts.

Alshara does not budge.

Well—if that is to be the way of things, then Shefali will simply simmer with excitement from where she is.

The scent of peonies grows thicker. Yes—fire, steel, and flowers. Her wildfire woman. Does the world outside seem brighter now that she knows Shizuka is in it?

Two minutes pass between Otgar's speaking and Shizuka's appearing at the door. For Barsalai Shefali, it may as well be two years. Any time apart from her wife is too much time.

The air itself hails Shizuka's coming. A faint glow of gold heralds her arrival. The gold of her armor, shaped by the finest smiths in Xian-Lai, cannot hope to compare. What delight does the sun take in shining on simple metal? No, its true delight has always been to illuminate the eyes of Minami Shizuka, to lend her hair its luster and her skin its radiance.

Every single time Shefali looks at her, she is convinced of this anew: the sun exists solely for her wife.

Yet the moment their eyes meet, Shefali knows there is something wrong. As a dye maker can discern between Blush-of-Heaven and Maiden's Kiss at a glance, so, too, can Shefali discern her wife's moods. See the glower in her amber eyes! See how the amber flares!

When Shizuka catches Shefali's eye, she sheepishly looks away.

Sky—what could have happened? For instead of the amber Shefali has known all of her life, Shizuka's eyes are gold. Pupil and iris together are luminous bright; so, too, is her newly gilt scar.

Again Shefali tries to stand, but her mother eases her back down.

"Shizuka," Shefali calls as her wife nears the door. "Are you—?"

She cannot finish the question, for her wife crosses from the door to her side and kisses her.

A woman walks through a cherry orchard in the early spring. It is Second Bell, and she has left her lover's home only moments ago.

Her hair is in shambles. If anyone sees her blushing, or her disarrayed robes, they will surely know where she has been. The woman cares for none of this—she is lost in the memories of the night.

How many ways did he say he loved her? With his lips, with his tongue, with his fingertips each in turn . . .

Midway through her walk, a breeze caresses her much the way he did. So, too, does it caress the flowers. Hundreds of petals—thousands—allow themselves to be seduced, to be carried away from their mother's homes.

The woman thinks to herself: *Each of those petals is one of the ways he proved his love to me.*

Barsalai Shefali wandered eight years with only the thought of petals to keep her company. Now, to be so near to them again sets her mind aswirl.

How is she meant to think, when her wife is smiling against her lips? How is she meant to remember that she must breathe?

Soon—too soon—they part, and it is only then that Shefali recalls the look in Shizuka's eyes as she approached. By then, the amber's gone soft again; by then, there is only laughter bubbling beneath the surface.

"Dearest," says Shizuka, cupping Shefali's face.

"Hmm?"

"You taste *awful.*"

That laughter bursts out. What is Shefali to do but echo her? Yes, of course, the medicine must still be on her lips—and of course it tastes awful to Shizuka.

Let whatever angered Shizuka wait. For now, they are together.

War can wait an hour or two.

PACKING UP THE camp takes the better part of a Bell's time. Seeing the gold-clad Shizuka among the Qorin in their embroidered deels fills Shefali with a sense of nostalgia. She's shed her war mask to better hear the calls—all kneel, all lift, set the pegs down over there, make sure the foreigners don't touch Burqila's mares. It is good work, honest work—the sort that Alshara used to insist Shizuka do when she lived among the clan.

"It'll be good for her character," Alshara said, though it was Otgar who voiced the words. "Do you think that girl's worked a day in her life before this?"

And she hadn't, of course, but in those days, she threw herself into whatever was put in front of her. Within two weeks of travel, she knew the routine so well that it did not matter if she did not understand the calls.

Back then she wore Shefali's childhood deels and pants. Now she stands clad head to toe in dragonscale armor. She's keeping her hair back, too.

A married woman, grown.

"Keep staring at her like that, and your eye's going to melt out of your skull," says Otgar.

Shefali shoves her. Otgar—stout as a Hokkaran gelding—does not move.

"At least your wife's helping," Otgar teases. "Not standing around, mooning over a pretty girl."

"I helped yesterday," Barsalai says. Not that Otgar is *wrong*—she has been standing in the same spot, watching Shizuka for the better part of five minutes. It's only that she can't let Otgar get away so easily. With one hand she hefts the bundled ger her aunts and uncles have laid in front of her. Shefali puts it onto the cart, claps her hands free of imaginary dust, and shrugs at Otgar. "That better?"

"Think I like you better when you're the Beast," says Otgar. "No talking back to me."

Shefali has half a mind to stick her tongue out at her, but they are not young girls anymore. To do so would be absurd. Instead, she sets another of the packed gers onto the cart. A lock of hair falls into her face. She flicks her head to clear it away, getting a look at the assembled Hokkaran army as she does.

Strange to see them so close to a Qorin camp—but the feeling is mutual. Though there are plenty of them standing around, looking imposing, none offer to help with breaking down the camp. Had they made such an offer, this would go by far more quickly.

But Shefali isn't sure she wants it to, and she doesn't know that Shizuka does, either. While they break down the tent, they don't have to worry about the mountain pass.

She can see the mountains from here, too, if she just turns her head. As a child, she thought Gurkhan Khalsar was the highest peak in the world—the closest place to Grandmother Sky. Journeying to the east has taught her otherwise. The White-Winged Palace in Ikhtar gets its name from resting atop the Shalakai Mountains. For the better part of the three months she had been forced to stay within its walls, Shefali hated that place for many reasons; the altitude was the first, and the most chronic. Looking out the window always made her dizzy.

The Tokuma Mountains are not so tall as the Shalakai, but they're closer to the Sky than Gurkhan Khalsar. The horses are already complaining about the trip. Later, when they are about to leave, Shefali will try to talk to them about it. It's easier to convince Qorin than it is to convince their horses. They're uniquely aware of their own importance, Shefali's found, compared to other horses. She can hardly hold a conversation with Axion war-steeds.

All of this is to distract from the reality of the situation: There is no Wall of Flowers here. It ends abruptly at the eastern foot of the mountain. As they go through the pass, the only things keeping their joint army safe will be the gods that lead it.

Perhaps that is why the Hokkarans are so stoic.

There are exceptions. Shizuka's second-in-command, a wiry man named Munenori, is trying to herd the sheep. The dogs are doing a far better job than he is. Uncle Batbayar leans on his walking stick and watches in amusement—but he offers no assistance.

And there is Sakura. Shefali had been surprised to see her, and more surprised still that she had not been able to pick her scent out from Shizuka's. They'd arrived at the same time. As a pheasant among sparrows, that woman. She flits from group to group with a portable lectern balanced on her arm, asking in very loud Hokkaran for everyone to tell her what they're transporting. An inventory. Shizuka mentioned them briefly when she spoke of going north, but . . .

They truly are an army now, aren't they?

"What do you make of that one?" asks Otgar.

Shefali tilts her head. Otgar jerks her finger toward Sakura, who is approaching with a look of indignant frustration. With her Xianese jacket and those smudges of ink on her fingertips, she reminds Shefali of Baozhai.

That is not a comparison she will be making out loud.

"Roots," says Shefali. "Like Barsatoq, but sensible."

"No such thing," says Otgar. She sniffs. By now, Sakura is close enough to hear them, and so Otgar decides to be as loud as possible. "Hey! Minami-lao, was it?"

"Sakura-lun, please. Minami-lao makes me sound like Shi—like Barsatoq's aunt," she answers. "You must be Dorbentei."

"Technically, it should be more like Jurgaghantei by now, but I won't put your soft western tongue through all that work," says Otgar, standing a little straighter. "Dorbentei will do."

Sakura raises a brow. "Right," she says flatly. "Everyone kept telling me you can answer my questions."

"That depends on the question," says Otgar. "You're keeping track of logistics, aren't you? Dalaansuv's husband is the one in charge of that. If you're looking for how to swear in as many languages as you've got fingers, though—"

Sakura rolls her eyes. Without so much as missing a beat, she curses up a streak so blue that Grandmother Sky mistakes it for a ribbon in her hair—and then repeats it in three different languages.

Otgar whistles.

"I grew up in a pleasure house," says Sakura. "What the fuck did you expect?"

"A Hokkaran," answers Otgar.

"You've got one," says Sakura. She sets the lectern down on the cart. Out of habit, Shefali dumps out the ink bowl; Sakura does not stop her. "I don't actually care about logistics, either. A lot of other people do, though. Can't crack open a scroll about the Five-Province Period without someone going on and on about how many soldiers there were, and how many horses they brought, and all the captains with their absurd titles . . ."

Shefali's eyes glaze over a little.

". . . and it's the strangest thing, I haven't met *anyone* who actually gives a shit about any of that when you're telling a story."

Shefali smirks. She picks up another bundled ger and sets it in the cart, careful not to disturb the lectern. Yes, this is why she likes Sakura.

"And is that what you're here to do?" says Otgar. "Tell a story?"

"Tell *her* story," says Sakura. Shefali does not need to be able to see her to know where she is pointing. "I'm her historian."

Otgar laughs—two quick bellows from deep in her stomach.

When Shefali turns to rejoin them, Sakura's crossed her arms. "What's so funny?"

"You being her historian," Otgar says. Otgar might be half Surian, but the other half must be wolf—just look at the way she is smiling! "What with your being a westerner, and all. Barsalai's story is ours to tell. There's all sorts of nuances you wouldn't understand."

Sakura purses her lips. Here is the difference between her and her cousin: Shizuka would've said something outright. No—that is unfair. The Shizuka that Shefali had left behind would have snapped at her. This Shizuka, the one she knows now, would listen.

"And if I tell you I've been invited to write the story, by your cousin?" Sakura says. The tip of her pen slips between her lips. Shefali wonders if that is on purpose—it reminds her of the sort of thing Ren might do. "If I tell you that I am doing this as a gift to her?"

"She has already written her story," says Otgar. Notes of anger in her scent, a rumble in her voice. "What use are you? What do you bring? Barsalai's been listening to Barsatoq recite poetry since they were knee-high. She's got that in her soul by now. What's your writing like?"

Sakura's brow twitches. Shefali fears what will come if the two of them are left to their own devices like this. "She's a scholar," says Shefali.

"And?" says Otgar, hands on her hips. "Your wife's grandfather was a scholar, too, and see where that got us."

"Sakura isn't like that," says Shefali. Now she is the one getting angry. "This is a gift she's giving me—"

"And what kind of gift is that?" says Otgar. "We've got your letters, Barsalai; *we* can tell your story for anyone who wants to hear it."

"If you treat anyone who comes asking to hear it the way you're treating me, then she'll die out in the Empire within a generation," says Sakura flatly.

Otgar sucks her teeth. Shefali can almost taste the thought brewing in her cousin's mind: *Then let her die in the Empire, let her be ours.*

Yet Shefali is not only Qorin. Loath as she occasionally is to admit it, she is Hokkaran, as well—and would it not do well for the Hokkarans to have their own version of events? For surely they will want to hear Shizuka's story, surely they will keep her name alive forever. Wouldn't it be a good thing to give them as few reasons as possible to deny Shefali's presence?

All of this crosses Shefali's mind, and yet she speaks none of it.

Otgar knows only her own image of Sakura; only a woodcut, and not the woman. To her she is nothing more than a fashionable scholar stepping outside her borders.

But Shefali knows her as a friend.

*You aren't what I expected you to be,* Sakura said to her once.

"Let her tell a story," Shefali says.

"What?" say Otgar and Sakura at once.

Nothing unites people like having a common enemy. The unconscionable deeds of Shizuka's grandfather galvanized the Qorin, allowing Burqila Alshara to unite the survivors of the blackblood into a single army.

Shefali does not hope to make herself an enemy—but she does hope to allow Sakura and Otgar to consider someone other than themselves.

"If you're so concerned," says Shefali, "then have her tell a story."

"We're leaving in two hours, if you hadn't noticed," says Dorbentei. Her hands stay planted at her hips. She looks like a perfect caricature of a displeased housewife.

"The *army's* leaving in two hours," says Sakura. From the lightness in her voice, she's catching on to Shefali's plan. "One third of you are going back to the steppes. They're not packing at all."

Otgar glances in the direction of those returning to the steppes. Older couples, mostly, with the children and a few youths unwilling to gamble their lives on this fool's venture. Most of them are sitting outside their gers, playing anklebones or wrestling.

She sniffs. "They're not going to give up their gambling for you."

Sakura scoffs, and this time, Shefali joins her. "Like I haven't had to charm people away from dice and cards before," Sakura says. She shoves her lectern into Otgar's hands—and Otgar, to Shefali's surprise, does not immediately drop it. "If no one in that group rolls a single anklebone the whole time I talk, will you stop giving me shit?"

"Like hell Yorogei's going to sit quiet the whole time," Otgar fires back. Everyone in the clan knows Yorogei will gamble away his grandmother's felt if you let him.

"I asked you a question," says Sakura. "Will you leave me alone or not?"

Otgar shifts Sakura's lectern so that she is holding it beneath one arm. She spits on her palm and holds it out to Sakura. "You get Yorogei to stop gambling, and I'll do whatever you want."

Sakura laughs. "Follow me, then," she says, "and you just fucking *watch*, Dorbentei."

For three heartbeats, Shefali wonders if Otgar will listen—if she will do as a Hokkaran tells her to, even if that Hokkaran is doing her a favor.

Three heartbeats is all it takes for Otgar to follow after her.

Strange. She doesn't smell angry at all anymore. Is that . . . Is that excitement?

Shefali purses her lips. The day is full of surprises, it seems—even more than the sight of her wife doing manual labor.

"Shizuka," Shefali calls. The Empress of Hokkaro looks up from her work. Sweat glistens across the surface of her scar, lending it the look of burnished copper.

"I'm going to take a break," Shefali says. She nods toward Sakura. "With your cousin."

Shizuka laughs, shaking her head. It's delightful to see—and yet not entirely genuine. Something in that smile does not reach her eyes.

Shefali flares her nostrils. Is it her, or does Shizuka smell more . . . ? There is more char to the flames now. As if someone has just thrown wood on the fire.

"Enjoy it," Shizuka says. "And make sure she does, too!"

There is something behind those words, something her wife is not telling her. After hearing the horrors of Ink-on-Water, Shefali is hardly about to ask her wife what happened out in the bay.

But she will wonder, all the same. And perhaps someday her wife will tell her.

THEY CROSS THE pass that same night, after Sakura makes Otgar dance like a singing girl in front of the whole clan. Watching her cousin fumble through the steps is ridiculous. Watching her do it with the Tokuma Mountains rising up behind her, knowing what the rest of the day will bring . . .

The Qorin take their comfort where they can. Shefali is no exception. She watches her cousin dance, and she laughs until her ribs ache. For an hour—let her not think on the mountain, or on her wife's strange behavior of late. The children steal Little Mongke's drum and beat a rhythm. The older folk join in, clapping their weathered hands. Otgar complains that the movements are too strict—that there's no room to be herself.

Sakura bops her on the nose with her fan. "That's the point, Dorbentei," she says.

Otgar tells her that sounds stupid, and it is about then that Burqila leaves her meeting with the sanvaartains. Shefali smells her scent on the air and turns to look—Burqila's heading right for them. She carries a large skin of kumaq in each hand.

Skins that large have one purpose and one alone: blessing horses before a long journey. Shefali idly wonders whether there was any need for her mother to consult the sanvaartains at all. Could she not have performed the blessing herself? Would it hold?

Ah, but that would be breaking tradition, and there is untold power in traditions. The Qorin have been doing things the same way for two thousand years, at least. To change on the whim of a young god—that has never suited them.

Blessing the horses this way had worked for every long journey of her life before her exile.

It would work now.

"Dorbentei," Shefali says. "Aaj is coming."

Like a hunting dog snapping to attention, Dorbentei rights her foreign posture. Sakura pouts, but only for a moment; she recovers just as soon as she begins to fan herself.

"Well," says Sakura. "Suppose we've all got to start dancing for our audience now."

HERE IS HOW they cross.

Shefali rides ahead with the scouts—her mother's five quickest riders. The rest of the clan lies in wait. Shefali does not need to be among them to know how her wife wilts away with worry—she can smell it on the winds, even as they approach the pass.

The mountains rise up around them like the hands of a massive sculptor. Shadows cross their faces as the Tokuma peaks scrape against the ash-gray sky. Two of the other scouts spit on the ground at the sight of them. The horses, despite Burqila's blessing, do not want to look at the mountains either.

Yet they have been summoned here to look, and so look they shall.

Shefali rides at the forefront. Her fingers are stiff around her saddle horn; she hopes that she will not have to draw her bow today. As the wind whistles through the pass, she flares her nostrils and breathes deep.

When Shefali was twelve, her uncle Ganzorig forgot to empty the pot before they broke camp. For three days, they wandered. It was the middle of summer, and so it did not take long for mold and rot to stake their claim on what was once a splendid stew. By the time they opened the pot back up, the smell was so rank, Temurin threw up on the spot. She swore the pot would never be clean again—it was better to throw the whole thing away.

"Steel won't hold a scent, you idiot," Burqila said in Otgar's voice. "Wash it out, and it'll be fine."

Temurin, in spite of the wisdom of her years, was skeptical. Yet she was the one who threw up in the pot and so she was the one tasked with cleaning it. On her hands and knees, with wads and wads of old felt, she scrubbed away. The pot was free of its tyrannical oppressors—but the smell lingered in the air for the rest of the day.

The wind here is like that pot. Shefali can smell neither blackbloods nor demons, but the scent of corruption remains. Perhaps it is the bodies of the beetles—some half-crushed beneath cannonballs, some pierced through—that produce it; perhaps it is their proximity to the Traitor's Lands. What soil remains beneath their feet is dry as bone. The trees clinging to life by the rocks more closely resemble errant brushstrokes than anything alive—and there's no livestock to speak of, either.

It is the lack of livestock that most worries her. Those who go where goats will not are foolish indeed.

Yet worry alone cannot stop her; she must continue. Farther and farther between the mountains ride the five scouts. As a tapestry left out in the sun goes paler and paler, so, too, do the mountains and the earth, the farther along they go. By the time they've traveled five li, their deels, their horses, the brown of their skin and the green of their eyes—these are the only colors in a world of gray.

After the first hour, Shefali sends back the other four riders. It's safe enough for the army to follow, after all, though she means to find the exact point of entry. She and Temurin are the only two remaining.

Eight years ago, she would have pressed on alone. Now, Barsalai is wise enough to know it is good to have company, and she trusts Temurin's sword more than her own right arm.

Two hours of riding with no sign of the enemy, save their rotting bodies; two hours of riding with no sound save those caused by the horses. To wander into an inkwash painting—that is what it is to scout out the pass.

At last, the air grows thicker; their ears pop as they begin their descent. The scent of flowers overpowers the rot of their surroundings. Her gray comes to a stop just as a thick fog rises up before them.

Shefali thinks to herself: *Here*.

A deep breath. The fog rushes down her throat and into her lungs. She can *taste* it—the rot, the salt water, the ashes of a broken promise.

Him.

"I don't trust this, Barsalai," Temurin says. Her horse stomps his hooves, shakes his head. Shefali does not comfort the poor gelding—how could she? They are driving him straight into the Traitor's clutches.

"You shouldn't," Shefali answers. "String your bow."

Temurin sucks her teeth. "Can't shoot what I can't see," she answers.

"Then stay close," Shefali says. "We have to go through it."

Temurin curses. Shefali wishes something as simple as thought would bring her any relief. She tries it, all the same, but it does nothing for her pain and less for her fear.

For she is afraid then, as the fog grows thick around them. Shizuka spoke of demonic marionettes, of possession, of brutal slaughters in fog just like this. Fear is a stern parent.

Not that Shefali will let her fear rule her. Even fear is no match for Burqila Alshara—and Shefali spent sixteen years disobeying her mother.

*I'll give you a sweet if you go ahead,* she says to her gray.

*There aren't enough sweets in the world,* says the gray, *but I suppose you're going to hop off and go on your own if I refuse.*

Beneath her mask, Shefali smirks. She says nothing, because there is no need for words.

Her horse sighs—but she goes on. Shefali holds on with her thighs, reaching for her bow with her stiff right hand. Normally she holds it with the left and strings it with the right. Today, it is her left side that is behaving; today, she awkwardly braces the bow against her body to get it strung.

But it is strung, the bow that no man can fire, and the arrows are within easy enough reach. The prospect of drawing with her right and nocking with her left doesn't excite her, but the necessary does not need to be exciting.

Deeper and deeper they go. The silence wraps about their throats and squeezes. Around them, nothing but the gray, nothing but the fog—they have stopped seeing even the bodies of the fallen.

"Barsalai," Temurin calls.

Shefali grunts. There is something prickling at her nose, something like the rot in an unwashed cauldron.

"Barsalai, how much farther do we have to go alone?"

*Only a little,* Shefali wants to answer, for the fog is about to break. With her free hand, she holds out a skin of kumaq to Temurin—one of the ones she has spent her nights working with. Frost rimes the skin even now.

"If there's trouble," Shefali says.

Temurin sniffs. Her brows come together, but she takes the skin all the same.

Together, they continue.

Up ahead there are shades of green, of violet, of red. The fog is as a veil before them—Shefali cannot make out what is truly behind it.

From reading Sakura's letters, she's got some idea: a bounteous, scintillating land of lies.

Those lies must be what's rankling her nose.

"When we cross," she says, "don't trust your eyes."

"Never have," says Temurin.

# TEMURIN, THE IRON WOMAN

## ONE

So rarely does one get the chance to outrace a god—not that Temurin pays any mind to that. The god follows, close behind, as Temurin lets her lungs sing a war cry. It's been years, she thinks, since she's made a sound like that. Temurin is the first to pierce the veil.

It had always scared the Hokkarans; maybe it will scare the demons, too.

But the true purpose of the Qorin war cry is to lend its bravery to those who hear its call and join. So it is with this: as Temurin's voice echoes through the valley, Barsalai kicks her own horse into a quicker gallop.

The sky is bruise-violet, the sun an angry wound; the brilliant flowers an assault on her eyes.

It strikes her as the work of a child given a basket full of exotic beads and told to make whatever they like.

A river cuts across the landscape, ending just to the right of the two Qorin. In the face of all logic, it flows directly into the fog. Something tells Temurin this won't be anything like the Rokhon—she does not look on it. That much water's never sat well with her, anyway. You could trust the Rokhon—you cannot trust anything west of the wall.

She directs her gaze to the horizon instead. There was supposed to be some sort of castle where the Traitor was keeping all of the other Qorin, from what Barsalai had said. It boils her blood just to think on it. Years ago—when the girls were young—she'd gone with Burqila to the Jade Palace. The ceiling in that place was painted to look like the sky. She wonders if the ceiling in that terrible demonic palace is the same—if the Qorin trapped within have any idea what the sky even looks like anymore.

She can see the castle. Temurin's never liked Hokkaran castles, with their roofs stacked on one another like autumn leaves, but even Fujino pales in comparison with this place. With Iwa. If her eyes do not betray her they are hundreds of li away from it, and yet she can count its roofs from here if she wanted to. Seventy-four adorn each of the six towers of Iwa.

Perfectly spaced, perfectly arranged—it is a wonder to behold.

But Temurin does not go far into this world, this creation. No more than ten minutes of riding into the strange world, she sees the child.

Eight, perhaps, or maybe a little older. Difficult to tell—he is tallish, but his face is younger than the rest of him, his cheeks still round and full. In any other instance she might find him adorable, for there's something endearing about how perfectly round his face is, or the dimples in his cheeks when he smiles.

But she does not find him adorable in this instance.

For he is a Qorin boy beyond the Wall, a Qorin boy with his white hair cropped at the pate, a Qorin boy in Hokkaran robes, a Qorin boy who speaks with a man's voice. Worse: when that voice—and how awful it is, how deep and echoing!—speaks, it is in Hokkaran.

A language she has never learned.

Temurin grips her bow. She notches an arrow and yet cannot bring herself to draw the string all the way back, not when faced with a child. What was he saying? What did he mean? She knows from his blackening eyes, from the sharp teeth she now sees within that smile, that this is no mere child. She knows this is the Enemy.

Temurin Baterdene Enkhjaryya rode to war at Burqila's side when she was twenty-two. By then she'd already lost all of her brothers, her father, and three aunts to the blackblood. She had seen some of them die with her own two eyes: she knew the suffering it brought, knew how it twisted the body into a perverse parody of what it once was.

But she had never seen the blackblood affect a child.

And being confronted by one now . . . she cannot bring herself to fire.

Even when the child splits down the middle into a giant mouth and launches itself at her.

As it flies through the air Temurin raises her arms and thinks to herself: this is what I get for riding so far ahead of the others. Her body braces for pain; her mind braces for the possibility that she may die here.

But in the end it does not come. She stays with her arms up for what feels an eternity, and when she lowers them there is nothing before her except flowers too bright for the season and a river that should not exist.

There is no boy.

Temurin's tongue sticks to the roof of her mouth. Her teeth are clamped so tight together that it would take five men to pry her jaws apart. Fear . . . she is not used to fear.

It was there only a moment ago.

When Barsalai comes riding up behind, Temurin tries to open her mouth to say something. She cannot. How is she to say it? There was a demon here and then there was not—and worse, she wasn't even able to fire upon it.

What sort of bodyguard, what sort of company is she?

Temurin swallows. As Barsalai studies her she feels uncomfortably as if she's being appraised, as if Barsalai can read her thoughts. The wind through the flowers sounds too much like the wind through the silver steppes; she wants to plug her ears and run from this place.

"Go and find the others," Shefali says.

Temurin tilts her head. "And you?"

"Don't worry about me," Shefali says. "Go. The kumaq will keep you safe."

She does not stop to explain *how* it will do that. If she does, there might be questions, and questions might shake her faith in her own abilities. Without faith, her abilities are nothing.

Temurin's brows come together. The corner of her mouth rises up in a smirk. She waves a finger at Shefali. "You're telling, not asking," she says. "Wherever you went, Barsalai, it made you a better leader."

"Go," she repeats.

Temurin gives her horse a kick. Together, they turn; together, they go into the fog.

TWO HOURS LATER, Temurin finds the army. From three li away, she can see them: thousands of horses and the proud Qorin atop them; the swaying banners and feathers of the Phoenix Guard making up the rear. She can hear them, too, in the perfect silence of the pass: the clattering of their armor, the thunder of their hooves and footsteps. The Qorin are singing an old war song—and the Phoenix Guard sing along to the melody, though they do not know the words.

She returns, as she has for the past thirty years, to Burqila Alshara. It is easy enough to find her—there is no other woman in the world who wears a war mask of her own face, no other woman in the world who rides a liver mare like hers. This is to say nothing of Burqila's bearing: she holds herself at all times as if she were listening to the groveling of her enemies.

Yes, it is easy enough to find her, and to find Dorbentei, too. Temurin rides up to them with hardly a thought.

Yet the moment she lays eyes on Temurin, Burqila calls for a halt. All at once, the army stops. Clouds of dust clot the artery of the pass. She holds up her hand to sign something. Temurin squints to try to make it out.

*What did you see?*

"Burqila wants to know why you took so damned long," calls Dorbentei, riding as always at Burqila's side. That girl acts as if Temurin does not understand Burqila's signing. Too cocky, by far.

And yet there is something strange about all of this. Closer, Temurin comes, and she sees that Barsatoq is not riding with the Qorin. Fine enough, she has her own army to lead, but . . .

"I had orders to follow," Temurin answers. She is close enough that they can talk now. She flips up her war mask. Dorbentei and Burqila do the same. Good. Temurin wants them to see her smile. "Your girl's gone and become a Kharsa while she was away."

And that is when it happens: Dorbentei and Burqila blink. Silence, as their brows furrow; silence, like an arrow landing in the base of Temurin's throat.

"Temurin," says Dorbentei. Burqila has not signed anything—whatever she is about to say is her own. "Who are you talking about?"

They can't possibly mean . . . "Your girl," Temurin says. "Barsalai Shefali." Her voice wavers. Demons wear the skin of mortals often enough—what if she's wandered back into a trap? Her eyes dart from Burqila to Dorbentei, to the confused faces of her clanmates. The air doesn't smell of evil, but she doesn't have Barsalai's nose.

But this awkwardness is a cloud drifting on the wind. Dark and strange though this moment may be, it is fleeting. Burqila's posture relaxes; realization dawns on Dorbentei's brown face.

"Ah, Barsalai," she says. The name sounds strange, as if she were speaking it for the first time. "How could we forget that oaf?"

Dorbentei laughs.

Temurin does not. She reaches for the skin of kumaq Barsalai gave her. It is cold in her hands, unnaturally so, and she wonders whether or not that is Barsalai's doing. Her palm sticks to it as she uncorks it, as she tips the skin to her lips and drinks.

Kumaq has a particular taste. Sour and sweet, the scent of it pricking your nose long after you've swallowed. It coats your tongue and stays there for hours.

This tastes nothing like that. Cool and smooth, it's more reminiscent of water—if water were transcendent. The rivers of the Rokhon are not so refreshing as this. The cool spreads through her chest and settles into her stomach.

Burqila signs. Her hands move quickly, expertly, and her eyes are as clear as ever. *Where the fuck is my daughter?*

"Burqila wants to know why she didn't come back with you. Has she gone off to be a hero on her own?"

Temurin takes a breath. A cool mist leaves her nostrils as she does.

"She's waiting," Temurin says.

*And you let her?* Burqila signs. There—the fire, the way she is stabbing at the air with her fingers.

Yes—the cloud has truly passed now.

"I'll tell you all about it," Temurin says, "but let me smell you first."

They agree quickly enough, and it is only when she is sure they smell like themselves that she tells them of what she saw.

But they do not speak of the woman left behind—the woman they forgot.

# BARSALAI SHEFALI

## SIX

Barsalai Shefali waits for her wife in this land of her enemy's making. She does not know how long it will be before Shizuka and her army arrive. The only thing to do—the natural thing to do—is to tend to her horse. If anything dares to attack Shefali, she will kill it; if nothing does, then she will at least have repaid her horse a little for all this trouble.

And so she dismounts, and fumbles removing the saddle with only one good arm, and then retrieves the brush. The world does not want her here—she can feel it in the wind, hear it in the sway of the flowers—but as the feeling is mutual she pays it no mind. The scent of rot grows stronger with every passing moment—Shefali wonders if she'll be able to smell anything at all over it.

But she continues to work. It's difficult work, to massage one's horse with only one working hand, but Shefali throws herself into it. Hard work builds character. Her mother always told her so.

*You're mad*, says the gray.

Her own blood tells her the same thing. Shefali can feel her heart beat strangely in this place—just off rhythm, scrambling to catch up. The veins and arteries, so stuffed up with black, pain her now more than ever; she can feel her own blood straining against her flesh.

*Stop resisting*, it says.

But Shefali continues to work. It is not the first time he has tried to assert himself, and it will not be the last. With her stiff right hand, she caresses the golden flower her wife gave to her, and she thinks to herself: *I am the master of my own body.*

HOW LONG IS it before she sights the army? It is impossible to tell in a place like this. The sun—if you can call that open wound a sun—does not move at all. Does that mean it has been less than an hour, or that time here holds no meaning? For she finishes dressing her horse and takes to tending to her bow. Surely it's been more than an hour, more than two. It must have been a Bell.

And yet the sun does not move.

She thinks of hunting. For a long while Shefali considers her surroundings, both the real and the imagined. What is there to hunt here? The creatures in the river, and the creatures roaming farther in—but she knows the former will not give her any usable meat and she has seen no trace of the latter.

Deep breaths, she takes, of the air around her, hoping to find some trace of life—but the rot here is too strong.

She takes to counting, to have a vague sense of how much time has passed. She reaches five hundred thousand with no one for company but her horse.

The sun does not move.

What sort of insult is this? The longer she looks on it, the more it rankles her. The Sky is not his domain. It has never been his domain. Why does he seek to exert himself in this way, to claim what is not his? So he and the other gods stopped the sun from falling to the earth—that does not give him the right to pluck it from the sky!

Too long. Too long has Shefali endured this. Anger makes her head spin. She takes her bow from its case and strings it once more, never mind the agony it causes her.

He thinks he can cage a wolf and name it his dog.

She nocks an arrow, draws back the string, and takes aim at the sky. She looses without much thought for how far it will fly or where it may land—only that she wants him to know what she thinks of him.

As the arrow launches past the curve of her bow, it goes ice white.

As it arcs through the sky, it leaves a silver trail behind.

Shefali stands and watches, wondering, wondering—can it reach that wound?

In the end, it is an errant breeze that dislodges it. The arrow sinks to the ground, far enough away that she cannot see where it lands.

Shefali grunts.

Next time—next time it'll strike true.

But she's wasted enough arrows on childish outbursts today. She sets down her bow and sits on the grass, the skulls, instead.

It is then that Shefali sees the approaching army. Like an inkwash painting of a forest somehow lurching to life—their spears and banners against the gray. Her heart feels near to bursting—she can see the faint golden glow of her wife.

Barsalai Shefali pushes herself up to her feet. How long has she been here, in this place? Too long already, too long. Her remaining days are precious to her—how many has she sacrificed sitting here, waiting for her wife?

Too many, too many.

THE QORIN ARE the first to break through the fog—Burqila and Otgar leading the way. Shefali expects them to make straight for her—but when Burqila's eyes fall upon her, it is five heartbeats before she makes any sort of motion.

How long those heartbeats feel. Why is her mother looking at her in such a way, as if they have never met? As if she is trying to remember something. What happened while Shefali stood here waiting?

A whisper of a thought soon becomes a shout: *What if it's been years already? What if she does not recognize me?*

"Aaj?" Shefali calls. She flares her nostrils, but it is no use—she cannot smell anything at all. The rot, the rot! If the Traitor had torn her right arm off, she would feel less out of sorts. How is she meant to navigate if she cannot smell? The true sight of this place overlays the false—that is all her nose will grant her here.

No explanation for her mother's confusion.

On the sixth beat of Shefali's withered heart, Burqila Alshara nods. She raises a hand and signs, and Dorbentei speaks for her.

"Needlenose, you're an idiot," says Dorbentei. Shefali lets out a breath. That must be her cousin, to address her in such a way. "Sending Temurin back on her own! Barsatoq near died on the spot. Worrying us like that!"

Burqila's eyes flick over to her niece. Shefali has the feeling not a word of what she said was actually translated.

"Sorry," Shefali manages. "How long?"

"A few hours," says Temurin. There's something in the set of her jaw—a residual discomfort. "Not long at all."

A few hours?

All of that—and it had only been a few hours?

Shefali presses her eyes closed. Around her the landscape assumes its true form. Is it her mind playing tricks on her, or are the skulls facing her now?

"Nothing's come for you?" says Dorbentei. "Burqila says she'd fought five of them, lost a horse, and fallen into a pit by this point."

"Nothing's come," Shefali echoes. "Everything here is dead."

"Not everything," says Dorbentei. "Remember why we're here?"

But how is Shefali meant to forget? Not once in her time here did she spot any of the trapped Qorin. Sayaka's letter mentioned they lined the river, in particular—fishermen and washerwomen all the way to Iwa.

Shefali sees none of them now.

What if this is a trap?

No, no. Even if it is, Shefali would rather have her head torn off again than let the Qorin suffer for her mistake. She will save them. No matter the cost—she will see to it that her people return to the steppes.

"Shefali!"

She opens her eyes in time to see her wife clearing the last column. What a sight she is, in her golden armor! The phoenix feather Shefali brought back dances atop her helmet; matching enamel decorates her phoenix war mask. She looks nothing at all like the pampered princess Shefali left behind—this, without a doubt, is a general.

Except that her horse is half as tall as the Qorin steeds surrounding it, and so she looks a little childish all the same. The sight brings a smile to Shefali's face.

She does not stay mounted long. With a swing that makes Alshara beam with pride, Shizuka leaps from the saddle. Shefali is quick to catch her. It is a good thing her condition has made her so strong—she can hold Shizuka up with only her left arm.

And how wonderful it feels to hold her! What did the eternity Shefali spent waiting matter, when this is her reward? She holds her wife close and nuzzles against her, as much as the armor will allow. How tightly Shizuka holds her! And listen, too—how sharply she's breathing, how the scales of her armor tremble with her hands!

"Please," she whispers. "Please don't worry me like that."

Shefali can only lift her mask and kiss her forehead. In truth, she had not considered that she might be worrying anyone. Her only concern had been Temurin and the wolf.

Yet how can she admit that now—that she was worried about an attack that never came? Like a child constantly crying out about wolves. She felt silly.

It is better to say nothing at all. She holds Shizuka until her wife gently hops out of her arms. Shefali wonders what the army will make of the sight—their general so small and vulnerable.

Perhaps it's best to make Shizuka look a little more powerful.

Shefali pounds her fist to her chest in a Hokkaran salute. "General Dog-Ear," she says. "Your orders?"

Shizuka's smirking, but Otgar's rolling her eyes. Let her.

"Report, Captain Steel-Eye," Shizuka says. She does it in her best general's voice.

"I waited an eternity," says Shefali, "and didn't see a thing."

"Not a thing?" asks Dorbentei. "You're sure?"

Shefali nods—but she does not look away from her general.

"Well," says Shizuka. "This place is as awful as I remember it—though much emptier. That changes nothing of our plan. We continue, toward Iwa. Toward him."

"And when we find our people, we set them free," says Dorbentei. Now she is reading Alshara's signs, now at last she is not simply speaking for herself.

"Yes," says Shizuka. "When we find them."

There it is once more—the harshness, the char to her voice that has turned up so often of late. It cannot be that she's forgetting why Shefali has come. It cannot be that she is forgetting the sacrifices involved in Shefali being here. An easy life was well within their reach—they could have stayed at the Bronze Palace with Baozhai.

Instead, they chose to do what was right and rescue those beyond the Wall.

Surely, the woman who holds Shefali's heart would not disregard a thing like saving the Qorin.

Shefali shoves the thought away—it is not worth the dignity of consideration.

"We continue," says Dorbentei. This is her rendition of two solid minutes of Burqila's signing. An oath of silence is difficult to keep when your translator vexes you like this—Burqila lifts her mask just to pinch her nose.

Shizuka nods. That is all the convincing Shefali needs—she hefts her horse's saddle off the ground with her left hand. Her gray knows well enough what is about to happen, and trots over to Shefali's side.

Yet as Shefali throws the saddle on over her gray's blanket, she cannot keep herself from glancing back at her wife.

The Phoenix Empress, looking out on the flames that sought to consume her.

SHIZUKA WAS NOT exaggerating when she spoke of the miseries of riding with an army. Back in Xian-Lai, Shefali could not imagine how it would be much different from traveling with a clan. There are several thousand of you all going to the same place. Some of you are mounted. Every night you make camp, and every morning you break it down again. In all respects, it seems exactly the same.

It is not.

To start with, there is the issue of pacing. The Qorin are accustomed to traveling with their horses, the warriors and their herds riding off ahead of the noncombatants. With three horses apiece, they could cover a hundred li in a single day easily.

That is a fine pace, a commendable one, and one that is absolutely unsustainable by the Phoenix Guard. The Hokkarans have only two horses each, if they have horses at all—most of them trudge across the skull-ridden landscape on their own two feet. To see so much gold approaching, to see their spears like the spines of a massive creature—these things are intimidating.

But to see how slowly they move . . .

It is only two days before the Qorin begin to complain. In the Burqila clan's ger, on their second night beyond the Wall, Uncle Ganzorig spits on the ground.

"We'd be knocking that bastard's teeth in already if it weren't for the—"

"For the infantry," says Shizuka. She is speaking in Hokkaran, though no one else bothers to switch languages for her. Shefali wonders idly how often she has seen the Qorin. How is it that they know Shizuka can understand them? Eight years is long enough to learn a language, she supposes; better still if she spent much time tracking down Qorin messengers to ask if they'd seen Shefali. And poor Sakura, sitting near Otgar with a book, unable to follow the conversation save for Shizuka's interjections. "You'll have to forgive me for taking care of my soldiers. To face down the Traitor is bold enough; to do so with bloodied feet and flattened arches is more than I can ask of them. We continue at the current pace."

Shefali sits on a folding stool, her eyes flicking from her mother to her wife. There is a saying about this—there must be. Enough Qorin kept their wives, lovers, sisters, aunts, and mothers all under the same ger that there *had* to be a saying about this.

Eight years abroad have dulled her mind.

She sniffs at her kumaq and waits for one of the queens to crack.

In the end, it is Burqila who relents. She leans back onto her seat and signs as if she is swatting away insects.

"If that is what your softhearted people require, who are we to argue?" says Dorbentei in her best imitation of Burqila's voice.

It is a joke, told in good humor—but Shizuka does not find it funny. The paper she'd been folding into a crane ignites; her soft face goes hard as she sets her jaw.

"Aaj," she says, her voice a blade. "Say what you will about me. Mock me for my softheartedness, if you must—but leave my army out of it."

There is no such thing as silence in a ger—there are too many mouths, too many stomachs, too many hands and feet. This ger is no exception. In the aftermath of Shizuka's challenge, no one speaks—but Ganzorig's stew continues to bubble in its cauldron, and the dogs growl as they fight.

Shefali bites her lip. Starting a fight with Burqila Alshara—what is Shizuka thinking? Though she is not wrong; Burqila should have known not to joke about a thing like the army.

But what does Shefali say at a time like this?

Nothing, thankfully—with Sakura around, there is never much empty air.

"If you two are going to start posturing, I'm going to need you to do it in Hokkaran," says Sakura. "Xianese works, too, if you're feeling saucy."

Dorbentei scoffs. For her, this is a joke—no more, no less. How often has she teased Shefali about having such a sensitive wife? "You think Xianese is saucy?" she says. "Try Surian sometime."

"I'd rather not," says Sakura flatly.

"Are you sure?" Otgar says, smirking. "If Surian doesn't work for you, I know Ikhthian, too. Fair warning, Needlenose *hates* Ikhthian."

"Yeah, well, I don't blame her," Sakura says. "Had to translate it once. Never again. Twenty-five different ways to say 'I.' Puh!"

The subject's gone by now. Though Burqila glances at Shizuka over the flickering flames of the cauldron, she signs nothing more.

Shizuka flings her burning crane onto the fire. She, too, has nothing more to say of armies.

And nothing to say later that night, when the others have gone to bed. When Shefali pulls her close and asks her what happened in Nishikomi, her wife presses a fingertip to Shefali's lips. Shizuka's head rests on Shefali's chest. For three breaths, she says nothing.

Then, quiet as a whisper: "I'll tell you about it after your birthday."

To be bitten by the dog you raised—what misery.

Shizuka will not speak about it, and Shefali will not force her.

She lifts Shizuka's wrist. When she brings it to her lips, she imagines the blood coursing through her—red, red, red.

And, eventually, when the nightmares come for Shizuka—Shefali holds her, and does not question where they came from. Shizuka has enough to contend with. Three hours of rest are all that she can manage before she starts to scream, before she starts to thrash, before Shefali carries her out beneath the stars and sings to her a song without words.

Even that does not soothe her. Not beneath this sky, not beneath these stars. When Shizuka wakes, her eyes scan the horizon and she curls up again, doubled up in misery.

"Get him out of me," she whimpers.

Shefali would forge a chain of silver and bring down the sun, if that was what Shizuka wanted—but she has never enjoyed lying to her. And it would be lying to say that it was as simple as piercing a vein and letting the skulls drink.

What can she say to assuage her wife? That it is not the first time she's had to acknowledge her bloodline's atrocities? Yoshimoto, who sent the Sixteen Swords and Sixteen armies to their deaths; Yorihito, who spread the blackblood to the Qorin.

What is one more stain?

No—she cannot say this, no matter how much it rankles her to think of her wife's lineage.

"You are not like him," Shefali says.

But these are only words, only words. How can she convince her wife of such a thing, when she is so lost in the forests of her own emotions? All she can do is show her the north star—it is up to Shizuka to navigate.

Shizuka is in no mood for it. Curled up in Shefali's arms, she looks steadfastly at the violet sky, at the sun that is not a sun.

She says nothing more until morning.

Or, at least, what they are calling morning here. Time has little meaning in a place where the sun does not move, and yet it is of vital importance to Barsalai Shefali. Thankfully, surrounded as she now is by people who have need of sleep, it is a little easier to keep track. One day is the amount of time they can travel before Alshara calls for a stop.

There is one problem with this: by Shefali's count, this leaves her only five more days before she will die.

Five days.

Her wife is heavy in her arms, but Shefali does not care. She holds her. With every breath, she tries to commit the smallest things about her to memory: the way her sleeping robes crinkle up, the rise and fall of her breathing, the exact way this false light falls upon her lips.

Five days.

If they are five days spent holding Shizuka, then they are well spent.

Even if Iwa seems to be getting no closer.

Every morning, when they break up camp, Shefali holds up her hand to the distant towers. Every morning, their height remains unchanged.

They are making no progress.

By this morning—the third—Shefali's stomach is starting to turn.

Not once in her life has she gotten lost. Her mother used to joke about it when she was younger—that if being a Kharsa did not work out for her, she might become a messenger instead.

Her arrows never miss, the cold never truly bothers her, and if you ask her which direction southwest by south is in the middle of the day—she will know. All these things have been true since her childhood. As a sparrow thinks nothing of flying, so she thought nothing of these talents. They do not require her to think of them.

It is the same here, or so she'd thought—easier, even, with something like the towers to guide her at all hours. She points her mare in the direction of Iwa, and the army follows.

Yet they are getting no closer.

Her blood is thick in her veins.

The captains come to find Shizuka as the Qorin go about breaking down the camp. Munenori—the tan man with the crane-shaped mask—stands foremost among them. Shefali tries not to listen in as her wife takes her morning war meeting, tries to focus on hefting the disassembled gers into their carts, but it is easier for the sun to set in the east than it is for Shefali to look away from her wife.

Munenori holds his hands up to the tower. He says something to Shizuka—Shefali cannot hear it from this distance—and Shizuka's aura flares again. When she answers him, it is with a firmness he does not deserve from her.

Shefali swallows.

This life of hers is wind; how can she be expected to contain all of it?

"Stubborn, isn't she?"

Shefali starts. Hokkaran, from behind her—but she hadn't smelled anyone coming. Her first instinct is to swat at the voice of an unseen demon. Thankfully, Minami Sakura spent most of her life learning how to avoid wandering hands. She sways to the side, and Shefali's claws rake only air—leaving Shefali herself gray faced with embarrassment.

"Good morning to you, too," Sakura says. "If you can call any mornings here good."

"Or mornings," says Shefali. That Sakura does not immediately condemn her is a weight off her shoulders.

"You're onto something there, Barsalai," Sakura says. She slips the tip of her brush between her teeth again. "Have you had your rice? Your proverbial rice, I mean. Your cup of stew that you sniff at a little while the rest of us listen to your relatives argue."

"They don't always argue," Shefali says. Though it must seem like it to someone who can't speak Qorin—Hokkarans tend to think of it as an aggressive language. The people who think so often haven't heard Qorin lullabies.

"Could have fooled me," Sakura says. She sighs. Up ahead of them, the air around Shizuka shimmers. If Shefali narrows her eyes she can almost see a shape to the haze—an arc floating a little bit above her. Though Sakura says nothing, she wears an expression Shefali's seen often enough on her wife.

"You're worried," Shefali says. "I am, too."

"There's a lot to worry about, between the two of you," Sakura says. "At least with her it's obvious what's wrong."

Shefali lets the silence speak for her. She watches as Shizuka grows angrier and angrier—as she jabs her finger at the map her captains have cobbled together of the surrounding area.

"She fell into the water," Sakura says. She keeps her voice low, as if she is worried the winds will carry the words to Shizuka's cropped ear. "The bay, I mean. At Nishikomi. I got my ass out of my mother's pleasure house to save her, but by the time I got there, she was already . . ."

Who is the unseen god who twists Shefali's heart in their vise? For even hearing those words causes her agony. Imagining Shizuka beneath the water, reaching up for help . . .

And where has Shefali been as her wife confronted her nightmares? Transforming herself into a giant wolf. Did they not swear they'd face their demons together?

"She hasn't been drinking, at least," Sakura says. "So I'll give her that. But I think she's going off anger now, instead of doing what's right."

*If we find them.*

Shefali frowns. The pain of having abandoned her wife mingles with a new ache—Sakura is right. Anger rules her now.

"Keep an eye on her," Sakura says. "She'll listen to you."

*Will she?*

Shefali hums in affirmation. She does not like lying—so she chooses not to think of this as a lie.

"But, like I said, at least I know what's fucking with her," says Sakura. She turns now, to look Shefali in the eyes. That she has to crane her neck to do so does nothing to diminish the fierceness of her gaze. "You're a different story."

Shefali purses her lips. She'd rather talk about Shizuka, but she knows better than to try to throw a Minami off topic.

"There's something about this whole venture that doesn't make much sense to me," Sakura says. "You're leading all your people here to liberate the rest of you, right? But we don't see anyone here. And we haven't, for days now. What makes you so confident we'll find your people out here?"

It is difficult not to find the question insulting. Shefali tells herself that Sakura means well, that she volunteered to come along as Shefali's historian. At least—that is why Shefali assumes she is here. It is a little unclear to her why Sakura chose to follow Shizuka when it came time for battle—but she is glad that Sakura made that choice. Who else would have dared to save Shizuka's life?

She means well. This is important, for historical record.

And yet Shefali cannot tell her that she knows the Qorin are here because Maki Sayaka wrote in great detail of their torture. In the letter that her daughter could never see.

"Something I read," Shefali says. It is true enough.

"And what was it that you read?" Sakura says, narrowing her eyes. "People care *an awful lot* about citations."

Shefali shifts. Sakura wants the truth of the letter—but who wants to know their mother came to such an ignoble end? Minami Shizuru's death left cracks in Shizuka's soul that, to this day, have not been mended. Sakura never knew her mother—but to know her through that letter . . .

"A story," Shefali says. She picks up one of the gers, grateful that her condition has granted her another functioning day.

"What kind of story?" Sakura asks. There's an edge to her voice, an insistence. She sets down her lectern just to help gather up the pikes and ropes for the gers. "I just find it *weird* that you'd gamble your people's lives on something like this, but you won't even tell your personal historian where you got the idea."

"I did," Shefali says. "Something I read."

*Please don't ask me anymore,* she thinks, but she knows this plea will go unanswered.

"But if it was something you read, you have no way of knowing whether or not it was true," Sakura says. "You said so yourself: you can *smell* lies. It's my pleasure-house cousins who can spot a cooked book from twenty li away."

"Sakura—" Shefali begins, but the clatter of pikes and rope hitting the cart cut her off.

"We're in the middle of enemy territory, Barsalai," she says. "You told me that we'd be surrounded, but there's no one else here. What am I supposed to think? The *most reasonable answer* to this is that they know we're here, and they're waiting for a good chance to strike. How am I supposed to feel about that, besides scared shitless? I've got no clue what's going on, because you conduct all your meetings in fucking Qorin."

Fear and anger mingling together—Shefali's ears tell her what her nose cannot. Sakura's voice is near breaking toward the end.

Shefali swallows. Words fail her, as they so often have. She picks up the pikes and ropes Sakura dropped instead, and squeezes her shoulder with her free hand.

The contact upsets Sakura more than it comforts her—she closes her eyes and takes a long breath. Shefali remembers too late what sort of life she led, and what touch means to Hokkarans. Quickly—as if she's burned herself—Shefali removes her hand.

"Thank you," Sakura says. She regains a little of her proud posture now that the hand's gone. Once again, she stares Shefali right in the eyes. "I'm not asking for you to move mountains. All I ask is that you tell me what's going on here, so I can try and figure out a plan."

"A plan?" Shefali says. But she's a—a scholar. That's what she is.

"What did you think I was doing all this time, getting married?" Sakura says. When she is met with a blank stare, Sakura shakes her head. "I meant—ask my cousin later, all right? I'm just saying, I've been busy. Burqila knows war, Shizu-lun knows war. *I* know history. And I'm the only one in the Empire who knows what happened the last time a bunch of gods ran up here."

Kenshiro's influence on that girl is obvious—but it is not entirely his voice Shefali hears in Sakura. He'd be more preoccupied with the numbers and absolute facts of the march than its purpose.

Sky, why didn't Shefali think to ask Sakura? She feels a fool and a half now. *You've been here once before*. Of course she has. Or, rather, Tumenbayar has.

"There was a wolf," Shefali says.

"Yes, I've heard the story," Sakura answers. "You became a huge wolf and ate a bunch of the enemy—"

"When I got here," Shefali says. The prospect of getting answers emboldens her. "It was the only thing I saw."

Sakura narrows her eyes. She looks to either side of them and leans forward. "Did the eight-fingered scowler see it?"

"No," says Shefali. "It spoke to me. Said I'd forgotten."

"That's because you fucking have," says Sakura. "Both of you have. Did it say anything else?"

Shefali shakes her head. If only apparitions were more useful with their warnings. They've brought Shefali nothing more than confusion and misery.

"What did it look like?" Sakura asks.

"Black," Shefali says. "With silver fangs."

"Well—that isn't much, but it's something," Sakura says. She picks up her brush again. "If you see any other shit like that, let me know. I have some ideas about killing him, but I need to be sure."

Was it the Minami blood, and not the Imperial, that lent Shizuka her obsession with godslaying?

"And one other thing," Sakura says.

"Hmm?"

"I *will* need to know what's in that letter sometime," she says. "Don't think your wolf can throw me off."

She breaks her stare only to look down at her paper. Characters form beneath her brush. Shefali cannot read them. Even if she were familiar with the language, Sakura's handwriting is . . . creative.

"Sometime," Shefali answers. She fights the urge to say that she will tell her in five days. This talk has taken far too long already—she wants to return to her wife's side.

Sakura knows well enough when a conversation is over, though she is fond of ending them herself. "If she gets rowdy, call me over," Sakura says, eyeing her cousin. "If not—I'll see you in the ger tonight."

Shefali nods to her. "Don't trouble the surgeons."

She's been riding with the surgeons in the Hokkaran army—that is the safest place for her, or so Shizuka claims. Shefali's convinced there's no safer place than with the Qorin engineers. Aunt Dalaansuv would rather be cracked open like a deer than let the enemy anywhere near her precious cannons.

"And don't die before you tell me what was in the letter," Sakura says.

Shefali watches her saunter off. She turns her attention to the makeshift Hokkaran war table, where Shizuka glows like a Jubilee firework.

Hm.

Come to think of it, it's the first day of Jubilee, isn't it?

Five days of celebration.

Five days from now is the First of Qurukai, after all—Shefali's twenty-fifth birthday.

Perhaps she will make time to enjoy the holiday—perhaps the two of them can watch Dragon's Fire burn.

NOTHING ASSAULTS THEM for most of the day.

Nothing about the landscape changes.

Nothing, apart from the river, makes a sound; nothing, apart from the traveling army, lives and breathes. In her desperation, Shefali has started to look on the river, to see if they are as alone as she thinks.

She finds only water.

Her stomach twists. It is one thing to ride into enemy territory, dust clouds rising up at your back and thunder between your legs, and find the enemy waiting for you. That's a deed as foolhardy as it is heroic. To drag half your people through Hokkaro and up over a mountain pass only to ride for three days in utter silence . . .

When she was young, the clan whispered that she was not fit to be a Kharsa. That she was too soft; that she'd been born with roots sprouting out from her ankles.

They do not whisper such things now, but they whisper all the same.

*Where has Burqila's girl brought us?*

*Load of horseshit, this whole trip.*

*Why'd we even come out here?*

She does not hear these words often. To speak ill of Burqila's daughter is to invite Burqila's wrath, after all, and that of her sisters. One of Shefali's aunts rides with each of the major companies. They, too, would brook no slander of their niece's good name.

Yet it is not slander if it is true, and the truth lends bravery to cowards.

Five days remain.

If they do not find something soon, Shefali worries the Qorin will leave as soon as she has died. What, then, of Shizuka? Alshara would never abandon her—but how many of the Qorin can she convince to stay just so Shizuka can have her revenge on the Traitor? Shizuka is family in more ways than one—but will saving her hold any water for the Qorin?

Shefali swallows. She feels sluggish, all of a sudden. Her vision blurs. Is the Traitor sapping at her strength to lend it to his own army? This is his realm, after all—does he not control everything within it? Perhaps she is the marionette in the fog, perhaps she is the scourge that will tear through this camp.

She rolls up her sleeve. Tiger fur on the deel gives way to charcoal black of skin—the only brown remaining is in her palms and fingertips. Thick, her veins, like cords beneath her skin, waiting to be deployed.

When did she become this person? She is surprised anyone in the camp recognizes her at all after so many years in Sur-Shar, so many years fighting this curse. Pointed ears, teeth more like fangs than not, skin so much darker and hair going whiter with every passing day—what is it that she is becoming? What is it that he wants to make of her?

They say the blackblood twists you according to your failings. Knowing as she does its source, Shefali doubts that. It must work according to what he *thinks* your failings are.

And what does he imagine to be hers? Why has he granted her such strength?

*Keep your eyes on the horizon,* her horse says to her. At first Barsalai thinks it little more than her gray's maternal instincts kicking in—but soon she hears the reason.

The scouts have returned.

Temurin leads them, riding hard, cutting straight across from the northeast. Or is that the southeast?

There's no time to dwell on her faltering sense of direction. Temurin's coming quick. Shefali glances to her left, where her mother leads the clan; Burqila nods. It's all the permission Shefali needs. She gives her gray a kick, riding out to meet Temurin halfway—

Temurin, who bolts right past her.

Shefali half stands in the saddle. Temurin didn't even *look* at her. What is going on? Is the enemy coming? Shefali turns to face the horizon once more. There are no blackbloods, no demons—only idyllic hills, only the towers of Iwa.

Realization dawns on her. Where are the other scouts?

She swallows. With her hips she urges her gray back toward the clan, toward the army, toward the lone returning scout. Temurin is dismounting already, pointing over in the direction whence she came. Now that she is standing still, Shefali can see gouges in her three-mirror armor. Deep as her fingers and as long as Shefali's arm, the gouges wrap around from right breast to left kidney. Were it not for the armor, she would not be standing.

". . . head of a bird . . ."

"Slow down," says Dorbentei. She waves to their aunt Khadiyya, one tumen over, who sends out the call to halt. "What's going on? Where're the others?"

Temurin earned her name during the Qorin invasion. She hadn't been much older than Burqila at the time—but she'd been angrier, and stupider. During their initial attack on Oshiro, Temurin broke from her tumen and took it upon herself to claim as many Hokkaran ears as possible.

She did not return to camp until she had fifty ears, a dagger embedded in her shoulder, and two stumps where her fingers should have been.

*Temurin*, Alshara named her. Iron woman.

For all Shefali's life, Temurin has lived up to her name. It seems it shall remain that way until the day Shefali dies—though Temurin's sword is bent back like a misstruck nail, she holds it up with more anger than fear.

"I'm going to kill it," she says. "Whatever that thing was. We're going to kill it. Give me twenty men, Burqila—"

Burqila makes a cutting gesture. Temurin shuts up. The signs come quickly after that.

"Burqila wants to remind you that I asked you a question, Temurin—"

"I know what she's saying," says Temurin. "And I meant what I said. Give me twenty men, and I'll have our scouts back."

"So it took them," says Dorbentei.

A murmur starts to spread. Shefali can watch it happen, if she cares to—but she watches instead for Shizuka's arrival.

"Where?" says Shefali. The creak of bows, the rattle of arrows being drawn—her people will soon be out for blood.

"Don't," says Dorbentei. "I don't care if you are a god; we're not risking you."

"I'm not dying today," Shefali says. There—the dazzling feather is making its way toward her.

"Did I stutter?" Dorbentei says. "I don't care if you're dying today or not. I'm not watching you get your throat torn out again."

Shizuka is nearly with them now. Shefali decides to let that argument lie before her wife arrives—it's best to decide what they will do about the missing scouts with Shizuka present.

"Let Barsalai come, if that is what she wants," says Temurin. "We'll need the wolf to kill that damned thing."

Not Barsalai—the wolf. So this is what her people think of her?

Five days.

Whatever they think of her, they will not have to think about it for long. Let her be useful to them, if that is what they want.

"Stop complaining and tell us what you saw," says Dorbentei. She's gone back to reading Burqila's signs. Burqila, for her part, is leaning forward in her saddle, as if she means to strike at Temurin.

"Wait," Shefali says. "Shizuka."

Burqila's eyes narrow. Nevertheless, she nods, and the Qorin wait on broken eggshells for Shizuka to join them. She brings Captain Munenori with her—a man who keeps his eye on the horizon while Shizuka does all the talking.

"Where are the rest of the scouts?" Shizuka asks as she arrives. It is the first thing she says. Her abruptness should not bother Shefali—the Qorin prize getting to the point—but it stings that Shizuka does not address her in any way.

Then again, they are dealing with the Phoenix Empress now. She has not raised her mask. The queer violet light plays upon the enamel and bronze, making her look more a peacock than a raptor.

"Temurin was just getting to that," says Dorbentei. Then, more sharply: "Wasn't she?"

Temurin doesn't bother to acknowledge Dorbentei's needling. She delivers her report facing Burqila, and not her interpreter.

"We were thirty li out, maybe thirty-one. A half hour's ride, no more than that; Checheg wanted to start heading back, and I thought it wouldn't be a bad idea. An hour of scouting's plenty when there's nothing to report.

"We turned back, and we were pretty sure of the way we were going—Jolorkai was casting some of Barsalai's blessed kumaq behind him, and that was what we followed. He was the first one to realize something was wrong. There was a bit of milk that landed right on a mountain flower, a violet one. The sort you see on the mountain back home. He called me over when he realized he'd seen that same flower five times.

"I told him he was being an idiot, but I kept my eyes peeled in case he wasn't. Turned out, he had a good head on his shoulders—the flowers kept repeating and repeating. We were going in circles.

"I knew something was wrong, and I knew our priority was to return to the army. I figured if we all rode out in separate directions, at least one of us would be able to make it back. Maybe one of our two gods could tell us what was going on, maybe that spot was important to the northerners, I don't know—but I knew the information was important.

"We took off in different directions, each of us, as close to the cardinals as we could figure out. Khadiyya gave us a compass, but that thing doesn't work out here—you see how it keeps spinning around like a scared marmot. We picked a direction and we went, and I hoped at least one of us had picked the right one.

"Maybe a quarter of an hour later, it started to rain.

"I knew nothing good was going to happen. Rain on the steppes is one thing, but rain out here? Could be the Traitor pissing on our heads, for all I know. I drove harder, looking to get through it as quick as I could. The clouds got thicker and thicker overhead—and then the fog showed up. Unrolled in front of me like felt, Burqila, I swear it did.

"Barsalai gave me a skin of kumaq the last time we rode through the fog together. I took a drink from it as I pushed through the dark, and held it in my mouth the whole time. That way I could hold my sword, I thought.

"It took another two minutes before the fog cleared. When it did, this shit? The river, the flowers, the field? Gone. We were at the base of a mountain. It wasn't one of the Tokuma; it was covered in pine trees. Not Gurkhan Khalsar, either, though it was about that tall. The pine trees were all around, wherever I looked.

"And so were the horses. All four of them, without their riders.

"I looked up at the mountain, at the horses, and I thought to myself, 'You don't want to die here.' So I turned behind me, expecting to see the fog.

"The fog was gone, too. There was nothing but forest around me, and the horses, and the mountain in front of me.

"Between a mountain and a forest, I'd rather have the mountain. I tied the other horses' saddles to mine, and tried to find some way up the path. Maybe that's what took me so long—I must have been gone for days."

"Only a Bell and a Half," Shizuka says, her Qorin jarring after the rumbling rhythm of Temurin's. That she can follow a story told in Qorin surprises Shefali. In spite of the circumstances, her chest warms with pride. "Continue."

Temurin wipes at her nose with her thumb.

"Up the mountain I went, worried the whole time that some twisted creation was going to jump out of the trees. My hand's still cramped from holding on to my sword so long. I didn't stop until my horse needed to, and even then—I didn't sleep. Kept my back to a tree and waited for something to try my patience.

"But nothing did. Nothing in this place moves, nothing in this place breathes, nothing in this place . . ."

Temurin's voice goes rough. She takes a moment to collect herself.

"I kept going. It was too quiet, and it rained the whole time, but I kept going. I don't know how long it took me to get to the top, but I did, and when I got there, he was waiting.

"Shaped like a man in Hokkaran robes, but he had the head of a bird. It. That thing. It was sitting in front of a firepit roasting meat.

"When it laid eyes on me, I felt as if it were seeing *inside* me. I reached for my sword, knowing I had to try to kill it. Bird-headed men on mountaintops can't mean well, not when they're looking at you like that. I charged, swung at it, and it caught my blade barehanded. Bent it back—look at it!—like it was a twig. Worse than a twig!

"I drew back to punch it, but with its other hand it caught my fist. The demon yanked at me so hard it's a wonder I didn't fall off my horse. The stirrups kept me on—that and my own two legs.

"Maybe that amused the demon. It sat back down and clapped its hands together. When it spoke, I expected to hear . . . squawking. Hokkaran, if not squawking. Qorin was what I got.

"It told me that it wanted to have a meeting with Barsalai and Barsatoq, and asked me if I thought all of this would get their attention."

Shefali chews the inside of her mouth. All of this—four dead Qorin—just to get her attention? *We need the wolf,* Temurin had said at the start of all this.

She can feel Dorbentei's eyes on her, feel the eyes of the forward riders. How many Qorin have died because of the Hokkarans already? How many uncles and aunts and cousins have they given to the Sky? Today, four more join them—just to catch Shizuka and Shefali's attention.

"What did you say?" asks Shizuka. If she, too, feels the needles of their eyes, she shows no sign of it. Four years at war and four on the throne have likely inured her to such things.

Temurin glares at Shizuka. She presses her lips together, wipes her nose again. Then her temper breaks; she looks away.

"I told him to go milk a stallion," she says.

A few chuckles from the forward riders. Good that they can laugh at a time like this—Shefali can't.

"Tough talk, to a demon," says Dorbentei. "But you're here in front of us without a scratch on you."

There's an uncomfortable silence, a question left unasked. Shefali sniffs. No answer comes to her—everything here smells like rot. If Temurin's changed, it is Shizuka who will have to spot her.

"He laughed at me," Temurin says. Her eyes are dark for a Qorin; they go darker now. Shefali gets the feeling that Temurin is staring *past* her. "He laughed at me, and told me to keep riding down the mountain. I'd find all of you at the bottom. He told me to tell you he wanted to talk."

"So you're saying he just let you go?" says Dorbentei. Burqila's signs were, for once, far shorter than this.

"Looking at him—something happened," Temurin says. She's shaking her head, as if trying to shake away the thoughts. "He took off his bird head, and underneath there was a man's, and he had this flute . . ."

A serpent awakens from its winter hibernation. Hunger drives it more than thought. It slithers forth, the writhing soothing the ache in its muscles. For two li, it crawls along on its belly; for two li, it tastes the air for any sign of a marmot. When at last it knows it has come to the right place, it coils in amid the silver grass and waits.

For an hour, for a day, for a week, it waits. Still as a statue, it waits, its heartbeat like the occasional clatter of a bamboo noisemaker. So still that the marmot has no hope of seeing it.

The marmot races by.

Mid-stride, it stops.

Two fangs sink into its throat; coils tighten around its body.

Shizuka, the serpent; Temurin, the marmot. A blazing arc of gold sears itself onto Shefali's vision. The strike itself happens so quickly that Shefali cannot follow it—the light swallows the motion whole. One moment Shizuka is seated atop Matsuda; in the next, she is sheathing her sword and Temurin is bleeding across the cheek.

The cut is as long as Shefali's thumb, as thin as a strand of hair, but it bleeds well. Red covers the dusky brown of Temurin's cheek.

A heartbeat of confusion. The others are trying to figure out what has happened. Temurin's reaching for the cut even as she turns toward Shizuka. Mounted though she may be, Temurin's tall enough to jab one of her remaining fingers right at Shizuka's chest.

"What the *fuck?*" Temurin snaps. She jabs her finger again, harder this time.

Shizuka remains not only upright but unmoving. Coals burn from the eyes of her mask, casting shadows on what little is visible of her face.

"We needed to be certain," says the Empress.

"Shizuka—" Shefali starts, but her wife's burning glare immolates the rest of her thoughts.

"We do not intend to have our army *infiltrated* by the enemy," says the Empress. She speaks in Hokkaran as precise as it is long-winded. "This wretch has vexed us before. Are you not a warrior? Are you not *accustomed* to such injuries? Bear it with pride, for the color of your blood is your savior."

Most Qorin speak Hokkaran. Temurin is the rare exception, thanks to a conscious decision she made many years ago. To speak the conqueror's tongue is to allow them into your soul, and Temurin will never allow such a thing.

And so it is that without faltering she stares right back at the Empress who has so demeaned her.

Temurin Baterdene smears her blood across the Phoenix Empress's war mask.

"That red enough for you?" she says.

There are parts of the steppes so cold and so barren that even the wolves do not risk them. To stand where the grass has given way to tundra is to stand five li away from any other source of life.

Shefali has been to those places, fond as she is of solitude and cold. She has sat among the withered grass and the tundra to look out on the stars, and she has heard there only the wind, only the music of the heavens above.

Those patches of celestial silence—all were noisier than this.

To breathe is to flow from one moment to the next, and in the next, Shizuka may well draw her blade again. Who can stop her, if she does?

How it pains Shefali to imagine her wife might do such a thing! Worse than the poison clotting her veins, worse than the blades between her ribs and the hammers that once crushed her hands. She would face the Queen of Ikhtar and all her punishments a hundred times if it meant she could avoid this ache.

"Shizuka," Shefali says. Now she, too, must become a hammer. "Temurin is family."

"Ask my mother how well it went for her, to trust in family beyond the Wall," says Shizuka. "Ask your mother, or Sakura's!"

Burqila Alshara urges her horse between her two daughters; Burqila Alshara, her mask a mirror for the face beneath it. She holds her hand high enough that the whole clan can see her signing. Dorbentei waits until she is finished before she dares to begin translating—in Qorin.

"Barsatoq Shizuka Shizuraaq—you're tearing at wounds that have never healed. The Qorin shall be safe because I will keep them safe *my* way. Do not forget that I cracked the skulls of Oshiro beneath my boots before your parents laid eyes on each other. If you were anyone but Naisuran's daughter, I'd have you dragged for what you did. You *do not* strike my people."

Shefali watches her wife's eyes, watches for any sign of regret or shame or guilt.

Instead—only the coals. "Understood, Burqila."

What torment in Shefali's breast at the sight! At the sound of those words! Who is this woman atop her wife's horse, in her wife's armor, wearing her wife's mask? For it is not Shefali's Shizuka; Shizuka would never dream of being so rude to her mother-in-law, to her own mother's best friend—let alone as one ruler to another.

Who is this, standing here, looking so familiar?

Sanvaartains are on their way to look at Temurin's cut. The woman herself stands there glowering, looking over her shoulder at a mountain that is not there. Sweat mixes with the blood dribbling down her cheek.

"Temurin," Shefali says. When Temurin turns, Shefali flicks up her war mask. She drags the sharp nail of her thumb in a line beneath her good eye. Yes—there. Nail breaks skin. Black seeps forth from it like winter sap.

The whole clan is watching. So, too, is Shizuka. Let her. Let her see what a mess she has made of things, that it should come to a gesture like this.

Temurin's dark eyes go soft. She sniffs, jerks her head in the direction of the mountain. "We've got to get going," she says, "if we're going to catch them."

Shefali isn't sure what's more endearing—that she is willing to set aside what could have been a major conflict, or that she thinks there is any chance they will find those four scouts alive.

After all, there is no one who knows better than Shefali the succulent taste of flesh.

Their scouts are long gone—but perhaps, if they hurry, they might find something to give to the Sky.

# O-SHIZUKA

## FIVE

Shizuka is going to kill him. Sure as the sun rising in the east—she is going to kill the Traitor.

Why is that so difficult for Shefali to understand? It puzzles Shizuka. Why is she showing such sympathy toward the creature, toward the demon lord? For that is the way she's been acting of late: as if it were a *bad* thing that Shizuka wants to see them wiped from the earth.

Is that not why all of them came out here—to rid the world of the enemy? To drive their swords and arrows into the bodies of the enemy until none rose; to snap the Traitor's head from his shoulders—is that not why they are here?

And yet Shizuka shows a little precaution, and suddenly all the Qorin hate her.

Madness. It's madness.

"*You* understand, don't you?" Shizuka says to Munenori. He rides at her right as the joint army follows Temurin and the forward riders. After the . . . incident with Temurin, Burqila and the Qorin elected to ride ahead of the Phoenix Guard.

That should not bother Shizuka. It's practical, after all; it isn't as if her infantry and artillery can keep up with the Qorin cavalry. And *they* don't ride in formation. Without the Qorin muddying things at the van, the Phoenix Guard can focus on their unbreakable formations.

Yet Shefali went along with them.

They're going off to confront a demon, and Shefali went with her family instead of staying with her wife.

It should not bother her. Truly, it shouldn't; this isn't the first time Shefali's had to decide between Shizuka and her family. Last time, she chose Shizuka. This is only fair.

But they'd said they'd be *together* for this, and Shefali acted as if it were the most terrible thing in the world to check if Temurin had gotten infected. As if Shizuka were some sort of monster.

When a sharp sword cuts you, you do not feel it until the air's gotten into the wound. So it is with this—it does not hurt to be abandoned until she is.

Captain Munenori is as silent as her wife. Most days that is a boon, a thing that warms her heart, but today it rankles her. Today, she needs the affirmation.

"Don't you?" she repeats.

"The necessary is often unpalatable," he says. The long beak of his crane mask distorts his voice.

"That's exactly what I mean!" says Shizuka. "How were we to know she hadn't turned? How were we to trust her?"

She and Munenori ride toward the back of the army, flanked on either side by two units of infantry. Ahead of them five more companies march, gradually coming together to form an arrow. Arrow, Shizuka reasons, is best when you are expecting trouble.

And it keeps her far from the Qorin.

For twenty minutes they've been marching. The Qorin are a massive smudge of gray and brown and black along the horizon. If Temurin is right, soon they very well may end up separated.

Shizuka grips her saddle horn a little tighter.

"General," says Munenori. "Did you draw your sword to strike down evil, or did you draw it out of fear?"

*What sort of question is that?* Shizuka nearly snaps at him, but she masters her temper enough to grit her teeth instead.

Before she can answer, the signal fans go up from the van. Shizuka squints—the eyeholes of her war mask leave much to be desired when it comes to visibility. Gold, red, green. A message for Shizuka in specific, danger, and a request to charge ahead. Had the enemy shown himself already?

The Daybreak Blade burns in its sheath. So it has since their second day here, as if burning away the corruption trying to seep into it.

"There will be time for self-examination later," Shizuka says. "We've word."

A small grunt, echoing within the beak of the mask into something greater. "The fog is coming," he says.

And so it is—she'd been too distracted by the war fans to notice. Fog is coming down from the confounded sky like an aggressive cloud bent on swallowing them up. Just as the landscape here changes when she closes her eyes, so, too, does the cloud of fog. When she blinks, it goes dark and grotesque; when she blinks, it is a mass of black feathers clotted together with blood.

Yet if *that creature* is inside it . . .

She draws the Daybreak Blade. Fire courses through her veins and into the sword itself. A brilliant gold, it glows, for a brilliant general.

Or so she likes to think of herself, anyway.

"Forward!" Shizuka shouts, her sword held aloft. "Heaven marches with us!"

Is there any feeling greater than commanding an army? In truth, she's come to enjoy it: Bellow one word, and thousands will listen. Look—the fields of gold and scarlet charging ahead! Watch them move in perfect unison, their weapons clutched tight, the false sun playing on their war masks!

Watching them thrills her—for everywhere the Phoenix Guard goes, the Phoenix Empress is sure to be among them. She is in every fall of their feet, every sharp breath, every heartbeat.

The clatter of their weapons, the earth shaking with their steps—all of this is to her as standing on the edge of a cliff face.

How sweet will be the fall, how exhilarating the wind whipping through her hair!

And yet, the horrible ground rising up to meet her: some of her soldiers will die today.

An unavoidable truth, a weight to stymie her celebrations.

Where they go, she will go; when they die, so, too, will something die inside her.

Yet it was her decision to bring them all here, and their decision to come. This is the life they've all chosen to lead.

A bird-headed man atop a mountain. Who knows what awaits them in the fog?

She thinks of Rihima—of the marionettes and the lives they took. She thinks of Daishi, of the hollow look in her eyes after years of war; she thinks of her mother, Minami Shizuru, drinking herself halfway to an early grave and hoping her daughter wouldn't follow.

As the fog descends, as the feathers descend, she sees the churning seas of Nishikomi, the dark depths of the Kirin.

Terror is a monster, feet beating against the earth, reaching for her heart.

Shizuka gives Matsuda a kick.

Let her fear try to catch up—she is going to kill the bird-headed man. Whatever her wife thinks of her for it.

HER HEART IS a thunder drum.

Closer they come, closer and closer. The Qorin disappeared into the fog five minutes ago. Her *wife* disappeared into the fog five minutes ago.

*She has faced worse than this,* Shizuka tells herself, *and today is not the day she dies.*

Fear, worry, anxiety—these are impurities that threaten to shatter her resolve. She must burn them from her soul.

She must become the Empress.

Closer.

The arrowhead, soaring across the earth, aimed straight for the cloud.

She grips her sword tighter.

The gold-tipped spears of the vanguard pierce the gray.

"Forward!" she calls again, stoking the fires within their hearts. Forward they march. Three steps and the spears disappear inside the cloud; four, and the vanguard joins them. Terror claws at Shizuka's back, but she does not falter.

"Forward!" she calls again. Forward they march—the flanking companies and the forward archers, the bannermen and the drummers. Once the fog swallows them, she sees only the barest traces of them within—thin gray lines where her proud gold banner once flew.

Her company is next. The fog is so thick that, had she the urge, she might cut straight through it. Shizuka has seen Qorin felt with more translucence. Looking on the fog—on the feathers and blood—fills her with an unspeakable trepidation; she tastes rot.

Yet Heaven rides with them, and where her soldiers go, she must follow.

Forward.

The fog smacks against her as they cross it, a wet and warm slap across the face. This is not the cool fog of morning, nor the salt-soaked kind so common in Nishikomi—this is the breath of the jungle, the breath of the south. By Matsuda's second step, Shizuka can feel the sweat clinging to the back of her neck; by the third, her chest heaves with the effort it takes her to breathe; by the fourth, it is over.

Four steps and they are through.

So quickly does it happen that she hardly has time to think, hardly has time to realize the scenery's changed. One moment she is enveloped in gray—and at the next, she is at the base of a mountain. Temurin was right—it is not so large as the Tokuma, but larger than Gurkhan Khalsar. Thick forests coat it like fur on a slumbering bear. At the top, a single plume of white smoke coils up into the violet sky.

The first thing Shizuka does is look out onto her army. All five of the forward companies seem to be in good shape, with no notable blurring of the formation. The pride she feels at this realization is second only to the worry that follows it—she cannot see any of the Qorin. Not ahead of them, at the base of the mountain; not behind them, where there is only forest to greet them; not on either side, where the green stretches into forever.

*Shefali.*

If that big oaf got herself captured while they were upset with each other . . . No, painting it that way does not change the starkness of the image.

Her terror's catching up to her. She licks at her lips beneath her mask.

"Munenori-zun," she says, "give me a spyglass."

She does not know that he has one until she asks for it.

Of course Munenori carries a spyglass—he bought it himself during his days as a sailor. Or perhaps he'd traded for it? The tesselated patterns suggest Surian craftsmanship, and so far as she knows, Munenori has never been to the far East.

However he came by it, she is grateful that he did. She holds the spyglass up to her eye and turns her attention to the mountain. There—racing between the trees! A streak of gray, a streak of red, a streak of yellow.

Shefali, Burqila, and Dorbentei.

Shizuka lets out a breath she did not know she was holding. She imagines that all her fears are contained within that breath, that they are leaving her now to mingle with the air.

"The Qorin are climbing the mountain," she says. "We will follow."

Her voice echoes through the cold, dry morning. She wonders briefly if it will carry all the way to Shefali's pointed ears.

# LAI BAOYI

## ONE

You can tell much of a man from his walk: whether he keeps his shoulders in line with the rest of his body or sways them speaks to his confidence; if he is a little bowlegged, then he must be a skilled rider; you may read all his military history in a limp at his right ankle.

Lai Baoyi learned to read the signs of men before she learned to read characters. Her very first memories are of her mother cradling her on one of the Bronze Palace's many balconies, pointing here and there to the servants. "Do you see, my precious gift? Look at how he holds his hands. . . ."

She is not surprised at what she sees of this man in this moment: the exaggerated curve of his puffed-out chest; the bold, costly violet of his robes; the clatter of his armor and the way he struggles a little beneath its weight.

This is their first meeting—but she has long known his reputation. The Empire agrees on few things these days. That Fuytusuki Kazuki is a retrograde fool of the highest order is one of them.

Or, as the Young Empress would put it, had she more people in whom to confide—Kazuki's a big, mean idiot.

That he bows at all is surprising to her, much less that he bothers to get in proper seating before doing so. Tradition is carved into the bones of all the provincial lords, it seems.

But then—he bows to her father, and not to her.

"Lord Oshiro-tul," says Fuyutsuki. He taps his forehead against the bamboo mats. "I have come, as summoned. Your palace servants have treated me well."

Her father stands a horselength away from her, cloaked in the black and gold robes of his station. A black hat sticks up like a shark fin atop his white hair. When he smiles it is warm, and it reaches his eyes, but Baoyi knows well enough that it is not genuine.

"Young Lord Fuytusuki-tun," says Father, "you have indeed come as summoned, but you must have gotten the wrong idea somewhere. Didn't you read your invitation?"

There is a pause. Kazuki cannot see the soft smile—the genuine smile—father and daughter exchange.

"Your Imperial Highness, I read it three times over. You summoned me to tea because you wanted to talk about the rebels."

"You are incorrect on three counts," says Father, "but I will let our gracious host do the rest of the talking—I've already overstepped my bounds." He claps his hands together and bows from the shoulder to Baoyi, who responds with a warm nod. "Your Imperial Majesty, Most Serene Empress, I leave you to your guest. Should you have need of me, I shall be right at my desk; you need only yell and I shall hear you."

And it is then, of course, that Fuyutsuki realizes precisely the error he has made. He doesn't sit up from his bowed position, but Baoyi hears him swallow. The idea that he might be afraid of her is a saddening one; she doesn't like being frightening. Rulers should be likeable. She sets about righting it the moment her father leaves for the desk he has set up in the back part of the chamber.

"Kazuki-tun, you can sit up," she says. "There isn't any point in staying down there if we're going to have tea."

He does as he is told. She notices, without really wanting to, that he is a little slow in doing so, as if he were a puppet that must be pulled into position by an unskilled hand. This, too, saddens her.

"Are you disappointed?" she asks. "Father isn't any good at making tea."

"I heard that!" her father calls.

"Well, he isn't," Baoyi affirms. "No matter what he said."

Kazuki's eyes flick over toward Father's desk. When they come to rest near her again, she realizes that he is staring at her mouth. Someone must have prepared him for talking to the Empress. Still, you weren't supposed to *stare*.

"Kazuki-tun?" she says. "I heard that your Hokkaran was very good, but if you'd like, I know three other languages. My tutor even tells me that my Ikhthian isn't bad."

Her mother taught her that one—it never fails to jolt the lords from their proverbial horses. "Hokkaran will do, Your Majesty. Did you say you'd be making the tea?"

"I did," she says. She sits up a little straighter. The kettle, cups, and supplies are all gathered on a small wooden platter before her. "But you didn't come dressed for tea, did you?"

"I thought this was a military meeting—" he starts.

She doesn't let him finish. "Please don't say such silly things," she says. "It is. But it's also tea, and we can't start with you dressed like that."

"Your Majesty," he says. "It would be immodest for me to change in your presence."

He's speaking so much more stiffly now than he was in the halls, as if he didn't think she'd ask her servants what he was like away from her sight. She doesn't like it. "That isn't a problem. Odori-lun, would you set up a screen for him? And Juzo-zun, would you help him out of his armor?"

Odori and Juzo—the Phoenix Guardsman standing to her right—move at once. The screen is in place before Fuyutsuki Kazuki can summon another argument against it. The clatter of hooks and latches soon follows, punctuated by heavy thuds. Baoyi can hardly enjoy the painting—*Minami Shiori and the Fox Woman*—before the whole process is over with. Odori folds the screen to reveal Fuyutsuki in his robes and wide trousers. He's still wildly unprepared for tea—he isn't wearing any seasonal patterns, he hasn't brought any candies for her, he clearly hasn't purified himself. There are dark stains at his chest and beneath his arms; hair like a forest peeks out from his lapel.

Her mother would have taken one look at him and demanded he go bathe before he earned the privilege of another minute in her presence.

But her mother isn't here, and sometimes you have to meet people halfway. If she sends him to go get properly ready, he'll have the time to gather his wits.

"That's much better," Baoyi says. "Don't you feel better, Kazuki-tun?"

The teapot is a solid bronze dragon with enameled scales—a gift from her mother for her tenth birthday. The heat is such that Baoyi must wrap her hand in the bottom three layers of her robes when she grasps the handle.

"Your Majesty, with all due respect, shouldn't I be speaking with your father about this? It's a military matter."

The Empress must never let anyone know what she's feeling—but she really wants to pout. He isn't paying any attention at all to the tea. Green powder, dark as a forest night, sits in a carefully chosen bowl. Once the lid is off the teapot, she hands him the bowl of powder. He doesn't even sniff at it—he just lifts it to his nose.

"How do you like the tea?" she asks.

"It's . . . It's well chosen, and exquisitely tailored to the season," he says.

It is, in fact, pointedly out of season. She was trying to send a message. Her disappointment overcomes her etiquette and she sighs a little as she pours the tea into the pot. Stirring is her least favorite part of the ordeal to begin with.

"A lie expressed sincerely is as good as the truth," says Baoyi. "I don't really like that saying, but a lot of people do. I don't think you're one of them, though, because you aren't a very good liar."

It hangs in the air between them—the silence, the soft whisking of the water. Silence like this scratches at Baoyi's soul.

"You can be honest with me," she says. "I like it when people are honest."

Fuyutsuki swallows. "I can't talk about quelling the rebellion with a child." The last word leaves him like a bit of shell found in his morning egg and rice.

Baoyi leaves the tea to steep. There are many thoughts dancing through her mind; keeping track of the seconds will give them something to dance to. "I'm your Empress; it doesn't matter how old I am." *Twelve isn't a child*, she thinks all the same. "And what's happening in Hanjeon isn't a rebellion."

His fingers twitch. He wants to make a fist, she thinks, but it'd be impolite to do that. "Insubordinate" is the word Father would use, but that isn't quite right. People should be free to think whatever they like, and free to say whatever they like to the Empress—so long as they are polite enough about it. "You think I'm wrong," she says, her tone a little bit warmer.

"I do," he says. "Respectfully . . ."

He glances up for just a moment. She nods, her bangs swaying in front of her eyes.

"For *generations*, we took care of those people. The Old Empress was a drunkard, everyone remembers that; cutting them loose at all was a mistake—one that history will scorn, mark my words. But who are we in this glorious empire if we don't keep our word? So—let them go, then; let them struggle and come begging for us in a few years. But then they go and declare themselves independent before the treaty's finished!" Now he really does clench his fingers. "It's an insult to you, an insult to Hokkaro, and it's an insult to decency. It *proves* they aren't ready to be on their own. Marching in to Hanjeon and teaching them a lesson is our only option."

It always strikes Baoyi as strange, the way some people speak about others. Something in her wilts, and it takes her a little while before she can think of something worth saying to this foolish, odious man. Maybe it is good that he is afraid of her.

"The High Council of Hanjeon sent me a letter a few days before their declaration. I approved it. I don't know where you got the idea that they insulted me."

"It's an insult to act—they're still your subjects!" Kazuki answers. The redness is starting to spread up to his face.

"They aren't," says Baoyi, "and, really, I never thought of them as my subjects to start with. They're their own people. It's right for them to rule over themselves, wouldn't you say?"

Fish-egg bubbles boil in the pot. Baoyi reaches the end of her count and pours Kazuki a cup.

He does not answer.

She thought this would be easier. "You aren't going to drink the tea, are you?"

It's frustrating, it really is, when he picks up the cup and takes a sip. No one drinks tea that way. You need to give it a little time to cool; you're supposed to smell it and compliment it in that time. He's flinching, so she knows that it hurts to hold the cup. When he's done, he puts it back down on the tray. "We had a deal, Your Majesty," he says. "They've turned their backs on it."

Like dogs set loose to hunt tigers, she thinks, he will not turn away from the pursuit of his goal.

But perhaps he doesn't realize exactly what sort of hunt he's on.

"But if you invade, that will bring war," she says. "You must have read all my declarations, Kazuki-tun. War is expressly forbidden. I want my reign to be a peaceful one."

He does not flinch now. "Hokkaro's history is written in blood."

"And it doesn't need to be," says Baoyi. "All we want—all anyone wants—is a safe place to live. Food in their stomachs and friends at their side. Some want to marry, and some don't; some want partners to share their lives; some don't. The only thing *everyone* wants is safety. Why would you risk that?"

There's too much fire in her voice as she speaks, but she supposes that's unavoidable. Her mother wouldn't be happy with her, but her mother isn't here.

This blow at least seems to have landed. The big man before her glances off to the side before he answers. "You must, at times, wrest safety from your enemies. The Jeon hate us. Who's to say they won't rally to attack us?"

A second refusal. She will explain to him one last time. It's only proper. Blowing softly on her cup of tea, she thinks of the best approach to take. A faint memory comes to her: the acrid scent of alcohol, a wash of bright red and gold. *Political games are for cowards. You've got to be direct.*

Terrible advice, especially from a half-remembered source. But there is some truth in it.

"Hanjeon at present has the smallest standing army west of the Wall of Stone," says Baoyi. "If you attack them, there will be no honor in it. Everyone will know you as the man who attacks a newborn instead of giving it room to grow. To say nothing of the sleeping giant just to their south. Haven't you considered what an invasion of Hanjeon would look like to Xian-Lai?"

He's back to staring at her mouth. She hopes that it helps her words sink in. When he says nothing, her hopes grow wings, and she allows herself a sip of her tea.

It is natural that he should tear those wings apart the moment the tea fills her mouth. "They shall know me as the man who seized what is rightfully ours. They shall know me for a scion of the golden age of Hokkaro, who hews close to the old ways. A man who is unafraid of ten thousand farmers with pitchforks and scythes."

She closes her eyes. An old trick—you can look quite serene with your eyes closed, so long as you make sure to keep your lids and brows relaxed.

"And if you are defeated?" she says.

He scoffs. "Your Majesty, do you doubt your retainers? I will not lose with Fuyutsuki's stone men at my back."

She wants to correct him. He said "stone men," but the Fuyutsuki army comprises women, too. It's been that way for as long as there's been an Empire—a fact some people are all too quick to forget.

"I'm sorry to hear you speak like that," says Baoyi. "Really, I am.

I thought that maybe if I spoke to you, you'd come to your senses. No one wants a war, Kazuki-tun. No one wants any more families broken up."

"We have to prove our worth," says Fuyutsuki. "If we let them traipse off like this, what sort of idea are people going to get? That they can just split off whenever they want? It isn't right. I'm doing this to maintain the celestial order, Your Majesty. I hope you can see that."

Appealing to her sense of righteousness—or at least, his idea of her sense of righteousness. Baoyi does not remember much of the old Empress—no one does, except her father the historian—but she knows they aren't anything alike.

"I have no army to stop you," she says. "I thought asking nicely would work."

There it is: in the shadow of his averted glance, she sees the guilt start to take hold, the shame.

"You didn't even finish your tea, and you didn't bring any treats, either. Lords are supposed to be people of reason and good manners. I'm a little sad, if I'm being honest."

She isn't afraid to let her youth work to her advantage—she perches her head on one hand. With the other, she waves him away.

"If you don't think peace is what's best for the Empire, then I don't think I want to have tea with you. At least, not right now. I think someday you'll see my side of things. You are dismissed, Kazuki-tun; Tsukiko-zun and Juzo-zun will see to your lodgings."

If he takes offense at being given the same rank as her guards, he says nothing. No—from the way he stands and the way he eagerly clutches at his armor, Baoyi reads only relief. Somehow having tea with a young girl has made him more uncomfortable than anything he's had to face before.

When the door closes behind him, she lets out a heavy sigh. "I *really* hoped that would work."

"You did your best, O-Yuuka-shal," says Odori. Already she is picking up Kazuki's neglected cup; already she is removing all traces of him from the room. "You spoke reasonably, and with such great empathy—anything he does now, he must do knowing it is his own decision."

Odori has been working for her since she and Father were named regents. Baoyi does not remember much of those first few months, but she does remember the serving girl who always sneaked her treats, always told her the gossip she'd picked up in the kitchens. Servants heard all sorts of things.

"Odori-lun is right. You did what you could. I told you it would be difficult to sway him." Father sits with his writing desk where Kazuki once was, replacing him as easily as actors replace one another onstage. He gives her a soft, consolatory smile. "Not everyone is going to understand your vision for the world, sprout."

*That's stupid,* she wants to say. Everyone understands peace. But her chest feels a little tight, and her cheeks hurt, and she is having trouble coming up with the words even now that it's just Father and Odori.

Father is as adept at reading her as she is at reading everyone else. He sets down his brush and his ink in favor of embracing her.

"It's going to be all right," he says. "We can send the Dragon Guard to Hanjeon. There aren't many of them, but—"

"We aren't fighting," says Baoyi. "We aren't!"

He says nothing, only smooths her hair. She feels like a child, and she hates that she feels like a child. Aren't these Empress's robes? Isn't she in charge of things? All those people in Hanjeon celebrating their newfound liberation—how can she sit here in her father's lap, knowing their happiness is at stake?

The knot in her chest is what drives her, the painful thread laced through her body: Anyone who dies in service of the Empire is a stain on her own hands. Anyone who dies in war at all—they will haunt her, she is sure of it.

Only decades ago, the Empire lost an entire generation of youths to the Toad's maniacal whims.

Baoyi *cannot* let a single person die.

Fuyutsuki won't listen to her, and she has only a few thousand in the Dragon Guard at her disposal. Father's suggestion is just going to lead to more fighting—Kazuki isn't going to be convinced to stand down unless the odds are truly against him. Failing in this endeavor would be political suicide. Anything else is a triumph.

And so she has to make sure he never raises his war fan.

Baoyi gets up. The morning light's warmed the mats beneath her feet—she enjoys the feeling for the scant few steps it takes her to reach Father's writing desk. The scroll he's working on is packed tight with his blocky characters—another history of the old Empress, another story Baoyi does not quite believe. She carefully sets it aside, opens the lectern, and retrieves a fine piece of silken paper.

Father's brows come together. "Baoyi? What are you working on?"

"I'm not going to let him win."

ON THE FORTIETH of Nishen, Oshiro Kenshiro receives two letters. One, bound with an amorous strand of red silk, is from his wife. Thick as his finger, it holds within many treasured promises, many treasured admissions—but also something that stands out to him. Near the end of the letter is a postscript.

*Ken-lun, let our daughter know I'm proud of her, but that if she's going to ask me for any more favors, I might not be able to grant them. A mother may love her child to excess—but my fondness for the north must have its limits. This is not Yangzhai asking for a toy. I love her, Ken-lun, but we must be rulers before we are family.*

This puzzles him, for he has no knowledge of Baoyi's asking her mother for any favors at all. She's a friendly girl, but a proud one; she likes to do things herself whenever possible. It's made finding tutors for her a difficult task. He purses his lips and tugs his beard and reaches for the second letter, which will doubtless hold more answers.

This—bound in violet and written on pale green paper—is from the Thorned-Blossom Queen. She sends reports every two months in hopes of fostering a positive relationship between their two nations, as if they are not all bound by love and blood to begin with.

Normally this letter is several pages long, addressing in reverse order the points made by Kenshiro's previous missive—but this one is only a single page, and only a few columns of text at that. That his wife goes so far as to adopt a different style of calligraphy when she is the Queen still amuses him.

But her words, this time, are far more surprising.

*Honored Empress Yuuka,*

*We of the South agree—the freedom and liberty of Hanjeon are precious things. To that end, we dispatched General Lai Xianyu to see to their instruction. It is our hope that this gesture of unity drives away any who might hope to shatter it.*

*We hope, as ever, that your reign continues to be a peaceful one.*

*Her Eminence, the Thorned-Blossom Queen*

He reads it three times—Baozhai likes to play with her character choices to conceal messages, and that's when she doesn't outright use a cipher. More than once he's realized there's been a hidden set of characters visible only by candlelight. His wife is as clever as she is paranoid. Naturally, the first thing Kenshiro does is hold the letter over a candle, where he finds that there are a few more lines hidden away.

*Lord Regent,*

*It's shrewd of you to check for additional messages. There are none this time—but you would do well to ensure the Young Empress knows these methods. The day is coming—soon, I should think—when her commitment to peace will be tested.*

*Your loving wife,*
*Queen Lai Baozhai*

How is it that he smiles even reading this? For the pieces are all coming together now in his mind: Baoyi has no army of her own, so she sought the use of her mother's. And of course her mother could not deny her—no matter how strict Baozhai likes to be with her, she is never denied anything of importance.

But instead of using the Bronze Army as a bludgeon, the way Shizuka had done so many years ago, Baoyi used them as a shield. Who could look on them and attack? They, who have so few defeats to their name? When Hokkaro took Xian-Lai, they did so without ever raising a finger against the Bronze Army; had they gone to war, the language of the land may well be Xianese. And to put Xianyu in charge of them! Even Kenshiro balked at saying an ill word to that woman. Fuyutsuki would know, too, her history in the Northern Campaign—if he attacked her, he was betraying all the goodwill that joint mission had left behind.

If anyone can call Ink-on-Water something that engendered goodwill.

Still—it is a masterly stroke, and one he can hardly believe came from his own daughter. After rising from his desk in the archives, he walks to her chambers. The guards announce him, and he enters as soon as she gives him permission to do so.

Lai Baoyi, Empress of Hokkaro, sits playing a game of poetry cards with Odori. Her sleeves are so long, they pool around her; she must hold them out of the way whenever she lifts her hand. Her white hair she wears long and unbound. There are some who say she does not resemble her mother at all, but these people cannot see beyond the color of her skin: that knowing look on her face is all Baozhai. Odori is about to lose whatever it is she's bet.

Seeing her like this—playing a childhood game in her childhood robes—strikes him with an awful sense of inevitability. Already she's playing political games—how long is it before he will start having to keep suitors away? He cannot fail her the way he failed his sister; Empress though she may be, he determines then that she will marry only someone she cares about, regardless of their standing or gender.

How could he promise her any less? When she humbles herself enough to ask her mother for help in behalf of others, when she invites brutish men to tea to try to convince them to set down their arms, when she cares for no one the way she cares for her horse—how could he promise her any less?

So many things he has ruined in his life.

He shall not ruin this.

"Father," she says, "is something wrong?"

King Oshiro Kenshiro, Lord Regent of Hokkaro, can think of only two things wrong: that his sister and sister-in-law are not here to see the sort of woman Baoyi is becoming; that his mother is not here to see what they have done.

Nevertheless, he takes the third seat at the table.

"Nothing," he says. "Please deal me in."

"But we just started this game." Baoyi pouts. She says that as if she doesn't have four cranes in hand ready to win.

"Ah," he says, smiling warmly. "Then I'll wait for the next. But in the meantime, you should know your mother wrote."

He lays the Queen's letter on the table—away from the piles of cards between them. Baoyi drops her hand immediately, scooping up the letter instead. As she reads it, Kenshiro leans toward Odori.

"She's got all four cranes," he says.

"Oh, I thought as much," says Odori. "Fate's always been kind to her."

She's wiggling in her seat by the time she finishes reading it.

Kenshiro takes a deep breath of the morning air. He does not know where his sister is, or Shizuka, or even his mother.

But he has his daughter, and he has his wife.

Fate's been kind to him.

# O-SHIZUKA

## SIX

To catch up to the Qorin is a fool's task. Easier to catch the moon in a saucer of rice wine—the Empire learned this lesson twenty years ago at Oshiro.

And yet Shizuka has captured the moon in a saucer of rice wine before. The memories are more precious to her than Surian gold, than her fine clothes, than the phoenix feather atop her head. How many times have she and Shefali sat on the veranda in Xian-Lai? And every time the full moon reared her head, Shefali would pick up the saucer with a smile.

"Here," she said, giving the saucer to Shizuka. "The moon."

The moon's reflection on the surface of the cup; the cicadas; Shefali's self-satisfied smile.

Yes—all these things are precious to Shizuka, and thinking of them cools her blazing temper.

So, too, do the trees. Well—the trees and the rocks. Hokkaran horses are used to such things, but quick Qorin steeds are not built for the mountains. Just as the rocky earth slowed them when they entered through the pass, this mountain slows them now.

Catching up is much easier than it would have been had they all been on flat ground.

Oh, it's difficult, still. This mountain is a steep one and the ground treacherous—more than once a soldier stumbles, skidding down a horselength until his fellows help him back up. And it is nerve-racking, too, to march in the silence of a forest like this. All the evergreens put Shizuka in mind of the Imperial Hunting Grounds, which teem at all times with life.

They've heard not even a single bird cry.

Farther and farther up the mountain they go. Shizuka calls for a change in formation before they get too far up into the woods—the trees will make it impossible for most standard types. With no way of knowing what angle the enemy will take in attacking, she settles for Yoke and advises the companies to keep in columns when marching through the trees.

It isn't ideal. Xianyu would ream her for marching in the woods at all.

But she is going to kill that demon, and he is waiting at the top of the mountain.

It is only twenty minutes by Shizuka's count before they meet up with the back half of the Qorin army—the cannons and carts being dragged laboriously uphill. Shizuka catches sight of her cousin atop a spotted brindle she has little idea how to command.

Something in Shizuka eases then, for the sight of her cousin is so ridiculous. Who gave Sakura armor? And not even Hokkaran armor. Not even *Xianese*, for that matter. She wears a mail shirt over a deel that does not quite fit her; a pair of vambraces decorated with falling leaves; two shin guards over her Qorin-style boots; a domed helmet that sits atop her head. What she does not wear is a war mask, and this makes her easy to identify.

And easier to target, if the enemy were to take that tack.

"Munenori-zul," says Shizuka. She points to her cousin, easy enough to spot even without the spyglass—hers is the only horse that's bucking. "I'm going to go fetch Sakura-lun before she gets herself killed. Mind the army."

Munenori nods in affirmation. Shizuka tosses him the golden war fan hanging from her belt—he will need it if he is to make any formal orders.

The army parts for her, if the trees do not already part them. As much as Shefali likes to brag about her gray—and indeed, it's warranted most of the time—it's Matsuda's plodding pace that wins here. In all her life, her gelding has not once missed a step. His reliability is what endeared him to her father, who bought him for her on her tenth birthday.

To think of her father at a time like this—she pushes the thought away.

Ducking the low-hanging branches, her eyes scanning every shadow for signs of life—it is not a pleasant ride, but it is a quick one. A good thing that it is—Sakura's horse has gone from bucking to outright thrashing. Horsemanship is not among a singing girl's many skills: she is barely clinging on to the saddle horn when Shizuka grabs her by the back of her collar.

"Oh, thank the fucking Sister—"

"Wrong god," Shizuka says. "Get on mine; he's used to pampered girls."

She offers Sakura her arm as a brace. Two of the engineers have doubled back now, to try to calm the spotted brindle. They dismount and Sakura soon follows; Shizuka then pulls her up onto Matsuda, sitting in front of her.

She wants to feel relieved. She wants to feel comforted by her cousin's presence, as she so often is—there are few people who know her better.

But the woods around them are bone, not wood; she can see their spines when she blinks. At the top of this mountain the enemy awaits them; at the top of this mountain, there will be blood.

And her cousin is getting herself thrown off a horse?

"You look ridiculous," says Shizuka. "Who gave you that horse? And that armor? You don't even have a weapon. You're going to get yourself killed—"

"I look stylish, thank you," says Sakura. Whatever happiness she felt at being rescued is slain by Shizuka's tone. She turns away from her, setting her eyes squarely on the ground up ahead of them. "And you were the one who asked me to come along. Who knows? Maybe I'll save your life again."

Like stepping on a shard of clay—a sharp wave of anger shoots through Shizuka. Yes, Sakura saved her life; yes, she had been the one to ask her to come.

But that did not mean . . .

Sakura is whoever she wants to be first and a scholar second. She has never been a warrior. For her to be marching through these dreadful woods because her cousin asked it of her is an act of bravery. Shizuka has been too used to the bravery of warriors to recognize any other kind.

Sakura takes advantage of her silence. "From the way the Qorin talk about you, you just might need me to."

"Have you learned Qorin, too?" Shizuka says. It comes out harsher than she intended; she curses herself for being so sharp. "So quickly?"

Sakura tuts. "Anything's possible with a good enough tutor," she says. "I don't speak much, but—"

A shrill whistle cuts her off—and lands with a *thunk* in the tree nearest them. So closely does the arrow pass that the beak of Shizuka's mask rattles in its wake.

All at once the world falls into a different sort of focus. There is no room for her ruminations, no room for her burning self-loathing, no room for anything but action.

If they're being fired on, the best course of action is to move.

Shizuka kicks Matsuda into a gallop as the Qorin sound their warhorns. Sakura slams back into her, jolting her just enough to annoy. No time to dwell on it.

"Move your hips and keep your head down!" Shizuka says, hoping that will be instruction enough.

Two more arrows fly through the air. One clips Shizuka's sleeve; the other soars past them. The engineers are swinging into their saddles as Shizuka turns Matsuda back toward the Hokkaran army.

And it is then that she sees them.

The shadows given life, the black fog in armor.

The demons she fought once before, on the other side of the Kirin.

Shizuka's heart drops into her stomach. There are so many of them, peeling off the trees themselves, bows in hand and arrows at the ready. Three hundred? Four? A thousand? More? Everywhere her eyes settle, the shadows stir to life.

And they're readying to fire.

The arrows are in the air the moment she recognizes them. Like a flock of birds in flight—there are so many, and from so many directions at once! Firing not just on her but on the army, too; not just on the army but on the Qorin as well—how are any of them meant to avoid such an assault?

She sucks in a breath. Solutions, not questions.

For now—she has to keep Sakura safe.

So Shizuka draws her mother's sword. Two cuts sever ten arrows before they can reach her or her horse—but only on her right side. Three glance off her armor; two pierce through to her leg; one cuts across her forearm. Pain is a starburst between her eyes—and yet somehow she cannot truly feel the wounds yet.

There is no time, no time. So long as she is breathing, she can fight, and so long as she can fight, she must protect her family and army.

If the Qorin are afraid, they do not show it. Without any word from their commander, they break off into small groups, galloping into the woods with bows drawn. Only when both their horses' front hooves leave the ground do they fire; their arrows punch through the shadow and land uselessly in the trees behind them.

Galloping horses, flying arrows—it is well and truly chaos now, well and truly a cacophony.

"Did they just—? Are you all right? Holy shit, are you all right?"

"Not now!"

Every movement strains her left leg. It's starting to go numb, but that does not matter—if they can make it through this battle, there will be surgeons to mend her. If she can be mended. If not, well—she has always healed faster than usual.

At last she breaks from the Qorin; at last she nears the stretch between her and the Phoenix Guard. Her soldiers may not have faced the enemy before, but they are impeccably trained—when one lances a shadow, he digs in his heels and tries to lift it overhead. That his spear is then empty is no fault of his—but it does distract him, and then—

Shizuka curses. Not all the shadows have bows, but all of them are dangerous. She cannot tear herself away from watching: the shadow re-forms and swallows the soldier.

People are dying because of her.

Fear, guilt, shame—they pain her more than the arrows. *Your fault*, *your fault*, *your fault*. The puffed-up Empress dies with the soldier.

Only the girl remains.

Another wave of arrows. She can hardly raise her right arm in time to cut them down. Sakura yelps, covering her head with her arms, as if that will save her. Three shadows dash out from the woods, their hungry mouths open wide as a tiger's. Again Shizuka raises her arm; again she makes her cut.

Her sword meets flesh and bone where she expects only mist. The shock reverberates through her shoulder—three shadowy heads hit the ashen earth.

She takes a breath. This is not the Kirin, and this army is not made of farmers who deserved better. The Qorin ride with her. Her wife rides with her.

Heaven rides with her.

Yet Shizuka is only one woman, and the enemy number in the thousands.

"Do not falter!" Shizuka calls, for she is among her army now, amid the melee of soldiers and shadows. Already there are bodies; already the air glimmers with departing souls.

Earlier she'd thought that loss of life was inevitable. Now that she is among it again, it is all that Shizuka can do to keep from crying.

What a fool she'd been to think she was hardy enough to be on the battlefield again, even so many years later.

*Do not falter.* She repeats it to herself under her breath, as if repeating it will make it true. Do not falter.

The shadows are closing in, but so is the army. As Shizuka takes her proper place among them, the lancers form a circle. She and Sakura sit atop Matsuda in the center. Another wave of shadows bursts forth from the forests.

"Steady!" she shouts, though her hands are anything but.

Like beetles, like serpents, like the bloated corpses that haunt her imagination—they are coming.

How many can she kill in one stroke? Shizuka does not know their names. Sky above, she does not know their names; the demons will be up again in a Bell at most. So many, so many, and how are they meant to fight in a forest?

Shizuka blinks, closes her eyes.

The pines give way to bamboo; the grit of the earth lies beneath a blanket of white snow. It is early in the winter, and her army has perfect faith in her. A capricious breeze tears the flowers from their stems. Softly they spiral down, down, red on white . . .

The memory is so vivid that she can feel the breeze against her cheeks, the winter chill. How cold her mask was in that forest! Her fingertips stuck to it when she reached for it then, and now—

Four sharp notes, played on a distant flute.

Shizuka's blood goes cold. For one horrible moment she cannot breathe, cannot think—

She forces herself to open her eyes.

The shadows hang suspended in the air. Gone, their nebulous mass—they float like strips of paper, like shadow puppets. As if someone sucked the life out of them, as if . . .

She thinks of Shefali's episodes, of her arm going flat as these shades, and something in her dies. To recognize her wife in these creatures . . .

She presses her eyes shut again. When she opens them—the paper shades are still there, still hanging motionless before them. The nearest one is frozen with three of its four arms extended. Two spears pierce through its chest, and through these holes the unnatural sunlight pours down upon the soldiers.

The confusion lasts only an instant. These soldiers are trained to endure horror, even if their general's throat is sealed shut in fear. As one, they raise their catches high; as one, they impale them; as one, they slam them down upon the earth.

"General! Your orders?" shouts one of the lieutenants. A brash young woman, her voice full of fire. How excited she sounds to have killed the enemy. The answer she expects to hear is "kill them all."

But that is not the answer the Phoenix Empress can give.

Not now. Not when the flute is playing that melody, the one from the bay of Nishikomi. Its lilting tune is like grinding glass between her teeth. Hackles rise at the back of her neck.

Her eyes dart around the forest. Nothing but black, nothing but shades and trees and death, nothing but her failures coming back in new armor—

There. Balanced on a wooden sandal with only one block to support it, standing atop the tallest tree in this forsaken forest, flute to his lips—the demon.

Shizuka's mind is just as much a battlefield as her surroundings. A company of fear charges, lances lowered, at the cavalry of her wrath. Her jaw aches; she can hear her blood echoing in her ears.

"You," she snarls. It is the only word she can manage. Anger and fury trample the lancers underfoot—she raises her sword and levels it at the demon. And then, finally—"All archers, fire!"

The creak of a thousand bows at once—like a massive creature howling awake. Arrows fly—but Hokkaran bows are built for distance, and not altitude; they have no true hope of reaching the demon.

And less, when the demon brushes them away. A gust of wind follows the gesture, scattering the arrows like autumn leaves. Only then does it lower the flute from its lips; only then does Shizuka see its wicked grin.

The demon is wearing the man's head today, with its thick, bulbous nose. Had it taken this body from a wrestler? For it is wide at the shoulders, and barrel chested; its torso is thick as the tree it rests upon. Long, dark hair kept tied back in a warrior's horsetail; brows that speak of determination—were it not for the demon's nose, it would be sure to win the hearts of love-starved noblewomen everywhere.

That smile. Shizuka hates it already.

"Four-Petal," it says, "is this any way to treat a man who has twice saved your life?"

Sakura swears under her breath. "So it is him."

Hearing her cousin's voice cuts through some of her anger, but not all. Much as she wants to jump off this horse and demand a duel, she cannot. The demon is not likely to accept, for one thing; she cannot leave her cousin's side, for another. If Sakura comes to any harm during this journey, Shizuka will never be able to forgive herself.

Yet she cannot tolerate the demon speaking to her in such a way. *Four-Petal.* At last the name makes sense to her—all this time, they've been taunting her. A flower, true—but one under the Traitor's sway. Four. They knew what stained her blood; they knew the cost of the jade she so proudly claimed.

"You've saved nothing," Shizuka says. "How can you claim to be saving me when it was you who set these demons upon us? You who cast me into the water—do not speak to me in such a familiar tone."

The Phoenix Empress speaks as formally as she can, using pronouns and articles considered obsolete by most—in this way, she sets the distance between them. In this way, she dares it to try to close that distance.

But what will she do if it does? It is atop that tree, and she is far beneath it, on her horse.

The demon laughs. It claps its hands once, and all its paper underlings start spinning as if a child is rolling their string between her fingers. With a single yank, the paper demons go flying toward it, settling like Poem-War cards onto its outstretched palm.

"There," it says. "Are you feeling safer now, Four-Petal?"

It laughs once more. The whole army around her stiffens; Shizuka hears their footsteps and the rattle of their armor. Munenori is cutting through the crowd on his way toward her. This is the terrible thing about war masks—she cannot see his expression.

And yet—why is it that she still hears the sounds of battle? She glances to her right, where the trees are thickest, but her war mask blinds her.

"Sakura," she whispers, for the demon is so high up that it cannot possibly hear her, and it cannot see her mouth moving. "Sakura, are they all gone?"

The Sister is the goddess of music, the hearth, and friendship—Sakura's always claimed her as a patron and used her pronouns. It is the Fourth who is the god of cleverness and deceit. Still, there is a saying: A singing girl can make the bitterest lie into the sweetest dreams. Sakura must have learned that from her fellows, for she quickly hides her mouth with her fan. How natural she makes it seem, to be fanning yourself on the battlefield! As if the stress has broken her spirit and she might, at any time, depart to the floating world.

"The Qorin are still fighting," says Sakura. Is she slurring her words more than usual on purpose? She must be; Shizuka's never known her cousin to sound like such a drunkard.

But it is the substance of her words that chills Shizuka to the core. The Qorin are still fighting. If she turns to look, the demon will know she is worried. She cannot let it have that power over her.

And yet Shefali is there in the woods, somewhere, fighting. . . .

Shizuka's throat is closing up again. This, too, is unacceptable.

"Well?" says the demon. It crosses one leg over the other and sits as if on some invisible bench. "I am not a patient soul to begin with, and after all the trouble I went through to set things up for you—"

"To *kill* my soldiers?" Shizuka says. Anger, yes, the anger will free her. "To threaten my people, to bring such pain and misery to my wife and her family—you call this 'setting things up for me'?"

It tilts its head. "Yes," it says. "Wouldn't you? We're talking now, the two of us."

Petulant. A child tugging on a mother's sleeve, demanding that she pay attention to a sand-drawing.

"I didn't expect him to be so fucking annoying," says Sakura. Maybe there isn't much difference between talking over rowdy sailors and an army at war—she has no trouble making herself heard. "All the stories say big-nosed types like him are arrogant."

Perhaps this was arrogance, in a way. No one in Hokkaro knew more of arrogance than Minami Shizuka. If she were in the demon's place, she'd be throwing a tantrum that her victim wasn't listening. That's what she'd done plenty of times before. Well, that and challenge people to duels—

Hm.

The Qorin are still fighting, and the demon wants her to listen.

"General," says Munenori, "the army is ready. To treat with this creature is to invite disaster. Now is the time for decisive action—"

"I'm aware," Shizuka says.

Burqila Alshara said one must always greet an army while mounted. If she saw Shizuka hopping off her horse to talk to a demon, her brown face would go red with rage. It is a good thing, then, that Burqila is so preoccupied with her own people and their fighting across the fog.

Shizuka does not hop out of the saddle; her injury makes it impossible. Instead, she lowers herself slowly onto the ground. Arrows sink their teeth farther in; blood wells out and soaks her riding pants. When at last she touches the ground, it sends a wave of pain shooting up into her; for a moment, her mind goes red. If she hadn't thought to hold on to Matsuda with her right hand, she would have staggered over.

And yet even this pain is a small fraction of what her wife deals with every day.

She thinks of Shefali, trapped in the woods with the shadows that could not die, and steels herself. Pain is temporary.

"General—"

"Don't," Shizuka says. Her voice is a blade. "Whatever happens, I need the two of you to pay attention. This will work, but if it doesn't, then you need to remember."

Sakura nods. Munenori bites down on whatever it was he was going to advise her to do.

A good thing, because there is no way he'd approve of what she's planning.

Shizuka grips one of the arrow shafts in her leg and yanks. Blood flies, red as fruit, from the wound. The world is starting to teeter, but the demon does not need to know that.

The demon needs to know that she is unbreakable.

And so Shizuka calls on the fires burning deep in her soul. She stokes them with her anger, with her worry, with her shame, until they threaten to immolate her. Only when the tips of her fingers glow like a smith's tongs does she know she is ready.

She jams her thumb into the wound.

*The pain.*

Biting down on her tongue is almost enough to make her bite it off. The taste of copper fills her mouth; her whole body shudders, and she struggles to breathe.

But Shizuka keeps her eyes on the demon as she cauterizes her own wounds. Steadfast and unyielding. A nation, and not a woman—a god.

"You wanted to talk?" Shizuka says. "Come down and talk. Unless you're afraid of me?"

The demon leans back, arms crossed behind its head. Its robes open to reveal more of its torso.

"Four-Petal," it says. "Do you think I'm a two-bu villain? I won't. The Eternal King has a generous offer for you—one that boggles my mind, if I am being honest with you. Here I am thinking perhaps we can put all of this—" He gestures broadly toward the army. "—behind us, and here you are acting the same as you always have."

What is more painful—snapping the second shaft and cauterizing the wound; or knowing that the demon is right?

She takes another step forward. Sakura sucks at her teeth.

"I won't hear your offer until you withdraw your . . ."

"My cards?" the demon offers. It tuts, as if she has asked it to sit properly at dinner. "I've removed them from your army."

"They are still attacking the Qorin," Shizuka says. Seething, the words leave her—she allows her pain to color her tone. "Remove them, and I may listen."

The demon leans forward, head perched on its hand. "Why?" it says. "They aren't your people. A phoenix need not concern herself with rabid wolves."

Shizuka wishes Shefali were here—*her* bow is strong enough to hit the demon. Two arrows in each eye and a fifth in its throat, that is what it deserves.

Sky, she hopes her wife is safe. What horrors have beset her? Though Shefali cannot die until the first of Qurukai, she *can* be injured—and her great foolish love won't hesitate to throw herself in harm's way for her family. The number of scars on her . . . Shefali has not told Shizuka much of what she did during her travels, but some of the stories are plain to see.

Stories best left unspoken.

Her brave warrior—how many more scars will she earn today?

"They are my family," Shizuka says, "and so long as they are my wife's people, they are mine as well. Leave them be, or return empty-handed to your master. I refuse to listen to you otherwise."

It is difficult to see from here if the demon is narrowing its eyes. In the silence that follows, Shizuka tries to get a better sense of it, to spot the golden characters of its name. Something gold gleams on the inside of its right forearm. She will need the demon to come closer if she's going to get a good look.

*Come down*, she thinks, as if it might somehow hear her. *Come down and let me show you how bright a phoenix burns.*

So quiet has it gone around her that she can hear the clattering of the Qorin's hooves, hear the shouts and the horns and the drums they use to frighten their enemies. Shadows know no fear—but that does not stop the Qorin from trying. Somewhere in that cacophony is Shefali. Somewhere in that cacophony, a death cry—one of the last Qorin leaves to join their ancestors in the sky.

They cannot continue to sustain losses. Only one-third of them remained in Hokkaro—they cannot die here.

And yet they might, if Shizuka fails to convince this demon to let them go. To send her own army would be a fool's errand; the shadows will not be harmed by mortal weapons. Perhaps if she had time, she might properly bless their spears—why had she not thought to do this?—but there is no time now.

Every second that passes, another life is snuffed out.

How much longer can she bear that knowledge? How much longer can she pretend she does not care? Even the strongest steel will snap if improperly handled.

Shizuka grits her teeth. "Answer me!" she shouts. "Will you retreat, or must I cut you down myself?"

Fear and anger overwhelm her efforts at polite speech. Gone, her formal conjugations; she speaks only slightly more formally than her cousin.

The demon tuts again. It wags a finger at her. "That is no way for an Empress to speak," it says. "Ask me once more, and ask me properly."

"And if she does, will you grant her request?" says Sakura.

Shizuka didn't expect her to chime in—what is she doing talking to demons? Well, if anyone is going to muster the will to do it, it'll be a Minami.

Shizuka worries that interruption will earn the demon's ire, but instead it smirks. "More of you? My, that blood does keep," it says. "Yes. If Four-Petal addresses me properly, then I will withdraw my army, so that we may talk as equals. Let no one say that Rikuto is an honorless dog."

Rikuto?

Is that its name? Shizuka has never heard of a demon simply offering it up before. Being tricked into naming themselves, yes, but this was delivered smoothly. Knowingly.

There are those in Fujino who imagine that Shizuka would balk at such a display of humility. That it would rankle her to address a demon in formal speech. To refuse on principle in favor of cutting down the tree and cutting the demon in two—that is what these people expect of her.

In truth, it is an easy decision to make. The lives of the Qorin and the lives of her army are worth more than the ego of the Phoenix Empress.

"General Rikuto, who watches the North. We of the Hokkaran Empire entreat you to withdraw your forces."

She speaks as formally as she can—yet she does not bow. The demon did not ask it of her, and she shall not be known as the woman who bowed to one of its kind.

Still, this seems to please it. Rikuto preens atop the tree for a moment, hemming happily, before snapping its fingers. Wind gusts through the forest. The trees strain to stay upright; more than one of her spearmen drop their weapons; even the Qorin are having trouble staying upright if those sounds are any indication. Shizuka raises her good arm to shield her eyes from the falling pine needles.

When the gust is over, Rikuto stands before her. In its hand is another deck of cards. Grinning, it drops the deck into a pouch at its belt.

"Was that so difficult?" it says.

She does not indulge the demon—there is no need to. The spearmen around her have given it a necklace already. Fifty spearheads glitter at the demon's throat. If she were to glance behind her, she would see the archers aiming straight for the creature; if she were to glance to her sides, the infantry are fondling their swords.

How many has she lost already? It is natural they want vengeance. She, too, wants to see this thing's brain dashed against this unnatural earth—but there is something different about this demon.

All women learn from a young age to discern those men who might hurt them. By the time a girl has reached eighteen years, she is as much an expert on the subject as the priests are on the Heavenly Mandates. A passing glance is all it takes—see the way he holds himself, as if he has something to prove? Look, his hungry eyes; witness the cruel curl of his lips! She will cross over to the other side of the street rather than be near him—and even then, she may change the route she takes to reach her home, lest he follow.

Shizuka knew that sort of man well. His example was the twice-damned Kagemori. The scar across her nose is not the only mark he left upon her. The closer this demon comes to her, the more Shizuka thinks of him, of his blackened teeth and his wandering hands.

*You're a wild mare, but I'll break you.*

The demon has not spoken those words—but it might. And knowing that sickens her.

If it so much as lifts a finger . . .

"Captain," says Shizuka. "Ride to the Qorin and see that they are undisturbed. Find my wife, and bring her here."

Munenori does not need to be told twice. He shouts in affirmation and kicks his horse into a gallop.

The demon growls in response—Shizuka can practically see its chest rumbling. "I came to speak with *you*," it says.

"Then you shall have to wait," Shizuka answers. "Without my wife, I am only half a woman. I must see that she is unharmed before I listen to your nonsense."

"Nonsense?" the demon roars. The very tip of its nose reddens. "I am offering you a reasonable—"

"So you keep saying," says Shizuka. "But killing my people isn't reasonable."

Redder, redder, its cheeks now like apples ready to eat.

The demon takes a step closer.

The first thing any duelist must learn is the length of their sword. The Daybreak Blade is two shaku long. Anything within that radius lives only because she allows it to.

The tip of the demon's nose crosses the sun's radius.

Gold, blinding bright—Shizuka's hand moves without her having to think of the motion. To think of the motion is to yield to doubt it; to doubt it is to fail; to fail is to sign the death warrants of her army and family.

And so she does not think of the motion.

The hilt of the Daybreak Blade chimes as it returns to its sheath. Shizuka stands a little taller as the tip of the demon's nose falls to the ground. Black drips from it, reminding her of a brush dipped handle first in cheap ink.

"You . . . ," it says, raising its hand to the wound.

"I," she says, "made myself clear. We are waiting for my wife. If you take one more step, then it shall not be your nose I cut."

"I could crush you," it seethes. "I could have killed you. Twice, I could have. You owe me your *life*."

"And every breath you take before me now is a favor I am granting you," Shizuka says. She cannot let herself falter, no matter how angry the demon becomes. If it strikes at her, so much the better—if it is angry, it shall not be fighting properly. She will take any advantage she can get. "You wanted to meet as equals, and so we have—you can summon your army whenever you like, and I can cut you down in response."

Shizuka regrets speaking the words as soon as she's stopped. What if it takes her advice to heart; what if it does summon its army again?

But if it came here to talk, then it won't. If it came here to talk, then the Traitor might have bound it to that purpose by oath. It may not be attacking her directly, because it *cannot*. The Traitor's control over his minions is difficult to fight off, if Shefali's struggles are any indication.

The demon glowers. Blood drips onto the border of Shizuka's realm. The lancers hold steady in spite of all that has happened. They, too, have hungry eyes.

If the demon attacks, she will kill it.

If it does not, then she will listen to its offer, and then she will kill it.

Her mother always had said that Shizuka should think things through before she did them.

"Bring your dog, then," says the demon. "If that is what it will take for you to listen. The Eternal King is right—you are an *insolent* little girl."

And perhaps this demon is right, perhaps the Traitor is right—she *is* insolent.

But it has been years since she was a girl.

"Someone fetch me a chair," Shizuka calls. "I can't stand this wretch's insults."

Sitting in the proper style is the respectful thing to do—but only if both parties are doing it. If one is standing, then the one sitting on their ankles is in a position of submission.

To sit on a Qorin or Xianese-style chair during a meeting, however—there are few things Hokkarans consider more disrespectful. It says to the other party that they are not worth the pain of proper sitting or the pain of standing stock-still; it says that you see them as utterly unworthy of your efforts.

Shizuka has never sat upon a Qorin chair at court. To do so might well stir Lord Shiratori into declaring war. A dais, always, made specifically for the Empress, or else her throne.

But today, before this demon?

She calls for a chair.

It is one of the infantry who brings it to her, one of the infantry who unfolds it behind her. Shizuka stares the reddening demon down as she lowers herself onto the seat.

And then, the moment she's seated, she breaks eye contact to study her nails.

Let it attack her, if that is what it wants to do.

# MINAMI SAKURA

## FOUR

Minami Sakura is beginning to think her cousin's been drinking again.

It's the only explanation she can think of for the way she's acting. That demon, there—the uncomfortably handsome one with the huge nose? It's the one that nearly drowned Shizuka. It's the one she drove away with five columns of fire and a sword of pure flame. The sight of her cousin in . . . in that state terrified her. Not because of the glowing eyes or the way the air shimmered around her; not because of her painful radiance; not because of anything physical.

But because it was her cousin—who sleeps sucking her thumb and never touches her horseradish at meals—as a god.

And now the thing that pushed her into such a state stands two shaku away, and Shizuka is not killing it. Instead, she's taunting it. Sakura's seen singing girls degrade clients who enjoyed such things—it's similar to what she's seeing now. She doesn't need to see Shizuka's face to know how satisfied she is that the demon cannot hurt her.

And it cannot. Sakura figured that out a while ago—if it could, then surely it would have struck at her when it called the winds. Surely it would have taken the field itself. All the literature on demons like this is clear: they make *excellent* generals.

In the old days of the Hokkaran Empire, when Iwa was the capital, it was said that Emperor Yusuke often sought the wisdom of long-nosed demons. He climbed to the very top of the Kyuuzen Mountains to find one in particular and beseeched it to tell him all it knew of war.

The demon promptly cast him off the mountain.

It is one of the many stories of Yusuke's mysterious death.

Still, apocryphal though it likely is, the story makes it obvious how much the old Hokkarans respected creatures like this. Why bother hauling your ass all the way up the most inhospitable mountains on the continent otherwise? It's the sort of thing that leans on the listener's knowing everything the speaker knows, the sort of thing that makes sense only when taken in context. Climbing a mountain to speak to a demon is unthinkable unless they were not demons at the time and they had something they could grant you.

There are snippets of older stories, too, quoted in books to teach young scholars about archaic characters. Someone named Koremori claimed to have learned their secrets and wrote an extensive book on the subject. The book itself was lost when the capitals shifted, but references to it survive, including some truly unbelievable claims about flight. And there are enough references to Koremori himself to know that he was a fierce warrior, responsible for slaying an entire enemy army with only twenty men and his own two arms.

If this demon wanted them dead, they would be dead by now. Sakura would be, at least—perhaps not Shizuka. She'd try to duel the damned thing.

Which is why Sakura is so confused by her cousin's actions. Why is Shizuka *not* just dueling it? She's cut off the tip of its nose already; it has killed several members of the Phoenix Guard already. It can't be because Shizuka is seriously considering the Traitor's offer—she'd never dream of it.

Could it be that her hotheaded cousin has finally learned discretion? That Shizuka will listen to the offer only to discover what it is the Traitor wants from her?

It's the sort of thing a hero in a story might do—a wily one. Shizuka has never been wily—but then, this is the first time Sakura's ever followed her into war. Perhaps having so many lives on the line brings out a different part of her bold cousin.

Or perhaps there's some prophecy in those arcane characters—one that Sakura still is not privy to. There's a bitterness in the back of her throat—perhaps this is Koremori, and perhaps Shizuka's only so comfortable because her mother's letter told her what to expect.

But to Sakura's displeasure, she doesn't regret coming North anymore. Not if she gets to see things like this. If only she'd thought to pack her drawing pad and brush—Dorbentei had said it was a fool's errand to carry such things around if a battle started up. Insisted on it, at that; said that Sakura was liable to get her head chopped off her neck if she was looking down to draw.

Sakura's convinced Dorbentei's being an idiot—but only about this. Watching Shizuka sit before the demon; watching the demon's skin go from pale to red to a swollen, turgid violet; these things fascinate her. The palms of her hands itch for a brush. What if she forgets some of the details before she can get them down?

It is only when she hears horses approaching that she remembers she isn't supposed to be Shizuka's biographer at all. Captain Munenori rides into the clearing with Barsalai Shefali, Burqila Alshara, and Dorbentei Otgar in tow. The right side of Shefali's deel is streaked with black blood; so, too, does black drip down the chin of her war mask. It looks as if she has fallen face-first into an inkwell. Her eyes are the only exception, the one greener for all the dark around them.

Burqila Alshara is unharmed. She holds a sword in hand—a curved one, in the Surian style—but otherwise looks no different than usual. There is not even any blood on her, save that which limns her blade. She does not so much as look at Sakura as she passes.

But Dorbentei does. Flicks her war mask up, even though Sakura can think of few things more unwise than to flick up your mask in a battlefield. She, too, is free of blood, but there is a weariness in her bearing that Sakura is not used to. There are bags under her eyes already.

"Glad you didn't die," says Dorbentei as she passes. Her voice is as heavy as her eyelids.

"That horse tried its best," Sakura says. If Shizuka hadn't gotten to her, she'd have been trampled; of this, Sakura is sure.

And she is also sure that she hates to hear Dorbentei sound so tired. As annoying as she may be.

Barsalai leads them, of course. She rides right to her wife's side and jumps out of the saddle with a surprising amount of agility. For a brief moment, Sakura wonders whether all that blood covering her has numbed her pain. It wouldn't be unheard of—there were plenty of stories about bloodthirsty—

No, no, this is her cousin's wife she is thinking about. It's impolite to suggest a thing like that, even in thought. Shefali's been nothing but devoted and determined in the face of her deteriorating condition.

Shizuka's red gelding whinnies and shifts. Sakura holds on to the saddle horn a little more tightly. She'd ridden on this horse before; *he* didn't intend to kill her. "Behave," she mutters. "They're getting to the interesting part."

Is it callous of her to think of this as the interesting part? When already some have lost their lives—is it callous of her to feel such excitement at watching whatever is about to happen?

The answer is irrelevant—whatever is about to happen will not be slowed by Sakura's moral crisis.

"Steel-Eye," says the demon. "What a *pleasure* it is to have you here."

Shefali says nothing in response. Indeed, she does not pay the demon any attention at all. She kneels in front of her wife instead. Sakura cannot hear what she is saying to Shizuka from here, but the posture's clear enough: she wants to know Shizuka is all right.

"Steel-Eye," repeats the demon, but still Shefali does not address it. She and Shizuka are having a conversation, it seems, though it is impossible to say for sure when both women are masked.

Dorbentei and Burqila are happy to fill the silence. "She's busy," Dorbentei says. "We have you to thank for that attack, hunh? You're lucky Burqila doesn't cut your head off."

The demon stays put. Is there some sort of magic afoot, that it cannot come any closer? Or is it so terrified of Shizuka's sword? Sakura reaches for answers she knows she cannot have. Theories form and fade.

"I don't recall Four-Petal asking for your presence," says the demon. "Leave."

Burqila responds with a sharp, unmistakable sign. Dorbentei doesn't bother to translate it—some things are understood just as well in Hokkaro as they are in distant Axiot.

"Burqila Alshara has killed your kind before," Dorbentei says. The weariness is still there, but buried now—she is forcing herself to sound more confident than she is. "She will not hesitate to do it again if need be."

"Ryoma was young," says the demon. Rikuto—that was its name, wasn't it? "I am not."

"And you aren't attacking us right now, either," says Dorbentei. She's gone back to reading Burqila's signing. "So you must want something from Barsatoq. Kill us and she'll go all gold on you, won't she?"

The demon grinds its teeth. If Sakura squints, she can see the air by its ears go hazy. This is not good. Shizuka taunting the demon is one thing, but Dorbentei and Burqila are mortal women. If the demon decides to punctuate its point . . .

"Rikuto here has come as a diplomat," says Shizuka. She remains seated—though Shefali is now standing next to her, arms crossed, like some sort of bodyguard. "It means to make me an offer on behalf of the Fourth. Sakura-lun, what are the characters for a demon like this?"

"Heavenly Dog," says Sakura. Doesn't Shizuka know that? It isn't as if stories about long-nosed demons are rare.

"And so we have it. A heavenly dog. That is what you are, isn't it?" says Shizuka. "A servant of this broken Heaven?"

Rikuto grabs its flute. With its eyes boring into Shizuka, it lifts the instrument to its lips and begins to play.

Sakura read once a detailed account of Narazaki Yuu's journeys through the Xianese jungles. Three weeks into her journey, Narazaki-kol's caravan was attacked by bandits. She survived only thanks to her quick wits—but afterwards, she was left to wander the jungle alone. That same night she unknowingly stepped into the coils of a python.

The passage has seared itself onto Sakura's memory—the muscular coils tightening and tightening, the great serpent's mouth opening impossibly wide. Though Narazaki-kol struggled, there was no escaping the serpent—bringing her fists down on its coils was like bringing her fists down on stone.

In the end, a bandit saved her by chopping off the serpent's head.

There will be no bandit now, Sakura imagines, for the serpent that holds her now is invisible. That makes it no less tangible. Rikuto's melody coils around her and tightens, tightens. With her ribs compressed, she has trouble breathing. Gasping for air, Sakura holds each breath as long as she can, and her heart races. All around her the army's weapons clatter to the ground. They, too, are wrapped in an embrace from which they cannot escape.

Squeezing tighter, tighter—Sakura feels she is going to burst at any moment. Fear sinks its fangs into her: What if this is how she dies? What if Rikuto kills her and the whole army because Shizuka cannot stop insulting it? So far from home, so far from those she knows, with no published work to her name—is this how she wants to die?

"What are you doing?"

She can hardly hear Shefali's voice over the music, hardly hear her over the pained groans of the army.

It hurts. Why does it hurt so much? To be strangled while staring up at a cloudless blue sky—how strange, how surreal!

A flash of gold; she closes her eyes to get away from the pain of it. When she opens them again, Shizuka's sword is embedded in the demon's hand. A thin line of black drips onto the ground.

*Sister's tits, it caught it,* Sakura thinks.

But no sooner than the thought crosses her mind, the coils loosen. Her whole body slumps over. She gasps for breath as if she were breaking the surface of the bay again, her hand around her throat. The air rushing into her lungs hurts almost as much as the coils did. She doubles over, reaching for the saddle horn to keep upright, and vomits off the side of the Empress's prized horse.

She is not the only one to empty her stomach. All around her, the army shifts back to life, looking around, grasping for their throats. Within the two-shaku boundary, Burqila is hacking, beating at her own chest.

And Dorbentei's gone nearly violet.

Sakura half throws herself from the saddle. A Qorin she isn't—were it not for her armor, she would have torn open her forearm on the rocks. Even so, there are bruises already forming, Sakura knows. She curses. When she tries to push herself to her feet, she stumbles; one of the soldiers must offer her a hand up.

And by then the argument's progressed.

"So you see that I am no paper tiger," says Rikuto. "Continue to goad me all you like, Four-Petal, but know that your actions have consequences."

Something smells like burning meat. Sakura cringes at the thought—it must be Rikuto.

"I should cut your arm off," Shizuka says. Why she does not puzzles Sakura. Surely, if she follows through on the cut—surely all of this will be over?

But then a thought occurs to her as she hurries to stand with her family: *This mountain is of Rikuto's making*. It must be. It did not exist before the scouts found it, and long-nosed demons are commonly found near mountains. If the Traitor exhibits control over the land beyond the Wall, as Shizuka claims, then perhaps his subordinates can do the same on a more limited level.

They are in this demon's world.

And if they kill Rikuto before leaving it . . . well, who knows where the fog will leave them?

That is why Shizuka is not killing it—because she needs the army safely delivered from this place.

"But you won't," says Rikuto. "Now—let's speak properly. All of us, if you insist on letting your dogs stay."

Shizuka withdraws her sword. Another spurt of black flies into the air, landing on Barsalai's horse. Barsalai is quick to wipe off her gray with her own deel. Dorbentei coughs, Burqila slaps her on the back; Captain Munenori stands stoically one shaku behind Shizuka. The army watches the gathering—as Sakura makes her way to Dorbentei's side, she is acutely aware of all the eyes boring into her, of the questions left unasked and unanswered.

"I'm glad you didn't die," Sakura whispers to Dorbentei. Curse these boots. If she were in her sandals, she'd be able to reach Dorbentei's ear without trouble. Now she must tip herself up as much as she can. She looks ridiculous, like a child in her older sister's armor.

Dorbentei's eyes flick over to her. She coughs again as she dismounts.

"Demon tried its best," she answers. There, again, that weariness!

But there is no time for the two of them to discuss this further. Negotiations, such as they are, must proceed. If they don't, Barsalai may well bite Rikuto's head off and see about finding a way back on their own. The way she's pacing back and forth—how like a wolf she is. That mask is misplaced on her.

The sound of the Daybreak Blade hitting its sheath is the cue for the meeting to start. There are no actors in black to arrange the pieces, no music to set the tone, and only war masks to describe what the main players are feeling.

But to hear two gods and a demon speak—Sakura can think of worse shows than this.

"The Eternal King," begins Rikuto, "is a patient and righteous king. For two thousand years, he has ruled over us. In two thousand years, we have known neither war nor hunger. The peasantry support the gentry; the gentry support the king. All things are in their proper place under Heaven, as the gods of old instructed us—and for that reason, we have prospered. There are creations in Iwa that would rob you of speech, Four-Petal.

"We are in all ways a perfect people. The Eternal King assigns each of us our career, and as we till our fields or shoe our horses, he is with us. He is Father to a nation—and yet the most humble man I have ever met."

"Get to the fucking point," says Dorbentei. "Unless your point is to feed us horseshit and call it Surian chocolate."

Sakura fans herself to hide her growing smirk. Is there anyone on the continent more fearless than Dorbentei Otgar?

Rikuto fingers its flute. Dorbentei quiets.

Perhaps not so fearless, after all.

"My esteemed relative has the right of it," says Shizuka. "You came speaking of an offer. I have not heard one. If you continue to waste our time, then we will have to settle this with steel."

"You know how well that ends for your people," says the demon. Nevertheless, it sets the flute down. "What the Eternal King is offering you is this: your freedom."

Shizuka's hand tightens around her sword. "A phoenix soars where she will."

"Unless she is caged," says Rikuto. "The Eternal King knows you well, Four-Petal. He knows that you are a willful girl, unsuited to the throne. He knows that you want nothing more than to roam the continent with your horsewife. He knows how you *detest* being told what to do. Being a god. And so, in his infinite wisdom and grace, he is offering you—both of you—a way out."

Both of you? Sakura glances to Shefali. It's difficult, as always, to read Empress Wolf, but there is a recognizable stiffness to her shoulders. Is that simply her condition? No—she swung from her saddle earlier. This must be something else.

Neither god says a word.

They can't seriously be considering . . . ? Though—Rikuto is right, Shizuka has hated the throne from the moment she won it. Few things irritate her more than going to court. For a god, every second of every day is court—they must weed through the prayers they receive, deciding who deserves to have their favor. Returning to the mortal realm only once every eight years . . . Shizuka is a woman of earthly pleasures.

This is bad.

Sakura scrambles to think of what the offer will be before Rikuto can speak it. What did they uncover about the previous cycle of gods? Why did the sun decide to fall? Because she could no longer bear her own existence without the moon; because she grew tired of it all; because she thought that if she consumed the world in purifying fire, no one else would ever have to suffer the way she had.

These were the rumors at the time.

Sweet Sister—she could imagine Shizuka throwing a tantrum like that.

But . . . But she has to have faith in her. Even at her most selfish, Shizuka can never fully abandon her duty.

"The Eternal King's offer is a simple one: return your upstart Empire to its proper ruler. Hokkaro has been the dominion of the Eternal King from its inception, granted to him by his brother. Call your flowers and open a path so that he may reclaim it—that is all he asks. In return, he grants you both your freedom. Do what you will; he shall never again lift a finger to stop you, so long as you never lift one against him."

"He wants to infect them," says Shefali. The quietest people know well the value of raising their voices—when Shefali speaks now, it's with all the venom she can muster. "He wants to control them."

"Freedom of thought is a small price to pay for the peace we enjoy," says Rikuto. "And those among us who are worthy are granted independence, as he sees fit."

"Freedom of thought?" says Shefali. She steps forward, taking the mask from her face. The false sunlight here casts shadows on her now-gaunt cheeks. When she speaks, her pointed teeth peek out from between her lips. "He's changed me into *this*."

"It isn't the King who shaped you, Steel-Eye," says Rikuto. From the curl of its lips, it seems it was expecting this question. That makes Sakura all the more worried—if Shefali's form isn't a result of the blackblood, then . . . "That is just the form you were always meant to wear."

Shefali seethes. "Horseshit." The word sounds all the harsher when she says it—Sakura's never heard her swear before. "It's him."

Rikuto crosses its arms. "Think him a liar all you like," it says. "This is the form you were meant to wear once you'd shed your mortal ties. He has granted it to you while you yet live as a gift. You are a living god, Steel-Eye. Is it the fault of the Eternal King if your fragile mortal body cannot handle the strains of godhood? That you've had so many years to accustom yourself to these abilities is a kindness, make no mistake of it—a kindness you've obviously squandered."

Shefali's nose starts going longer, and her mouth soon matches it—Sakura cannot make herself look away as Shefali, in her anger, begins to shift form. Bones cracking and re-forming, sinew stretching, skin going taut as muscles shift beneath—all these things are incredible. All these things are true. All these things must be remembered.

Barsalai Shefali, the Wolf, stands twenty-five hands tall at the withers. The others exist only in her shadow. When she growls, the ground beneath them shakes; when she bares her teeth, each one is the size of Sakura's forearm.

"Is this the form of a god?" says the wolf. Sakura's ears ring.

Yet the demon does not falter. Rikuto looks on the wolf with a curled smile. "Yes," it says. "Aren't you grateful you've had such time to master it?"

Now the earth really does rattle. Burqila and Dorbentei's horses start; the whole forest echoes with the sound of metal clattering. Dorbentei shouts something to her transformed cousin in Qorin, something Sakura cannot follow, but it does not seem to calm her. Burqila signs quickly. Dorbentei glances over to read it—but these words are useless as her own.

Barsalai takes one loping step forward.

Shizuka lays a hand on her wife's massive front leg.

Only then does Shefali's growling cease.

"We will not be taking your offer," Shizuka says. Yet that is not her personal speaking voice—it is the one the Phoenix Empress adopts while presenting court. "Whatever dreams we might have for ourselves are irrelevant. The lives of our people are our greatest concern. To live controlled by a man like the Traitor is hardly to live at all. We must ensure that our people are happy, but most of all, we must ensure that they are free. If they are free, then they may strike down what makes them unhappy, and build something better in its absence."

Some members of the army begin to cheer—Shizuka silences them by lifting her hand. How quickly it rises, how quickly she quiets them! Sakura cannot see her cousin's face—what expression is she wearing beneath that mask?

And it occurs to Sakura then what Rikuto said. *The Hokkaran Empire has been the Traitor's from the outset.* But that does not make much sense—the histories are very clear: Yamai was the First Emperor, a beloved son of Hokkaro, lost to time. He was born off the coast of Hirose, the son of a fisherman and a dried-seaweed maker. From such humble beginnings—well-documented humble beginnings!—he rose to prominence. He and the Traitor are two different men who could not be less alike.

Except—aren't all the sources on Yamai hard to find? Kenshiro once showed her a fragment of an old noble's diary that spoke of him; they could look on it only at night, and only with a mirror. The paper was so brittle that their breathing was enough to ruin it.

The stories—the many, many stories—on the Fourth's betrayal are in a much better state. It seems anyone who was anyone two thousand years ago wrote their own version. Only the most key elements remained the same: The Traitor grew jealous of his brother, who ruled over the oceans, and accosted him in anger. The Father tried to reason with him. "You rule the minds of people," he said, "and I only the rising waves." The Traitor would not listen. He struck at his brother with a knife, only to find that his nephew had jumped in the way.

And it was from that moment that the war between the gods truly began, for the Traitor felt no remorse at having killed his own nephew.

*Given to him by his brother.*

Strictly speaking . . . strictly speaking, nothing in the stories is contradictory, and Yamai's death is a mysterious one. She's read fifty different versions at least.

Like Tumenbayar.

They say that if a warrior does not keep his mind sharp and his quiver full of knowledge, then he is lost.

Sakura feels lost now, as the realization hits her: The Traitor founded the Empire. The First Emperor they all worship is the Traitor himself.

Which meant that Shizuka . . .

"Tell your master that we have allowed you to live," says Shizuka. "And if this so-called meeting is at an end, then return us to the lands outside Iwa."

The demon's eyes are hard now. The red-violet of its skin makes it look like a man-sized bruise.

"You know that I can kill your army whenever I like, Four-Petal," it says.

"And I can strike you down the moment you summon your shadows," Shizuka answers. "Your flute trick does not work on my wife and me."

"Still," says the demon. "I was given clear orders. If you refused to listen to sense, then I was to make you a second offer: Leave with me and I let your army go. Refuse, and they die."

Now this is what Sakura had expected to hear initially—but that does not make it any more palatable.

Shizuka is going to deny the offer. She's going to strike Rikuto down, and Rikuto is going to summon its shadows. Assuming they outlive it, the army will perish—only Shizuka and Shefali can reliably kill them. Assuming the shadows die—well, they are still in this pocket of reality Rikuto created. They won't be able to find their way out until it allows them to leave.

And it can't do that if it's dead.

If Shizuka draws her sword, they are all going to die, one way or another. Given more time, Shizuka and Shefali could properly bless the army's weapons; that would give them a fighting chance during their next encounter.

But they'd need time.

The life of a singing girl, painter, and scholar little resembles that of a duelist—and that is a good thing. When there is a sword in your hands, every problem looks like a duel waiting to happen; when you have a brush, or fan, you must learn to see things differently.

And so it is: the scholar recalls that long-nosed demons love games; the singing girl knows how to tempt it; the painter knows how to make the whole thing dramatic.

"I've a counteroffer," Sakura says, taking a few steps forward. She keeps the fan fluttering in front of her face—with her nose covered, she more closely resembles Shizuka. It'd be easier to look seductive if she weren't wearing all this armor; she makes do with fluttering eyes and swaying hips. "We play a game. If you win, my cousin goes with you. If you lose, you set us on the proper path to Iwa and leave."

Everyone is staring at her. She's acutely aware of it—the eyes both green and amber fixed on her. She does not need to see Shizuka's face to see the question written upon it: *What are you doing?*

That question is echoed in Rikuto's eyes—but so, too, is a hunger Sakura knows quite well. "And why should I agree to such a thing?"

"Because you're *excellent* at games," Sakura says. Keep your voice pitched just a little higher than usual—men love delicacy, perhaps demons do, too.

She takes another step closer, another. Her heart's hammering as she gets within striking distance of the demon—but she can't let on how nervous she is. It's just another cocksure client, she tells herself. This is no different from pretending she has no idea how to play painted tiles.

Minami Sakura touches the demon's chest. Then, quiet as a caress: "And you want to put my cousin in her place."

She can hear, distantly, the army asking one another what the fuck is going on. She doesn't care, so long as no one interrupts her. The demon's surprisingly easy to ply—perhaps it's all that arrogance. Perhaps it wants to believe that Sakura would throw her cousin under the cart like this.

Rikuto is an easier mark than many of her clients. "I *am* undefeated in most of your mortal games," it says. It touches her chin. Sakura laughs, as she's been trained to laugh, and closes her fan. Rikuto throws an arm around her shoulder. "Four-Petal! You never told me your cousin was so sensible. We will play a game before I take you to your new home."

"Why not wrestling?" Sakura offers. It has been her plan all along. "The horselords, they're always bragging about their wrestling—"

"We taught men all there is to know about wrestling," says Rikuto. That laugh! The laugh of a creature who thinks itself untouchable.

Sakura can hardly believe her luck. She glances meaningfully at Dorbentei before giving Rikuto the side-eye. Dorbentei never can shut up about being the clan's best wrestler. Sakura just has to hope she is good enough to beat a demon.

That twinkle in Dorbentei's eyes—it is as if Sakura has lit the candle within a lantern.

"Wrestling?" Dorbentei says. "Well, Needlenose here can turn into a wolf, but she can't throw me even when she's that big. Isn't that right, Needlenose?"

Shefali, still in her wolf form, tilts her head toward her cousin. Her ears flop a little. Sakura wonders if she is doing that on purpose—all of this is already so ridiculous.

"That tilt, that means yes, when she's like this," says Dorbentei. "If you want to wrestle, then I'm the best around."

"You?" says Rikuto. It scoffs. "I could crush you with my own two hands. Why should I bother with you, when Steel-Eye has the strength of a god?"

"Because my wife is in too much pain to change back to her usual form," says Shizuka. Her posture has relaxed. It's difficult to discern her exact emotion—but she sounds less suspicious than Sakura thought she would be. "And I am no wrestler."

"You must think you're going to trick me," says Rikuto. Like cold water down Sakura's spine—she bites her lip to keep from making any unusual sounds. "You've picked wrestling because you've got confidence in it. Painted tiles would be a true game, or Kingdoms."

"We've no boards," says Shizuka quickly. "This must be a game that can be played with only what we have already present."

"The horselords do not carry Kingdoms with them? They are more uncivilized than I thought," says Rikuto. Burqila's horse shakes its head. "And none of the soldiers?"

"Gambling is strictly forbidden among the Phoenix Guard," says Shizuka with some measure of pride. "We recruit only the most upstanding members of the army. Drinking, gambling, all these things are forbidden. Ask any of them you wish."

That not a single member of the army has a pair of dice is difficult for Sakura to believe—but Shizuka does not like to lie. She's a *terrible* liar. Her eyes always give her away—she can never look directly at you when she's lying.

But she is looking straight at Rikuto now.

Rikuto spits on the ground. "You would stake your life on this horselord's skills?" it says to her.

Shizuka does not hesitate. "Yes," she says. "Absolutely. What my cousin proposes is fair."

Dorbentei has trouble disguising her surprise. From what Sakura has seen, Shizuka does not often speak kindly of her. It takes an elbow from Burqila to get her to reply. "You aren't afraid of me, are you?" Dorbentei says. "I *did* wrestle a woman with a stone arm once. Heavier than a cart full of shit, but I did it. Bet you're lighter than a cart full of shit."

A well-considered approach. Rikuto abandons Sakura in favor of strutting forward. With a pitfighter's panache, it shrugs out of its robes, letting the sleeves hang from its waist.

"Tough talk," it says, "soon defeated."

Dorbentei dismounts. Sakura has read about Qorin wrestling practices—it does not surprise her when Dorbentei flat out undoes all of her deel. She tosses it behind her, knowing that someone will catch it.

That someone is Burqila Alshara.

No one is going to believe Sakura's account when she writes this—but she can only do so if she survives. If they can win.

Underneath her deel, Dorbentei Otgar wears a thin linen shirt. This, too, she removes. A small jacket is all that remains. It covers her arms and shoulders, but leaves her chest and torso bare.

Rikuto may be thick as tree trunk, but it does not have the body of a man who does any actual labor. Dorbentei's shoulders and arms show a bit of definition—that is all. She, too, is thick about the middle—but her stomach is smooth thanks to her fat. The same fat that speaks to her work ethic. You cannot have muscles if you do not feed them.

Sakura wonders quickly whether Dorbentei's stomach would be hard or soft to the touch—and then brushes that aside.

Dorbentei slaps at her chest. "Lucky for you, I came prepared!" she says.

"What are the rules?" says Rikuto. "I'm unfamiliar with your barbaric ways."

Barsalai paces around the two-shaku perimeter. Every swing of her tail is a small breeze. Somehow, though she has changed her form so drastically, her eyes are still gray and green.

"First one to the ground loses," says Dorbentei.

"Is that all?" says the demon. "No illegal holds?"

"Wrestling is about crushing your opponent," answers Dorbentei. "Fuck no, we don't have illegal holds."

"Then I hope you are prepared to die," says Rikuto.

Sakura keeps her eyes on the two of them as she walks toward her cousin. Shizuka glares at her only a little. "You'd better have a plan," she says once Sakura is close.

"I don't," answers Sakura. "We really are trusting Dorbentei on this one."

Sakura can see Shizuka's brows coming together even under the mask. It isn't like Shizuka to curse—her upbringing was far too delicate—but she sounds as if she is coming close.

The two wrestlers sink into their stances.

Rikuto's is older, more Hokkaran—it places one hand on each knee, then raises its leg and slams it back down. With Barsalai circling as she is, the force of the gesture is lost. Still, it shouts loud enough that Shizuka's red gelding whickers. When it is done with its show of force, it remains squatting, its knuckles touching the ground, leaning slightly forward.

Dorbentei doesn't waste any time with theatrics. She bends over, her elbows near her knees, hands at the ready, and knees slightly bent.

"Before we begin," says Sakura. "We should have the oaths of the participants. Shizuka-shal, do you swear that you will go with Rikuto-yon if Dorbentei loses?"

"I do," says Shizuka—but she does not sound pleased about it.

"And Rikuto-yon, do you swear you will free us—the entire army—from this infernal maze, if you should lose?"

"I won't lose," says Rikuto. "But for the sake of this, yes, I do swear it. Do you swear that you will come with me, too, when I win?"

All those years of life and it has not learned when a woman is not interested. "Of course," says Sakura. She glances at Dorbentei—whose face has gone, for some reason, a little sour. *Don't lose,* she mouths.

Dorbentei beats her chest again.

"On the count of three," Sakura says. Barsalai stops pacing in favor of getting a better view—she's standing at her wife's s side, and Shizuka is petting her haunches.

"One."

Burqila drapes Dorbentei's deel over her horse.

"Two."

The creak of metal as hundreds of guards flick their masks up to watch.

"Three!"

Rikuto shoots forward. For a figure so well defined, it is quick—in three steps, it's closed most of the distance between the two of them. Like a bull it charges; like an arrow shooting through the air; like a colt struck with summer.

Dorbentei does not move.

*Come on,* she thinks, *win this for me, you lug.* Rikuto is taller than her, broader than her. If they make contact, its momentum alone is going to knock her to the ground, isn't it? Sakura hasn't seen much Qorin wrestling, though she's counted a few Hokkaran wrestlers among her clients. They told her how often the match is won in this initial charge.

If Dorbentei doesn't get lower, it's going to bowl her over.

Sakura bites her lip again. Gamblers and singing girls are like sharks and the fish that clean them, yet gambling has never excited her.

Why is it, then, that she has decided to gamble with thousands of lives and the future of an Empire?

It must be her Minami blood.

Rikuto lets out a howl. It's almost reached her, almost bowled her over; it ducks its head to get a better grip—

And at the last possible moment, Dorbentei strikes. In one smooth motion she steps to the right and grabs Rikuto's shoulder. When she pivots her hips, its momentum carries it the rest of the way to the ground.

Sakura's heard of this move. It's illegal in Hokkaran wrestling. Worse than illegal—anyone who attempts it is forbidden from wrestling again. Considering the ordeals many of them go to in order to get their bodies ready, it is near to a death sentence. There are dozens of former wrestlers who work for the Gem Lords of Nishikomi. Who else will employ them?

No Hokkaran wrestler would think to sidestep.

But a Qorin wrestler? A Qorin wrestler who knows how many lives are at stake? The Silver Steppes taught Dorbentei to survive, and that is precisely what she has done.

She throws up her hands with a grin. "Dorbentei Otgar, Demon-Wrestler! Hah!"

Burqila claps, tipping up her mask enough to let out an ear-piercing whistle; the army behind erupts into cheers. This time, Shizuka makes no motion to stop them. Sakura hears her let out a sigh of relief. Even the wolf Barsalai relaxes, settling at last on her forepaws.

But Sakura cannot bring herself to cheer, for there are plumes of smoke rising from Rikuto's ears. Darker still goes its skin—it is the color of Axion wine now, a thing Sakura has seen only twice in her life.

"You . . . ," it says as it pushes itself off the ground. Dirt streaks its face; its nose is bent at an unnatural angle. "You *cheating mongrel*!"

Dorbentei is smart enough to take a few steps back—but not smart enough to keep her mouth shut. "I told you there weren't any rules," she says. "When it comes to the manly arts, it isn't cheating if you win."

Rikuto screams wordlessly, its throat and shoulders going taut with the gesture. For a moment Sakura thinks it is going to charge at Dorbentei. Shizuka must think the same—she reaches for her sword once more.

And Rikuto does indeed take a step toward Dorbentei, arms raised, mouth open with wrath.

Yet it is only the one step. Its body goes stiff as it tries to take a second. Again, it screams. It steps back and claws at its hair, stomping its feet like a petulant child.

"What's the matter, Rikuto-yun?" says Otgar. "Can't go back on your oath? What a shame!"

Blind with rage, the demon makes no answer. Before Sakura realizes what she is doing, she finds herself pressing up against Barsalai. The safest place to be in a situation like this is surely with the immortal wolf.

Shizuka is braver—she positions herself between Dorbentei and Rikuto, tilting the hilt of the Daybreak Blade so that it will be easier to draw.

"You swore an oath," she says. "Best to fulfill your side of the bargain before your body turns on you."

"Your master will hurt you," rumbles Barsalai. Sakura feels each word in her lungs.

Still, Rikuto seethes. It is frothing at the mouth now, raking its own cheeks in its fury. "Cheater!" it repeats. "You cheating—"

"You agreed to the rules being 'no rules,'" says Shizuka firmly. "Now, take us back to Iwa."

Rikuto jabs a finger into Shizuka's chest. Barslalai springs up. It does not take her more than two steps to reach Rikuto—and it takes her no effort at all to pick it up by biting the robes that hang at its waist. It dangles from her mouth like a dumpling in a wrapper.

"The next time we meet, Four-Petal, you shall die," it says. The threat is less intimidating given the demon's current position—but no less forceful. "I will see it happen. My oaths prevent me now, but I won't make the same mistake twice. I will kill you. The Eternal King has no use for a pompous brat—"

Barsalai whips her head back and forth. Rikuto's body twice slaps against the ground. Another wordless howl leaves it—but it reaches for its belt, and it pulls a fan from it.

"Go to Iwa, if you must," it says. "You'll never leave that city alive. Just you wait, Four-Petal, just you wait . . ."

The demon begins waving the fan over its head like an oversized sword. A gust of wind follows. Sakura staggers as the wind threatens to push her over.

". . . Rikuto will have its revenge."

It must be magic that transports them, for Sakura can hardly follow what happens. *You must remember,* she tells herself, but how can she remember this? The winds swirl stronger and stronger, until at last one final gust does knock her over. Out of reflex, she closes her eyes; out of reflex, she throws out her hands.

But when she lands, it is not on the dry ground of the mountains.

When she lands, it is on the banks of the river. Something lands with a heavy thud next to her, and something heavier a little distance away.

When she opens her eyes, she sees them.

The Qorin, the Phoenix Guard, and her family, all borne to the earth by violent winds. They hit the ground like overripe fruit—some will no doubt be hurt by the impact.

And yet they are alive.

It worked.

Her plan worked.

What she wouldn't give for a sketchbook.

# BARSALAI SHEFALI

## SEVEN

Round ears.

That will be the easiest thing, Shefali tells herself, and so it is what she turns her attention to first. Already sweat clings to her forehead; already she can taste it on her lips. Still, she sits atop the grass-that-is-not-grass and focuses.

Round ears.

Rounder than Otgar's, which are two gourds on either side of her face; not so round as Shizuka's.

Cold pricks the points of her ears. Good. She closes her eyes, breathes in, draws the cold deeper and deeper into herself. Her lungs are full of it now.

*Round ears.*

A thought, a command. Cold shoots up her throat and blossoms in her skull. If she touched her eyebrows, she swears her fingers would stick to them. Plumes of vapor rise from her nostrils, curling up toward the false sky.

Shefali screws her face in concentration. Round, round, round. Closing her hands around wet sand and forming it, shaping it, becoming—

It hurts. She winces, her focus faltering for a moment; the cold leaves her and she must draw it back in with a hurried gasp.

*Focus.*

The ears are shaped. The rest must now follow: full cheeks, perfect for holding sweets; teeth shaped for properly biting into them. The cheeks are simple and do not pain her; each moving tooth is an agony that threatens her focus.

But she holds on. She must prove him wrong.

Brown skin, and not this sodden ash; she cannot risk opening her eyes to see if it is working, but she must assume that it is. She can feel the cold spreading out over her skin like frost over the Rokhon.

Hair the color of good hay, and not this limp, dull mess; a straight back and joints that do not pain her. Gone, the scars at her rib cage and throat; gone, the talons she calls her nails.

Everything falls into place.

*This* is the form she is meant to wear.

"There!" says Sakura. "You've got it, Barsalai, now just hold—"

An errant child wanders onto the ice. To impress his friends, who watch from the riverbank, he jumps up as high as he can. When his feet meet the ice, they kick straight through. The river swallows him.

So it is with Shefali's focus, so it is with Sakura's voice. The moment she thinks anything other than *This is my body,* she loses control. Her body shifts, changes: growing fangs puncture her gums; her spine bends like a reed; her joints go stiff, and her ears . . .

Even her ears are gone.

Stars burst behind her eyes, glass lines her throat, everything aches all at once. She doubles over before she knows what she is doing. The grass beneath her is not truly grass, but it is cool enough to remind her of what she has lost—she lies down, cradling her head. To breathe is to crack open her chest, to speak is to tear herself asunder—and so Barsalai Shefali whimpers.

Shizuka is with her in an instant—the warmth of her hand on Shefali's back is unmistakable. Shefali sniffs. It's no use—she cannot get Shizuka's scent in this place. Another blow, another inhumanity inflicted upon her.

She musters all the strength she can to lay her head on Shizuka's lap.

"Shefali," her wife whispers. "Oh, my brave Shefali . . ."

"That's the longest she's managed to hold it," says Sakura. "Thirty seconds, by my count."

Thirty seconds? All of that for *thirty seconds*? If she had not already been doubled over in misery, that would have pushed her over the edge.

"Again," Shefali rasps. "Held the Beast of Rassat for three minutes."

Shizuka runs her fingertips through Shefali's hair. She is careful not to muss the braids. "This is not the Beast of Rassat."

"No, and that's the fucking weird thing," says Sakura. "The Beast, that's shaping herself into whatever people call out and putting it all together. Impossible combinations. Creatures people have never seen. Should be harder to do that."

"Her condition's gotten worse," says Shizuka, her voice going firm. "Is it necessary to perform these experiments? Look at how much pain she's in—"

"I'm fine," Shefali says. To convince the others, she tries to roll over—but it is only an attempt. Halfway through the motion, her shoulders cry out in agony, and she soon follows. It is a good thing they have gone half a li away from the army—surely the clan would have heard all her screaming otherwise.

"My love, I know you are as enduring as the mountains, but even mountains can crack. Please. We must rest." Shizuka's voice goes soft as she strokes Shefali's cheeks, as she wipes the sweat from Shefali's upper lip with an Imperial finger.

Shefali scowls as much as she can. It pains her. She does it anyway. "It's my own form."

"It's your *old* form," corrects Sakura. "If what Rikuto said is correct, then this is your new one."

Shefali grunts. That demon—she understands now why Shizuka is so intent on killing it. The smugness, the arrogance! Worse than any northerner, worse than the Queen of Ikhtar, worse than anything Shefali faced in the Womb. Sakura's explained to her by now her reasoning for the wrestling contest—she had to explain it to *everyone*—but something in Shefali still longs for its blood.

"Fuck Rikuto," Shefali says.

"Plenty of people willing to do that, I'm sure," says Sakura. "But I think it has a point, Barsalai. I think it might be right about all this god shit. The blackblood makes people into the worst versions of themselves—it exaggerates their flaws and sends them running north to join . . . to join whatever this is."

They did no more traveling after their return from the mountain, but it has been hours and they've yet to see anyone else.

"But that's not what happened to you. You got stronger, you got faster, you learned to change your shape. You didn't grow any extra limbs, you didn't go running off to the North—"

"You can't seriously be suggesting that Shefali's condition is a gift," says Shizuka. How grateful Shefali is to have a wife who can read her mind. "Every day she is in agony. Every day she must fight with him for control over her own body. It is only my presence or the flower's that allows her to remain herself—it takes two gods to thwart him. Two."

With her eyes closed and her nose not working as it should, Shefali has no way of knowing what is going on between the two Minami women. It is quiet, whatever it is. A mutual glare, perhaps.

After a small span, Sakura sighs. "Well. We won't find any answers if you're in that much pain, Barsalai, and we need you in good shape for tomorrow. The Hokkaran scouts say the landscape's actually changing when they move now."

Hokkaran scouts, because they'd already lost four Qorin. Strange to celebrate a victory when you'd lost soldiers. On top of the scouts, they'd lost sixty Qorin and fifty Phoenix Guard.

No—there were no celebrations, no true ones. Even Dorbentei settled down when it came time to count heads. Even Dorbentei had cried when they realized sixty Qorin were never going to return to the Sky.

The numbers would have been worse if Shefali had not torn through so many of the enemy, if she had not become the wolf. Munenori found her with ten shadows in her massive jaws, a pine tree snapped under her forepaw like a matchstick. Adopting the form a second time when Rikuto taunted her had felt like the right thing to do—but, Sky, it had left her so drained.

"Your leg," Shefali mumbles, for it is then that she remembers Shizuka's injuries.

"Healing well," answers her wife. She picks up Shefali's taloned hand, lays it on her thigh. Even beneath her riding pants, it should be easy to feel the wounds—but Shefali feels only smooth skin. "There are benefits to our state. But don't let that give you any ideas—you're done for the evening. No more shifting."

"But—"

"No buts," says Shizuka. "I'm the Empress, you know. That means you have to listen to me."

It is a joke, but one she does not quite have the spirit to land.

Shefali smiles anyway. She cannot think of anything to say, any joke to diffuse this miasma surrounding them, but she smiles. It is what her wife needs.

"I'll tell everyone to get their shit together," Sakura says. "Me and Dorbentei, we'll get all the weapons sorted out for you two. In the morning, you'll bless them, however it is you think you can do that."

*Kumaq*, Shefali thinks, *but will there be enough?*

What is she talking about? With thousands of Qorin in one place—of course there will be enough. But what will Shizuka use? She's been conjuring fires and light beyond the Wall, but no flowers—has she lost her link to them so far to the north? The flowers surrounding them are aberrations to the word; Shefali can see their true forms well enough when she blinks.

What is it like for her wife—being surrounded by such a blatant perversion of her domain?

A thought for later. Shefali can deal with only so many injustices at once.

"Sakura-lun," says Shizuka. Shefali can feel her voice. "Thank you for today. Truly. You . . . I would have killed it, given one more moment."

"And trapped us all on the mountain," says Sakura. She sounds smug, and so Shefali imagines her as such, fanning herself despite the perfect weather. "I know."

Again, Shefali does not want to open her eyes—whatever is passing between the two cousins is lost to her.

But she does hear Shizuka swallow, does feel her take a breath, does instinctively squeeze her hand.

"It was wrong of me to insist you come," says Shizuka.

A pause. "Worked out all right, in the end."

"But this isn't the end," says Shizuka. "This isn't even near to the end. We're beyond the Wall, where anything might happen, and all of us may well—"

"We won't," Shefali says. Speaking hurts, but the pain is worth it. In the same way that a blade is sharp until wear makes it dull, Shizuka is confident only until reality wears her down. Shefali has always been her whetstone. It is a role she is happy to play even now.

"Listen to your wife," says Sakura. "Aren't you the one saying you're always certain? Be certain about this. You'll kill that bastard demon."

"We will," echoes Shefali. She forces herself to squeeze Shizuka's hand again. At least the contact of their scars grants her some small relief. "We promised."

Shizuka's breathing goes ragged. If Shefali did not know better, she would assume her wife is crying—but those tears will never come. Only this rough gasping, only the sniffing.

To move her own body is to sling Gurkhan Khalsar across her back and carry it for twenty horselengths.

And yet—let no one doubt Barsalai Shefali's strength: she pulls herself up higher onto Shizuka's lap, her head against her wife's chest, and squeezes her as tightly as she can.

"We did," repeats Shizuka. "Together."

And in that word there are promises, in that word there are oaths, in that world is a pact sealed by sun and moon. Together. Across the sky, one chasing after the other, the stars trailing in the wake of their eternal dance—together. Through the heavens and beyond, cloaked in darkness that could not conquer them—together. In these mortal bodies, on this mortal plane, after the lives that they'd lived, steeped in regret and exultation . . .

"Together," Shefali repeats.

But the cosmic, the universal, the eternal—all of these things wear on her. Perhaps it is as the demon said: perhaps this flesh cannot hope to contain the truth of her power, perhaps this was always meant to be her fate.

Five days until the first of Qurukai—and by her reckoning, it is already Last Bell. Breaking down the camps, riding to the mountains and then through the forest, the battle, the shifting—how much can a dying woman stand in a single day?

Her pain is a weight. Down, down, she is sinking; her eyelids are starting to droop. When did she get so *tired*? For she feels it now the way she felt her old form only moments ago—how aware she is of this sudden lethargy! At her joints and along her back, as if some creature has sapped the strength from her very bones!

"Shefali," Shizuka says. Her voice is low, little more than a whisper, and Shefali has the distant thought that Sakura must have left them. Close as she is, Shefali can hear her wife's breathing—the staggered intake, the ragged out—her thundering heartbeat. What troubles her so, that she should feel this way even when they are alone together?

Shefali sniffs the air, but there are no answers to be had. Only rot.

"Shefali, I failed today."

"You didn't," Shefali mumbles. Ridiculous of her to suggest it. Loss of life is never to be celebrated—but all of them could have died today, instead of only some. If Shizuka had acted on her more rash impulses, they would not be here beneath the false sun, Shefali would not be listening to that beating . . .

"I . . . When the battle came, I couldn't . . . I froze. I let my fear win."

"It didn't," Shefali says. She'd muster more of an argument, but a fogbank has consumed her thoughts. *Thud-thud, thud-thud, thud-thud . . .*

"But it did," says Shizuka. "If I'd been thinking clearly, I would have mustered us all at the foot of the mountain and waited for it to come find us. No one would have died, then. That's what Xianyu would have done. But instead, I—"

"We went first," says Shefali. Splitting into smaller groups so that they could more easily navigate the strange forest had saved the lives of many of the Qorin—but condemned others. It had been Burqila's decision. The right one, so far as Shefali is concerned; the forest is no place for cavalry.

"I should have—"

"You survived," Shefali says. "We survived. Tonight we mourn; tomorrow we fight again."

Shizuka says nothing to this. She does not need to. Her breathing is getting steadier. She traces circles on Shefali's open palm.

"Shizuka."

"Yes, my love? Is something wrong?"

How concerned she sounds. If something were wrong, there is not much Shizuka could do. Hold her hand and whisper to her, perhaps.

But . . . but perhaps that will be enough. The two of them.

"I'm falling asleep," Shefali says. The words come out garbled—and in Qorin, at that.

She hears Shizuka smile. "Rest, then. I'll keep you safe."

Her Qorin is almost as garbled as Shefali's.

They are half a li from the camp, half a li from their ger, half a li from their bedroll, but there is no use fighting it. Sleep is coming for her like a pack of hunting dogs, and she is backed into the corral already.

"I love you," Shefali says, switching to Hokkaran.

"And I love you, bright star," Shizuka says. She kisses Shefali's forehead. "Sleep. We can talk more in the morning."

It does not occur to her then that Shizuka is saying she won't be sleeping. It does not occur to her what effect that might have on a general, on a warrior. It does not occur to her that perhaps Shizuka does not want to sleep because she knows—she *knows*—how bad her nightmares will be if she attempts it.

All that Shefali thinks, as she drifts off to sleep, is this:

*She called me her bright star.*

# DORBENTEI OTGAR

## ONE

The Qorin language assumes all singing girls charge, for a single night of their service, their own weight in gold. Altanai is the word for them—golden women—and Dorbentei has never liked it until just recently.

When the Altanai comes to visit, Dorbentei Otgar is reading. She likes to read. Not in the way Halaagmod does, or the way the Altanai does: they're always neck deep in some scroll full of some old Hokkaran's ranting. There's too much of that in the world already, so far as Otgar's concerned; she doesn't need to read a book about how the Hokkarans came to power to know the ramifications of it. Even as far as Ikhtar, Hokkaran prejudices and propaganda outweigh reality: more than once, she and Shefali were asked if a horse had given birth to them.

Of course, that is why Grandmother Sky gave them each two fists and strong arms. People only say that sort of thing once.

But Sakura—it feels odd to use her name, even in Otgar's own thoughts—is different.

When she opens the door, for instance. Hokkarans don't have solid doors the way the Qorin do; they have no real concept of knocking.

But Minami Sakura, who spent several years in a Xianese palace—she knows what knocking's all about. Three quick raps, a pause, and then: "Roast meat your bones."

Otgar guffaws before she can stop herself; the air leaves her as though she'd been kicked in the gut. *Roast meat your bones!* The woman's Qorin is worse than a Surian merchant's. Only when her shoulders settle and her cheeks start to hurt does she realize how badly she needed a laugh like this.

"What? Isn't that what you say?"

"It's close enough," Otgar answers. "Come in."

The door opens and shuts. Otgar sets down her book on the small folding nightstand she picked up in Salaam. Sakura's still in her oversized armor, though she's left the war mask and helmet aside. The sight nearly kindles another laugh from Otgar; it is only by biting the inside of her cheek that she keeps it in check. What is it with Hokkarans and wearing so much metal? No wonder their horses are so small; they are weighed down by living boulders.

Yet the look on Sakura's face does not lend itself to laughing at her. It's hard to see, in the dark, but there's something a little frantic about her. That she is carrying a bottle of rice wine and two saucers—instead of her usual lectern—only emphasizes this. The bottle clinks against the saucers as she steps into the ger. Sakura's head turns as she sweeps the place: the makeshift bed; the few carved wooden sculptures she carried back from her father's homeland; the books; the little figurines Barsalai whittled during their travels scattered like ants wherever best struck Otgar's fancy at that particular moment.

Things to be proud of. Her things. She admits, she is excited to hear what Sakura thinks of them.

"You have only one chair?"

Otgar sucks her teeth. "I'm only one woman. I don't often have guests."

"Well, tonight you do," Sakura says. "I need a fucking drink." She sits right there on the carpets. Otgar half expects her to sit cross-legged, like a Qorin, but she sits on her ankles instead. Must be an old habit. Likewise, when she pours the wine, she does so in practiced, graceful motions—including holding back a sleeve that is not long enough to require holding back.

It's presumptuous to walk into a woman's ger and announce that you're visiting, to leave no opportunity for argument. A woman beats her ger into existence; she should have some say in who gets to stay within it.

And yet Otgar cannot summon the will to argue the point. She, too, needs a drink. Standing, she folds her chair back up and leans it against the nightstand. Sakura's shoving the saucer of drink at her before she's even sat back down.

"I thought you were the one who needed to drink," Otgar says.

"I can't drink alone," Sakura says. "You start drinking alone, that's when you have a problem."

"So you came to me," Otgar says. With a smirk she tosses back her head and drains the saucer. Rice wine is boring and flavorless; a lingering burn. At least that makes it easy to drink. "What can I say? I'm a popular woman. They should start calling me Demon-Wrestler Otgar."

It's an easy, casual brag, the sort of thing that would invite banter from Shefali or any of the others. On a better day, it might have done the same for Sakura.

But today is not that day. Today, Minami Sakura shrinks; today, she pours another cup the moment the first is done. "I saw people die today." As silk on silk, her whispered words.

Dorbentei Otgar, woman of many tongues, finds that all of them have now fallen silent.

Sakura finishes her second cup. "No one told me about the smell. Or the screams. Well, you hear about the screams, everyone writes about them, but you don't really *know* what they're like until you hear, and . . ."

The first time Otgar saw a man die she was five. One of her cousins was dying of the blackblood in the sanvaartains' ger. She remembers distinctly that her mother told her not to watch—but how was she to stifle her own curiosity? The man was screaming day and night, howling like an animal, and she could not believe that it was her cousin causing all that racket. In the middle of the night, she'd left her mother's ger. Cloaked in two deels to keep out the cold, she waddled over to the sanvaartains' ger and opened the door just a crack.

She heard him then. The sound. It so horrified her that she screamed and fell backwards onto the grass. The sanvaartains took her to her mother, who switched her so hard she could not sit for two days. In truth, there was no need for such punishment: Otgar had learned then that death was not something you sought out.

That it has taken Sakura so long to reach this point—she finds herself thinking Hokkarans live pampered lives. Otgar's story is not unique; she has heard similar from the mouths of everyone her age. Everyone who lived, at any rate.

And here is Sakura, tears falling like glittering rain onto her saucer of rice wine.

"The sound's awful," Otgar says.

Sakura nods, too plagued by her memories to say much of anything. She pours Otgar another saucer full of wine.

What to say in a situation like this? Otgar knows what Burqila would do: tell Sakura that she is being a child, that she has chosen to be here, and that she must accept the consequences of that choice. She knows what Barsalai would do: sit and listen the whole night through, stopping here and there to say something so insightful you almost hated her for it.

But she is neither of them. "Can I ask you something?"

Sakura's brows come together. ". . . yes," she says. "You know, normally you let a person talk about their problems more, before you start asking them things."

"If you wanted that, you wouldn't have come to me. You would have gone to Barsalai," Otgar answers. This she does not need to think about. "You came to me because you wanted someone to talk to. So, I'm talking to you the way I'd talk to anyone else."

Silence. Then, spoken over the rim of her third cup: "You got me."

Otgar nods. She continues only when Sakura finishes that third cup, when their eyes meet in the relative dark of the ger. She half expects to see a touch of yellow when the candlelight catches Sakura's eyes—but they are as brown as the earth itself, brown as soft soil.

Otgar has always liked brown eyes.

Perhaps the vehemence with which she shoves aside that thought comes across in her voice, for the next sentence leaves her more sharply than she imagined it would.

"Why are you here?"

Sakura sets the cup down. She does not refill it, not immediately; instead, she traces a fingertip along the rim. Otgar follows it while Sakura gathers her thoughts. "I told you I came here as a historian. That's only part of the story."

Her shoulders go tight. If Sakura is about to admit she's here as some sort of spy . . . But no, Shefali would have caught that. Needlenose likes her.

And Otgar doesn't believe that she could be. She's too different.

"I never knew my parents," Sakura says. "When I was a baby, my mother left me in the entry hall of a pleasure house in Nishikomi. I was raised there."

Otgar doesn't see the connection, but she won't say so. Now's the time to let her talk. She sips from her cup.

"A few years later, a woman in a ratty cloak stopped by in the middle of the night. She knew who I was—knew my name and my father's name, and even the color of the silk I'd been wrapped in. The woman who raised me—my real mother—told her that if she didn't want to be back in my life, she should go away. The woman gave her a letter for me and left. No one ever saw her again."

"What did the letter say?" Otgar asks.

Sakura bites her lip. "I don't know."

Otgar tilts her head. "You don't know?"

"That's the whole reason I came!" Sakura says. Her voice cracks. "I can't read the fucking thing. I've tried, and tried, and tried, but the letters just keep moving. I brought it to *everyone* I could. Our scholar clients couldn't read it; Ken-lun couldn't read it; Baozhai couldn't read it. Twenty years I've had this thing, twenty years I've kept wondering why she left. It's got to say something, right? Why did she come all the way back for me, just to leave this letter no one can read?"

The tears are flowing like rivers now; it's getting hard for her to talk.

Otgar sits next to her. It feels more like the right thing to do than the wrong thing. Sometimes that level of comfort is all a person needs. In a ger everyone would be embracing her, patting away her tears; they'd all work through it together. Hokkarans aren't like that. If Otgar embraced Sakura, she'd probably skitter off, and that would do her no good in a state like this.

And so she simply sits by her side, fully expecting Sakura not to acknowledge her.

It is surprising, then, when Sakura loops her arm through Otgar's.

"That letter's the whole reason I left Nishikomi. I have to know why I wasn't good enough."

Otgar's throat feels tight all of a sudden. "You are good enough."

"Not for *her,*" Sakura says. There's venom there; Otgar finds herself surprised by it. "She could have taken me back, and she didn't."

"Then that's her failure," Otgar says. "She and my father can go milk stallions together."

A beat. Sakura sits a little straighter, turning at last toward Otgar. They are close enough that Otgar can smell the wine on her warm breath, the sweat, the dried blood of some unfortunate soldier. "Your father?"

"It's different for Qorin," Otgar says. She clears her throat of something painful. "You can sleep with whomever you like, so long as you've gotten the permission of everyone involved. Ganzorig, he's around my mother all the time, but he isn't her husband, and he isn't my father."

"I thought—"

"They get along well," Otgar continues. She can't stop. "I'm happy for my mother, I am, and it isn't as if my father was her husband, either. We don't care about that. Ganzorig's here for the kids they've had together—that's what I care about. What any of us care about, with how often we don't make it to eighteenth birthdays."

"I didn't know," Sakura says. She's sniffling, her hand on Otgar's shoulder like a warm weight.

"My father was a Surian merchant who sold us cut-rate scrolls and spices. After he left, we never saw him again. When Needlenose and I were in Sur-Shar, I thought about tracking him down, but I don't have much to go on. He probably doesn't even know I exist." Another swallow. "Shame for him, as far as I can see, but I didn't need him. I don't need him."

There's a long silence then: the two of them sitting in the relatively bare ger, a half-empty bottle of rice wine before them. If she tries, Otgar can hear the rise and fall of Sakura's breathing. That armor must be overheating her. She thinks of saying something about it, telling her she can get more comfortable if she wants, but she knows what it's like to want that layer of safety.

"You're good enough," says Sakura.

Otgar smirks. "I threw a demon today, of course I'm good enough," she says. "And you decided to wade knee-deep into this fucking mess because . . ."

Otgar falters. Why, exactly, had Sakura come? She hadn't quite answered.

"Because your cousin was able to read my letter," Sakura answers. "And she won't tell me what it says. Because I couldn't leave Shizuka alone, after all of the things she's done to herself. I watched her light herself on fire, Otgar."

Otgar frowns. The letter struck her as a cipher of some kind, a puzzle—in truth, she wants to get a look at it herself. And it's a fine thing to focus on instead of the feeling in her stomach when Sakura calls her by her childname. But if Shefali is the only one who read it, Otgar has the sneaking suspicion it wasn't meant for just anyone's eyes. Shefali attracts trouble like corpses attract flies—just look at whom she married.

"I asked her, and she just . . . she keeps avoiding it."

There's got to be a reason for that. The furrow in Otgar's brow gets deeper the more she imagines what it might be. If Shefali knew it was the only thing Sakura's mother left her . . .

"Do you know why?" Sakura says. She's leaning her head against Otgar's shoulder now. If she's trying to make it harder for Otgar to dodge the question, then it's working. Otgar doesn't want to believe that's the case—not when Sakura's voice is as ragged as a washer-woman's cloth.

"She's never brought it up with me," says Otgar. "But if I know that big oaf well, she's probably trying to protect you from something in it. She likes to . . . If you put two jugs of kumaq in front of Barsalai and tell her one of them is poisoned, she'll drink them both. It won't hurt her, so she thinks: 'I will save people.'"

It is then that Sakura reaches for another cup. Otgar hands it to her. They clink their saucers together and tip them back at the same time.

"Your cousin's an idiot," says Sakura. "I'm a grown woman; I deserve to know."

"It might change things if you do," says Dorbentei. "You people care so much about your bloodlines."

"It isn't even about that," says Sakura. "I don't care who she was—I care why she left."

"She'll tell you," says Otgar. "When the time's right, she'll tell you."

It's a weak assurance, but it's one that Otgar is confident in all the same. Barsalai is convinced she's going to die soon. She won't go to the Sky with so many loose ends; it isn't like her.

"All she said was that it was nothing good, that my mother wasn't well. . . ."

*So she's dead,* Otgar thinks. Odd that Sakura hasn't caught on to that—but a horse with blinders misses much.

"Barsalai will tell you when the time comes," Otgar says. She shifts a little; Sakura readjusts her position to match. "But that's the last I'm going to talk about my cousin tonight, and the last we're going to talk about all this sorrowful shit. We're two hundred li away from anything like civilization and we might die tomorrow. That's time to drink, not time to mourn."

Sakura pours them another round. Otgar's head is starting to swim. She wonders what she is doing alone in her ger with some puffed-up Hokkaran girl, and she decides she doesn't care.

"Then, please," Sakura says, "let's drink until I forget."

# O-SHIZUKA

## SEVEN

Shizuka has been staring at the same morning glory for a Bell.

A sort of feeling deep in her guts: she has been doing this too long. Three hours, at least—an entire Bell spent staring at a flower beneath an unchanging sky.

And yet she cannot look away. That morning glory—violet, with its central white starburst—fascinates her. It is not the flower itself that does it. Morning glories are astoundingly common; she's never been fond of them, for that reason. There are hundreds of morning glories swaying in these endless fields, thousands maybe. Rarer flowers, too—azalea without rocks to cling to, chrysanthemums the size of her head growing well out of season, striped peonies and asphodel from distant Axiot—and yet it is this tiny morning glory that wins her attention.

When she closes her eyes, this morning glory—this single flower—is the only one that does not change. The rest show their true forms: spines of forgotten animals, strange bones and stranger faces. Ten thousand eyes watching her wife fall asleep on her lap. It's enough to make her skin crawl, though she has been here so long already that she has forgotten what it is like to be completely at peace.

But this flower . . .

Shefali talks to her horse. She's spoken to Shizuka about it before—the tongue of swaying grass. More than once Shizuka's tried to hold conversation with daffodil and hydrangea, with sagisō and gardenia, and not once have they answered. Whether that is because flowers have no mouths remains to be seen. Still, when she summons them, they appear; when she gives them a task, they grow to accomplish it. She supposes she should not be too upset that they've never actually spoken.

And yet . . .

A li away from the rest of the camp, a li away from any prying eyes, unable to escape the warm burden of her wife's sleeping body—well, what is she to do but speak to the flower?

It begins simply enough. She feels preposterous trying, but if she stops to second-guess herself, then the whole venture will be lost before it begins. She was the Peacock Princess, she is the Phoenix Empress—it is natural that the flowers should speak to her. This is the thought she holds in mind, this is the idea to which she clings.

"Have you always grown here?" Shizuka asks.

It's a ridiculous question. Wisteria can grow to be thousands of years old—there is one such tree at the center of Horohama village—but not the humble morning glory. It can be only a few years old, at most.

Yet she leans in as much as she can with Shefali's bulk in the way and waits for an answer.

The flower is silent.

Shizuka counts to eight hundred before trying again.

"You are the only true flower north of the Wall," she says. "Since my birth, I've enjoyed a . . . relationship . . . with your kind. Well. Not your kind specifically—I mean it in the broad sense."

She sounds like a fool. Her ears are going red. What if Shefali hears her? Oh, what does it matter?

"Everything here is under Yamai's control. Everything, I think, except you," Shizuka says. Naming him summons a gust of wind; she worries that it will muss the morning glory. If only she were closer, she could properly shield it. Instead, she can only watch it and—yes! It is still standing.

"Try as he might to influence you," says Shizuka, "you've blossomed bright and colorful. Truly colorful. You've not bothered another flower's petals, and you've not decided to bloom in green on a lark. Whatever was here before he was—you were there, weren't you?"

Another count of eight hundred. She worries, part of her, that the Traitor can hear whatever it is she says. This is akin to worrying over spilled ink—the Traitor's eyes and ears dot the landscape like blades of grass. He is always with them.

Let him listen, then.

Shizuka narrows her eyes. She stares at the flower, stares at its creases and the tips of its petals, at the curve of its stem. When she was younger, it was a simple thing to change the color of a flower. A single touch was all it took.

There is a chrysanthemum blossoming in mocking gold within arm's length. She drags a fingertip along its thick petal. *Black,* she thinks, in the way she used to think when she was a child. Is it her imagination, or are her fingertips glowing gold?

The flower does not turn.

She tries this with every flower she can reach. None listens to her, none bothers to indulge her in the slightest. These are the Traitor's flowers.

Except for the morning glory.

Shizuka loves her wife more than she has the words to say—but Shefali is heavy. Incredibly heavy. There will be no going anywhere with her on Shizuka's lap, unless she finds some way to extricate herself. Yet Shefali's sleep is such a rare thing—would she dare disturb it?

She thinks back to their shared years on the steppes. Qorin all sleep in the same ger, regardless of who else is still awake. It had been an awful time for Shizuka, who by then had not learned how to sleep wherever her feet left her. Shefali, however, had more than once slept through a horsehead fiddling contest.

Moving her probably won't wake her, and Shizuka isn't going far. The morning glory is within two shaku, even. She can protect her wife and study it at the same time.

Shizuka slips her arms beneath Shefali's shoulders and pulls her up. Shefali snores, mumbles something about being hungry, but does not wake. It takes a lot of effort and some decidedly unregal grunting, but at last Shizuka manages to lay her wife down on the false earth. She even peels off her armor and arming coat, balling the latter to form a makeshift pillow.

"Please sleep well," Shizuka whispers to her. She kisses Shefali on the forehead—how serene she looks!—and goes to the morning glory.

Closer up, it is no different from any of its neighbors. Shizuka reaches out for it with a cautious hand. Perhaps it would be safer to use the Daybreak Blade, but she does not want to frighten the flower.

What sort of warrior is she? Frightening flowers . . .

The air around the flower is warmer than usual. Shizuka waves her hand around to be sure—the border around it is about the size of a summer melon.

"Hmm. Are you playing tricks on me?" she says to the morning glory.

And when she touches its petals, the morning glory answers. In Xianese.

". . . Sister, what's come over you?"

Shizuka's brows come together. She does not know that voice, but she does know that accent. The speaker is a woman from Xian-Lai. Well-to-do and properly educated. She sounds nothing at all like the acolytes Shizuka spent her time with at the temple—but she does sound like . . .

"Nothing has 'come over me,' Third Sister. I resent your choice of words."

Baozhai.

Shizuka's heart catches. What is going on? She does not know, but she cannot bring herself to tear her fingers away from the flower. Baozhai. Is this . . . ? Of course, there are morning glories all over the gardens at the Bronze Palace. Baozhai loves them. Vines of them decorate every gate in the garden—and there are plenty of gates to walk beneath.

"All this talk of the North!" says the other woman. Baozhai's third sister. What is her name? Shizuka racks her memory. She remembers the characters. How were they pronounced? It's fixed, in Xianese, isn't it? Wangzhi. That's it. She works at the temple in Xian-Lun—what is she doing back home?

"And is it so strange to speak of our neighbors? Of my husband?" Baozhai excels at concealing her own emotions, even from her sister—but there is no mistaking the tiredness to her voice. "He has been away for too long already."

Too long? Shizuka finds herself smiling. It's been less than a month—Kenshiro must only now be settling into Fujino. For such a serene woman, Baozhai is a worrywart when it comes to her husband.

"Didn't you see him last year?" Wangzhi asks.

*What?*

Shizuka's mouth opens. Her fingertips tremble; the sounds of Xian-Lai fade in and out. Desperate now—incredulous—she wraps the vine around her wrist.

The effect is immediate. It is as if she has peeked her head through a curtain separating rooms. All around her she can see the gardens of Xian-Lai, but she cannot *feel* them. The oppressive humidity and gentle breeze do not touch her.

Yet there is plenty to harm her all the same. Baozhai sits on a bench, wearing one of her more reserved dresses—solid emerald green with no embroidery to speak of. Though her hair is gathered into an elaborate style, there is a streak of white at her temple. Softness has crept into her features.

She looks older.

"For three days," she says. "Baoyi is not yet old enough to be alone for very long, and he cannot abandon Fujino with those sharks circling. Yangzhai is more concerned with catching frogs than policy; he'd love a journey like that—but we've our treaty with the Lady of Flowers to think of. This is the safest place for him."

How long has it been? Is this a dream? It must be a dream. Surely it is a dream, a vision of the future.

The woman sitting next to Baozhai more closely resembles

Xianyu—they have the same hardness to them. She keeps her hair close cropped. As Shizuka watches, she carves a length of wood into a shape something like a flute.

"And why not recall him?" she says. "A nonsense dream? That is precisely what I mean. Something's come over you. The northern gods will try to distract you, Sixth Sister, but you mustn't stray from the path."

Her hands are steady as she carves, as if she has done this a hundred times before. Perhaps she has. She does not even need to look—Lai Wangzhi keeps her eyes trained on her younger sister.

And so, too, does Shizuka. The way they're speaking—strange dreams and northern gods. No one spoke of the Hokkaran gods the entire time she served at the temple. No one wanted to worship gods they knew to be dead—and gods that had been forced on them besides. To hear them mentioned in this context perplexes Shizuka.

But it does not perplex Baozhai. "It was a vision, Wangzhi. You of all people should understand that."

"A blazing phoenix and a great black wolf swallowing the heavens," says Wangzhi in the sort of tone one might use for poetry one does not like. "Yes. Quite insightful, that. You've read too many novels. The real gods are more obscure than this. Phoenixes and wolves are all the North ever speaks of; it is one of their idols that plagues you."

Baozhai's brows twitch just slightly. It is as good as a frown on anyone else. "Third Sister," she begins, "you may choose to disbelieve me if you wish, but do not accuse me of being seduced by foreign influence. My mind has always been my own. Kenshiro must remain in Fujino."

"So spoke your foreign god," says Wangzhi.

Does she mean . . . ?

Shizuka swallows.

"So spoke . . . ," Baozhai begins, but the sentence trails off. A look comes over her then, as if she were trying to recall something someone said to her in passing. "So spoke the Phoenix."

The Phoenix?

Two words like two blows: the Phoenix. Baozhai's come up with creative ways to address her in their years together, but never "the Phoenix." "O Phoenix," on occasion, when they met as equals—but never when introducing her to others. Never so casually. Baozhai's lines were as clearly drawn as her eldest sister's battle plans: she never mixed Shizuka the Sovereign with Shizuka the woman.

And the Phoenix is certainly the Sovereign.

"Baozhai," she calls. Her voice cracks. "Baozhai, please. Can you hear me?"

Wangzhi continues her carving—but Baozhai does look up. Not at the morning glories—at the sun.

"Did you hear something?"

"A bird," answers Wangzhi. "Your Phoenix, perhaps. No one has seen a Phoenix in years, Sixth Sister. Including yours."

"The Phoenix was never mine," Baozhai answers, but her brows are coming together; the ringed fingers of her right hand rise to her temple. "Can we speak of something else? My headache's returning."

"You only get a headache when we talk about this," says Wangzhi, sucking her teeth. "Very convenient."

"I have no control over my health," Baozhai says. "We shall speak of another matter or we will not speak at all."

Wangzhi sighs. "Tell me about your violets then. You're always eager to brag about them."

The violets. Ah, what pain—the violets! As Baozhai glances in their direction so too does Shizuka. There, a little up on the hills, protected from prying eyes by Baozhai's prized wisteria tree: the violets. Only a week ago they'd stood at that very spot, only a week ago Baozhai had taken her hand and said—

Shizuka's throat aches. *Remember,* she pleads.

But Baozhai's eyes narrow. "In my mind they are so vibrant," she says. "But when I look on them now . . ."

The air thick with rain yet to fall. Baozhai's eyes, the color of the giving earth itself, as her mouth shaped the words: *Will you promise me more pleasant days?*

"You sound like one of our groundsmen," says Wangzhi. "Seems all the flowers west of the Wall are giving up on bright colors."

"They'll bloom again," Baozhai says. "The way they used to. Perhaps for Baoyi's coronation."

How the corners of Shizuka's eyes ache; how her head pounds! Her lips tremble and once more she calls out: "I swore to you!"

But only silence follows.

Shizuka's breath is starting to go ragged again. What does any of this mean? If it is a vision—then from whom? If it is not . . .

She does not want to consider what it might mean if it is not a vision. If it is happening at this very moment, then . . .

When is this moment?

How long have they been over the Wall? There's talk of Baoyi's coronation, which can't be until Shizuka returns—but no one seems to remember her. If she is old enough for a coronation she must be a young woman already.

Shizuka swallows. Baozhai cannot hear her—it's no use sitting here with the flower, hoping to catch her attention. If there is something wrong, it is better to know sooner rather than later.

And she knows exactly how she will find her answer.

Shizuka unwraps the vine around her wrist. In a small pouch she wears around her neck, she keeps the violets, the ones she grew that day at dinner. In spite of its musty home and in spite of how long it's been in the dark, they're as bright as ever. She plucks one of the flowers from the bunch.

There are centuries of texts on Hokkaran swordplay, and centuries more of techniques passed solely through word of mouth. Every minute of every day of her youth, she studied whatever she could find. How to hold her sword (as if she were holding a bird in hand), the proper distance between her and her enemy (two shaku), the five stars and three points by which all men might die—Shizuka knows all of this.

But there are no scrolls on how to be a god, no wizened old women to beat her with switches until she learns.

Holding the violet does not seem to have the same effect as holding the morning glory. Frustration mounts. What is she meant to do?

"Show me my niece," she says. Commanding things is in her nature.

Yet the violet is cheeky, and does not listen immediately. Her vision swims with streaks of gold and jade; she sees strips of the palace she called home for so many awful years. There: her grandfather's headless statue; there: the spot where her bare feet scorched the tiles.

*"Show me,"* Shizuka repeats. She draws a breath, reaches for the fire, clears her mind as much as she can. All of it is right there within her reach if only she can—

There.

Her duelist's calm rushes over her. The image stills.

She knows this room, but that is a foregone conclusion. She knows every room of the Jade Palace. Even so, this one is particularly close to her heart, for it is the room her parents once shared. There on the wall is the saddle Burqila Alshara gave to her mother. Her father's writing desk sits in the corner to the right; what remains of one of his writing sets lies atop it, clean and free of dust. Visions of Nishikomi decorate the screen that separates the sleeping area from the eating. Nishikomi lives, too, in the painted swamp lilies that decorate the room.

Though she cannot truly feel this place, her memories fill in for her senses—the faint scent of incense from the censers as the priests call the Bells, the mat against the soles of her bare feet. Her throat closes, though she is not sure why—perhaps it is the aura of this place.

Perhaps it is the girl who kneels in front of the shrine at the center of it. Poet's Promise Violet robes are expensive enough, but to dapple them with Xianese patterning? In Imperial Gold? Shizuka shrinks to think of the cost. And on one so young! Pale hair, worn childishly loose, pools onto the floor behind her. Bent over as the girl is in obeisance, Shizuka cannot see the color of her skin—but she does not need to.

Baoyi.

But taller now, older. Somehow.

A familiar sensation—pressure behind her eyes, her nose watering, Minami Shizuka takes a single step forward before falling to her knees. Baoyi was scarcely knee high when they left, and this girl—this girl must stand twelve hands tall. In another year, she will tower over Shizuka.

*How long has it been?*

"Baoyi," Shizuka says.

Baoyi shoots up, her hair fanning out behind her. The sight of her face! Shizuka's heart aches. Her niece is only a girl of six—this girl is at least ten. And already she has begun shaving her brows, already she wears the ornaments of her station, already she—

What has Shizuka done to her? For she knows that weight better than anyone—and she has laid it upon a child? Did she, in her longing to secure her Empire, ruin Baoyi's life? How could she have done this—?

In Baoyi's shocked expression, Shizuka sees her own self.

And so when her niece asks her who she is, she does not at all register the question. Her own sorrow consumes her, overwhelms her senses: she has shackled Baoyi to a throne she never asked for.

"Who are you?"

It is the second repetition that breaks through to Shizuka—the second repetition that wounds her. The fear in Baoyi's voice! She has scrambled backwards, her hand raised as if to fend off a knife, her green eyes wide.

"Who are you, and how did you get in here?"

Is it—has Shizuka manifested as something strange? She glances down at herself. No, she's manifested in the same armor she wears at the present moment beyond the Wall. She isn't even wearing her war mask. Why is it that . . . ?

"Baoyi," she repeats. It is a difficult thing to keep her voice calm and soothing when her soul is in such disarray. "Don't you recognize your aunt?"

"My aunt?" says Baoyi. Her brows are coming together over her eyes—far darker green than Shefali's or Kenshiro's. She is reaching for something on the table, something Shizuka cannot see given the distance between them.

A distance she does not dare close.

"Yes," Shizuka says. It hurts to have to say it at all. "Your father's sister's wife. Minami Shizuka." How cold it sounds to phrase it that way. "Aunt Zuzu. You remember, don't you? I . . . I picked out your name."

Shizuka's soul hangs on a thread. Baoyi holds the knife. With one word she can sever it, if she so choses.

*Remember,* Shizuka thinks. All of her self she pours into that singular thought.

Who is she if her family does not remember her? If her people do not remember her? Minami Shizuka has never existed—only the Empress, only the Phoenix, only the woman they needed her to be. How much has she sacrificed to the Empress?

And now, for her own niece to fail to recognize her . . .

Shizuka waits. She waits, and she watches, for that is all she can do.

Baoyi gets to her feet. She is taller than Shizuka imagined, broad about the shoulders. All the commotion's made one of her hair ornaments slip. And then, like a kite slowly lowering to the ground—confusion gives way to recognition.

"Aunt . . . I . . ." Baoyi stares down at her hand and Shizuka sees, then, what it was she was reaching for: the violets. One of which has shriveled in her palm. "You gave me these, didn't you?"

"I did!" says Shizuka. "Before I left for the Wall. I told you that if you ever needed help, you only had to call, and I would hear you."

The young regent continues looking at the flowers. That furrow in her brow, that tension in her posture—much as Shizuka's heart leaps at the barest memory, they are not yet truly reunited.

"The Phoenix gave me these violets," she says quietly.

"I did," Shizuka says. Her voice cracks. "Baoyi, it was me. O-Shizuka-shal. Empress Yui, if you prefer—aren't I in the records?"

Another long moment passes. If she wanted to, Baoyi could have called for the guards—that she has not is a good sign.

*Please,* Shizuka thinks but does not say.

"My aunt is the Phoenix," says Baoyi, more to herself than to Shizuka. Still, there is no doubt to her voice.

"Yes," Shizuka says. "I was the Phoenix Empress when I left, but what is another new name? None of them matter to me." Now that she has begun, it is hard to stop—she has uncorked a bottle and she will pour until it is empty. "My people matter to me. My family matters to me. I was . . . I visited your mother, just now, and—Baoyi, tell me. Please, I must know: How long have you been living in the Jade Palace?"

Baoyi blinks. She lays the living violets back on the table, pinching the dead between two fingers and holding it up in front of her. She sniffs at the blackened flower and frowns.

"Father keeps track of it better than I do. Eight years, I think. I heard him say the other day that he hadn't seen his sister in that long, and I thought that was odd. I didn't know he had a sister. Are you her?"

*Didn't know he had a sister.*

Shizuka starts. The Jade Palace bubbles around her as she struggles to keep focus. Shefali is within two shaku—what if she heard? It would crush her. Only force of will is keeping Shizuka together at all.

"I . . . I see," says Shizuka. Like fireflies flickering in the night: questions blinking in and out of her mind. How is she meant to choose? Why has she come? If Baoyi is not in danger—and it does not seem as if she is—then what else is there to say? Look at how she's holding herself—this visit isn't bringing her any comfort. Shizuka isn't bringing her any comfort. "Eight years. How . . ."

Pain contorts Baoyi's face, as if a blow has struck her from behind. Every corner of Shizuka's body goes taut with trepidation—but the moment passes, and Baoyi fixes her in her gaze once more.

"You went away," she says. "You . . . you and Aunt Shefa. You told me to watch for the sun and moon."

The corners of Shizuka's eyes ache with tears she cannot possibly shed. Her nostrils flare. "Yes," she chokes out.

"Why haven't you come home?" Baoyi asks. "You and my aymay—my father's sister. All of the other Qorin, too. If you're a god, now, why haven't you come home? There are so few of us left that sometimes I wonder how long we will even last."

Conversations are much like duels.

Baoyi has just attacked with an unknown stroke.

Shizuka falters. She opens her mouth and nothing comes out, for how is she to explain the reality of the situation? She would come home if she could, but going back to Hokkaro now would take as much time as going to Iwa. And she cannot allow the Traitor to continue living—not when his hands are stained with the blood of countless Qorin. Not when her own veins are clotted with his rank influence.

She cannot come home.

But how is she to explain that to her niece? To a girl who has had her childhood torn away with her eyebrows?

"I am sorry," Shizuka says. Her throat aches. "I can't."

"You can't?" says Baoyi. A sneer rises on her lip. "Papa must have lied about you. He said you're a hero."

Even as a child, Baoyi had been far too like Shizuka. It should come as no surprise that she has a sharp tongue.

"Baoyi—"

"That isn't my name anymore!" says the girl, her voice full of fire. "My people call me Princess Yuuko, and since you won't come home to your family—that's what you can call me, too."

Yuuko. How does she spell it? Courageous, permanent, reason, leading? So many ways . . . and yet it is not the name Shizuka gave her. It was not *precious ambition*.

The vision of the Jade Palace flickers around her.

"O-Yuuko-shan—no. O-Yuuko-shal. Forgive me for abandoning you. I had no idea it would take this much time—but you must understand I cannot give up on my mission. The arrow's already in flight."

Baoyi's eyes are glistening. Shizuka swallows down a wave of envy and shame. "That means more to you than we do?" says Baoyi.

No. No, nothing could ever mean more to Shizuka than her loved ones.

But duty is not about what is important to a single person. It is not about wants and desires; it is not about personal pleasure.

It is about doing what is right. Too long Shizuka had put her own selfish desires before the right thing, the just thing. Those four years she could have been fixing the Empire, lost instead to drink and her own nightmares.

But now, in the distance, she can hear the horns that wake the Qorin every morning.

"Call for me if you have need," says Shizuka. "And I will answer."

Like the rippling water of a pond—the room around her. Even as the image flickers, even as she feels herself growing distant, Baoyi remains.

"You won't," she says. "And neither will I."

Shizuka closes her eyes.

When Shizuka opens again, she is once more beyond the Wall. Death surrounds her in its blossom mask. The air smells of rot. On the horizon are the towers of Iwa, where her ancestor lies waiting for her.

*He wants to speak to you*, Rikuto said. *You can roam wherever you like*. . . .

She knows now the cruelty of this offer. Even if she accepted, the world she returns to will not remember her.

Minami Shizuka has never existed.

Soon, Empress Yui won't, either.

The crown that she's worn all her life has passed to another.

Why, then, doesn't she feel any lighter?

# MINAMI SAKURA

## FIVE

Sakura's never dealt with an army before, but she's dealt with a mob of angry sailors, and those are basically the same thing. At least the army's sober. Mostly. The Qorin *are* fond of their rotten milk.

Wandering from camp to camp, from ger to ger, wearing her Imperial Gold robes and asking people to surrender their weapons—it shouldn't work. It really shouldn't. What if she's one of the enemy wearing someone else's skin? Why aren't they more suspicious of her?

Probably because they've been out here for a week or more already, and there's been only one battle. Because the Qorin are busy mourning their dead and the Phoenix Guard are listening to their captains outline exactly what went wrong in the woods. Because they have better things to do than worry about Minami Sakura. Because if an attack happens, their unblessed weapons are worthless, anyway.

But Sakura doesn't say any of that when she comes to ask for their weapons. All she says is that it needs to be done, and most of them are content enough to listen. Say something nicely enough, and most people will go along with it—that's the greatest secret there is when it comes to social interaction.

The trick is that "nicely enough" varies from group to group.

The Phoenix Guard want you to come to them and bow and speak properly, without any of the slang Sakura's used to. They want honorifics and arcane pronoun use and recognition of their ranks. She isn't fond of that—not by any stretch—but she can make it work. Captain Munenori, after all, started life out as a sailor. Sakura wheedled that bit out of him before they left Nishikomi. Two cups of rice wine was all it took.

And she knows how to work sailors.

So it's all smiles and innuendo with him, all false modesty. *Why, Captain, what are you talking about?* That is what he expects from her—perhaps what he expects of all women who aren't the Empress—and so that is what she gives him.

Because she has convinced him, she has convinced all the others—it only takes mentioning that First Company has already surrendered their weapons. Those transactions go much quicker; she hardly needs to use her fan for them at all. "Honored Lieutenant, her Serene Imperial Majesty the Daughter of Heaven asks that you follow First Company's lead . . ."

Easy as scallion pancakes.

But the Qorin? Oh, the Qorin are a different story altogether. The first ger she visits is overseen by a woman two years short of a hundred if she's a day, so wizened and small that Sakura assumes at first she is a wooden statue her family has inexplicably chosen to bring beyond the Wall. Her first words startle Sakura right out of her skin. There she is, talking to a lumbering man who insists his name is Big Mongke—which is not the same as Fat Mongke, and certainly not Strong Mongke—when that old woman pipes up.

"You people took six of my children," she says. "Now you want our weapons? Puh."

Sakura's never taken *anyone's* children, except if one of the girls at the shrine asked her to hold her baby for a moment or two. She feels offended—but it passes. This woman isn't talking about her, in specific; she's talking about *all* Hokkarans.

"It's Barsatoq and Barsalai who are asking," Sakura says. She feels as though she should bow to the woman, but given the circumstances, that might be taken as an insult. "I'm only delivering the message."

"And why hasn't Barsalai come herself?" asks the old woman.

"Because she's resting," Sakura answers.

Big Mongke laughs. Sakura feels it in her lungs—just how big is he? It's hard to tell when he's leaned over in the ger. "Barsalai doesn't rest."

"She does, sometimes," Sakura says. "You can go look if you don't believe me."

"I don't," says the old woman.

"Neither do I," says Big Mongke's wife, a woman only a little taller than Sakura. "You want us to surrender our weapons so you can take us as prisoners. Use us as shields. Defile our horses. We're onto you."

*They are right to be upset*, Sakura thinks. Over and over, she thinks this. She tries to think of what to say, of what could possibly be nice enough to a people who have lost more than half their number because of Hokkaran hatred.

Thankfully, she does not have to think long.

"Eresheyya, are you giving Barsatoq's cousin trouble?"

That voice—it's Dorbentei. Sakura's caught between relief at having sympathetic company and consternation at being caught in the midst of failure.

Eresheyya—the old woman—answers in Qorin. They all do. Six people in the ger, and all of them are talking at once in a language Sakura can only vaguely understand. Big Mongke's voice drowns out all the others, and yet somehow Dorbentei is ignoring everything he says, standing there with her arms crossed and near shouting at Eresheyya. Louder and louder the discussion gets. The dogs wake and run off. Sakura wonders how long it will be before one of them punches another—and then, just as quickly as it all started, it's over. Dorbentei claps the old woman on the wrist and sniffs her cheeks.

"They'll give you their arrows," Dorbentei says, turning to Sakura.

"Just the arrows?" says Sakura. "What about their swords?"

"This family doesn't have any," says Dorbentei. "They have arrows, we get arrows."

Sakura writes this down in her lectern. Big Mongke's gathering the quivers from around the ger—she figures she might as well give him some privacy, and steps outside. Dorbentei follows. Somehow, Sakura is not surprised.

"Don't you have better things to do?" Sakura says. "Some old woman to translate for?"

"Burqila's resting," Dorbentei answers. She leans against the bright red doorframe. "I thought you'd probably need help with this, being a northerner who doesn't understand us."

"Wasn't aware Burqila Alshara needed to sleep," Sakura says, though she's been aware of that for weeks now. It's all the answer Dorbentei's going to get from her.

"Everyone needs to rest eventually," says Dorbentei. "Even my cousin. That what she's up to now?"

Sakura nods. "Tried to keep her form. Her old one."

"With the cheeks," Dorbentei says sagely.

"It didn't work," says Sakura. "But it took a lot out of her, so she's resting now. Probably the last time, if I don't miss my guess."

Dorbentei gets off the threshold. She starts walking toward the next ger, and Sakura follows, knowing full well it'll be useless to try to argue her away.

"Don't talk like that," says Dorbentei. "Barsalai's not going to die before she's good and ready."

"You sound like *my* cousin," says Sakura. "The wording was very clear on the prophecy Shefali was given: she won't live to see her twenty-sixth year. It's almost her birthday, now."

Dorbentei sniffs. There are four dogs running outside this ger, all of which are carved into the red door leading in. Dorbentei kneels down to play with them. One, a fat old hound with a gray muzzle, starts licking at her face.

"Ask her, when she wakes," says Dorbentei. "Ask her what the Mother said to her."

It's a preposterous thing to say when a dog's licking your face. More preposterous to smile while doing so. Yet there's something easy and charming in Dorbentei's casual arrogance. She doesn't need to assert herself, doesn't need to boast. Yesterday, she wrestled a demon. Now she pets a dog and talks about visiting the underworld.

"You went along with her, didn't you?" says Sakura. This particular story is not one Shefali has told her. "To the Womb."

"I was with her through almost all of it," says Dorbentei. She reaches into her deel's pocket for a lump of fat and sugar; she feeds this to the dog and stands. "Talked to her right after, when she was starting to go that color. Ask her to tell you about it, *historian*."

"Don't tell me how to do my job," says Sakura.

"Just a helpful suggestion," says Dorbentei. "I'm a very helpful woman."

"To whom?" says Sakura.

"Everyone. That's why I'm Burqila's favorite niece," she says. That's no brag—it's a simple statement of fact. She isn't wrong in the slightest: Burqila is distant with most of her other nieces and nephews. "Why don't you let me handle my clan? You're tired, aren't you?"

She is. She's never been this tired in her life—if she stands too still, she might well fall asleep on her feet—but she has a job to do.

And besides, where does Dorbentei get off making suggestions like that?

"I can handle myself," says Sakura. "It isn't my first sleepless night."

"So you're going to sleep in the saddle?" Dorbentei says. "If we get attacked in the morning, you're going to miss the whole battle. Sleep in a litter, and it's the same—not to mention you'd have to find someone to carry you."

"I can think of a few volunteers," says Sakura. The words leave her softer than she intends them to—and yet Dorbentei's eyes narrow a little all the same.

"That so?"

"That's so," says Sakura. What is it with Dorbentei? Who allowed her to look so damned self-satisfied? "But I've got to make sure this gets done. I can get some sleep while the two of them are blessing all this metal and bone."

Dorbentei lays a hand on Sakura's shoulder. "Or you could go get some rest now, and ask Barsalai to tell you her story while she blesses the weapons . . . and that way, you wouldn't miss out on anything interesting." She smirks. "If I didn't know better, I'd say you don't trust me to finish this job. I mean, you must be tired after all that drinking last night."

She is. And objectively speaking, Dorbentei's the better choice for it. The Qorin will listen to her without much question. Having Sakura go around and ask for weapons might unintentionally foster distrust among the ranks.

But that doesn't mean she has to tell Dorbentei that. If she does, the woman's head will swell up like a puffer fish.

Sakura's pouting, her eyes drooping closed. Dorbentei taps her—and takes the lectern from her hands as gently as it's possible to do such a thing. Sakura's too sleepy to stop her.

"All that rice wine got to you, didn't it? Go, rest," says Dorbentei. "You know where my ger is."

"Aren't you tired, too?" says Sakura, but it comes out as more of a mumble than she'd like. Dorbentei sleeps in Burqila's ger with the rest of Barsalai's immediate family; Sakura has a vague memory of her leaving in the middle of the night.

"Less tired than you are," Dorbentei says without missing a beat. She taps Sakura's shoulders and points to it. "Go."

Sakura frowns at her. If she had more energy, she'd argue that she isn't a child to be sent to bed—but she is exhausted. Truth be told, having someone else tell her it's time to sleep is the sign she needed, as to stop on her own would have been to show weakness.

"You'll get all the rest of their weapons?"

"As many as they're willing to give," says Dorbentei. "Important distinction."

"And you *promise*?"

"On my horse's mane," says Dorbentei with a smile. An honest, warm smile. "Now will you go? Your eyes are glassier than an Ikhthian cathedral."

Sakura's never been to an Ikhthian cathedral. She wants to ask Dorbentei what they're like, wants to hear her tell a story, wants to listen to her talk in that accent of hers that's five different accents put together.

But she's tired.

"Fine," she says. "Don't ruin my ink."

"I won't!" says Dorbentei.

Sakura walks to the ger—come to think of it, wasn't it unusual for a single woman to have her own ger?—and does not look over her shoulder. This is a conscious choice she makes, one that takes much of her fast-fading focus.

If she looks over her shoulder, she will see Dorbentei waiting until she's safely in the ger.

And she does not know how to feel about that image.

SHE'S THE ONE who goes to talk to Shefali and Shizuka in the morning. It's something the three of them—Burqila, Dorbentei, and Sakura—decide on over breakfast.

Having breakfast with Dorbentei and Burqila is surreal enough. Having a *Hokkaran* breakfast with them even more so. Sakura doesn't know where they got all this fish from. Have they held on to it since Nishikomi? Perhaps they have; most of it is salted and ready to travel. It occurs to her the army must be saving it for Shizuka, or must have been trying to.

The joke is on them. Shizuka only likes salmon. She *hates* all other fish.

But Sakura's free to fill up her stomach, and she does. There's no way of knowing what awaits them today.

"We've got everything in carts," says Dorbentei. She's eating fish, too, much to Sakura's surprise—she pours extra sauce onto her bowl. "Once you've got them awake and presentable, just have Barsatoq do something fancy with that sword of hers. We'll see the light and bring over the carts."

Burqila nods. She isn't touching fish at all—her bowl is full of stew they've reheated over the fire. Sakura isn't sure what to say to her. Dorbentei's the one doing all the talking, after all, and she doesn't see Burqila signing.

"What about breaking down the gers?" Sakura says.

"That can wait until they're done," says Dorbentei. "Gives everyone more time to get themselves ready. Rough shit, the other day. Some of the older people—the ones who remember the blackblood—they're getting cold feet. Burqila's going to talk to them."

Sakura meets Burqila's eyes. They're hard and sharp as always. She wonders—how old is the woman? Did she lose any siblings to the blackblood? What of her parents? So many questions, and so few answers. She isn't about to ask. There are some answers she knows she isn't entitled to.

"Is this place the way you remember it?" Sakura asks instead.

Burqila's brows come together; her right eye narrows. Dorbentei purses her lips in surprise. When Burqila's signing comes, she translates it in a clear voice.

"Yes. I hated it then, and I fucking hate it now."

Does Burqila swear? It seems hard to believe, and yet there's a hardness about her—yes. That must be a direct translation; she isn't faltering in response to it at all.

Before Sakura can ask her another question, Burqila signs again. This one's easy enough to read—she waves Sakura closer.

When the Terror of the Steppes asks you to come closer, you do. Sakura sits and tries not to move as Burqila studies her face. Eventually, she sniffs Sakura's cheeks. Shit. Should she be returning the gesture? She tries, only for Burqila to draw away and sign something.

Dorbentei's stifling a laugh—though it dies down as she has to translate.

"Naisuran's brother is your father, isn't he?" says Dorbentei. "Burqila says she knew him. She says you look a little like him, but more like your mother."

Sakura's heart drops. *My mother?*

"My . . . You knew her?"

Burqila nods. She keeps her eyes on Sakura as she signs.

"Burqila says that she hated your mother," says Dorbentei. Her tone's starting to waver, and she pauses before translating the next part. "She says that your mother was . . . overly cautious. Angry. That she did not accept her responsibilities with an open heart."

None of that is what Burqila said. A cold desperation seizes her. She sets down her bowl of fish and rice. "The exact wording, please."

Dorbentei sighs. "You won't like it."

"I've heard a lot of shit in my time," she answers. "Try me."

"Burqila says your mother was a coward who never should have gone on the mission to begin with," says Dorbentei.

*Never should have gone on the mission to begin with*. But that means . . .

Sakura swallows. A woman who leaves her child at a pleasure house rather than attempt to raise her—Sakura has never wanted to believe she could be a coward. And yet, for so many years to have passed without a word . . .

"One of the Swords?" she says. "My mother was one of the Swords?"

Burqila nods.

Dead, then.

She's always known, on some level, that her mother must be either dead or callous. It is good to know it is the former—though if Burqila named Sakura's mother a coward, then the latter might still be true. But what sort of coward joined the Challenge of the Sixteen Swords? Everyone knew what the end result of that tournament would be. Everyone had known the "reward" was a suicide mission.

So why enter at all?

Sakura runs through the list in her mind: The letters left with her are all from Sayaka—so her adoptive mother claims. Thirty years before Sakura's birth, you could not have thrown a stone without hitting a Sayaka—the name was as popular as Keichi had been for men. And there *was* a Sayaka among the Swords: Maki Sayaka, an assassin of some renown. They still speak of her in Nishikomi.

Her mother had been an assassin and a coward.

She presses her eyes shut.

But where does an assassin learn to write in an ever-changing cipher? Sakura's intellectual curiosity overpowers her shame. Barsalai read a letter from Sakura's mother—from Maki Sayaka—before they departed—a letter that Sakura herself has tried time and time again to decipher to no avail. How is it that Barsalai read it without difficulty; how was it that Maki Sayaka learned to write in such a way?

Except . . .

"Did you see her die?" Sakura asks. A surprisingly easy thing to say. If Sayaka had been one of the Sixteen Swords, then she is dead, and nothing Shizuka can do can possibly bring her back.

Burqila shakes her head.

The pieces begin to fall together. This is no longer a personal tragedy—it is an intellectual one.

"If she was one of the Swords and you did not see her die, then she must have died here—over the Wall," Sakura says. "Did O-Shizurumor see her die? You two were separated for a little while, weren't you?"

Burqila's eye twitches. If Sakura didn't know her better, she'd say that Burqila Alshara was flinching. That, however, is impossible; everyone knows Burqila fears nothing. Why should she? She slew a demon with her own two hands when she was younger than her daughter is now. And without any of the benefits of godhood! No, Burqila Alshara would not flinch.

And yet.

She signs an answer, though Sakura was careful to keep it open enough that she might nod or shake her head. Dorbentei's a little sullen as she translates.

"Burqila says that your mother ran off on her own after they crossed the fog," says Dorbentei. "Shouting about Iwa."

Like the last stroke of a paintbrush—yes. It's all obvious to her now. Maki Sayaka, for whatever gods-forsaken reason, went off to Iwa. That must have been where she wrote the letter, and that would explain why it was impossible to read—something happened to her in the Lost City. But why would they have left her alive?

Sakura reaches for her lectern. Dorbentei was kind enough to clean it before she returned it—it sits atop a Surian-style nightstand within arm's reach. Flipping through the letters, she sees with some relief that none of them have changed. All remain written in Hokkaran—even the ones that Dorbentei filled in last night. Sakura leaves aside the thought that Dorbentei's calligraphy is much finer than she'd have expected. If these letters, written beyond the Wall, have not changed, and only Shefali can read them, then it must be exposure to the blackblood that had made Sayaka's swirl in such an accursed way.

And if her mother contracted it in Iwa, she would have been close to the Traitor. Who is to say it was not he guiding her hand the whole way? It is little wonder Shefali reacted in such a way. Already the Traitor harried the flanks of her mind. To read his words delivered through the hand of another, to know beyond a shadow of a doubt that what had happened to Sayaka could also happen to her . . .

A difficult thing indeed.

But even this is not answer enough. What was her mother doing here in this infernal land? Where had she gone, and what had she seen? If she'd sent the letters after her exposure, then what if . . . She dares not think it. Better to assume that her mother is dead.

Sakura sniffs.

"Thank you for telling me all of this," says Sakura. "Don't know if I've ever had a more educational breakfast. I think I need to go speak to Barsalai about something."

Dorbentei's eyes narrow. "Are you going to be all right?" she says. "It's a lot, what you've just heard."

"I told you before: I can handle myself," says Sakura. She scarfs down the last of her meal and sets the bowl aside. "Besides, you're the one who kept telling me how interesting the story about the Womb is. If I don't get going, I'm going to miss it, aren't I?"

She smiles, but it isn't a friendly smile, and it fools neither of the women across from her.

Dorbentei sucks her teeth. "Suit yourself," she says. "But you want another drink, you come find me."

Sakura learned at a young age how to keep her cheeks from going red—she employs that skill now. Dorbentei's cut to the quick of it. Sakura loves her cousin dearly, but there is too much at stake for her to ask for Shizuka to listen to her worries. Barsalai is an excellent listener—but in four days, she will die, and Sakura's already asking enough of her. Munenori's out of the question, as much as he'd perhaps like to be in it.

Which leaves Dorbentei.

She doesn't like the well of emotion she feels at the thought. Sakura doesn't like attachment in general, and that is what this is: an attachment.

Sakura opens her fan as she stands. "You're going to need another chair," she answers.

She does not stop to listen for the answer.

Barsalai has a story to tell her.

SHIZUKA ISN'T IN the best mood when Sakura arrives. Sakura doesn't expect her to be. Whatever Shizuka saw in Nishikomi Bay has changed her. The stories of a headstrong princess no longer match up to the woman she's become—still confident, but only so long as it can counter her own terror.

And she is afraid this morning. Sakura isn't sure of what. She knows better than to ask. The only thing Shizuka hates more than going to court is talking about her own emotions. To ask her now would only agitate her—the answer will come out soon in one way or another.

She'll tell Barsalai, perhaps, and Barsalai will, out of concern for her wife, tell Sakura.

That is the way of things.

But even Barsalai looks as if sleep's gotten the better of her. She sits facing Iwa, with one arm wrapped around her wife. There are circles beneath Shefali's eyes still, and the points of her ears now poke out past her hair. Has it gotten whiter, or has she gotten darker? For she looks more monochrome than ever. Are those dapple marks on the backs of her hands? Like stars, Sakura thinks, like a starry saddle blanket across her skin.

It really won't be long now, if Rikuto was right. If this is the form Shefali was always meant to take.

Sakura's curious. Of course she is. But she knows better than to pry, knows better than to ask why her cousin is lying with her head against Barsalai's shoulder, the two of them reaching toward the lost city.

Instead, she simply calls out to them.

"Good morning," she says. "I hope I'm not interrupting."

Both of them turn toward her at once. A strand of snot drips from Shizuka's nose; she is quick to clear it. When the Phoenix Empress speaks, her voice is little more than a rasp.

"Good morning, Sakura-lun," she says. "Have you had your rice?"

"I have," says Sakura. She holds up the wrapped stack of bowls. "Brought some for you, too. Would you believe Burqila's had fish this whole time?"

The corner of Barsalai's lips turns up in a smirk. "Aaj hates fish," she says.

"More for me," Sakura answers. She sets the bowl down in front of Shizuka, wishing that she'd thought to bring a bowl of tea leaves for Barsalai. "Don't worry. It's all two-day-old stew for you, Cousin."

"Delightful," Shizuka says. It might be sarcastic, but Sakura has the feeling it isn't. Shizuka does genuinely enjoy Qorin stew. The trouble's just . . . whatever's wearing on her. She uncovers the bowl and unhooks the spoon from its handle, but does not yet start. "How did it go?"

"Well enough," says Sakura. "I handled all the Hokkarans. Dorbentei insisted on talking to the Qorin. Everything's in carts now, just waiting for the signal."

She pauses, waiting for Shizuka to eat. If left to her own devices she'll neglect her meals more often than not.

Shizuka takes a single begrudging spoonful of stew. She swallows it, licks her lips, and then taps her spoon against the rim of the bowl.

"How were things here? No attacks?"

"None," says Barsalai.

"Well, don't you tell me that," Sakura says. "You were asleep the whole time."

"Only part of it," Barsalai answers. Sakura doubts her, but does not call her out on it in front of her wife.

"No attacks," Shizuka echoes. She points with the back of her spoon toward . . . something. A flower, perhaps. That's all there is in that direction. Which one she means is beyond Sakura's ability to grasp at a moment's notice. "I spoke to our niece."

"Did you?" says Sakura. She tilts her head. "What'd she say?"

Not how, or why, or anything like that. If she starts questioning Shizuka's motives, they won't get anywhere at all.

"That she doesn't remember me."

Sakura stops fanning herself mid-motion. This is . . . Well, it isn't entirely unexpected. All the research does lend itself to this conclusion: Barsalai and Shefali will be forgotten in time. She just . . . never expected it to happen so soon.

"I'm sorry," Sakura says. She starts to speak more, but Shizuka cuts her off.

"It's been six years—in Hokkaro, I mean. Six years have already passed since we left."

*Six years?* But it hasn't even been six *days*! Sakura swallows. The timing beyond the Wall of Flowers—she'd suspected as much back in Dorbentei's ger, but to hear it confirmed out loud . . .

How much of her life has she given away for this mission?

How many years will pass between her departure and her return—if she returns at all? When Sakura returns to Nishikomi, how many of her friends will greet her, and how many will have long since given up on ever seeing her again?

Sakura, her knees suddenly a little weak, sits next to her cousin.

Shizuka sucks in a breath, as if she is caught in the middle of crying. "I'm sorry, Sakura-lun," she says. "I didn't know. I wouldn't have asked—I would have let you stay behind. I've—"

"Don't worry about it," Sakura says, though her throat is shattered glass. What a day for discoveries. Her birth mother was a coward, and the woman who raised her may well be dead by the time she returns to the Empire—along with most anyone she ever knew. If Sakura even does return. "Nothing we can do about it now."

"We can win," offers Barsalai. She points to the distant towers with her lips. "We can kill the Traitor, reclaim history for ourselves."

"Baoyi . . . ," says Shizuka.

"She'll understand," Barsalai says. "One day."

It is just like that woman to stay so practical at a time like this. Six years already, and six more likely to pass before they return—by then Baoyi will be a woman grown. The Empress in truth, if that is what she still wishes to call herself, styled after an aunt who has ceased to exist long ago.

And Kenshiro sitting in his library the whole time, going grayer and grayer, keeping record after record of his sister's disappearance. How long will it be before he forgets what he is recording? How long will it be before the other lords label him a madman?

When all that is left of Shizuka is the legend of the Phoenix Empress—what makes Baoyi's claim to the Hokkaran throne legitimate?

Again, Sakura's curiosity overpowers her despair. She knows of no other situation quite like this. In the Imperial Records, how is Shizuka's reign recorded? Has she become a mythic figure, like Yusuke the Brawler, or has her name merely disappeared, leaving Baoyi as the successor to the Toad's awful reign?

"I don't want Baoyi to have to understand," Shizuka says. "I meant for her life to be better than mine, Shefali. All I've done is ruin it."

"You've given her a nation at peace," says Barsalai. "Or you will, once this is done."

"And Shiratori? Fuyutsuki? Even your father—what if they turn on her? She does not think of me as a hero, Shefali, nor does she seem likely to ask us for help. And we will be here beyond the Wall, unaware any of it is happening—"

Barsalai kisses her wife's forehead. She says nothing more, for there is nothing more to say on the subject. This price they are all paying grows steeper by the day. Surely that is the Traitor's intent—to separate them from the people they love, from the place they're fighting so hard to defend. A wolf in isolation fights twice as hard but bleeds twice as fast, as the Qorin saying goes.

When Sakura returns to Hokkaro, it is likely no one will remember her. Who was she to those people but the Empress's cousin, the forgotten Minami? That is all that had lent her authority in Hokkaro. In Xian-Lai, at least, she might be able to prevail upon her reputation as a scholar. . . .

The lectern balanced in the crook of her arm is heavy as a mountain. She promised Barsalai an accurate record of her life. If Shizuka is right and they have already faded from memory, that record is more important than ever now.

Six years. Fuck, what if her favorite fried octopus stand is gone when she gets back?

Sakura pushes the thought aside. There is so little time here for her, for her own thoughts and wants and needs. A small taste of what Shizuka is dealing with—but a bitter one, all the same. Perhaps she can talk about it with Dorbentei later.

"When she is older, and when you've returned to Hokkaro with that bastard's head in hand, she will understand," says Sakura. "You aren't acting for yourself, you're acting for your country."

"But . . . ," says Shizuka. She sniffles again.

"You can't all be Tumenbayar," Sakura says. "Running off to have adventures. That shit fills novels, but it doesn't improve anyone's life. Just remember—that's why we're out here."

She doesn't quite believe it herself. What's her presence going to do? Whose life is she bettering? But then—and this was the worse thought—whose life is she hurting? No one back below the Wall knows her well enough to miss her. Baozhai's probably throwing parties dedicated to Sakura's absence.

Maybe Kenshiro remembers—when he isn't busy being Regent.

Sakura had better not go back to him empty-handed.

"I suppose you're right," says Shizuka. "But it feels . . . it feels awful."

"They never tell you about that part," says Sakura. "How much it hurts, being a god."

Barsalai shifts in her seat. She lets out a small sound halfway between a grunt and a sigh—and that is how Sakura knows she has an opening.

"Or has someone told you otherwise, Barsalai?"

Barsalai fixes her with her steel eye. The thin film of black that covers it makes it strange to behold—although, is it shining brighter than it used to? For the sheen on that metal more closely resembles silver than steel.

"You haven't told me what happened in the Womb," Sakura says. Barsalai's always appreciated directness—and from the way Shizuka perks up, this isn't a story she's heard either.

"You met her, didn't you?" says Sakura. "The Mother. The two of you spoke. I asked Dorbentei about it, but she said I should hear the whole thing from you."

Barsalai does not answer—only stares at the towers in the distance.

"Did she say anything?" says Shizuka. "About him?"

Barsalai presses her lips together. After a moment's consideration, she lets out a true sigh.

"Yes," she says.

And it is as if a fire's ignited in Shizuka: gone, her maudlin expression, consumed by her burning need to *know*. She sets her hands on

Barsalai's shoulder and leans in close. "What did she say?" she asks, and even Sakura is surprised at the desperation in her voice. "Did she tell you how to kill him?"

Barsalai's shoulders stiffen. It does not take a former singing girl to know she is uncomfortable with her wife's . . . enthusiasm over this particular subject.

And yet there may be answers lurking there, in those memories of her. Answers. If they are trapped here in this time-that-is-not, far from home in every way that matters—why not learn all they can about their enemy? Why not use every tool available to them?

Barsalai undoes the first clasp of her deel. Silvering scars overlap at her neck—a thick one that runs straight across and a large starburst on the right side. Given the darkness of her skin, they look like galaxies, like heavenly bodies trapped within her flesh. And yet—what was it that gave her those injuries? For any normal person would have died of these wounds.

But Barsalai Shefali is no normal woman.

"It is a long story," says Barsalai.

"We'll signal the carts," says Sakura. "All my cousin has to do is light up her sword or something—they're watching for something like that."

"You told them I'd use my powers as a signal flare?" says Shizuka.

Sakura shrugs. "What, are you saying you won't? You make light, Shizuka-lun. It's the easiest way."

Shizuka does not suck her teeth, but only because that is the sort of thing she would never dream of doing. What she does instead is raise her chin, so that she is staring imperiously down on her own cousin.

"I can't believe you," she says.

"You don't have to," says Sakura. "Everyone else will."

And that is the great joke of this—however ludicrous Barsalai's story, it is Sakura who must make it palatable to the general public. But what does that mean? What does that mean in a Hokkaran context? Is she to strip the elements of the story that might offend her own people at the expense of Barsalai's? In the face of all of this—what is her mission when it comes to these histories?

That is a question for her future self. For now, Sakura prepares her writing set.

"Go on," she says to Barsalai. "Whenever you're ready. You can bless while you tell the story, right?"

Barsalai narrows her silver eye. "Yes," she says. "But you'll have to write quickly."

# O-SHIZUKA

## EIGHT

Shefali isn't doing well.

It isn't something she has to say for Shizuka to take notice. So rarely does Shefali *have* to say anything at all. A lifetime trapped between two nations all too happy to mock her accent in both languages—this has taught her the better part of silence. Shizuka has always been a little astonished at how efficient Shefali can be when it comes to communication. Most of their conversations aren't vocal.

Now, for instance.

It is, by Shizuka's reckoning and Sakura's, the first of Qurukai.

The appointed day of Shefali's death.

Earlier, before they broke camp, Shizuka caught her wife sitting on her own three li away from the others. What horror had seized her when she woke without Shefali at her side! For she knew the day, she knew the day, and to imagine that already Shefali might have left—that she might have scattered like funeral ashes to the wind . . .

Is there a single thought more crushing than this?

If there is, she has no will to think it.

And so in search of her wife Shizuka had gone, and her wife she soon found. Three li she had gone, and after three li she found her.

"Shefali?" she'd called to her.

Shefali did not move. She stared with a sort of steadfast resignation at the towers of Iwa. They were close now. Two more days, and they'd be at the walls—that was what the scouts were saying.

But they did not have two more days.

Shizuka could not help but feel like a failure as she beheld them.

Together, she'd promised, like two pine needles. But no matter how hard they'd driven the horses . . .

"We can get there today," she said, but the words felt wrong even then. Lying had never suited her. "If you and I help them breaking up the camp, and if we drive the horses into the night—"

"They'll die," said Shefali. "I won't kill any horses." She let out a quiet sound, a sort of pained grunt, and leaned back in her seat. When she clucked, her gray mare trod on over as if bearing the weight of the world upon her back. Shefali stood only so that she could start rubbing the gray down. How near white that horse was! The moon itself was trapped beneath her hide, constantly shifting from phase to phase.

Shizuka could only stand and watch her. She knew how to help, she did—Burqila Alshara was insistent that Shizuka look after her own gelding when she traveled with the Qorin.

But wandering with the Qorin had also taught her the intimacy of this moment.

Today was the day that Shefali was ordained to die.

Neither of them needed to announce it. It was clear in the way she had to lean against her horse for support, in the stiffness of her arms and elbows as she worked the tension from the gray. It was in the barely concealed agony on her face; it was in the quick, hissed breaths as she overexerted herself. So stiff, so stiff—a warrior forged wholesale from silver.

And yet there was no fear to her.

As Shefali worked, she glanced every now and again to the towers looming ahead of them—but never with anything less than determination.

"I won't kill any horses" turned out to be the only thing Shefali said that entire impossible morning.

They were the only five words Shizuka heard from her wife for hours.

TRAVEL TREATS THEM no better.

It is a difficult thing indeed to see a Qorin struggling to stay upright in the saddle. Shefali has been riding horses since two weeks after her birth, when her mother tied her to her middle as she rode across the steppes. Such is the way for Qorin children—the motions of riding are more familiar to them than breathing.

And yet now Barsalai Shefali cannot seem to manage them. Stiff, she sits, as if an errant breeze may unseat her. She isn't even breathing—or at least she isn't when Shizuka glances over to her. As if doing so might burst her lungs from within like overripe fruit . . .

Sky, what is she to say?

She's tried things. Many things.

"Today is the day of our triumph," was first among them, spoken at an ill-fated rally before they truly departed for the day. The troops took to it well enough—a fair amount of cheers—but you can hear the same sentiment expressed only so many times before it becomes a chore. Even the most grandiose statements will seem trite if they are all you hear, day in, day out.

"We will be all right," Shizuka ventures, when it is only the two of them, riding with their armies like interlocked circles around them. "I promised you we would do this together, Shefali, and I am a woman of my word."

This earns her a green-and-steel glance, a muted nod, this reply a sort of resignation that is somehow more painful than if Shefali had said anything at all.

"Can I help you?" she tries again, after it has been Two Bells and they have made only the normal amount of progress. If they are going to reach Iwa, they'll need to be twice as far as they are now. But if they travel into the night . . .

*I won't kill any horses.*

But what if they don't use the horses? What if Shefali transforms herself into that massive wolf? She is large enough in that form to carry a rider, surely, and perhaps the two of them can sort out this issue all their own?

But that is a child's dream. Shizuka knows, on some level, how unlikely it was. What will the Traitor do? Walk down from his ivory towers and duel her? This is not a matter that can be settled with a single sword stroke. And even if they do kill him today—what, then, will happen at the end of the day?

When will O-Akane rise from the caverns she calls home to claim Shefali?

Shizuka is more nervous about it than she cares to admit. For the first time in all their travels, they are beginning to see birds. Each one that passes overhead—each shadow—puts her in mind of arrows. She finds herself flinching over and over in the saddle, finds herself wondering when the enemy will appear.

For they will appear today; she is sure of it.

That is the way of these things.

Minami Shizuka rides through the lands beyond the Wall with one hand on her mother's sword, waiting—just waiting—for the chance to slay her wife's murderer. A serpent buried in the sand.

But for all the pain she's in, for all the stiffness and obvious agony, Shefali has not slowed one bit. To do so might kill her, Shizuka thinks, in a way more painful than having her heart stop in her chest. If the Qorin see her falter on horseback, she is lost to them.

So, as the hour nears Fifth Bell, Shefali kicks her horse into a gallop.

"Where are you going?" Shizuka asks her, but if Shefali hears her, she does not think to say a word. Off she goes—a lightning bolt on four legs.

Should she follow? What if something were to happen to her?

Could she bear the burden of having hung back? But perhaps Shefali simply wants to feel the wind through her hair, perhaps she will return.

Shizuka half stands in her saddle.

Just as she decides to go, Burqila Alshara and Dorbentei Otgar do, too. There is Dorbentei fully standing, beating her chest as she rides around the rest of the Qorin army. She starts to bellow a song. The melody is an ancient one—rising and falling like the lamented weep of a widow—and yet something of it cuts to the core of Shizuka's being. She has heard many Qorin drinking songs and fighting songs and even songs for coupling—but never something like this.

Never something so profoundly sorrowful.

And it does not long remain Otgar's song. The others pick it up, one by one—Alshara's sisters first among them. Voices mesh but do not quite meld—some start at a different point in the song altogether, some sing a countermelody, lending the song yet more sorrow for all the contrast.

Five thousand voices. Ten thousand.

The Qorin army stand in their saddles as Barsalai Shefali pulls out in front of them.

Yes, Shizuka is standing in her saddle now, though it does not lend her much in the way of a view. There is her wife, racing across the impossible landscape—there is her wife, a fleck of silver and black beneath the towers of the lost city.

"General," says Munenori. He's ridden up to her side. "General, the Qorin—if the enemy are present, this singing will surely alert them. There might be some sort of trap up ahead."

She shakes her head, though she does not bother to look at him. "The scouts said no such thing."

"The scouts have been wrong before," Munenori offers. "On today, of all days, should we not be exercising caution?"

Does this not move him? How can he hear this swelling song and speak of such things? She has half a mind to tell him to milk a stallion until all of it is over with.

And yet she is still a general, though she may no longer be an Empress—there's a certain amount of decorum involved.

"On today, of all days," she says, "let my wife do exactly what she pleases."

And it is then, of course, that the screaming begins.

The screaming is not the first indication that something is wrong, although it is what draws Shizuka's attention. Had she been watching only a moment earlier, she would have seen the cloud of dust rising up from the earth; she would have seen the horses tumbling down, down. Like a wave, she thinks—the sight of it is so like a wave. One moment the Qorin are there, and the next they are sinking farther, farther into the yawning mouth that has now opened up beneath them.

Horror sets in. The pit's as wide as the Jade Palace and perhaps just as deep—she cannot see where the Qorin are going, and more of them keep funneling in, like ants piling atop one another. She cannot see an end to it.

And somewhere in that mass of people tumbling to what must be their deaths—somewhere in there is Shefali. Desperately her eyes scan the horror-struck faces of the Qorin. Where is she? Darker than the rest, her horse so bright—where is Shefali?

Shizuka cannot see her.

Shizuka's body moves without her having to think; she raises an arm to halt the approach of the Phoenix Guard.

"Munenori, you're in command!" she says.

The right thing to do—the just thing—would be to stay and watch over her army.

And yet what is more right, more just, than saving a people who have suffered too much already?

Shizuka kicks her horse into a gallop. She must find her wife.

Up ahead the Qorin scramble to keep their horses under control. Some are lucky enough to skid to a halt just short of the pit; most are not. The pained cries of rider and horse alike assault her ears as she pushes forward, forward. She doesn't want to think of how many of these animals will have to be put down; she does not want to acknowledge the woman screaming that she can no longer feel her legs. The Phoenix Guard will watch over them.

Only Shizuka can save Shefali.

Forward, forward, her horse's hooves beating against the earth. She draws her mother's sword though no enemies have made themselves known—if Shefali sees the familiar golden light, perhaps she will know which way to go. Sorrow sinks into Shizuka's stomach as she approaches the pit itself: even holding the sword aloft, she cannot see the bottom.

*Where is she?*

The howling, the screaming, the cries of the fallen—all of these are a distraction. Deep in the darkness of that pit is her wife, if only she could get a better look. Shizuka dismounts, giving her horse two quick pats before walking closer, closer. A pebble by her foot tumbles into the black. She kneels down, her heart hammering in her head, and thrusts her lit sword into the darkness.

But this is no ordinary darkness—it is a living thing. The moment her sword pierces its veil—and how awful it feels!—the darkness ignites. Like black cobwebs, the darkness as it burns, revealing the horrors concealed beneath: corpses piled high as a festival float. The stench of it! How far down are they? There is no way she can make her way down there without hurting herself, no way she can do anything but die if she falls—

No.

Shefali is down there.

It is the first of Qurukai, but it is not the day her wife will die—Shizuka won't let it be.

"Shefali!" Shizuka screams. Everything she is, everything she will be—she throws all her focus into her mother's sword. A blazing arc shoots up into the false sky. Daylight—true daylight—shines into the pit. She can see the narrow winding walls; she can see the things stuck to them. . . .

It is customary for the Hokkaran royals to raise silkworms. Shizuka was no exception to the rule. She's been around them for much of her life.

The Phoenix Empress knows well what a cocoon looks like.

And in front of her now are cocoons, lining these horrible walls. She is too far up to see what is contained within them, but the husks are tall and broad and plentiful and . . .

"Shefali!" Shizuka screams again. There is some movement at the base of the pit, where all the others fell. Surely, Shefali is among them; surely, she will hear.

But there is no answer from her wife—only the trapped Qorin.

"Naisuran!" they scream. Her mother's name. "Naisuran, something's—"

The ground beneath her rumbles, rumbles—*cracks*. Shizuka scrambles to keep upright as the two halves of the earth beneath her spread farther and farther apart. Her head is swimming with stress already—she is so close to the edge—

She takes a steadying step.

Her foot meets empty air.

She is falling—

And then she is saved. A strong arm grabs her by the back of her jacket and yanks her to safety. She falls backwards; the air's knocked out of her as she hits the ground. A shadow looms over her. She reaches for her sword, ready to cut—

But when she looks up, Shizuka sees only her mother-in-law.

Burqila Alshara, wan, her viper green eyes wide in the holes of her scowling war mask.

Burqila Alshara, who has just watched her sisters, her niece, her daughter, her people—all of them—tumble into the pit.

There is a half-mad fear to her.

Shizuka swallows. "Aaj," she says, getting to her feet. "Aaj, I have to—"

Burqila shakes her head. Even now she will not shatter her oath, even now she would rather shove Shizuka further toward safety without having to speak. The shove is enough to almost send Shizuka tumbling back again, but—but can't she see they don't have time for this?

*"Let me go!"* Shizuka shouts. It is the only time in her life she has ever raised her voice to Burqila Alshara. The backhand that meets her is expected; it does not daunt her even as she feels the bruise beginning to form. Burqila signals to two of the survivors. They rush forward and seize Shizuka around the shoulders.

But Shefali is at the bottom of that pit and the ground keeps rumbling and—

"Naisuran! Burqila! Whoever—there's a *spider*—!"

The abject fear, the hopelessness of that cry! She has not heard its like since Nishikomi. And to be audible from so far down—the speaker's lungs must be burning. Trapped, with no way to climb up—

Shizuka rushes forward as much as she can. One of the Qorin holding her staggers.

"I'm going!" she shouts. "You can't keep me—! *She needs me!*"

Now it is Burqila who has her by the shoulders; now it is Burqila who pushes her back and back and back. The fear is still there in her eyes, but there is something more besides, something deeper. Recognition, perhaps—realization? Love?

Shizuka does not have time for it, whatever it might be. Her wife's life hangs in the balance.

She tries to push forward.

Burqila digs in her heels. Taller than even her daughter, Burqila is a wall of flesh and muscle.

The ground rumbles, rumbles; Shizuka looks beneath Burqila's armpit to see a nightmare approach.

To name it a spider is to name a dragon a dragonfly. The demon emerging from the dark is ten times the size of the Qorin before it. A thing that size defies nature. Look! The cruel angles of its legs as it skitters down the tunnel! The mandibles chittering as it nears its prey! Hear the laughter—the throaty joy of a woman who has found some new entertainment. Watch as the spider crosses the line into the light—see the woman's body growing out from where its head should be! Its hair wild and unbound, black as the night they've long since left behind. Eight eyes gleam blood red on its face; its grin is unnaturally wide and lined with sharp teeth.

"My, oh my," says the spider woman. "What have we here?" Its deep voice climbs up the pit; the surviving Qorin freeze in place at the sound.

Yet what controls the others only galvanizes Shizuka. Fear and determination lend her limbs the strength she needs—she shoves Burqila out of the way. Her feet beat against the earth. Two steps, three—she's at the very edge of the mouth—

Arrows are flying through the air. The Qorin at the bottom of the pit, broken though they may not be, are not going out without a fight. They sink into the flesh of the spider woman, though they do not slow its movement. Careful, careful, like plucking a fallen eyelash from a sleeping lover's face—the spider plucks a body from the wreckage.

A woman in a tiger-striped deel.

Before Shizuka, a fall that left even proud Qorin horses crippled; before her, a mound of bodies and flesh and dying and dead; before her, a fall that will kill her. But there—her wife, too.

Heart like a war drum, Shizuka launches herself.

Falling is not difficult. No one in the history of the Empire has ever claimed as much. Any child might fall, any dying man, any lovers in the dead of night. It is the landing that is the problem.

And so as Empress Yui, the Daughter of Heaven, Light of the Empire, Celestial Flame, The Phoenix Empress herself falls—as this worthy woman tumbles, as her jacket flaps in the air above her, she tries to think of some way she might save herself.

The bodies—they could break her fall. Yet what blasphemy, what desecration, for the Empress of Hokkaro to break her fall on the bodies of Qorin—Shizuka refuses to be anything like her ancestors.

Then perhaps a flower might save her? Flowers are her dominion, and to call on them would hurt no one—yet what flower can save her here?

If only she were a true phoenix, if only—

It's a matter of will, isn't it? Whether or not she is a phoenix?

*I am,* she tells herself. *I am, and my wings shall save me.*

And yet Shizuka knows that she is no shape-shifter, knows that it has never been among her talents. No matter how hard she focuses on the image, wings do not come to her. Today shall not be the day she takes flight.

Even the gods can be slain—and even the gods are beholden to gravity. The ground rises to meet her.

In the moment before she slams against the earth, she thinks: *I won't die today.*

But the black takes her, and she thinks nothing more.

# BURQILA ALSHARA

## ONE

Burqila Alshara is a symbol. In times of distress—which, for the Qorin, means all the time—her people look to her for guidance. For strength. For answers.

She has none to offer them now—only her own guilt.

She knows what the lands beyond the Wall are like. She knows how pits can open up at any moment. She should have told the girls about it, should have broken up the army better, or made sure they were not all charging at once.

All of this is her fault. She stands at the lip of the pit and looks down on her slaughtered people, their limbs rising at unnatural angles—and she thinks: *This is my fault.*

This land took her first horse from her—and in the end, it had also taken the only woman Alshara had ever loved. Now it is trying to claim her daughters. She should have known.

Shizuru had asked her to take care of her daughter, and what did Burqila do? Let Shizuka run off to war and get herself traumatized, let her mourn alone while the Qorin were away, let her go on this suicide mission. And what of Shefali? After so many years apart, after she at last earned back her name—the day has come, and the Mother is going to get her due.

Shit.

She hates this.

But the trouble with being a symbol is that you cannot indulge these thoughts. The Qorin do not expect to see Burqila Alshara, grieving mother; they hardly know that woman. They expect only Burqila Alshara, the Wall-Breaker, leader of her people since she was old enough to know they needed leading.

And they need it now. All the clan riders have scattered in wake of the horror before them. Moments after Shizuka leaped to her— No, she won't think of the word, that's bad luck. Moments after Shizuka landed, the spider woman had dragged much of the mound of bodies away, setting them on its back as if it were carrying its own young. There's been no further sign of the enemy, but there doesn't need to be—the idea of dying in a pit so far from the sky is enough to strike fear into the hearts of the Qorin.

What needs doing? Burqila forces herself to think on the practical questions; they can figure out how to save the girls later. They have each other, now. If the armies remaining above do not keep themselves united, the enemy is going to trample them into the ground. She forces herself to look away from the pit. *What needs doing?*

There. Dalaansuv is shouting for her company to set up the cannons in case they're attacked. Trust her to have her head on straight—Burqila breathes a sigh of relief, knowing she's safe. Khadiyya is missing, Zurgaanqar and Dorbentei, too—but at least she has Dalaansuv.

And it is a good thing that she does—there aren't many people she'd trust to translate for her.

Burqila runs to her youngest sister; it's no use getting her horse when she'd only be trampling her own people. Easier to avoid them on foot, easier to tug up the fallen and give them the stern slap on the back they need to keep going. Qorin are hardy; they will survive nearly anything given the proper motivation.

Knowing that Burqila Alshara has taken the time to get you back to your feet—that is proper enough for most of them.

The ground shakes again beneath them. Has the spider woman left?

Burqila does not look over her shoulder to find out. Dalaansuv's weaving between the cannons, shouting directions. She's got some Surian contraption hanging from her hands, something that helps her measure distances. It's as foreign to Burqila as anything the sanvaartains have ever crafted; she knows better than to question how it works.

Dalaansuv catches her coming from the corner of her eye. She hops off the cannon she's calibrating and runs, throwing her arms around Burqila in full view of the rest of the clan. Much as it pains Alshara, this isn't the place or time for such displays—after sniffing her sister's cheeks, she sets her back at arm's length so she can sign.

[[Barsalai, Dorbentei, Barsatoq, they're all in the fucking pit,]] she signs. [[Any word from the northerners?]]

Dalaansuv shakes her head. She hasn't spent much time learning how to read Alshara's signing—by the time she was old enough to talk, Alshara had already sworn her oath of silence. It takes her a few moments to process what's being said.

[[Fuck,]] Alshara signs.

"Tell me about it," says Dalaansuv.

Again the ground rumbles beneath them. Warhorns go up from the back—now the front—of the Qorin array. Burqila draws the sword from her hip.

[[I need an interpreter,]] she signs. [[Come with me.]]

"I've got the cannons to work on," says Dalaansuv. She's speaking louder than she needs to. People often forget that Burqila is not deaf. Her own sister is not making that mistake—only shouting to overcome her own fear. "We're going to need to recalibrate after each—*Shit!*"

Burqila follows her sister's pointing finger. A single li to the south, an army spreads across the horizon. Alshara cannot make out their banners from this distance, but she does not need to—only one army rides in a place like this.

And they *are* riding. Cavalry make up the forward right and left flanks. In the center, pikemen; behind the pikemen, archers.

All of them—every single one—a living shadow.

*What can be done?* Again she asks herself the question, for if she allows herself to focus on what any of this means, then her people are lost.

[[Keep your shit together,]] she signs to Dalaansuv. [[Barsalai blessed all of this. It should work against them.]]

She wishes Dorbentei were with her so she wouldn't have to actually say any of this. So often she is able to sign her own thoughts and let Dorbentei make them palatable to others. Alshara and Dalaansuv have always lived at a remove from each other—Kharsa and clanmate, not sisters. She probably could have phrased that better.

But the trick to getting her family back is to live through this barrage. And for that—much as it pains her to admit—she's going to need the Hokkarans.

She runs to her horse and swings into the saddle. If she's to reach them in time, she *will* need the horse. Her liver mare lets out a distressed sound as Alshara turns her around; she strokes her mane and thinks to her: *You can cry later.*

But Burqila is not her daughter, and so her horse cannot hear her thoughts. Progress through the fallen is slow and, at times, painful. The civilians are doing all they can to pull the wounded out of the way, but they can do only so much. Alshara tries to avoid trampling over anyone, but . . .

A wave of arrows shoots up from the enemy army. Within the confines of her own mind, Alshara curses as loud as she can. In reality, she ducks her head beneath one raised arm and hopes for the best. Grandmother Sky is kind to her this day—none finds her or her horse. Her clanmates are not so blessed. She watches as the earthbound Qorin scatter like ants around her. Howls of pain pierce the air as arrows pierce their skin.

Shit, shit, shit.

When Burqila looks up, she sees them: sanvaartains and elderly, running out along the battlefield to haul the fallen out of the way. One of the oldest women in the clan is limping her way to a wounded warrior, an arrow piercing her right through the calf.

Another wave is coming—but how is she to warn anyone? Burqila swore she would never speak again, swore that her tongue would lie as silent as that of her old friend's—but people are going to die if they aren't warned. That old woman can't possibly hope to find cover in time . . .

A figure up ahead jumps up and down like a child, waving her hands above her head. Somehow, the arrows missed her. Burqila doesn't recognize the armor—borrowed and cobbled together as it is—or the mask. A doe? On a battlefield?

She's of a mind to leave her in the dust—at least until the figure speaks.

"Burqila! Burqila, you're alive!"

Barsatoq's cousin. The Altanai. Burqila sniffs. The girl isn't cut out for a battlefield—if she's left to her own devices, she's just going to end up getting herself killed. For the Sky's sake! She can't even ride on her own, can she? She's fallen off every single horse Burqila has given her. If Barsatoq returns and her cousin is dead . . .

Leave her. The practical thing to do is to leave her.

She's set her mind on doing just that when—like a fool—Sakura tears off her war mask. Burqila nearly brings her liver mare to a halt.

Barsatoq takes after her father, the poet.

But this girl, she takes after . . .

She is nineteen, barely a woman, already a mother. The two of them sit in a pit only a few li north of the Wall. Shizuru's nose and mouth are streaked with red.

*My little brother . . . I can't believe he's gone*, she'd said.

And Burqila, who had killed her only two brothers, sat and listened and squeezed her shoulders. They were not fated, the two of them—but that did not mean she could not comfort her friend. In that cave, Burqila, for the first time in her entire life, broke her oath of silence.

For Shizuru's sake.

This woman, this Altanai before her . . . She had failed Keichi in the fog. She could not fail him again. She could not fail *Shizuru*.

What a woman, to hold such sway over Burqila Alshara even years after she'd died.

Burqila holds out an arm. The Altanai takes it. The movement isn't so smooth as it used to be, but Burqila scoops her up all the same. It feels dirty to have someone else on her horse, some pale-faced northerner who has no hope of understanding her, but she tells herself it is a favor to Shizuru.

*I hope you're watching,* she thinks, *you pampered git.*

The Altanai cannot hold herself properly; by the horse's third step, she is clinging to Alshara for dear life. Her fingers dig in at Alshara's shoulders. Did she not think to trim her nails? Alshara can feel them even through the hide of her gloves. How did she get them on to begin with?

"Fuck," she says. "The earth just . . . they're all . . ."

Burqila nods. Isn't she meant to be a scholar?

But there's no time to tease her about it, even if she had the words to do so. Another wave of arrows soars through the sky. Burqila raises her arm again, this time leaning forward, shielding the historian with her body. This time she is not so lucky—an arrow finds her forearm. She grunts, closes her eyes, hopes that her mare will know the way to the Phoenix Guard. In truth, she cannot feel much in the way of pain with all this blood rushing through her—only the imposition of a foreign object into her shooting hand.

They're going to need to do something about all those archers. About everything, really, but the archers are the foremost problem. They wouldn't be if the Qorin were still around in large numbers—their bows can shoot farther than the Hokkaran ones the enemy are using, and they are stronger besides. Yet of the thousands of Qorin they've brought with them, only a few hundred remain aboveground. Most of them are too busy trying to soothe their horses, and rescue those who haven't been as lucky.

*Dalaansuv,* Burqila thinks, *now would be a good time for the fucking cannons.*

But it is not a thing she can voice.

"What's the plan?" says the girl in her arms. Her helmet knocks against Alshara's chin, a small sunburst of annoyance. "There's a plan, right? Tell me there's a plan. My cousin . . . Your daughter's in there!"

Is it the nature of scholars to state the obvious? If a bird shits on your head, complaining about it isn't going to help. Burqila opens her eyes. Sakura's gone pale.

*Calm down,* she wants to say.

But she cannot.

And so she simply slaps her, and hopes that is message enough.

Sakura clutches her swelling cheek. Her eyes narrow in anger and disgust—but she says nothing more. Good. It's hard enough to think amid the horns and the arrows and the wails of the dying.

They pass Big Mongke trying to lift a horse off his younger brother. It isn't going well—only Shefali can lift a Qorin horse with any ease. The boy trapped beneath—his lips are going blue. Ganzorig is slumped over a little ways away with an arrow in his gut. Tsetseg is bent over him, trying to spread a poultice on a wound they both know is going to go sour. He's looking up at the old sanvaartain with a smile. Saying something. There's no way for Alshara to know what.

Her eyes see these things, but she does not allow herself to recognize them. The deaths of her people. Her family.

Shefali . . .

The Phoenix Guard is rising up ahead. They move like perfect toy soldiers into place, spreading out into two overlapping crescents. How the fuck is that meant to help? The arrows will get more of them this way. Anger roils in Alsahra's gut; she's going to crush that captain's skull beneath her boot once this is all over.

But only when this is all over.

The ranks of the Phoenix Guard do not give way for the Kharsa on her liver mare. She cannot shout for them to leave, and so she must slow—at least until the Altanai decides to make herself useful. Sakura cups her hands over her mouth and starts screaming.

"General Burqila seeks Captain Munenori!" she says. "Get us Captain Munenori!"

She is no general, but now is not the time for correction. Enough of them get out of the way to allow her something like a path between the ranks. Why do they insist on flying those banners even here? The enemy army knows whom they are facing. They're almost here. What use does a banner have save to stoke the fires of its owner's glory?

Honor and glory are going to get them all eaten by fucking demons.

All around them, the Phoenix Guard sink into their readied stances. The forward army—most likely to face the rain of arrows—carry long tower shields. These they raise overhead, that they might save their companions from the onslaught. It's worked for them so far—there are fewer dead Hokkarans in the ranks than there are dead Qorin farther back. Maybe they're going to have to look into this shield business.

Captains shout; companies echo. Burqila's ears ring with it: *positions, ready spears, brace . . .*

They cannot mean to field only lancers. Hokkarans favor them when dealing with the enemy, and favor them in dealing with the Qorin—but lancers are slow. You plant them in one place and hope for the best, while your infantry cleans up whatever makes it over the line. They're going to break the cavalry charge, but what then?

"Oshiro-zur!"

The name does not register as her own—it takes three tries and Sakura tugging on her deel for Burqila to realize she is being called. Oshiro-zur. All this traveling, and they have not learned to properly address her.

It is the captain who is calling her—Munenori. He's astride a stout brindle, his war mask clamped on tight. Despite the hopelessness of the situation, his eyes are clear and fearless. Good. At least Barsatoq knew well enough whom to leave in charge.

"What's going on?" says Sakura. Is she trying to interpret? Let her.

Shadow passes over them as another wave of arrows takes to the sky. Two of the shields shift so that they block Alshara and Sakura from the onslaught. Sure enough, *thunk thunk thunk*—arrows find wood and steel instead of flesh.

"I'd think what's going on would be self-evident," says Munenori. "They're coming."

"Right, but what are we going to do about it?" says Sakura. "There's a plan, right? I was just telling Burqila, there's got to be some sort of plan."

They cannot see his face beneath the mask, and can see little of his eyes as he turns to glance at the oncoming army. By now the ground beneath them trembles more often than not.

"Crane's Wing will blunt their charge," he says. "We'll close in around them. With blessed weaponry, we'll have a chance."

He sounds as if he is trying to convince himself more than Alshara.

She does not like that. A general must be absolute; a general must be iron. For him to waver even the slightest bit speaks ill of the whole affair—

The shrill notes of a flute cut across the din of war. Though there is no way she should be able to hear it so clearly, Alshara can hear every note, every swell.

There it is at the head of the enemy army: the Demon General Rikuto. It is impossible to mistake it. An antiquarian would consider that armor outdated: the massive helmet adorned with a radiant sun; the laminae that cover it in panes of gold and leather. It wears no war mask, for it has no need of one. It's the one playing the music—the flute's held to its mouth, just beneath its bulbous nose. Trails of smoke rise from its burning eyes.

Burqila's seen that look before. Her elder brother gave it to her after she'd killed their younger brother. Hatred is a simple thing; you cannot varnish it or adorn it. You know it the instant you make contact with it.

And that look—yes, Rikuto hates them.

"You have a plan to deal with that, too, right?" says Sakura.

Captain Munenori does not answer. He stays turned away from the two of them, surveying his army—the war fans rising to signal readiness or the lack thereof. Though there is no fear in his eyes, he is breathing quickly.

How old is he? Thirty, thirty-five? Was he of fighting age when Alshara invaded? She does not think so, and she does not remember any captain by his name. Is this his first true war, then?

Hmph. He has good instincts, but . . .

The music's swelling. She takes a breath to assure herself she still can—that it has not taken hold of them the way it did on the mountain. For now, they've been granted their freedom.

"Munenori-zul," says Sakura. Panic strains her voice. "We know his real name. If we can sever his head as we name him, he'll be dead. You're going to send your finest straight for him, right?"

He does not hear her.

Munenori, Alshara, the entirety of the Phoenix Guard—they watch the demon with the flute. Anticipation settles like miasma over the army.

The music stops. They are fifty horselengths away from the enemy at most. How insulting their armor! All Hokkaran-styled shadows, all armed to the teeth. Every one of them is practically bristling with weaponry. It will make them slow—but will it truly? There are no laws in this place other than the ones the Traitor imposes.

"Errant children," it calls. "This is your only opportunity for surrender. You have lost your gods; what hope do you have against me and mine? The tacticians among you know that this battle is not winnable. Lay down your weapons, and the Eternal King, in his mercy, may find use for you." Its voice is clear and deep; it sounds every bit the old General.

Alshara expects to hear more murmuring from the army—but they are for the most part silent. Only their breathing, only the gentle rattling of their armor and weapons, fills the air. No one speaks of acceptance. No one considers it.

Perhaps there is something to be said for honor and glory.

"We haven't lost them," says Sakura quietly. For the first time, Alshara's inclined to agree with her. They haven't lost Barsalai and

Barsatoq—not yet. She will believe that her daughters have died only when the sky cracks open like an egg.

But they will need time. Her daughters—if they are facing the spider, they will need time to deal with it. They can hardly deal with Rikuto's army and it at once.

And that means they will have to hold out here for as long as possible.

*Send your finest,* Sakura said. Is there sense in that, too?

Ten thousand Hokkarans, a couple hundred cannons, whatever horses and riders the Qorin can scrape together at the very last moment. Last time, she'd had to do this alone. If she were either of her daughters, she might still consider dealing with it alone. Dueling it.

But Burqila Alshara knows better than to attempt a thing like that—at least outright. She is going to go straight for it once the battle is joined, but only once the battle is joined. If she has any hope of taking its head, it will be in the din and chaos of a melee.

Burqila reaches into her deel. To survive is Qorin, and to be prepared is near to it—she's got a roll of gauze tucked away for emergencies. An arrow through the forearm hardly qualifies as an emergency, but it might if she's going to be wading into battle with those things.

She shoves the roll into Sakura's hands and stands in the saddle. The burning eyes of the demon threaten to consume her, but she stands fast. Only when she is sure that it and its army are watching does she make her move.

Burqila Alshara snaps off the arrow embedded in her forearm. She tosses it, like a drumstick of meat, onto the ground. Then, after clamping her mask into place, she gestures as if milking a stallion.

Steam comes out of the demon's ears as she sinks back into the saddle. Sakura's caught somewhere between flush admiration and flush confusion; either way, she's as pink as her namesake.

"What the—? Did you just—?"

Burqila nods. She points to the roll and then to her forearm. Much as she's satisfied that her act of bravado had the desired effect—the demons are preparing to charge—she does not want to waste any time. Thankfully, Sakura gets the hint; she rolls up Burqila's sleeve and gets to clumsily dressing the wound. A scholar, a painter, an Altanai—but no surgeon, this girl.

"I can't believe— I thought my cousin was a fucking idiot, but you're—"

*I'm Burqila Alshara*, she wants to say, *the Terror of the Steppes.*

But she swore her oath of silence. Instead, she points down at the saddle twice and tilts her head.

"Are you asking if I want to stay?" says Sakura. Her hair's shaking from the coming assault.

Another nod. At least she isn't stupid.

Sakura looks from Burqila to the coming army. Thousands of them—shadows swirling with gleaming weapons in hand. They've no feet to speak of, and so they do not trample the flowers as they pass. A small mercy. Burqila's never been fond of flowers, but Shizuru . . .

*Flowers have many uses.*

That damned woman. There is something of her in the way that Sakura's expression settles, something of her in Sakura's determined eyes.

"I think I do," she says.

They are so close now that a thrown lance could hit the enemy.

Burqila draws a finger across her throat. It's important she knows the decision she's making—there's no guarantee that either of them will make it out of this alive.

Sakura is the one who nods. She bites her lower lip. "Yeah," she says. "Yeah, I know. But someone has to remember."

*The Qorin will remember*, she thinks, *we don't need your twisted histories.*

But she does not say this.

To look on a wave of unrelenting darkness and stand resolutely on the seashore, to plant your feet in the face of a charging bull, to greet your death with clear eyes and a clearer heart—all of these are to be commended.

And scholar though she may be, Minami Sakura is doing it.

Burqila draws her boot knife. She sets it in Sakura's hands, closing her fingers around it. The girl is shaking worse than ever, but she asks how to make the cuts all the same. Burqila shows her the motions. In the precious seconds before the wave hits them, Sakura finds something like confidence.

"I've got your back," she says, more a whisper than a promise.

It will have to do.

Burqila draws her sword.

The shadows crash into the tower shields; the lances pierce the dark clouds. Behind them—so far behind that Alshara hopes they will be safe—the cannons sing.

Burqila kicks her liver mare into a gallop.

She has a demon to slay.

# BARSALAI SHEFALI

## EIGHT

Pain is nothing new—but this infernal stench is.

This is not simply the scent of this place, above even the rot and corruption to which they had become accustomed. There's something else lurking beneath the surface. Sour milk, perhaps. Shit.

Barsalai Shefali groans. She tries to remember where she is as consciousness returns to her, but it's difficult to think when that smell is distracting her. Puts her in mind of a ger, for some reason; puts her in mind of—

"Are you awake? What a nap you took, Steel-Eye. I was ever so worried about you."

*That voice.*

All at once, the memories come back to Shefali: the pit opening up before her, the earth itself swallowing up the army. The fall did her in—she'd cracked her head against the ground when she landed. What use were her godly powers if she was unconscious?

Spider?

When Shefali forces her eyes open, she sees the demon. Yes, a spider, but also, a woman: the legs and thorax take up much of the room they're in. A woman's torso rises from where the head should be. This wave of revulsion—is this what the others feel when they look on her, transformed? The angles of its legs, the gleam of the dim light on its teeth—Shefali cannot bear to look at it for very long. The details are too grotesque: the stitch where skin meets spider-flesh, the mandibles, the legs, the dripping silken threads . . .

And yet that is not the worst of it. Shefali cannot see most of the spider's body, but she can see all of the woman, and there lies the true horror. Clad in old-fashioned layered robes, its hair a wild mess, it looks every part the lady. That only makes its grinning maw with its snapping pincers seem all the more alien—to say nothing of the eight eyes now blinking, each in turn, at Shefali.

Shefali swallows. She averts her eyes. Where is she? She does not remember coming here, does not remember arriving in this place, does not remember what this place is. The darkness is no impediment to her, but when she tries to move her head, she finds that she cannot. Something sticky holds her in place.

She curses.

Of course—she sees it now: the silvered threads of a massive web, spun in one of the upper corners of the room. Were it not for the web, Shefali would be dangling several horselengths up in the air, or else dashed upon the craggy rocks below. The spider woman's silk lines the walls of this place, too, coating it in white like a perverse parody of a ger's felt walls. Lumps here and there lend the rock some of the texture the webs took away. How many of them are there? Like larvae, Shefali thinks. Are there more of this creature waiting to be born?

And yet Shefali knows there cannot be—it is not how demons breed. And to warp the landscape in such a way—this can only be one of the Traitor's Generals. Was it the one who had trapped Shizuru and Alshara so many years ago? No, it can't be—Burqila had slain their captor.

Who, then, was this? And how was Shefali meant to figure out its name if she cannot scent it?

The more she awakens, the worse the situation becomes. It is not until she has fully scanned the room that it occurs to her spiders make webs in order to catch their meals. And, yes—the spider woman holds a severed arm in its hand, gore dribbling onto its chin. Red slowly darkens its white robes. When it catches Shefali looking, it covers its mouth like a demure noblewoman.

"You mustn't stare at a woman while she eats," it says. Its words come out a little slurred, and Shefali has the sickening realization that it is trying to speak around a mouthful of Qorin flesh. "It's terribly impolite. Although I suppose I shouldn't expect much from a barbarian like you."

Shefali tries once more to pry herself from the web. In her life, she has broken steel and flung boulders; she has lifted twenty men at once and held them dangling over a cliff.

But this web—this web vexes her. The more she struggles against it, the more it tears at her skin. If Shefali is going to sit up—and she does not know that she has it within her aching body to muster that strength—then she will lose strips of skin in the process. Her deel can protect her from only so much—the back of her neck, her wrists, the right side of her face, they will all suffer.

And yet that is a small price to pay for her freedom. Shefali focuses what strength she has on her aching limbs, on lifting her arm from the muck.

But it is simpler to bend the spine of an iron sheep than it is to raise her arm. Her body simply will not heed her; her shoulders and elbows are swollen to the point of uselessness, and she feels heavy enough to begin with. There is no strength left to her.

"Don't bother struggling," says the spider woman. *Crunch*. "You won't be going anywhere unless I want you to."

"Who are you?" Shefali says. Much as she is loath to admit the demon is right, she does not see herself being able to get up anytime soon. And yet—there was an entire army at her back. Even if . . .

No. To survive is Qorin. There will be others who lived just as she did, and then there is the Phoenix Guard besides. There is no way that Shizuka would suffer an attack like that without returning it in kind—and less chance still that Burqila Alshara would.

"If you think you're going to get my name, I'm afraid you're sorely mistaken," says the Spider. It shoves the last of the arm into its mouth with another sickening crunch. A small laugh leaves it as it wipes its mouth on its snow-white sleeve. "I'm not a fool like Rikuto."

The edges of the web tremble just slightly; the Spider purses its unnatural lips together.

"Bother, bother," it mumbles.

Bother, bother? That trembling—what does it mean?

Shefali remembers, all of a sudden, her aunts beating felt into shape in the ger. When her cousins would run around, the loom would sway along with their footsteps. Perhaps this is the same?

The army. It must be the army.

Shefali closes her eyes. There's hope still.

"Where's my wife?" she asks.

Weight shifting along the web—the Spider creeping closer to her. Drops of warm blood land on Shefali's cheek. A disgusting thrill courses through her—if she could lick some of it off, it might give her the strength she needs to break free.

But to feast on the blood of a cousin—no. She is no monster, though she is plenty monstrous.

"Four-Petal is such a *brave* little girl, wouldn't you say? Always trying her hardest," says the Spider. Now it is really slurring its words. Slurping, almost. When Shefali opens her eyes again, she sees that the Spider is working up its spittle. "She'll be coming for you any second now."

A distant *boom* up above; rocks and dust fall from the ceiling. The Spider's frown deepens. Nevertheless, it slathers its human hands in its spittle and lowers itself toward its prey.

"You're going to die," says Shefali. She is too weak still to sit up; too weak to move very much at all. Speaking is taking much of her concentration. Two more drops of blood land on her forehead. If she opens her mouth . . .

"Oh, perhaps," says the Spider. "But today is your day, isn't it? It's terribly rude to keep the old hag waiting. You've met her, haven't you? What a bother she is."

With all the tender affection of a lover, the Spider lets its fingertips dance along Shefali's exposed flesh. Caressing her cheeks, smoothing her hair, pinching her nose—it even traces Shefali's collarbone. How foul its touch! Everywhere its fingers go, Shefali finds herself going numb.

As if her lack of strength were not bad enough to begin with.

Shefali swallows. Shizuka is coming for her; she is sure of it. Today may be the day she is fated to die, but she had thought they'd be together when—

Another *boom*, closer this time.

One of the stalactites to which the web is lashed cracks, cracks, and finally plummets to the ground, taking a third of the web along with it. The segment they're on remains attached only just barely—it swings from one side to another like a moody mare.

All at once, the Spider's cool, collected manner shatters. Its face contorts into a hideous mask of revulsion; as it skitters toward the falling web it lets out an unholy screech.

*"Rikuto!"* it shouts. "This was not in our agreement!"

So it is working with Rikuto? But that means . . . Those loud noises are not simply the army marching on the pit, lowering themselves one by one so that they might get to Shefali. If Rikuto is involved . . .

The pit is the corral, and Rikuto's army the hunting Qorin. The Demon General means to drive them in for the slaughter.

Shefali looks around. Where is the corridor? She remembers seeing a corridor before the darkness took her, before she became this useless hunk of flesh. There—a great mass of webs crisscross over something that *might* be a corridor. Difficult to tell from this angle, but she can hear the distant moans of pain that emerge from it.

There are people in that direction.

If she can get to them . . . If she can get to Shizuka . . . How far down are they? If she can shift her form to something useful, the two of them may be able to climb up out of this at least.

And now is the best time to strike. The Spider's distracted, reweaving its web in a panicked effort to keep them elevated. Shefali can feel the web starting to give beneath her. She won't even really need to move—just get her weight moving, and let the laws of nature do the rest.

It's going to be another long fall. That will be all right—so long as she does not hit her head again, so long as she stays awake.

She sucks in a breath. Her lungs feel as if they're going to burst. Wiggling her shoulders as much as she can, she tries to get her hips to follow along. The stickiness of the web holds, but with one good roll, she might be free.

"What do you think you're doing?" says the Spider. The web isn't yet fully re-formed but it skitters closer all the same, its eight legs now adhered to the roof of the cavern. Its hair falls down like some sort of macabre brush. "Do you think you can get away from me like that?"

Shefali closes her eyes and throws all her weight into another roll. Yes! The skin on the back of her neck peels away, and so, too, a strip at her cheek. It aches—but it means she is free. Another roll, and her top half is over the edge; only her legs remain adhered.

*Pull yourself free*, she thinks, but her limbs do not listen—her arms hang stiff up ahead of her, dangling over the edge of the web. Black blood drips onto her tiger-striped deel.

It is then—at the very edge of the precipice—that she realizes where she really is.

The lumps lining the walls are not larvae at all. They are Qorin. And not just any Qorin—Lost Qorin. Two of them wear their braids in the intricate fashion favored by the southern clans; one of them has the geometric embroidery of the northern tribes at his collar. So many of them! She has not seen more than a handful of southern clansmen—the blackblood hit them the hardest.

The Spider left their heads exposed so it could watch them suffer. That is the only possible reasoning there might be for this—the Qorin are awake, but their eyes are glassy, their cheeks gaunt, their hair stiff as straw. How long has it been since any of them ate? How long have they been lashed to the walls? She finds herself hoping that it has only been a few days, a few weeks perhaps—that they have not had to wither for long.

And yet to see them! To see so many of them trapped where the sun and stars cannot reach them, to see them locked in a place their ancestors cannot see them . . .

How many of them are her relatives? How many of them are her friends?

The more her eyes scan the walls, the sicker she feels. Not all these Qorin are from the lost tribes. A few of them are from clans she's encountered before. There's Sarangaarel's cousin, from the pine wanderers; there's Aunt Baykhaal's husband.

Awful. Awful, awful.

There, to what feels like the east: a fresh new cocoon, still glistening, enshrouds her aunt Khadiyya. Her head is lolled back, her tongue dangling out of her mouth like an overheated dog.

Shefali lets out a whimper. Go. She needs to go; she needs her limbs to listen. As hard as she can, she throws herself forward and kicks against the webbing. Tumbling, tumbling—she's hurtling toward the ground. The spider woman is rushing toward her, but how can it hope to beat the laws of nature? Shefali is going to hit the ground. She turns, draws her elbows up to brace herself—but the impact never comes.

A wet, slimy cord wraps itself around her waist. She jerks to a halt midair. Her Laughing Fox mask slips from around her neck and clatters to the ground, shattering an old skull in two as it lands.

"What did I say? What did I tell you?" says the Spider. It is laughing now, and the webbing it's caught Shefali in rises and falls with the motion. "Did you think I was that much of an idiot? That you could get away from me so easily? Oh, no, no, no . . ."

It draws Shefali higher, higher. Wriggle though she might, this web is stronger than steel, stronger than iron, stronger than even her own will. What is she to do in the face of it? The pained cries of the Qorin below her lend her strength, but even that—even that—is not enough.

They are going to watch her die.

Her aunt Khadiyya, her cousins, her uncles, the distant relatives she never got the chance to meet—they are all going to watch her die.

Numbness, brought on by the Spider's venom, begins to spread through her body. She can no longer feel her heart beating. Even that she might be able to withstand, but—but she can no longer feel herself drawing in breath, either. And if she is not breathing . . .

Closer and closer to the Spider's lair, closer and closer to its grasp. Thick globs of venom fall onto her face, mixing with the blood of her family, seeping into her own open wound. Were she not infected before, she surely is now. Her arms go limp.

*Move,* Shefali thinks, *struggle, fight!*

But her body will not heed her.

Closer and closer. She can no longer feel her legs. Even the serpent women did not affect her in this way, even Jiyun—she fought them off. Why is it that today is the day she fails? All her will, all her concentration—she throws it into imagining herself smaller. Shaping her skin and bone into something that might be able to escape.

But what use is that when she cannot even imagine herself?

The cold. Perhaps the cold can save her—

Except that Shefali cannot feel her own breathing, and if she cannot feel her breathing, then how is she to feel the Ninth Winter?

She forces herself to try to take a breath as the Spider draws her up, as it cradles Shefali in its arms. Breathe. Is she breathing? She cannot tell. It does not sound as though she is. Breathe, breathe, breathe . . .

"I do love the look of panic in your eyes," it says. "But I need to keep you safe. Yes, yes . . . with Rikuto reneging on his deals like this."

Slowly, slowly, the spider turns her—like roasting a goat over the fire. Shefali is unable to do anything but blink her eyes in horror. Even her mouth fails her—she cannot keep from dribbling like a child. Layer after layer of silk wrap her tight. It would be impossible to move now.

"You see, Steel-Eye, I never actually wanted you," it says. It drags a fingertip along Shefali's aching cheek; Shefali wishes she had the strength to spit on it. "You taste terrible. Like death. Pah! But your wife . . ."

The Spider laughs, again, covering its mouth with its sleeve. With its other human hand, it pulls on the cord it's made. Barsalai, cocooned, rises yet higher and higher into the air. Hanging upside down as she is, the blood starts rushing to her head.

"Well, the Eternal King thinks he can tame her. And me, for my part . . . I've never had an Empress's heart before."

*And you never shall!* Shefali thinks. Fury within her breast. To trap her in a place like this! Even if her body would not heed her, her own heart would not fail her—any moment now, Shizuka is going to cut through the swath of webs and barge right on in.

Shefali closes her eyes to imagine it: the arcs of gold giving way to radiant flame, the Qorin warhorns sounding behind her. Shizuka, clad in her enameled armor, raising her blade with an arrogant shout.

"Drop my wife, or drop your head!"

So Shefali imagines.

Her body may no longer be heeding her, but her mind . . . She can will her wife to come.

# MINAMI SAKURA

## SIX

Minami Sakura didn't ask for this.

To her left, a shadow-clad warrior slices a Phoenix Guardsman in two. The sword digs in at the guardsman's waist. It takes him a little while to die; it takes the sword a little while to cut all the way through him. Sakura watches it go—like a dull pair of scissors trying to cut through thick cloth. She can smell his death: that acrid blend of guts and blood and refuse spilling out of him.

And yet he does not stop fighting. The guardsman lets out a shout that would make any instructor proud. With what little force remains to him, he pivots his hips and drives his sword into the shadow-warrior's chest. The warrior dissolves into the air like ink in a water bowl.

Only then does the soldier slump over; only then does he try to take a moment to rest. As his eyes close, Sakura knows that rest will be an eternal one. The crows will come for him, as the Qorin say.

Sakura cannot tear her eyes away from this. Even if she could, where would they land? For on her right this scene is playing out over and over as well: soldiers advancing with shields raised, driving lances into shadows; shadows leaping like fleas onto the soldiers, tearing heads from bodies.

She does not want to look at any of this. She does not want to see it. The horror of it all has her vomiting off the side of Burqila Alshara's liver mare. Worse, still, as Burqila pushes her way through the melee and the demons start to attack *them*. Burqila's sword rings as it parries away those of the enemy.

Sakura's got to keep herself low if she wants to be useful, got to stay out of the way as much as possible. She wraps one of her arms around Burqila's waist and presses herself against the warlord. It occurs to her that she's made herself into a human shield. There are still arrows flying—their whistling is part of the unholy cacophony of war—and surely some will find her. They've found Burqila, already. What if she gets hit, too?

It doesn't matter now, does it? This is the decision she's made. The two of them on this horse racing toward . . . racing toward the General? She doesn't know what Burqila's plan is, and she isn't sure she needs to. Her job is to watch Burqila's blind spots.

She's doing a shit job of it.

Like flies nibbling at a rat's body, like wolves on the attack, the demons. A dozen of them surround Burqila's horse at any given moment. The soldiers are doing their best to clear a path, but there is only so much they can do without harming Burqila's horse.

A shadow swipes at them from the right as Burqila cuts a demon's head off on the left. A nasty one, too—it has more weight to it than most of the other shadows; the light does not pierce it all the way through. Patches of its darkness are flesh-solid. Instead of driving Burqila's boot knife into its shoulder, Sakura . . .

She is a scholar. Before that, she was a painter. She's had to fight some men in her life, certainly. This isn't the first time she's held a knife, or the second, or the third. She knows perfectly well what to do—catch its outstretched arm and drive the knife in at the elbow. There's never any armor at the joints.

But it's one thing to defend yourself from a man who hides his cruelty behind his coins; it's another to strike at a demon. Its smoldering eyes bore into her and she falters, knife in hand, her mouth hanging open. Its claws come nearer, nearer—

Burqila twists her body. The demon tears through the deel her daughter made for her. She hisses in pain, but the pain does not stop her—she twists back with a heavy downward cut. Her Surian sword chops the shadow's arm off. Only then—only when Burqila has already hurt herself—does Sakura find the courage to sink the dagger into the demon's eye.

She doesn't expect the resistance. She doesn't expect to feel the length of the knife scrape against bone and muscle, doesn't expect the sensations that reverberate up her arm. She wants to be sick, she wants to weep, she wants to run from this place and hide—but there is nowhere to go.

The demon dissolves around her dagger. The triumph does nothing to soothe her mind, nothing to soothe her racing heart. She can't think, can't breathe, can hardly process what is going on. Two more demons attack, and Burqila makes the first cut in both cases, the heft of her sword cracking open their skulls. The motions tear open her wounds—Sakura feels Alshara's blood against her back.

Burqila's bleeding in a place like this. That isn't good. Any general would recall her, any captain would demand they return to the camps for proper treatment. Infection was no laughing matter. Sakura's never seen it herself, only the aftermath—and only Shefali, who had survived.

"Your wound," she says. "We need to get it cleaned—"

She's cut off by a demon pulling itself onto Burqila's liver mare. The mare, knowing full well the corruption it now bears, starts to buck. Sakura's head thumps against Burqila's chest. The world spins, and it occurs to her in a distant sort of way that she should probably be stabbing at the enemy.

It's lunging forward, arm outstretched, just like the one from earlier. Sakura swallows. If she keeps failing, if she keeps hesitating—Burqila is going to get hurt again. And she can't let that happen when they've already lost so much.

*You're a Minami, aren't you?* she thinks to herself.

Sakura pushes the breath out of her lungs. There—grab the arm, pull it forward, get it off balance. The demon tumbles forward, leaving its neck exposed. Sakura plunges the knife in before she can allow herself to think about it. This feeling's even worse than the last—the knife slips in between two vertebrae, and she must put so much of her weight onto it to keep it digging in. When the demon dissolves, she falls forward herself. Her face slaps against the liver mare's neck just as she returns to proper footing.

"I did it," she mumbles. "I did it."

But it feels hollow.

Especially when the demons keep coming. How does anyone think like this? How can anyone possibly pay attention to what's going on around them when they're in the belly of death? It makes sense to her now, why Shizuka was in such a state after the war.

She's earned them only a moment's reprieve. Hands and swords and spears and teeth continue to plague them; Burqila's cuts are getting messier and messier. It's impossible to see her face given the war mask, but there's no need when her body is showing such signs of exhaustion.

Where is the General? Where is Rikuto? Burqila wanted to attack it earlier. If they kill it, then all of this will end—won't it?

Dodging out of the way of a spear thrust, Sakura sees it. It isn't very far, if they can just—

Far behind them, the cannons ring. She's never been so grateful for the abominable racket they cause—the demons aren't fond of noise. The sound alone unseats them; many raise their hands to their shadowy ears in an effort to fend it off. The Phoenix Guard presses their advantage. She can see, in the distance, the flanks of the army closing in around the enemy. Soon, there won't be anywhere for them to run.

And they will want to run.

Like meteorites, the cannonballs fall, the air itself growing heavier in their wake. One lands not two horselengths away from them; the liver mare recoils a little from the point of impact. Shadows scatter to the winds. Like campfire smoke, she thinks—like campfire smoke.

The Phoenix Guard's war drums follow. Have they finally gotten ahold of themselves, then? Have they gotten sick and tired of dying like dogs? If these were truly the finest soldiers the Empire had to offer, there was much to fear—for even they struggled against the Traitor's forces.

But they marshal again all the same. Sakura sees them—their banners flapping in the wind. She feels them, the war drums, in her lungs, and she thinks to herself that she finally understands why the Hokkarans have insisted on taking drummers into battle for the past two thousand years: There's thunder rumbling in her chest. She feels a little more invincible.

But only a little. An arrow whistles just over her head and she buries her face in Burqila's shoulder again—only for Burqila to shove her back upright. Is there going to be another slap? She might even deserve it. Useless, useless.

The least Sakura can do is try to remember. O-Itsuki's lines on Minami Shizuru will live forever—if the story of Shizuka and Barsalai can join them, then Sakura can die happy.

And so she keeps her eyes on Rikuto. To her surprise, as the cannon volley dies down, Rikuto seems to be heading straight for them. Plumes of smoke rise from the corners of its ears. The tip of its nose is a bruised violet.

"There!" says Sakura. "He's right there. Keep the horse going!"

It isn't useful—but then she isn't very useful, either. Keep it together. The only way to shake the disgust coming off Burqila in waves is to prove that it isn't a mistake to bring her along.

There's courage deep within her—courage she must have locked away as a child, courage that will flower only twice in her lifetime.

She reaches for it now.

The demons are getting over their momentary shock. Five guardsmen have surrounded Burqila's liver mare, swords at the ready—but Sakura is ready, too.

Demons meet guardsmen; claws rake armor. The awful scraping of metal only makes her headache worse. She wants to close her eyes and pinch her nose, but that won't help, and there's the very real possibility she may die if she tries it.

Shit.

She hates war.

But at least the guardsmen have finally regained control. Together, they advance, the horse by necessity going slower than usual. Swords meet flesh on both sides. Burqila grunts. In this brief moment of reprieve, Sakura looks over her shoulder at her savior.

"My cousin isn't going to let us fucking die here," Sakura says. "And neither is your daughter."

Obvious, obvious—but sometimes you need to hear the obvious things. Sometimes it lends you strength to hear things you already know. Burqila seems like the sort of woman who doesn't get comforted often.

Her eyes soften, and for a moment her posture is stiff and uncertain. But is that because of Sakura's words, or is it because of the demon flying toward them?

Sakura sees it too late to help. Following Burqila's line of sight, she turns, knife clutched in a white-knuckle grip, and there it is: arms spread wide, mouth hanging open to the waist, a shadowy tongue tasting the air. It's high up enough that it won't be landing on the horse, oh no—it's aiming straight for the two of them.

*Be brave*, she tells herself. *Be fearless*.

But in that instant, the flower of her courage withers. What is she to do? Kill it? She couldn't possibly, couldn't possibly—its teeth will find her no matter what she does. Throw it out of the way? Sakura isn't strong enough. She isn't . . . She isn't meant to be here.

Her limbs go tense.

She promised Baozhai that she would keep Shizuka safe, and instead she's going to die here beyond the Wall. She's going to die here, far from the seas of Nishikomi, far from her library, far from her home, far from her family.

Minami Sakura buries her face against Burqila's shoulder a third time.

But Burqila does not falter. A wordless warrior's shout thunders against Sakura's ears as she thrusts her blade into the demon's gut. The weight of her body carries through into the blow—she twists her hips and pushes the already-fading corpse off her weapon.

How many times has Burqila saved her already?

How many times has Sakura died this day?

She keeps waiting for the pain, keeps waiting to feel her flesh torn asunder, but it never comes. This can't be real. None of this can be real—

"Burqila Alshara."

Rikuto. Sakura's sure of it. Has Burqila's infamy spread even beyond the Wall? For its voice is deep with fury, deep with rage. It is only two horselengths away now, towering and powerful.

"We never should have let Ryoma deal with you," it says.

Burqila is still standing in the saddle behind her. Breathing's getting tougher for her—Sakura can hear her swallowing air.

"If we'd just killed you, like I asked back then, then none of us would be here today," it continues. "Ah, but the Eternal King—he wanted to be able to speak with your daughter. Yours and the Minami woman's."

It lifts its flute to its lips. Two notes. Sakura flinches, but the paralysis she fears never comes. Instead, when she manages to work up the courage to open her eyes again, she sees that it has conjured itself a massive sword. How can it hope to use a thing like that? It's nearly as long as she is and just as wide. The heft of it alone—how can it lift it? The muscles of its neck strain.

Rikuto lets out a warrior's shout. Slowly, at first, it twirls the massive sword at its side. Weight builds momentum—by the time it is right in front of them its sword is a whirling wall of steel.

"Got any tricks up your sleeve?" Sakura asks.

Burqila's been watching the display without a word. Sakura isn't sure what else she expected from a woman so famously mute.

Well—that isn't quite the case. She didn't expect Burqila to dismount, and that's exactly what she's doing, jumping fearless from her saddle. Before she has even landed she has drawn her sword: a thick, curved scimitar more akin to a jungle chopper than to a Hokkaran blade.

"H-hey! Where are you going?" Sakura calls, but Burqila does not turn to look at her, does not acknowledge her at all. "You can't just go fight it. It's a General! You're going to get yourself killed!"

Nothing.

Burqila takes three steps forward. It occurs to Sakura then, as an arrow whistles over her shoulder and leaves her ear ringing, that Burqila does not move the way her daughters do. Shizuka, say what you will about her and her habits, is graceful and light—she's practically gliding whenever she's fighting. Shefali doesn't have the same delicacy, but there's a quiet confidence to her, too. To those watching her stride through the streets of Xian-Lai, it was clear that she knew she could kill anyone around her if she wanted to—and clear that she had no great want to do so.

But Burqila is different.

Burqila Alshara stalks through the melee like a hunter. Her shoulders hunch a little, as if ready to strike a blow; she holds her sword at a slight angle away from the rest of her body. Every one of her steps is slow and steady and inevitable. There is no grace here, there is no arrogance: only the knowledge that you are her enemy, and Burqila does not suffer the existence of her enemies.

There are no flourishes here, no tricks—only a mother and her sword. Only an uncrowned sovereign. Only a woman who has seen the worst the world had to offer and come back for second helpings.

"The Eternal King made a mistake granting your daughter her strength so early. She could not handle it. She broke. You shall break, too."

It raises its sword to eye level and holds it out with one hand. Sakura realizes with a sickening twist: it is *saluting* Burqila. As if this were a duel they are fighting, as if they were meeting in the confines of the arena and not in the middle of a melee. It cannot be serious. The battle would be won easily if Burqila and Munenori were to die. Munenori's banners are safe at the very back of the army. Why not strike Burqila down here?

Ah, but it is too honorable for that. Yes, that makes sense to her; her stress-addled mind can put together these pieces at least. Long-nosed demons are not inherently evil—but they are inherently proud. Dorbentei's deception had enraged it, and yet it had kept its word.

Burqila Alshara escaped once before. Rikuto wants to kill her itself now, and it wants to afford her the respect a worthy opponent is entitled to.

But it is a shame that Burqila has never cared about honor.

Instead of returning its salute, she charges forward. Sakura's surprised at how much force she's got to her—like a bull rampaging through its pastures, Burqila through the melee. The bodies of the fallen don't trouble her at all; she tramples them underfoot as she brings her sword down in a heavy slash. The blow lands—but on the flat of Rikuto's blade, which it has turned to use as a makeshift shield. Sparks fly in her wake; Rikuto's body shifts from the weight of the blow. If it were human, it'd be laid out on the ground by now.

And Burqila means to get it there. A forward kick lands on the sword flat. It takes a step back to better handle the force, and she meets it with another slash.

Sakura has always liked watching Shizuka go through her sword forms. In the early hours of the morning, with that glow around her and the rosy-fingered dawn above, it was better than any dancer's show. Shizuka's morning sword forms were a frequent painting study for the sheer fluidity of her movements.

This is different.

Burqila's slashes are more like a butcher chopping at a corpse. Heavy, brutal, quick—there is no time to recover in between them. The low growls that leave her only add to the impression. One, two, three more cuts—each heavier than the last, each with the entire weight of her body behind it. If it pushes back at her, she might be in trouble—but how can it push back when she has offered it no respite?

Further and further they go, Burqila's relentless assault propelling them along. The shadow army fill in the gaps they leave; the Phoenix Guard are quick to engage them. As the curtain of black falls before her, Sakura knows she can't stay where she is. The demons aren't attacking Burqila, but they might attack her.

"Come on," she says to the liver mare. She's learned only a bit of

Qorin. Command words, mostly. Qorin are very vocal with their horses. "Forward."

The horse whickers. To her right, a demon leaps toward her, only to be caught on the spear of a guardsman.

"We have to catch up to your mother," she says to the liver mare. This time she slaps her a little, hoping that will serve as incentive enough. Perhaps something about the gesture is reminiscent of Burqila, for the horse finally starts moving.

And Sakura clings for dear life. Leaning forward, her torso pressed against the horse's neck, her feet barely in the stirrups—she does not want to take any chances. Thankfully the horse is moving at a canter, at best, and the guardsmen can keep up. Plumes of blood paint golden armor red; the smell threatens to empty Sakura's stomach once more. She does not allow herself to look to her sides. If she does, she might see her countrymen dying.

The horse's heartbeat is strong and steady—the only stable thing in this forsaken mess. Sakura clings to it as best she can.

The swords and spears of the guardsmen part the curtains. There: Burqila's wild onslaught continues. Every slash brings with it a new war cry, a new burst of sparks, a new *clang* as metal meets metal. Relentless.

And yet . . .

Sakura almost doesn't want to watch. Burqila's blows are coming slower and slower. The back of her deel is dark with sweat—to say nothing of the blood seeping out from her shoulder wound. Rikuto has more and more time to prepare for the next slash, the next kick, the next bull rush. It hardly has to move the sword anymore.

To the people of Hokkaro, and of course to the Qorin, Burqila has always loomed large—but she has never been anything more than mortal. Even the Terror of the Steppes tires. And why shouldn't she, after today? After all she's been through?

"Did you think this would work?" says Rikuto. Its sword-shield rises and falls with its bellowing laughter. "You can't keep relying on Dragon's Fire to win your battles."

The taunt works. Burqila lets out a guttural scream and swings—but it is a sloppy one, without any of her usual force to back it up.

Rikuto pushes forward at the moment of impact. Two, three charging steps—the sword slams against Burqila.

And it is she who tumbles backwards, falling, falling—

Sakura screams.

All around her the shadows are chanting, chanting: "For the Eternal King! For the Eternal King!"

All around her the sounds of war, all around her the death and destruction she has feared all her life, all around her there are thousands of souls and hearts and bodies being forged and broken.

Burqila Alshara cannot die here.

Rikuto raises its sword. Burqila's feet are in the air; she's going to try to kick the sword from its hands as it comes down. Sakura's seen Dorbentei do it as a trick.

But Dorbentei is younger, and Burqila's twice wounded already—

Sakura should throw herself from the horse. She knows this. Deep in her heart she knows that the thing to do is to try to help, to save Burqila the way Burqila has saved her.

And yet she cannot move. Fear is a sculptor. From cold stone it's carved her. The likeness is so fine that her soul has abandoned her body for the statue—she cannot move.

Rikuto remains unscathed.

A smile spreads and spreads across its lips. The sword's impossible weight makes it quiver at the apex of the blow, and Sakura thinks to herself that the strike will not cut Burqila at all—it will crush her. Like a melon beneath a stone.

*Move,* Sakura thinks. *Move, move, move.*

But her self-preservation outweighs her honor. If she throws herself atop Burqila, the two of them will both die.

Down, the sword, down! Dropping like a boulder to the earth! Burqila kicks at its wrists but the sword keeps coming, as inevitable as death itself. Desperate, she tries to roll, but she's too off balance, she's wasted too much time on the kick—

Sakura cannot look.

She shuts her eyes and buries her face in the crook of her elbow, for she knows what is coming, knows what she will hear: the cracking of bone, the squelch of flesh that was once Burqila Alshara.

One breath, two breaths, she waits.

The sound does not come. Only the usual cacophony of war.

Her heart throws itself against the walls of her rib cage. Sakura can feel it even in the tips of her fingers. When she opens her eyes, she thinks that perhaps an arrow caught her in the temple and she is already dead.

For Burqila Alshara decided that if she could not roll *away,* she would push herself *toward* the demon. Her whole body is curled around its leg, well out of the way of the trench created by Rikuto's misshapen sword.

And yet this is a short-lived victory. Burqila doesn't have the energy to stand. She *can't* have the energy to stand, not after all that. Her chest puffs like a croaking frog's throat. Dirt and Hokkaran blood alike have dug into her wound. She's lifting her legs as if she means to jump back to her feet, but she does not have the energy, does not have the strength—

Rikuto leaves the sword where it's dug itself into the ground. It plucks Burqila up by the collar, as if she were a child and not a giant of a woman. Her feet dangle in the air. She's trying to kick at it, but perhaps she really has become a child—the blows do not even make it to Rikuto's torso before losing momentum.

High, it lifts her, so that the whole army may see her huffing. With the palm of its massive hand, it tears off her war mask. The face beneath is not much different—Burqila Alshara scowls. She spits at it. The spit lands in its eye, and for an instant it winces.

"I expected better from you," it says.

"No," says one of the guards near Sakura. "It isn't— That's *Burqila Alshara*—"

Its hand on her head. Barsalai Shefali once tore a man's head clean from his body just outside the Bronze Palace. Sakura has been to the spot. Even Baozhai, ever the mistress of her own home, has not found a way to get rid of the stain. A splotch of darkness on the cobblestones—that is all that remains of him.

It is this memory that shatters Sakura's stone cage. She cannot fight it; she has no hope of winning.

But she might be able to distract it.

Sakura stands in the saddle. The horse keeps going forward and Sakura knows, she knows, that she will have only one shot at this before she topples backwards like a fool. With all the strength remaining to her, she hurls the knife straight at it.

The blade lands straight in its chest, wobbling like an arrow shot into a tree. Black blood seeps from the wound. Rikuto turns toward her. When its eyes lock on hers, her throat clenches shut.

*"You?"*

The disbelief, the *fury*! The hairs at the back of her neck stand on end. Run. She wants to run, wants to get far away—but this is the life she's chosen. The death she's chosen.

It is only looking at Burqila that calms her: the warlord's scowl has broken into a shit-eating grin.

Rikuto drops Burqila. One step, two steps—its footfalls echo the way the cannons do when they land. Sakura stumbles backwards trying to get away from it. If she were a Qorin—if she were Dorbentei or Burqila or Barsalai—she could have managed it on the liver mare.

But she is a northerner through and through, and so she falls from the horse with little ceremony. One of the guardsmen manages to catch her and set her upright, but she is too panicked to thank him, too panicked to do anything but run, run—

"You would interrupt a duel?"

A scream. She makes the mistake of looking behind her only to see Rikuto picking up a guardsman with one hand. A single squeeze of its hand and the man's head bursts like rotten fruit.

"I thought you knew better."

So many people dying because of her, so many people—

The guardsmen surround her, telling her not to worry, that they will get her to safety. But she knows that is a lie. There is no such thing as safety beyond the Wall of Flowers.

They are all going to die.

A shrill whistle behind her. The horse's hooves, moving. At least Burqila could get away. At least there is—

Shouting, screaming, cracking bones and squelching flesh. Bodies falling useless to the ground behind her. It is so close that she can see the shadow of its nose overlaying on her own.

And so when it grabs hold of her, that is no surprise.

She's crying. Sakura always thought that if something like this happened, she'd be brave enough to say something cutting, brave enough to make some snide remark, but words fail her as the demon's eyes bore into her. She is crying so much that her skin is more salt than flesh; she is whimpering.

Minami Sakura is going to die like a coward, thinking of her mother and her home and the people she will never again get to see—

A hand atop her head—

The whistle of an arrow, the thunk as it digs into its shoulder. Sakura can see Burqila half-standing behind it, her bow in hand, and a nervous smile breaks out across her face.

The same trick won't work twice.

But she's grateful. She's grateful.

Sweet Sister, she doesn't want this to hurt.

She sucks in a breath as it starts to squeeze. The pain of it! As if she were trapped in a vise rapidly tightening. Her eyes feel as though they are bulging from their sockets; her skull threatens to give—

Four notes on a flute. She wonders briefly if everyone hears them before they're taken. Why four? Isn't five the appropriate—?

It occurs to her that it's stopped. Though she's in agony, though she still feels as if she will burst at any moment, it has *stopped squeezing*.

She opens her eyes. There's a distant look on its face; it's focused on something back in the direction of the pit. More plumes of steam shoot from its ears. It grunts like an animal before flinging her to the ground. Her head cracks against the earth.

But before the darkness takes her, she swears she sees it disappear into the wind.

# O-SHIZUKA

## NINE

*BOOM.*

What is that?

*BOOM.*

Her head . . . her head . . . who's hurt her head? That sound—is it someone trampling on her? A boot coming down, over and over? She can't think. Where is she? Can't remember, can't think.

*BOOM.*

That sound again! No one tramples her, but the sound is enough to make her wish they did. If someone were trampling her, at least she'd have some idea of where she—

"Barsatoq! Barsatoq, if you don't wake the fuck up—"

*Barsatoq?* Her Qorin name. The Qorin! In a rush of horror and agony, it comes back to her: she's at the bottom of a pit filled with dead Qorin. Shefali? No, that wasn't Shefali's voice—

She jolts up, one hand on her forehead and the other closed around her mother's sword. Darkness surrounds her—she banishes it as she ignites the sword. Light blares painfully into existence.

She wishes it hadn't.

Minami Shizuka sits at the very foot of the mound of bodies. From here, it seems impossibly tall, impossibly cruel: hundreds of horses and a thousand bodies all mashed together, some not yet dead. Plaintive cries rise from the mass, which writhes here and there. Everywhere her eyes land, there's another wriggling limb. Any relief she feels at seeing survivors is soon trampled by the knowledge that she will not be able to save them. There simply isn't time.

"Save me," wails a woman, "please, Sky, it hurts."

"Just kill me. My horse is dead, just kill me and finish it."

Her throat swells. It isn't her head that hurts anymore.

"Barsatoq, look at me."

Someone's at her side. She can't tear her eyes away from the mound, can't tear her mind away from what it represents. How many of these people did she meet? All of them swearing to come on this mission, all of them wanting only to rescue the Lost Qorin . . .

And now they are going to die beyond the Wall.

Her fault.

This is her fault.

She should have known. She shouldn't have let Shefali run on ahead. They should have . . . It was the first of Qurukai, they should have stayed put until the day was through. To march forward knowing it was the fated day was a fool's decision.

"Barsatoq."

She doesn't deserve that name—without her wife, she is lost. Her companion's tugging her by the shoulders, but she cannot summon the will to move, cannot force herself to look away. To look away would be to hide from the horrors of this thing she's done, these lives that she has ruined with her childlike dreams of godslaying.

"Barsatoq!"

A palm atop her helmet physically turns her head. Dorbentei Otgar is kneeling next to her. At least, she thinks it's Otgar. Her face is swollen on one side—it's impossible to see her right eye for all the swelling. When Shizuka looks her up and down, she realizes that Otgar is bracing herself with one of her arms—her right leg is bent at an unnatural angle beneath her.

Shizuka wants to close her eyes, but she cannot. She forces herself to look at Otgar's leg. She forces herself to think of what it might mean if Otgar cannot walk after this.

"I said at *me,*" says Dorbentei. She lifts Shizuka's chin. "Fucking northerners can't listen to instruction. Look at me, listen to me."

She does. A swollen face, near beyond recognizing—but her unharmed eye is the same as it has always been. The fall might have broken Dorbentei's leg, but it did not break her.

"You have to get up," she says. "I won't call it a miracle that you didn't really get hurt, since you're . . . what you are. But if we're going to get out of this alive, we need you."

*We need you.*

But they do not need her—they need the Empress. They need the god. The guilt-ridden girl is hardly going to be helpful here.

Shizuka presses her eyes closed. Up ahead, another distant explosion. The cannons? But if the cannons are firing, then that means . . .

"Shefali?" Shizuka says. Her wife's name is the only thing she can trust herself to say, and even that comes out in a rasp.

"Farther down the tunnel," says Dorbentei. Shizuka hears it now—she's slurring her words a little. No wonder, with the falls they've both taken. "The spider woman carried her off after . . ."

The rest remains unsaid, and perhaps for the better. When Shizuka is brave enough to let her eyes wander, she sees puddles of blood and gore on the ground.

"We can get her back," says Dorbentei. "Needlenose isn't going to go down without a fight—not while she knows you're all right—but she can't do all the work herself. She needs you."

Pebbles fall on Shizuka's head. Whatever is going on aboveground is . . .

She swallows. If she saves Shefali, maybe she can save everyone else. The two of them, together. Gods. What use is being a god if you cannot even save your people?

"Can I lean on you?" Shizuka rasps. She's so slurred, she can hardly understand herself.

Dorbentei seems to get her point. She reaches for Shizuka's hands and sets them on her own shoulders. "C'mon," she says. "Up you go."

Standing may have been a mistake—the room around her spins and spins, and she must put all her weight on Dorbentei's shoulders if she is to remain on her feet. Nausea twists her stomach into knots. She raises her war mask just in time to keep from getting any vomit on it.

"Let it out," says Dorbentei. "Won't have time for that once we get going."

It doesn't bring her any relief to vomit. She hasn't had much to eat, truth be told, with all the other things she's had to worry about. As children she and Shefali took all their meals together. These days . . .

Shizuka wipes her mouth clean. Her head's starting to steady. Her healing at work? She hopes it is; she cannot imagine fighting in such a state. Even if her mind isn't involved in the process at all, her body's too shot for any kind of swordplay.

*But Shefali fights like this all the time.*

Her wife . . . Her wife is too good for her.

Shizuka clears her throat. She blinks once, twice, as her vision settles. Webs surround them—coating the walls and crisscrossing the ceilings. Intricate designs trap the eye as readily as the webs trap their prey. There is an awful lot of the latter: cocoons dot the walls every few horselengths, each one a trapped Qorin waiting to die. Shizuka's stomach threatens to empty again. For once, she wishes she hadn't been right.

"Throw an arm around me if you need to," says Dorbentei.

"Your leg," Shizuka says. It comes out a mutter.

"I'll be fine," says Dorbentei. "Had worse wrestling. Don't worry about me when there's so much at stake."

Before Shizuka can protest, Dorbentei takes her arm and slings it around her shoulders.

"C'mon," she says again. Desperation leaves her sounding rough.

One step. Dorbentei has to lean on her, but Shizuka needs Dorbentei for support. What an awful pair they make! Wobbling this way and that, the world spinning, the cries of the dying and the distant din of war the only music granted to them.

The farther into the tunnel they go, the narrower it becomes. Shizuka wonders how the Spider managed to fit through this at all. Sideways, perhaps? For there is not enough room even for her and Dorbentei to stand side by side—they must turn, both of them. The walls are like the pages of an old book, and they the unfortunate pressed flowers. Neither of them can tell how high up the ceilings go—there is only dark, only web above them.

Shizuka leads. It is the least she can do, she thinks—to brave this impossibly narrow passage herself. At least there's plenty for Otgar to lean on.

Except—if they simply walk through, the webs will trap them.

*Fire,* she thinks, and her mother's sword answers her: when she touches the blade to the webs, flames soon consume them. The two women stand heaving what breaths they can amid all the smoke.

"They're going to know we're coming," Dorbentei says.

"Shefali always knew," says Shizuka. She can't imagine Shefali has kept quiet about that either. Her wife is a romantic at heart—bragging about her impending rescue is absolutely something Shefali would do.

"Barsatoq."

"Yes?" Shizuka says. The fires are still burning, but she takes her first steps into the passage all the same. Fire has never frightened her.

"I don't understand what she likes about you," says Otgar.

Shizuka frowns. As she slides into the dark, the flames lick at her cheek. She imagines the fiery woman from Shefali's story—would they have gotten along, the two of them?

"You don't have to," says Shizuka. Is it the dark playing tricks on her, or does she sound louder? Warmer. As if she's become a forge.

"I just wanted you to know," says Dorbentei. She sucks in a breath and follows, the flames now dormant in Shizuka's wake. Is she breathing heavily? Ah, but this sort of confinement cannot be healthy for a Qorin who craves the wide-open sky. Her lower lip's trembling.

"In case one of us dies. It's not honest, to let someone think you like them."

Perhaps the joking is the lifeline keeping her from absolute panic. Strange, to discuss a thing like this as they make their way to a ravenous spider woman's chamber. If Shizuka were younger, she'd have told Otgar to milk a stallion, as the saying goes; they have work to do.

But seeing her this afraid . . . No, she cannot.

"I never thought you liked me," Shizuka says as warmly as she can. She holds out her hand. "And neither of us is going to die."

Smoothly, with no trace of doubt—the same way she has spent all her life speaking. Shefali's always thought of Shizuka as confident. Dorbentei might still, too.

There is a moment of hesitation: Dorbentei's eyes flick over to her, and then down. Twice, three times this happens.

And then she takes Shizuka's hand.

With careful steps they continue, step by perilous step. Rocks fall onto their heads. The farther they go, the worse the sounds of battle become; Shizuka swears that she can hear Qorin warhorns. Good. They haven't given up yet.

Neither will she.

Her wife is at the end of this tunnel.

It is the first of Qurukai—she cannot allow Shefali to die. Not without her.

As the jaws of a hunting dog open to drop its quarry at its owner's feet—so, too, does the passage open. They are through the narrowest part, but not through the horror. A long chamber awaits them. There are more Qorin strapped to the walls here than there have been in all the previous sections combined—so many that Shizuka must stop to empty her stomach once more. Like ticks on the hunting dog's ear: the white bumps, fat with flesh.

And not all of them are along the walls. Some, too, hang from cocoons over their heads. Dozens of them, at least, swaying with every distant round of cannonfire.

Worse—some here are awake. Some are newly captured. The web

is fresh around them, glistening, and they look on the two women with the horrified disbelief of war prisoners.

Dorbentei's whimpering. She's trying to hide it, but Shizuka can hear her: her ragged breathing, her nose stopping up with snot and tears. As terrible as the sight may be for Shizuka, she does not know these people personally.

Otgar does.

Staggering steps she takes toward one of the cocoons on the walls, her arms outstretched before her. She says no words as she walks—yet that does not mean she does so in silence. Pained sounds leave her; the agonies of a tortured daughter.

For Shizuka knows where Dorbentei is going. She can see the object of her mission strung up. It's easy to recognize her from the colorful patterns adorning her deel, from the deer embroidered at the collar.

But it is not easy to recognize her by her looks, for her face is . . .

Bite into a plum, but do not bite all of it. Half, perhaps. Draw your head back as if you are some sort of wild animal. Spit out the sweet flesh of the fruit; feel the juice dribble down your chin.

Zurgaanqar's head is the plum. There is little left of it. Parts of her bottom jaw; the blood streaking down over the webs, painting the white a grisly red. She is not the only Qorin so mangled—the Spider must have been hungry—but she is the most familiar. Shizuka's heart aches at the sight of her.

And aches, too, as Dorbentei wanders closer and closer to her mother's headless body.

This is a pain Shizuka knows all too well. A soiled bed, bones poking out of familiar flesh, the agonized wails of the dying. "Dorbentei," she calls. "Dorbentei, you don't want to see her like this."

But Dorbentei cannot hear her, or else will not. Forward she goes, the tears on her face an echo of the blood on her mother's. She opens her mouth, but no words come out—only agony.

"Dorbentei," Shizuka repeats. Her voice cracks on the name. "You don't want to—"

Dorbentei grabs hold of her mother's body. The webs stick to her arms, to the backs of her hands. She does not seem to care. As Shizuka watches—powerless, made weak by the sorrow of another—Dorbentei braces herself against the wall. With her broken leg, she will need all the leverage she can get. Practical, even now.

She pulls, and pulls, but the body does not move—the webbing holds fast to the stone just behind it.

"Aaj," Dorbentei whimpers. "Aaj . . ."

Minami Shizuru's sword burns in Shizuka's hand. A dirtied pillow, a single cut.

Her throat aches. It's going to have to be her, isn't it? It's going to have to be her.

Shizuka walks to Dorbentei's side without a word. They've gone past the point of needing them. She lays a hand on Dorbentei's shoulder, as if to tell her that she can rest, that she can stop pulling—but Dorbentei continues all the same. There's an increasing desperation in how hard she's pulling, her whole body jerking with each movement.

One cut. It would be best to keep this painless.

Shizuka gets as close to the wall as she can. She breathes in, stoking the fires within herself, and—

There.

A flash of gold in the pits of despair.

Zurgaanqar's body slumps over onto her daughter. Dorbentei, leg broken, cannot quite manage to catch her—the weight sends her tumbling backwards. Before Shizuka can help her, Dorbentei falls flat on her back in the spider's cavern.

And for a while she says nothing, only weeps, only throws her arms around her mother's body and holds her tight, only covers herself in her mother's blood like some awful remembrance of her own birth.

*Itsuki? Where's Itsuki?*

Shizuka cannot bear to watch the scene play out anew. She turns her back, her own breath a jagged tear at best. Everywhere her eyes fall, there is more of this. More bodies half-eaten, more mothers and fathers half-digested. Here and there, their bones dot the floor. Scalps, too. The Spider isn't fond of eating hair.

Shefali.

Any of them could be Shefali.

And yet, is that not a selfish thought? The sight of this is horrifying enough without having to tie it into her own suffering. Dorbentei's shrill cries should not make Shizuka worried for Shefali—she should be pained enough knowing Zurgaanqar is among the fallen. With so many dead Qorin in one place . . .

How many of them will make it out of this campaign?

How many of them has she killed?

Zurgaanqar survived war with Hokkaro. She survived the brutal deaths of her eldest sisters, and Burqila's revenge on the brothers who had caused them. As the blackblood spread through the Qorin camps, twisting relatives and friends into cruel monsters—she had endured. And she'd raised a family, even! Her eldest daughter was Burqila's personal interpreter; her youngest son a master mapmaker at such a young age. What pride she must have felt in her family!

And now she is dead.

And now her lifeless body crushes her daughter beneath its weight.

Shizuka tries to swallow down the dagger in her throat. It isn't much use. She cannot leave Dorbentei here—who is to say whether or not the Spider has any underlings? If a demon finds them here, she will die. Though Dorbentei might want to at the moment, Shizuka has no plans of letting her.

It is not Shizuka, however, who turns back to facing Dorbentei, nor Barsatoq. It is not the Empress who kneels down next to her; it is not the Peacock Princess or the Burning Dawn who slings Zurgaanqar's arm around her shoulder and lifts.

It is General Dog-Ear, who has seen too much of this already.

Zurqaanqar is—was—a large woman; it is difficult to carry her alone. Thankfully, she does not have to for very long. Dorbentei gets to her feet and takes her mother's other arm. A woman with a broken leg and a corpse between them—what an awful sight they must make, the three of them, and yet they continue.

What else is there to do but continue?

What else is there to do but see this through to the end?

Dorbentei says nothing. Shizuka does not expect her to. Suffering's clamped a hand around both their mouths. It is one thing to speak like a brave hero when everything is going well—it is quite another to do so when your friend has just lost her mother.

Forward.

One step, another. Dorbentei leans on her mother's corpse for support, and the corpse leans on Shizuka.

Forward.

Up ahead, the chamber opens once more. She thinks it might, at any rate: it is difficult to see anything at all beyond the massive wall of demonic silk. An intricate pattern rises before them, as wide as the palace gates and at least as high. To see the top, Shizuka must crane her head backwards—but she is not particularly interested in the pattern. She's caught enough of it near the base. Crashing waves. Who ever heard of a spider weaving a crashing-wave web?

She feels sick, sicker even than she's been since the day after Daishi died. Beyond the webbing, she can hear the Spider's voice.

"What's the use in struggling? This was always going to happen to you. Why not be a dear about it?"

Shefali.

Another round of cannonfire, another starburst of pain behind Shizuka's eyes. She guides Dorbentei and her mother to the wall. There, she cuts away enough of the web that they might sit together—as together as they can be at present. Slowly, silently, she helps Dorbentei to sit.

"It isn't as if she's going to listen to you, you know," says the Spider. "That woman is awfully insistent."

Dorbentei's one good eye fixes on Shizuka. General Dog-Ear kneels in front of her wife's best friend, her wife's cousin, trying to think of what she might say. The words do not come to her.

But they do come to Dorbentei. "Kill it." Like a rock shattering.

"I will," says Shizuka. It pains her to speak even that much.

"I mean it, Barsatoq," says Dorbentei. "Kill it. Take its fucking hea—"

Sorrow swallows the rest of it. Dorbentei hiccups as the tears take her again.

Shizuka's never been good at comforting others. Too much of herself gets in the way. Even now, as Otgar weeps into the shoulder of her mother's corpse, Shizuka can think only of her own mother. Of Minami Shizuru. How long had she held on to that body? How long had she cradled it in her arms? . . . In truth, she cannot remember. The funeral, such as it was, is a painful blur.

"This is a wound that will never heal," Shizuka says. "But over time, it might . . . it might hurt a bit less. You'll get used to it being there. And some days, you will think of her, and you'll feel the warmth of her memory before you feel the coldness of her absence."

It feels right.

She gets to her feet. The wall of webs towers before her, but Dorbentei's still eyeing her with fear and anger and hope.

"I'm going to get your cousin back," she says to Dorbentei.

Shizuka ignites her mother's sword.

She makes the cut.

Flames consume the crashing waves of Hirose, the delicate image destroyed before Shizuka can bring herself to appreciate it.

There, the Spider, as horrifying as Shizuka remembers from her brief moments of awareness after her fall. It sits on a web as large as the palace courtyard, lashed to three stalactites which give it shape. All around it hundreds of Qorin bodies hang like wisteria blossoms. The walls, too, are lined with them. Everything in this room smells of fear and death and wrongness.

But it is not that which troubles her.

The demon, at the peak of its power—it has wrapped Shefali in its web. Shizuka can see her from here. Her wife desperately tries to wriggle out of the silk bonds holding her in place, but it is no use; she throws herself into swaying from the ceiling in an attempt to work herself free.

But that, too, is no use.

Shizuka thinks of the morning—of Shefali's being too proud to admit she needed help getting into her saddle, even with the medicine.

And still she tries, still she tries.

As Shizuka crosses the threshold—the webs still burning around her—the Spider turns toward her. A grin spreads across its woman's face.

"My, my," it says. "Four-Petal's with us."

In a cruel mockery of court behavior, it bows—both the normal way with its human body and by lowering its spider's body. The fires in Shizuka's stomach flare with anger. Higher, still, when the Spider grabs Shefali's cocoon and bends it in half, forcing a woman whose body has gone stiff to bow. "Don't be rude, Steel-Eye. Bow to Her Majesty."

The howl of pain that leaves Shefali stops Shizuka in her tracks. No enameled armor, no war mask, no sword can protect her from her wife's suffering. Before . . . Before Shefali left, Shizuka swore she wouldn't . . . She swore that this would stop.

How many people has she failed already?

"There, there," says the Spider. "Was that so terrible? You're such a complainer, Steel-Eye. I've been waiting to meet your little toy for *years*. You've only had to wait a few minutes."

"Let go of her," Shizuka manages. She holds aloft her brazen sword—flames dance along the blade. "Let go of her, or come down and face me."

The Spider covers its mouth, the very image of a shy court maiden from the shoulders up. It's laughing at this—at the suffering it's caused. Only when it speaks does it drop its hand back to its side. "And why should I do that? It seems to me that I'm the one in power here, Four-Petal. Steel-Eye's too far gone to fight back, and you do know what day it is—"

"Let her go!" Shizuka repeats.

One step forward, two, fall into stance—she slashes the air and the Daybreak Blade obliges her. An arc of flaming gold sears through air toward the Spider.

But the demon skitters out of the way, and the arc succeeds only in lighting the web on fire. A useful thing in most other cases—except that before long, those flames will be licking at Shefali, and Shefali is not fireproof.

The Spider laughs again.

"So eager!" it says. "You two were made for each other. The Eternal King told me how impatient you were, but I wanted to see it for myself, you understand."

The Spider shoots a strand of web up at the ceiling. From this it suspends itself, eight legs skittering and chittering above its head. Shizuka slashes and slashes as the Spider creeps toward her wife, but none of the arcs hit their mark—she is too dizzy to aim properly.

For the first time in what feels an eternity, cold seizes her.

And yet Shizuka cannot stop fighting.

Forward, ever forward, until she is standing right beneath Shefali and the Spider. She raises her sword to cut—

And the Spider's dribble falls right onto her. Three fat drops—the size of small children—land atop her head. Viscous liquid rolls down her shoulders and covers her armor, seeping in at the wrists. Her hand starts to go numb.

The sword. She must keep hold of the sword.

And yet she is frozen in place, frozen in this pose, her sword raised like a statue of some forgotten hero.

The Spider cannot stop laughing. "What fun you are," it says. Shizuka can only watch as the Spider flings Shefali's cocoon onto its back. The thought occurs to Shizuka that, wrapped in white as she is, Shefali's become little more than a roll of felt slung across a horse's back.

She hates herself for thinking it. Look—Shefali cannot even hold her head up straight, but still, she stares pleadingly at Shizuka.

*Live,* her wife mouths. *Get away from here.*

But how is she to do that?

How is she, when—?

Will. It takes concentrated will to break out of situations like this. The fires within her haven't died away yet. She stokes them one more time, burning the venom from her veins. It aches, but she can move again. Five steps back, she takes, sword in hand, as the Spider descends toward her.

To her surprise the Spider makes no move to attack her, no move to restrain her. It wears that self-satisfied expression without alteration. This is all so very amusing to it—watching Shizuka struggle to breathe, struggle to think, struggle to keep her footing.

And it *is* difficult to keep her footing. The dizziness she felt earlier has returned now with an army at its back. It is all she can do to keep from scrambling backwards, all she can do to keep herself focused on the Spider. Another slash would throw her off-balance—perhaps catching her breath will allow a more perfect cut later. And the Spider will be closer then, too.

When it is only four horselengths above Shizuka, the Spider speaks again. Its crimson eyes glimmer with self-satisfaction. It looks, Shizuka thinks, far more feline than arachnid.

"He really does want the best for you, you know," it says. "The Eternal King is nothing if not noble. He wants the best for *all* of us."

"I'm not dealing with him," Shizuka says. The words come out slurred and sloppy; she sounds the slattern more than the Empress. "Let my wife go."

"Or you'll what?" says the Spider, tilting its head. "Attack me? You're in no state to do that. Oh, your sword is fast, and you must think you can cut me down before I kill her. Is that so?"

Shizuka does not grant it the dignity of admitting it is right. Another wave from the cannon—a rock dings against Shizuka's armor. Shefali squirms, her green eye burning, as if sensing what is coming.

Shizuka does not actually see it happen—she blinks. In the time it takes her to do so, the Spider drives one of its legs into Shefali's torso. A scorpion could not hope for so fine a stinger as this—the whole leg is as wide as Shizuka's hand. It stays there, buried just below Shefali's ribs, as the Spider laughs again. Sweat streaks Shefali's pallid face; her mouth is open and she is sucking in every breath she can, her eyes now closed as she tries to deal with the pain.

"I'm pretty quick myself," it says. "Would you care to reconsider? I've a very attractive offer for you."

The sight of Shefali struggling—how that wound must pain her! Shizuka feels its phantom twin on her own stomach. No—what if it *were* her stomach? She thinks to Arakawa, to the forest, to the soldiers she put down as they desperately tried to keep their entrails inside their bodies.

Shefali.

Her Shefali, unable to move, unable to get away—and here Shizuka stood, too dizzy to cut properly. Useless, useless.

"What is the offer?" she says.

"Shizuka!" says Shefali. It is the first word she's spoken all this time, and it leaves her like an arrow.

Because, in truth, she knows what the offer will be.

The Spider's grin goes feline. It chuckles. "The Eternal King has decreed that you are not to be killed. We are to subdue you and take you to the palace instead, where he might show you the proper way of things. . . . I'm sure you've heard it before."

Shizuka blinks once, twice—her vision is starting to blur. All she can see of Shefali is a smudge of gray and black and white.

"And I would *never* disobey the Eternal King, you understand, I'd never *dream* of such a thing. But, well, you're here now, and I'm ever so hungry. All my meals lately taste the same. You must know what that's like? Four years straight of nothing but rice? How terrible that would be, how terrible—"

"Shizuka, *please,*" says Shefali. "Don't listen to her. Get away from here!"

But she is listening.

"And here before me is an honest-to-goodness *princess,*" continues the Spider. It drives the leg into Shefali's torso a little deeper. "What variety! What exotic flavors! Surely no one in creation loves anyone so much as you love *this dog*. And I got to wondering if any of that love had seeped into your flesh. What you would taste like."

It speaks so casually, so calmly, as if the two of them were discussing the merits of one poet or another. The words don't feel real.

And yet . . .

"Speak plainly," says Shizuka. "My patience is wearing thin."

But it is not her patience that is thinning—she is not certain how much longer she can remain standing. Her right knee's wobbling and she cannot seem to keep it in place; her head aches so badly that she cannot think. Though she has burnt the Spider's venom from herself, the effort has turned her fires to cinders. It was like this after Nishikomi, too, but she has no divine shroud here, no crown of fire.

"Give me your heart," says the Spider. "And I will let your wife go. I won't hurt her or her mongrels for half a year by our reckoning—a generous offer, I assure you. It takes only a few weeks to get back to your former Empire, after all, and that's where they're bound to go without you to guide them. Give me your heart, and all of this will be over."

A heart. How large is her heart? What a strange thought to have—no larger than her hand, in all likelihood. A small lump of dark red flesh. She could feel it pounding throughout her whole body. She'd given the Kirin her tears. Could she give up her heart, as well? What would be left of her then? A body that did the Empire's bidding. A shell, and not a woman.

And yet—she'd still have her lungs. Shefali did say a person's soul filled their lungs. You fed it every time you breathed.

One heart, her heart. A bit of pain, and all of this could be over. She thinks of the woman in the fox mask and wants to laugh. *Will you give them your heart?*

She closes her eyes. It won't kill her, giving up her heart. Somehow she knows this—what happened at Nishikomi kindled something within her; the gold where her scars were once speaks to this metamorphosis.

"And the Qorin?" Shizuka asks.

"What of them?" says the Spider. It moves its hands as if closing a fan—of course, it does not actually have one. "I already said I won't attack any of them."

"I meant these Qorin," she says. She gestures with her left hand to the cocoons all around them. "The ones you've been feeding on."

"Oh, you can't want them," says the Spider. "My leftovers! It would be so unseemly, Four-Petal, to scrounge for scraps."

"They aren't scraps," Shizuka says. "Let Shefali and her family take the Qorin from this cave. And call off the battle. That's what's going on above us, isn't it? A battle?"

The Spider purses its lips. Shizuka shuts her eyes again, sucking in a breath. Her chest already hurts in anticipation of what is to come—but she must be sure. She must be certain.

"Shizuka—you can't be . . . ," Shefali says. How her voice cracks! To speak at all must be such agony given her position, and yet she's ventured it all the same.

But everything will be fine.

This is the best way, isn't it? No one else has to die this way. She can stop the killing. Minami Shizuka can take responsibility for once in her life—she can put an end to all of this herself.

Shizuka can't let Shefali die today. She can't.

"My colleague's gotten the toy soldiers out, yes," says the Spider. "I can't make any oaths for Rikuto. How impolite, to do something like that! No, no, you'd have to negotiate directly. Rikuto will be the one taking you to the Eternal King's residence, at any rate. If you agree, I will do the summoning, and perhaps that can buy your dogs the time they need." It claps its hands. "How generous I am! A woman of endless virtue."

There is nothing polite about this, nothing generous, nothing courtly. It is negotiating the terms of war, yes—but the ultimate prize is a woman's heart.

Shizuka looks over her shoulder. Dorbentei rocks back and forth with her mother's corpse. The Qorin lashed to the walls—the ones who live—have the same haunted expressions.

And there is Shefali.

Shizuka cannot see her well, because she cannot see anything well, but her mind can paint the picture of her expression. Shizuka knows Shefali's face better than her own. No matter how far apart, no matter how long the separation—she would always remember Shefali's face.

She is a child again. Her mother is kneeling in front of her in a place much like this—a place of death and cold and wrongness.

*This is a warrior's end,* she says. *This is all that awaits you.*

She is a woman grown. The woman in the fox mask is kneeling in front of her in a place much like this—a cavern that calls for death.

"You will suffer," she says.

It won't kill Shizuka, she thinks—but it might be worse. The Eternal King said he wanted to speak with her, but what if he tries to control her? What if he feeds her that mixture of ink and seawater? What if she becomes like him?

No.

He'd never think of accepting an offer like this. He'd never think of sacrificing himself for the greater good, and neither would any of his progeny—her cursed bloodline, her awful ancestry.

*This is right,* she thinks. *I can kill them all later. It's only my heart.*

"I accept."

# BARSAL AI SHEFALI

## NINE

When Rikuto appears before them, Shefali knows that all of this is real.

She doesn't want to believe that it is. No more than anyone who knows the day of their death is coming, no more than anyone in her position. She is lashed in place on a spider demon's back, too weak to move, as her wife offers herself to the enemy.

Why?

She cannot understand it. Why go with them? Why agree? Today has always been the day Shefali was meant to die—why would Shizuka throw away her life on the hope that it might not be? They are dealing with *demons.*

But as Rikuto dusts itself off, as it cranes its head to observe the Spider's work, it occurs to her that she already knows the answers to these questions.

Shizuka is doing what she thinks is best for the Empire—and she is convinced that she can change destiny simply by believing that she can.

"Let's make this quick," says Rikuto. "I have a duel to get back to."

*Let's make this quick.* As if all of this is simply a chore to it, a thing it was coerced into doing. A dagger juts from its chest, weeping black blood onto its fine robes. Whoever it was fighting was giving him more trouble than it had bargained for.

Shefali hopes it's her mother. She hopes her mother is safe and not part of the pile of bodies—but that is useless. Even if Burqila avoided falling into the pit, she wouldn't be staying anywhere safe. She'd be on the front lines of the battle that was surely raging above their heads, the battle that rattled the ceiling.

As if to punctuate the point, dust falls on Rikuto's head.

"Oh, far be it from me to intrude on you, General, far be it from me to remind you of your *duties,*" says the Spider. Its words reverberate through its body; Shefali feels them against her back. When the Spider lowers itself in a mock bow, Shefali slides a little up her back. She lets out a hiss. The wound in her stomach's getting wider.

Of all the things to fell her. Web and venom and a gut wound. What a hero she is, what a god! Her self-resentment is second only to her determination to leave, but even that cannot help her here. Attempting to move herself is . . . It is staring at a wall and telling it that you would like if it walked somewhere else. Thanks to the Spider's venom, she cannot even feel her limbs anymore.

Ah, but she feels the wound. Every few seconds, the Spider will toy with the edges of it, like spreading its noodles to the edges of a plate. Whatever's coating its legs nullifies the venom—it must delight in seeing its victims squirm.

And Shefali would be squirming, if only she had the strength.

Instead all she can do is watch. Shizuka—her Shizuka, her wife!—cannot bear to look her in the eyes. She stands a little ways away, swaying this way and that. Like a drunkard, Shefali thinks. This would be easier to deal with if it were something so simple as a drunken lark.

But it isn't. Shizuka might be dazed, but the look in her eyes is one of determination, of resignation. This is the path she's chosen.

"What are the terms?" Rikuto grunts. "Her life for Steel-Eye's?"

"Precisely that," says the Spider. It chuckles. Hatred rises like bile at the back of Shefali's throat.

"But not just that," says Shizuka. How she slurs! Shefali's heart aches—no, no, she cannot think those words anymore. If she thinks them, they will come true. "You're attacking the army up above, aren't you? Withdraw at once. That is my second condition."

She sounds so determined—but what a terrible tableau this is. There is Shizuka, unable to stand at her full height, wrung out like a washerwoman's rags; there is Rikuto, towering above her, looking a little annoyed. A cat making demands of a tiger.

Rikuto raises a brow. "Is that all?" it says. Then, before she can answer the rhetorical: "Yes. I agree. I give you my word that I will withdraw my army the moment you formally surrender to me."

Shizuka's eyes flick over to the Spider. Anyone who saw her might mistake her for a confident woman, for an empress, for a general—but Shefali sees her brow quivering and knows the truth.

She's afraid.

If it were simply a matter of willpower, then Shefali would've burst out of this cocoon by now. If it were simply a matter of willpower, she would have become the wolf, would have torn out the spider's throat, would have chased the meal down with Rikuto's clotted blood. All of her—all of her—is focused on this.

If she does not burst free, then Shizuka is going to sacrifice herself.

*Heed me*, Shefali says to her limbs. They do not listen. Still, she lies, still as the grave, still as the trees her cousins so often said she fell from.

*Heed me*, she says to the cold. Snot clogs her nose; tears streak down her face. *Please*. But to chase after that sensation is to loose an arrow at the clouds and expect a downpour. Shefali cannot close her hands around something that is not real; cannot draw it into her lungs when she's in such agony.

If she had . . .

If she'd had some . . .

No, no, no.

She will find some way out of this that does not involve defiling the dead Qorin. There must be.

"Lovely, lovely, how nice to have it all settled," says the Spider. Shefali hears it clapping its human hands together. "If you would bare your chest, Four-Petal? Silk always gets stuck in my teeth."

Shizuka's shaking.

Shefali shuts her eyes. The cold, the stars, even Grandmother Sky—whatever will hear her now, she calls out to them in the confines of her mind. If she is a god, then something will answer. If she is a god, then . . .

Armor falling to the ground. The memory returns unbidden: Baozhai explaining in detail all the features she'd commissioned. Beaming with pride as she pointed out the reinforced kidneys, the subtle brace for Shizuka's bad knee. A suit the smiths of Xian-Lai poured their very souls into—now piled at Shizuka's feet.

"Scars chased with gold!" exclaims the Spider. "How decadent!"

"What are you doing?" asks Rikuto. Shefali thinks she hears footsteps, but Shizuka's always had a light step. It's impossible to tell without opening her eyes.

And she does not want to open her eyes.

"Oh, don't concern yourself," says the Spider. "She'll live. I'll be sure she does."

"You can't—" Rikuto begins in exasperation.

"Nothing in the rules says that I can't," answers the Spider.

"Will you both stop bickering?" says Shizuka. Now, at least, she sounds forceful. A pity that it is coming so late—but what if this is all some sort of ploy? The thought lends Shefali a little hope. It *would* be canny of her. Get close enough for the Spider to eat her heart and then drive in the Daybreak Blade . . .

"He's going to have your head," says Rikuto to the Spider. Then: "Sheath your sword and hand it over."

She won't. Shizuka would never give up her mother's sword. In all the world, nothing means more to her than that.

So why is it that Shefali hears metal against wood? Why is it that the light across her eyelids dims?

"You will return it to me when we reach his palace," she says.

"If the Eternal King commands it," says Rikuto. "He won't let us hurt you, but that might change if you take advantage of him."

Take advantage of him?

Shefali cannot fathom how this creature sees the world. This demon. How is it that it thinks they could possibly take advantage of the Traitor? If the four of them were together looking on a statue of a ram, the demons would name it a bull.

She has to burst free. She has to.

But as soon as she has that thought, the Spider once more moves. What it does now is worse than simply playing with the wound. Shefali watches, helpless, as it raises the leg up into the air again. Shefali's own blood drips onto her forehead just before the leg pierces through her chest. She gurgles. Breathing air is like breathing underwater—though she sucks in as much as she can, it never seems to reach her lungs. There's something caught, something stuck in her chest . . .

When she coughs and sees the flecks of black blood that leave her mouth—then she knows the truth.

The Spider has pierced her lung.

Even if she had managed to draw in the cold, where would she keep it now? She can't breathe, she can't breathe—

"Stop hurting her!" says Shizuka.

"I said I wouldn't kill her, didn't I?" says the Spider. "My, oh my, what little trust. I'm only making sure she doesn't interfere."

"Hurt her again and I'm leaving," says Shizuka.

Shefali wants to tell Shizuka not to worry about her. She wants to tell her that it's more important that the Empress lives; Shefali's death has been a foregone conclusion since that day in the Womb. If Shizuka dies, who will lead the army? Who will guide them?

But Rikuto says it for her: "Oh? And will you sprout wings to leave this pit? Will you fight us? You can hardly speak, and I've your only weapon. No. I think you will stand where you are and trust in us. We've already given you our word."

*Move, move, move;* Shefali says it so much to herself that the word begins to lose all meaning. It is only a sound—only a useless plea. Worse, with her lung pierced as it is, she cannot bring herself to focus on anything else about her body. She cannot see them for all the webbing, cannot feel them for all the venom, cannot think of them for all the pain.

She is an insect. Less than an insect.

She cannot open her eyes. The silence that fills the air is awful. She'd rather be aboveground. At least on the battlefield, she knows she can be of use. Surrounded by the fallen Qorin, by her own trapped family, and no strength even to save her wife.

Why had they ever thought they were gods?

Silence, silence, and yet she knows well enough what's happening. The Spider's weight is shifting. It must be picking Shizuka up. It must be holding her, must be dragging those awful hands—

Shefali doesn't want to think of this.

And yet even that is not her decision to make. The leg piercing her withdraws, only for her to feel the distinct weightlessness of being lifted up. It's over in a moment as the Spider tosses her to the ground. Gravel and bone dig into Shefali's gaping wounds; if she could writhe in pain, she would, but that, too, is denied to her.

The world is still spinning when someone—it must be Rikuto—grabs her by the hair. Its fingers dig into her braids, pulling them out of shape, leaving her proud hair a mess. It lifts her up. A pair of fingers spread apart the lids of her good eye.

"You're going to watch," it says.

Lovers' eyes will pursue each other as naturally as the sun pursues the moon. So it is that Shefali meets her wife's gaze, though it is the very last thing she wants to do. Green and amber, united once more. Two pine needles. How afraid her wife looks! Shizuka's eyes are more yellow than ever, impossibly yellow—

"Shefali," she says. "Look away."

And what a cruel joke it is that her strength does return to her then—but only enough to turn her head away, and only for an instant. Rikuto's grip forces her back into place. Yes, the Spider's holding her wife, drool dripping from its mandibles and mouth. Coming closer, closer . . .

"Shizuka," Shefali says. It is all she can say; there isn't any air left in her for more.

"I love you," says Shizuka. "Please, always remember that—"

What's left is lost. The Spider opens its mouth wide, wide, and sinks its teeth into Shizuka's chest. How long, those teeth! How sharp! The blood's running—

She doesn't want to look, she doesn't want to hear her wife screaming, doesn't want to be here—

She wants to die.

For the first time since her encounter with Ren in Shiseiki nearly ten years ago, Barsalai Shefali truly wishes for death. Today is the appointed day, isn't it? Let the Mother take her now. Let her die, rather than face any more of this.

Rage fills her belly, rage and hate and bitter, bitter agony—and even these are not enough to overcome the failings of her body. Still as the great trees of Fujino, she cannot break her bonds.

By the time it is over—by the time the thick red is bubbling down the Spider's throat, by the time the gaping hole in Shizuka's chest finishes pulsing—Barsalai Shefali knows two things.

First: much as she wants to, she cannot let herself die—not until she has torn the heads from both these demons and pulped them with her bare hands.

Second: there is a part of her, however small, that will never forgive Shizuka for agreeing to this. Which is not to say that Shefali loves her any less—she does not, could not, will never—only that some wounds ache long after they're healed.

When it is done, the Spider licks at its long fingertips and laughs.

"She's all yours, Rikuto," it says. "What delectable flesh. Take her, before I eat the rest."

Shizuka isn't meeting her wife's eyes anymore.

Shefali wants to call to her, wants to tell her that she will find her, that no matter what happens, she will find her.

But she doesn't have the air left to speak.

"Got to get rid of this one first," says Rikuto.

*What?*

It wrenches the dagger from its chest, holds the point to her throat.

And in spite of all that has happened, in spite of her missing heart, Shizuka struggles. She slaps at the Spider, bats at it as the anticipation rises.

"No," she says. "You said you wouldn't. You swore. You *swore*—"

"That's right," says the Spider. "*I* swore. Rikuto made no such oaths about her safety. What a shame, what a shame."

And so in the end, it does not matter whether or not Shefali wants to die that day. It's funny, in its own way—struggle all you want, but fate's hunting dogs will always find you.

The last thing Barsalai Shefali sees: her mother's knife in the hands of a demon, cutting through her throat.

The last thing Barsalai Shefali hears: her wife's screaming pleas.

The last thing Barsalai Shefali thinks: *I'll come back for you.*

# O-SHIZUKA

## TEN

So long as she lives, Minami Shizuka will never forget the sight of her wife's death.

She wants to. Already she does. As the demon Rikuto hauls her along the winds to the towers of Iwa, the world spins around her; Shizuka's stomach empties and empties, two boulders clap together on either side of her temples, the wound on her chest drips Imperial blood onto the earth her ancestors stole. She is in agony, and yet it is not the physical wounds that trouble her.

It is the memory.

Shefali's green eye going wide. Her gasp as she realized what it was Rikuto was about to do. Her hand, outstretched, falling limp. The sound of the knife . . .

The loss of her heart is little in comparison.

In truth, the wound itself does not bother her as much as she thought it would. It aches of course, and an intolerable coldness has settled in its wake. All her breathing, all her rage, cannot melt the block of ice where her heart used to be.

But then her anger is not so hot as it was before the Spider ate her heart.

"I will kill you," she mumbles to the demon carrying her, but the words are paper tigers. It is the right thing to say. She knows it is. But . . .

But she's having such trouble feeling. As if she is trying to light a fire with wet tinder. There are sparks and smoke—but no heat.

"Is that so, Four-Petal?" Rikuto says. It is holding her as a husband holds a bride. The cold is heavy, too heavy—she cannot summon the strength to squirm away from the demon. Even if she did, where would she go? The world is passing in a blur around them, beneath them. Wind fills her ears. She can't afford to open her eyes—the nausea would again overwhelm her—but she feels the wind pressing against them. Arrows in flight could not hope to catch them.

Except for Shefali's arrows.

But Shefali isn't here anymore, is she?

A quiet gasp, an outstretched hand, the anguish of knowing there was nothing she could do to change Shizuka's mind . . . if Shizuka were to look on her hands, her wife's black blood would coat them.

"I will," she says. "For what you did to her."

"For what I did?" It scoffs.

The wind stops. She lurches forward, almost falling out of its arms, and it presses her back to its chest with a firm hand. After ten heartbeats, the world comes to a halt—and that is before Rikuto begins to walk.

Feet on mats. The hushed flap of clothes—courtiers bowing. A familiar, nostalgic melody, played on a biwa and complemented by a flute. The smell—ugh, the smell—of peonies and incense.

Court.

This is court, isn't it?

"This is the problem with you," says Rikuto. It's walking, its steps long and confident; she feels her body bobbing along with every footfall. "If you'd made me swear to leave that mongrel alone, I would have. You did not, and so I had no reason to. Whose fault is that?"

*Yours,* she thinks. In spite of the headache, the exhaustion, she forces herself to open her eyes. What she sees sickens her once more—the entranceway to the Traitor's palace is a perfect mirror to her own. There, two lion dogs rampant near paintings of previous rulers; there, carefully arranged flowers speaking to the season. Chrysanthemums. It was winter when they left, and yet the Traitor is displaying chrysanthemums. Everything—from the dark finish on the maple rafters to the gold tiled floor—is the same. Even the uniforms worn by the dead-eyed Qorin are an exact match for those used in Fujino—although they are several generations out of fashion.

"If a man shoots another man with a bow, we do not blame the arrow," says Rikuto. "And yet you are blaming me."

How tired she is of listening to the demon already.

She closes her eyes again. If the layout is the same—and that is impossible, given the towers' construction—Rikuto will turn right in twenty-five steps. This will take it to the throne room. It will go eight hundred eighty-eight steps through there and make a left. Up the stairs and to the right—the Emperor's chambers.

"You do not accept responsibility for your actions," it says. "You never have. That is why you shall never be the Eternal King's equal."

Twenty-five steps.

It turns right.

She opens her eyes out of curiosity, out of spite for the ancestors whose blood courses through her veins. Yes—even this is largely the same. The jade columns, the massive statues on either side of the Dragon Throne, the coiling dragon wound throughout the room. A perfect replica.

Which came first?

It must have been this. Once Iwa fell to the Traitor, his children must have tried to make a new home for themselves in Fujino—one exactly like the old. *His children*. She'd looked up to Yusuke the Brawler in her youth. To know that his unnatural strength came from the dark blessings his father must have given him . . .

Nothing about her is pure.

Not with Shefali . . .

She can't bring herself to think of the word.

If she does, then it will become real, and what is left of her world will shatter like a pot struck by an arrow. Calamity—that is the word for it. If Shefali is . . . really gone, then Minami Shizuka has failed utterly at everything she ever set out to accomplish.

The ice is a boulder on her chest. Breathing is hard. Her lungs can't expand.

*Kill it for me,* Dorbentei had said.

*Keep her safe,* Kenshiro had said.

But Shizuka couldn't do either.

Some Empress she is—some god.

Perhaps Rikuto is right about her.

Perhaps the Traitor is right about her, too. Perhaps she is the worst Empress Hokkaro has ever had, perhaps she is an insult to her parents. Perhaps it would be better for everyone involved if she lived out the remainder of her life in a garden somewhere, tending to the flowers she has never betrayed.

These are the false thoughts of her sorrow, the knives searching for her in the dark. Shizuka knows them for assassins—but she has not the strength to fight them off.

Eight-hundred eighty-eight steps. Up the stairs.

The palace is staffed entirely by Qorin. They move in perfect harmony—every footfall lands the same across the palace. They blink at the same time. They wear the same antiquated Hokkaran hairstyles—shaved pates for the men and wide fans for the women—and they greet her with the same phrase, over and over.

"Welcome home, Four-Petal. We will treat you kindly."

The same phrase delivered from a hundred different mouths, at least. They all turn to face her as Rikuto passes, all bow from the shoulders to *just* the right angle. Not a hair out of place.

Shizuka hates it.

She does not want to watch it happen, for she knows what it would mean for a Qorin to work in a place like this—to work beneath a fixed ceiling, to stay forever in this place, to wear the clothes of a people who did their best to wipe them from existence.

In each one she sees her wife. Here, a woman passes with eyes that are precisely the same shade of green. There, a man who wears his braids the same way.

Shefali.

Her Shefali, cold and alone, lying headless on the floor of the cave . . .

Despair rushes up her nostrils as the water did four years ago; she sucks it deep down into her lungs. It is this feeling alone that has not been dulled, this feeling alone that hits her at full force.

Shefali.

All her life she's . . . At least . . . At least Shizuka will never be able to hurt her again.

Rikuto's turning to the right.

Two tall, broad guards clad in green enameled armor stand on either side of the carved jade door. They wear no war masks over their brown faces; they wield Hokkaran straight swords and not elaborate glaives.

The Emperor's Chambers.

"The Eternal King is gracious and merciful," says Rikuto. "He thinks you can be taught. I have told him otherwise."

The guards bow to them. To her.

"Welcome, Four-Petal. We will treat you kindly."

They speak with the same voice.

"If you continue to be so stubborn, if you continue to throw a fit over the consequences of your own actions—well. One way or another, he will bend you to his will."

She thinks of Shefali's vision—of Minami Shiori arguing with him when he was still Yamai, of his blood under her nails, of the fury burning in her stomach.

But in the end, she lost to him as well.

In the end, the Traitor stamped out her ancestor's fires, and she became his servant.

Hopeless. Even her childhood heroes, even her favorite stories—all of them end the same way.

*Together we will slay the Traitor.*

What a childish thing to say.

She sees that now. Her mother, her father, her army, the people of Shiseiki, and now her wife—yes, Rikuto is right.

She's never truly accepted responsibility for what she's done.

Knives in the dark.

The door opens. Rikuto carries her over the threshold. There, in the eastern corner of the room, is Emperor Yamai—her ancestor.

The first thing she sees of him are his irises, like two golden crescents in the relative darkness of the room. They shine in stark contrast to the rest of him. The rest of him is plain and understated—nondescript, even. He wears four layers of robes, with only the innermost bearing any hint of Imperial Gold—all in solid colors with no patterns to be seen. Though he wears a beard, it is kept closely trimmed, as if he once saw a painting of a scholar and now strives to replicate it in perfect detail. In truth, he has a scholar's face—thick brows meant to furrow over lost texts, a mouth shaped for recitation, the sharp cheekbones that speak of his refinement. The thin Dragon Circlet he wears is hardly necessary when he carries himself in such a way.

He sits in the proper, courteous style, though they are the only people in the room. When the door closes behind them, he does not incline his head, he does not smile, he offers her no visible trace of kindness.

Rikuto sets her down on the mats in front of this man—the Eternal King. It places her forehead right against the ground, places her hands in front of her, bends her knees. Prostrate. Proper. Only then does it do the same.

"Your Imperial Majesty, Eternal King, True Light of Hokkaro," it says, "I have brought to you your errant descendant, Yui."

If there were anything left of her that could feel anger, she would have felt it then. Her Imperial name, bestowed by the Toad.

Even here, she could not be Minami Shizuka.

She tries to look up at him from where she is kneeling, but it is difficult to get a good view—her hair obscures much, and her dizziness the rest. Blood drips onto the mats. Her fingers brush against the edge of the wound, against the hole in her chest. The macabre urge to stick her own hand inside it is strong.

"We thank you for your service, Rikuto. You are dismissed."

His voice, too, is terribly nondescript. Deep but not too deep; cultured and well accented, but only in the same way all other scholars are. If Shizuka walked into the White Leaf Academy with her eyes closed, she would not be able to discern the Traitor from any of the other instructors.

Rikuto hesitates. Shizuka notes this, for it is at odds with all its talk of the Traitor's wisdom. Still, it leaves all the same, taking her mother's sword with it.

And then they are alone—the First Emperor and the Phoenix Empress.

All her life she has dreamed of this moment. In the haze of her condition, she reaches for a sword that is not there. Some part of her still thinks she can solve all of this with one cut. They're close enough that she could, even prostrate as she is.

But if she strikes him down, what will happen to all the Qorin in the palace? Will they die, too, linked as they are to him? What will happen to the palace itself? For the Octopus King's dominion faded once it died. If she kills him here, elevated as they are—will she fall to her death afterwards?

It would be worth it.

It would.

Ending all of this. Cleansing the stain that her family has laid upon the land. Avenging her wife, her Shefali—yes, it would be worth it.

If she had a sword, and if she could draw it in her current state.

But Shizuka doesn't, and she can't.

She won't endure his presence alone for long—this she swears. The assassins have not killed her yet—there is still some of the fire burning deep within her. A single flame, flickering but still there.

Shizuka presses her fists into the mats to prop herself up. Almost immediately she starts to waver—but she does not find that she cares. It is meeting his eyes that is important, and it is meeting his eyes that she does as she sits upright, in the Qorin style.

It pains her—how it pains her!—to do this. Blood seeps into her armor, and she knows she does not have long before she loses consciousness; the cold is starting to sink into her stomach.

But for the moment she is awake. And so she will meet his eyes—for they are equals here, two gods alone in a room, two sovereigns, two scions of lost families.

"You will not break me," she says. The words come out scarcely louder than a whisper, but that does not lessen their strength. A blade wrapped in silk may not be able to cut—but it is still a bludgeon.

Yet if the Traitor feels its impact, he makes no sign of it.

"Child," he says as the world begins to go dark around her, "I already have."

# THE FATHOMLESS SEA

Darkness, cool and sweet. Waves rise and fall at the surface. Up above, Grandmother Sky's fine studded cloak covers the heavens. The stars—the ancestors—look down on the eternal ocean with trepidation.

*She has joined the others.*

*Wasn't she meant to be with us?*

*A tragedy, a tragedy.*

So they whisper to one another. Trapped for eternity within the bounds of their orbits, their celestial bodies hurtling along practiced routes, they nevertheless take the time to speak of the fallen god.

Of the ocean that has swallowed her whole.

But the ocean, too, looks up at them. Beneath the glassy surface—beneath the mirrored waters—life is teeming. The souls of the dead have no eyes, no ears, no skin, no self—and yet in their pining for the Sky, they are united.

In all things, they are united.

But one thing drives them more than any other, these fallen souls, these discarded hopes and dreams: the shore.

For there *is* a shore. A distant one. A fine ship could carry you to it within the hour—but no one could swim it on their own. To do so would be folly. You would begin strongly enough, as they all do—you would swim with confidence, your legs kicking the swirl of souls, your arms cutting through them as you propelled yourself forward.

But it would not take long for the burdens of those lives unlived to weigh you down. The water that rolls down your back is heavier than molten iron—though it does not burn. Instead it is cold—but not the cold of winter, nor the cold of a scorned lover's glance—it is the inexorable cold of time. Of age.

You will not notice it at first.

Farther and farther you will go. As your muscles start to fail, start to scream, you will think that you have trained all your life to swim this distance—to reach the distant shore. How can you fail now? No, you must keep going. You must reach it. Otherwise, what have your family's struggles meant?

Farther and farther you will go, and slower and slower in the going. It is dark here with no moon to guide you. You forget why you entered the water; you forget when you entered it. You have been swimming all your life. The wrinkles you see forming on your skin must be your own imagination.

Farther and farther, slower and slower, your limbs heavier and heavier, until . . .

Ink in water. Fat sizzling on a pan. Your self melting away.

The water embraces you. You join it. You become it. You have always been in the water, and the water has always been in you.

So it is.

The water never loses its lust for the shore. Not the eastern shore—it knows that one well enough. From there the swimmers are born, from there they emerge, from there they make their ill-fated journeys.

It is the western shore the waters want. The western shore, its banks lined with red flowers.

Up, the waves! For this is their breath, this is their will. Forward, forward! What they could not reach as individuals they may yet reach as a whole—multitudes of drops forcing themselves forward with no wind to guide them, rushing and roaring with their thousands of voices—

Only to meet a wall of wind.

For there is such a wall around the western shore, around the western island. A woman in an old boat conjures it by twirling her scythe. Around and around the island she goes, spinning the scythe in hand—and the waves meet their untimely ends against it. She hums to herself a song as she does, an old melody she heard before all this began—and she looks on the eastern shore with an unspeakable longing.

And what lies beyond the wall? For there is water there, lapping at the very edge of the island. The ocean knows the taste of it. Those souls are the luckiest of all, for if they could only wake, they would know . . .

They would know what lay on that distant shore.

But it is not the place of the water to wake. It has never been the place of the water to wake. We are born, we rise from the mouth on the eastern shore, we try to reach the west, we die.

So it has always been.

Not everyone is granted the chance to make the swim. On occasion, the crane-headed guardian will emerge from the mouth of the cave with a clay jar in hand. This is full of souls who could not pay the toll. He will walk to the water and he will dump the jar into it, all the while shaking his head.

It has not always been the crane-headed guardian, but it is at the moment. There were others. They joined the water.

And there is the matter, too, of rain. An uncommon occurrence, but not unheard of—rain in the dark landing like a punishment against the ocean. Souls joining the water with no idea of where they are or who they are—and soon all their ideas are wiped away.

On this day—the first of Qurukai—it rains.

On this day, thousands of fat drops slap against the surface; on this day, there is a single drop of silver.

The silver does not know where it is—only that it is sinking. Silver is far heavier than water, one must understand. The natural thing for it to do is to sink. At the very bottom of the ocean, where no light can dream of reaching, there is more silver. There is gold. There are gems, and jade, and precious things that can never join the water.

If this silver drop continues to sink—as all the other silver drops have before it—it will join the others. It will lie there, in the dark, feeling the motion of all the other souls against it, locked away forever from the sky it once loved.

But this drop . . .

This drop does not *want* to sink.

And yet what is a drop to do when submerged? Sink or dissolve into the surface—those are the only two choices. Those are the only two options to speak of. If it will not sink, then it must dissolve.

The water strains to tell it this. The silver feels the water around it as it sinks farther down, feels the ripples and the eddies offering it another path. *You do not have to go to the bottom,* they say. *Join us.*

*But I have something to do.*

And there, yes, there—that word! The silver refuses to sink, refuses to dissolve, refuses to see itself as anything but silver—and refuses to speak of itself in any other way. *I have something to do.*

Ripples strengthen into something more, something like the waves but farther down. If the silver had eyes, it could see the shock running through the water—large circles shooting out in the four cardinal directions as the silver's words reverberated through the sea. I have something to do.

Don't they all?

Bubbles rise through the water. Some intercept the drop of silver, buoying it up further, but the sea cannot tolerate their existence for long. The bubbles burst beneath the pressure and weight of the water.

*Stop. It's futile to try. We all have, and it's gotten us nowhere.*

*I'm not you,* is the silver's answer.

And yes, yes, the water is truly boiling. I'm not you! What a thing to say, what a thing to think! They are all the same here, they are all one, they are united and perfect in that unity.

Who is this drop to speak otherwise?

And yet the thought's already been loosed. That is the trouble with being so united—there's no way to stop the spread of ideas. This one, now spoken, becomes an idea they've all entertained. I am not you.

Again the eddies and the currents rise—but this time, they pull the silver drop upward. And—look! Watch how a sphere forms around the silver drop! Watch it grow, as the others feed itself to the silver! For they, too, are not the same as the rest. These are the souls that remember their swim, these are the souls that remember what it was like to strain against the inevitable.

Growing and growing, and yet crushed by the weight of the sea—the silver starts to take shape.

*You are all of us,* says the sea to the silver. *We cannot leave this place. The wind will stop us.*

*It won't stop me,* says the silver.

And what a flurry! The once smooth surface of the sea is choppy. Waves form only to break long before reaching the wall of wind. The woman on her boat staggers—this is the first time in thousands of years there's been such a disturbance in the water. She turns toward the east and narrows her eyes, but it is no use—she cannot see the cause in all this darkness.

The cause is growing. The silver's thoughts become those of the rest of the ocean, awakening them, calling them to action. *It won't stop me.*

Why had they surrendered? For united as the sea, they are unstoppable. Anything that tries to face them will surely drown.

And united as this silver, united in this form . . .

Like wildfire, the idea spreads. Join. Join the silver.

She grows.

And it is "she," now. She's remembering herself.

*All around you are those who have tried. Millions of us. More of us than there are grains of sand in all the world. You think you can succeed where we have failed? Cease your struggling; you are only going to get hurt.*

*I don't care,* she thinks.

And she doesn't. She's never cared about getting hurt. Pain is an old friend of hers and cannot possibly scare her.

Two arms, a little long, but well defined from all her years of archery.

Two legs, thick around the thighs, bowed out from all her years of riding.

How the sea roils! For those who cannot join the silver woman nevertheless pull her upward, upward. It is only the desolate souls who do not assist her, do not assist their brethren that have joined her.

Thousands of years and no one has reached the shore.

This woman can.

The thought spreads and spreads: she can. *She can do it, and if we join her, then we can do it, too.*

She feels it in the stomach now forming, feels it in her kelp-ridden guts, in the castaway wood of her bones. *We can do it, too.*

But how bitter the oldest souls! How deep their hatred for this hope that now lies within their midst! For if they could not reach the shore, then why should this young upstart? Have they not flung themselves against the wall of wind for thousands of years? Have they not struggled? She cannot know, she cannot possibly know—

The sea tears itself apart for her.

Higher and higher up the currents carry her. The bubbles that propel her are the size of horses. She remembers horses now. She remembers the steppes. She remembers, with a bit of a laugh, that she never learned how to swim.

Two eyes, two cheeks, two lips, two lungs.

*You are going to drown,* the sea says to her.

*You will not drown me,* she says in return. And she is sure of that now. It is impossible to tell how close she is to the surface, but in truth, it does not matter—she will kick and she will pull herself higher and higher.

For she is not only herself anymore.

Her blood is full of seawater, full of the souls of the departed.

She cannot betray them; she must take them to the shore.

Higher and higher, stronger and stronger.

The water is heavy with souls but it will not weigh her down. All her life she has borne it. From the moment two pine needles fell between her brows, from the moment she took her first breath, from the moment her mother decided she wanted a child of her own. Yes, she knows that now—she knows how she came to be. That secret is part of her.

Burqila Alshara kneeling in a ger with a clipping of her husband's hair.

Five sanvaartains gathered around her.

Magic, thick as smoke, clinging to the felt.

*She gave up your brother,* her body says to her, *she had no child of her own. No one to inherit.*

And so her mother enlisted the sanvaartains. And so those six women defied nature to create her.

Is it any wonder that a woman born in such circumstances should refuse to die?

Higher and higher, stronger and stronger, the name at the tip of her tongue.

*This is the weight I have always carried. This is the weight of my people.*

A weight that is not a weight, a weight that is a lightness—for her people are among her now. So many of them, drops that had joined the ocean, so many of them who longed to see the sky once more—she cannot let them down.

Her hand breaks the surface. The cold of the water cannot compare to the cold of the air above—that her hand isn't immediately rimed with frost is a miracle. The memory of how to swim rises to the surface of her mind just as she rose to the surface of the water. A gift of one of the souls from which she's forged herself.

One arm over the other, kicking forward. Water fills her mouth and she thinks to herself that it is blasphemous and foul, but she must keep her mouth open if she is to breathe. Currents tug at her body, threatening to pull her under, but she will not allow them to. She is stronger—they are stronger—than the bitter souls that wish to see her fail.

Darkness has never deterred her, never hidden the world from her. She can see with perfect clarity the woman on the boat twirling her massive scythe. As she comes closer and closer to the shore, she thinks of what she might say, thinks of what she might do. A guardian, to be sure—but what price can she pay?

It does not matter. She will reach the western shore.

Forward, forward. It is not until she is nearly at the wall that she realizes she is in no pain. Her shoulders do not trouble her; there is no stiffness to her joints. In this place beyond creation, she is free of the agony she's known so long. Strangely, it feels as if she's lost a part of herself—as if she is less herself because it is no longer there.

But she does not miss it.

The choppy waves slap against the wall of wind. With no care for whether or not it will stop her, she throws herself against it.

Wind may stop water, wind may waylay arrows—but it cannot defeat a daughter of the steppes. All it can do is carry her soul further, make her legend more well known. So it is, let us hear the name: Barsalai Shefali passes through the wall of wind and lands on the white sand of the western shores.

The woman on the boat sees this. Her breath catches in her throat and she thinks for a moment of stopping her eternal dance. If she does that, the waves will surely overwhelm the shore—she cannot. Yet it is her job to guard the shores, and she has clearly let someone through . . .

But it will be such effort to catch her.

Better to stand on her boat and keep the others from getting any ideas.

Barsalai, for her part, lies catching her breath on the sand. The starlight granted to her by her ancestors allows her to get a good look at herself for the first time. She holds her hands up in front of her face. Black, her skin—black as the night that surrounds her. Silver, her nails.

But her nails—they are human nails. Not talons.

The corners of her mouth rise into a smile; hope blossoms in her heart. She touches her face. The plump cheeks of her youth sink a little beneath her fingers. When she laughs, they rise up; she can feel them hurting a little from all the smiling.

She's her old self, isn't she?

And yet when she touches her left eye, she knows she isn't—there, her steel eye, still in place. Tugging at a handful of her hair reveals that it has turned to silver.

Her smile shrinks.

If she goes to the water, if she looks on the mirror of its surface, she knows well the image she will see. She knows that her teeth will be silver, and her left eye, too.

This—*this*—is the face she had always been born to wear.

But this isn't why she came here; this isn't her focus.

Her wife needs her help more than ever.

Thinking of Shizuka brings all her old pain to her at once—though this time concentrated in her heart.

There is no time to waste.

Barsalai Shefali stands among the red flowers of the western shore. Thin, graceful things—like chrysanthemums but more delicate. Though she cannot remember the name for them, it soon springs to mind: spider lilies.

Shizuka never liked them.

Akane. She needs to see Akane—the woman must be around here somewhere. Her eyes trace the horizon. There: an old Hokkaran castle.

She starts walking.

It occurs to her then, as she tramples a flower underfoot, that she is naked. Her hair, too, is unbound. She was not raised Hokkaran, she has no shyness about her nudity—but it would be preposterous indeed to confront the Mother this way. She must be ready for anything.

"Grant me my mother's deel," she says to the stars above her.

And they listen. When she next blinks, a deel is sitting a little ahead of her, neatly folded atop a pair of riding pants, with a set of boots standing next to it. It is not her mother's deel—perhaps it was foolish to ask for a thing that belongs to another. Black, its color, with silver embroidery so delicate that no mortal hand could have made it.

She stops to put it on. It fits, of course. There are pockets sewn into the chest to make it easier to carry things. The thoughtfulness of her ancestors returns the smile to her face—she has never owned a deel so nice in all her life.

The boots and the pants fit just as well, with no need for breaking either of them in.

Five more steps forward. She stops.

"I have no bow, and no arrows to shoot," she says.

In the same way, she takes two steps and sees them.

Sees *it*.

Resting atop the flowers is a bow of purest silver. How luminous! She cannot look away from it, cannot bring herself to, for she knows in truth what it is. With reverence, she drops to her knees before it. It is then that she sees the lightning dog leather quiver, then that she sees the windcutter arrows tucked within.

Tumenbayar's crescent moon bow and sacred arrows.

She swallows. Though she has died now and re-formed herself, she is, at her core, the same girl. The same drop of silver. To be in the presence of something like this is humbling. She looks up at the Sky above and mouths a question: *Why?*

*They have always been yours,* is the answer. The voice sounds familiar to her, though she cannot quite place it. The accent . . . *We have only been holding them.*

She picks up the bow. It flares bright at her touch, cold shooting up her arm and into her heart. When she breathes, a cloud of vapor leaves her. Such power courses through her that her hands start to shake.

But she does not let go. This is hers now. This has always been hers—it's only that she forgot. With every breath, more of the memories return to her: she and the others looking up as the sun plummeted toward the earth. Her husband's stern expression, and the softness of his stomach against her back. Thousands of gers gathered at the base of Gurkhan Khalsar, tens of thousands of brown faces watching her as she sounded a horn . . .

Yes. This has always been theirs.

She isn't the same woman anymore. She isn't Tumenbayar, just as that Tumenbayar was not like her predecessor. Their lives are too different for this. The Tumenbayar of her childhood is all jokes and riddles, all cunning and laughter, for she was raised in a time of relative peace. This Tumenbayar—Barsalai Shefali—was raised with determination and yearning in her belly, knowing she could never fit into either of her parents' domains.

But enough of her is the same that the bow sings to her. She strings it, noting how thin it is, noting its delicate curves and almost-invisible bowstring. How a thing like this can hold more power than her old bow perplexes her—but ah, she remembers. She remembers.

With the quiver belted around her hip and the bow in her hand, she feels nearly complete. It gives her some small joy to see that Tumenbayar fletched her arrows with starling feathers, the same as her mother did.

"Thank you," she says to the stars above.

*Go and meet her,* they say to her in turn.

And so she does. Step by step, Barsalai makes her way to the Mother's castle. It strikes her that the gates are much like those of the Jade Palace: two lightning dogs rampant holding a bar between them. She braces herself for any guardians, but they never come.

This place is abandoned.

There is a holy stillness, though, a sacred lack of life.

She passes a garden where every flower has withered—and yet every flower remains on its stem without drooping. Petals curled and dried, but eternal.

She passes the stables, where there are no horses—only their bones stood up as if eating from a hostler's hand. This sight fills her with dread, for she can think of no worse omen than a dead horse, and yet there is something reassuring about it as well. The horses seem so at peace—and there are so many blankets, so many treats left uneaten—

that she cannot help but conclude they lived good lives. And with no meat, every part of them found a use.

She passes into the palace itself soon after. There are no courtiers here, only bones. The halls are silent, the halls are still, the halls are dark. Only the bow in her hand provides any light at all. Its silver light bounces off the polished walls, casting the skeletons in an eerie glow. As she walks among them, she swears that she sees them whole—but only from the corners of her eyes, and only briefly.

Up and up she goes, sniffing at the air around her. There are no scents here—or perhaps the problem is that she cannot smell anything over the souls she now comprises. Nevertheless she continues, picking her turns out of instinct.

There is no way for her to know how long she has wandered—only that it is too much time spent away from her wife. She thinks of her body lying headless in the cavern, thinks of Shizuka trapped within the Traitor's clutches, and finds herself running through these foreign halls. Her footsteps, her breathing, her heart—these are the only sounds.

Five floors up, she catches the scent of burning. This she follows like a dog hunting a fox. Three turns later, a heavy iron door confronts her, its handles wrought into the twisting coils of a dragon on one side and painted gold into a phoenix on the other.

She grasps it by the dragon handle and pulls.

The room before her is a parody of Shizuka's—there is even a clock taking up most of one wall. Hokkaran robes hung for display take up the opposite side. The wall directly across from the door—the eastern wall—has a circular window in the center that spans the height of the room. From it she can see the eastern shore—the campfire where she first met Akane so many years ago.

But the woman herself? Yes, she sits by a fire now, too. There's a firepit in the center of the room. Akane herself sits on western side of it, her back to Shefali. She does not turn when the door opens; she does not turn when a draft whips her fire higher and higher.

"You have come to argue with me," she says.

Shefali crosses the threshold. There is nothing to fear from this woman, this god—not when her wife's life hangs in the balance.

"I have," says Shefali.

Akane's right shoulder slumps with a sigh. The left remains stiff. "Sit. Let us talk like equals, Moon."

*Moon.*

When someone calls your name, it knocks against your bones. Shefali can feel the knocking, now, stronger than ever.

She walks to eastern side of the fire and sits cross-legged on the floor. From here she can see Akane clearly: see the melted flesh that remains from Yamai's successful attempt on her life. The first time she saw Akane's face was shocking—now it is routine. This is not the first or the second time they have spoken, but it is the only time they have spoken in this tower. The light of the fire lends her brown eyes an Imperial look.

And so, too, does the set of her mouth, the narrowing of her remaining brow. "You want to save her."

"I'm going to save her," Shefali says.

Akane smacks the corner of her lips. "So determined. Just as you were four years ago."

Shefali says nothing to this, for there is nothing to say, and Akane is not yet done speaking besides. It is just that she will need some time before she addresses the subject at hand.

Shefali spends that time studying her. She flares her nostrils, hoping to catch a secret or two from Akane's scent, but the fire conceals it.

At length, Akane sighs. "Everything dies. Everything. We are no exception. Your proper place is in the sea, or in the stars if you'd prefer. The latter is the only kindness I can grant you."

The thought of returning to the sea fills her with dread. She'd been so close to forgetting who she was—and now she can never return. Not when she'd used the lives of the dead to revive herself.

Perhaps it is the silver bow in her hand that calms her, perhaps it is the whispered wisdom of the lost souls that guides her, perhaps it is simply her own stubborn refusal to let Shizuka be hurt that clears her mind—but she has an answer. "What about you?"

Akane's eyes go hard. She reaches with her right hand for a bit of firewood. "I am Birth and Death," she says. "I cannot leave."

But Shefali will not take this for an answer. "Cannot or will not?"

Akane throws the twig on the fire. "The answer is the same," she says. "So long as I am here, holding up a slot, I will remember the rest of you. All of you."

"How many?" Shefali asks, for the question has long vexed her.

"You are the fifth," Akane says.

"And the other four?" says Shefali. "Are they stars?"

"Some," answers Akane, with a dismissive wave. "Their stories are old, Moon—older than you by far. This is the way things have always been. You will die, and your Sun will too."

Shefali does not need to think to answer. "Together."

"Hm?"

"We die together, or not at all," Shefali says. Her voice is firm, but polite. "I won't die now."

Akane laughs. There is a bit of a wet sound to it, with half her mouth sealed shut as it is. "Ridiculous. You are a ridiculous woman, Moon."

If that was meant to be comforting, it's missed the mark. Remembrance will mean nothing if her wife is dead, if her people are dead. The souls within her roil at the very thought.

"I can swim to the other shore," says Shefali.

Akane's lip curls. "Ah, but that will lead you up the cavern. You'd be on the other side of the world, if you did that. And that's presuming you got past the guards."

"I can get past them," Shefali says, a little too quickly. In truth, she had no great want to kill the crane or the stoat, but if she had to—well. To survive is Qorin. "I could kill you, too."

"You don't want to," says Akane. Then, with another sad laugh: "And you couldn't if you tried. I'm already dead."

Another pause between the two of them. Shefali's patience, practiced though it may be, is wearing thin. Every moment she spends here is another moment her people are dying and her wife is suffering. Just as she opens her mouth, Akane speaks once more, looking over Shefali's shoulder.

"Listen to me, Moon," she says. "The sea swallows whatever passes across it. You can no more reach that shore than a sparrow could."

Barsalai stands. She turns toward the window, nocks an arrow, and fires—it surprises her how smooth the draw on the bow is.

It does not surprise her how far the arrow travels. She watches it soar higher than it has any right to. Cold trails in its wake, giving it a tail much like a comet's. Ice falls on the ocean of souls. For one hundred heartbeats she waits—until at last the arrow lands on the eastern shore.

It is then that she turns. Akane glares at her.

"You have some nerve," she says.

"The starling made it," Shefali says. She holds up the quiver, the fletching of the arrows plainly visible. "Sparrows are bad luck."

"So it did," says Akane. "But that means—"

"The starling made it," Shefali repeats, "and you remain. If you have special rules, then I want the same."

Akane closed her good eye. Barsalai could see that she was thinking it over—it was written there on her face. If she spoke any more, she might upset the matter, and so she simply waited with the arrows in hand.

But at length the silence grew too much to bear—and looking on the bow gave her an idea.

"Let me be like the moon," Shefali says.

Akane tilts her head, her one good eye still closed. "How do you mean?"

"You said we all must die. I will die. Every month, for three days, I will die. But the rest of the time—the rest of the time I will be alive."

"Poetic of you," says Akane. She opens her eyes and beckons Shefali over. She cannot stand under her own power without great difficulty—Shefali knows this well enough.

Shefali helps her, for she knows what it is like to struggle in such a way. Akane loops her burned arm through Shefali's and points, with her good hand, to the window. Together they make their way toward it.

"It will hurt every time," she says. "It will hurt the way it hurt this time."

"I don't care," says Shefali. "She needs me. You'd do the same for your husband."

"And that's another thing," says Akane. The mention of her departed husband unhorses her; her voice wavers a little. "I can tolerate this only while she's alive. The moment she goes, you're coming here with her."

But she *can* tolerate it. Shefali's heart swells, disregarding the latter part of Akane's statement entirely.

"Swear it to me, Moon," Akane says, half-turning toward her. There is a surprising amount of fire in her earthy eyes. "Swear that you will stay here forever when the time comes. That you will let your successor take their rightful place without a struggle."

At that moment Shefali would have sworn to almost anything. "Yes," she says. "You will put us in the Sky?"

"If that's what you've earned," says Akane. She sniffs. "The two of you are making me go soft in my old age."

"How old are you?" Shefali asks. The question springs to her lips before she can stop it.

"You won't be getting your old body back, either," says Akane, dodging the question. "It will be this one. You'll be tied to the phases of the moon—your condition will worsen as it wanes."

All of this was sound, all of this was logical—though she admittedly had no great want to see her old body. And where would she manifest? It had to be somewhere near enough that she could help the army, that she could save Shizuka.

As if reading her mind, Akane continued: "Your birth was a strange one, and so it's easy for me to find your body. That will be where you reappear. I can't control anything that happens after that, do you understand? If you get yourself killed, you'll be dead until the next waxing phase rolls around."

Shefali nodded. So she will have to see it. Well. It is a small price to pay.

"And you will get yourself killed following her."

"As long as she's safe," Shefali answers. "Is she . . . Will this happen to her? Will she have to die, as well?"

Akane glances to the window. A small harrumph leaves her. "No," she says. "Did you know, of all the five in your place you're the only one who has needed to die to figure things out?"

It should not be surprising. "I'm stubborn."

"So you are," says Akane. "But she is worse. It will not take dying for her—she is so near to her powers already. All she has to do is stop sabotaging herself."

She thinks of Shizuka—of her bragging, of her arrogance, of the shards of herself she so desperately keeps together. Akane's proclamation sounds strange in the face of that at first.

But only at first.

The more she thinks of it—yes, Shizuka has spent all of her life loudly proclaiming things that she fears to be true. Acceptance is far rarer with her.

And it is acceptance that she will need.

Akane gestures toward the cabinets along the western wall. Shefali helps her to them. Under her direction she picks out two saucers and a bottle of what must be rice wine. Akane pours one and gives it to Shefali before telling her to do the same.

"We're going to throw these on the fire," she says. "I will throw mine first, and then you will throw yours. When the wine touches the flame—then you will be birthed again. Do you understand?"

What is it with her and asking for understanding? She might've been speaking old Hokkaran, but communication between gods is a simple thing, as Shefali learned in Ikhtar. She herself is speaking Qorin, and Akane understands everything she says.

But, regardless, she understands—and she is eager to return.

"Thank you," says Shefali.

"Don't tell the others," says Akane.

She empties her saucer into the flames. They leap high, so high that Shefali worries the roof will catch and the whole place will be consumed. But that isn't her concern, is it? That Akane would work so closely with fire after what it has done to her . . .

*Fire cleansed me,* she'd said four years ago. *It burned away what I didn't need.*

What will Shefali lose in these flames?

She does not care. If all the gods that have ever lived materialized before her then and challenged her, she would kill every single one with her bare hands.

She is going back.

Barsalai Shefali tips her saucer into the flames.

# MINAMI SAKURA

## SEVEN

It happens quickly.

The shadows are there, and then they are not. The wind scatters them as easily as it scatters dried petals.

It happens all at once.

The sky is bright violet, and then it is not. Night comes for the lands beyond the Wall.

It happens . . . it happens in the way that dying does.

The waxing silver moon hangs in the sky at daybreak.

Minami Sakura, scrambling to Burqila Alshara's assistance, stops in her tracks to marvel at it. Never has she seen the moon as close as this. Every crater, every canyon, every crest is clear to her. If she were to reach out, she would surely feel its crevices beneath her fingertips. Curiosity compels her to do so.

All around her, the army shifts. The drummers falter and hesitate before finally coming to a stop. So, too, the horns. The initial celebrations at the enemy's sudden retreat die down as the darkness falls, as the impossible moon swallows the spires and the castles on the horizon. No one dares to disturb this silence—for it must be the work of the gods.

And there is this feeling at the back of Sakura's mind, as if there is something she is forgetting.

She isn't sure what it is, and she isn't sure she cares.

A pillar of moonlight shoots down from the sky like a battering ram. The earth shakes. Another pit—this one far smaller and far deeper.

This—this sight—is what she came here to remember.

# THE WARRIOR MOON

## ONE

The earth craters beneath her. With her first conscious thought as a woman reborn—as a god—Barsalai Shefali apologizes to the Grandfather for hurting him. Her second thought is one of amusement, for she knows now that the Grandfather has never really heard her—some other person among the stars must be hearing her instead. No matter. She is sorry to them, too.

Her third thought—and this comes to her only as she opens her eyes—is that she is going to kill the Spider.

She draws herself up to her full height as the Spider skitters backwards. "Skitters" is the word for it—all eight of its legs move at once, carrying it at full speed away from Shefali, away from what she represents. The horror that's dawned on the spider woman's face is almost as delectable as the sweet fear in its scent.

"Y-You've returned?!"

The spider hides the blood-slicked bottom of its face behind its white sleeves.

Shefali's words are precious; she does not grant them to this demon. Forward, forward, nocking a windcutter arrow to her crescent moon bow.

"But your head . . . !"

Backwards, the Spider—its back legs carrying it up onto the web that lines the walls.

Barsalai looses. She does not stop to look at the crumpled mess of her own headless body; it does not matter at present.

This is the thing that hurt Shizuka.

It will die.

As simple and inevitable as that.

And so, too, is it a simple thing for her to control the arrow. She wills it to circle the room, to sever the webs that bind the spider to its perch.

Tumbling forward now, the spider shoots a desperate strand up at the ceiling.

Shefali makes a cutting motion with her free hand. The arrow heeds her, slicing clean through the new strand before burying itself in the spider's chest. Black blossoms on the white. As its fine robes stain, Shefali thinks to herself that it looks quite like a chrysanthemum.

The Spider thumps against the ground. Its body curls in on itself, a bit like a scorpion, and Shefali nocks another arrow. Frantic, now, the Spider pushes itself back up.

"W-wait," it says.

Shefali does not heed it.

The second arrow does not soar across the room. It does not need to. It lands square in the Spider's throat.

It cannot speak now, and that is likely for the best. Howling in pain, the Spider thrashes. Its sharp legs slice through web in search of Shefali—who continues walking straight toward it.

A desperate lunge, a desperate swipe. Shefali avoids them. The same is true of the venom the Spider spits out, mixed as it is with its own demonic blood.

Shefali's right in front of it.

"You," the Spider says. "You *dog.*"

There is little lower to a courtly Hokkaran than a dog. Shefali's never understood why—but she is in a generous mood. A giving mood.

And what she wants to give—well.

With her eyes set on the Spider's, she sets down the bow and quiver in front of it.

"The moon isn't a dog, Hiba," Shefali says. The Spider's name was hiding in its scent—how clearly she can breathe now that her blood is free of the Traitor's influence.

A thought is all it takes to shape herself, all it takes to summon the wolf. To her surprise—to her *delight*—it does not hurt when she shifts. She is one thing and then she is another, as simple as that. Her bones and body are happy to rearrange themselves.

The great black wolf looms over the Spider.

Fear in its eyes, fear in its scent, fear in the quivering of its eight legs—but not a drop of regret, not a drop of contrition.

It tries to run, but eight legs cannot outpace four.

One leap and Shefali has it pinned. Her stomach rumbles.

A Spider makes for a paltry meal—but it fills her belly all the same.

# MINAMI SAKURA

## EIGHT

They go to the pit.

What else are they to do? With that column of light shining down upon it—what else are they to do? It is a sign. All the Qorin agree on this point, and Sakura is not keen to argue it.

And so while the surgeons and the remaining Qorin set about gathering the bodies, Sakura, the Phoenix Guard, and Burqila Alshara visit the pit.

Sakura does not know what she is expecting. Shizuka, perhaps, but then Shizuka has never been associated with moonlight. Sunlight and fire have always heralded her cousin. This must be something else—but what?

The answer is as coquettish as a singing girl—she can glimpse it only over a well-painted fan.

Weaving their steps so as not to disturb the bodies, they make their way. There are more now than there were before the battle started. Such things are natural. Sakura can recite at length the death tolls from all the major battles in the Empire's history—thousands and thousands who laid down their lives for the sake of something greater. And yet—what a profound difference it is to be walking among the dead instead of simply seeing the number. What a difference to know how and why they died, to see their bodies, to smell them, to know that so few of them saw this as a romantic venture.

What will history make of Ganzorig's slumped body? What will it make of the Qorin who died with their horses rather than be parted from them?

The thought nauseates her, even more than the sights have, but there is nothing left in her stomach to throw up.

She wonders how large the pyre will be. She wonders who will even light it, or if they will have time to do so at all. Shizuka. Shizuka will have to do it, but—she's seen enough of death. Sakura spent enough time with her cousin to know how little she slept—to know how often she woke in a cold sweat, screaming about the blood that stained her Imperial hands.

She's going to blame herself for this, isn't she?

Sakura presses her lips together. They can deal with that after they find her—and they will find her in the pit, beneath that column of light.

At the mouth of the pit stand the Qorin: the sour-faced woman with missing fingers and Burqila's youngest sister are the only ones she can recognize. The rest of Burqila's family must be in the pile of bodies at the base.

Dorbentei included.

Sakura's throat tightens.

"Is there any word?"

It is Captain Munenori who speaks, pulling off his war mask as he does. He addresses them in Hokkaran, because that is the only language he speaks. The sour-faced woman turns and sneers at him. She spits something back in Qorin—something about a stallion—and Burqila has to break the tension.

Yes, Burqila, with two arrows sticking out of her still, wounded as she is—it's she who breaks up the fight. That she is walking at all mystifies Sakura, that she is *breathing* at all mystifies her.

Burqila makes a sharp cutting gesture. Her fingers fly as she speaks in shapes and forms. The sour-faced woman and her sister, of course, both understand her—but Sakura and Munenori are left bathed in confusion and moonlight.

"I don't suppose you know what they're saying," Munenori says to her.

"I don't," she answers.

"Dorbentei would," says Munenori. There's a surprising amount of worry in his voice when he says this. "But she's—"

"She's down there," says Sakura sharply, "waiting for us to find her."

She refuses to believe anything else.

Two steps forward, she takes, while Burqila continues speaking with her family. The conversation—such as it is—is only getting more animated. The sour-faced woman's joined in on the signing; Dalaansuv is fighting back her own set of tears. Not one of them wants to look into the light of the pit.

But that is the thing about Minami Sakura: she has always been too curious for her own good. It is what has made her such a natural scholar, such a natural historian; it is what has propelled her from a pleasure house in Nishikomi to the battlefield of the new gods.

The light is bright, almost solid. She bites her bottom lip. There are stories about this sort of thing, about mortals coming in contact with the work of gods. If she stuck her hand in, she'd either gain something of them or die.

Well.

That is hardly a choice at all, is it? Someone's got to do it. Why not her? She's been enough of a coward for a lifetime.

She reaches with her right hand—her nondominant hand—and touches the column of light.

Cold—that is the first thing she feels. This is not the light frost of a Hokkaran winter, not the cool silk of chilled wine. This is the cold that lives atop mountains; a hoary chill that saps the marrow from bones. Sakura draws her hand back only for the cold to remain—it's shooting up her arm and down into her stomach.

If this is how she dies, then it will be a slow death—she must hope otherwise. The cold isn't hurting her, only cooling her. This gives her enough hope to cling to. As she takes a calming breath, a cloud of vapor leaves her, and in its shape she remembers what she has forgotten.

"Barsalai," she says. "It's Barsalai!"

Burqila's hands drop to her sides. Without so much as a parting gesture, she abandons her friend and sister and runs to the column—but by then it has already begun to fade. Desperation colors her as she lunges for it all the same, as she attempts to gather an armful of light and cold. For the barest moment, she's limned in blue—and then the light is gone.

Burqila stares down at her hands, breathing heavy.

"Did you feel it, too?" Sakura asks. "The cold?"

Burqila nods. She clenches her hands into fists and closes her eyes.

"She lit up as you did," Munenori says. "You're saying that was Barsalai-sur?"

"It was," Sakura says. "Her . . . I think she's ascended."

"Ascended?"

She finds herself wishing he wasn't here—she doesn't want to have to explain everything. What's happening to Barsalai and Shizuka is great and terrifying—how is she meant to condense it for a man who knows nothing of it?

But as her eyes adjust to the lack of light, she realizes she will not have to. The answer is loping in from the cavern: a wolf the size of a siege engine, black as night, its pelt shimmering with silver at the tips. One green eye and one silver shine even in the dark.

Barsalai Shefali.

Burqila's mouth hangs open. Even the sour-faced woman is forced to acknowledge what she is seeing. Wonder breaks across her face as Dalaansuv curses in Qorin.

"That's her," Sakura says. If only she had her lectern! She has to remember this, has to remember the shape of her, has to remember all the details of the moment. When it comes time to write the history of this battle, she cannot shy away from the realities: yes, her cousin's wife has transformed herself into a giant wolf, and this is to be commended—but they are surrounded by death on all sides.

If she has come to save them, then it cannot be argued that she has come too late for many.

Still—the sight of her is a balm. Sakura pushes two fingers into her mouth and curls her tongue. When she whistles, it is shrill enough to pain the ears of everyone around her. The wolf looks up at her with its mismatched eyes and lets out a low, playful rumble.

Yes—that must be her.

Burqila falls to her knees at the mouth of the pit. Dalaansuv is behind her, holding her back, so that she does not fall.

The four of them wait. Barsalai enters the chamber at the foot of the pit in full—she really is massive. If she stands on her hindpaws, she will reach the lip.

And so, of course, she does.

Two forepaws the size of horses rest on the flower-strewn earth. Barsalai's head soon follows—her mouth is a little open, and she's panting. Close as she is, Sakura can see that the silver tips of her fur are not silver at all, but the flickering lights of the stars. A sort of giddy disbelief overtakes her at the sight. A wolf! A wolf this large, her mouth slick with the enemy's blood, her eyes as kind and quick and hard as ever.

Burqila runs to her, but Dalaansuv again pulls her back—if she embraces her daughter's head, she will surely catch the blackblood. Sakura does not need to understand Qorin to realize that's the remonstration being given. Even so, Burqila struggles against her sister's grasp. Such emotion on her face! Pride and amazement, relief and fear!

"That creature . . . ," says Munenori. He's narrowing his eyes, his grip on his polearm tightening at the sight. "That's Barsalai?"

"You saw her like this in the forest," Sakura says, although that isn't quite true. That wolf had not been half so magnificent as this.

If he has any more arguments to make, he stifles them when Barsalai lifts her paw. She sets it down on her mother's head. Burqila, overcome with emotion, reaches overhead to cradle her as much as she can.

Sakura looks away, offering them what privacy she can—but in truth, her curiosity is getting the better of her again. Where is Shizuka? For she leaped down after Shefali, and she, too, is a god. The fall could not have killed her. To see Barsalai returning alone and covered in blood . . .

Sakura's heart twists in her chest.

Shizuka will be here at any moment.

Sakura stares at the opening to the rest of the cave, stares at it and wills her cousin to return. Any moment now, a flare of bright gold, any moment now an intolerable line. "You cannot kill a phoenix," or something equally uncreative—her cousin's never had the mind for that sort of thing, no matter her famed father.

Shizuka will walk up to them, and she will have Dorbentei with her, and together they can all figure out what comes next.

Sakura waits, and waits, and waits—but her cousin does not come.

*Please*, she thinks, *please*, *Shizu-lun*.

"Her Majesty is still missing," Munenori says.

"She's coming," Sakura says. "She has to be."

Barsalai's ears twitch at this. She turns her head toward Sakura. Her eyes! They are tall as a man, each of them! If Sakura is not careful, she will lose herself to them—but she is pulled back to reality when she sees the calligraphy upon the steel.

*Peony*, written in Shizuka's own venerated hand.

She'd often wondered why Shizuka chose a peony for the eye, but never thought to ask. Mountain flowers are endemic to the steppes—they make a more appropriate choice for a Qorin. Peonies are the province of sovereigns and pampered courtiers.

Who ever decided that the peony should stand for bravery?

And yet it is bravery that Sakura thinks of now, bravery that she tries to summon, for it is clear to her from Barsalai's expressive green eyes that Shizuka is not here.

She opens her mouth. Her voice fails her as she tries to find the words to ask, to confirm this great fear of hers. What will she do if Shizuka is gone? She can't be dead. They'd know if she were dead, wouldn't they? There'd be some sign or portent. Fires would go out, perhaps. Swords rust in the hands of their owners.

They'd know, wouldn't they?

Once, twice, she shapes the question—but she cannot give it air. She cannot make it live.

In the end, it is Munenori who finds the courage to ask. "Is the Empress with you?"

Green and silver—earth and sky.

Barsalai shakes her head.

Sakura does not feel her knees give away, but they do—she crumples to the ground, covering her mouth to stifle her cry. Munenori catches her—but in the Hokkaran way, he does not look at her while he does so, and he says nothing to soothe her spirit. He only ensures that she remains standing as the two of them stare down the wolf—the newborn god.

"What happened?" she manages to say. "What happened to . . ."

Sakura does not know why she expects that a wolf will be able to answer her. It makes no sense at all—how would she shape any of the syllables?

A frigid wind carries the words to her; Barsalai's silver eye flares.

"She made a mistake. We will save her."

*We will save her.*

But will they? Can they? When the shadows cut through so much of the army—can they save Shizuka? They've lost a third of the guard and at least half the Qorin, if not more. The numbers are stacked against them—to say nothing of the enemy's treacherous tactics and unnatural abilities.

Barsalai sounds so confident. Why?

Even with their weapons blessed, even fighting as hard as they could . . . If Rikuto had not disappeared, they would have lost the battle. Burqila would be dead.

*We have come here to die,* she thinks, and the thought is like a stone in her stomach.

A weight on her head. Barsalai's paw. "Trust me," she says.

And Sakura wants to, truly she does, but she has read all the stories. She knows how this all ends: an impossible last stand against an army five times their size. They may well kill the Traitor, but they will all die doing it, their names lost in the fog, their lives twisted into a romance of some young author's creation.

But there is nothing romantic about this. There is nothing romantic about the mud that coats her, the aching in her ribs, the horror that has left her feeling like a shucked oyster and not a woman. There is nothing romantic about the bodies stacked high in the pit, nothing romantic about the bodies littering the battlefield; there is nothing romantic about the scent of shit and despair that pervades this place.

This is war. This is what she agreed to.

She closes her eyes. One question remains to her, one thing she must know if she is to have any hope of keeping herself together. "Did Dorbentei make it?"

A quiet nod. Barsalai lowers herself into the pit once more. When she comes back up, it is with two Qorin hanging from the backs of their collars. One is . . . one does not have a head, and Sakura must avert her eyes lest her stomach attempt to betray her again. The other has a leg bent up at a forty-five-degree angle from her body—and that side of her is so swollen she is nearly unrecognizable.

But Sakura would know those dark eyes anywhere.

Dorbentei Otgar.

Barsalai sets her down; Dorbentei catches the body in her arms. For long moments she does not move. Her hands are shaking; her eyes clenched closed. Tears stream down her face and onto the body.

Silence among the Qorin, silence from Otgar, silence from even Munenori. No one has seen Dorbentei in such a state. A few days ago, Sakura would have said it was impossible to imagine. Dorbentei, bold Dorbentei, crying like a child with a body in her hands? Reduced to worldless sorrow, the woman who has a joke for every occasion? Dorbentei could never shut up, and now . . .

Sakura takes a step toward her, but she is too slow. Dalaansuv and Burqila have already flanked her. Burqila throws her arms around Dorbentei and the body, Dalaansuv whispers to her.

Sakura knows a moment of profound intimacy when she sees it. However acute her own sorrow, however much she wants to help Dorbentei bear her sorrows—it is not her place. Not now.

For she thinks she knows now who that body once was.

Zurgaanqar. Dorbentei's mother.

The romantic in her wants to say that at least Ganzorig and Zurgaanqar died at the same battle. Their spirits will find each other in the Womb, and they will journey together to the stars the Qorin hold so sacred.

But Zurgaanqar lost her head, and Ganzorig his entrails, and so how can they possibly meet? How can they possibly journey anywhere at all together?

The stories she so treasured growing up are lies.

Sakura knows that now.

The tears come for her again. Her shoulders tremble.

It occurs to her that her sorrow will get her nowhere. This despair is akin to the fear she felt in the melee, the worries that paralyzed her.

Useless. She does not want to be useless anymore.

There is Minami fire in her blood yet. She turns a little away from Dorbentei—Sister, she's started to howl—and toward Barsalai.

"There are more of them, aren't there?" she says. "Could you bring them up? They don't deserve to rot down there. We can set up a pyre for them. There's been enough fighting for tonight. We need time to mourn."

Silence, and then another nod. Leave it to Barsalai to be no less taciturn as a god. Down she goes once more—and when she returns, it is with a body gently held by its deel. A woman, no older than Sakura, her head bent backwards.

This is awful. Truly awful. The whole day has seeped into her soul; she will never be free of the stain it's left upon her.

And yet however much she is suffering just from being here, the Qorin suffer twice as much. To them these are not merely casualties of war—they are cousins and daughters and sons and mothers and lovers.

Family.

Families, even, some of them wiped out in one fell swoop.

Yes—they have a god on their side.

But what good will that do the dead?

"Lay them out properly," she says to Munenori. That she is commanding a captain does not occur to her—only that there is a thing that needs doing, and he is the man who can do it. The pieces are falling into place in her mind. She does not want to be useless—and there are only so many things she is good at.

"What?" he says.

"You heard me," Sakura says. "Lay them out, you and the guard. Make sure their faces are visible. Later we'll try to get their names."

Munenori's eyes go hard. He looks on the body at their feet the way some men look at women who speak of their monthly bleed. "You mean for us to handle the bodies?"

"Yes," says Sakura. "Soldiers cause enough of them, wouldn't you say? It shouldn't be anything out of the ordinary for you. Lay them out."

It surprises her how firm she can be about this. She feels . . . not like her old self. She will never be her old self again.

But she might wear her mask now and again.

"Why not build the pyre now?" says Munenori. "We can find out who is missing later, if we have the time for it. Names of the departed are hardly the most important—"

"To you, maybe," says Sakura. Fury fills her. "But when their ashes scatter to the winds, the Qorin will want to know who is being carried away. Do you have any idea how many of them died in the last generation? How many families *we* ended? Some of those people . . . Some of those people were the only ones left who remembered the fallen. We aren't just mourning those who died today. We're mourning *all* of them."

Her voice cracks in righteous indignation, in sorrow and misery. She can no longer look him in the eye.

"Lay them out so I can get their names," Sakura says. "Please. They have to be remembered."

She does not wait for his answer. The caravan where she kept her things thankfully survived the battle; she needs her lectern and good paper.

As she leaves the pit, she hears Dorbentei's howl grow louder and louder.

Every step away from her is an arrow.

# O-SHIZUKA

## ELEVEN

When Minami Shizuka—Empress Yui, Mother of Hokkaro and all her children, Light of the Empire—awakes, she is in her own room.

The phoenixes carved into the rafters tell her that these are meant to be the Empress's chambers.

Except that it is not her room.

The Emperor's chambers and the Empress's have always been separate, with the consort visiting the sitting ruler. So it has been for the course of Shizuka's life, so it has been for twenty-two sovereigns. The same is true of Iwa—the Emperor's chambers are at the other end of the hall. Rarely did she spend any time in her uncle's quarters, but she knows these well.

Here, for instance. The first thing she sees with her bleary eyes: a screen painted with the story of Minami Shiori, a screen that has been in Shizuka's room almost longer than she has had one. In the first panel, Shiori is born to a weaver beneath a full moon on the double fifth. In the second, she saves the First Emperor from drowning. In the third, she tricks the sun into giving her a beam of light, and makes from that a sword. The last panel features her confronting the fox woman.

But the painting is wrong.

The second panel. The drowning figure isn't wearing the Dragon Circlet—it must not be the First Emperor at all. The clothing is all wrong for an Emperor, too; he wears no thread of gold.

The sight of it fills Shizuka with anger. It's easier to feel angry now that she's had some time to rest—now that her head has mended the wound it suffered falling into the pit. Her aches remain, but they are distant and dull compared to the memory of what has happened.

The sheets are heavy, and she is tucked in tight. Swaddled, almost. She works her way free of them and sits up. The screen stands right at the side of her bed, so that anyone entering her chambers is spared the sight of the Empress's rumpled bedding. When her toes skim the ground, she realizes there are slippers already prepared for her—red with gold trim. So, too, does she realize that she is not wearing her warrior's garb: instead she is wrapped in a soft red under-robe. It is as plush as it is unwelcome—the touch of it against her skin feels like a violation.

Disgusted, she unties the robe and throws it across the room. It lands on the replica of the clock that Baozhai gave her—a clock whose hours are all labeled "contemplation." Standing to the right of it is a statue of the many-faced god one of the Ikhthian ambassadors gave her, but this one has been replaced with the faces of her ancestors, the Imperial Line. Their eyes bore into her now as she sits bare chested before them.

She wants, more than anything, to cut the statue down. To burn it. Without thinking, she reaches for the fires within herself. The smell of burning wood soon fills the room and her lungs, bringing with it the memory of calm.

Because that fire—that tiny fire, that little blip of orange at the tip of Yoshinaga's nose—means she is not yet broken, no matter what the Traitor might say.

He can break her army, he can send her wife away, he can put her spirit into a vise—but he cannot break a god.

She refuses.

The fire begins to burn in earnest. Cinders drop from Yoshinaga's nose onto the mats. Shizuka could quell them, if she chose. It wouldn't be a difficult thing to do—one thought and one breath to suck the fire back into herself are all that it would take.

But she lets it burn.

She stands as the fire rises. Almost immediately, she falls back onto the bed. As much as her wounds might have healed, she has still lost a lot of blood. Cursing her own weakness, she tries again—more slowly this time—and manages to stand of her own power.

Outside the window, the walled city sprawls out before her. This, too, is like Fujino—she knows all the streets, all the thoroughfares. Eight main avenues surround the palace like spokes on a wheel, with the Imperial Hunting Grounds as a hub. Time has no meaning here, but she thinks it must be their version of Fifth Bell—there are scores of Qorin clad in white making their way down the Mother's Lane, toward her temple.

"Praise the Eternal King," they call, "who grants us life and protects us from ignoble death."

Their voices weave together. She can hear them with perfect clarity even from her tower.

How many of them are there? Moving in perfect unity, a sickening puppet show made from a people who have suffered so much already. That he chose to use them for his mock capital and not the Hokkarans . . .

To survive is Qorin, she tells herself. When she finds a way to kill the Traitor safely, she will free them. She isn't certain of how. She isn't even certain that it's possible.

But she chooses to be certain that she will do it.

It is the least her wife would ask of her.

Shefali.

Shizuka's fingers rise to the place where her heart once was; she staggers, knocking over the screen in the process. Shefali. Why is it Shizuka alive in this gilded cage? Why not Shefali?

"Your Highness, Princess Yui—have you woken?"

The voice is one of three the women here all share. What relief, that it is not the Spider! And yet even that is fleeting, for she is trapped without a sword, and it will surely be a Lost Qorin who is made to wait on her.

She does not want to dignify the Traitor's servant with a response, and so she does not.

What she wants to do is curl up and weep at the prospect of what she has done, to crumple beneath the weight she must now carry—but this is denied to her. She cannot weep anymore, for one thing; she cannot allow herself to break, for another.

And so she gets back to her feet, the Phoenix Empress beyond the Wall, and she steels herself for the consequences of her actions.

"I can dress myself," she calls. There are four sets of four robes hanging along the far side of the wall. Plain, all of them, lacking the patterns, prints, and paintings she so enjoys. Only one in each set is gold—the rest are in subdued reds or cool blues. Robes for a scholar's wife and not an Empress.

But then—he has not addressed her as an Empress, has he?

The doors swing open. Out of reflex, she tries to duck behind the screen, having forgotten that she has already knocked it over. Shame claws at her bare back—the guards can see her, which means *he* can see her. The blankets are her only cover. She wraps them around her shoulders as quickly as she can.

"Your Highness, we understand that you may *believe* you can dress yourself."

It is not until she turns toward the speaker that she realizes there are four of them—four Qorin women wearing rictus grins, four women speaking all at once with the very same voice. The way they move reminds her with a sickening lurch of the marionettes at Rihima—they each pick up one of the robes on the first display.

"I can," Shizuka says. "I am no girl of ten; I can and have dressed myself before. You can tell the Eternal King I refuse to shed my modesty for him."

The women all turn toward her, all tilt their heads at precisely the same angle. Though their faces are different, there is an awful sameness to their expressions—to the smiles, the dead glint in their eyes. Dolls, all of them.

Shizuka has never been fond of dolls.

"Your modesty?" say the four women. "Don't be preposterous. You have never been a modest girl; why be a modest woman? Let us dress you."

Closer they come, the robes held up before them like a washerwoman's work. Outside, the guards watch with something like interest. The fire—tall enough now to fully consume the statue—does not seem to bother them.

Shizuka gets to her feet once more, the blankets draped around her. The cloth rubs against the open wound on her chest; it hurts, but not enough to distract her. Already gold is filling in the cracks. How long before that is all that's left of her heart? Mended like a shattered pot and just as empty.

No, not empty. There's fire, still. Shizuka draws her arm across her face in a sharp gesture. The flames follow, pouring out from the statue to form a wall between her and the handmaidens.

"No," says Shizuka. "You shall leave, or I will burn you."

This at last gives them pause. The four women blink all at once. For an instant, their smiles crack; for an instant, she can see the hinges and joints that make their faces contort in such a way. His own anger showing through.

"Insolent, insolent, insolent," say the four women. "But the Eternal King is merciful. He knows you cannot change your ways with only a day's worth of lessons. Dress yourself today, if you are so inclined. You will be present for breakfast within the hour, or you shall be made present."

Breakfast?

After all of this—*breakfast*?

The raw audacity of it stuns her. He wants to . . . simply have a meal with her?

After killing so many Qorin, so many Hokkarans?

And yet the bitter truth is that Shizuka does not have much choice in the matter. If she does not attend, he will send Rikuto, and it has her mother's sword. The fires in her veins may not have abandoned her—but what good are they when the Daybreak Blade is in the hands of another? If that sword is raised against her—can she break her mother's sword? Her ancestors' sword?

No, no. She must have it back.

True, she might have left her army behind—but that does not mean the war has ended. This, too, is a battle. The Eternal King thinks he can conquer her.

Shizuka will show him otherwise.

But she must do so when she is ready. Prudence is a virtue Xianyu did much to teach her.

"Are we understood, Yui?"

Breakfast.

*Puh.*

Shizuka stares back at them over the wall of flame.

"Yes," she says. "You are understood. Will we be breaking our fast on the terrace?"

"The Pine Terrace," say the four women. Her lip curls into a sneer at the name. Of course. Everything in this place is meant to taunt her. "You shall dress yourself and wait for your escort. Should you leave the chambers the Eternal King has so graciously provided, there shall be consequences."

She has already lost her heart, her soul, her tears—how can the Traitor threaten to hurt her any more than she's already been hurt?

But that is asking the knife how sharp it is.

"Leave me already," Shizuka says. "I've gotten the point."

She holds their gaze as she speaks to them, in hopes that the Traitor knows she is staring him down. Perhaps he does—the handmaidens bow only so much as necessary before leaving her. The door closes behind them.

She is alone with her fire.

The statue's consumed already. There's little left of it. Flames lick at the rafters, at the phoenixes carved with such loving care so many generations ago.

Shizuka draws in a breath. She will need it all if she is to survive this. The flames return to her. There's no trace of the cold she felt earlier, no trace of the ice—only a dull ache where most of her feelings should be. Her fingers trace the rim of the wound. They did not bother to bandage her.

She sighs.

For the first time in years, she sets about dressing herself. The process does nothing to calm her. This cloth—who would pick cloth like this? It is coarse and awful, and not at all befitting of someone of her station. Even the golden robe is *too* well waxed; it feels tacky against her skin.

Her movements are careful and precise—nothing at all like those of a woman with a gaping hole in her chest. Under-robe, first belt; the heavy weight of the other three, and finally her second belt. It is difficult to tie it properly on her own, but she manages, tying it on the bed and slipping it over her head before pulling the knot closed. Tight but not too tight—she truly does hate the feeling of the gold.

At the mirror there are pots of various kinds of makeup. Thick white paint and sticks of charcoal for her teeth; a small tin of rouge and a set of small brushes with which to apply it. Perfumes, too, lie in wait for her there, helpfully labeled with their scents.

He wants her to wear them—to cover the thick scar across her face, the notch in her nose.

Minami Shizuka will not.

Baozhai had given her a phoenix ear cuff to wear four years ago. It lies somewhere in her old chambers in the palace now; the Traitor has not replicated it here. To see the work of someone she loved so perverted would have been a blow indeed—and yet she knows that even if the cuff itself were here, she would not choose to wear it.

And so she tucks her hair behind the stub of her ruined ear. She catches sight of herself in the mirror: amber eyes smoldering with anger, with determination, with hatred; her clenched jaw. A woman unbroken.

She thinks to herself that Shefali would not like the look of hatred.

She flinches.

Five hundred heartbeats Minami Shizuka is alone. She counts, for she has little else to do save ruminate on the mistakes that have led her here, little else to do but remember her wife's last moments. Counting does not stave away the assassins for long—but it helps. She tries to focus on the numbers, on the arcane meanings her tutors assigned to them based on their roots and multiples, but she finds she cannot remember any of them now.

Her mother was right—they really had been wasting their money paying those stuffy old men to ramble at her.

Minami Shizuru would have fought her way through the towers by now, sword or not.

Minami Shizuru would have had the Traitor's head for her rice wine saucer, as Burqila Alshara would say.

She tells herself that she is not weak for waiting until the right moment. She does not believe it. Shefali thought of her as a decisive hero, and here she is . . .

The doors open. There is no knocking here, for there is no expectation of privacy. What use is it to knock when everyone shares the same mind? Four guards march into the room, Dragons all, with Rikuto standing at the center. It wears a deep blue robe beneath a white coat emblazoned with the Traitor's seal. Waves. Revulsion takes her at the sight; she wrinkles her nose in disgust.

The demon crosses its arms. "All the kindness he's shown you, and still you act like this."

"Who changed me this morning?" Shizuka asks.

It scoffs. "Why does it matter?"

"Because I don't want him touching me," says Shizuka, rising to her feet from her place of contemplation on the mats. "If he has, then he has not done me any kindness at all."

Contempt flares behind the demon's eyes. The tip of its long nose reddens a little; it waves a hand dismissively. "One of the servants," it says. "Women and their modesty. You wear it only when it suits you. Come. The Eternal King hates lateness."

The guards—all men, she notices—leave the room. Rikuto stands right where it is, staring at her. They are duelists, the two of them, appraising each other's strengths. She knows that she is quicker—but it is far taller. Any blow she strikes at it would have to come after a parry, when it is off-balance. Its size will work against it then.

Shizuka imagines sliding her sword between its ribs. She imagines the tip piercing its heart. She imagines the feel of its blood spurting out onto her; she imagines the rattle of its dying breath.

But she cannot imagine taking its head.

"The longer you wait, the later you will be," it says. "And the later you are, the worse the punishment."

Punishment. That word again.

She begins to walk. As she passes it, she does not look back for it. Long, confident strides—an Empress and not a princess. She does not bow her head; she does not meet the eyes of the Qorin who greet her with their mechanical smiles. Shoulders back, neck straight, head held high. Walk and think of all the tributes you've received—so Baozhai once told her.

And so Minami Shizuka walks through the halls of this impossible palace, this place that does not map to its outward appearance at all, this echo of her previous life. Turn right. Marvel at the statue of Empress Yumiko—or in this case, a woman she does not know wearing seven swirling cloaks. Down the hall, taking the back stairs, toward the terrace. The servants are preparing to call the hour—she can see them lined up in sets of four along each of the major paths. The haze of incense stings at her eyes.

As she walks down the stairs, she chances a look over her shoulder. Rikuto is following eight paces behind her, watching, watching. It catches her eye and smiles mirthlessly.

Her chest burns again, and she thinks to herself that she is really going to kill it if she has to endure it much longer.

But how?

The answer presents itself as she reaches the landing. To reach the Pine Terrace, she must pass the Imperial Gardens. To her surprise, the Traitor has replicated it, too—but more important, he has used real flowers. There can be no mistaking them. Outside, the scintillating fields have a false gleam to them—but here there are some that are half-wilted, here there are spots and blemishes among the perfect blooms. His influence poisons everything it touches.

And yet the flowers hold on. The rosebushes, the dogwood tree whose branches were so often her home, even the gentle hill upon which the golden dandelions once grew—all of them are here, all of them are waiting, and all of them turn toward her as she passes.

To keep real flowers in a place like this is an intolerable vanity. A weakness. An opportunity.

*If I call, will you heed me?* she asks them as she passes.

*If you call, we are yours*, answers the marigold.

Men have long discounted flowers. Rikuto seems like the sort to follow in their footsteps, though it is not quite a human man. If she calls for the flowers to strangle it, they will listen.

Ah, but it does not have her mother's sword. Where is the demon keeping it? Shizuka cannot kill it until the Daybreak Blade is back in her possession.

But it is a comfort all the same, as she passes the garden, to know this will be the place it dies.

The terrace rises ahead of them. A cool wind whips through her hair, and she realizes she has not bound it as a married woman should. Guilt is a poison at the back of her throat: Has she forgotten her vows already?

No, no.

Vengeance for her wife, justice for her people—these are her goals now. These will keep her warm at night.

Eighty-eight steps up to the terrace itself, each engraved with a line from the Mandates.

*On Earth as in Heaven, the will of the Father is supreme.*

*Death comes for all warriors. Do not falter when you hear the nightjar sing.*

*Never bare your teeth.*

Shizuka knows them, all of them, and she hates them, all of them. There is so much hate within her that she fears it will consume her as the fire consumed the idols. What will remain of her once all of this is over with? Once she has slain this man and his cohorts, once she has righted the wrongs of her ancestors?

Does it matter?

A melody, achingly familiar. *View from Rolling Hills*—a crack in her soul. How dare he? Her father's most famous poem, written on the subject of returning home after war, set to music by a famed pacifist her uncle had executed—playing in a place like this?

She hesitates on the next step—but she takes it anyway. An Empress continues when there is nothing left.

At last she summits the stairs, at last she sees them: the Traitor sitting on the northern side of the squared table. The biwa players on the eastern side, accompanied by flute and shamisen.

Her father sitting to the west in deep blue robes.

Now, truly, she stops; now, truly, she staggers. Her mouth hangs open at the sight of him. It cannot really be him—she knows it cannot really be him. Twelve years her father has been dead, twelve years since she took the Daybreak Blade to her own mother's throat. It cannot be him.

And yet she knows that it is. The years have put gray in his hair; the crows he wrote so much about have left their prints on either side of his eyes—but it is him. Twelve years and he still wears his pate unshaved; twelve years and, when he looks at her, his eyes are the same shade of honeyed amber.

And he does look at her. Their eyes meet across the expanse of the terrace and he rises, the wind whipping his hair into his face. A smile—his smile, his easy grin—disarms her more surely than any enemy she has ever faced. Instead of bowing, he waves, and when he speaks, her feet of clay shatter.

"Shizuru," he says. "You've finally returned to me."

It is journeying eight years for a phoenix feather only to discover that you are dying and the phoenix cannot help you.

It is avenging your cousin only to drown a province in the process.

It is her childhood hero, her mother, lying on a soiled bed and crying out for her husband.

For the second time that day—that hour—the pressure behind her eyes is almost too much to bear; for the second time that day, she takes hiccuping breaths to try to steady herself.

Her father's joy dissolves into concern. He rushes to her side and throws an arm around her. With a lurch, she realizes that he even smells the same as he used to: old paper and floral perfumes.

"Shizuru?" he says. "Zuru, what's wrong?"

The worry in his voice! The concern! Shizuka is trying to breathe, but there is only water to fill her lungs, only this awful false relief. Her father is here with her, but he doesn't . . .

He wraps his arms around her as she hiccups, as she starts to shake.

"Listen to me," he says, stroking her hair. "Whatever happened in that cave is behind us. We're together now, you and I. Nothing will tear us apart again. I'm going to have a word with my brother, Zuru, I swear I will. What he did to you—"

"Father," O-Shizuka croaks, though she cannot bring herself to tear herself away from, cannot bring herself to leave the embrace she has missed for so many years.

O-Itsuki, Poet Prince, lets out the quiet laugh he was so well known for. "Father?"

Tearing herself away from the comfort and safety of her father's arms is tearing her heart out anew. She does it all the same, because it must be done, and holds him at arm's length. Her eyes meet his. It occurs to her that she takes after him far more than she's ever taken after her mother—his delicate brow, his cheekbones, his eyes. There is so little of her mother.

How can he mistake the two of them?

For recognition does not dawn on him even as he studies her. His brows narrow over his Imperial eyes, and he purses his lips. "Zuru," he says, leaning forward to whisper behind his hand. "Is this about our guest?"

Guest?

Like a moth drawn inexorably to a flame: Shizuka's gaze and the Traitor's self-satisfied eyes. He sits in the proper style, having not moved at all during this exchange, save for the slightest quirk of his lips.

"Pay me no mind," he says.

For once, she is inclined to listen to him—the issue of her father is more pressing to her than the Traitor's presence. There are shards in her throat as she swallows, as she tries to summon the words.

"Father," she says, "It's me. Shizuka. Your little tigress."

Using the old nickname feels like baring herself before both men. The pleased sound the Traitor makes! The way he opens his fan in spite of the wind! He holds it before his face to hide his wolfish grin, she can tell. The flames of her hatred burn hotter than ever—and yet she cannot give them any control when her father is before her again.

This is a trick of some sort. She knows it must be and yet hope has conquered her good sense like Chen Luoyi conquered the South. There is little left of reason, little left of the Empress—only the child-like need for her father to call her name.

To recognize her.

If all the others forget her—that is the price she was born to pay. If her names are struck from the Imperial records, if no shrine ever bears the characters for "quiet" and "excellence"—then that, too, would be bearable. It would be fate.

But for her father to return to her . . . The way he's looking at her now! As if he is trying to consider whether or not she is joking—and if she is, then he must consider what to do with her.

"Please," she says when he does not answer her. "Please, Father. You remember, don't you? Your daughter?"

*Please*. She thinks this word over and over until it becomes a prayer, though she knows there is no one to hear it but she herself.

"How could I ever forget my morning sun?" he says, and for a moment her heart leaps—but the next sentence is the arrow that finds the bounding hare. "She is safe on the steppes; Burqila-lao will be returning with her any day now."

Careful, his words; cautious, his tone. If he were speaking to a madwoman, he might use the same voice he uses now. So much is unspoken: *You haven't forgotten, have you, Shizuru? She is safe and we are not.*

And it is the most awful thing in the world to know that her father is speaking from a place of perfect earnestness. This is no illusion she wears. There is no magic cloaking her.

He simply doesn't remember.

He has been to war and war has broken him, and now he contents himself with living in this mockery, this farce. She knows that distant look in his eyes; she knows the way he hesitates before speaking; she knows that tremble in his fingers.

He is afraid of the things she has forgotten—just as she is afraid of the water.

And it would be a simple thing to tell him the truth. *I am not my mother, because my mother has been dead for twelve years. She died screaming for you, mistaking me for you. I am your daughter. That man is the Traitor, and we are both his prisoners.*

Yet Shizuka knows that he would not listen. He has sealed himself up in some chamber of his mind where he can see only one part of the world, one part of reality, and if something should come by to shatter that window—well. He will have it repaired.

As her father stares at her, as the Traitor looks on in amusement, as the servants lay out the rice and light broth—has she ever felt more alone?

Her only home lies headless in a cave hundreds of li away; her people live on in bliss without her over the Wall; her family has forgotten her.

And it occurs to her then, in all its bleak glory, in all its austere truth: this is her punishment.

Itsuki takes her hand.

"Come to breakfast," he says. "Our guest was just telling me about his theater company. You must have seen the puppets in Nishikomi—it is he who invented them! What marvels!"

He takes her to the table, where he helps her sit on the southern side before taking his place on the west. He kisses her on the forehead and he places a hand on the small of her back.

She draws away from him as if from a hot iron. Struck, he shrinks, his shoulders slumping.

"Shizuru?" he says. There is such hurt in his voice.

How long has he been waiting for his wife's return?

She can't even cry. What sort of horrible person is she if she cannot even cry over this?

"She is just hungry," says the Traitor. "Women have flighty spirits, O-Itsuki-lor; it is important that we tether them whenever possible."

His eyes find hers again. Her skin crawls and something in her dies, even as Itsuki defends her.

"I am not in the practice of tethering women," he says, "nor do I think it a man's place to do so."

He is a good man, Shizuka thinks, and that is the worst part of all of this.

The servants set a bowl of rice before her.

By the time breakfast is over with, she has not eaten a single grain.

# THE WARRIOR MOON

## TWO

Barsalai Shefali has never been much for talking—or at least she never had been before she died. She finds it comes to her easily now. Perhaps it is because she is no longer telling only her own story—perhaps it is because she speaks for the souls of all those who granted her this new body. It is always easier to do something unpleasant when you are doing it for someone else's sake.

For the better part of a Bell she has spoken, and Minami Sakura has listened. The two of them sit in Otgar's ger, away from the others, to record the story of the first of Qurukai. Barsalai Shefali's voice is clear as the night sky above the Silver Steppes.

"The Mother said to me that I could not hope to reach the far island. You may be inclined to agree with her. It is well known that the Qorin have never been fond of swimming, and I am no exception—"

"Catch your dogs."

The voice is as abrupt as it is exhausted. Otgar, it must be—and a quick sniff of the air confirms it. Shefali stops mid-sentence, a stoic sort of resignation overtaking her pride, her serenity when it came to the story at hand.

Sakura, too, stops transcribing mid-motion. The long hours of sleeplessness have not worn on her. There is a simple reason for this: Shefali has not allowed them to. Within the confines of this ger, they are within her domain, within her realm of night, and she has decided that Sakura will not tire here. That is all it takes: a decision, an exertion of her own will. Sakura will not tire.

And so she doesn't.

But there are other forms of exhaustion. Though her body is hale and her mind is clear, the memories eat away at her behind her eyes. Shefali can smell her despair, her fear, her worry. They mingle on the back of her tongue. When she looks up to the door, it is not with the sardonic grin she so often wore before they were attacked on the first—it is the face of a soldier's wife awaiting the worst.

"That's Dorbentei, isn't it?" she says. Her voice is scarcely more than a whisper.

Shefali nods. She reaches out and squeezes Sakura's shoulder, forgetting for a moment how Hokkarans feel about physical contact. When Sakura flinches, Shefali draws back her hand.

"To survive is Qorin," Shefali says to her. "Otgar will be all right in time."

The words don't seem to soothe Sakura much—but there's a lightening in her scent all the same. At times like this, that's all Shefali can ask for. She stands, looking on the marvel of the ger with pride for a moment before calling her cousin in. The starry skies of the steppes replace the white felt walls Otgar beat into existence. Comets streak across from one side to the other and back.

Some might say that it is sacrilege, what she is doing, that it is blasphemy to trap the Sky, but she knows better.

She is the Sky.

It is only fitting that her surroundings should reflect this.

And yet she knows it will be an overwhelming sight for Otgar in her current state. Her cousin has never been fond of Shefali's godly antics. With a sad thought, Shefali dismisses the vision of the heavens. Sakura slumps over a little on her chair, struck by a sudden tiredness.

"There aren't any dogs, Otgar," Shefali says.

The red door opens. "I know there aren't," says Otgar. Not in the mood for any banter, it seems, and Shefali cannot blame her for it—but that does not make the look on Otgar's face any less painful. The roundness that is so well suited to bawdy jokes makes her look childish now in the depths of her sorrow. She wipes at her runny nose with her blood-streaked sleeve.

And it is a strange thing, to be a god—to be the god of the Qorin especially. Barsalai Shefali, who was Needlenose and Laughing Fox, wants to comfort her cousin. The Warrior Moon knows it is better to let her find her own path—to point out the proper paths to her and hope that she will follow them.

The newborn god takes the middle route: she embraces Otgar only long enough to sniff both her cheeks, and then sits across from Sakura near the firepit. It does not escape her notice the way Otgar and Sakura look at each other—the way Sakura averts her eyes. Much is unspoken between the two of them.

Today will not be a day for speaking it.

"Are there any reports?" says the Moon. It is strange, to be so forward, but she finds that it is easy now. She feels as if she has been wearing blinders for years. Why had she ever feared this? These are her people. They love her. They always have, in their own way.

"Do you think I'd be here if there weren't any?" Otgar says. A cutting tone. Barsalai tells herself that it is not Otgar speaking but her anger, not Otgar but her grief. It is a simple enough thing for her to accept—she has lived a life surrounded by grief—but Sakura flinches at the sound of Otgar's voice.

"No," answers Shefali. "What have the scouts found?"

Like diverting a river to flood a battlefield—it will take time, but being direct is the best path.

Otgar sniffs again. She reaches into the chest pocket of her deel for a Surian pipe stuffed with kuulsar. Sakura is the one who gives her a light—she takes a branch from the firepit and holds it out to Otgar, who throws it back into the cinders when she is done with it. The sweet scent soon fills the ger. It is enough to overwhelm Shefali's senses—she can see not only the plant but also the woman who picked it—and yet she says nothing to dissuade her cousin. Otgar needs her comforts.

"The city's a fucking waste," Otgar says. "Half-empty."

"Half-empty?" repeats Sakura. "But that can't be. We saw that demon's army, and we know the Traitor has more Qorin working for him within the walls of Iwa. How can it be half-empty?"

"I don't know," says Otgar, chewing on the stem of her pipe, "but I'm telling you what they told me. I think maybe he's planning for something. Another fucking trap. Burqila and the crane are talking about it."

And yet if Otgar is here, that means Dalaansuv is the one interpreting for Burqila, and Shefali knows that cannot mean anything good. Dalaansuv can hardly keep up with her older sister's signing. That Otgar would choose to be here and not in the Kharsa's ger . . .

"We should join them," says Shefali.

Otgar shakes her head. "Got a problem just for you, Your Eternal Majesty." The honorific leaves her like a curse.

*This is not Otgar talking*, Shefali tells herself again.

"Needlenose," Shefali corrects.

Otgar does not laugh—but something behind her eyes softens and she lets out a sigh. "Needlenose, then. Do you want me to bring them here, or do you want to come out and see them?"

She isn't sure to whom Otgar refers, but she is sure of what she means. If Shefali leaves the ger, she may be mobbed again. Word of her transformation spread quickly—how could it not?—and the remaining Qorin were eager for Shefali's blessings. Eager to see her at all, really. She'd done what she could to help the survivors. Healing was not within her realm of command, but hardiness was; she could grant her people the strength to endure their injuries with a bit of kumaq and some kind words. She'd done this for everyone who asked. It had taken the better part of her evening.

If she leaves the ger again now, they may ask her for another helping.

She would be fine with that in any other circumstance—but the army must be moving soon. Shizuka is somewhere within the city, trapped somewhere in the towers of Iwa. To think of the horrors she might be enduring sours Shefali's stomach to no small end; they cannot simply sit idle while it happens.

They have to save her.

And, more important to the Qorin and the world at large, they must kill the Traitor and his foul servants.

"Bring them in," Shefali says.

Otgar nods. She stands again and heads for the door. Sakura hops up after her, though her tiredness lends her limbs a clumsiness Shefali isn't used to seeing from her. The two of them don't talk about it as they leave—Otgar simply glances over her shoulder and nods.

Shefali is alone for only a few minutes. Soon, someone else calls for her to catch her dogs. This time it is Sakura, making a valiant effort at a notoriously difficult Qorin phrase. It shares no syllables at all with anything in Hokkaran—all voiced deep in the back of the throat, wet and alive.

"There still aren't any dogs," Shefali calls in Hokkaran.

The door opens once more. Otgar and Sakura are there, but so, too, are five Qorin Shefali has never met before, dressed in Hokkaran robes. She realizes who they are the moment she gets a whiff of them: castoffs from the Northern Qorin, who lived just south of the pine forests. They'd given in to the Traitor's influence, and it had led them over the mountains to this foul place, where he had given them these clothes. Their eyes are glassy and distant, focused on the struts of the ger instead of the silver god within it; they do not move except when Otgar shoves them forward. One by one, the captured Qorin stumble into the ger, and one by one they stand stock-straight as if nothing has happened.

The Queen of Ikhtar could not hope for such wonderful pets.

The sight of them brings Shefali to her feet at once. The heat of her anger threatens to melt the chill of her divinity, and yet this passes in a flash of vapor from her open mouth. His time will come.

But until it does, she has her people to care for.

"Where?" she asks. The lost Qorin all turn toward her as she speaks, though she cannot say any of them are looking at her.

"The scouts picked them up from within the city walls. They were going on about that wretch, but they shut up and went limp the second they left through the gates."

The second they left the Traitor's most potent sphere of influence. All the lands behind the Wall were his creations—Shefali could feel his putrid touch in all things—but only the towers were the seat of his power. He might do anything he wished there.

"Are you going to help them?" says Sakura. In her tiredness, she is slurring. "Maybe the kumaq would help?"

Shefali nods. "Get me three skins."

Sakura bows from the shoulders and heads back out. Otgar stays, watching Shefali as she circles the five lost Qorin.

The scent of the Traitor is upon them like a burial shroud—but they are not dead. Something of their old selves, their old scents, remains underneath. Her nose itches. Shefali pulls the nearest one close to her and sniffs his cheeks.

Barshikigur, that is his name, of some northern compound Shefali can't quite make heads or tails of. She hears it all the same when she breathes of him, though—she sees him stalking through the forests in the dead of night. Her stomach rumbles along with his. It has been twenty days since his wife had a good meal, and ten since they were able to feed his son anything but a mouthful of jerky.

Hunting so late at night has its own risks. His clanmates have a false bird cry they use to differentiate between a night stalker and a night predator, but Barshikigur has never been fond of it. You start crying like a bird in the middle of the night, and you'll scare away the stags.

But he's willing to risk being shot by someone else's arrow.

He's heard the others whispering, too. Something else lurks in the forests these days. A spider, they say, as tall as the tallest pine. He doesn't believe such talk. The people who believed that sort of thing also believed there were still dragons and lion dogs if you knew where to look.

And so he hunts.

Hours it took him to find something worth killing—and even then, it is a wolf. To kill one would bring bad luck and misfortune down upon him. Eating a wolf is the same as eating a Qorin, so far as the sanvaartains are concerned.

But he cannot care. He has lost too many children already.

Forward.

He draws his bow, nocks an arrow.

It looses into the night as the spider's mandibles hook into the back of his neck.

All of this Shefali sees as clearly as if she were Barshikigur, all of this she experiences. She rubs at the base of her spine, half-expecting to feel two scars there, but this new body of hers has only a few. Her missing eye, the half circle on her palm, the starburst at her shoulder, and the line around her neck—only these remain to her.

None from the Spider.

She presses her lips together.

"Barshikigur," she says to the man. He does not move, though his ears jog up and down as if he is unclenching his jaw. "You may not be able to hear me now—but hold on."

"Is that his name?" says Otgar. "You just know names now?"

"I can smell them," Shefali says.

Otgar puffs. "Guess it's convenient," she says, "for a demonslayer."

Not for a god. She can't bring herself to say it, Shefali knows. Not even when her cousin is so drastically transformed.

Another call to catch their dogs. Otgar answers this time, telling Sakura that she can stop trying so hard. It's Otgar who opens the door and Otgar who gingerly takes the skins from the much smaller Sakura, setting them down at Shefali's feet. The lost Qorin stand unmoving through all of this—even when Sakura bumps into one and hastily bows in apology. It is a little strange to Shefali: in many ways Sakura is nothing like the uptight courtiers she's known in Fujino, but in many, she is not so different at all. Shefali cannot imagine a Qorin apologizing for that light brush against someone's shoulder. In a ger, there is no such thing as privacy.

And she is in a ger now—that will make this easier. She thinks it will, at any rate. To aim at an iron ring suspended from a branch atop a mountain and know you will not miss: this is godhood. As impossible as the thought of freeing them may be, she is certain that she can do it. Not certain in the way that Shizuka is: all bluster and arrogance, all fire and denial of her own fears. No, this is the quiet certainty that never needs to assert itself.

Shefali picks up one of the skins of kumaq. With her thumb, she pops off the lid.

"Bowl?" asks Shefali. Otgar walks to her nightstand—a tiny thing scarcely used. After a few seconds of rooting around, she produces a Hokkaran-style rice wine saucer. Shefali and Sakura both tilt their heads.

Otgar glowers. "It was a gift."

"From whom?" Sakura asks before she can stop herself from asking such a question.

Otgar looks straight at her. The air goes thick with the weight of things she wants to say but, for whatever reason, will not. She smells of hardwood and regret. "It doesn't matter anymore," she says at length.

Sakura's shoulders slump a little.

They really will have to talk, the two of them, when they are ready. But that is a concern for another day. Shefali swirls the kumaq in the skin before pouring some out into the bowl. The Traitor created his affliction with blood, seawater, and ink. The seas have no influence over the Silver Steppes, over the Qorin people, and so Shefali will forsake its inclusion. Blood and kumaq—that is all she will need.

It takes only a thought to grow her nails into talons. How it still surprises her! There is no pain, no stiffness accompanying the small transformation. The Mother spoke of her body mirroring the Moon—perhaps the full moon is what grants her such comforts. She thinks for a moment of what the waning moon will be like. A shudder overtakes her.

But it is a sacrifice worth making.

Pain is never something to aspire to, never something to desire—but sometimes, just sometimes, it is something to accept.

The cut Shefali makes along her forearm is one such pain. Quick and sharp, already burning a little. It occurs to her just before she wipes her finger along its length that she has not seen her own blood since her ascension.

She tells herself that if it is black, it is the depths of night, not the shade of the Traitor's influence. She tells herself that she is ready for whatever the outcome may be.

When Shefali holds her bloody hand over the bowl of kumaq, she sees silver. Bright silver, at that, swirling with potential and power. A smile spreads across her face.

This body is hers, truly hers.

A deep breath fills her lungs with cold. For eight heartbeats she holds it there. For eight heartbeats she thinks of what it means for her to be here, in a ger her cousin beat into existence, among people who would give their lives to save one another. She thinks of her family: of her mother's pragmatic decision to kill her brothers if it meant uniting them; of her grandmother's recalcitrance; of her great-great-grandmother, an Ikhthian storyteller who longed for silver and blue; of her brother, trapped in Fujino, and the niece she does not really know, and in Xian-Lai, the nephew she has never met.

The souls that granted Shefali this new body hum like strings in perfect tune. They, too, know these things. The note they play is one that cannot be sounded by mortal voices—but it is one that leaves Shefali's lips as easily as her wife's name.

And as it leaves her, so, too, does her breath; so, too, does a small part of her fathomless soul. The temperature in the ger plummets. Hackles rise on Otgar's and Sakura's skin; the lost Qorin shiver though they do not know why; a thin layer of snow coats Otgar's nightstand. Ice floats atop the milky white in the saucer.

Two drops of blood land atop its surface. How like the moon, this image! Yes, it is ready.

Shefali stands. Barshikigur does not move, does not look at her, but she can smell something in his scent quickening. Hope, perhaps. She dips two fingers into the mixture and smears it across his upper lip, where the scent will reach him.

One breath, two. She watches with the saucer in hand, eager for the moment of severance. To ease the pain of another, to shift her form—these are simple miracles.

To break the Traitor's control? If she managed that, she may well live up to being Tumenbayar's successor.

Three breaths, four. Silence in a ger is a strange thing, as foreign as an Axion sword, and yet that is what prevails now.

Five breaths, six. Her heartbeat is heavy as a horse's.

Seven breaths, eight—*there*.

It happens quickly enough that if she had not been studying Barshikigur, she would have missed it. Like the last snowfall of the year melting off the branches of a pine tree—a silver rim around his eyes dissolving into green. His lips part as he sucks in a breath, as he lets out an awful groan. His hands fly out to his sides to grasp something that is not there—and he falls backwards as his legs give out from under him.

The Warrior Moon is quick to catch him. She slings his arm around her shoulder and helps him up. Shaking, quivering—is this a man who has been liberated, or a man who has discovered he is accused of murder? Her heart sinks at the sight, at the sound.

"Barshikigur?" she says. "You are safe here."

"This is my own ger," Otgar offers. The sight of one of their countrymen in distress is a catalyst for her; she's tucked her pipe back in her deel. "Beat it with my own two hands. You're welcome here, as long as you'd like to stay."

Barshikigur's eyes flick from Otgar to Shefali and back before settling on Shefali. It is as if he sees her then for the first time—he quiets as he realizes it is no ordinary woman who holds him up. Once more the snow melts for him, but this time it is the frost of his own fears, leaving only awe in its wake.

"Tumenbayar?"

Shefali smirks. "Something like that," she says.

But it is Otgar who shakes her head, Otgar who sucks her teeth. "I just told you, you're in my ger, and there you go insulting my cousin. This is Barsalai Shefali Alsharyya, and she's our new god."

"New . . . ?" he says, but he uses an old word for it—one Shefali hasn't heard since she was a girl and her grandmother was flinging it about. *New, new, new, that's all you care about, Alsha.*

Yet revulsion is the farthest thing from Barshikigur's face. Awe, yes, but joy lends color to his cheeks as well. A wide grin breaks out across his face like the first rays of dawn. He looks her up and down—really seeing her this time—and squeezes her around the waist.

"Let me smell you," he says. "The woman who came to save us."

HEALING THE OTHERS is much the same.

The finest painter in Hokkaran history is Yusumi Shoteikai. In the Jade Palace, there are two of his originals framing either side of the entrance to the Emperor's chambers. Both depict the pine forests of Shiseiki in an abstract fashion—dramatic smears of ink, with the white of the paper suggesting morning fog. Both are as tall as Shefali. The differences between the two are slight—the slope of the branches, the curl of the unseen fog clouds, the tiny needles falling in one of them. Such simple images should not be able to stop one in their tracks as readily as they do—but there is beauty in that simplicity. There is confidence in it, there is faith, there is the sublime wonder of nature itself.

The woods on a cloudy morning, perfectly captured.

Yusumi Shoteikai painted nothing but this image. There are hundreds of them scattered all over Hokkaro—black trees, white fog. Twenty years he painted them, until his fingertips carried a black stain no matter how often he washed them. Thirty years, forty—when his eyes started to give, the trees grew as fluffy as the clouds they suggested, and yet he kept painting.

Shefali often wondered how anyone could do something so many times and still love it.

She does not wonder that anymore.

Two hundred Qorin she heals that first day—and she delights in meeting each one for the first time. In learning their names and hearing their stories. In telling them that she is here now; that she will not be leaving them; that together, they will crush the man who did this beneath their horses' hooves, and they will drink kumaq from his skull.

She speaks two hundred promises—and she means every one.

In and out of her ger, they come, filing in like ants. The scouts find more and bring them to the ger just as Shefali finishes freeing the latest arrivals. Burqila and Captain Munenori had intended to move out that day, but confronted with the stream of incoming Qorin—what are they to do except accept them? To argue otherwise flies in the face of common decency and notions of honor both.

But it is not just the lost Qorin who gather outside the ger. The clan does, too. It is a Bell before Burqila Alshara is called away from the war room, a Bell before she goes to see for herself what all the commotion is about. When she does, the sight almost brings her to her knees. There is her daughter, her own flesh and blood, silver-haired and shining in the darkness of the ger. There is her daughter, who suckled at her breast, freeing her ancestors and clansmen with the milk of a mare.

Astonishment and pride, nostalgia and hope, these things color her scent. One breath, and Shefali can see her own birth playing out across her eyes. Her mother stayed in the saddle until the very last moment. Two legs spread out in front of her, two knobby brown knees; the night sky stretched out above, hoary with winter frost; Tsetseg and Zurgaanqar telling her when she needed to breathe and when she needed to push. A wrinkled, purple child emerging. Two pine needles falling from a clear sky onto the girl's forehead.

It is a strange thing to see one's own birth. Stranger still after shucking off her old body. She tells herself that it is still her, still Barsalai Shefali, and the way her mother throws her arms around her confirms this.

Burqila runs her fingers through her daughter's silver hair. The lost Qorin Shefali has just freed—a messenger from the eastern clans—grins.

"This," she says, "this is why our people will survive."

And perhaps she is right.

For there is something to be said about it, this closeness. Later that night, when Burqila braids her daughter's hair, she binds together more than those wild shocks. The whole clan is gathered around.

All of them.

Those who survived the great pit only a few days ago, those who survived the Qorin Invasion of Oshiro, those who fell to the plague only to break free of it—all of them gather around Burqila's folding chair. Shefali sits between her mother's knees with her head inclined a little forward as her mother twists and twists. The braid she earned for killing the tiger, the braid she earned for mastering herself, the braid she earned for killing a demon—each is as wide as her thumb.

But these new braids are thin, almost impossibly so.

There will need to be room for two hundred.

Her mother's deft fingers fly through their work. She speaks not a word through the Bell and a half it takes her to braid what remains of Shefali's hair, though Shefali does not expect her to. The songs of their people fill the silence. There is a song for this occasion, a song for a warrior getting a new braid, but it is a short one, and they will be here for hours. It is the song that begins the occasion, but not the one that ends it.

One of the younger Qorin sings a song of Burqila's long-ago military victory: of the flames licking at the walls and the explosion that broke them, of the Qorin pouring into Oshiro like grains of rice through a funnel, of the rage that lent their sword arms strength, and the sorrow that bound them for surrender. It is a powerful song, a familiar one, and though the lost Qorin do not know the words, they lend their voices to the melody. But this is not the song that ends it.

A dirge rises from the weary souls of the lost Qorin. The melody is as old as it is heavy—a plodding thing, each syllable landing like the foot of a mourner walking to her mother's grave. Heavier, still, for the voices singing it. Shefali heard this song often as a child—sung whenever one of the infected was put down—and often wondered at the archaic turns of phrase it used. All her life she had thought it distant from real emotion—but hearing it now from the throats of those who wrote it convinces her otherwise. The doubled voicing, the buzz of traditional singing—these pierce her to her soul, and her shoulders shake with tears at the thought of those who could not join them here. But this—this is not the song that ends it, either.

The song that ends the evening is the mortar of their resolve.

It is a song about Tumenbayar, a song about the falling of the sun.

And it is her cousin who starts to sing.

Dorbentei, who has lost so much already. Her cousin, tears streaming down her face, her voice as boisterous as it is raw from the tears.

What is Shefali to do but join her? For her heart catches at the sight, and she knows this song as well as she knows her own names. The words come naturally to her. They fill her lungs with their old magic, their old stories, and they pour from her throat like proclamations, like prophecies.

*Teach us to saddle thunder,*
*Teach us to fly!*
*When the veil is torn asunder*
*We'll follow you into the sky!*

The chorus rises higher and higher. Part of her worries that the enemy will find them and attack them in the middle of all of this, but this is the human part of her, the mortal part of her. She knows they will not. Rikuto swore its eightfold oath. And even if it were to break that oath—the Warrior Moon can break the Demon General.

She is confident of that now.

As the song rises to the false heavens, violet and pink give way to the deep blue and silver. Barsalai Shefali's veins prickle with the cold.

Her mother finishes her last braid.

Shefali stands. She whistles for her horse, and her horse trots up to her. Shefali formed her anew herself from clay and milk.

It is the third day of the full moon. Tomorrow, she will start to ache again. Tonight, she can swing into the saddle. Tonight she can draw herself up and sit tall upon her horse's back. Tonight she can ride at full gallop around the camp and throw kumaq in her wake; tonight, she can bless the entirety of the Qorin.

Her people, her family.

Their voices rising into the night, their hopes swelling in her breast.

Tumenbayar's song is an old one.

But it is the one that Shefali sings that third night as she makes her rounds, as she looks on her people the way Yusumi Shoteikai looked on his paintings.

# O-SHIZUKA

## TWELVE

She does not sleep.

It isn't because she doesn't want to. She does want to, very much so—but the idea of sleeping in this place terrifies her more than she is willing to admit out loud. If she sleeps, she will leave herself vulnerable to him. He will slink into her room, and he will pour ink and water and blood in her ears, and she will lose all that she has worked for.

So no—she does not sleep.

But she does try to count the hours as well as she can. Every Bell, the Qorin servants recite their own strange versions of the Mandates. Her mother always told her routine is important—the same way she'd talk about cleaning or taking control of your own space. She cannot control her space here, not really, and so she counts the hours.

It has been sixteen Bells since she woke. Forty-eight hours. Two days, and too much of all of this already. Her head injury's healed, for the most part, but the sleeplessness has taken hold of her. By the first day without rest, she was a groggy, sluggish mess; somewhere along the line, a second wind had seized her and now refuses to let her go. *Awake,* her body tells her, *we must be awake—if we are not awake, then we are dying.*

And she has done enough dying for now.

So she is awake, and she is doing, doing, doing. The Traitor likes to keep her busy, she has learned. All proper women are busy in his point of view—idleness leads to wandering minds, and wandering minds list ever toward rebellion. For the first time since her childhood, she must endure the lectures of tutors—but he has not even sent her anything amusing.

Rikuto teaches her history in the morning, or tries to; she pays no attention to its ramblings. The cities it speaks of and the peoples it refers to have no bearing on her and her life. Her Hokkaro exists below the Wall; her Hokkaro always has. The lost cities are no more than curiosities; the people who now fill them a twisted insult. The rice and plain soup it brings her at the start of the lesson remain uneaten. It leaves on both mornings with plumes of smoke coming from its ears.

Her father visits afterwards. He asks her why she is not eating. "Shizuru," he says, leaning close, "are you . . . are you well?"

She tells him that she is, and she holds the rice in her mouth. She even mimes swallowing. The thought of him worrying over her is too much to bear, which is of course why Yamai has sent him.

"And you? You won't leave me to break my fast alone, will you, Father?"

She knows that it's a mistake as soon as she says it. He does not think of her as his daughter; he is expecting his brash and unkempt wife. If she tells him the truth of where he is—where they are—it will break him. See how he purses his lips!

"Is it the air here?" he asks. "There's a chill to it I'm not fond of. It's Nanatsu; it should be warmer than this."

Shizuka flinches at the mention of Nanatsu, at the memory of the ninth.

"It must be," Shizuka says. "Never had this problem in Nishikomi."

She's been to Nishikomi perhaps twice in her life, both times at the behest of her mother, and both times in the middle of the summer, when it was about as hot as Hokkaro ever got. But it seems like the sort of thing her mother would say.

"Your accent's fading," her father teases her, and she pretends to laugh along, murdering a little of herself in the process. "If your mother were here, we'd never hear the end of it."

Shizuka never met her grandmother—Shizuru had never been fond of her to begin with, and visiting was a difficult thing to do given all their collective responsibilities. She'd gotten word at fifteen that her grandmother had died and thought little of it save to send handwritten prayers to the family estate.

How cold that feels now. How final.

She watches her father eat. Part of her wants to find some flaw in it. If this man is not really her father, then she has no obligations to him, after all, and can proceed with her plans unbothered.

But—there. He drops a grain of rice onto the back of his left hand. Instead of simply raising his left hand to his mouth and scooping it up with his tongue, he picks it up with his chopsticks—a single grain of rice.

Yes, he really is her father.

There is so much she wants to say to him. So little of it are things she can actually say, given the circumstances. She wants to tell him that she begins every day by writing his poetry for practice. She wants to tell him that she is grateful that he is so famous, for she sees and hears him everywhere, and in some ways they have never really been apart. She wants to tell him that is a lie, and that she has missed him the way she now misses the heart that used to beat in her chest.

But all he wants to do is plan out the rest of their year.

"Yuichi's boy is getting married soon," he says. "He sent me an invitation. I know how you feel about weddings, Zuru, but it would mean the world to him. . . ."

"Will there be wine?" she asks. This lie, at least, comes effortlessly.

O-Itsuki chuckles to himself. He finishes the last of his soup. "Somehow I doubt there will be enough to appease you," he says.

An animal craving settles in her gut. She wants wine. If she drank enough, perhaps her slurring would come close to her mother's accent, and he would not question her so much.

"Well, they can try," says Shizuka. "And so long as Burqila is there, it is bound to be enjoyable."

He tilts his head. "Burqila?" he says. "And here I used to worry about how close the two of you were."

Like stepping into what you think is a puddle only to sink in knee-deep. Shizuka drinks of the tea on her plate. Eating is the terrible thing to do when you're in another world, so the stories go—but drinking is fine.

It does nothing to clear her mind.

"I . . ."

Four knocks at the door. Her next tutor has arrived. She wonders briefly what her father thinks is going on. O-Shizuru never took meetings and did not have any tutors at all.

"Your Eminence, Prince O-Itsuki-lor," calls the servant in her borrowed voice, "your next appointment awaits the honor of your presence."

Ah. So that is how the Traitor is playing this.

Her father sighs with resignation—only partly exaggerated. He scoops the last of his rice into his mouth. As genteel as ever, he waits until he is done chewing to speak once more.

"I am coming," he says. Then, more quietly: "I am sorry for all of this, Zuru. I'll be with you as soon as I can, but there's so much to deal with. You know how everyone hates discussing anything important with Iori."

"I hate even to look on him," says Shizuka, "and so I cannot blame them."

"Is that why you think they're after me? My good looks?" Itsuki teases.

Shizuka's stomach twists. She does not know what to say. Tears well up behind her eyes, the pressure mounting without a suitable escape. Her head hurts.

Every day since his death, Shizuka has wished for her father to return to her—but as her father. Not like this.

The words catch in her throat. Overcome by shame and revulsion, she can say nothing to him at all. This, too, is its own suffering: to see his eyes narrow, to see the smile melt off his face, to know that she is the cause. In all her memories, he is so happy, so serene . . .

"Try not to get into any fights while I'm away," he says, rising. Shizuka recognizes this, at least—it is an old joke her parents used to share.

"So long as you don't seduce any of your fans," she answers.

"I'd never dream of it," he says, but the words leave him like a strained reflex.

The door slides open. She watches him go, biting her finger to keep from making any sound.

It is then that she smells the burning.

Something about the scent of burning has always fascinated Shizuka, from her childhood. She does not remember her early attempt on her future wife's life, but she does remember the scent of her own burning flesh as she knocked over the nearby brazier in her passion. How young she had been then—her resistance to fire had not yet blossomed within her. There is something precious about that awful smell, something transient and mortal.

And there is something precious in this scent too. Shizuka checks to see if she is burning now, with a level of resignation most often seen on provincial bureaucrats: *what is it this time?*

Fire will not hurt her—but it might entertain her.

Yet when she looks down, Shizuka sees that it is not her own flesh that is burning but the flowers tucked into her belt: the violets she'd given Baoyi.

*If you ever have need of me . . .*

Can Shizuka even do much to help from a place like this? Yamai's power may well override her own; it may be that she is forced to watch as Fujino burns.

But her niece is calling for her, and Shizuka has so little family left. If this fails, at least she will have tried.

With her bare hands Shizuka plucks the burning violet. She expects that the fire does not burn her, and it doesn't—but she does not expect for it to feel so cool against her skin.

Shizuka tilts back her head and drops the flaming flower into her mouth. When she swallows, she feels the cold flames tickling their way down her throat.

A blink.

When she opens her eyes, she is in Fujino.

Two things occur to her.

First: this is not her parents' apartment within the palace. This is a room she's visited perhaps twice in her life—the archivist's quarters. Tall stacks of scrolls line the walls, with some unrolled and displayed. The air here is stale; she smells old paper and older ink.

Second: it is not her niece who called her.

The years have been kind to Kenshiro. The close-trimmed beard he now keeps has filled in, giving him the look of an old general. Crow's-feet make the green of his eyes more vibrant. For some men, time is a sculptor, and it seems as if that is the case for him. Where is the shy young father Shizuka left behind? Even his bearing has changed: he sits straight-backed and imperious, his robes trimmed with Imperial Gold.

"Shizuka-lun," he says. "It's really you."

Before she can say anything to this, he has stood from his proper seat and thrown his arms around her. She expects that he will pass right through her—but instead she feels his arms as if he stood with her beyond the Wall. He has gotten *more* solid, somehow.

She isn't sure what to do. Embraces are not . . . She hasn't had to deal with them very often in her life, and particularly not embraces from men. She finds herself going stiff in his arms simply because she does not know how to hold herself. When at last he holds her at arm's length, she almost wants to sigh in relief—but to do that would be heartless.

There is such wonder in his eyes, after all. And that he is able to touch her . . . her mind is beginning to buzz with possibility. Whatever hold the Traitor might have on her, he cannot stamp out the embers of her power.

In that way, it is thrilling to be here among the things he cannot touch.

"You haven't aged at all," Kenshiro says with a broad smile. "The scar! Your ear . . ."

"I'm happy that you remember," says Shizuka, for she can think of little else to say. Was there a reason Kenshiro used one of the three remaining violets, or does he just miss her? She finds that she does not care either way. If he has need of her then she has an excuse to stay, an excuse to leave the false Palace behind for a few hours. How long will it be before she is noticed? Time passes slowly there. She might be here for days, poring over old tomes, having tea with her niece . . .

And if Kenshiro simply missed her? Well, for once, she would not mind his wanton abuses of privilege.

"I drew you," he says. He shuffles through some papers on his desk. Shizuka notices, as he walks to it, that there is a stiffness to his right leg. She's seen that sort of limp before—on rainy days she develops it herself. An old war injury.

But Kenshiro, with a war injury?

Just what has happened in their absence?

At last he finds the page he was looking for. Pages, really. He holds up four large sheets with portraits drawn upon them. Kenshiro is no artist—the likenesses are clumsy, at best, but he's gotten the important parts. Shizuka's scar and mangled ear, her dark hair and sharp features, large whorls of orange for eyes. Shefali's face, though . . . It is different in each image. In some she has the full cheeks of her youth; in some . . .

"Every week," Kenshiro says, "I draw the two of you. It forces me to remember what you look like. I also write out our family history every month and reread all the previous entries, checking for any discrepancies. I . . . it's been so long. I thought . . ."

"I stand corrected," Shizuka says. "If you're doubting me, you mustn't remember me very well at all."

He laughs, the sort of laugh that draws tears in the midst of it. How precious this laughter is to him! For his eyes go wide, as if he has seen something more sacred than the god manifesting in his archives.

And in this earnestness he does at last what he has tried to do for all of their lives: he wins Shizuka over, and makes her smile. For in spite of where her body may be, her soul is still with her family.

Though, she supposes—something of her body, too. It is strange, being partly corporeal.

Curious, she begins to pace around the room. Or, well, attempts to. She has manifested in her war boots and she does not dare walk around in them. Shefali spoke of will being paramount in situations like this—she looks down at her armor and wills herself into something more suited for the occasion. Imperial Gold, Sunset's Promise Amber, Light of Morning Yellow . . .

One moment she is in armor; the next she is in her robes. Gone, her boots. She may wander at her leisure.

How strange. This doesn't feel at all like manifesting for war, or when she'd done so to raise the Wall of Flowers.

"Look at you!" Kenshiro says. "How did you do that? Come to think of it, your scar—it's gone gold now, and the tips of your hair . . ."

Shizuka pinches a few strands between her fingers. Small fires swallow the ends. Watching the colors move reminds her of the feather Shefali had brought back from Sur-Shar. Part of her is sad she cannot see her hair swish about as she walks; it must be mesmerizing.

"I told myself to, I suppose," Shizuka says.

"Oh, you can't say it as simply as that," says Kenshiro. He's scrambling for his brush, grinding up the ink. "There must be *more detail*. For the records."

She takes her first steps through the room. The mats feel cool against the bare skin of her feet. As she approaches a desk stacked high with texts in Old Hokkaran, she lets her knee knock against the corner. Her robes absorb most of the blow—but she feels it all the same.

"Is that why you've summoned me, Kenshiro?" she asks. "For your records?"

He stops grinding his ink. His shoulders slump, and for a moment, he looks like his old self. "It isn't like that," he says. "I thought . . .

I hadn't seen you in so long. I didn't want to forget. And there's so much we need to talk about."

"Yes," she says. She had only meant to tease him earlier—but she should have known better, given their past. "Much has changed, no? I'm sure you are eager to tell me everything."

Down, the brush and the ink—he sits near his desk and shrinks. "Yes and no," he says pensively. "No one remembers your name, or . . . Is my sister with you?"

Shizuka busies herself looking at a stack of old poetry scrolls so that she does not have to look at her wife's brother. With one finger she pushes at the edge of one and it goes tumbling down, unspooling itself along the way.

"She is elsewhere, Kenshiro, and if you question me any more about it I will leave."

When he makes that face, he looks just like Shefali. "Shizuka-lun—"

"Don't make a habit of questioning gods," Shizuka says. She makes herself sound confident, sound assured.

He could press the issue—she does not have it in her to leave, in truth. Not when she is so desparate for real company. That he allows her time to gather herself instead is a testament to his growth.

He runs a hand over his beard. "Do you want the news of the Empire first, or news of your family?"

"The Empire," says Shizuka. She hates herself a little already for saying it, but it is the more imperative of the two. What use will saving the Empire be if there is nothing to return to?

"Dao Doan's independent now," he says. "When we attempted to establish trade with them, they posted armies along their borders. The formal response was that we had taken too much already for any sort of trade to be meaningful."

Expected. It stings, though in truth, that's a perfectly reasonable reaction from them, considering how Hokkaro seized their nation. "What is their relationship with Xian-Lai?"

"Good, so far as I can tell," Kenshiro says.

Shizuka narrows her eyes. "So far as you can tell?" she says.

He frowns. "Baozhai has . . . things are different when we meet as sovereigns. She must guide her people."

Shizuka thinks of the garden. "She misses you terribly."

"Did—have you seen her?" he says. His expression is a flickering lantern—bright at first, and then darker than before. "Of course you have. The two of you were always close."

"I . . . She couldn't hear me when I visited her. Interaction was not possible," Shizuka explains. "It . . . it hurt, to see her so close and be unable to touch her."

She picks up one of the scrolls as a demonstration. To her surprise, the paper goes gold beneath her hands—but thankfully, the characters are still readable beneath.

Kenshiro's eyes widen a little. He swallows. "You're really here, though," he says.

"So it seems," answers Shizuka. "Perhaps because you called the flowers for this. When I visited Baozhai, it was through a morning glory I found beyond the Wall."

"Interesting . . . ," says Kenshiro. He tugs at his beard. "This isn't your physical body."

"Isn't it?" Shizuka says. She bites her foreknuckle—it does hurt. "I can feel perfectly well, interact with my environment—"

"I can see straight through you," Kenshiro says. "This is only a manifestation. There aren't any texts about this, you understand, but we have some records of what it was like when the Heavenly Family visited their temples. In all cases, the gods were described as 'gauzy.' As you are at present."

He's gotten started. She wants to know more about the world without her, and he wants to know more of what being a god is like. The two of them are like two duelists running through different drills.

"There were exceptions. I have it on good esteem that the Daughter manifested in the flesh more often than not; her priests claimed it was because she wanted to feel the world in the true way. Perhaps the same is possible for you, under the right conditions. The right flowers . . . should I be planting daffodils?"

"Kenshiro," Shizuka says sternly. "This visitation won't last forever." Though she cannot bring herself to tell him the reason.

He looks up, having lost himself in thought.

"Right. Well. The trouble is that there's so much to tell you and so little time to do it all in. Shiratori hasn't been doing well, and Ryoujitul's been talking my ear off about invading Dao Doan. I had to put a stop to that. We just granted them their freedom; we can't go repeating our past mistakes."

Shizuka tilts her head. "What do you mean 'put a stop to that'?" she says. "I've never known you to be firm."

He laughs a little. It is the laugh of a much younger man. "You haven't known me recently," he says. "I may not be a duelist, but I remember a bit of wrestling." There is a proud glimmer in his eyes as he continues. "He called me weak in front of the entire court. Red in the face, frothing at the mouth—the man was an animal. He said that if the Phoenix herself had not granted my daughter and me the throne, he would mutiny."

"Is that the story?" Shizuka asks.

"Yes," says Kenshiro. "You're quite a mythic figure; no one seems to know where you came from, and most allege you brought the Empire a thousand years of peace before Yamai took the throne—"

Now it is Shizuka who flinches. The scroll in her hands burns to ash. "Don't say his name," she says.

"That . . . that scroll was . . ."

A pang of guilt. She hadn't meant to destroy the thing; it was only that her anger welled up like a flame, consuming, consuming . . .

"Sakura-lun will bring you better records from her travels," Shizuka says by way of apology. "Please. Continue your story."

It is a little while before Kenshiro heeds her. Even then, he does not quite recapture his earlier enthusiasm. "I told him that if he wanted to mutiny, he was welcome to try and kill me."

"You *what*?" says Shizuka. "Kenshiro! If I had said that in court, your wife would have flayed me alive!"

"Well, I wasn't thinking about my wife at the time," he says. "It's my thinking that if I am your regent, for your heir, then I should be as much like you as possible. So I did what I thought you would have done."

He's smiling a little as he speaks. Shizuka isn't sure what to do with him.

"He stabbed you," she says flatly. "In the leg."

"So you noticed. Yes, he charged the throne and stabbed me in the leg, so I picked him up and drove him face-first into the floor."

Who is this man that sits before her? For he is not the scholar she left behind. So much has happened.

How many years has it been? She's loath to ask, lest he realize how little control she has over her own situation. Baoyi was a young teenager the last time they met. Kenshiro and his wife were of the same age, which was uncommon enough in the courts to be well noted. Of course, Shizuka knew Baozhai's age well, it being a common teasing point between the two of them: she was seven years Shizuka's elder. Being that Baozhai gave birth (auspiciously, just as she'd planned) on her own twenty-eighth birthday . . . Kenshiro would have been just nearing forty during her last visit to the palace.

He was past that, now. Forty-five, perhaps.

Which meant they'd been away for eleven years already.

Shizuka finds herself leaning on the table for support, unable to summon the words for the isolation in her heart.

He draws himself back up, regaining a bit of his confident posture.

"He hasn't troubled me since," says Kenshiro. "But I have, ah, earned a bit of a reputation for violence as a result. It's a good thing Baoyi does most of the ruling, these days. Seven years ago when Hanjeon left the Empire, she kept everyone in line without lifting a single finger. There's nothing better she loves than peace. Watching her negotiate tax rates and write new laws, watching her visit other lords, watching her flourish . . ."

Shizuka can hardly think of ruling as flourishing.

"You would like her," says Kenshiro. "You would be proud of the work she's doing. She's reduced our army by a third. All Baoyi wants is peace on the continent—peace between all the parts of herself."

As Kenshiro continues, his voice grows more and more tender. His eyes glaze over a little bit and he looks over Shizuka's shoulder rather than straight at her.

An Empire of Peace. Shizuka had never bothered to dream of such a thing. That her niece has made it her foremost concern . . .

How sweet, how bitter, this wine.

"Kenshiro," she says. The lump in her throat surprises her. "Is there anything else I need to know? About the Empire?"

It's a specification she doesn't want to have to make. She wants to hear more of Baoyi and Yangzhai, of Baozhai, of their friends and family. Her heart is in knots, wondering what might have happened to them.

But you cannot rule with your heart.

And yet Kenshiro has himself sat on the throne, or behind it, for thirteen years. He, too, knows something of duty. "Your Wall has held," he says.

"Even in the mountains?" Shizuka says in a hushed voice.

"We've patrols there," he says. "Since you left, we've seen far less of the enemy coming through. I used to think it was because you'd killed him—but you haven't, have you?"

*Have you?*

What a weight those words have! How harshly they land on her ears! Anger flares around her; the flames licking at her hair and skin go blue.

"I'm going to kill him," she says. "You have my word on that. I will crush him, I will keep Baoyi safe, and I will preserve our country."

Kenshiro gets to his feet and walks over to Shizuka's desk, laying a hand on one of the books. "Do you mean to take the throne again when all of this is through?"

The question knocks her breathless. Does she mean to take the throne again? Obviously, she does. She is the rightful ruler of Hokkaro and its provinces. She and Shefali have been able to rule together for only a scant few months—and that just barely. There's so much left for them to do—so many functions to attend, so many proclamations she still wants to make. A festival in honor of her mother. Reworking the Challenge of the Sixteen Swords to *truly* allow anyone who wants to join, instead of charging a registration fee. Forging a stronger relationship with the Qorin—one that they can both benefit from, one that is safe for the riders of the Silver Steppes.

So many things left to do.

And—with a sigh—she realizes how many of them she hates. Arguing for a new festival would mean arguing with all the priests at once. That is difficult enough as an impartial sovereign; she cannot imagine what it will be like as a god. Her mother's birthday had been the twenty-eighth of Nishen; that's already the Festival of Lanterns. The arguments . . . *Why does this woman deserve greater attention than the fires of Heaven?*

*Because Heaven would not be burning without her.* That is what she wants to say to the conjured courtiers, to those who cannot hear her and will not listen.

Reworking the tournament would mean speaking to the governor of Fujino, and that woman never gave a single hairsbreadth in concession. The Qorin like her well enough now, but will that change when their numbers swell with the saved? Will that change if—and she hesitates even to think it—if Burqila Alshara does not return from beyond the Wall?

Thinking on it all gives her a headache.

This is her duty, she thinks. This is the weight placed upon her at her birth, when two pine needles fell on her forehead and declared her a god.

And yet—is it?

For the needles are their own burden, separate from the issue of her black-flecked blood. She was a princess before she was a god, but she will be a god long after she takes the throne.

Long after everyone she knows has forgotten her.

And they *will* forget. Kenshiro is staring at her now as if he cannot bear to imagine that she will leave, as if he is trying to memorize the jagged edges of her scar and the way her mangled ear curls in on itself.

Already she rules a people who do not love her.

Can she rule over them if they forget her? If they see only the Phoenix, eternal and brilliant, as dazzling to behold as a thousand suns turning in their heavenly revolutions?

If they forget Shefali, if they forget Shizuka—can she truly abandon herself to that degree?

Kenshiro watches her. He's been kind, allowing her this much time to think over her answer.

Life on an eternal throne—or shackling her niece's lineage to that same fate forever.

Which is cruel, which is kind?

Shizuka swallows. "I named Baoyi my heir," she says. "It has been years since I last saw the Empire, and it will be many yet before we return. This land is . . ."

*No longer my own.*

But it never was, was it? She has only been its custodian.

Kenshiro, as if sensing her difficulty, softens himself. "They say that the Phoenix will return to Hokkaro when our need is greatest."

Something like a smile tugs at the corner of Shizuka's lips. It isn't a particularly happy one. "How romantic," she says.

"I'm glad you think so," says Kenshiro. He winks. "I was the one who started the rumor."

Minami Shizuka has known Oshiro Kenshiro all her life. In truth, she cannot remember the first time she met him—he was simply there, lurking in the background of Shefali's existence, with a friendly smile and an ill-timed joke. This has always been his way—but the two of them have never truly been friends.

How could they be?

Kenshiro, the eldest son of one of her vassal lords, charming and well learned but utterly friendless.

Minami Shizuka, his sworn sovereign, charming and daring, but utterly friendless.

What have they *ever* had in common, aside from Barsalai Shefali?

But in that room, in that moment, something transpires between them. The air shifts. His eyes go a little softer and perhaps hers do, as well.

Shizuka looks out onto the archives, and she wonders: Will she ever behold this place again? Perhaps she should try to memorize the maps here, perhaps she should take the time to read the papers laid out onto the table, perhaps she should . . .

She has so many questions, but already her focus is starting to waver. She does not belong here, in this place, at this time.

Whatever home the palace once was to her—let it be Baoyi's now.

She swallows. Out of reflex, she reaches for her mother's sword, only to find she did not consciously manifest it. Her hand meets only empty air. She starts, drawing back, afraid of looking the fool in front of her own brother-in-law.

"Then let's hope you won't be needing me anytime soon," she says. "I have work to do."

Kenshiro nods. He glances down at the papers on the table, at Shizuka's hands, her palms made rough by the life she's chosen to lead. At last his eyes land on her face.

Their eyes meet.

"I'll keep the Empire as safe as I can for you," he says. He shifts his stance once, twice, and she knows that whatever he is about to say pains him. "Will you tell my sister I said hello? And that I'm thinking of her? Tell her that I spread kumaq in all four directions. Tell her that I remember."

Shefali is gone and Shizuka is not strong enough to tell him; his sister is gone and she cannot bring herself to say the words . . .

But Kenshiro is still a liar.

But he is lying.

She knows he is lying: it is as clear as the pale aura of silver around him, the light of lies that has plagued her since her youth. He does not spread kumaq for her. He does not remember. The sketches, the names, these are all that remain to him. All it will take is . . .

There is a bowl of ink and water on the table. Her eyes fall on it and, for a moment, she is lost to her own fearful memories, but a destructive thought overpowers them: all it will take for Kenshiro to forget his own family is the spilling of this ink.

Once those drawings are gone . . .

"Please, keep remembering." Shizuka closes her eyes.

"Shizu-lun," Kenshiro says. "Wait, there's something else I want to tell you—"

There is always something else he wants to tell her, there is always another complication. How foolish of her to think she could get away from them for very long.

"Don't go yet, it's about—"

It is time to go.

Within her soul Shizuka makes a cut.

When she opens her eyes, it is her prison that awaits her. She is alone in the false palace, alone eleven years and thirteen thousand li from the only home she has ever known.

Minami Shizuka hugs her knees tight to her chest and sobs, knowing full well the tears will never come.

# THE WARRIOR MOON

## THREE

Shefali does not sleep.

This does not surprise her. There is much to do, much to be done, much to see about doing. The scouts have tucked in for the night; there will be no more Lost Qorin tonight. She sits in the ger with Burqila Alshara, her aunt Dalaansuv, and Minami Sakura. Dorbentei, her cousin, snores on the floor. Captain Munenori is three gers away with the Hokkaran commanders, sharing the plans they've made, the information they've gained.

The very same thing that Burqila, Dalaansuv, and Sakura are doing now.

Burqila's gestures are heavy and a little languid; Dalaansuv's translations come slow; Sakura's sketches of Iwa lack her usual attention to detail. They are, all of the mortals, tired, and Shefali thinks to herself that it is strange that she isn't.

"Here's the deal," says Dalaansuv, gesturing lazily at the sketch. "Scouts say this wall's a little higher than the Wall of Stone. Not so tough, though. Brittle stuff; chips if you punch it barehanded. Circles the base of all the towers. Lookouts every four li."

The sketch reflects all of this: a wall more stately than functional, gates engraved with two unknown men holding up the arches. The doors—wood?—are shut. The lookouts themselves are squarish platforms. Sakura's done a separate sketch of them—they are scarcely wide enough for a single Qorin to lie in. Four of the possessed nonetheless take their positions on it. One on each side, two facing the front.

"How'd we get this?" Shefali says, pointing to the sketch of the lookout.

A small smirk tugs at Burqila's hard face. She tosses something onto the table: the tip of a Hokkaran-style bow.

"Our scouts are stupid," says Dalaansuv, "but brave."

The guards pictured must have been among the returned. Shizuka would be able to tell who they'd been from the strokes of the brush—but Shizuka isn't here.

"We can't kill them," Shefali says.

"That goes without saying," says Dalaansuv, who is saying it anyway. "Makes things harder, but there's no other way to do it."

"Can we capture all the guards?" asks Sakura.

"We're working on it," says Dalaansuv. "Scouts say they got half of them down, but no telling if there will be more in the morning."

Shefali rubs at her chin. Yamai held thousands of them beyond those walls; he would not hesitate to fling as many at the problem as were necessary. If they had a long time, they might be able to steal more of the lookouts, however it was the scouts were managing to do so—but Yamai wouldn't tolerate that for long.

A direct attack would force his hand.

But there is the question of direction.

She taps the door with one finger. "Strong?"

Burqila gestures, and Dalaansuv speaks. "Strong enough. Thick, too. The walls are a better shot, if you ask me; he won't be expecting us there."

Shefali nods. She reaches into her deel for the horses she painted in Xian-Lai, only to realize those had belonged to her old body. Looting her own corpse had seemed a blasphemous thing to do—but Shefali spares a thought for the keepsakes now lost in that grotesque cavern.

And so instead, the Moon breathes into her curved palm and wills the cold to form into a horse's shape. Her mother's eyes go wide; Sakura smiles in spite of her tiredness; Dalaansuv, it seems, cannot yet be bothered to summon any wonder.

Shefali places her little horses down—one at the gates and two eight li away.

"We blow the wall here," she says, gesturing to the two. "If we have explosives."

Dalaansuv's answer is hers alone: she huffs in mock offense loud enough to stir Dorbentei. "We *have* explosives. Don't you worry about that."

Burqila laughs a little as she signs something. Before Dalaansuv can interpret for her, Sakura speaks.

"Like mother, like daughter," she says.

Burqila's fingers fall still. She jerks her head in Sakura's direction, looking pleased with herself.

"Oh, is that what you were saying?" says Sakura. "I think I might be getting the hang of this."

It feels comfortable in a way that it perhaps shouldn't, considering all that has happened. Already she thinks of everything before her death as her former life. Keenly she feels the wants and desires of the Qorin—but the personal tragedies are a distant consideration.

Except for getting her wife back.

Burqila's hands are moving again.

"The foreigner says he will lead the forward army," says Dalaansuv. "We don't need to send our people there. Focus them all on blowing the wall."

The Hokkaran army *did* move as a single organ. It would be good to have them front and center, where they might absorb the brunt of Yamai's welcoming party. Shefali nods—and only then realizes that her mother is taking orders from her, and not the other way around.

Yes—this really is strange.

"Inside?" she asks, rather than focus on it.

"Not many people, from what we saw," says Dalaansuv. "A few

thousand, maybe. We think there are more in the towers, and more farther back in the city itself. At least one of those things has got to be a barracks."

"We will find it," says Shefali, "and destroy it while they sleep."

"They don't," says Sakura. "At least, they won't if they're anything like you. Once infected, it's rare that a blackblood sleeps at all."

Shefali purses her lips. "Then we destroy it while they're awake."

"Or," says Sakura, "you use some of that godly power of yours to conjure up darkness. You're able to see in it because you're the moon. My cousin doesn't have the same gift, so he won't either, and that means none of his people will."

Well considered. The Moon nods. Conjuring a darkness—a task insurmountable not long ago, now as easily conceived as opening a jar.

"You've blessed all of us already, so with any luck, the whole . . . darkness thing . . . won't bother us," says Sakura.

Burqila gestures again. "My sister says that we should test it," says Dalaansuv.

Cold still clings to Shefali's lungs. She expels some of it in a breath, and the fire they're gathered near is extinguished. It is dark in the ger then, but it is not absolute darkness. The false sun still shines in through the roof, for Shefali has not been extending her will to countermand it.

But she does then, at that moment, the way she had earlier while her mother braided her hair.

*Come, night,* she says, and the night heeds her. The sky above goes near black.

And yet the moon hangs in the sky! The ger is not truly dark. To banish the moon would kill her, Shefali knows this, but the army will need true dark if this is to work.

If she cannot banish the moon, then she can steal its light into herself. She pops her silver eye from its socket and holds it in her mouth. Nothing tells her that this is the right thing to do except her own instincts—it feels right. If her eye is the moon, then she need only swallow it.

But the human part of her is terrified at the idea of swallowing the moon.

So she simply holds it instead, and waits. The smooth metal of her eye goes craggy the longer it is in her mouth. Cold seeps into her like mint. She lets out a breath through her nose and it, too, is chilled.

Slowly the light of the moon fades. A deel thrown haphazardly over a lantern suppresses most of its light: so it is the case here. A fuzzy ring of silver surrounds the celestial body, but it banishes no shadows.

Darkness takes the ger.

But it has never troubled Shefali, and so she has no idea if her blessings are working. She crosses her legs and waits. There: her cousin shifts in her sleep, and Minami Sakura frowns at her for it—not with displeasure, but in sympathy. Only a moment later, Burqila begins to sign and Dalaansuv speaks for her.

"We can see," says Dalaansuv. "It's still dark, but . . ."

"It's as if we've been in the dark for years," says Sakura. "As if we know it."

*Because I have lived in the dark for years,* Shefali thinks. *Because I know it.* She does not say this, for it would be a smug sort of thing to say, and she does not want to be a smug sort of god.

"It works, then," Shefali says.

"Your mother says that she will do all her hunting at night, with the eyes that her daughter has given her," says Dalaansuv.

It's enough to rattle Shefali's focus. The night flickers; Sakura flinches and raises her arm.

"Barsalai?" asks Dalaansuv. "Did you mean to do that? If you want to give us cover, you can't have it giving out. The enemy will see us."

Burqila Alshara shakes her head with a bit of a smirk. She signs again. Dalaansuv rolls her eyes. "She says she'll try to be meaner to you on the battlefield."

The thought brings a small smirk to Shefali's lips. Even so, she does not allow the happiness to touch her overmuch—Dalaansuv has a point. Her focus will need to be absolute.

And so it shall be. She cannot disappoint her people.

"So—under the cover of your darkness, the Phoenix Guard attacks the gates while you and the Qorin make a gate of your own," Sakura says. "What happens when you get inside?"

"We free our people," Shefali says. She holds up a skin of kumaq, one she has already blessed. At her touch, it glows silver. Dalaansuv is still not impressed. "Using these."

Sakura's face goes hard. It is then, when she is scowling, that she looks the most like Shizuka—but perhaps that is because Shizuka has not done much else of late.

"And what is to stop the Traitor from killing my cousin in the meanwhile?"

Shefali sets down the skin of kumaq. The light goes out from it like an extinguished lantern.

"Shizuka will," she says.

"You said that demon took her sword," Sakura argues. "What's she going to do without a weapon?"

It is Shefali who looks a little self-satisfied now. "She's the Sun. When she awakes, she will make her own."

How sure she is of everything. It is . . . Shefali cannot see the future. To do so would go beyond her domain, beyond the realm of her powers. What is yet to come approaches like a beast in the night—but Shefali can see the shape of it.

And she has always been an excellent hunter.

"When she ascends?" Sakura asks. "You mean she hasn't already? But out on the bay—"

"Sleepwalking," Shefali says. Tapping her lungs, she continues. "She needs to wake *here*."

"Regardless of whether or not Barsatoq wakes from her nap," says Dalaansuv, "we need a workable plan. Who gets those skins? How do they use them? You're going to head straight for the palace—"

"No," says Shefali. "People first."

Sakura tilts her head at this—and it is then at last that Shefali earns her aunt's wonder. Dalaansuv's mouth hangs open to catch flies. Burqila's brows furrow, the green of her eyes muted in the shadow.

"You're not . . . You're not rushing headlong into danger to save her?" says Sakura. "After all she's done?"

They do not understand. They cannot feel the cold; they cannot hear the song of the stars or the rallying cries of the moribund sea.

"You were not listening," she says. She does not feel tired, but there is tiredness in her voice, as if she were explaining astronomy to a toddler. "The Sun needs no one to kindle her fires. So, too—she does not need me to save her. She will save herself."

It's the sort of grandiose statement Shizuka might make. A pot remains hot long after the flames have left it. So, too, does Shefali feel her wife's warmth out beyond the city's walls. She lives. She will live. She will burn bright, if only she remembers how. This flickering she's doing ill suits her.

"I will go to her," Shefali says. "She is the light of my soul—I *will* go to her. But if I neglect my people to do so, I am lower than shit."

Sakura clenches her delicate hands into fists. Shefali does not blame her for this. To her, it must look cold and distant, this decision. As she speaks, her shoulders tremble. "She would run to you. She did. When the pit opened up, she was . . . There wasn't any stopping that dumbass. And now you're going to take a detour before you save her? I thought you loved her—"

"I do. Gurkhan Khalsar will crack in two before I stop loving her. The rivers will flow to their sources, and there they will freeze, if my love for her should ever falter," says Shefali. "But you are treating a wolf like a dog."

Her voice is calm and level, but in her green eye is a queer fire, cold burning. Mist forms about her shoulders like a cloak.

And yet Sakura does not falter. It must be the Minami blood, holding as true as ever.

"I don't know if I like you as a god," she says.

Dalaansuv speaks, reading signs that Burqila shapes as she stands between Sakura and Shefali. "She isn't your god."

Like tearing a painting in two—the look on Sakura's face.

And yet Shefali cannot say her mother is wrong. She'd hoped that Sakura would be able to understand.

Perhaps that simple statement is the slap she needed. Sakura bites her lip. "I . . . ," she begins. She looks away, pinching her eyes and nose. "You're right. I just . . ."

Barsalai Shefali stands. She squeezes her mother's shoulder. Something in her is laughing—even as a god, she is not taller than Burqila. Burqila turns. The same thought must occur to her, for she smiles a little as she steps aside.

The Moon walks to her wife's cousin. She does not embrace Sakura this time—but there must be some gesture.

It is Shefali's Hokkaran blood that guides her. She bows from the shoulder. Her new braids shift against one another.

Sakura's scent goes sharp with disbelief. Shefali remains there long enough for that to fade—for the swell of emotion to overwhelm it.

"She and I will be as inseparable as two pine needles," Shefali says.

She means it, of course.

She has meant it every day of her life. She has meant it even when she did not know the words for it.

And it is that sincerity, in the end, that wins Sakura over.

More planning follows—but there passes not an hour in that ger without Shefali glancing to Iwa, to her wife's faint light.

# O-SHIZUKA

## THIRTEEN

A new tutor walks in—a Qorin woman in five lush robes, white hair styled into a Hokkaran fan. Shizuka dislikes her on sight.

"Four-Petal," she says, "I am your zither instructor."

*Play the zither for your mother, won't you? It'll make her so happy to hear you.*

He knows what he is doing, sending in a zither tutor so soon after her father has left.

Shizuka swallows. She hates this woman. No—that is not quite right. This woman is not acting of her own accord. Those eyes, that voice, these clothes—all of them are borrowed from the root of this evil.

It is the Traitor who looks on her now.

"I know how to play the zither," she snaps. "Leave me be."

"Four-Petal," says the tutor, smiling in the way of court women, "it would so disappoint your father if you did not take your lessons. He is so proud of—"

The fire gets the better of her. She flips the serving tray. Her anger tells her to do something, anything; the thought of immolating the servants occurs to her.

No.

They are only vessels for him.

Teeth clenched tight, she pulls at her hair and walks to the burning column.

"Do not speak to me of my father," she says. "You, who have muddled his memory!"

Rice, sauce, and clear soup darken the woman's robes. She smiles all the same, having not moved at all during Shizuka's outburst. "Is that any way to speak of a gift? Your ungratefulness knows no bounds."

"Ungratefulness?" she says. "You have taken my mother, you have taken my wife. Now you give me this shadow of my father and expect me to bow before you? To thank you?"

The woman stands, straight and abrupt, as if pulled by a wire over her head. She walks in small, delicate steps toward Shizuka. The column of flame roars louder the nearer she comes.

Once more, Shizuka thinks of burning this intruder. Once more, she decides it would be an unacceptable crime.

"We expect you to behave in a manner befitting a ruler," says the tutor. "We expect you to listen. To learn. To care for your father, as is any child's place in the world, regardless of his condition. But if you would prefer your freedom from him—that can also be arranged."

The woman's smile does not change at all. Footsteps in the hall, a struggle outside, a strained shout from what must be Itsuki—but she does not stop smiling.

Not when the doors slide open again.

Not when Itsuki is thrown in and lands on his knees, his hair falling from its bindings.

Not when he draws the short sword all nobles carry.

His bright eyes are cool and distant—he is staring at the window and not at Shizuka. His hands do not tremble at all as he holds the short sword to his throat—

"Stop!" Shizuka shouts. It is too much to bear—her father holding a blade to his own throat! She pushes past the tutor and to the kneeling man. He does not fight her when she pulls the dagger from his hand; he hardly even keeps himself sitting up. Her father's eyes roll back in his head; he slumps, limp, against her.

Now panic truly closes its hands about her neck. "Father?" she says. She starts shaking him by the shoulders, but it is no use; his head lolls to and fro. "Father, please—"

"He cannot hear you," says the tutor—but though her mouth is shaping the words, it is not her voice that speaks them. "Not that you'd want to reach him. Weren't you complaining just now, Four-Petal, of how much you disliked having to care for him?"

If she had her sword . . . But no, no. Even that is secondary to seeing if her father is all right. She presses two fingers along the side of his throat. Steady, if weak, his pulse.

"What have you done to him?" she asks.

"Reminded you of your place," says the tutor. "There are consequences to your actions, Four-Petal. Somehow this has escaped you all your life. Take this as a lesson: if you contradict us again—if you let that childish rebellion rule you—then it is he who will pay the price. We have no need of him save to keep you in line."

She'd known, of course. Itsuki's existence here beyond the Wall is a miracle—but it is not one freely granted, not one freely earned. How long has the Traitor kept him here? How long has he waited for Shizuka to arrive? All the while thinking he was waiting for his wife . . .

Her father, who has never done anything wrong in his life. Who hesitates to swat flies.

She bites her lip. Copper fills her mouth. It aches, this weight; it aches. "Bring him back."

"Will you take your zither lesson in peace?" asks the tutor.

Her father stirs in her arms. His lips shape a single syllable. Ow? He is in pain, and she is the cause. A fresh wave of shame fills her lungs.

How low she feels.

"I will," she says. "Just . . . restore him."

The tutor taps her fan against the butt of her palm. The motion is jerky and unnatural—just as the way her father sits up straight in her arms and turns toward her. This is not the way people move.

And yet in spite of this, there is something in his eye that is different now. O-Itsuki cups his daughter's face, his touch light. In a voice as low as the whisper of silk on silk, he speaks to her.

"Am I forever to gaze upon the blue sky and dream of better? The memory of the sun keeps me warm through the winter."

"Father?" Shizuka says, for her father had been fond of saying such grandiose things when he was . . . When he was well, and perhaps this is a sign. Her soul grows light at the idea. She hopes, she hopes—

But then that hardness returns to his expression, and he looks on her as if he is seeing her for the first time. "Shizuru? What are you doing here?"

Minami Shizuka screws her eyes shut. She takes her father's hand and sets it down into his lap. It is heavier, she thinks, than the crown she has borne her entire life.

"Your Eminence," says the tutor. "Everything is well. Her Excellence the Mother of Dawn only wished to see you again before departing. The rice wine must be getting to your head!"

The rice wine . . .

"Ah," he says, "that is what I get for trying to keep pace with Minami Shizuru!"

He scratches the back of his head, as if this were all some funny joke, and gets to his feet. He offers a hand to Shizuka, who looks back on it the way a woman in search of death might look on a venomous serpent.

The tutor is watching. If she does not take his hand . . .

She wants to close her eyes, but she does not. She looks her father right in the eye as their hands meet.

And it is then that the lights flicker. Outside, the perpetual day goes dark—a curtain of night drawn across the horizon. The room is plunged into black within an instant. To her right, the tutor crumples to the ground, her tongue lolling out of her mouth.

What?

A curious feeling fills Shizuka's chest—a familiar cold. She takes her father's hand as she flies to the window. There, in the distance—plumes of white smoke, and at their center a single figure in silver.

Like water to the dying.

She has never been so happy to be so cold.

For she knows that silver as well as she knows her own gold.

Barsalai Shefali.

Her wife. She's alive!

Shizuka covers her mouth to stifle the sound that comes out of it. The reasonable part of her knows that she must move quickly—for how long will this darkness last? Yet this is at odds with the part of her that wants nothing more than to stay at this window and speak to her wife forever. If she opens the window, then surely the winds will carry her words.

But what will she say?

The words come to her. She throws open the shutters. Cool wind musses her carefully prepared hair, caresses the scar that she earned so many years ago.

"Shefali, I—"

But just as soon as the moment begins, it ends—the false sun returns to the sky, the tutor stands behind her. Two guards rush into the room.

"Four-Petal!"

"There is nothing to see. Come with us—"

"She isn't going with you," says Itsuki, his voice low. "You are guards. Do not forget your place. If you touch her, then you will have to contend with Imperial justice."

He stands slightly before her, this wispy poet, his arm spread out in front of her as if he will be able to stave these guards off single-handedly. It's a farcical gesture. If she were seeing this onstage, she'd laugh.

But there is nothing to laugh at now. Her father might not know who she is, but he is still there, buried beneath the dirt the Traitor has laid upon him.

She risks another glance over her shoulder. Sure enough, the plumes of smoke are still there. No wonder she missed them earlier: the Traitor has tried to mask them as clouds, but a shimmer of silver gives them away as anything but. And there is the silver shard at the base of them.

Her wife.

Minami Shizuka has not slept in two days. She has not dreamed in longer. But at that moment, while her father argues the guards down, she allows herself a moment to do just that.

*My wife is alive*, she thinks, *so I will free my father, and I will return to her.*

Order is restored shortly thereafter. She pretends she has not seen anything. Her zither tutor tells her it was only a trick of the light, and nothing to concern herself over.

But she thinks of the garden she saw on the way to the terrace.

And she knows exactly what she's going to concern herself with every minute of every hour until Shefali arrives.

Together, they swore.

# THE WARRIOR MOON

## FOUR

Barsalai Shefali has heard in her travels the music of many nations: the delicate melodies of Ikhtar, lively Surian drumming, even the strange paeans of Axiot. If you were to ask her what she liked best, she might answer her wife's zither playing, or her cousin's throat singing, depending on her mood.

But on this day there is no zither, no throat singing, no horsehead fiddles nor bamboo flutes.

On this day there are the drums of war and the roar of the cannons, and she finds this suits her well.

All through her childhood she had wondered what it would be like to ride in her mother's stirrups, to see the Wall of Stone come crumbling down before her. How dizzying to wield such power! And yet now that this and more have been granted to her, she feels like a child granted a toy.

*Did you really think that would stop me?*

She does not speak the words—for if she does, he will hear, and she is not in the mood to speak with him at present. But she does think them as loudly as she can. Let the cannons drown her out.

And they are doing so. Dalaansuv's precious creations bring light to the divine darkness with each bark. This to say nothing of her aunt's laughter, the peals of which hit Shefali's ears the way the cannons hit the walls.

"I fucking love these things!" she says.

And, well, Shefali is not going to argue the point.

"On your order, Needlenose!" Otgar shouts from behind her. A passing breeze carries her scent to Shefali's nose: bitter hatred and resignation, but also something light and floral. Sakura, no doubt, joining for history's sake.

But it is difficult to think of this as history. Someday it will be—but today, it is only a series of obstacles to overcome before her people can be free. Before she can save her wife.

There: a shimmer of gold to the north. Pulsing in time with a frantic heartbeat, beautiful and fragile and unyielding. Shizuka. The sight of her fills Shefali's cold chest with warmth.

And it occurs to her then, as she gazes on the towers of Iwa and the army rushing to defend them, that this is the moment she has been waiting for all her life. This: the arrows whistling through the sky toward them, the cries of the enemy, the chants of the Qorin behind her. The Qorin—she can feel the thrill of their hearts like goose bumps against her skin. Two thousand, three thousand, all of whom have already endured so much to be here—all of them wait for her command.

This realm—everything beneath the night sky—is her creation, and so the breeze that tousles her hair must have come from her as well. Nevertheless, it surprises her—not simply the breeze but also the way her braids sound as their beads clink together. When she turns her head, they sing: *Today is the day, Barsalai.*

It is a song, but it is one that lurks beneath the surface of things, hiding in the bray of horses and the creak of bows, the whisper of leather and felt, the rasp of thirsty blades calling out for blood.

And there is one woman who sings it louder than any of the others—one woman who sings in perfect silence.

To Barsalai's right, atop a liver mare, is Burqila Alshara. The wind's sending her braids clattering, too, but the rest of her is as solid and unyielding as ever. Her eyes are fixed on the explosions ahead of them, on the massive hole that will soon welcome them. The bronze war mask so many have learned to fear sits atop her head, yet undonned.

Barsalai Shefali, the Moon Incarnate, presses her tongue to the roof of her mouth. Then, in the voice of a girl seeking a new blanket in the depths of winter: "Aaj. Attack?"

And it is then that her mother turns—but only her head. Burqila's gaze fixes on her daughter's. Godhood has done nothing to inure Shefali to the intensity of her mother's eyes; she feels at once as if she has been caught doing something untoward.

But it lasts only a moment. Her mother shakes her head, a small, sad smile tugging at her lips.

"Needlenose? You can't keep us waiting," says Otgar. "The forest clans are champing at the bit."

Otgar is, too, though she won't say it. Shefali can smell her thirst for vengeance. It's a common scent among her people.

No, she really can't deny them much longer.

Barsalai stands in her saddle. From the quiver at her hip, she draws a windcutter arrow—this with one hand. With the other, she raises the bow. Arrow meets bow. She draws back the string—see how the shoulders of a god strain to draw it!—and aims.

To the north. To the shimmer of gold. To the sky she has reclaimed, and its blanket of stars.

She looses the arrow.

Silver streaks out, trailing ice in its wake. High, high, higher it soars! See the snow landing on the faces of the Lost Qorin—the blackbloods—who cease their snarling to stare upon it! See the flakes fall upon the mimicked city, upon the food stalls and the houses and the eaves of false temples! See it fall on the tips of the towers, on the pine veranda!

Yes—see it as the Qorin see it, feel the cold as the Qorin feel it, know it as the Qorin know it:

The Warrior Moon has come to Iwa.

# O-SHIZUKA

## FOURTEEN

There is no night here. Not consistently. That does not stop Shizuka from imagining one, or from longing for it. Not an hour passes without her looking out her window, where she sees that shining silver on the horizon.

*I will wait*, she thinks.

But in truth, it is not waiting—it is planning. With Shefali still alive, there's no doubt in her mind that the two of them can kill the Traitor. How she lives is irrelevant; why she lives is also irrelevant. If she can see her wife's smiling face one more time, it will erase the other memory.

The Traitor calls her for dinner at a little past Fifth Bell. The meal is a sedate one, perhaps because of the earlier incident. She expects him to lecture her on the finer points of rulership, or to enumerate her many mistakes, but he does no such thing. Instead he simply sits on his side of the table upon the terrace and eats his seaweed rice in silence. Distantly, Shizuka wonders where he got the salmon and tuna that complement the dish. Neither species is native to the northern reaches of Hokkaro as far as she knows.

But then, there is no guarantee the food here is real at all.

She will not risk it. Before her is the very same meal—seaweed rice with glazed salmon and four tuna rolls—but she eats none of it. If the Traitor notices her holding the same mouthful of rice for two minutes before discreetly spitting it out, he says nothing.

Silence from him. Terrible, contemplative silence. He is watching her every move. She is conscious of his evaluating her—the angle at which she holds her chopsticks, the amount of rice she scoops into her mouth, how she holds the hem of her robes back so that they do not get dirtied. She is conscious of these things and so she pretends to be the sort of woman he wants her to be: delicate and precise.

Yet that sort of woman is a difficult sort to be. Even Baozhai—so often lauded by the Hokkarans and her own people alike for her delicate nature—does not come by it naturally. It is a concerted effort. Theater, like so much of ruling is.

Shizuka is not well suited to the role. She drops her rice more than once, and more than once speaks with her mouth still full. With every breach in etiquette, the Traitor's lip goes a little stiffer; his eyes go a little harder. The tension on the terrace is thick enough to drown in.

To everyone except O-Itsuki, who wants nothing more than to discuss his day speaking to imagined courtiers. Shizuka indulges him, for Yamai certainly won't, and Rikuto looks as if it would rather die than exchange words with the Poet Prince. She is practiced at these sorts of conversations. She can keep them going without really thinking.

And she can watch the Traitor and his General as she does so.

They have to have spoken about what happened. Rikuto is holding itself awkwardly, as if the seat is burning it, constantly glancing in the direction of the steppes. It does not drum its fingertips on the table—to do so would be impolite—but it does sniff far more than anyone should, even with a nose that large.

The Traitor, too, occasionally glances toward the clouds. He has the look of a man trapped in a conversation he cannot escape. Shizuka wonders—if his domain is the mind, then how many conversations is he having at present? How many eyes does he see through, how many ears is he hearing with?

Dueling is about assessing your opponent—their weaknesses, their openings.

As her father concludes his story about a Minister Fujiwara of the Interior, Shizuka decides it is time to do a little testing.

"Honored Ancestor," she says, for she does not want to lend the man the courtesy of his name, "there is something that weighs heavily on your mind. I don't suppose you'd care to share it?"

He does not respond. Indeed, he makes no motion as if he has heard her at all.

"Honored Ancestor," Shizuka says more firmly. "You would not turn away your descendant when she seeks your wisdom, would you?"

"Ancestor?" says Itsuki. Shizuka curses her own lack of guile.

"We share one, he and I," she whispers to her father. "In the Minami line. A little playful teasing."

Itsuki nods as if he believes this, and Shizuka thinks to herself that her father would believe nearly anything her mother told him. Then, to Shizuka's amusement, Itsuki taps the Traitor on the shoulder. Only a prince could be so bold, and only after years of marriage to Hokkaro's least polite woman. "My dear guest! Share your problems with us; they're clearly burdening you."

The Traitor starts. In that instant, Shizuka realizes something vital: he is not a warrior at heart. This she knew on some level from Sakura's stories, from Shefali's visions of the man, but it is possible to be a scholar who has hardened to battle. It is possible to wear that armor. The Traitor does not; even a simple unexpected touch is enough to make him jump.

Twice, the Traitor blinks, before the reality of the conversation and its particulars seep into him.

Rikuto clears its throat to try to draw attention. "His Lordship does not like to be touched," it rumbles.

Itsuki's smile is easy and carefree. "Ah, you must forgive me! How often I forget my manners. With my wife once more at my side, I find all the more onerous details slipping away. Please, I beg your pardon."

He inclines his head. The Traitor watches him, eyes burning, and

Shizuka thinks for a moment that he will say something harsh. Instead: "Freely forgiven, so long as it does not happen again."

"You've my word," says Itsuki. "As a gentleman and a poet. The word of a poet is worth much."

Perhaps it is her father's lack of concern for the danger at hand, perhaps it is the knowledge that her wife is coming—Shizuka feels bold now. It is time for more testing.

"I was curious," she says. "You've spoken so much of giving me advice, and you've done so little of that. Is it my stern demeanor that's throwing you off?"

She's trying to sound like her mother, but it's difficult to imitate Minami Shizuru's precise swagger. The woman had a way of speaking as if you were at once her closest friend and utterly irrelevant to her.

"Your demeanor has nothing to do with it," the Traitor answers. His tone says otherwise. Still, there is a softening to him, as if he has been waiting for her to ask this question. He drops a piece of tuna into his mouth and waits until he is done with it before continuing. "You must open a scroll before you may write upon it. Minds are much the same."

There is a perverseness to the way he says "minds," a barely masked arousal.

"Do you not think my mind is open?" Shizuka says.

"It is not," says the Traitor. "You are too focused on yourself. There is an old poem—"

"'It is the mind that is the enemy of the mind,'" Itsuki says. Shizuka has not heard the poem but despises it already—one of those built largely upon repetition. If you are given thirty-one syllables, you should endeavor to use different ones where possible.

"Thank you, O-Itsuki-lor," the Traitor says, his words clipped. Shizuka notes that he does not like being interrupted. "I have found wisdom in those words, albeit with one important modification: It is the mind of the common man that is the enemy of progress."

"That line needs work," says Itsuki. The Traitor squirms. She wonders with a sort of childlike hope whether her father is doing this on purpose.

But it does not last. The Traitor's squirming soon changes to something else, something sharp and awful, and with a snap of his finger, her father falls silent and still. Itsuki's expression is frozen on his face; an awful mask of what was once genuine mirth. The Traitor meets Shizuka's eyes.

"Let this be a lesson to you," he says. "Do not interrupt me."

Shizuka swallows. She knows now where the line is. Her father . . . It was a joke. A good-natured joke. He'd said worse than that to his brother on many occasions, and everyone loved him for it.

"As I was saying—your mind is closed. You do not see the greater good, you see only yourself. In this way you are much like the commoners subsisting harvest to harvest, wondering only where their next meal will come from. You have not risen above your base instincts—and so I cannot share my wisdom with you."

A man so selfish as to kill his own brother because he did not get the kingdom he wanted is telling her about selflessness. The irony of it is a knife, but she cannot feel the cut of knives anymore, not when her heart is missing from her chest.

Shizuka is trying to think of what she might say to him—of how she might temper her own anger, her own disgust—when darkness falls upon the terrace. How suddenly it happens! As if the hand of an unseen god drew the shades of the heavens! Yet it is not an unseen god at all—a needle of silver light pierces the dark just to the southeast.

Shizuka's breath catches in her throat.

*Shefali,* she thinks.

"Your Majesty," says Rikuto, standing.

"Take care of it," the Traitor grumbles, waving the Demon General away.

"As you command," it answers. Without so much as a bow to Shizuka, it walks to the edge of the terrace. She expects it to fly—to ride the same winds that brought her to this place—but instead it simply leaps off into the dark of the city. She does not hear it land.

"This is exactly the sort of thing I mean," says the Traitor. "The conquered people thrive under my care. You have seen them yourself. Are they not cared for? Do I not provide for them? They are free from the burdens of their harsh lives, Four-Petal, and immortal under my care besides. And how do they repay me?"

She cannot peel her eyes from the wall, from the silver light coming closer and closer. The Traitor's words pour into her ears only to pour right out the other end, and yet Shizuka dares not interrupt him, for fear of what he might do to her father.

"Rebellion is in the nature of the common man. They know no peace. If you give a man eternal life, he will ask you why you have made him suffer, for in his mind he has already realized that his sorrows will ever increase. But only if he has to think about them. If he simply severed his ties to the world, he'd be happier, but he clings to the false happiness of the here and now instead. He does not know how to experience without thought. That is the gift I grant. That is what I will provide to my kingdom in the South. But you are too busy thinking of your freedom to accept it."

He is right—she is not paying attention to him. As she watches, every house in Iwa opens its doors. Hundreds—thousands—of Qorin pour from their doors. Some do not bother using the doors at all and instead leap from the windows of teahouses and libraries. As one, they move, coalescing into a column in the center of the city. In the dark, they do not look like people at all—only shadows.

"My wife is coming to kill you," Shizuka says.

"So she thinks," says the Traitor. He, too, rises, pulling his outermost robe tighter around him. Vapor curls from his nostrils. "Our dinner is over, Yui. We will quash this rebellion—and you will watch it happen from your chambers. Guards!"

The four Qorin at the foot of the steps turn at once. Like clockwork dolls, they march up the stairs—raise one foot knee high, bring it down onto the step, raise the next. Her father, too, stands.

Shizuka presses her lips together. Her wife is coming. There are only four guards here. Though she has no weapons of her own and Rikuto has taken her mother's sword, the guards have four. Their swords are comically short for them—but perfectly sized for her. With sword in hand, she could kill all four of them.

It is so easy in her mind: The Traitor must focus on orchestrating his army—he will not be able to respond to her cuts if she makes them quickly enough, and the Qorin will not be able to parry what they cannot see. She can cut them down without killing them. Three strokes and the deed is done—tendons severed at the wrist, combatants rendered casualties. If they continue, well—she tells herself that her wife will forgive her defending her own life.

Revulsion courses through her, but she continues to imagine what might happen if she chooses. The Traitor, isolated on this terrace without his faithful General, could not hope to hold her off. Not truly. He wears no armor and carries no sword—what will he do? Borrowed blade in hand, she strides in her mind across the terrace, moon painting her silver. Like a coward, he backs away from her. His hands find the banister behind him—there will be no escaping her, and she tells him this as she prepares for her cut—

—and the Traitor smiles as her father's blood spurts onto her face.

Breath stops. Her throat closes. A soiled bed, a woman without arms or legs who once was her hero, a woman fever mad and agony blind. The sword felt the same gliding across her throat as it had impaling Daishi. Would it feel the same to kill her father?

Flowering dogwood. Poetry read in the gardens, near the golden daffodil, where no one dared to bother them. *My little tigress.*

No. She cannot attack him while her father is so close. What Yamai lacks in martial prowess he makes up for in cunning; the guards are there for show. Itsuki is his real shield.

And, perhaps realizing her line of thought, Yamai forces Itsuki to speak for him now. Her father snaps back into consciousness as if waking from a nightmare. His mouth hangs open as his brows come together over his eyes.

Yet he does not hesitate. Let no one name O-Itsuki a coward: confronted with the unknown and with guards approaching, he reaches for Shizuka's hand. "Are we staying, or are we going?" he says. The tremble in his voice smooths out as he speaks. "Whatever you wish, I will follow."

How ridiculous. How *ridiculous.* Vowing to follow her though he knew not the danger . . .

Shizuka's throat is a vise.

"This isn't a night for fighting," she says.

Her father tilts his head. If he were not confused before, then he must be now—Minami Shizuru never backed away from a fight, not a day in her life.

But Shizuka is not her mother—and she knows well what will happen if she tries anything here.

Before her father can question her, she starts walking toward the guards. He falls into step beside her. The two of them are down the steps before the guards are, and soon a few spans ahead of them. The Traitor stays on the terrace. When she chances a look over her shoulder at him, he is facing the wall.

Good.

"Shizuru," says her father. "What's gotten into you?"

"You asked if I wanted to stay or go," Shizuka says. "I want to go."

"But—"

"I thought this sort of thing happened without question," Shizuka says. "Isn't that what marriage is all about? Implicit trust?"

Her mother never would have said "implicit trust," but she doesn't care so long as the tone is close. Righteous indignation is a note they both knew well.

The gardens are coming up before them. The Traitor will be too busy with the oncoming battle to pay attention to the guards—or at least, that is her hope. She yanks on her father's hand and pulls him into the gardens. Before he can realize what is happening, she shoves him under the rafters holding up the walkway. There the darkness is true, there he won't be able to see what she is about to do.

Yet he grabs her by the shoulders with confusion and hurt mingling in his expression. "Zuru, what are you doing?"

"Telling you to stay put," she says. It hurts to be so sharp with him—more when she sees the turmoil her tone sows—but it is the way her mother would have handled things.

"This erratic behavior isn't like you. What's—?"

"Listen to me," Shizuka says. She takes her father's hands and sets them back down at his sides. To do so kills something in him, she is sure, for he sees only his wife standing before him. His wife, whom he followed to certain death. To be a pot crushed beneath a potter's heel—that is the feeling she sees in him then. And yet she continues, straining to keep her voice level, straining to sound like the woman he misses, and not like the daughter he has forgotten. "If you have ever loved me, you will stay right where you are."

O-Itsuki stares back at her, stricken.

She does not give him time to argue. If she does, he is sure to say something that would have melted Shizuru's heart, and will only pain her own.

Shizuka jumps up and grabs hold of the walkway. As she hangs there, the thud of passing steps rumbles through the wood—the guards are coming. She had hoped to have a little more time—but hopes mean little on the field of battle. Closer, closer—she waits until they have already passed before trying to haul herself up.

"Trying" is an apt word for it. She was not raised on a diet of meat and disappointment, as Shefali was. Her hands tremble and she groans, trying to force the air out and summon as much of her strength as she can. It is not much—but it is enough to get her halfway up. Pride swells in her breast, but it does not come alone; she whimpers as the stitches holding her chest together burst.

And that whimper is enough to draw the attention of one of the guards.

One, of course, means both.

Together they turn on their heels, together they lock eyes on the woman clawing desperately at the planks of the walkway.

*Damn it*, she thinks. Every breath brings more pain; every breath makes her head spin a little more. If she is going to get one of their swords, she will need to act decisively—but how can she when she's in such an embarrassing position? Some hero she is; she can hardly keep hold as it stands.

Farther and farther she slips. If she hits the ground, they will come down to fetch her, and if they do, they will see her father hiding away.

And she cannot let them go anywhere near him.

Two guards approaching. One reaches for her sword.

"Four-Petal," says the other. "Were you trying to get away from us?"

"I . . . I fell," Shizuka lies, but it comes out strained. Staying up is taking so much of her focus, so much of her energy; if her concentration falters, she is sure her arms will give out. They still might regardless.

"You are lying," says the one with the sword.

Hanging from the side of a walkway, barely able to keep herself up—why did she think this would work? And yet it must. Not for her own sake, but for her father's. From the set of that guard's feet, she is readying an attack. There'd be no better time for one.

But the Traitor has shown no signs of wanting to harm her. Lecture, yes; oppress, yes; but physical harm? In three days, he has not once had her tortured. It is more than she'd expected from him.

If an attack comes, it will be a bluff—a show of force, not meant to do anything but dissuade her.

Pain and determination stitch the plan together in her mind.

"We do not take kindly to liars," says the other guard, the one who has not yet gone for her weapon. "It is behavior unbecoming of a ruler."

Ruling is lying, more often than not—but she detests it all the same.

Two steps closer. The edge of the unarmed one's boots brush against her knuckles; the one with the sword is pivoting backwards at the hip.

"A childish thing of me to do!" she says. "You are right, you are right—I wanted to see the flowers before the battle ruined them—"

The lie is not a convincing one. Stilting, it leaves her, as if she has endeavored to explain a concept she does not understand. If she were a student and the guards her instructors, she would have been laughed out of the academy.

But thankfully, she is not a student, and this is not an academy. She is a god, and this is a war, and in war there are such things as explosives. *Boom!* Even from several li away, the shock wave carries—the guards stagger as the ground beneath them jerks.

And Shizuka is no exception. Her tenuous grasp fails; her hand rises for just a moment, and that is enough to set her falling. She lands with a painful thud on her upper back. Though the breath's been knocked out of her, though the pit in her chest is covering her with wet blood, she cannot stop the smile from forming on her face.

Trust the daughter of Burqila Alshara to blow a hole in a wall whenever she sees one. Her Shefali—what a woman.

# THE WARRIOR MOON

## FIVE

As a boulder heralds an avalanche, so do the cannons herald the coming of Barsalai Shefali's army.

She needs say no more words to stoke them—only to squeeze her horse's ribs and set off ahead of them all. The next time she draws an arrow, it is not for a symbol, not for a gesture—it is to slay a demon.

There: just beyond the hole, the First Company! Twenty lost Qorin—twenty blackbloods—under the sway of a demon. The demon holds a small drum, no larger than a man's hand; this it beats in an unholy rhythm as it shouts its orders to the lost Qorin. Like overripe fruit, the stolen Qorin, swelling and like to burst into their more monstrous forms. The scent of them—how painful to her! And yet the nearer the draw, the more pressing the issue: the demon leaps up onto the wall, its feet adhering to it like a spider's. With one clawed finger, it points to the coming army.

Berries beneath the foot of an angry child: the first blackbloods bursting from their skin, becoming beetles, charging straight for them.

Shefali does not wait to see if the arrow will find its mark in the demon's skull—it will. Instead she reaches for the skin hanging near to her quiver; instead she flicks the cork from it with her thumb; instead she leans over in the saddle.

"Don't let me down," she whispers to her horse.

The first of the beetles is so near that Shefali feels the buzzing of its wings in her eyelashes.

*As if you can get anything done without me,* the horse answers.

Black, black—the shadow descending upon her. Hear the clicking of its mandibles, the chittering of its legs!

Barsalai dips her finger into the kumaq. When the beetle lands on her broad shoulders, she thrusts her hand up, up, into its jaws. The moment its proboscis flicks over her fingers, the deed is done—it lets go of her and drops flat onto the ground. Insect reverts to human, gasping, kicking at the air.

A victory.

But there are more where that came from.

She stands in the saddle. Like locusts in the desert, they fly toward her, but she meets them with drops of kumaq smeared across their carapaces. One by one, the blackbloods drop—and one by one, the Qorin scoop their brethren onto the backs of their horses.

They didn't come here to kill their own.

Through the hole, into the city of Iwa itself—Shefali and her army ride their thunderbolts. The Traitor's army is arranged in dark columns through the streets. At their forefront rides the long-nosed General, the giant demon Rikuto. The shadows they once faced march to meet them once more—but this time there shall be no trickery; this time, the blessed blades and arrows of the Qorin shall not miss.

Not when their god rides among them.

The kumaq skin in her hand glows silver. She tosses it, over her shoulder, to her mother.

The command need not be spoken.

Burqila catches the skin with an outstretched hand. She holds it aloft, and three dozen riders—similarly equipped—break off to find their way through the city. Shefali can see them if she tries, flying up the streets like lightning bugs.

They will be attacked. They will be hunted. To send their fastest and cleverest out on a mission like this—the Hokkarans turned their noses up at it.

But that is the difference between Hokkarans and Qorin, between generals and Kharsas: doing what needs to be done to save their people.

A lump rises in her throat as she watches her mother ride off. There is a feeling in the pit of her stomach, a wrongness that she cannot shake, but she cannot let it intimidate her. Not now. Her mother will be all right.

And if she isn't—what better way for Burqila Alshara to die than this?

The harshness, the distance of her own thoughts frightens her. Barsalai swallows deep of the air, drinks of the hopes and dreams of her people. Her mind clears just as a wave of arrows comes crashing down against them. Two find their homes in her chest. Silver drips onto her starry deel, but she feels no pain, only a slight discomfort.

But the rest of the army is not so lucky. Death's scent comes to the Qorin, smothering courage and bravery wherever it finds them. She does not glance over her shoulder, but she hears them, smells them, feels them dying.

Three more volleys between them and the shadows. How many can survive?

From the depths of her lungs, she summons one word: "Break!"

The Qorin, accustomed as they are to these tactics, do not need to be told twice. The command passes from ear to mouth to ear. Soon, they've scattered like ants, turning down the streets. Temurin, Ogordolai, and Big Mongke—they will all converge on Rikuto.

But only once the vanguard's been softened up.

"Where the fuck are the—?" says Dorbentei.

"Giving their lives," is the curt answer from Sakura, and so it is true. Death has come for the Hokkarans, too. When Shefali chances to look over to the main gates, she sees them dying in droves, sees them killing in equal measure. The crush of gold against smears of black reminds her of droplets of paint swirled together. Above them the air glimmers with souls bound for the fathomless deep. How cruel, how futile their efforts must seem! And yet if the shadows abandon the Phoenix Guard, the guard will surely push straight to the palace.

As the first of the three volleys takes to the air, Shefali makes a promise to herself, to the Qorin, to the guards.

*No one here shall die in vain.*

Silver drips onto her saddle horn. The whistle of the enemy's arrows pierces her ears. She will lose more riders to this volley if she does not do something. But what? Death is a natural part of war; shouldn't she—?

No.

To survive is Qorin.

And Tumenbayar had named these arrows "windcutters" for a reason. She pulls one from her quiver now and breathes silver onto its tip. When she fires, she aims up, toward the peak of their arc.

Like birds against stone, the arrows of the enemy! For Shefali's arrow summons with it a wall of wind, and the enemy cannot puncture it. Thousands drop from the air and onto the ground, where they are soon trampled underfoot.

A soft gasp behind her, a chorus of whoops and cheers.

Barsalai smiles to herself.

Yes, this is the day.

Steam leaves the ears of the Demon General. Shefali nocks and releases again, aiming straight for it. Who among the Qorin would dare such a shot as this? For it is far enough away that only Barsalai can make out its head, only Barsalai can see its face going ruddy.

And only Barsalai, as it happens, can hit it.

As if struck by a battering ram, it staggers backwards, clutching hold of its nightmarish steed by the barest of margins. More steam rises from it, a cloud dense enough to obscure the faces of its soldiers.

With a voice like the spheres of Heaven, she speaks. "Rikuto! We have business!"

"You sound just like your wife," Dorbentei says, drawing alongside her, but even so, she's got her sword out. "Leave some for me, won't you?"

Closer and closer they come to the shadows, closer and closer to the real battle. Behind her, in ill-fitting armor, Sakura is clinging to her for dear life. That is true bravery, isn't it? Making the decision to be here among the whistling arrows, though you want nothing more than to be safe at home.

Twenty horselengths. The others can see it now—and they can see, too, the shadows bracing conjured lances. Shefali glances to the east, to the west, to the alleys the others went down. Any moment now—

There!

Like a dam bursting, like a vengeful river—the Qorin pouring from the streets to harry the flanks of the enemy. How beautiful they are! Like the moonlight on glassy night waves, and the shadows are the rocks. Curved blades find their homes in necks and heads, arrows sink into eyeless sockets. Attacked from the sides as they are, the spearmen cannot turn to defend themselves quickly enough. Qorin steeds trample them as readily as they trample anything else.

Shefali's heart sings watching it—sings to be part of it.

She draws her bow. Another shot, another—the movement is as familiar to her as stroking her wife's delicate cheek. Here, an arrow lands in the skull of a shadow mid-swipe, and one of Temurin's riders gets to live another day. There, another pierces the hand that holds a fatal lance.

One by one, they are falling.

Close, now—so close that she can see the hairs of its chest beneath the layers of its robes. Its nostrils flare, its lips curl, it lifts a finger to point at her. *"Moon."*

Shizuka would boast in a situation like this. "I am the Sun, great and terrible," she'd say, and in a single beautiful stroke, she would part its head from its body.

But Shizuka is not here at the front. A bright flash of gold to the northwest is all Shefali can see of her wife, and all she needs to see—her love yet lives.

There is time, then, to give Rikuto a proper punishment.

And so Barsalai does not reward it for recognizing her.

Silver streaks from her bow and buries itself between the knuckles of its outstretched hand. Howling, it draws the hand back. Two shadows leap to its defense, hurling javelins at her—she catches them and flings them back as easily as a child skipping stones across a lake. The javelins find the heads of their former masters and impale them.

Barsalai draws herself up—now standing not only in her stirrups but atop the saddle itself. Her horse whickers, but bears her as she has all their lives.

Rikuto reaches for its sword.

Barsalai leaps. A mountain goat could not hope to match her, nor a hare or gazelle—five horselengths she leaps, and the whole while stays eighteen hands in the air. Rikuto readies a slash to greet her—and it is then she realizes precisely the mistake she has made.

If it were a normal blade, Shefali could bear its kiss, but it is the Daybreak Blade, and only agony awaits her.

Yet it is too late to turn away from the path she's chosen now.

Any swordsman would be proud of the blow the demon lands. It is said that to practice the simplest slash one million times can transform one into a sage—and Rikuto is, if nothing else, a sage of war. Clean and crisp, the arc: it cuts the descending god from forehead to navel. Silver sprays over gold.

This, she feels; this, she hates. If only it were a sharp pain! That at least would be bearable. The edges of her flesh bubble and simmer like fat on a griddle. She'd intended to land on the demon's shoulders, to tear its head from its shoulders the way she'd torn foul Nozawa's, but the cut throws off her focus—she lands curled on the ground before it instead. The ground drives the arrows farther into her chest. She coughs. Should have snapped them off.

"I don't know what sort of bargain you made with the hag, but consider it ill advised." Pride and arrogance—how giddy Rikuto is to have struck her. "You are a dog. You have always been a dog. The heavens chose wrongly when they anointed you."

Around her—around them—the battle rages on. Two horses go down to her right—she knows them well, a dusky spotted Surian and a white gelding named Lumps who had always been too meek for his own good. Their cries of agony echo the ones she must now swallow. She is a god; who ever heard of a god crying out in misery?

No, no, she cannot.

Nor can she fail here.

Two spears thrust in at her from right and left. The right finds its home in her shoulder, but she grabs hold of the shaft. She takes a sharp breath. Cold fills her lungs. Pain dulls in its wake. With a howl to match any wolf, Barsalai Shefali swings the spear—and the attached shade—into the opponent on her left.

And yet that is no true respite. More spear tips lunge for her; these she rolls to avoid. Dirt and wildflowers dig into the cut across her middle. A tear bites at her green eye. Another sharp breath. In the way of fighters and soldiers, she kips up to her feet. Silver once more stains her deel, dripping from her split lip.

Rikuto fixes its eyes on her. A circle's formed around them, though only wide enough for two horses strung together. Outside its bounds, the Qorin swing their blessed swords against the spears of darkness; within it, the demon wields its stolen blade. The shades on either side of it retreat back into the melee when it nods in their direction.

"You bleed well," it says.

She half coughs, half laughs. If only she didn't hate Rikuto so much—it is a very Qorin joke to tell someone she bleeds well when you are yourself wounded. Evil ink smears itself across the rayskin handle of the Daybreak Blade.

The Demon General falls into a dueling stance—the blade held at its side, the tip nearly touching the ground.

Ah, so that is its game. It must think itself terribly clever.

One step, two steps forward, she takes. From the corner of her eye, she sees Dorbentei's familiar shape. A heartbeat *later*, she hears her cousin's famous war shout as she drives a sword into a shade's neck.

"I had wondered about your blood."

*So do most Hokkarans,* Shefali wants to say to it. "You are not special." The words come out clear in spite of her injury. Part of her takes pride in this, and part of her finds it amusing she'd take pride in something so superficial.

On her third step forward, she staggers—it is only partly artifice, only partly the wily fox at work. A wide upward slash across the chest is her reward. Pain blossoms in her breast.

But Barsalai Shefali is old friends with pain, and so she continues onward, the old demon warrior's face growing more and more self-assured.

Fourth step. It's returned to its proper stance, whipping the Daybreak Blade clean of silver.

Fifth step. "Again you are mistaken." Like a man of middle age, the demon has a way of sounding as if it knows everything. "There is no one like me."

Sixth, seventh—

On the eighth, she mocks stumbling toward it.

Rikuto seizes the advantage: it raises the sword and holds the blade straight out before it, the tip level with Shefali's eyes. From this position, it lunges forward.

Here is the trick of it, the trick of its stance, the trick of its strike: Rikuto does not think she knows the length of the Daybreak Blade. Forged as it was in older times, it is shorter than most Hokkaran swords; to conceal this failing, the Minami family often used this very stance. Shizuka thus rails against it. Why wield a godly sword if one cannot do so proudly? Its length is not a failing, not something to be ashamed of, so far as she is concerned.

And so whenever she had sparred with Shefali, she used far more open stances than this. Barsalai Shefali sparred with her wife every morning for the better part of three years. You learn quickly, in those circumstances, the length of your opponent's weapon—not that it ever helped her win a bout.

But that was when they'd both faced each other with swords. The things always felt so clumsy in Shefali's hands. She'd never understood why until her infection: there is a particular rush to fighting unarmed, a particular thrill to using your own two hands to end your enemies.

Rikuto lunges for her—but the demon is a little too far for the blow to be a comfortable one, a sure one. She has more room to maneuver than it wants her to believe. Leaning forward as she is, she conceals her own movement until it is too late for Rikuto to do anything about it: she clamps the sword in her armpits and twists from the hips.

It is said that you must hold a sword the way you hold a bird: lightly, but so that it cannot escape. In its confidence to strike at her, Rikuto relaxed its grip. The Daybreak Blade falls to the ground after Barsalai twists. She plants herself over it and grins.

"Wrong," says the god to the demon.

Such consternation! See how its nose grows longer, see how its skin goes violet with fury! It wastes no more time trading barbs. Boulder strong and bull quick, it ducks its shoulder and charges her, raising its arms as if to grab at her leg. It means to take her down? Why attempt something so amateurish? All she must do—and what she does do—is lower herself to anticipate it. She slams her shoulder against the demon's to stop the charge, grabs it about the waist, and lifts.

And it occurs to her then, as she sees its eyes widen in fear and realization, what its strategy is.

It thinks the steel eye has affected her vision—that she cannot judge distances. In such cases, straight strikes are brilliant, but ah! It is funny, truly, that the demon has overthought the issue.

That eye is no longer simply steel. Of course she can see through it. Not *well*, but well enough.

There is a grin on her face as she hefts it overhead, one hand knotted in its hair and the other grabbing the waist of its wide-legged pants. The awful clatter of battle goes silent if only for this. Shades flicker in place as Rikuto's focus—its will—falters; the Qorin turn toward her, hungry for hope, hungry for vengeance. Among them: her cousin and Shizuka's, watching with wide eyes.

Were she the many-splendored dawn, it would be time for a speech.

But she is the Warrior Moon.

Five women emerge from a ger clad in their celebratory best. One of them holds in her hands the spine of a ram. A young couple, newly married, sits on a hastily prepared dais festooned with gifts. The bride smiles as her friends approach.

"We've come to test your husband's strength," says the girl with the spine.

"A husband must be able to defend you," says another.

"Let us see if he can bend a ram's spine; you deserve no less."

The young man picks up the spine. Its heft shocks him, for he has slaughtered his share of livestock and knows the weight of a spine. This is far heavier. All the same, kumaq makes him a braggart: he tries to break the spine over his knee.

Unbeknownst to him, the young women ran an iron bar through the ram's spine. When he tries to break it, he succeeds only in hurting himself. The women laugh.

Shefali has seen this happen half a dozen times at least. After her infection, when she in her daydreams entertained the idea of her own wedding to Shizuka, she'd imagined being handed the iron spine. It would not be difficult for her to break it. She was, in fact, eager for the opportunity.

Rikuto's spine breaks over her knee as easily as the ram's spine would have. *Crack!* The sound of it! The howl that follows! Were it the voice of her own general, it would curdle her blood, but it is the voice of the enemy, and so instead it thrills her.

Smiling, the god surveys the battlefield, holding her enemy by the scalp. Half the shadows wink out of existence as Rikuto continues its howling, as it claws up at her like a child. That is the trouble with immortals, she thinks: so few of them understand pain.

The Spider begged, too, in the precious seconds before Shefali swallowed it.

She will give Rikuto more opportunity to do the same—not because she means to grant it mercy, but because her people deserve to see this. A thousand years and more as the enemy, a thousand years and more as the uncivilized scourge of the world, a thousand years of hatred and oppression—to survive is Qorin.

She would see them thrive.

And—loathe as her people would the metaphor—for them to thrive, she must water them.

How it struggles, this barrel-chested sack of water.

The battle is dying down now as the combatants fade away. One by one, her army lowers their weapons; one by one, they turn to watch her. Their eyes upon her make the souls within her sing.

High, she holds it, high and by the hair: the General who caused them so much trouble. The creature of shadows. Steam rises from its ears. Its nose, swollen and purple tipped, looks malformed on its once-handsome face. Its hands bat at hers, but it has no more hope of disturbing her grip than a child has of dislodging a boulder.

"How should I kill it?"

The air goes sweet with their hunger, with their joy. Let them remember this always.

"Roll it in felt and drag it behind your horse!" shouts a woman in a stoat mask. Age is a varnish on her voice.

"Lash it and let us trample it!" cries a young man, one of her cousin's cousins, if she does not miss her guess.

But it is the third voice that catches her attention, the third voice that wins her. Like an old friend returned after many years, that voice: transformed by the things it has seen, the things it has done.

"Give it to me."

So speaks Dorbentei Otgar Bayasaaq.

There is a moment of silence between them, a moment where their eyes meet. Dorbentei has asked her for so little during the course of their time together. Shefali cannot recall another time like this.

"Its head, or its heart?" Shefali asks her.

Minami Sakura squirms behind Otgar. The mask might hide her expression, but it does not hide her soul: this turn in Otgar disgusts her. Violence disgusts her. She has no stomach for it, yet here she is. What has happened here will change her.

Brave, Shefali thinks again.

"Its head," Dorbentei says. The word comes out like smashed pottery.

A Kharsa does not turn away her people when they come to her; she grants their requests when they are reasonable and boldly sought. So it is with Barsalai.

"Sharpen your sword," she says, "and come."

Now fear sinks its claws into Rikuto. Though it cannot move its legs, the demon digs its nails into her arm. Silver drops fall onto its forehead. Barsalai does not let go.

"Unhand me," it demands.

Dorbentei dismounts. An errant spear lunges for her; her younger brother chops the arm off the offending shadow. There is not yet hair on him. Barsalai feels a pang of regret for the childhoods she has ruined.

But she does not let go.

"You would throw away eternity?" says the demon.

Dorbentei reaches in her deel. When she withdraws her hand, there is a whetstone in it. This she uses to stroke the long, curved blade she favors—a sword from her father's nation. Sur-Shar.

"If you strike down the Eternal King, another god will take his place. There will be six others, Steel-Eye. One of them will try to kill you eventually."

There is a harshness to Dorbentei as she walks to them. Shefali tamed her own wildness with butchers and hunters; she forged it in the fires of the desert.

Her cousin will have to tame it at blade's point and forge it from this demon's blood.

Its nails hit bone. Still she does not let go.

"You cannot love the sun," he says. "She will burn you."

And it is this at last that inspires her to answer. Her cousin arrives, laying her sword at the demon's throat. Barsalai shifts her grip—she holds Rikuto in a great bear hug so that Dorbentei may hold it by the hair as she makes her cut.

It is broad in her arms, broad but not strong. It does not struggle.

"Who can burn the eternal sky?" she whispers to it.

Dorbentei knots her fingers in its hair.

"Please—"

Dorbentei hears it. Shefali sees a flicker across her wide, dark face.

And she sees, too, the spurt of black as she makes the cut.

# O-SHIZUKA

## FIFTEEN

"What was that?" asks Itsuki. He's rushing over to help her up, and she is too much in pain to refuse help. As she gets to her feet, she turns toward the south. There, rising from the wall: two licks of flame, dancing like singing girls. "What's going on?"

"My friends are here," Shizuka says to him. She does not chide him for leaving; there is little time for that now. The Qorin—Shefali's Qorin—will be pouring into the city now. Yamai will be distracted. That means . . .

The guards are frozen in their positions atop the walkway. What a cruel joke! The woman with the sword is stuck with her arms splayed behind her, and the other is doubled over. Like two figures from a woodcut, forever trapped in their positions, never moving no matter how the woodblock itself did. Their eyes stare unblinking out on Shizuka—but she is confident they are not really seeing her.

Good, good. It is just like her wife to save her.

And yet they do not have long. Shizuka knows well the sound and rumble of an army—and there is one afoot somewhere near her. She can feel their footfalls if she lays her hands on the rafters. Arakawa taught her she has no hope of fighting off an army alone—it will have to be now.

"Your friends?" says Itsuki. "Shizuru—they just blew a hole in the wall, didn't they?"

"Yes," Shizuka says, "but trust me, they're friends."

With the guards frozen, there's little time to waste. Roses, camellias, lilies, and sunflowers—all turn to face her as she makes her way to the center of the garden. Another round of cannonfire sends all the flowers swaying; when she looks to the walls, she sees streaks of fire crashing over them. The trebuchets have joined in, too. How much longer will the Traitor be able to hold this place?

"You would let an army crash into Fujino while the two of us go for a walk through the garden?" says Itsuki. The hurt in his voice! She does not dare look back on him.

"I thought you said you trusted me," she says. Giving him any more attention than this will ruin her focus. The fires within her need stoking if she is to do what she means to do. "Please, Father. We'll be safe here."

Father—a crucial mistake. Just as she feels the fires rising in her breast, he pulls her back. "Why do you insist on impersonating my daughter?"

"I'm not—" she begins, but as the heat swells in her throat, the words leave her with a thundering resonance that is too harsh for her own father. Yet it is too late to stop herself—the words have already left her, the fire's filled her. Her soul is all flames now, and her eyes are the surest window.

What pain, what misery it is to see the realization on her father's face! The way his lips open in surprise, his mouth hanging open in shock! Slack, his noble features, as his mind races to find some sort of explanation for what he is seeing.

And what does he see? She cannot chance to look on herself, not now, but the air around her has gone hazy with heat. Everything, everything feels golden and bright; everything, everything, feels sure and right and true. Here beyond the wall, she cannot feel the threads that join her to her people, but she knows that if she looks, they will be there. If she looks on herself . . .

She will see a god.

And that is what her father sees—her father who thought he'd been spending all this time with his wife. Never in her life has her father looked on her in such a way, never in her life has she seen this look on him. Not even when the flowers first started turning toward her, not even when she handed him a sprig of hydrangea she'd changed to gold.

How well she remembers those days in the gardens! All the halcyon days of her youth spent at her father's side, listening to him read the works of others. Xianese long-form poetry, old Jeon songs to which the melodies had long been lost, Doanese meditations on justice—her father's tastes ranged the whole world across, so far as Shizuka had been concerned. But to her, it did not matter what it was that he was reading—only that it was the two of them alone in the gardens, only that no one would dare to interrupt them.

There is a dogwood tree in this garden, too. The Traitor's deception is complete—of course there is a dogwood tree here. Itsuki would have noticed its lack. Perhaps with its help she can convince her father of what he is seeing.

"Come with me," says the Phoenix. She takes her father's hand and leads him to the dogwood. He follows, his steps small and staggered. The Poet Prince left speechless.

"When I was young, you would hoist me onto these branches," she says, her voice like the ringing of temple bells. "You would read to me, at least until I asked you for a story. Then you would move all the heavens and earth to contrive one for me. Always, a young girl at the center; always, she did what was kind and just, no matter how difficult."

There is a part of her that cracks saying all of this, a part of her that cannot stand the weight of these memories—but her godhood fills in the break like gold on a shattered pot.

Another battery from the siege engines. The branches of the dogwood shake. Petals, now free from their bindings, spiral through the air to land on Itsuki's head.

"I am doing the kind and just thing now," Shizuka says.

And she is. Is there anything kinder and more just than this? Saving her father before the Traitor can further corrupt his mind, sending him home where Kenshiro can care for him? War is no place for poets, and it is war that is coming now. No matter how much she wants him to see her burn the Traitor to cinders—she cannot risk it.

Her father must be safe, and that must come first.

The Phoenix takes one of the violets she's carried with her. Though it has followed her to the depths of Nishikomi Bay and over the peaks of the Tokuma Mountains, it is as thick-petaled as ever.

*Serve me,* she says to the flower.

And so it does. Gold, it glows; gold, the flower that binds her to her family.

*Open,* she says to the flower.

And so it does. Like a knot in reality's fabric loosening—the flower unfolding, the flower becoming larger and larger, until at last the space between its petals is as tall as a Qorin and three times as wide.

This she casts to the earth. The moment the petals touch the soil, the gap between them springs to life.

Five years ago, she had gotten as a gift from the Hierophants of Axiot a mirror. As tall as this it had been, though more narrow. Transporting it across the ocean and southeast from Nishikomi—this alone would have been enough to beggar a smaller nation, but Axiot spared no expense when it came to grand gestures. Five men they had sent along with the mirror, their hair burnished copper, their skin pale except where flecked by red. All five of them it took to raise the mirror back up to its full height.

"A gift," they'd said. "The finest we can offer."

And in truth, she had never seen anything like it: the elaborate golden phoenixes framing the mirror itself, the shimmering surface of their feathers; the rubies of their eyes and the ivory of their talons. To say nothing of what they flanked! The surface cannot have been silver, for how could silver reflect her so perfectly? For the first time in her life, she saw every detail of her own form perfectly rendered: every thread of her thick robes, every strand of her dark hair, every striation in the scar the dog Nozawa had given her.

But it is a terrible thing to look on oneself, a terrible thing to confront the physical reality of one's being after so long trying to run away from it. Shizuka had left her physical self in the Kirin River. Drunk as she was, this fine gift did nothing but upset her—for there she was, eyebrows shaved and teeth blackened, sitting on the dais without her wife at her side.

She'd sent it back.

But the memory of it remains, and if she is to call the flowers, the mirror is the first thing she reaches for. As the violet grows and unfurls she shapes it with a thought: a great mirror of petals, a massive drop of dew for the mirror itself.

The garden shown on that smooth surface is not the one they currently stand in. There is no Itsuki to be seen, no blazing goddess behind him. Here it is spring, but there it is the first blush of autumn. The chrysanthemums Shizuka so prized during her time in the palace have just started to bloom. Two Phoenix Guards spring into action at the sight of the thing, debating what is to be done about the mysterious window that has opened before them. Shizuka can identify neither—but she knows their names, thanks to the gold characters floating before them.

"The enemy?" says Kusunagi Mako, the younger of the two—a girl with choppy hair and the rough accent of Fuyutsuki.

"Don't be an idiot," answers Genzo Hikari, a man with a sword hanging at his hip. "They've been defeated for years."

"But what do you call that thing?" says Mako, growing more distressed.

In a distant way, it is amusing to see them panic, when it is only their Empress returning home, only her father at last returning to the place he was born.

But this is not a distant sort of thing. Shizuka takes three steps toward her father. So elated is she with her creation that she no longer feels the ache of her heartlessness—or perhaps it is simply the rush of divinity that numbs her.

There is no way to see his reaction from behind him. His shoulders rise and fall with his breathing. *Yes,* she thinks, *he is remembering.*

"This place is a lie. You are in the Traitor's palace, not your own," she says. "The real Fujino—the place you've always loved—is right through that window."

He swallows.

Mako runs off to find a superior. Hikari stays planted right where he is.

"Who are you?" he calls. "By what means have you come to the Imperial Palace?"

How brave he is, how unfaltering! He does not draw his sword but stands tall and straight, his voice firm and yet not unfriendly. Shizuka is proud to have such people enlisted in her ranks—but then, these are no longer her ranks.

"Tell them," she whispers to her father, for she does not know how she appears to Hikari. "Tell them your name."

As the silence between a duelist and his opponent—so this quiet.

"Your name, Lord-tur!" says Hikari. "I can tell from the light upon you that you have the Phoenix's own blessing, but you must tell me who you are if I am to let you through."

*The light upon you*. She does not want to be seen by him, and so she is not. The comfort of anonymity is dizzying.

But so, too, is the anticipation.

"Father?" she whispers.

Another battery from the cannons. The army's footfalls are louder than ever—can Hikari hear them? Yes, he must be able to—his brows come nearly together over his head at the sound. It occurs to her that he is not wearing a war mask.

"Father, I do not know how long I can keep this open," she says. She squeezes his shoulder, plumes of smoke rising where her fingers burn against the cloth of his robes. "Please."

It is then that her father turns to her.

It is then that she sees the tears falling from his amber eyes, the misery writ plain across his face.

"You . . . ," he says, and something in her breaks in two, something in her is not strong enough to bear the sorrow in that single word.

"I see it now—your clever disguise. If my Shizuka were a woman grown, she would look quite like you. But she is only a child, and you are only a demon."

Has she been made of clay before this moment? All the fire she contains has done nothing but make her brittle. Here—see a god shatter. See her clutch at a heart that has long since left her, see her stagger for breath.

"You are not my daughter."

God though she may be, powerless she is to stop her father. Into his robes he reaches. His eyes still fixed on hers, he draws forth his inkstone—the one she'd given him as a gift just before the Ninth of Nishen—and casts it to the ground.

It—like her—shatters.

A thick sea scent envelops them; she cannot open her eyes to see what is happening, for she cannot summon the strength to confront the sight of her father in such a state. The hiss of smoke precedes a low, rumbling laugh.

She knows that voice.

No, no, no.

All she wanted was to save her father, all she wanted was for him to be safe—

—She is a child again, thirteen and at her mother's bedside, telling her that there is nothing she can do and she does not know where her father is—

—but she does know, and he is right there in front of her, looking on her as if she were a monster.

He does not recognize her.

A knife in her breast.

The cannons fire, and even this is not enough to bring her back to the reality of the situation, even this cannot serve as a tether. She cannot breathe, she cannot think—

"I was told the enemy would wear a familiar form, but this . . ."

That tone. The three of them in the throne room with her uncle. He casts down his fatal proclamation—that Shizuru must attempt to kill forty blackbloods on her own—and her father protests. *She will have a guard, won't she?*

That same hopelessness, that same betrayal.

She feels as helpless now as she did then.

"You did the right thing, O-Itsuki-lor."

The Traitor.

He is here.

Calamity rarely strikes alone.

She forces herself to open her unweeping eyes, to take in the sight before her. Hikari has gone for his sword now, but it will do him little good.

For it is not simply the Traitor who stands before her—his army has come as well. The footfalls she felt earlier weren't Rikuto's forces at all, but Yamai's: the palace guards gathered in columns along the boardwalk. Thousands, at least, packed tight as salmon roe. No human army could stand being so close together—but he controls them, and so they stand where he wills them to. He himself wears the lacquer armor of a general, trimmed with Imperial Gold. Four waves are stamped on his breast; strands of seaweed decorate his hair.

Looking out onto the window, Yamai is genuinely smiling.

"What fine work, Yui," he says. "Truly exemplary."

She cannot summon her fire with her soul in such a state, cannot make herself feel anything but sorrow and misery—but even so, there is anger in her voice as she speaks.

"Leave," she says.

"I see no reason to," says Yamai. He takes a few steps toward them, kicking at the shards of the broken inkstone with the tip of his boot. "I was summoned to dispatch a demon, after all."

Itsuki has said nothing—but he shifts as the Traitor kicks his inkstone. "You will . . . you will, won't you?" he says. "You promised that you would."

"Who do you think he is?" creaks Shizuka. "Whom do you think you've bargained with? Look on him and his army. Look at his eyes, Father!"

Yamai's smile shrinks only slightly. "Now, O-Itsuki-lor, you wouldn't take the word of a demon over mine, would you?"

Cruelty. Cruelty of the highest degree. He can simply rob Itsuki of his consciousness and be done with it if that is what he means to do, but no—the three of them must have this conversation.

She reaches for a sword that is not there.

"I . . . but why have you brought an army?" Itsuki asks.

Behind him, Mako has returned with ten more guards. Each has a sword in hand. If she is going to do anything about this—anything at all—she is going to need a weapon. Hokkaro is her realm as the Steppes are Shefali's—surely the Phoenix Empress can take a sword from one of them?

Two steps toward the golden frame. Her father jerks into motion, planting himself squarely in her path. Confusion colors his eyes.

"What are you doing?" he asks the Traitor.

"What I promised I would," is his answer. "Eradicating demons is best done by many." A fan hangs from his hip—he takes it now and opens it to the army. One by one, they begin to hop onto the gardens, walking in their mechanical way toward the window.

No, no, no—

Desperately she reaches for the calm, for the fire, for her power, but there is too much happening and she cannot think—

She tries to shove her father out of the way, to shove him into the window, but no matter how much of her strength she throws against him, he does not move.

The Traitor laughs again, and it is then—looking at him—that Shizuka sees it.

The dagger. Her mother's dagger. In her distress over losing the Daybreak Blade, she had not thought to keep track of the dagger. A fool! A fool she is, for now it is in the hands of the enemy.

She lunges for him, but her father's arm shoots out. By the throat, he's caught her. Horror in her father's face, horror in his eyes—a scream stifled by his grip.

"It is as I told you earlier," says the Traitor, walking toward them with the dagger in hand. "Your mind is closed. The moment you saw him, you had determined to save him. There was no possibility of failure in your mind, even when I showed you I see through his eyes as readily as anyone else's."

But Itsuki had not fallen into a trance when the battle started, he had not stopped, and there is no way the Traitor would hurt anyone of Imperial blood—

But this isn't hurting him, is it? Only controlling him.

With one hand, her father holds her by the throat. The Traitor presses the tip of the dagger to Itsuki's sternum, and Itsuki takes hold of it himself. A man choking his daughter with one hand and near to killing himself with the other—this was the Poet Prince.

"There is no use for a child on the throne, Yui," says the Traitor. She cannot see him waving his hands but she hears his fan snap shut, hears him tap it against his wrist. The possessed soldiers in their columns march down into the garden, their footfalls a constant rumble.

She cannot breathe. They are marching toward the mirror, toward the portal, and she cannot breathe. *Run,* she thinks to the two guards, but they do not hear her; *run and fetch the army.*

Perhaps they hear her, or perhaps their good sense prevails when they see the approaching column of empty-eyed, armor-clad Qorin. Mako and the others all unsheathe their weapons.

"Stop where you are!" they shout.

"How quaint," says the Traitor, "to be ordered by another."

Another tap of the fan against his wrist.

She does not see it happen, but she hears it: flesh stretching, bones popping, a sickening crunch. A howl of agony followed by ten war cries. How proud their ancestors would be, to hear the spirit of their voices! And yet those ancestors will soon welcome them—for there is no doubt in Shizuka's mind who wins when even two blackbloods face ten men.

She does not see it happen, but she does not need to.

Minami Shizuka knows well the sound of her own failure.

Squeezing her eyes shut does little to isolate her from it. With her father still strangling her, there is no hope to escape the knowledge that—once more—she has failed. Once more, she has brought death to the people she swore to protect.

That the world is starting to twist and roil around her is only right and just.

"You are thinking that there is still a way to stop me. That you can save your father, if you try," says the Traitor.

And yes, this is part of her thinking—but she will not give him the dignity of an answer.

"You can save him," says the Traitor. "All you must do is nothing. If you take any actions—any at all—before my army has returned to its home, he will die. It is as simple as this."

The Traitor laughs behind her.

Cannons firing in the distance. Soldiers pouring in like grains of rice from a sack, hundreds of them rushing through the portal, thousands, maybe—a stream of shining armor and white hair. The laughter of the old god, and the pained, rattling breaths of her father.

These are the only sounds.

She raises her eyes, but still she cannot bring herself to look on her father. Instead she looks to the soldiers—there are only three columns left. Three hundred? Of the thousands she'd seen, only three hundred remain, and the first of them is approaching the portal. The soldiers move with such speed—how many are already storming Fujino?

With a sickening lurch, she recalls Kenshiro. How proud he had been of his daughter, of her decision to shrink the armies and the guard! Shizuka took most of the Phoenix Guard with her on this madman's mission—how many remained? How many has Baoyi recruited in the intervening years? The only threats to her person being *human,* being mortal—what impetus did she have to see that they were properly equipped for dealing with the enemy?

The guards don't even wear war masks.

Years, they'd gone without her—and in her absence, peace has finally come to Hokkaro.

Ruined now, by her own making.

Bitter, bitter, bitter.

Is it for this she has struggled? For the destruction of her childhood home, for the massacre of her people? To sit idly by in the clutches of evil? When she swore her oath with Shefali beneath the white birch tree, she did not swear to lose.

Shefali journeyed eight years to return to a woman lost in her cups. Will she return now to a child unable to defend what she loves?

She closes her eyes.

The Traitor is right: what needs to be done is simple.

But it makes her want to die.

Yet it is the place of a god to die for her people, and the place of an Empress, and the place of any dutiful servant of the greater good. So long has she thought of herself as above these laws. So long has she thought of herself as the most important person in the room—but in the grand scheme of things, her suffering matters little.

The thought is a spark on the kindling of her soul; the flames rise again within her, burning whatever they find.

When she opens her eyes once more, they are no longer amber but a terrible, unyielding gold. Gold, too, the stitch across her face; gold, the insides of her mouth as her lips part and she speaks.

"You have mistaken me, Yamai."

As the gong in the center of the Jade Palace—so Shizuka's voice. How clearly it rings, though her throat is in her father's iron grip! This is not the voice of the Peacock Princess or the temple acolyte; this is not the voice of General Dog-Ear or the drunkard atop the Phoenix Throne.

It is the voice of the god.

Yamai is no longer laughing.

She does not turn her attention to him. He does not deserve any of it—not now—and he will have all of it the moment she is done with what needs doing.

She meets her father's eyes. Wide, they have gone, and though the Traitor holds his body, the awe on his face is plain.

So, too, the regret.

Shizuka covers her father's hand with her own. Within her, the flames burn white-hot; the whole of her soul is in absolute agony.

"Father," says the god.

He says nothing, for there is nothing he *can* say—but the bulb of his throat bobs as he swallows.

And she thinks, then, of the dogwood tree and the poetry, of the late dinners and the jokes that had always made her groan. She thinks of the mourners swarming Fujino—so many that it was impossible to move through the main streets at all.

The flames consume these thoughts like tinder. In their wake, there is only numbness.

But there is one memory more precious to her than all the rest, one she holds above the fire like a treasure: her father and her mother drunk in Burqila Alshara's ger, their faces red, singing a rousing song neither of them truly knew. Her mother leaning her head on his shoulder when it was done; her father taking her hand. The glance they shared then, so close to their doom, full of absolute love.

"Mother has missed you for too long," she says then, and anyone who heard her would say that her godly voice cracked on the words—that they heard only the orphaned girl instead.

"What are you—?" begins the Traitor, but Shizuka has no room for his words and his wants in her mind. She grabs the dagger and drives it into her father's chest.

And the gold fills *him* then, the way it has filled her: his eyes shine bright with it. The hand holding her throat goes limp and falls away. A sharp breath from him, another—gold spilling forth from his mouth, gold seeping from the wound.

The Poet Prince O-Itsuki slumps over, clutching at the dagger embedded in his chest with one hand. With the other, he holds the face of his daughter, and it is then that he sees her truly.

Pale as winter's first snow, he smiles at her.

"'Long sought and hard won, / Paid for in blood and sweat, the / View from rolling hills. / Home is calling to me now, / And who am I to refuse?'"

As the last words leave him, so, too, does the light: a shimmer in the air flies up from his lips to the false sky.

O-Itsuki falls—and his daughter is there to catch his body. She has never thought of herself as a particularly strong woman; apotheosis has not lent her any might. She kneels to the ground and cradles him.

As the gold leaves him, as the shimmer soars higher and higher, as his blood seeps onto her clothes—she cradles him.

*It needed to be done*, she tells herself. *You needed to save your people*.

But holding him now as she is, she cannot stop the Traitor as he bounds through the portal, cannot stop him as he plucks the violet on the other side. The whole of the window snaps shut behind him: the last thing she sees of him are his eyes, burning in anger.

# LAI BAOYI

## TWO

Lai Baoyi does not remember much of her birthplace, the Bronze Palace—but she's come to know the Jade as well as she knows her own hand. Surrounded at all hours by courtiers and advisers and guards, it is only natural that she learned to evade them. With excuses and feigned sickness at first: simple things, easily conceived of.

The hiding places came after: the apartments in the library, where only her father might find her; the scullery, where a maid of about her size and age had worked, and she might remain for hours until her accent slipped or the other girl showed up; the hunting grounds, where the Eternal Phoenix had once slain a tiger.

All of these locations served her well, but it was not until her investiture as Empress that she learned of the hidden chamber. Her father had pulled her aside after the ceremony. She'd thought, at first, that he meant to speak to her about her marriage prospects. They'd managed to go her entire life without broaching the subject, and he was half-drunk—this was the blow she'd expected.

But instead, he had taken her to the plaque, and he had shown her what lay beneath it, and he had called full-eight Phoenix Guard to lift it. No less than eight could lift the door from the outside, he said.

"But if you're ever in the position to need it, there will be at least sixty-four to defend you," he said. The smile was meant to be comforting. It was not. Her head hurt from the weight of all her clothes, from the music, from the questions carefully deflected.

"This isn't one of your puzzles, is it, Papa?" she asked.

"No," he said. "This is a safe room, Baoyi. The only thing that should ever drive you here is invasion."

How seriously he'd spoken! But the idea was as distant as Axiot: they would not be invaded. Young Lord Fuyutsuki had new eyes for her; her grandfather kept a tight hold on Oshiro; her mother ruled Xian-Lai to the south; Shiratori Rin disliked her almost as much as she loved her poetry; the North had not posed a threat since the Eternal Phoenix had raised the Wall of Flowers.

Hokkaro would not be invaded.

But she'd indulged her father all the same, and down into the chamber they went. It smelled of dust. An old suit of armor, a zither, eight waist-high jars of wine—were these meant to keep her company in case of the worst?

The next day, she'd asked Kobayashi-zun—the captain of the Phoenix Guard—to see to it there were books added to the chamber. Paper and ink, too. Rations came third in her mind; clean water, fourth. With this done, she was happy never to think of the place again.

On the first of Qurukai in her twenty-second year, someone grabs her by the shoulders and shakes her awake. She's so shocked by this—by the contact—that she thinks she must be dreaming. That it is her father in armor does little to dissuade the notion. This must be a dream. Her father has never been a warrior.

"You aren't going to believe this when I tell you about it later," she says, for surely the dream will not care what she does.

But it is about then that the first arrows land outside her window—*thunkthunkthunk*.

"We're taking you to the chamber." She has never heard her father sound so gruff.

Words catch in her throat. She looks around only to find that there is no one else in the room with her. Where are Akishika and Momiji? Her handmaidens sleep in the same room, only a little removed, but they aren't here. Outside, eight Phoenix Guards stand shoulder to shoulder, blocking the door. As she takes a sharp breath, she finds that the air tastes of smoke and metal.

"Papa, what's going on?"

He flinches a little when she calls him that—she had long stopped using such childish nicknames. The words leave her father now like wounded soldiers climbing a hill. "The enemy is attacking us."

"The enemy?" Baoyi says. "But the Wall of Flowers—"

She is on her feet, scrambling for something halfway decent to wear. Her robes are all near Akishika and Momiji's rooms; she grabs the first she sees as she peeks in. Their sheets are strung wildly across the room, their drawers open.

Baoyi swallows. Her friends. Where have they gone? No—she cannot think of them when the Empire itself is under attack.

"They've arrived in the gardens somehow," her father says. In the time it's taken her to find her robes, her father's gotten hold of her ceremonial armor. He holds the cuirass up now. "Come. We don't have much time."

"You can't be—" she begins, but she hears a howl from the roof outside, and decides it is best not to question him at the moment. On goes the cuirass, strapped hastily together; one of the guards produces her boots and the Phoenix war-helm. All of it feels heavy, all of it feels wrong.

"Your aunts will be coming to help," says her father. Hope soothes the frayed edges of his nerves—he is speaking to himself as much as he is to her.

But she does not want to hear him. "Who are you talking about? My aunts all live in Xian-Lai." There is a memory briefly there, tugging at the back of the empress's mind, a woman who smells of peonies—but the unfamiliar shape fades. "Father. I have to muster the army. No one can stand before the Phoenix Guard and live."

Those selfsame guards cluster in around her as they leave the room. A stench hits her, like rotting meat but worse. Tears sting at her eyes. In the distance someone screams; Baoyi knows that voice. The scullery maid.

Her knees are weak.

Kenshiro, though—her father is there to catch her. He slips his arm beneath her just as she starts to buckle. "The Phoenix Guard can hold for a while, but . . . you don't remember the enemy. No one does anymore. You've done such a good job of keeping the peace."

This does not feel like peace. The throne room is not far from her personal chambers, though it is well guarded—and even this distance has become one of ten thousand li. The halls Baoyi once thought of as properly cozy now show their true purpose: to force any attackers into as small a space as possible.

And there are attackers. An awful snarl comes to her ears from somewhere up ahead. The crunching that follows is worse, a wet sound that reminds her of the butcher's cleaver at work.

"Don't look," her father says to her. "Keep your eyes on your feet. One step in front of the other, sprout. That's how we're going to do this."

"Lances ready!" say two of the guards.

Her eyes fall to her feet. Forward, forward. They are coming to the stairs now. Whatever it is that's causing all this ruckus must be perched atop them.

Her father's quiet Qorin cursing tells her she is right. So, too, do the war cries of the Phoenix Guard, their feet on the ground as they charge. Arrows whistle toward the stairs. Something—it is not human, it cannot be human—laughs.

The creature speaks in old, heavily accented Hokkaran. It sounds like a man—like one of her old mentors—and yet she knows it is anything but. "Is that what she looks like? The pretender to *my* throne?"

"Lances, again!"

*Don't look,* she tells herself. She is dizzy already, dizzy with all of this, and she wants more than anything to wake from the nightmare she's found herself in. This cannot be real. There cannot be demons in the Jade Palace. How would they even get here? Through the gardens . . .

There was something in the gardens once, wasn't there? A golden flower?

Her head hurts.

More war cries, but they are short lived—one stops with an audible crunch. Red splatters the floor before her. It takes her a moment to recognize it as blood and not as ink—Baoyi had always thought blood spray would be brighter.

*Don't look.*

"Get her downstairs!" shouts Kobayashi. She's here? Baoyi hadn't recognized her in full armor—but of course she'd come, of course she'd be here. "We can hold it off for now!"

"May the birds find you," her father says, and she realizes in a distant way that he is talking about Qorin funerals.

None of this is real.

The shadow of the lancers as the creature lifts them. The sounds, the smells. These guards are dying for her sake, and she cannot even stop to properly honor them, cannot even stop to collect their bodies. Her father is pushing her forward, forward, down the steps. What she first takes for wind in her hair she realizes to be a swipe from the creature, foiled by Kobayashi's strong sword arm.

"Listen to me. Your aunts are coming. Even if you don't remember them, even if no one does—they would never let the enemy win. They'll save you, but you have to give them time."

The empress stumbles on the staircase—there is someone lying at the foot of it. Facedown, a sword just out of his hand, the bright red armor of the Phoenix Guard. Her eyes find the pit in his chest without meaning to. Like a brush rammed through paper. It is then that she realizes he is dead.

"Papa, he's—"

"I know, sprout. We have to keep moving."

But she can't. Her feet aren't listening to her. That soldier's dead, and the eight guards outside her room are dead, and Kobayashi's probably dead—

Her father scoops her up, as he hasn't done in years. Down the stairs they go. Baoyi looks up at him and tries not to look at anything else—the smears of blood on the walls, the distant shadow of the creature—but it is hard to ignore them. The creature especially. Just as her father reaches the foot of the stairs, just as he steps over the fallen soldier, the creature fills the threshold above them.

Two seasons ago, an awful plague spread among her hunting dogs. Many of them lost patches of fur, many of them wasted away, many of them became thin parodies of their former selves. The creature looks much as they did— but it is as tall as two men stacked together, and with eyes like red coals. Spittle dribbles from its toothy mouth onto the ground. The broken shafts of two lances are embedded where the collarbones would be on a normal dog.

*Don't look,* her father had said, but she cannot look away. This is the thing that is destroying her palace; this is the thing that is killing her soldiers. What sort of Empress would she be if she could not face it? The horrors of this place have reduced her to her childhood, but she will not let the enemy see her in such a state.

All at once, she jumps from her father's arms. At his hip hangs a wide sword, a Qorin sword, which she draws now from its sheath. The weight of it strains her arms—she cannot level it at the creature as she meant to.

"You shall never conquer us!" she shouts up at it.

But the creature laughs at her as her father pulls her by the collar.

"A fool, like your predecessor," says the creature. Its mouth does not move. "Conquest is the soul of Hokkaro."

Her father's hissing in her ear, but Baoyi cannot hear him. Dragging her farther and farther along, farther and farther from the creature. Her body tenses. It will follow. It will follow, and it will tear them apart, and—

An arrow whistles over her, passing so close to the bridge of her nose that she thinks for a moment she must have been hit. Her hands fly to her face and find only sweat there—no blood at all. In a daze, she follows the arrow's trail: another company of Phoenix Guard are up ahead, bows aimed at the creature on the stairs. Five arrows land in its chest, and it only smiles.

"Baoyi," her father says, taking the sword from her hand. "This isn't your fight."

"They're my people!" Her throat hurts. "Of course it's my fight, people are dying—the empire—"

"Baoyi," Kenshiro says again, this time shaking her. "If you do not get to the chamber, then you will die, and they will no longer be your people. Do you understand?"

The words are not what sways her: it is his tone that does, the half-frantic look in his eyes as he speaks of her death.

She swallows, looking at her army and the creature in turn. "I . . ."

He takes her by the hand. They are walking again, toward the army. When he holds the sword, it looks light. "There is no one in all creation bolder or more foolhardy than your aunt, and if she saw what you just did, she'd shrivel with worry. You are no god!"

*But I am the Daughter of Heaven,* she wants to say.

The words are lost as they make their way through the columns of Phoenix Guard. To her shock, they are wearing their masks, every one of them. More than one whispers to her as she passes: "Our lives for yours." "They will not pass." "Get to safety."

The last time she walked between their ranks like this, the newest recruits had just been formally sworn in. They'd looked on her with admiration then, with love.

It would be easier, she thinks, if they looked on her with hate now—but they do not. It is that same admiration, that same love.

They are all going to die for her, aren't they?

"Take courage. Hokkaro will remember you," she says, but this is not the voice of an Empress at all.

Beyond them, the throne room. Her father pulls her along toward it, his steps as sure as they are quick. Eight guards break off from the back of their column to join them as they make their way to the jade plaque. There aren't any bodies here, she notices, there aren't any dead. The air doesn't taste of death.

She is ashamed at the gulps she takes of it.

"Your Imperial Majesty, Most Serene—"

"Don't bother with propriety," Baoyi says. "What is going on? How many are there?"

"You won't want the answer to that," her father rasps, but Baoyi does not look away from the soldier.

She, in turn, does not look away from Baoyi. Perhaps the long shadow of doom gives her the courage to look Baoyi in the eye as she speaks. "We are not sure. Thousands, at minimum."

A crash. When she looks over her shoulder, the creature from atop the stairs is at war with the front of the column. Ten, twenty soldiers attack it from all sides, and yet it shows only mild fatigue.

"Thousands of those?" she asks.

"Yes," answers the soldier.

"The chamber," her father cuts in. "It's our only hope."

"Hope of what?" Baoyi says. "Am I to sit inside it and listen to everyone die?"

She can see the plaque now, with its remonstrations about wisdom. She wants to stamp on it, wants to crack it, but she knows that will do her no good.

"You are to live," says her father.

What he is asking of her is shameful—to live while so many throw away their lives for her—and yet there is a large part of her that wants to do just that. She wants to hide. Before this awful morning, the worst thing to have ever happened to her had been leaving the Bronze Palace.

She does not have a warrior's heart; she does not have a soldier's strong arms; she does not even have the eyes of an archer.

All her life, Baoyi has been a diplomat like her parents had hoped she would be.

What good is diplomacy here? Perhaps she has been kind enough to her people that they are willing to go to such lengths for her. But that only leaves her feeling worse.

The eight guards gather around the plaque. Up, the false tile.

"Your Majesty!"

"I told you—"

She cannot finish the sentence—the guard tackles her to the ground. Her head cracks against the tile; stars burst before her eyes. The world spins but her hearing is true: there's something skittering where she once stood. One of the enemy? But how had they gotten past the army?

Before she can sort out her thoughts, the thing in front of them—small and much like a turtle-imp—belches. From its beakish mouth comes a cloud of heavy fog, black as smoke, which at once sinks to the ground.

Blurry, blurry, but as she stares up at the ceiling, she can see them: dozens, maybe hundreds of scurrying creatures crawling along. Like beetles, she thinks. They are so like beetles, and she has never seen so many of them in one place before.

"Don't breathe the smoke!" her father shouts. "All of you, stop up your masks!"

She has no mask to stop up, but she holds her breath. One of her tutors told her all about the dangers of breathing in smoke—but this isn't the sort you'd get from a fire, is it? It tastes . . . It tastes of ink, and the sea . . .

Her father raises his wide sword and swings at the small creature. It makes a rude gesture and skitters away, laughing, laughing, and Baoyi thinks to herself that she has never heard a sound so terrible as that. But that isn't true—she has heard so much screaming today.

"Get me up," she slurs to the guard. True to her years of service, the guard obliges, grabbing her beneath the shoulders and lifting. The world moves entirely too quickly; it is all she can do not to vomit.

But the guard solves that problem for her by clamping a hand onto her throat. At first, Baoyi mistakes it for some gesture of reassurance—but then the squeezing starts. The choking. A scream dies on her tongue—what is happening? For her grip has gone stiff as iron, and her nails are digging into Baoyi's windpipe, and there is an awful rattle to her breath—

"Pa—"

Before the second syllable is formed, her father strikes. What horror in his eyes, what fierce determination! Once more he raises the sword, and this time his blow lands true: a vicious chop that takes the guard's hand right off her arm. Blood spills out onto her. Baoyi screams in earnest then, throwing herself against her father.

She wants him to embrace her. She wants to wake up somewhere that is not here, somewhere else. Sur-Shar, maybe. She's heard such lovely things about it. There hasn't been a war in Sur-Shar in years.

But her father does not embrace her—he only squeezes her a little before pushing her toward the chamber. The guards have already gotten it open.

And as Baoyi stumbles backwards to the waiting guardsmen, she sees two things.

First: the one-handed guardswoman's mask has come off. Her skin has gone clammy and gray, her eyes and lips pitch black. Though the stump of her arm yet bleeds, she draws her sword and lunges for her father.

Second: there is an unnatural shimmer to the smoke. How quickly it spreads! Already it nips at the heels of the column in the hallway.

Baoyi has been a clever girl all her life. Whenever her father told her a story, she'd figure out the ending long before the central players took the stage. It was a talent of hers, a thing he'd tease her about: *Politics will not be so easy as these stories.*

And so she knows already how this is going to end. All the soldiers who inhale the smoke—the same murderous intent will seize them.

Her throat goes tight.

She knows.

"My father," she says to the guards that catch her. "Please, we must take my father into the chamber!"

But the guards do not answer her. It is her father who does instead, as he brings his blade down on the one-armed woman. "Have I ever told you my Qorin name?"

"Halaagmod?" she answers. "Father, we don't have—"

"It means that I grow roots," her father says. He grabs the woman by the hair and cuts. So much blood, already, so much blood on him when he turns toward her. "Go into the chamber, Baoyi. I'll plant myself on top."

And it is this, at last, this that breaks her. Tears land on the backs of her hands as she reaches for him, only for the guards to pull her backwards.

"Come in with us!" she says. "Father, *please*, you're not a soldier—"

"I'm not. I'm an oak. That's what I've always been," he says. He smiles at her, the same smile he has always given her. "I'm happy to have given you shade."

It is the last thing she sees of him before the masked guardsmen pull her into the chamber, before they seal it shut and lash the blessed ropes about the entrance.

Baoyi does not hear the blow that takes him—she is too busy screaming herself hoarse. She has no way of knowing what is happening just above her, no way of seeing him plant himself there just the way he swore he would.

And she cannot hear the sounds of it over her own screaming.

# THE WARRIOR MOON

## SIX

The Qorin army, victorious as they have not been in years, rally at the Moon's back. What a sound, what a thrill: thousands of horseshoes beating against the polished tile of this mock Fujino. There is so much elation in the air that Shefali can hardly breathe; it stops her throat, like sticky-sweet fruit.

"Where are we going?" asks Temurin. There are two claw marks on her horse and three across her chest. The injuries have not stopped her, though they have left her sounding exhausted.

In reply, Shefali simply points at the column of gold.

Sakura eyes it with something like nostalgia, something like anxiety.

Forward, the army. The Hokkarans will follow along. With Rikuto dead, the shadows have vacated the city—only the blackbloods remain, and her mother will soon have broken the spell on them. With every breath, Shefali feels more of them returning to their old selves, each one a raindrop.

For an instant, she throws back her head and allows herself to feel the storm.

But it is over as soon as it has begun. Minami Sakura—her scent unmistakable—is tugging at her arm. Shefali opens her eyes to find that Sakura has removed her war mask. She keeps her eyes focused on Shefali, on the god.

"The flowers," she says.

Shefali follows her pointing fingertip. Fujino is rife with flowers; this original city is no different. This would be the Fujiwara district they are in: a great wisteria marks its center. The tree's branches are as gnarled and twisted as an old woman's yearning hands, but it has spent years in the care of the careless.

Except that the petals are falling from it like the shorn hair of a maiden as they watch.

"Kharsa!" shouts one of her clansmen. "Kharsa, look at the buildings!"

Near her is a teahouse, or what would be a teahouse. This one has a mural of Emperor Yusuke the Brawler wrestling a lion dog painted on its door. Easier to say, perhaps, that it once did: the paint is fading to nothing.

"Sakura," she says. "Can you explain this?"

"I . . . ," she starts. Her eyes wander. She sees the blood streaked on Shefali's deel. She remembers.

"Close your eyes, if you need." The Moon has her way of comforting.

Sakura takes her advice. It is still a struggle for her to get the words out. Battle has its scent, after all. "He's gone. The Traitor, I mean. Either he's dead or he's gone, somehow. Without a god around, anything too unnatural reverts to its old form."

"Gone?" says Dorbentei. Sakura flinches at the sound of her voice, though she has not deigned to get off Dorbentei's horse. "So we've won?"

"Only if he is dead," Shefali says. She does not feel as if he is. The passing of a god—surely a thing like that would have some sort of feeling to it. One brother knows when his twin has died.

There's a lurch in her stomach. If Yamai is not dead, then he has left, and if he has left—where has he gone? Axiot lies across the sea from here. He has ships that might carry him. Will it be another eight years' journey for them? And, speaking of time—has the Traitor's hold on it relaxed now that he is gone? Shizuka told her of their niece, of how much Baoyi's aged in the short time they've been gone.

That lurch travels up Shefali's throat.

*Where?*

The golden column has the answer; she is sure of it.

Fujino fades the farther in she goes. It is as if the passing army wipes a slate clean, for in their wake, all color leaves, all plants wither. Whole buildings crumble as if knocked aside by a child. Foundations rot; a temple collapses.

When she looks over her shoulder, she has left her family behind. Dorbentei's fat dun is hard to make out, although it is easy to spot Sakura in her Imperial armor. No sign of her mother. That is a hound at her heels; she will slay it later.

Forward, forward, along tile pathways that shatter long before her horse reaches them. Blood pounds like war drums in her ears. If she had dawdled too long, if she had wasted too much time with theatrics . . .

But still the column burns.

Through the gates, between the false maple and the true. The column is coming from the pavilion, or near to it—a place Shefali has never had cause to go. Up, up, onto the boardwalk. The first plank rots at her horse's touch.

She drives on.

Like two pine needles, they'd sworn. Together, they'd sworn.

Dread seizes her as she rounds the corner, as she approaches the column. What if . . . ?

The vision is clear: a woman in tattered robes, maggots eating at her eyes, her tongue a gray lump between her shriveled lips. "Come to me," she beckons, "and see what you have wrought."

The demons have long left her—but the scars remain.

Her heart is a stone. She opens the eyes she hadn't consciously closed.

There.

Sitting among the golden flowers, cloaked in the dawn itself: her wife, safe and well. Yet the relief that leaps to Shefali's breast withers like the conjured flowers, for there is a body lying in Shizuka's lap, its robes trimmed in Imperial Gold.

She half throws herself from her horse just to get to her wife faster. Like a smith's hammer against the anvil: her feet against the ground.

"Shizuka!" she calls, for even now, her wife has not looked up at her. Shizuka's precious hands run through the hair of the man in her lap. Now that Shefali's drawing closer, she sees the dagger jutting up through his back: a dagger tipped with gold.

Her feet hit the earth of the garden.

Shizuka finally looks up at her. Will Shefali ever tire of this sensation? The coldness in her melting, giving way to indescribable warmth; the whole of her soul filled with gold? God or mortal, wanderer or Kharsa, there is no greater thing in all of Heaven than this: Shizuka's eyes on hers.

And yet it is not a moment for joy, not a moment for exultation. Shizuka's smile is so muted, Shefali may well be imagining it—to say nothing of the pit where her heart once was. Seeing it sets Shefali's own aching. She kneels there, next to her wife and the dead man, among the flowers.

"Shizuka," she says. She reaches for Shizuka's face only to remember the blood on her hands—she wipes it on her own deel before touching her wife's holy cheek. How soft, how warm, this phoenix! Every breath she draws in Shizuka's presence is a gift; every moment they spend together is hard won and paid for in blood and suffering.

Together, they swore, and at last they are together again.

She laces their fingers together. Two silvered crescents meet in the palms of their hand. Just as it had been so many years ago, a thrill stirs her blood and settles—the rush of war and the elation of the journey home all at once.

What will she say? So many words spring to her mind all at once: *I thought you were dead. I've killed the other two. We're gods now, aren't we?* The latter nearly leaves her lips, for it is as clear to her that Shizuka has ascended as the steppes are from the mountains.

But the sorrow in her wife's eyes is just as clear to her. Shefali swallows the words she might have said in favor of cradling Shizuka's head. Slowly, slowly, she rocks them back and forth. The wind through the flowers cannot drown out the sound of the oncoming army—of their horses and their armor, of their cheering—but perhaps Shefali's whispered promises can.

"We're together now," she whispers to her.

Still her wife is silent.

"It's going to be all right," she whispers to her.

Still her wife is silent.

"Whatever . . . whoever this is . . ."

And it is then that Shizuka speaks, then that two words leave her like a death rattle.

"My father."

Like a boulder rolled before a cave—the words stopping Shefali's mouth. Itsuki? Shizuka would never lie to her; if she says it is her father lying dead in her lap, then it must be. But how?

It does not matter. Only that he is here, and he is dead, and it is Shizuka's dagger piercing through his chest.

The tragedy written here is a familiar one. She need not read it to know it.

Closer, the army. They will be here soon, and then there will be no time for delicacy, no time for the discussion they need to have. Together—alone—they may be women; when the army comes, they must once more don their crowns and divine mantles.

But how heavy the weight seems at present.

The words that stopped Shefali's throat broke down Shizuka's resistances: she sobs now, tearless and childlike, against Shefali's shoulder. How she clutches at Shefali's deel! How delicate, the voice that leaves her—broken already, raw and looking for flesh to cut!

What is Shefali to say to all of this?

She holds her wife. She holds her wife, and she sways, and in the quiet recesses of her mind, Shefali says her good-byes to the only Hokkaran man who was ever kind to her. O-Itsuki-lor never once mocked her calligraphy. When it came time for her to learn proper court Hokkaran, she did it through him—through her brother reading his poetry to her near the campfire. All through her life, his works have been her favorite; she'd been too shy to ever say as much, and by the time she found her courage, he had long since departed.

And now he is dead.

It feels wrong to let him lie here.

She kisses her wife's forehead. There is a thought in the back of her mind. Is this how Shizuka felt standing before the Kirin? For the prospect is dizzying and terrifying and—she realizes now—unavoidable.

Something must be done; Itsuki cannot be left here. If Alshara sees him, it will tear open the wound of Shizuru's death anew—to say nothing of what it might do to the Hokkaran army.

"May I?" she says, her hands hovering over Itsuki's shoulders. Shizuka nods.

So it is that Shefali turns him over. Swift and certain, she plucks the dagger from his chest and closes his eyes. The look on his face—what happened here? Where has the Traitor gone, and whither his army?

*After,* she thinks.

After.

"I had to," Shizuka whimpers.

"I know."

The approaching army sends the flowers swaying. This must be quick. Words said, probably, although words have never been her favorite things.

Barsalai Shefali breathes in the cold. She holds it there, in her lungs, as she lays her hand across O-Itsuki's nose and mouth. It builds behind her eyes until it is ready. Only when she sees fractal frost blossoming across her vision does she breathe out.

There, in her hand: a frozen star, its points reaching out from between her fingers. Clear as the pool near Gurkhan Khalsar her mother visited before making her journey to Oshiro. Its facets catch both Shefali's light and Shizuka's; their own faces stare back up at them. Shizuka's mouth hangs a little open.

"What is . . . ?"

"His name," Shefali says. She does not let go of Itsuki's nose and mouth—the cold is flowing into him, and already he has taken on a cool blue glow. "His name needs to be written on it, I think, and I can't . . ."

Something softens in Shizuka then. It is not quite a smile that takes over her face, but it is the potential for one. "Bring it here."

Shefali is happy to hold it closer to her. Shizuka traces the characters with a single fingertip. Though she cannot read them, Shefali watches all the same—there is a holiness to the way Shizuka writes. It is not unlike watching the wild horses that roam the steppes, their coats gleaming like burnished copper.

The moment she lifts her finger, it is done: the star pulses with light. As gently as she can, Shefali parts Itsuki's lips. Into his mouth, she drops the star.

What happens next happens quickly. The body of the Imperial Poet—Shizuka's father, Shefali's father-in-law—flashes a bright white. Even Shizuka flinches at the sight of it; even she must look away. When they turn their attention to him once more, only the star remains, pulsing brighter than ever.

Shefali picks it up and stands.

"He was a good man," she says, "and this way, the wolves will never find him."

With this, she flings the star into the sky. How impossible, its ascension! Watch as it soars straight up from her hand, as it careens upward and upward, as it winks out of existence only to wink back in hundreds of thousands of li away.

A star, in truth.

When she turns to Shizuka, she finds her covering her mouth, her face wrenched once more in sorrow—but she looks up at the sky, the place where the star now shines.

"Shefali . . ."

She wants to pick her wife up. She wants to scoop her up in her arms and carry her somewhere far away from here—the two of them wild horses.

But that is a mortal want, and the army is coming.

And so instead, Barsalai Shefali simply kneels in front of Minami

Shizuka, this woman for whom she has sacrificed so much: kisses her eyes, kisses the bridge of her nose, kisses her mangled ear.

"When this is over," she says, "I will find your mother and do the same for her."

"When this is over . . ." Bitterness returning; the last dregs of tea. "I have ruined it for all of us, I'm afraid. Yamai's army runs rampant in the palace."

As a sheep knocked with a club before its slaughter, Barsalai and this news. "What?"

Shizuka presses her lips together. Now, for the first time, she breaks eye contact with the Moon. "It is true. I . . . I conjured a portal there, with the flowers—I meant to send my father home, so that I might deal with Yamai myself. But he set my father upon me instead, and marched his own army through."

The dog you raised has the most vicious bite.

Bile rises at the back of Shefali's throat. How she loves her wife! How she loves her! For if anyone else had told her this news, she might well have berated them, but knowing what Shizuka had been made to do tempers her reaction. To think—if she had struck quicker, if she'd struck harder, perhaps they could have caught him in the act.

"Shizuka," she rasps.

"It is my fault," Shizuka answers. "He knew. He knew that I would try and save him."

Of course he had. Shizuka, for all her many virtues, is the most predictable woman in Hokkaro. She will always try to do the impossible thing, no matter the odds set against her; she will always try to save her family.

And, it seems, she will always end up killing them.

Such cruelty. How long did he keep O-Itsuki here, waiting for Shizuka to arrive? It was the demons who told the Toad to send the armies north—had it been demons, too, who told him to send Shizuru to her death?

For how many years did he plan this torture?

No, no, Shefali cannot truly be angry at her. She did what she has always done and will always do. Killing him after reuniting with him . . .

Shefali thinks of her mother. She swallows.

Temurin and Dorbentei—Shefali can smell them now. They will be here at any moment, and they will want to know where their quarry has gone. She cannot tell them he escaped, and she especially cannot tell them he has gone to Fujino thanks to Shizuka's actions.

She closes her eyes. The crown is there, if only she will reach for it.

It is then, in setting her hands on her hips, that the answer comes to her—for it is then that her palm brushes the golden flower she took from her corpse. An answer! "Can you make another portal?"

"I would need another flower from Fujino," Shizuka says. "I think whatever I use must be tied to the place I am going—and I used all the violets I gave Baoyi already—"

Shefali plucks the golden flower from her belt. She places it, stern but loving, into her wife's hands.

Fire blooms behind Shizuka; her eyes flare bright. It occurs to Shefali that her wife has not much transformed, physically, since her ascension: it affected her eyes and clothing alone. The armor she once wore has gone pure gold, the clothing beneath it scarlet and beautiful vermilion. "You kept it?"

"I keep all your gifts," says Shefali. She kisses Shizuka's forehead. "Qorin are coming now. We will take back Fujino."

Already the golden daffodil sprouts new roots, already it opens and turns in Shizuka's hand. She walks to a spot a horselength away and thrusts it into the ground. When her eyes meet Shefali's, they are like the sun on the ocean—but Shefali will never tell her this.

"Your mother," says Shizuka. "Is she—?"

"Nothing can kill her," Shefali says.

It is a simple truth. The sun rises in the east. There is a rider for every horse. The moon dies every twenty-eight days, and Burqila Alshara never will.

"Make the portal," Shefali says.

She refuses to dwell in this uncertainty.

# O-SHIZUKA

## SIXTEEN

In some ways it is fortunate that the Spider ate Shizuka's heart. If she hadn't, then the sight of Fujino under siege might well have ended her.

War is one thing. She knows war. She has seen both its heroic face and its true one; she knows its stench. If it were only war, then something within her, surely, would be able to comprehend what she is seeing.

But this is not war.

When the blackbloods burst from their mortal skins and descend upon their victims, they are not attacking soldiers. They are attacking servants.

And they have claimed so many already. Bodies like fallen leaves litter the gardens; the green ground has gone brown and wet with their blood. Here, a severed hand holding a sprig of laceflower; there, its half-eaten owner. Dull horror strikes her when she realizes that she recognizes the body, headless though it may be, by the tattoo on its bared shoulder: Hisao-zun, who once served as a temple guard in Nishikomi, and told her all sorts of tales about her mother. When she was a girl, he would sneak her saucers full of rice wine.

"It isn't fair that she gets it all to herself," he'd say.

Now he lies dead, a goat-headed blackblood tearing at his flesh.

The gardens are only one part of the grisly sight before her. Blood stains the walls of the Jade Palace; blood pours from its sloped roof. The enemy lope along the rafters with bits of flesh clamped in their mouths. A noblewoman is trying to force herself through a window meant only for arrows, and Shizuka cannot tell if she is doing so of her own volition.

*This is your fault,* she thinks to herself.

"You're sending us into that?" says Dorbentei.

Shefali—her Shefali, her moon!—crosses her arms. "I am," she says. "Anyone who does not want to fight can take the long way; the fog won't trouble them anymore."

There are a few murmurs of dissent, but mostly there is silence. The Qorin, better than anyone, know the horrors of the blackbloods. Yamai saved the worst obstacle for last—to go against them is as good as suicide. Their blessed weapons cannot save them from the corruption of their blood. Shefali may be able to break their hold—that is where Alshara has gone—but not before the pain sets in.

Shizuka thinks of Shefali sweating in bed—dying as Minami Shizuru had, years ago.

She closes her eyes.

How is it possible to hurt this much?

"How many?" says Sakura. To hear her—yes, it is possible to hurt even more. The fear in her voice, the distance! Something in her has broken through all of this.

Shizuka pinches her nose. "Thousands."

"Thousands?" says Dorbentei. "We barely have that ourselves."

"The Hokkarans will come," says Shefali. She gestures to them—Shizuka can barely see the tips of their banners. There are fewer of them. Did Munenori-zul fall, too? Will she paint her hands with his blood?

Temurin sucks her teeth. Clipped Qorin syllables leave her. Something about Burqila.

"Burqila will join us," Shefali says. How different she sounds—Shizuka keeps expecting her to sound as quiet as ever, but there is nothing quiet about the woman before her. So much of her has changed. Oh, her cheeks have returned, and her good eye is the same shade of green it has always been, but . . .

All her life, Shefali has been steady in the way of warhorses. Now she is steady in the way of mountains. It is impossible to look away from her. Shizuka's soul swells with pride and love to see her—her silver hair and her black skin—but she wonders, she wonders.

Will they be the same two women they were before all of this?

"You've lost your goddamned mind, Needlenose," says Dorbentei. "I'll follow you—of course I will—but I want you to know what you're asking for. We are going to die."

"Not if they kill the Traitor quickly enough," says Sakura. Her eyes flick over to Shizuka's, and Shizuka must force herself not to look away. *This is what you have done.* "If he falls, then his will does, too. It might be enough to stop them."

"'Might be'?" says Dorbentei. There is a head hanging from her belt. Rikuto's, no doubt. Perhaps that is what's making her bold again. "We're gambling our lives on a 'might be'?"

Voices rising. Shizuka does not need to understand the language to understand the tone of them. Knives, every one of them, each one held right at her throat.

"Argue later," Barsalai says. As if sensing Shizuka's distress, she squeezes her hand. Their scars touch. "To survive is Qorin. Shizuka and I will kill Yamai. Until then—we hold the palace."

Temurin says something then. Syllables leave her throat like cannonfire. Not for the first time, Shizuka wishes she'd taken the time to truly study Qorin—but her drinking habit had taken up so much of her precious time. She looks to Sakura out of reflex, as if she were already fluent, and is horrified to see the blood fading from her face.

More horrified still, when her cousin marches across their little gathering, her shoulders held low as a fighter's, her neck straining with anger. When she slaps Temurin right across the face, no one stops her—not Dorbentei, not Shefali, not Dalaansuv or any of the other war council Qorin.

Temurin stares back at her. No one speaks, no one dares—Sakura is on the verge of tears. Her hand trembles as she draws it back up. "Dorbentei. Translate for me." It is not a question. Dorbentei's eyes flick over to Shefali, as if for approval, before she nods. Minami blood is half flame, so the saying goes: all of it burns in Sakura's voice. "There are good people in that palace. Serving girls, students, traveling families paying a visit on an unlucky day. *Children*. Tell me again that they deserve to die. I fucking dare you."

Much must be said of a good translator: Dorbentei mimics Sakura's tone precisely. Shizuka learned the Qorin word for "fuck" long ago—it lands with all Sakura's venom.

"If she tries to kill you for that," says Barsalai, "I won't stop her."

That, too, gets translated—Dorbentei adopts a new voice for Shefali, though she cannot quite mimic the metallic tone her godhood has lent her.

The air goes taut as a wire, but Shefali does not wait for Temurin to snap it. There are more important things to settle. She whistles, and her horse comes—a stately gray nearly white with age. To see her swing into the saddle with ease warms Shizuka's heart.

Or it would.

How much has she given to this war already? How much more is there to give? Despair threatens to swallow her; she closes her eyes once more. When she opens them, Shefali's hand is outstretched before her.

And, yes, it is a god who reaches for her now. See her night-dark skin, see her hair and teeth and eye of silver.

But that smile, the one that hides her eyes behind her cheeks—that is her Shefali.

"Together," Shefali whispers.

For that had been the plan for the majority of her life: the two of them together riding against the Traitor, the two of them against the world, the two of them with an army at their backs.

All the mistakes of her life have led her, somehow, to this point. And there will be an eternity to fix her wrongs.

An eternity with her wife. An eternity with her people.

"Together," Shizuka answers.

She takes Shefali's hand. So quickly, so easily, Shefali pulls her into the saddle. From her horse's saddlebags, she draws the Daybreak Blade, and this she lays in Shizuka's lap.

How like a serpent, that sword. The sword Minami Shiori once wielded to save the man they are going to kill. The sword she reached for so often as a child—the sword her mother never wanted her to wield.

Shizuka swallows at the sight of it, at the weight of it on her lap.

So many years she fought to be able to use it—and now she wants nothing more than to cast it aside. If she never again drew the Daybreak Blade, that would be reward enough. Godhood paled in comparison to the idea of a peaceful life.

But she cannot have a peaceful life while her people are suffering—while her niece is in danger.

For they will be going after Baoyi as surely as moths to the flame.

She closes her hand around the pommel. A rush of warmth fills her, as if she has just drunk her fill of boiling tea. An ivory sheath cannot hide the sword's flare.

Palaces hold nearly as many secrets as spies. In the throne room, there is a jade plaque extolling the Father's Wisdom. Beneath the plaque, a wrought iron handle; beneath the handle, a heavy stone door. The chamber it opens into was installed twelve generations ago, during the war with Dao Doan, in case the palace should ever be taken. Shizuka herself has been there only four times in her life, and three of them were to get drunk in peace—so few people know of the place that she could lie there for hours at a time. The seals and statues meant to ward off evil and arrows never warded away her hangovers.

But they might ward off the Traitor.

In the grand scheme of things, it is a recent addition to the palace. The Traitor will not know it is there. What few artifacts remained to

Hokkaro of its former protectors—shards of the Brother's armor, a zither that once belonged to the Sister—are kept there. It will be the first place Kenshiro thinks of to keep his daughter safe.

And so it will be the first place she and Shefali will go.

The Traitor, after all, cannot truly seize the throne without killing its current occupant.

The sword flares once more in Shizuka's hand. She holds it at her side, the tip pointing to the ground. A line from Shefali's letter comes to her: *Hokkaran swords are awful on horseback*.

Perhaps that is true.

But she will have to try, all the same.

Shizuka wraps one arm around her wife's waist. "Let's go."

"Aunt Dalaansuv!" Shefali shouts. "When the artillery's through, let them sing. The rest of you, with us. Can I count on my cousins, or will I have to carry you all to battle myself?"

From the sound of it, she won't. By and large, it is a Qorin war howl that answers her. Shefali nods. "Stamp out the flowers once the army's through," she says.

And it is then that the thought occurs to Shizuka, then that she thinks to ask: "But what of Aaj?"

"She will go with us, or she will go the long way," Shefali says. She is not looking at Shizuka as she speaks, but instead at the carnage that awaits them.

The light lands on her good eye. As they ride through the portal into the bloodshed that awaits them, that eye is viper green.

# O-SHIZUKA

## SEVENTEEN

This place is not her home.

Together, through the portal—and the moment they are all through, Shizuka wishes she had instead kept her eyes closed. The shattered tiles, the smoke sticking to the roof of her mouth, the bodies like fallen leaves . . . This must be the banks of the Kirin, this must be Onozuka Village, even Iwa—but it cannot be the Jade Palace.

What remains of Shizuka's heart is caught in her throat the moment they pass through the gate. As Alsha's tail clears it, the two blackbloods nearest them rise from their macabre meals. Like lion dogs, both of them: short, four-legged creatures with stout chests and manes of rippling black smoke. Gore slicks their jaws; the low growl that leaves their throats speaks to their hunger.

She has just enough time to think to herself: *They're people, we cannot kill them*. In the time it takes her to have that simple thought, they pounce.

Her throat closes. In her hand is a sacred sword, a holy sword, but how is she meant to defend herself without harming them? The second thought comes like an assassin in the night: *The Daybreak Blade did not save Shizuru from these same horrors.*

One stroke and she can kill them both.

One stroke and Minami Shizuka can sever their arms, one stroke and she can draw blood however she wishes—but she cannot stop this assault without hurting the people committing it. Too many departed souls weigh on her already—she cannot raise her sword, cannot bring herself to strike them.

In all of the Empire there is no one more Hokkaran than Shizuka, after all—and hasn't Hokkaro tormented the Qorin enough? For not only were these creatures once people—they were more than likely Qorin. And it is a Qorin army at their back now, led by Qorin women, for the purposes of liberating those stranded beyond the Wall.

How, then, can Shizuka kill any of the blackbloods?

To do so would be to commit the same violence her ancestors had.

It is her wife who saves her, as she has saved her every day they've ever spent together. Shefali wields her skin of kumaq like a dagger; a savage swipe sends drops flying out onto both blackbloods. Their human eyes go wide as Shefali bellows a single word with a mountain's voice.

Ice covers their bodies as it does the ponds in winter. Within a heartbeat, they are encased; the next, they fall to the ground. Ice cracks. When Shizuka looks down at her would-be opponents, she sees only two Qorin flat on their stomachs.

"How did you . . . ?" she begins, but she realizes the folly midway through. Shefali is the god of the Qorin now, and there is little more Qorin than a harsh winter.

"Hold on!" Shefali shouts.

For to say that these were the only two enemies they faced was to say a woman takes only two breaths in her life. Shizuka takes another now as Shefali urges her horse forward. To her shame, she presses her head against Shefali's strong shoulders rather than confront the sight before her.

It is, after all, the sight of her own failure. The latest in a long line.

No, no, she cannot allow herself to think this way.

A spear of bone scrapes against her back; its owner is a skinless man joined to a skinless horse. Shefali tilts her head back—holding more kumaq in her mouth, most likely, as they are coming up on the gates from the gardens to the palace. There the Phoenix Guard made their first stand. Shizuka can see what remains of them now: twisted hunks of armor and chips of bone between the teeth of monsters. Shefali's attention is focused on what is ahead of her, and not on this spear-flinger. Already it is cracking one of its ribs off to use for another projectile.

Shefali will not see it coming.

She cannot let her wife do everything herself. Together, they swore, and together they must be—even if Shizuka cannot imagine a way to resolve this without killing the thing.

The person, she reminds herself. The person.

Shizuka is going to kill a Qorin; the pit in her hollow chest aches at this realization.

Her hands close once more around her mother's sword. Shefali relied on the cold within her to break the Traitor's hold—the answer must lie in mimicking her. Shizuka has no great control over cold, or over Qorin at all—but she has her fires.

She pricks her finger on the Daybreak Blade. Alsha leaps over a fallen body then, and so the cut is a little longer and more jagged than she'd intended. More blood for her to use. Gold, not red. Something in her mourns as she coats the flat of the blade in it. One breath, two: she calls the fires within herself and tells them to *ignite*.

And so they do.

Bright as the sun in a polished bronze mirror, hot as the depths of a smith's forge: the Daybreak Blade.

The creature hurls the spear with unnatural strength; Shizuka splits it down the middle as easily as cutting bamboo. The shards of it burn to useless ash—but still the creature remains.

And it is not alone.

Ten gather now, their shapes grotesque and twisted, but all of them intent on the sword. On her, and on her wife. Smiles spread across mouthless faces. She knows that look.

She cannot bear it. For a moment, only a moment, she glances at what lies before them. Ten blackbloods gather there, too, their arms interlinked and their mouths at the ready. Even if Shefali freezes them, how are they going to clear the wall they've formed?

The cut has to be perfect.

It is the least Shizuka can give them.

But how crushing—to fall from such a height! For as their heads tumble from their bodies she cannot help but imagine the people they had once been. Once more her throat stops, once more she crumbles.

A thousand years of Empire are alive and well, spurting from the heads of the fallen.

She cannot bring herself to look at her wife.

# THE WARRIOR MOON

## SEVEN

The world beneath the Moon twists and turns; the gray's hooves leave the ground. Shefali breathes a cloud of frost onto the blackbloods before them. Frozen as they are, they pose no threat save clearing the jump.

Qorin mares are not known for being high jumpers. The best high jumpers are from Ikhtar, where they treat their horses much as they treat their nobles. There must be some Ikhthian in Alsha's history—she has to be at least six hands in the air. When she lands inside the palace itself, it is with a pained whinny.

Shefali curses under her breath. She swings out of the saddle, taking her gray's head in her hands. Shizuka follows. With the ice wall on one side and a long hallway on the other, they'll have a clear view of anyone coming.

"Where are you hurt?" she asks her horse, speaking in their own hushed language. The great brown eyes that fix her make Shefali feel human once more.

*Everywhere,* says the mare. *But we need to keep going.*

"Not if you're hurt," Shefali answers her. The words come out strained. When she runs her hand over Alsha's foreleg a sword drops into her stomach. The torn strands of muscle are unmistakable.

Her gray mare—now her white—cannot hope to run like this. Her leg will give out from under her if she tries; it is perhaps because of Shefali's intervention that she is standing at all.

If they were on the steppes, the proper thing to do would be to ride her out to the mountain and see to her end there. The next day she would bring what remained of her to the ger and the whole clan would make use of her. Shefali has seen it happen more times than she can count; it is a solemn occasion, but a necessary one.

Everything dies. Flowers, kings, gods, and horses.

But not *her* horse, never *her* horse. Alsha and Shefali had been born together. What sort of god would she be if she could not find some way to heal her oldest friend? What use was any of this power if it could not do something so simple as that?

"Your horse?" Shizuka calls. She's peering around the corner, down another long hallway. This one branches off into the kitchens, from the smell of things.

But blackbloods savor the taste of human flesh—and there are few places more populous than the kitchens. It takes a small army to feed all the servants, let alone the Empress.

Baoyi.

The words stick in Eternal Sky, save her from this choice: saving her horse or her niece! Freeing the Qorin is one thing—she is not certain how long it will take to save Alsha. Speaking to animals has always been within her power, but healing them . . .

*Tell her I'm fine*, says Alsha. How insistent! She butts her head against Shefali's chest even as she sways. *We're wasting time standing around like this.*

But Barsalai Shefali cannot lie to her wife. The agony on her face comes through in her now-quiet voice. "She's hurt."

"She's hurt?"

"Her front knee," Shefali says. Shizuka looks at them, but at the sight of the injury she covers her mouth in sadness.

"Is there . . . There must be something we can do," Shizuka says. "We're gods, and your horse is earthborn, isn't she?"

Shefali pinches her nose. She paces back and forth, back and forth. A spear arcs above the frozen wall, landing where Shefali had just been. She sucks in another breath—this time thrusting her palms into her eyes. Another spear.

They do not matter. Nothing matters at the moment save Alsha and Baoyi. Let all the masked assassins of Ikhtar come against her: she would rather suffer the thousand swords of their hatred than lose her niece or her horse.

Sorrow twists at her heart; she cannot bear to look around, cannot bear to breathe the air and taste her horse's agony.

Her wife's gentle voice comes as a surprise.

"Freeze her," Shizuka says. "You can do it without killing her. When this is over with, we'll let the sanvaartains get a look at her."

"She's my horse," rasps Shefali. She lays one hand on the gray's flank.

Shizuka rushes to her wife and takes her hand.

"Shefali," she says, "listen to me. She'll still be your horse when this is done—but every moment we spend standing around, Yamai gets closer to our niece and more of your people die."

The Qorin warhorns are sounding now—the battle will be truly joined. With this gate sealed off, they will have to go along the pavilion. A bloody path, to be sure, and a loud one besides. The Traitor can put his armies on either side and slaughter them.

But only if they do not stop him.

One finger beneath Shefali's chin. Their eyes meet. She wants to kiss her, less from amorous intent and more out of fear that she may never have the chance to do so again.

"Please," says Shizuka.

Shefali closes her eyes—but she nods. Shizuka kisses her on the cheek. How cool, her skin, how like polished stone.

A whispered word, a tender caress. Shefali breaks with her wife to press her forehead against her horse's.

*You're really going to freeze me?* says her mare.

It is so difficult to speak. "Yes."

A whicker, a proud puff. Her mane flops in front of her eyes, and Shefali clears it away.

*You had better do it quick, then,* says the horse. *Burqila's daughter never hesitates.*

Already Shefali is sucking the cold into her lungs, already she is willing this to work.

*I will see you again,* she thinks, and she hopes Alsha can hear it.

One breath is all it takes: a cloud enveloping the proud gray mare, who rears up on her back legs as the ice coats her. There she remains, like a statue, as Shefali whimpers.

Tears on Barsalai's cheeks. An aching jag of a breath leaves her as she tries to get herself under better control—but why bother when her oldest friend is encased in ice?

Shizuka squeezes her hand. When she calls her wife's name, Shefali does not immediately turn—but instead stares longingly at the frozen horse.

"Shefali," Shizuka says again. "We will fix her."

Shefali swallows. "I wanted her to be with us."

"She is," says Shizuka. "She did well. But we need to go—we need to get to the throne room."

How small she feels standing near this statue of Alsha.

Her wife is right—they do not have the time for this. But Shefali cannot tear her eyes away from it. There is the scar from the arrow in the Golden Sands. . . .

A crack in the ice. They turn—there is a brute twice Shefali's size throwing its shoulder against the wall.

"Shefali, please." She tugs her wife's hand toward the second hallway.

Shefali stares at the brute.

At a time like this? *"Shefali!"*

But there is no stopping her.

Nothing changes in the first step. Nothing changes in the second, either, save the air around Shefali going ice cold. On the third step the ice shatters; on the fourth, the blackblood crashes through.

What has Shefali cost them with her single-mindedness? And yet Shizuka cannot look away: Shefali lets out a bloodcurdling howl as the creature rights itself. When it swipes at her with its brutal fists, she does not move out of the way—it is her bones that move for her. The sickening crack, the wet pops—Shizuka's stomach still churns at the sight. Shefali's spine stretches; her shoulders hunch; when the swing comes, she is already doubled over, mid-transformation.

Shefali forces herself up in time to grab the blackblood's elbow. Claws tip her human hands. As a wolf on a carcass, so does Barsalai Shefali bite into the arm of this blackblood, so does she gnash and tear at its flesh. Black dribbles from her muzzle—for it is a muzzle now, her nose and mouth. Gore and evil ink spurt and fall on the polished tiles of Shizuka's childhood home.

"Shefali!" Shizuka calls again. The wolf rears her head back in time to see two of the enemy push forward through the broken barricade: one swollen as a puffer, the other a twisted little goblin rolling it.

They are headed straight for her wife. Shefali has no hope of being able to reach her in time. Fortunate, then, that Shizuka knows well the ultimate gift of a ruler to their people. After all else has failed, a quick and merciful death is all that remains.

Two cuts. The arcs fly out, searing right through the two approaching blackbloods. The puffer bursts like a paper bag; the goblin is cleaved in half at the shoulders. Still the arcs fly, still they cut—two more pushing through the barricade lose their arms.

Her eyes settle once more on her wife—but this is an easy thing. All she must do is look on the great shadow that falls upon the room, all she must do is look up at what casts it.

A wolf only a little shorter than the vaulted ceilings of the Jade Palace—tall as ten Qorin stacked atop another, and wide as a team of aurochs. Fur dark as the new moon, one eye bright as the full; wicked, lustrous teeth—this is her wife.

The Phoenix Empress's mouth hangs open—though at the corners, she wears something of a smile. How like Shefali to casually do the impossible.

Their eyes meet. What unquestioned admiration Shefali finds in her wife's face! There, in the curve of her lips; there in the roses of her cheeks! And yet roses are soon to die away amidst fields of war; these are no exception.

"Beloved, they are coming."

How quickly the wolf turns! Her wife must duck out of the way of those tree-trunk legs. The padding of her feet alone would be enough to set most off their balance; at last, her mother-in-law's lessons on balance in swordsmanship are proving useful. Then the Moon breathes another cloud of ice from her muzzle—this one sealing the gate from floor to ceiling above. So thick is this ice that Shefali can barely see through it: it is white, through and through.

Shefali turns back. This time it is much more slowly, much more mindful of the Empress between her paws. Soon they are face-to-face again.

"You were incre—" Shizuka starts, but the rest is lost in a shocked yelp. As a cat picking up her kitten, so does Shefali pick up Shizuka. With the scruff of her armor pinched in her wife's muzzle, there is little Shizuka can do. Less still, when Shefali jerks her head upward and lets go.

Shizuka slaps against her wife's back with a groan. "There was no need for that!"

"Wrong." It is difficult to enunciate with this snout, but she's worn the wolf's shape before. There are ways.

As if to punctuate Shefali's point, two more blackbloods throw themselves against the barrier. It will hold—but not for long.

Shizuka grabs a handful of her wife's fur. It occurs to Shefali that a saddle would help, but they've no hope of making one now. Some god of the Qorin, to change herself into a giant wolf and forget to add a saddle.

They will need to move quickly if they are to reach Baoyi—and they must reach her. Shefali can smell her niece's fear from here, along with . . .

. . . paper, armor, blood . . .

Is that Kenshiro?

"Don't let go," says Shefali.

And who is Shizuka to disobey her wife's orders? Tight as an eel to a shark's fin, she clings to that clump of fur. The first bounding step toward the hallway lifts her right up out of her makeshift seat; the next sees her slamming down against Shefali's spine. Shizuka grunts.

"A bit more gentle, if you could!" she says between gritted teeth.

"Fast, gentle, steady," comes Shefali's voice. Qorin say you can have only two. One, perhaps, with so much at stake.

"Fast and steady it is, then," Shizuka mumbles. Shefali's ears twitch on either side of her.

As a child, she had looked on the ceilings here, on the height of the halls, and marveled. When she was eight, Shefali asked the Poet Prince why it was built in such a way, and he had told her that giants planned the place. Given how she had to crane her neck to see the ceiling at all, this sounded perfectly reasonable. Giants are the sort of people who paint false skies, especially in Hokkaran palaces.

Still—Shefali's divine form barely fits; there are only two hands of clearance between the top of Shizuka's head and the ceiling. She presses herself low against her wife's back just to avoid hitting her head.

And as they approach the kitchen, it occurs to her that the ceilings there are much lower.

"The next right," Shizuka says, "and make yourself smaller!"

Shefali whips herself around to make the turn—and in so doing, she shrinks by about a third. There's no more clearance here than there was in the grand hall. As a soldier nearly pierced by an arrow laughs, so then does Shizuka. There is a certain thrill to the sound, but it does not last long.

Five of the enemy await them in the kitchens. From the scent that hits her, there must be at least four times that many bodies. Disgusting—the whole palace smells disgusting.

Shizuka shimmies down the side of Shefali's back just to get a better look: yes, there—the bodies lie between the rows of tables.

Shefali watches her wife stagger as recognition hits her again and again. She knows the dead. Was this the face Shizuka wore at war? Shefali could live her life without ever seeing it again.

Anger wells within her. And yet as Shizuka grips her mother's sword the enemy come closer and closer. Two are perched atop one of the bodies.

The air is thick with blood about to be shed. She can smell some that is too familiar—her own brother's.

They do not have time to wring their hands.

"Do it," Shefali growls.

And so Shizuka does. As a scythe through the grass, her sword through the blackbloods. The shock runs up her arm; her shoulders howl with effort. The Qorin were right when they said straight swords were no good for mounted combat.

"Northeast corner," Shizuka says. "Behind the statue of the Sister. It's small; you're going to need to shrink again."

The third blackblood spits a foul stream of venom at them; Shizuka only just manages to jerk out of the way. Nonetheless, some lands on her robes. To her horror, they start blackening, as if burned by some unseen fire—she cuts the fabric off and lets it fall.

She is about to tell Shefali to watch out for that one, but there is no need. So many bold blackbloods today. She should be saving them, she knows, but she is out of kumaq—and no one can threaten her wife in such a way. She tells herself that she would still be killing them for it had they met on the steppes, or at least fighting them; she tells herself that they might not be Qorin at all.

But she knows that they are.

Quick, merciful deaths.

Mid-stride, Shefali snaps it up between her jaws. She does not bite, but whips her head twice in each direction. When at last she lets the body go, it is at the height of a swing—it flies out and lands on a table.

It is only then that she shrinks again. Shizuka feels as if she were riding a wolf made of ice in the summer, and that is not far from the truth. Shefali is hardly bigger than a horse.

Two more to contend with. One is a wolf much like Shefali; the other is human shaped, and that is worse. There's a spark in the eyes of the latter, a recognition—and a smile from ear to ear. For all the days of her life, Shizuka will remember that thing's toothy grin, the bright, beautiful green eyes in its sockets. The wolf lunges at them and Shizuka soon splits it, but it is the human that troubles her.

Shefali leaps a table. The statue of the Sister is less than a horse-length away—the human-shaped blackblood is the only thing barring their way. In its hands, a large pot of something or another. It meets her eyes with that awful grin, but it does not move, it does not move.

Not until the very last moment.

Then it throws the hot oil in the pot right at Shizuka.

Clever, it must think itself—but nothing has burned Shizuka in twenty years. When she swings her mother's sword, the oil catches all along its arc. Flames consume the creature; the scent of burning flesh meets Shizuka's nostrils. Another cut puts it out of its misery.

"Disgusting," Shefali rumbles.

Expert craftsmen gather around to drive a post into the ground. Six of them, hammers in hand, confront their task. The first strikes, and the next, and the next, acting in such smooth motion that their arms are like the waves of Nishikomi. So often have they done this that there is no need to speak, no need to say who comes next.

So it is with Shefali, Shizuka, and the statue. The prudent thing would be to dismount, to let Shefali move it aside so that they might proceed through the passage—but Shefali will not let her wife dismount. She knows how long it takes her to get back into a saddle, and knows well that she cannot ride bareback at all.

Shefali does not stop, and Shizuka does not question her: she simply splits the statue of the Sister in two—the arc of light coming from the Daybreak Blade makes quick work of it.

The passage is a narrow one, worn more by the steps of the servants than by any of her father's giants. How cramped, how dark!

And yet the faint taste of Kenshiro's blood drives her on. Something is wrong. Something is very wrong, and if anything has happened to her brother . . .

None of the blackbloods have found the passage—for a few brief minutes, they are free from the sounds of battle, free from the scents, free from the screams of the dying. And yet this is no peace. Is Baoyi in the chamber? Is she safe? What of her brother? Possibility is an army; Shefali is but one woman—even if she is a god. Their demonic knives find her back, and she can do little to fend them off.

Baoyi has the Phoenix Guard. They will keep her, if only for a little while—but who will save Kenshiro? The cherry-sweet taste of her scholar-brother's blood lands on the back of her tongue. Shefali wants to cry out, but what use would it be in this form?

She must save him.

Another statue of the Sister conceals the exit. Shizuka readies herself for another cut—and then they are through. Only one more hall between them and the throne room.

Yet when they emerge—when they see what lies before them—both women freeze. The Phoenix Guard are indeed here—but they are not the warriors they once were. Shoulder to shoulder, backs rigid and straight: in every way, they appear to be an army.

But they do not wear their masks, and their skin has gone the color of thousand-year eggs. Black veins crawl beneath the surface. Black their sclera, black the insides of their screaming mouths. Their teeth, too, have changed to fangs.

And the moment the two of them emerge from the tunnel, the army turns as one to meet them. So, too, do they speak as one.

"Good evening, Yui. I see you've brought your dog."

In truth, Shefali hardly hears him. Between the legs of the Phoenix Guard—just behind the Traitor—she can see her brother.

Oshiro Kenshiro is on his knees in a pool of his own blood, his eyes rolled back, his mouth open in a snarl. A spear runs him through from chest to foot. Like an errant puppet, he is nailed in place above the jade plaque.

He looks so little like himself in that makeshift armor that Shefali at first does not believe it is him, cannot believe that Tree-Mind would try to fend anyone off. What did he think he would accomplish? And yet . . .

The door is closed; his daughter is safe.

Because Kenshiro chose this sacrifice. Because he flung himself in the path of danger. Because he protected her the way he never could protect Shefali.

In a hundred years no one will remember this moment—save those who were there to see it. They will light their incense to the Warrior Moon, they will chant her name, they will beseech her guidance when the night is long and their bellies are empty. She will protect them, as she must; she will guide them, as she must. When this is through they will thank their god; when this is through, they will think to themselves that they are lucky to have someone so valiant, so vigilant watching over them.

But they will not know this: instead of rushing to her brother's aid, Barsalai Shefali let him die.

That is a weight the Warrior Moon will have to bear until the skies come down.

# THE PHOENIX

## AT LAST

“Good evening, Yui. I see you’ve brought your dog.”

His voice. Clouds of darkness leave their mouths as he voices them, coalescing into a knee-high fog at their feet. It smells of the sea, of iron, of death.

So much death—and now there will have to be more.

Her voice is a knife. “Let them go. Your quarrel is with the throne of Hokkaro, is it not? Challenge me if you will, but leave these souls out of it.”

It is one thing to see that awful grin on the face of a single black-blood—it is another to see it blossom on the face of all these soldiers at once. Like a field of flowers, she thinks, and she hates herself for the thought: all of them opening to the sun at once. “You do not hold this throne, Yui.”

As one, they move, drawing their swords and falling into their stances. Each wears the same expression, each holds their weapon the same way. The Phoenix Guard have specific height requirements—every soldier is of a size with the next, every soldier’s hair is cropped the same way. These things are meant to build unity, and so they do—but only when undertaken voluntarily.

This is something else.

The puppets at Rihima, the bodies rising to strike at their former comrades. A village reduced to cinders and ash, where the deer fear to graze and the bears fear to hunt.

The Jade Palace will soon be such a place if Shizuka does not strike down her own poisonous ancestor.

Shefali howls. She rears up on her hind legs and in so doing, grows larger again—when her front paws once more reach the ground, she is back to her towering size. So high up is Shizuka that she can no longer make out the details of the soldiers' faces.

"I may not hold the throne," she says, "but I act as Yuuko's champion in this matter. So long as I breathe, you shall not lay your foul hands on her."

The army laughs in two careful exhalations: *Ha ha*.

"Shefali," she whispers. "We are going to have to go through them."

There is no verbal answer—only something like a nod, and then five bounding steps. They are in the air once more before Shizuka knows what is happening. Over two, three, four ranks they fly—but even Shefali cannot jump them all. They land on the fifth rank, and the fifth rank is ready for them. Swords held aloft cannot compare with pikes, but they hurt all the same. Shefali howls and buckles as their weapons pierce her underbelly.

"You have no place here," the army speaks.

But they are wrong.

This is her home, this is her wife, this is her niece, these are her people. This is her place. This shall always be her place.

And it is bravery indeed to refuse to surrender it in the face of such odds.

The Daybreak Blade flashes in her hand; she swings it in a mighty arc. A flaming crescent flies from the tip. Fire consumes everything it touches—soldier and stone alike. Where once stood a rank, now there is only slag and ash. Mothers, sisters, brothers, sons, gone in a single stroke. When she looks on the heat glimmers of their souls, she finds that she knows them. Their names, their lives. If she cares to, she can hold a bead of light before her fingers and see the whole of it. Favorite foods, words whispered to one another in the dark.

Her people. She has killed her own people.

The horror of it rolls down her back like water—but the guilt she felt earlier does not find her here. There's a hollowness, a serenity instead.

She drops from Shefali's back onto the ground. All as one, the guards withdraw their swords from her wife's stomach. Drenched in molten silver, they turn toward her. She does not hesitate—if she does, she is lost. Her mother's sword flares. In a heartbeat, in a single brilliant stroke, it is over. Ten soldiers sliced in half. Ten lives gone. Why does she not feel them?

"I know that all of you can hear your Empress," she speaks. "Fight the darkness within you. Let my wife and me through, or we will be forced to go through you."

Let them call her the Heartless Sun. Let them hate her. So long as they can kill the Traitor here and now . . .

To look on a healthy plant and know what needs to be trimmed—this is what it means to be a god.

She lets out a breath, lets out a little of her fire. "Shefali. We don't have much time."

Her wife stands in spite of the wounds, in spite of the blood she has lost. Pain clouds her green eye, but she remains unwavering. With her great wolf's head, she nods.

That is all the peace they have before the army collapses in on them. Shizuka grabs hold of Shefali's fur, and Shefali flips her back into place. Another puff of ice buys them just enough time to take off down the molten path Shizuka created for them.

But Shefali isn't running so quickly as she was before, and Shizuka can feel her struggling to breathe. This—this!—is what brings her pain. The swords going in, the empty looks on the army's faces . . .

"Shefali," she whimpers, but if her wife hears her, she is too busy with the army to respond. That puff of cold has become instead a steady exhalation: with every step she takes, ice flies up around them, creating a frozen passage to the throne room. But they must have pierced her lungs: there are holes in the wall like those in a fisherman's net. Determined soldiers can slip through.

And so they do. Breaking their spines like reeds, snapping their arms, contorting themselves—they slip through. And it is then that Shizuka must strike, willing the light to leap from the tip of her sword.

How many die in that charge? For it lasts only ten minutes. Difficult to finish a meal in that span—but easy enough for a lance of light to pierce you, easy enough to wander into the jaws of a hungry god. Watch them as they fall! Watch them lurch toward their deaths, watch them raise their swords to slice at the undying! Yes—the wall is a net, and they are caught within it. In their wake, the bodies are like the kelp left ashore at low tide.

Still they ride.

Still, forward they go, as the crowd grows thicker and thicker. The broken statue of Emperor Yorihito towers like the Father's Teeth over the inky depths; the jade columns her ancestors so prized are torn apart and broken. There, the throne, the dais! How clearly she can now see them, how completely they've been destroyed! For the throne lies in splinters of gold, and the dais is a crater in the center of the throne room. Overhead, the rafters are full of bats that were once human. As one, they descend; Shizuka must avert her attention from her wife's flanks to cut them down. Worse—half of one lands on Shefali's back just in front of Shizuka. It twitches as it dies, its blood matting Shefali's fur.

A person.

With the flat of her sword, she pushes the creature aside. It topples over, landing on the head of an overzealous blackblood. To Shizuka's horror, the once-noble Phoenix Guard chomps down on it like a piece of fruit.

None of this will end if she cannot find the Traitor. Swallowing, she scans the horizon for him—for the particular tile that leads to the hidden chamber. In the northeast corner of the room . . .

There!

There he is. As a wolf among dogs, the Traitor, clad in his gaudy armor. That she missed him before now is a testament to the chaos of the moment. How casually he stands! One hand rests on the pommel of his sword as he orders his minions; he does not look toward Shizuka and the charging Shefali at all. Four blackbloods have planted themselves at each corner of the trapdoor. A body is slumped over atop of it, though beaten so bloody, Shizuka cannot imagine to whom it might belong.

"Unhand it!" Shizuka shouts.

It is then that the Traitor looks at her; it is then that he tilts his head toward her. As a professor eyeing an unruly student—Yamai and his descendant.

She does not wait for him to taunt her. With all her might, she swings. Wide and tall as an anchor, the arc that leaves the Daybreak Blade! Light slices clean through the arms of all four blackbloods; only stubs remain.

But they do not look at her.

Only he does.

Her blood boils in her ears. Standing in the shadow of Emperor Yorihito, looking so utterly pleased with himself . . . how can any sovereign find pleasure in such destruction? How can he possibly enjoy this?

But it occurs to her that she has killed many already and felt only passing guilt for it.

Her boiling blood is the same as his.

Red, her vision! Thunder drums between her ears, fire in her veins! Yes, a fire—how hot it burns! The smallest mote might consume the palace, a large one the nation. If she unleashes all of it, surely she could burn the world.

But she does not want to burn the world.

Cloaked in heavenly flame, the Phoenix Empress throws herself from her wife's back. She lands as petals land, slow and delicate, in the space the Traitor has cleared for himself. The Daybreak Blade is hot as a blacksmith's tongs. Even the air goes hazy in her divine presence.

Hear the god speak; hear the mountains crack; hear the fiery rain that leaves them!

"I am Minami Shizuka, daughter of Minami Shizuru and scion of the Minami clan. This is the name of the woman who will kill you."

Even the finest armies would tremble at the sound of her! Even Yusuke the Brawler would lay down his arms at the sight of her, her glowing eyes, the fires that lick the air around her!

And yet the Traitor born of the sea does not. He only draws his sword and lays it on his shoulder—the image of a gaudy vagabond. "When I look around with my ten thousand eyes, I see five thousand of my swords and only one of yours. You are foolish as always, Yui."

With his free hand, he snaps.

The armies turn to face them—an arena of flesh and evil ink. Shizuka's flaming aura glitters in their raised blades.

"They do not concern me," Shizuka says. She takes a single step forward. Still, the Traitor does not fall into his stance.

Another snap. Like rice through a funnel—the soldiers charging toward her.

But Shefali is there to meet them. Not once has she stopped running—and now is no exception. Before the army has taken five steps, she is running in a wide circle, breathing more ice as she goes. The wall of ice grows and grows—and Shizuka watches her wife fall away behind it.

Her fires flicker. When she said the army did not concern her, she hadn't meant . . . ten thousand against a single woman! And already she is injured, already silver blood mends the cracks in the ice wall.

A black shadow against the white—that is all Shizuka can see of her wife, her Shefali. Her name dies in Shizuka's throat; she cannot bring herself to call out for her. Together. Hadn't they said together?

Shizuka is the pot; doubt is a hammer.

And Yamai the man who wields it. His pommel cracks against her nose. Stars burst before her; blood pours into her mouth. Out of reflex, she reaches for her nose—and he meets her with a blow to the sternum. Her stomach threatens to empty. She coughs, desperate for breath, as he shoves her away.

"They should."

She twists quick enough to land on her shoulder and not her head—but even so, it is a struggle to get herself oriented. She cannot breathe, cannot focus, and just beyond the wall, she can hear Shefali's pained cries.

Yamai jabs her in the chin with his pommel. Her teeth rattle.

"You are selfish. You have always been selfish, and you will always be selfish."

Blood on the ground. The crunch of a body between Shefali's teeth. Her head, her head! As if someone has hollowed out her skull and filled it with liquid—everything is sloshing against everything else with only the slightest movement.

The sword. She must keep hold of the sword.

*Crack*. She knows that sound from the Qorin camps. No one ever wrestled Stone-Arm Batbayaar, because of his nasty tendency to break ribs. How strange, now, to recall such a thing instead of feeling any pain. How strange to think of the Qorin, and not the night she learned you can break a woman's ribs with a sheath.

A ragged breath escapes her bloodstained lips.

He answers before she can summon words. "You do not find solutions to your problems, you merely kill them."

*Puh*. Spit lands on her face, hot and then immediately cold.

And in this, the Traitor makes his first mistake—for nothing offends Minami Shizuka more than abject disrespect. The fires kindle within her once more. The daughter of Minami Shizuru, the Queen of Crows, letting a man spit on her! Lying here as he strikes her again and again!

The sharp song of a drawn blade; the clatter of his sheath against the tile. His next strike won't be so kind.

This isn't the first beating she's endured. She swallows a mouthful of blood. Her knuckles go white around the Daybreak Blade.

When he thrusts, so does she, striking up from underneath him at his sword arm. Blood wells from his wrist as he drops his sword. Whatever pride she feels is consumed by the sight of his blood: it is pale and blue, thick with bubbles.

Water. He bleeds seawater.

All it takes is the sight of it. All it takes is one glance, and already her mind has abducted her. So heavy, her armor, so dark the depths of the Kirin. The water, flowing up her nostrils and into her lungs; the water, claiming her cousin, her tears, her childhood self.

No sooner has she gotten to her feet than she screams. It is not a conscious outburst—it comes like a babe's, pulled from its mother. There is nothing more natural in the world than screaming because you are frightened.

Yet even over the sound of her own scream, she can hear her wife. Shefali's war howl pierces the screen of Shizuka's despair. This is not the Kirin. It cannot be, for her wife is here with her, and their two peoples are depending on them.

*Watch your opponent.*

This is the first rule and the north star of swordsmanship. Too long already has she neglected it. Touching the tip of her finger to the blade brings a sharp hiss of pain—this is enough to anchor her in the present. She focuses her eyes on him, though the world spins around her.

The Traitor staggers. He clutches at his bleeding wrist, his sword at his feet.

One cut is all it will take, if she can just—

Fall into stance, breathe in, step forward, cut—

He twists aside at the last moment. The arc of light flies into Shefali's ice wall, cracking it halfway. Shizuka's stomach lurches. An entire army lurks beyond that white, with only Shefali to fend them off—and now she's put a crack in their defenses.

Perhaps she really is selfish.

In the moment it takes her to glance at the crack, the Traitor has run to the trapdoor.

"You won't be able to open it," she says. "The ropes binding it were blessed by the Father himself."

An ugly look crosses Yamai's face—a storm cloud of an expression. "My brother," he says, "can never bar me for long."

He reaches for the body's hand, and it is then—yes, it is then—that Shizuka's world falls from beneath her.

That hand is smooth and brown; the cuff at its wrist green felt with white triangles embroidered. She knows that deel. His mother made it for him. During their winter in Xian-Lai, he'd worn it every single day, bragging of its warmth and many pockets.

Kenshiro. Dead with a Qorin sword in hand, dead atop his daughter's hiding place, dead after facing the same army that now threatened to claim his sister.

No.

He isn't . . . He is . . .

That *idiot* . . .

A young man may say he is the bravest warrior in the world, but that claim dies with the first friend run through by the enemy.

So it is with Shizuka. Frozen, the Sun, as Yamai closes Kenshiro's hand around the handle and pulls.

A scream shrill as metal on glass. Shizuka's hand flies to her ear, but she cannot drown it out. He's lifting, lifting—

Two spears jab at him, but he only laughs—

She cannot let this stand!

Forward, forward! Her second cut catches him across the back. Water spills from him as if his body were a dam—but he does not stop. Instead, he lets out a rattling laugh. "Haven't you forgotten something?"

A taunt, only a taunt. Another cut will end him. Straight down the line of his spine she slices—and yet still he continues. Two spears pierce his chest. He stands with a guttural yell, throwing the trapdoor fully open.

How?

Kenshiro—*Kenshiro*—said the Traitor isn't a warrior. How is it that he can withstand such blows? All her life, she has waited for this moment of their ascension; all her life, she has imagined killing the Traitor—and now her sword does not truly hurt him?

When weapons fail, your own hands will have to do. Shizuka lunges for him. He does not move to avoid her. Just as she throws her hands around his waist and sinks to her knees, realization strikes her.

The screaming has stopped. It is then she sees the water from his wrist dripping onto Lai Baoyi. Her niece's green eyes are foggy and wide, her mouth hanging open. The armor Kenshiro must have gotten her into is two sizes too big; a sword she has never used hangs at her waist. The two Phoenix Guard continue trying to kill the Traitor, oblivious to the state of their charge.

How can a man crush a heart that is no longer there? For "crush" is the word—her soul buckles at the sight. It is impotent rage that drives her, it is fury that compels her to continue her attack. She drops to her knees and lets gravity do the work of flipping him. When he clatters to the ground, a puddle forms around him—his seawater mixing with her gold.

He has the nerve to laugh. "You see? I've already—"

But she does not let him finish. He does not deserve to speak. Wretched creature! Kinslayer, betrayer of men! Who would suffer his words? She drives the Daybreak Blade straight through his throat and farther still. The tip of her sword melts through to the tile; he is doubled over backwards, with her right above him.

Yet he does not die.

The wound in his throat keeps him from laughing at her, but he does it with his eyes just the same. She raises the sword for another blow—only to stagger when a fist meets her temple. Shizuka's ears ring.

"A proper woman must be skilled in defending her home."

His lips aren't moving. He isn't the one speaking, but that is his voice, that is his voice—

She does not want to turn.

She has to turn.

There: her niece, her knuckles bruise-violet.

None of this was supposed to happen. "Baoyi," she whimpers.

"She can't hear you." Pinned as he is to the ground, he continues to speak through her niece instead. The pleasure in his voice is unmistakable. "How much of your own family can you kill in one day, Yui?"

To hear that from her lips! To see her face, to know that they are here only because of *her* failures!

Her hand flies to her chest as Baoyi reaches for Yamai's sword. "Baoyi, please—"

The slash comes quickly. Reflex alone saves her: she pulls the sword from Yamai just in time for a hasty perpendicular parry. Blade grinds on edge; her bones shiver. That strength is not her niece's.

"Ah, I forgot. You can't kill me." Now he is speaking for himself—she can hear him rising behind her, can hear the water pooling around him from his wounds.

Baoyi slashes at her again, wild and vicious. It is all Shizuka can do to parry with her flat and shove her niece's shoulder. A quick stumble is her reward—but the true treasure comes moments later.

Golden characters appear on Baoyi's chest as she recovers: *Precious, Righteous*. Shizuka chose them herself. It was—aside from Shefali's accepting her marriage proposal—the greatest honor she'd ever been given. Baozhai laid it upon her as thanks for formally severing the ties.

Her name. Shizuka still knows her true name.

But she does not know Yamai's. She sees them now, the characters, or the suggestion of them: they are so antiquated, she cannot properly read them. Even if she could—is this Yamai, or is this another name? It was not uncommon for nobles to adopt a new one upon taking the throne. Shefali had seen him in her vision as a grown man—but she couldn't have read his name.

Baoyi's assault continues. Farther and farther back she beats Shizuka, the blows heavier every time. God though she may be, Shizuka's arms scream for respite. They will find none here—no one will. Yamai's taken up a spear.

An awful sinking in her chest. Truth be told, she hadn't often defended against multiple opponents, even during the war. In those days, she was always surrounded by her own soldiers, by Xianyu or Munenori or Akiko.

But here? Here she is alone.

Baoyi's swings are heavy; parrying them is like trying to parry a bull. Five more swings, Shizuka endures, before she switches to swaying away from the tip of that thick Xianese sword. One, two, three steps she takes, watching her niece's shoulders and feet.

But Yamai is watching her.

One step backwards. Her foot lands on the severed hand of a guardsman; she slips, skids—and Yamai's spear is there to meet her. As easily as a needle pierces thread, his spear slips between her already aching ribs. It is the sight of it that jars her more than the pain, for she is by then so lost in the battle that she cannot feel any more pain. But see it—the crossguard of the spear pressed against her fine robes; the gold welling up like liquid light; the spurt when he withdraws it. Shizuka's side goes hot, and then cold as the blood leaves her.

If she was dizzy before, she is spinning now.

"What a shame you would not listen to reason, Yui. I think I could have made something worthwhile out of you."

He laughs near her ear.

*Your name, what is your name?*

When she tries to draw a breath, she finds that she cannot—something in her chest is no longer working. Blood shoots up her throat and fills her mouth. Shefali wrote so often of blood's sweetness—Shizuka tastes only copper.

Baoyi's blurry form lifts her sword overhead in one of the traditional Hokkaran stances. Another blow is coming: an overhead slash. Shizuka can see it in her shoulders. Yamai wants to split her from forehead to groin, and he will use her niece to do it. Swordplay is her mother tongue—she knows a quick thrust to the chest or stomach will end the attacker before they can finish the overhead swing.

And kill her niece.

No.

She refuses.

Spinning, spinning. The sword overhead, the spear somewhere behind her, waiting for her to back out of the way.

She cannot falter. Twenty years and more she has trained for this. If she fails, all of Hokkaro will be as glassy-eyed as her niece; if she fails, Kenshiro and her father will have died for nothing.

In her mind she sees it: she steps back, manages a hasty parry, and Yamai's spear pierces through the hard bone of her chest. This is what he wants, this is what he expects of her. Failing that, he expects her to go for the counterstroke—and so, too, will he.

Whether she steps forward or back, her fate is sealed.

It is a good thing, then, that Yamai has no actual talent with a sword.

Baoyi brings down her sword with a shout to make her ancestors proud. How heavy, that blow! A hardened oak could not withstand it, and so Shizuka does not try.

She twists toward Baoyi's sword arm, the Daybreak Blade held just overhead. As she dodges the blow, she slashes her niece across the wrist. Yamai might control her, but Baoyi's muscles will react without conscious thought. For a precious instant, her grip on the sword falters—and it is then that Shizuka drives the pommel of the Daybreak Blade against the hilt of Baoyi's, knocking it from her hand.

The idea comes to her like an old memory. With her free hand, she coats her fingers in her own blood. Baoyi comes for her like a wrestler—and Shizuka meets her with twelve strokes to the chest. All at once, the breath leaves her niece; all at once, her strength falters. She doubles over, draped around Shizuka's waiting arm.

Two characters, painted in divine blood on her chest: *Precious, Righteousness.*

Shefali has her kumaq—but Shizuka's domain has always been calligraphy. Whether it is the loss of blood that elates her or genuine relief—does it matter? She would trade nearly anything for more of this moment. Baoyi is safe. The glass has left her eyes; she is free from him. For once, Shizuka feels the hero.

Yamai cares nothing for this moment. Rage and anger drive him forward like an arrow, his spear questing for purchase on Baoyi's slumped body. Shizuka does not need to think—she drops Baoyi's unconscious body and throws herself in the path of the spear. That she manages to bat the spear off track surprises her almost as much as it surprises Yamai—his brows rise halfway up his head.

True swordsmanship happens without thinking. In this way, Shizuka drives the Daybreak Blade through Yamai's gut. Only when her hilt meets flesh does she stop thrusting; only then does she back away, twisting her wounded side away from the spurt of water.

A rasping breath. She stands, facing Yamai, her shoulders bowed. There are three of him in her vision: three spears at the ready, three rivers spouting from three men. Desperately she searches for any sign of the characters she needs. Legend and folklore said the Emperor bore the name Yamai because of an illness he'd overcome as a child—it cannot be his real one.

There! One of the characters settles into place—the second of the two. *Above*.

Above what?

"You're throwing away eternity." His voice is a washerwoman's rag. "The old hag lives forever because she cannot die. You and I—divine though we may be—can be killed. With the world under my control, they will never lift a finger against us. We will know when the new gods come, and we will drown them. The Hokkaran Empire shall stand forever, as inexorable as the tides. That is the world I envisioned. I thought my own progeny would have the good sense to join me—but here you are. Dying."

For all his talk, he, too, is dying—or will be, if she can figure out his name. Their makeshift arena is slick with his watery blood. When he levels his spear at her, it rattles; his shoulder trembles. This man is no fighter.

And yet neither can Shizuka stand. As a branch in the wind, she sways from side to side. No, her blade does not rattle in her hands, nor can she focus on the five stars of swordsmanship. How is she to pay attention to Yamai's shoulders when she cannot tell which image is the real one?

Two gods sealed in a chamber—and look at them. Ragged and worn. He was right. Either of them could die here. The sort of thing her father would have written a—

*Am I forever to gaze upon the blue sky and dream of better?*

That's it, isn't it? When the moon rose above the false palace, when her father spouted that poem—*he was helping her.* How did Shizuka not put it together sooner? Better than the blue sky—the wide, dark ocean. The blood he shed, the kingdom he so longed for. The fox-woman had tried to tell her to listen to her father!

Laughter takes her. Oh, it's all so *obvious*.

She will give the man this much credit at least: he takes her laughter for an opening, and one he is eager to seize. Another thrust from the spear, arrow quick and boulder heavy. She sways out of the way and slices the spear in two and grabs it by the shaft. Closer she pulls him with the last of her strength, close enough that she can hold him by the collars of his robes. His mouth grows into a grin. There is a dagger at his waist, and he is reaching for it. She does not care.

"What is it about incompetent gardeners? Always going on about their techniques while their flowers die around them," Minami Shizuka says. Already her fingers are tracing the characters onto his armor, already the fire is pouring into them. *Above the sea*. "Do not presume to tell the chrysanthemum how to bloom, Umigami."

THERE! HIS GRIN shatters. She has only a moment before the dagger pierces her, only a moment to do what needs to be done: she slashes over his arm at the air behind him.

"You *missed*," he says.

The dagger crashes into the side of her throat. She does not feel the pain, but she feels the impact. So, too, does she feel her fingers against his armor, tracing his name in her own golden blood.

All of this—all of this!—is so funny to her.

How common it is among the dying to laugh like this—and yet how perplexed he is at the sight.

"I never miss," she says as the darkness starts to take her, as the shadows start to swallow him.

And it is then, of course, that he hears the crack of ice. It is then that he feels the earth thudding beneath his feet, and it is then that he sees the wolf looming above him.

He drops her to the ground.

And, yes, though the dark is deep, though she has lost all her blood—she sees it happen. She sees Barsalai Shefali clamp down on him with her massive jaws; she sees her swallow him.

And she thinks to herself: *It is all right to die now, we are together.*

The rest can wait—

# LAI BAOYI

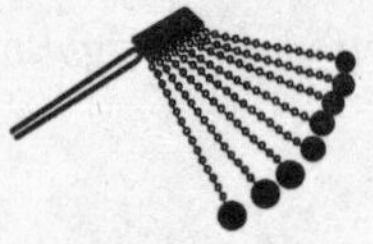

## THREE

When she wakes, Baoyi is cradled in a god's lap. Familiar eyes meet hers—but she cannot place them, does not know where she last saw them.

For a moment Baoyi thinks she must have woken from an awful dream—a dream where she forgot her own aunt, a dream where Barsalai wandered off for years and she lived her whole life without ever seeing her again, a dream where demons attacked the palace and her father decided to die.

This moment is one of the happiest in her young life. Indeed, the elation that comes to her then outweighs the elation she felt when her father placed the Phoenix Crown upon her head, the elation she felt the first time she met her mother in court as an equal and not as a subordinate, better than her brother carving his first bow and running up to show her. This moment, this joy, is better than all of the hills she has rolled down, all of the horses she has raced, all of the games of Poem War she won thanks to fate conspiring in her favor.

This moment, however, is transient. She cannot bring herself to think of it as beautiful—but it is transient.

The smell hits her first, compelling her eyes to look around. Bodies line the floor like rotting fruit beneath a tree. Some have burst, here and there, splotches of rust and wine seeping out of them. The eastern wing of the throne room is on fire; the west is clogged with the dead. The god who is holding her kneels in an ankle-deep pool of water. Blood and ink alike soak into their clothes.

The first beat of her heart is like a bolt through rice paper. The second is the fall of a hammer. So it is: she has swallowed a thunder drum, and now it wants to sing. Everything within her dances to its maddening song: her blood rushes to her ears, her breathing goes ragged; she must move, must do something to convince herself that this is not real.

She reaches for the collar of the god's deel only to see the state of her own wrist: a weeping gash of red. Somehow she expects it to hurt more than it does when she grabs hold of the deel. It is the fear, not the pain, that comes through in her royal voice. "My father. Where is my father?"

The god's eyes screw shut. She picks up Baoyi with little effort and holds her close, rocking the two of them, burying her head against Baoyi's shoulder.

And Baoyi, whose tears are not coming, thinks to herself that this is pathetic.

She hates herself for that thought, she does, but she has it all the same. This is pathetic. Whoever heard of a weeping god? Aren't there things this god should be doing? All those years she spent away doing who knows what—and now she can't even be strong when other people need her to be?

"My father," Baoyi says again. "Stop—I need to know where he is!"

"I tried," creaks the god. "We came straight here, but my horse was hurt, and I couldn't . . ."

Yes, it is pathetic to hear a god speak this way.

A horse. She can understand, on some level, what a Qorin feels for their horse, but . . .

The Moon had stopped in her tracks, and now Baoyi's father is dead, and her palace is full of soldiers who gave their lives to ensure that their young empress could be here, comforting a god.

"Tell me. Tell me where he is. Show him to me."

The god shakes her head. She has not let go of Baoyi, not once. "I have to keep you safe."

Baoyi shoves her. Despair is an open wound and every moment she spends pressed against that woman tears it anew. The hurt in the god's eyes, the hurt in her open mouth, the awful whimper she makes when she finds herself sitting alone: these things would have affected Baoyi mightily before today. Before today, she never would have imagined she could be this cold.

But she has to be cold now. Nothing is going to get done if everyone sits here weeping. These people—her people—didn't die so that Baoyi could sit here mourning.

She stands. Somewhere along the line she must have lost her shoes, for the water rushes over her feet and something in her is repulsed by the contact. She steels herself as she surveys the damage in truth, as she scans the dead for a mop of white hair.

It does not take long to find him. He is only a little distance away—just past the woman in gold.

Five steps, it takes her.

After the first, Baoyi can see what it is that killed him: there is a spear jammed right through her father's breast, piercing him through the legs beneath. He is doubled backwards like a doll.

After the second, the smell starts to fade, or perhaps she just becomes used to it.

After the third, she draws abreast to the woman in gold. A glance alone tells her who this is; a new wave of anger swells within her breast.

*I will come for you if you have need of me,* her aunt had said. Now she lies dying on the floor of the palace, her eyes clouded gold, her divine shroud soaked in water and blood.

Baoyi keeps walking.

Her father's body awaits her. She stands in front of him and it occurs to her that this is something like looking at a statue. This man, twisted backwards in his horrible pose, is not a man at all—he is a sculpture by some talented Axion. An offering sent to her; a testament to the bravery of the fallen.

If she thinks of him as a statue and not her father then perhaps she will not cry.

And she cannot cry now, not when there is so much to be done. When was the last time there had been such a funeral in the Jade Palace? The pyre they'd need for the fallen—you might even be able to see it in Arakawa. So many, so many.

And that is to say nothing of the political implications, the things she will have to weather in the days to come.

*This is why you needed an army*, they will say to her.

And she realizes with a crushing certainty that they will be wrong. An army of fifty thousand could not have avoided this fate—not when the enemy was so inhuman. But who will believe her if she says this?

There is a man in front of her, a man nailed to the ground. She must move him.

Baoyi wraps her hands around the spear and pulls. The lurch of it, the friction of his bones against the metal, disgust her, and she drops it after only a moment.

She hates herself for this weakness. After all her soldiers have done for her? After all he did for her? She cannot even . . .

Again she tries, and again her courage fails. She yanks and yanks and yanks but it will not move, it will not move, and somewhere in this, removing the spear becomes the only thing she can control, and—

And in the end, it is the god who must do it.

In the end it is the god who strides over and pulls out the spear, doing it as easily as one might remove a maiden's hairpin.

It is the god who scoops up the body of Baoyi's father into her arms, the god who carries him, the god who looks down on her and then says only: "I failed you."

Anger stops Baoyi's throat, for what is she to say to a thing like that? The god is right: she did fail. She failed everyone here. What is she to say? She cannot, will not assuage the god's guilt and shame. She refuses.

Lai Baoyi swallows. "Give him to me," she says. "You have your wife to carry."

IT TAKES HER an entire day to notice that the sun hasn't risen.

There's too much else to worry about. Soon the letters from the other lords will start pouring in, but until then the Empress has the people to deal with. Their horror, their revulsion, their confusion. On the evening of the first day she addresses them from the Pine Terrace. She is still in the armor her father strapped her into, his blood smeared all over her torso, when she tells the people of Fujino that they are safe.

That there is a god among them.

It pains her to say this, it pains her to make this announcement, but her own pain is hardly the thing that needs attention.

The people need hope.

And if hope comes in the unreliable form of her aunt Shefa, then that is what Baoyi will give them.

"The Warrior Moon arrived in our time of need," she tells them, "and it is the Warrior Moon who will see to it that we are safe."

Her aunt does not shift under the weight of this proclamation. Good. Perhaps this time she will not buckle.

She does not allow them to ask her any questions. There are only so many things Baoyi can say before the anger stops up her throat again, before she thinks to herself: *I liked it better when the gods were distant.*

And yet she cannot simply return to her room—the room her father wrenched her from just this morning, the room her handmaids have yet to return to. How is she to sleep after a day like this? How is she to lay in the silence, where she might hear their cries forever?

No, no. She cannot return to the room.

Her aunt asks her if there is any place for the Sun to rest, and Baoyi tells her that she does not care—she may use any room in the palace. She says this without looking at either of them; she says this on her way back down to the throne room.

It is dark. Overhead the moon shines through the broken ceiling of the Jade Palace, and it is in this silver light that she sees the bodies. The palace servants—those who survived—are at work already. Like puppets in a shadow play they move quickly, methodically: pick up a body, move it outside, throw it onto the pile. Tomorrow they will start the pyres. They do not see her standing there, in the threshold, watching. They do not know that it is her.

All the better.

Lai Baoyi takes a sword from the fallen. With it, she cuts her sleeves short and fashions herself a mask. This she ties around her Imperial face—and then it is time to work.

In Hokkaran thinking there is little more filthy than touching a body. Death clings to those it touches—or so she was told. In truth, the bodies do not cling to her at all. Many are stiff and unwelcoming; many do not want her to carry them, but she does. It is the blood that stains her, the blood that clings, but she is already covered in so much of it that she pays it no mind.

And so, engrossed in the necessary as she is, she does not realize the sun has yet to rise until the criers announce that it is Fourth Bell.

Fourth Bell, and the palace is still bathed in the dark.

THE SUN NO longer rises.

They know it for certain on the fifth day. At the hour appointed by her astrologers she watches the sky. Instead of the dark going light she sees only a purpling of the sky; instead of the sun, there is only a faint rim of gold around the moon.

This is the longest eclipse anyone can recall.

Lai Baoyi knows this because Minami Sakura has told her, and she knows who Minami Sakura is because the woman will not leave her study.

"I'm sorry for your loss," she says, by way of introduction. "Your father did so much for me. I don't know how I ever would have repaid him. He was a good man."

But Baoyi cannot imagine her father working with a woman like this. She's heard him talk about an old assistant of his here and there—a student who would bring back a life-changing tome—but Baoyi cannot reconcile those stories with Minami Sakura. How can she, when this woman showed up a day after everyone else in armor that doesn't even fit? When she arrives without a trace of blood anywhere on her?

"Thank you," is all she says to this, for an Empress cannot fall victim to her own emotions.

So her mother taught her. Her mother, who has yet to arrive; her mother, who has not yet received word of what happened here.

Minami Sakura sits in Baoyi's room wearing one of Momiji's robes. She alleges that all of hers got ruined in the fighting, and so she must wear those of her fallen handmaiden. Dorbentei Otgar—apparently one of Baoyi's Qorin cousins—sits not far from them, with her right leg stretched out in front. Between the three of these distant relations there is a tea set. Baoyi does not have the wherewithal to mind it; Sakura is the one serving them today.

"Have the others written in yet?" Sakura asks. "The lords, I mean. They aren't going to take this omen well."

Baoyi has received three letters: one from Fuyutsuki, one from Oshiro, and one from Xian-Lai. The first was precisely what she'd expected: a polite upbraiding, a bit of bragging that the Stone Men could have stopped the Fourth Army, an oath to send whatever aid they could, and a promised visit from young Lord Kazuki. This she left atop the lectern concealed beneath the other.

At first she thinks she must have misread the letter from her grandfather: she has never known him to dote. On the pale yellow of that paper he proves that he has something of it in him. *Your father proved his valor, but the valor of the dead is little comfort to the living. Should you wish to spend the coming months among the peaceable lands I keep, you are more than welcome. Mourning is a lonely thing.*

But she feels no need to tell this woman—this stranger—any of that. "Yes. You're right, they aren't."

"You're going to need to explain to them," Sakura continues. She pours until the kettle overflows, which tells Baoyi all she needs to know. What excess. "What happened here wasn't your fault. It wasn't anybody's fault—"

She cannot stop herself. At least the words come out coolly. "It's theirs."

Dorbentei and the Minami woman exchange a look. Baoyi can read it well: *She doesn't know what she's saying, this girl.* But Baoyi knows perfectly well what she is saying.

"My cousin gave her life to keep you safe," Sakura says, gesturing to the other room—Momiji and Akishika's room. Even from here they can see the faint glow of the Heartless Sun's repose.

"She isn't dead," Baoyi answers. It is a triumph that she says this and not what she is thinking: *I wish that she was truly dead, and that my father was instead alive, and that neither of my aunts had ever come back from their journey.*

"Well, she isn't getting up any time soon, either," says Dorbentei. "Listen to me, Baoyi. I lost my mother in this war; I lost the man who raised me; I lost cousins and friends; I lost thousands of my people. But those two, they did everything they could. You can't blame them for this. They didn't march the army to your gates. That was the Traitor, himself, and it began long before your birth. They love you, both of them—"

Something wells up inside of her, something awful and bitter. She cannot stop herself this time. "Why does it matter how much they love me when they've hurt me so badly? Leaving me behind in a place like this and returning only to ruin it."

Neither of the women has anything to say. Silence settles upon them, broken only by the bubbling of the tea. Minami Sakura pours it into their cups without a word. Unable to shed her years of training no matter her turmoil, Baoyi raises the cup to her lip and smells it.

"Fine leaves."

"Thank you," says Sakura. "They're yours."

Of course they are. She counts to eighty before drinking, as is polite. The tea is smooth; the taste coats her tongue. She tries not to think of how often she shared this variety with her father.

"Where is the Moon?" she asks. She tires of these niceties.

"Checking in on a friend," answers Sakura. "But she asked Dorbentei and I to keep an eye on you and my cousin."

Checking in on a friend at a time like this? Selfish, selfish. If it was Baoyi laid out in that room, her father never would have left her side.

"When's the funeral?" asks Dorbentei, and Baoyi is almost grateful for the change in subject.

"Tomorrow," Baoyi answers. "The pyres will burn on the Pine Terrace, where everyone may see them. It is the least that I can do."

"Tomorrow?" says Sakura. "But what about your mother?"

It is an abominable talent of hers to say the thing that will hurt the most. "My mother is in Xian-Lai. It will be at least another week before she's able to be here. The dead deserve their rest sooner than that."

Sakura takes a sip from her own cup.

They have their tea together, these women, mostly in silence. Here and there Sakura will attempt to start a conversation—but it never gets far before Baoyi finds the inevitable fault with it. She wonders why people pay for the companionship of singing girls at all if this is what they offer. Aren't they supposed to be better at conversation?

Dorbentei is better, but only a little—she knows that there isn't much to say in a situation like this on a personal level. It's she that steers the conversation toward the eclipse and what it might mean: to the fields soon to wither without light, to the cold summers and long winters if something is not done.

They are problems without solutions and questions without answers.

Lai Baoyi is tired.

LATER THAT NIGHT the Moon comes to her.

"I have something to show you," she says, appearing as she does beside the sleeping Empress.

(She cannot sleep in her own bed anymore. She sleeps in Odori's, instead, as it has been empty since the day of Mourning.)

Baoyi looks up at her. The silver disc hangs in the window just behind the god. The crown it lends her is unearned. "Why should I come?"

The Moon kneels down next to her and extends her hand.

"Please."

Against her better judgment, Baoyi accepts.

THEY ARE ON the Pine Terrace. Already the pyres themselves have been constructed; the bodies must be moved beneath them, and that will happen tomorrow morning. At the stroke of Fifth Bell Baoyi will light these delicate wooden constructs. The flames will consume the bodies of those who died, offering their souls as smoke to the Eternal Sky.

That is how her father would have put it. But her father is dead, now, and she will lay him first upon the pyres in the morning.

Fujino is no place for a sky burial.

The Moon next to her is silent. In the dark of the night—the true night, and not the eclipse—she looks more like her human self. A twinge of guilt runs through Baoyi. This is her aunt, after all, whom she has treated so harshly.

Her aunt—whose weaknesses got everyone killed.

But it would be unbecoming of her to be impolite. She breaks the silence of the moment, as awkward and wrong as it may feel to do so. "How did your visit go?"

"My visit?" says the Moon. She sounds surprised.

"In the city," says Baoyi. "Minami-lao said you were visiting a friend."

A pause. The Moon's face goes a little softer. "She is well."

Another silence. They stand there amidst the pyres, the jagged edges of their broken souls threatening to chip each other.

"Baoyi."

The Moon cannot say her name properly. Xianese tones are difficult; she tells herself that she should not be angry about it—but it is another of her failings. A simple one to remedy. Can a godly tongue not shape a syllable properly?

"Aunt."

"I failed you," says the Moon. "But I won't fail my brother."

Baoyi's stomach goes cold. "What do you mean?" she says. She cannot allow her hope to grow, cannot allow herself to be reckless.

The Moon raises a finger to the stars. Baoyi follows it, squinting at the constellation. Junko and the Tree, if she's not mistaken—but there is one star that does not fall in line with the rest. At the very top of the tree one shines brighter than all of the others, one she is certain she has not seen before.

"That is where he is," says the Moon. "And that is where he will always be."

Hope is a strange thing. Birthed quickly, it is doomed for either a life of fragility or one of incandescent greatness. Its death leaves behind a taste more bitter than any wine. Baoyi has nurtured hope for most of her life—but there are always new hopes to be born, new hopes to die in her breast.

But none feel quite so bitter as this death.

"I want him back," she says.

"I know," says the Moon. "I can't do that."

"You're a *god*!" Baoyi argues. She's surprised at how loud her voice is, at how it echoes around the terrace. To her utter shame there are tears in her eyes; to her utter shame, she cannot keep that same voice from cracking. "How can you say you can't? How can you . . . You just hang a star up and act as if that's meant to help?"

The Moon says nothing. As Baoyi rounds on her, as Baoyi thrusts a finger into her chest, the Moon says nothing—only listens.

"I cannot talk to that star, Aunt. It cannot talk to me. When I am alone at court with no defenders, I can't expect it to cheer me up. You have taken my father and given me a star, and you have the *nerve* to stand here and act as if I should be grateful?"

The Moon says nothing. As Baoyi beats her fists against the Moon's chest, as the tears stream down her face, she says nothing.

"He was your *brother,*" Baoyi says. The strength is going out of her and she hates that it is, she hates that she cannot keep raging, she hates that she is raging at all—that her aunt can see her in such a state.

The Moon tries to embrace her, but Baoyi bats her arms away. "Don't touch me," she says. "Don't you dare touch me. You *killed* him."

Her legs give out. The Empress collapses on the Pine Terrace, clutching uselessly at her aunt's star-spattered deel. Those three words keep leaving her: they are the only thing she can think, the only thing she can say, the only thing she is. All of her being, all of her soul, is encased in that accusation. She speaks it over and over, until her voice at last gives out in the cold air of winter. Sobs at last win out over words; she can only choke at the memory of the man who has left her behind.

The Moon says nothing—only sits next to her and bears it all: the accusations, the attack, the unimaginable misery.

Because in the end, she knows well enough that Baoyi is right: her brother is no longer here, and it is her own fault.

The two of them sit in the dark until morning, and when at last the Empress cries herself to sleep, the Moon carries her back to her room.

## MINAMI SAKURA

# NINE

When all of this is over—when the dead have been buried, when Empress Yuuka has given her speech honoring them, when the Qorin leave for the Silver Steppes—Minami Sakura decides she will return home.

She tells Otgar this on the night before her departure. They are together in the rooms Baoyi has provided them—gifts given with a polite smile and an unspoken desire for them to leave. Otgar is reading over the lines Sakura wrote that day at the lectern, her deel half unbuttoned. Her skin looks like polished wood when the light shines upon it, and Sakura finds herself thinking—not for the first time—that it would be lovely to paint her.

"I'm going back home," Sakura says to her.

Otgar smirks. She doesn't look up from the lines. "Which home?"

"Nishikomi." Sakura throws the contents of her ink bowl out the window. "It's been too long."

"Are you sure that's what you want to do?" Otgar says. Now she turns, her injured leg always bearing the least of her weight. "Places stay the same, but people don't. You go back there, and you're going to be a crone among children."

"I'm not that old," Sakura answers her, but there's little mirth in it. She is thirty-something when, by all rights, she should be most of the way to fifty. At least, that's what she thinks. Sometime during their journey, even the calendars changed: the years are counted since the departure of the Phoenix.

It has been eleven years since that day in Nanatsu.

"Old woman," Otgar repeats. Then, more quietly: "We're both old women."

Otgar makes no more arguments on the subject. It'd be pointless to when she herself is leaving in the morning for her own home. Perhaps that is why she gave such advice in the first place.

If it is, Sakura does not want to think about it, and neither of them want to speak of it.

So little of the world makes sense now.

That night they fall asleep in each other's arms. Otgar's never shown interest in anything beyond this, beyond the simple intimacy of sleep with someone safe, and Sakura has never pressed her. It is simple, and it makes sense, and it occurs to her that she feels safe here in a way she rarely does anymore.

In the morning, she sees Otgar off.

In the afternoon, she thanks Baoyi and leaves.

SHE TRAVELS WITH a caravan along the Threefold-Promise Road. North from Fujino, over the Sound of Stone to Arakawa. One week there while the caravan trades their textiles for lumber and craft goods, and then it's on to Horohama, where the remaining textiles fetch fine art and furniture. Weighed down as they are, it takes nearly a month to reach Nishikomi from Horohama.

There is plenty of time to think and to listen and to speak. Growing up the way she did has taught her the value of these things—people will tell you anything if you convince them you're a good listener. She ingratiates herself to them within the first week with gifts and compliments; in the second week, she becomes their closest friend. So long as they never ask her anything about herself—and they so rarely do—she is happy to listen.

Here is the truth of the matter: she cannot think of anything to talk to them about. All her favorite poets have long since fallen out of fashion; so, too, her favorite painters. She finds this out after quoting one and referencing the other only to receive blank stares for her trouble. They tease her for the patterns on her robes—doesn't she know no one's worn deer-dapple in ten years?

Sakura tells them she is a little old-fashioned.

By the time they reach Arakawa, they have all given her their secrets one way or another.

But she does not care about secrets. Not now.

She cares about the mundane. Kazuma-zul might be straining to impress Seijuro-zul, but it is not that which interests Sakura. It is that Kazuma-zul is from Shiseiki Province and is the most well off of the caravan guards. New armor, a new sword at his hip polished and bright, fine clothes beneath, leather boots and a mask of solid silver—what is a boy like that doing in a merchant caravan? And why is it that everyone expects this of him, given that he is from Shiseiki?

The answer does not come to her until she reaches Horohama. Then everything falls into place: Horohama and Kimoya are the only two cities left untouched by the Great Wave. Anything north of them was carried up and swallowed away—meaning that most of Shiseiki's population lived there, and now a generation had grown up there in the face of that tragedy.

Horohama had grown from a town of artisans and engineers to a sprawling metropolis that approached—but could not match—Nishikomi. Easily thrice as many people lived there as she'd expected. Those selfsame artisans and engineers had, in the wake of the Wave, realized the value of their craft—it was they who ran the city now. As they reached the city walls—walls around Horohama!—the guards wore the livery of the Craftsman's Guild, and not the province itself.

She had tried, of course, to look as if she expected all of this: the streets lined with food stalls and performers, the buildings rising twelve stories up, the clockwork and exquisite statues.

"Beautiful, isn't it?" Kazuma-zul said to her as they rode through the streets. "There isn't anywhere like it in the whole Empire. Above the Waves—that's Shiseiki for you."

The answer had come out of reflex. "It's nice," she said, "but it's no Nishikomi."

Through all her time in Horohama, she told herself that this was true. The fried food here was good, but there wasn't any fried octopus—you had to go to Nishikomi for that. So what if she could fetch a good price for her paintings here? She'd get a better one back home. And what did it matter if she couldn't even recognize the patterns girls were wearing on their robes these days? Nishikomi was the Queen of Cities; she was as timeless as the stars above.

After two months of travel, she awoke one morning to hear that they were near Nishikomi. With an unspeakable thrill in her heart, she thrust her head out of the carriage.

And there it was, the Queen of Cities: just as bright and beautiful as ever. From here, she could already see the massive ruby glinting atop the governor's manse, taken from Dao Doan; from here she could see the sprawling streets she knew so well, the old buildings with their old stone guardians; from here, she could see the docks, the Father's Teeth, the theater houses, and the campus of the White Leaf Academy.

The darkness brought on by her cousin's long rest only served to make the city seem more alive, somehow: there are lanterns hanging on lines down every street.

From here, by any account, she could see the shadow of her home.

And yet—from here she could see the bay, where Shizuka first ascended, and where Sakura nearly drowned; from here, she could see the Tokuma Mountains, where the Qorin had carved a path north through the Azure Pass; from here, she could see the thousands of sailors and merchants and street toughs, the assassins and the singing girls, so many of whom were children when she left the city.

They pass the gates.

She thanks the caravan guards for her passage. They smile. "We're leaving again in a week," they say. "In case you have any business in the capital."

"I won't be coming back," she tells them. If she tries, Baoyi will cast her out. What use does the Empress have for her? Historian for a woman no one remembers, record-keeper to no one of record. That Sakura changed Baoyi's bedclothes doesn't seem to matter—her memories of her childhood are muddled at best.

And so she leaves the caravan behind. It is early in the morning in Nishikomi, though she only knows that it is thanks to the criers. The air carries the salt and sound of the sea.

Her feet carry her forward. She does not consciously think of where she is going, deciding with a sort of duelist's serenity which way she will go at any given corner. Down the streets and up the alleys wanders the lost historian, surrounded on all sides by those who do not know what she has seen.

The first fried-octopus stall she sees is only a few streets in. She stops there and asks for three balls of it on a stick, her favorite way to eat them. The merchant looks her up and down with vague amusement—she has changed her deer-dapple for a geometric knot pattern—and smirks. "Ten bu."

"Ten bu?" Sakura protests. Maybe it's the sea air that brings her accent out in full. "For fried-octopus balls? Quit jerkin' me around, I'm a local. I'll pay ya five, at most."

But the man's smirk shrinks a little, fading like paint in the sun. "I said ten bu. It's ten bu wherever the fuck ya go. Don't like my prices, go argue with somebody else, lady."

Haggling can get you only so far when someone's staring at you like this. She knows she's lost. Resigned to her fate, she reaches for her coin purse—only to realize with a lurch that she does not have any properly stamped money. All through her travels, she's gotten by on an Imperial Writ Baoyi was kind enough to give her—but that only covers transportation and its associated costs. The caravan itself covered all her expenses.

All she has now are a handful of coins, stamped with her cousin's Imperial Name, coated in rusty brown flakes of blood.

Her stomach lurches. "Look," she says. "I'll make ya a deal. I'm a painter—"

"Don't wanna hear about a deal," says the merchant. He taps the stall with a forefinger. "Ten bu."

She puts the coins down.

He takes one look at them and sneers. "The fuck are these? Stop wastin' my time."

There are four people in line behind her. Two of them start to snicker; one sighs. Already she can feel the weight of their derision.

She takes her coins—her cousin's coins—and she tucks them back into her purse and she leaves without any of her favorite food.

It is another hour of wandering before she stops again. In that time, a hatred stews within her. On the mouths of sailors and thugs alike, she hears the words "Day of Mourning." Women gathered outside teahouses talk of little else except the Empress's proclamation, which has only recently reached Nishikomi.

"Idiot move to call on the Heartless Sun," she hears. "The price ain't worth it. How many did we lose?"

"Pretty much everybody that was there, way I hear it," answers her companion. "If it wasn't for the Moon, we wouldn't have a capital."

These words, exchanged behind the polite screen of fans, are poison to Sakura. She cannot stop herself from boiling over. "They saved the Empress together, Sun and Moon both. Watch yer mouth when yer talkin' about them."

The two women turn to face her, their brows rising halfway up their foreheads.

"What?" says Sakura. "If you want to fight about it, let's fight about it, but I ain't gonna stand here and listen to you talk about the Sun that way."

"You a sun-lover or somethin'?" says one of the women. "If you ain't noticed, it's been months since she showed up. She's probably fuckin' dead."

"This one's sick in the head," says the other. "Just look at how she's dressed."

*I painted these robes,* Sakura wants to say. *I made this popular.*

"I was fucking there," she says instead. The words come out like shards of crushed glass. Her throat's raw; she tastes copper. Blood rushes to her temples, and she wonders who the fuck they think they are to say something like that, to speak so casually when so many people have died. All at once, the memories return: the blood up to her ankles, the scent making her eyes water, the screams and rattles of the dying. Hands reaching out for her. The smoke that coated everything for days afterwards. All the bodies burned on a massive pyre.

And these women treat it like everyday gossip?

As a grape in a vise: her head, her emotions. She shuts her eyes and drives her palms into them—a vain attempt to calm herself.

". . . Sorry about that, then," says one of the women.

"Yeah, we didn't know."

Sakura doesn't want to be around them anymore.

There is an aching anger that threatens to split her apart from within. The violence of it shocks her—and it *is* violence. Never in her life has she been so overwhelmed by her own fury. Shaking her head, she leaves the two women and continues down the street, turning at the first alley she sees.

Minami Sakura, Imperial Historian, slams her back against the wall in an alley. She slides down onto her bottom. Leftover rainwater soaks into her fine robes. A little farther down, there are three thin vagrants sharing a single pipe of Blessing; she can smell it from here. Even this scent is enough to cut through to the quick of her. She is shaking, she is rocking back and forth, and she does not know why.

Only when she opens her eyes does she find some relief.

There, upon the wall, is the mouth Juzo told her to look for all those years ago. Man-eater Matsutake's sigil has faded since the last time she saw it—vibrant red to dusty brown, bright white to a faint gray—but it is unmistakable all the same.

*I'm safe,* she thinks to herself, and for a moment, she even believes it. Breathing comes easier; she stops shaking quite so much. With a bit of effort, she can even get to her feet.

But it occurs to her as she wanders closer, as she runs her hand over the painted symbol, that it must have been years since someone stood where she did now and created it. Eleven years north of the Wall, eight years in Xian-Lai . . .

She has been away from home for half her life, hasn't she?

A cold desperation seizes her. Swallowing, her stomach rumbling, and her head still pounding, she returns to the street. She pays little attention to the crowds this time, humming as she goes to try to drown out their chatter. One turn, another. Fate must work in mysterious ways—she is not far now.

One turn, another.

Past the fried-octopus vendor she gave most of her childhood earnings to, past the dye merchant who gave her her first paints, past the teahouse where her famous aunt wooed all her one-night companions.

*I am safe*, she thinks, *I am home*.

But when she rounds the last corner, she must lean against a cart to keep from falling over.

For the first twenty years of her life, Minami Sakura lived in a pleasure house—and the most famous pleasure house in the quarter, at that. The Shrine of Jade Secrets attracted even the young Lord Shiratori in his youth—along with all the gem lords and all of Man-eater Matsutake's people. Sakura's aunts fetched the highest prices outside of the capital.

But it was more than a pleasure house—it was a place that accepted women, a place that celebrated them, whatever shape they wore. Sakura grew up surrounded by them: the delicate flowers so often favored by the nobility, the guards with their hair styled short, the women who came because no one else would recognize them as women. Only a Qorin girl could say she grew up with more aunts than Minami Sakura.

If anyone could understand her, if anyone was willing to listen to what she'd gone through—it'd be them.

Where have they gone now?

For the Shrine of Jade Secrets no long stands around the corner from that old teahouse.

Nothing stands there. An empty lot, filled with weeds where the flowers once stood.

Once more she feels herself start to crack, once more she thinks: *I can't take any more of this.*

There's a vagrant sitting right outside the lot; she walks to her as if in a trance. "Excuse me—what happened to the place that used to be here?"

The woman's eyes are quick and alert. There are any number of reasons she might have ended up on the streets; Sakura doesn't want to consider any of them. "The brothel?"

"The pleasure house," Sakura corrects. "What happened to it?"

The woman's mouth perks up at the corners. "Where have ya been? It's been years that place ain't been here."

"Just . . . just tell me!" Sakura says. She can hardly breathe—her eyes keep going to the lot, to the emptiness of it. How awful to know where her room used to be—and to see only empty space instead.

"Fine, fine," says the woman. "There was a girl worked there by the name of Fujiko. Real popular. Got herself tied up with Matsutake's kid. The two of 'em really got along; it was more than just a work thing for them. Matsutake's kid starts talking marriage. Turns out, one of her other clients was Howlin' Hidamori, and he didn't take too kindly to it. Burned the whole place down in the middle of the night."

*Burned the whole place down.*

How is it that people speak so easily of tragedies?

"But the girls—"

"Most of 'em made it out okay," she says. "But it was years ago, like I said. Most of 'em skipped town to Horohama or Fujino after that. Ain't worth the hassle, they figured."

Horohama.

She was right there, and she hadn't known . . .

*Places don't change, but people do.*

Otgar is wrong. Standing in the empty lot, Sakura thinks to herself that Otgar is wrong. Perhaps there's an element of truth if you're a Qorin, your only markers the hills and river and mountain—but if you put enough people together, then they'll change any place over time.

Twenty-two years since she last set foot in Nishikomi.

Why did she ever think it could be home again?

SHE SELLS PAINTINGS for a day up by the Academy. What she really wanted was a chance to present her work on the Day of Mourning, on the journey she'd been on for the past fourteen years, but the dean has no great want to hear her.

"If you are truly Minami Sakura, you would have come with Queen Lai's recommendation," he says.

"I just got back from the North," Sakura says. "I haven't had time to visit the South yet."

He smacks his lips and strokes his beard. "It will do you no good to go now. The Queen is in mourning; her son is accepting visitors on her behalf. Prince Lai Yangzhai is not kind to those who mean to defraud his mother."

Yangzhai? Was that what they'd named him? She wonders if he takes after Kenshiro at all—if he is soft and kind and in far too deep. From the sound of things, he takes after his mother, which means this man is right: he will never accept a visit from her.

"Minami Sakura would be near fifty, at any rate," says the man.

She wants to tell him about the way time works over the old Wall, in the place that was once so thoroughly under the thumb of evil that the hours themselves could not escape.

He will not understand. He is simply here to preside over his students—a body of scholars to whom Sakura has never belonged.

She thanks him for his time, she leaves, she sells the paintings. In one day, she earns enough to have someone take her to the swamps.

To the Minami lands.

Though she has served as the steward of the manse and its surrounding property for eight years, Sakura has never been there herself. There was never any reason to visit as a child; that manse belonged to Minami Shizuru, and the Queen of Crows was known to make periodic visits. Woe betide anyone she caught lurking in the dark on such occasions. Later—after O-Shizuru-mor's passing—only her elderly grandparents remained, and who would rob an old couple?

But it has been years now, and they are probably as dead as all the other Minami.

She must see it for herself.

It takes less than a Bell to reach the Minami lands from Nishikomi. She feels guilty for commissioning this carriage at all—surely she could have walked. It is only when the solid ground gives way to filmy green water that she realizes she has been right all along.

The carriage driver knows a ferryman, and the ferryman promises to take her to the manse. It lies a little farther in, surrounded on all sides by nose-deep water.

"Careful, Sakura-lao. Lots of beasties in a place like this, ya know?"

So he speaks to her.

She sees them, the beasties: two golden eyes just above the water, a ridged back. She hears them: the snap of powerful jaws, the hiss of an unseen serpent.

"Frankly," she says to him, "I wish they'd try me. They wouldn't like what they found."

He laughs at this, and she knows that she has her in. She asks him a little of what he's heard. The ferryman's quick to tell her that Dao Doan's army grows by the day, that he doesn't trust them, that they must mean to seek vengeance—but she is just as quick to cut him off.

"Tell me about the manse."

"It's haunted," he says, as if describing the color of the sky. "Has been fer years, now. Kinda sad, ain't it, when a whole family dies out like that? I mean it's no wonder the last few of 'em never stuck around."

"The last few?" Sakura asks him.

"That old couple, and the historian, too. She had the same name you do, I think—Minami Sakura. Singin' girl, they said."

"It's a common name," Sakura says. "Especially with singing girls."

She asks him no more questions, and he gives her no more answers. When at last the manse itself rises ahead of them, she thanks him and tells him to wait. He gives her a bow from the waist.

"Whatever you say, Sakura-lao," he says. "Just remember, you gotta pay me again for the ride back."

It strikes her as unfair. Two weeks ago, she would have argued the point, but she no longer has the will for it. This is the way of the world now—everything keeps getting more expensive, and she has so little to pay with.

But the ferryman soon falls from her mind. Comparing the dilapidated pile of wood in front of her to the sketches she received every few weeks is a troubling exercise. The manse was never a large one, not even when it was granted to the family, but this . . . If a child dropped shattered tiles on a pile of twigs, it would have gotten a similar effect. Strangely, only half the manse has been so crushed: the western wing remains standing just as she'd imagined it.

She wonders if some unseen giant stepped on her ancestral home. There isn't any way to know—the trouble with invisible giants is that you die if you see them.

For a moment, she stops before the manse and admires what there is left to admire: the corner guardians, of which only kirin and dragon remain; the fine red lumber they'd used for the flooring; the lacquer on the door. Half a gilt fox head escaped the destruction: its single eye stares back at her as she approaches the door.

Within, it is dark; within, it smells like the belly of a whale. Sakura covers her nose and mouth with her unmarried sleeve. There is a lantern hanging by the door—she picks it up and, without thinking, asks for Shizuka to light it.

*Idiot*, she thinks.

A sigh.

She puts the lantern back on its hook. It swings, the hinge squeaking, and she resolves herself to stand in this very spot until her eyes adjust well enough to see.

The Shrine of Jade Secrets may have been destroyed—but she can salvage something here. These are her lands now. Baoyi would not deny them to her if she asked. It seems a tragedy to let a line as old as theirs die off. Hokkaro treasures its traditions; surely there is still a place for the Minami clan.

Of course, all of this means she'd have to have children, and she isn't certain how to feel about that. The idea of something growing within her for nine months makes her skin crawl; the idea of pushing it out . . . no.

Perhaps Otgar will want to speak to a sanvaartain.

She gives that thought no more room to grow, for if she does, she is afraid there will be a place for it. Already this one is ruined.

Darkness takes shape before her: a screen, crushed as if in some unseen hand; a flower vase dashed against the wall, the pebbles within it like the scales of a slumbering serpent; empty sheaths hanging from the wall. She notices with something like pride that the bamboo mats beneath her feet are perfectly dry. At least something in this place lived up to its name.

But this is only the entry room: there should be five more, with the servants' quarters in a separate building a li away. She turns the layout of the place around in her mind: What has the collapse ruined? The kitchen, of course; she realizes with a lurch that the reading room was beside it and must also be gone. That leaves two rooms of personal quarters and a small shrine.

There is a sliding door to her right—it leads to the shrine, which branches off into the two personal rooms. She steps toward it as carefully as she can—over the pebbles, over the chunks of broken wood.

This is the last place in the world that is truly hers; she must know what has come of it.

And yet Minami Sakura is no Barsalai Shefali: her vision at night is no more special than any woman's. So it is that she steps on one of the shards of the broken vase; so it is that she yelps with pain; so it is that she falls to the ground and more shards find their way into her shoulders.

As if the pain of having her homes taken from her were not enough, as if the pain of solitude were not enough, as if the pain of being forgotten were not enough: she must bleed.

She curses, sucks in a breath, and curses again. It does little to alleviate her suffering. She thinks to herself that the right thing to do is to get the shards out and find a walking stick to stand with, but that seems an insult after all she has been through. For four minutes, she lies there as the tears well up, as she cries onto the mats her ancestors wove, as she wonders what it was she did to deserve all of this.

In truth, she knows the answer: she made the choice to leave with her cousin.

And now she lies bleeding in their clan's own broken manse.

But it is the fifth minute that truly drives despair into her heart—for five minutes after her injury, she first hears the breathing.

A dog that has run for three li in search of its master, only to find him a corpse on the battlefield; a murderer, slathered in the viscera of their passion; a demon leaping onto the back of Burqila Alshara's horse.

All of them made this sound.

Cold familiarity strikes her. Her heart has fallen into a vise; her body has turned to stone. She cannot move for fear of what she might find if she turns around. "Who is that?" she asks.

There is no answer—only more of that rasping.

Worse: it rises and falls, rises and falls. A bellows emptied over the fire; the snort of a boar on a lance; the death scream of an oak tree: all these things resemble the laugh of the creature. "Company."

"I don't want any company!" she shouts back. Her voice has gone shrill as glass. The thing's voice is enough to kindle her body's survival instincts: she scrambles backwards, the shard driving itself farther and farther into her flesh. Her hands land on something hard and smooth, and she thinks that it must be a table—she tries to hoist herself up only for the shelf to give out beneath her weight.

*Thud, thud, crack.*

Whatever it is, it's coming closer.

Sakura swallows. There is no Burqila with her now, no Shizuka; the evil that lurks here is something she must confront alone. Only the ferryman even knows she is here, and he won't be able to hear anything that happens in the manse—he's too far off.

"You're *my* company."

What will happen to her if she dies here?

What manner of creature is this?

She feels for something else to stand on even as she trains her eyes before her, where the shards of pottery shatter beneath the unseen footsteps of the creature. It occurs to her then that she has already seen it, that it was here all along: the darkness itself is marching toward her, solid as ink, a shadow living and hateful.

A scream dies in her throat, for she realizes then what this is—not a demon, not a god, but a ghost of formless hatred. If she could make it outside the manse, then she might have some hope of escape, but even that would be short-lived: this thing would cling to her no matter where she went. She had shed blood within the Minami clan's mansion.

At last her hand finds a solid plank of wood. Thrusting it against the ground, she pulls herself up. The exit is close enough, she could probably run it; she needs to run it, she did not make it through fourteen years of demon warfare only to die here in an old abandoned manse; she does not want to die; she cannot make that run.

*Crack, crack, huh huh huh.* Rank breath washes over her; she can feel its evil coating her skin, her hairs standing on end.

"It's been too long," says the creature. "Too long since I tasted—"

The last word is lost in a scream—the creature's. Sakura plugs her ears as a silver bolt pierces straight through the center of the dark. Like string around a spool, the silver bursting forth. Though she covers her eyes and turns away, she knows somehow that it will not harm her—even as the temperature in the room drops to a winter chill. Soon she can no longer feel her injured foot at all, for the cold has sapped away all the feeling in it; soon she is breathing in daggers and breathing out desperation.

Only when she hears the next voice, only when the evil has left her skin, does she open her eyes once more. "Always a Minami to save." Like temple bells, like quicksilver.

The Warrior Moon stands before her.

For the second time in only a few moments, Sakura swallows. "Barsalai," she says. "I thought . . . thank you."

The Moon tilts her head. "No jokes?" she says.

"Don't have any in me," Sakura answers. How could Barsalai think this was a time for jokes? Even Otgar would have held back. But, then—who can know the mind of a god?

Barsalai says no more. She kneels down in the ruins of the manse—the moonlight filtering in through the windows—and reaches into her deel. The pungent smell of kumaq conquers the wet musk of the manse. Eight white drops land on Sakura's injured foot.

Sakura waits for something to happen, anything. Though the shadow of death has left a bitter taste in her mouth, there's a morbid curiosity to this. What will it feel like to be healed by a god? Kenshiro told her once that Shefali had helped him in this way, and that was before she'd fully ascended. What will it be like now? Will it leave a scar?

But in the end, nothing happens.

Barsalai purses her lips. "Sorry. Only Qorin."

Sakura winces. Disappointment after disappointment. "Can you keep it cold, at least?"

A nod. Barsalai's hand skates over Sakura's skin, leaving a thin layer of frost in its wake. Then she sits up and looks around. In silhouette, her nose stands out like a needle—she has not left that part of herself behind. "Why here?"

The question comes as a surprise. It's a fair one, she supposes, and deserves an answer. "This place is mine. My cousin left it to me. I . . . I wanted to see what was left of it. If I could make something out of it, you know?"

She hates how childish she sounds—but Barsalai does not make her feel childish for saying it. Instead she nods once. "Two bodies," she says, pointing. "Get a priest to lay them to rest."

It is then that Sakura laughs, for the idea of a god—her personal friend, the god—asking her to summon a priest is preposterous. A smith asking someone else to make him a nail.

"Death isn't mine," says Barsalai. "It's Akane's."

"Yeah, it's just . . ."

"Silly."

"Yeah," Sakura agrees. "All of this is silly."

Another small silence. Barsalai Shefali, the Warrior Moon, clears away the shards and sits next to her wife's cousin. Her friend.

Sakura has found it easy to speak to others her entire life, but no words come to her now. The food merchant, the shrine, the Academy, and now this: four defeats have left her cracked and broken. Tears flow through the cracks now; gulping cries soon follow. Barsalai listens as her sorrows carry her away—but she says nothing, for there is nothing she *can* say.

"I just wanted to go home," says Sakura. A child, a child—that is all she is. "I just wanted to go home, for once, to have some time for myself . . ."

"Home isn't a place," Barsalai says.

"It was *once*!" Sakura answers. "You don't understand. You didn't grow up the way I did. For you, it was always the people, wasn't it?"

Barsalai nods.

Sakura sniffs. "It wasn't just that for me. It wasn't just the people I knew. It was the city itself. Nishikomi was a friend to me. It had its salty side, sure, but . . ."

Another stretch of silence. Barsalai's white brows are knitting together over her eyes, as if she's trying to imagine how anyone could possibly love a city.

"Wherever I went, I kept thinking: 'When this is done, I'll go back home to Nishikomi,'" she says. Her voice is a creak. "I kept planning it out in my head, the places I'd go, the things I'd do, the people I'd see. But none of it . . . None of it's the same now. Everyone got old and left without me. My favorite place is gone because some asshole couldn't get his temper under control, and even this *stupid fucking wreck . . .*"

She can't keep talking; her throat's closed. Thankfully, Barsalai doesn't press her. There's another silence, another chance for Sakura to catch her breath.

And it is in that moment—with the moonlight shining into the wreck of the Minami manse—that a question slithers its way up her throat. In voicing it, she makes real a thought she isn't brave enough to name.

"Barsalai," she says. "Was it like this for my mother?"

This time, there is no silence. "Yes."

Days folding into years, a city whose face you no longer recognized, the ruins of a dream long gone. She understands. At long last, she understands. "She killed herself, didn't she?"

"Yes," says Barsalai.

Sakura laughs, but there is no mirth in it. Her head hits the wall; a snow-devil of dust coats her shoulder. "You told me to light prayers."

"Everyone deserves to be remembered," Barsalai says. "In any way they can be."

A pause. The words hang in the air, echoing as they always do, and Sakura wonders how she is ever going to capture the sound of it.

"I could take you home," Barsalai says.

Sakura chuckles again. "After all that, home?"

Silence.

Sakura wants to ask her what she means—where she could possibly say is home. Does that mean the steppes? Some ger half-frozen in the wilderness? Does she mean Oshiro, where she spent part of her youth? What is home to a god?

She doesn't care.

It's better than here.

"Yes," Sakura says. "Take me home."

# DORBENTEI OTGAR

## TWO

Dorbentei Otgar Bayasaaq is no idiot—she sends word ahead.

It's the sensible thing to do. Fourteen years separate her from the Qorin waiting on the steppes. Given that many of them were elderly when she left, she doesn't know how many there even are. The Qorin dwindling down to just under a thousand must have been a tempting opportunity for Oshiro, too—part of her worries there won't be any left at all.

If that's the case, then she and whoever rules Oshiro are going to have some words.

But if there are remaining Qorin—and she refuses to believe there won't be—they will all be adults by now. The newborns will be fourteen, old enough to start paying their bride-prices or entertaining the courtship of whatever snot-nosed brat was picked for them. It is these new adults who truly concern Otgar, for they will have grown up in a world without Burqila Alshara—a world with so few of their fellows.

She tells herself that it can't all be bad for them. A life without the fear of infection is a good one, for one thing. With fewer people competing, there'll be plenty more marmot and lamb to go around. Fewer arguments over campsites, too.

To survive is Qorin, as the saying goes. They'll find the good wherever they go.

Nevertheless, she sends her letter.

*To the acting Kharsas and Kharsaqs of the Qorin,*

*I am Dorbentei Otgar Bayasaaq, niece of Burqila Alshara Nadyyasar and her chosen heir. You might remember I went north with the rest of us fourteen years ago. You probably thought you were rid of me.*

*You aren't.*

*I'm hereby announcing my return and that of the Burqila clan. On the authority granted to me by Burqila and her daughter Barsalai, I'm calling a meeting at the base of Gurkhan Khalsar.*

*We have some matters to settle.*

She hands it to the first Qorin messenger she sees: a girl of about twenty sat atop a wiry gray that reminds her too much of a young Shefali. The girl squints at her a little when Otgar calls to her—more so upon receiving a stack of letters in Qorin.

"I don't know you," she says. "Are you from the northern clans?"

Otgar tries not to let it stick in her teeth, but those three words are a chip of bone digging into her gums. "You know me," she asserts.

"Patterns on your deel are so . . . simple," says the girl.

"Because the Burqila clan doesn't need to scream out who we are," answers Otgar. She can't help but notice the needlework at the girl's collar: intricate knots and vines. Vines, of all things.

The girl whistles. "Burqila clan, huh? Thought you guys disappeared."

"Then you thought wrong," Otgar answers. "Get those to whoever's in charge these days. Might want to hang around the mountain yourself; there'll be a show."

The girl tucks the stack of letters into her deel with a wolfish grin. "Yeah, I bet there will be," she says. She gives that wiry gray a solid kick, and off she goes, the forests outside Fujino swallowing her like a hungry fish.

It isn't until she's left that Otgar realizes the girl never introduced herself, never offered her cheeks. What is the world coming to? She leaves for a little while, and now the youths think they can go gallivanting around like that, disrespecting their elders. Never would have happened in Otgar's day. The fear of Burqila alone was enough to keep anyone in line.

But Burqila isn't here anymore.

*She'll be back*, Otgar thinks. The alternative isn't worth considering.

The trip to the steppes goes by quicker than she thought it would—though that isn't very quick, considering the sheer number of people that are moving. Many of the liberated Qorin don't have horses, and many of the Burqila clan lost at least one when the Spider attacked. Half of them move on foot. Those mounted can't leave behind their trudging companions, and so the whole process slows to a painful extent.

But they are able to cross the river without issue, and no one in Oshiro gives them any real trouble. The night they camp within sight of the palace, Otgar gathers the older Qorin and tells them about Burqila's conquest. She points to the Wall of Stone, to the seams still running through it after all these years, and she tells them this is the mark the Qorin have left on the world.

"And you say everyone followed her?" asks one of the old hunters. "You're not feeding me a skull with the cheeks carved out?"

"I'm not," says Otgar. "Everyone followed her. Northern clans, the Arslandai. Even had a couple of defectors from the Rassat."

"Why follow some punk who couldn't even talk?" asks another.

Otgar's mouth twitches. Who in creation thought of Burqila Alshara as a punk? "Because she was right. Because too many of you had died for us to keep going the way we were, raiding one another and dying in droves. Because we needed to make the Hokkarans feel the way we had when we lost more and more of you every day."

The hunters go silent. She's won them back over, she thinks, and continues with the story: Burqila's marriage, her daughter's birth, Shefali's childhood encounter with the tiger.

Let the sanvaartains say what they will: there is a magic in storytelling more powerful than any they can call upon. Look on the gathered Qorin and see. What draft could enchant thousands at once? What poultice could hold their attention? Place a stick of incense at the center of the gathering, dip it in the elixir of immortality, set it alight: the crowd will not look on it with half the wonder they look on Otgar as she tells this story.

For it isn't just any story—it is the story of a girl who lived among them, the story of a girl born in Ninth Winter, the story of a girl who became a god.

Their god.

They know her, all of them. Memory may dull much, but it cannot blunt the image of Barsalai Shefali: of her silver hair and eye, of the stars shining above her, of her silver bow and earth-crafted horse.

They listen until the early hours of the morning. Not once does anyone see the moon—overhead or otherwise. As Otgar comes to the end of her story—Shefali's death in the cave and mysterious rebirth, for which she had to invent a few details—someone raises their hand. A boy of perhaps eight. How did he end up infected? Otgar decides not to dwell on it.

"Why isn't she here with us now?" he asks.

"Because it's the new moon," Otgar says. "My poor cousin's dead. She'll be back when the next phase starts."

It bothers her a little that, after all of that, they should ask her where Shefali is. It isn't a reasonable annoyance. Of course they'd ask about her, she's the god of the Qorin; of course they'd want to know where the woman who saved them has gone.

But there is this small voice in the back of her mind: *They won't follow you.*

She doesn't need them to for very long. Burqila will be back, and when she is, she can take control once more. Even the young Qorin wouldn't dream of overruling her, not when her memory looms so large in their minds. All she needs is a little bit of buy-in; all she needs is for them to hold on until Burqila can make it back from over the Wall.

The farther they travel, the more she finds herself asking what Burqila would do. Kill the usurpers, likely enough, and from their bones forge something new. But that strikes Otgar as the wrong thing to do here—to the young Qorin, their new Kharsas and Kharsaqs are the only ones who have any hope of understanding them. To kill them would be to galvanize the youth against the whole. After all, Burqila herself didn't take up arms until her elder sisters were murdered, and she was about their age at the time.

So she can't kill them—but she can't truly allow them to continue claiming their titles, either. Feathers serve a purpose when they're on an arrow or a bird, but you scatter them everywhere, and they're just fluff. So it will be with the Qorin: the Hokkarans will see an opportunity. No—it will be the Surians. Otgar can't imagine Baoyi will allow her grandfather to muster an army against her grandmother's people.

She cannot kill them, she cannot let them continue.

The idea of what to do follows at her heels like a hungry dog the whole way through Oshiro. All thought promptly falls out of her mind, however, when she sees the gate.

Nearly as tall as the Wall of Stone, with two massive wooden doors, it is a mountain among doors. Two teams of aurochs are yoked on either side simply to pull it open. Not that there is any need to do so now: the gates are wide open, providing an excellent view of the farmland outside them, and a touch of silver on the horizon beyond that.

Where are the guards? There are so few that at first she misses them: four by the doors, a dozen walking the parapets with bows in hand. Sixteen guards for the most hotly contested border in all the Empire.

Or at least, what was once the most hotly contested border.

It can't possibly be so now. The last time Otgar was here, the gates were hardly wide enough for three mounted; now the whole army can march right through with no trouble at all.

There's a sinking feeling in her stomach. It must be some sort of mistake, some sort of trick. She searches the gates for any sign of hidden blades, searches the ground for trapdoors. After the Spider, she never wants to feel the ground give way again.

She sends Temurin and the scouts out to investigate—but they come back with trays full of dumplings instead of any dangerous tiding. "Gifts from Oshiro Province," says the scout who brings them.

"From Lord Oshiro?" Otgar asks. "Oshiro Yuichi?"

A stamp on one of the trays gives her the answer: they are indeed from Oshiro Yuichi. How old is that man? Seventy? She forgets, at times, how much longer people live when they don't have to struggle against the steppes.

But why is he giving them gifts? Her first thought is that they must be poisoned; her second thought is that Oshiro Yuichi, for all he hates his wife's people, has never lifted a finger against them. And now they are not simply his wife's people—they are his granddaughter's, as well.

When Otgar catches Temurin's eye, the older woman gives her only a resigned shrug.

They might be poisoned—but they probably aren't, and Otgar isn't going to risk losing anyone in case they are. She picks up the first dumpling herself. Soft meat and spices melt in her mouth; she thinks of her uncle's stew and feels a wave of guilt for even thinking of the comparison. There will never again be anything like Ganzorig's stew.

But these dumplings are good. She gestures for the others to help themselves. How Oshiro managed to make so many of them in such short notice boggles her mind, but she will not argue the comfort they might bring.

She picks up a second dumpling from the top tray—the one she and the captains are eating from—and realizes there is something smudged on the cloth. Ink? Waving Temurin and the scouts away from having any more, Otgar pinches the cloth between her fingers. One character is only the start—there is a letter there, written in Oshiro's own hand. Otgar recognizes it from his letters to Halaagmod.

*To Burqila Alshara,*

*We of Oshiro heard of your service during the Day of Mourning. As you return home with your people, please accept a small token of our gratitude.*

*In my old age, I can no longer bear you a grudge. You have kept our granddaughter safe, and you are the reason my son died a hero's death. Though I shall feel his lack the rest of my days, I have you to thank for knowing him at all.*

*And so—a token.*

*Your husband,*
*Oshiro Yuichi*

Reading it staggers her. She thinks of Halaagmod dying to keep his daughter safe—thinks of Baoyi's anger when Shefali said there was nothing she could do to save him. She thinks of Burqila and her twenty years of loneliness—her devotion to a woman who could never love her, and her disgust for the man who was the same.

What will Burqila do, reading this? Has age softened her?

No, Dorbentei decides. It hasn't. If Burqila were here, she'd send all the food back the instant this letter was discovered.

But Otgar looks out over the Qorin biting into this gesture of goodwill, she watches them laugh and smile and brag about their own cooking in comparison. She hears the lift in their voices. When she turns, the gate lies before her, larger and more peaceful than ever.

Dorbentei folds the letter and tucks it into her deel.

"What'd it say?" asks Temurin.

"Don't worry about it."

THERE ARE, AS it turns out, three new Kharsaqs and one new Kharsa.

Ganbatar Khurchig Batbolor is the first to arrive, and with good reason. His clan is the smallest of the five. Only twenty gers between them, compared to the hundreds of banners atop the Burqila camp. He and his people arrive two days after Otgar and the Burqila do, and the first thing he does is visit her.

Or ask to, at any rate. Otgar's stationed Temurin outside. Burqila said it was always better to make people wait a little before they talked to you, so it seemed as though you were busy. Burqila spent that time complaining to Otgar about whoever it was she thought it would be; Otgar spends it now getting in a few more lines of reading.

When she calls for him to come in, she doesn't bother moving the scroll. It's some of Sakura's work in Hokkaran. If he can read it, then let him take heart: they've been through too much to endure any foolery here.

He's short for a Qorin boy, maybe Barsalai's size, but with the husky build of someone who has never had to struggle for a meal. White dusts his skin where he's attempting to grow a beard. In his hair—close-cropped, for some reason—there is a single braid. Otgar cannot imagine how he might have earned it. Still, he wears it proudly as he strides into the ger. His eyes land on the book with curiosity; they stay long enough that Otgar knows he can read Hokkaran. He comes with no guards and no sword at his hip: a good sign.

"Dorbentei," he says. "We got your message."

"Try starting out with something less obvious," she says.

He clears his throat. "Like?"

"Like what you're going to do about our return," Otgar says. "You're Kharsaq, aren't you? Or at least think you are. How'd you earn that braid?"

"I fought off twenty Surian raiders," he says, straightening his shoulders.

"Twenty?" Otgar says.

"I am a good wrestler."

"I wouldn't go that far," Otgar says. She can't stop herself from bragging. "*You* haven't wrestled any demons. So. The Surians are raiding us? What have you done about it?"

"Killed a few of them," says Ganbatar. Talking doesn't come easily to him; his words are rough and clumsy. "They don't come so often now."

That they're coming at all is decent enough knowledge. "That's good work, but we'll need more than that if we're going to keep ourselves safe. You don't have that many people. Why is that?"

"Because I left Sarangarel's clan," he says. To his credit, he doesn't look away when he says this.

"Sarangarel, she's running one of the others right now?"

He nods. "The largest."

"Why'd you leave?"

"She wanted to raid the farming villages," he says.

The farming villages? When they have so much more food available to them? On the way here, Otgar saw more marmots than she had in her entire life. Did kids these days not like marmot?

The confusion on her face must be obvious: the boy continues. "She said it's what Qorin do."

"What Qorin *did*," Otgar says. "What we do is survive, and we don't need to attack some poor farmers to do that anymore. If that's true, I can see why you left."

He says nothing. She wonders for a moment if this isn't Shefali in disguise. It isn't like her cousin to test people, though. "So—what are you going to do, you and your little band? Are you going to stop her?"

"No," he says. His eyes are the green of the northern forests. "You are."

She has to chuckle. He knows how to ingratiate himself, at least. "Share this kumaq with me, and I'll consider it."

He has no problems doing so. She has to admit, it's a bit of a relief that he doesn't recoil from the smell—with no one sniffing anyone else's cheeks anymore, it's hard to predict what traditions have fallen by the wayside. When she asks him to swear that he holds no power over Dorbentei, and none over Burqila Alshara, he repeats after her with a heavy sort of determination. Like a hammer, this boy.

But hammers can make excellent tools. Over the next three days, she puts him to use, questioning him about the current state of things. It's simpler than she thought. Sarangarel was fourteen already when the Qorin left; she rose to prominence not long after their return to the steppes. Ganbatar says she's beautiful, but Otgar doesn't believe that's all there is to it. He doesn't seem to know what else it might be. She's beautiful, she speaks well, she's a fast rider.

None of those make for a good leader.

Otgar listens all the same. Sarangarel came to power by fending off the first Surian raid. Ganbatar was there with her, as were the other three new Kharsaqs, but she got the wolf's share of the credit for it. Her tactics, she argued, and her having spotted them while she was out on a ride. Ganbatar didn't argue, because he got a braid; the others very strongly did. This was the first and most significant split: Borma Nergunser Montaq, the eldest of the boys involved, said he could not conscience such behavior, and took with him half the new Qorin.

Borma arrives within three days. Otgar half expects that he will demand to speak to the nearest man in charge; she gets the feeling he must not be fond of women from the story.

But it is a foolish assumption. It is not women that Borma dislikes, it is *a* woman. He arrives with two scarred lieutenants, both girls, and asks if he may have a meeting with Dorbentei.

She grants it, of course, though she does make him wait. When he enters, he sits cross-legged on the floor and bows from the shoulder.

"Dorbentei Otgar," he says. "We met once when I was a young boy—or I met Burqila, and you happened to be there."

"Honest of you," Otgar says. "Did I make a good impression?"

"You threatened to box my ears in if I didn't help loading the carts."

"And did I?"

"No, you didn't," says Borma.

"Then we're off to a good start," Otgar says. "So—tell me. Are you going to cause me any trouble?"

He has to think about the answer. That would have upset Burqila, and probably Barsatoq, too—but Otgar likes it when people think things over. It's a rare sight in her family.

"There are so many of you, I couldn't," he says.

"So many of us," Otgar corrects. "We're all Qorin. The old-timers might be a few generations off, but Ganbatar's people are already teaching them the latest drinking songs. But agreeing just because you hate our number won't do. I hear you have problems with this Sarangarel woman?"

"I want her dead," is his simple answer. "You would, too, if you had been there. Burqila Alshara was never thirsty for glory the way this woman is. She'd take credit for lighting the sky if she could."

"My cousin would beat the shit out of her if she tried," says Otgar. It occurs to her that she probably should not speak of her godly cousin so easily, but then she was thinking of the flesh-and-blood Shefali. All her life, Barsalai Shefali has been willing to fight a war at Barsatoq's slightest indication. "Is it true she wants to raid the farms?"

"She wants to raid *everyone*," he says. "Sent riders against me and mine, too; had to kill some of our own people. It's foul, what she's doing. That kind of thing spreads sure as horserot."

Otgar's mouth is a hard line. Worse and worse, it seems.

"I'll deal with her," she says. "So long as you share this kumaq with me."

Borma's quick to agree, just as Ganbatar had been. Otgar thinks herself lucky for this. That there haven't yet been any fights is some sort of miracle—but there has always been a spirit of acceptance among the Qorin. Burqila was even taking in Hokkarans before they left.

The next two to arrive are brothers: Adarakar Khalja and Begutei Narin. Begutei's the elder of the two, but only barely—Otgar thinks he is a little younger than she is. Or, rather, than she was when she left.

Here, too, she expects some friction: Adarakar and Begutei served as Sarangarel's lieutenants when she went after the Surians. It was only after an armed regiment came after the clan that they started having doubts; a rout only solidified them. When Sarangarel ordered a raid on the Rassat, Adarakar and Begutei left with four hundred

Qorin and twice that in horses. In doing so, they stymied Sarangarel's more warlike ambitions, for without a sizable cavalry, there was little she could do.

She expects them to be quarrelsome, expects them to tell her that she cannot beat Sarangarel—that sort of thing. If it were one of those novels Sakura likes so much, that is how it would go. But life is not so predictable as this: Burqila Alshara once saved Begutei's life; he would never dream of betraying her. So it is that both of them swear fealty without much trouble.

And this, of course, leaves only the woman herself.

Otgar does not trust that she will come of her own accord; neither of them are idiots. She dispatches three hundred and twenty Qorin as scouts, split evenly among the eight directions, and while she waits for their tidings, she speaks to the boys. Ganbatar wants her imprisoned; the other three want her dead. She listens as they enumerate her crimes. While her blood boils, her mind also starts to wander—there is a mundaneness to these audiences she hadn't expected to find when she was the one conducting them.

It takes eight days, but the scouts return. Sarangarel is coming with an army: five hundred, bolstered in places by desert wanderers.

And it is this, in the end, that seals her fate.

Dorbentei Otgar rides out to meet this woman with five thousand of her own—the core group of Burqila's most loyal soldiers, with the four-Kharsaq army added in for good measure. She finds them on the field—and they do not slow down upon seeing her. How Sarangarel inspires five hundred to fight against ten times that number is beyond Otgar's ability to comprehend, but she does not *need* to comprehend it. She only needs to stop it.

Under a white banner, she sends Temurin. To her astonishment, Sarangarel has enough tact not to shoot her on sight, and the message is safely delivered. Otgar awaits the answer atop her fat dun. Always meet the enemy mounted.

It comes after only a few moments. The woman on the seal bay must be Sarangarel; she's got the tallest banner, and she's the one who hops off her horse when Temurin speaks. She, too, is the one who walks alongside Temurin's horse to the center of the battlefield.

Otgar calls for felt as she, too, dismounts. Ganbatar carries a roll of it on his shoulder, walking with her to meet Sarangarel. The other three follow—empty-handed, as a sign of good faith.

Sarangarel is taller than Otgar expected, with a wiriness to her that suggests a withered plant. Still, she must begrudgingly admit there is something beautiful to her, in an otherworldly sort of way: her eyes are the size of Surian karo, her lips full and well-formed. She's no Sakura, but she's no Temurin, either.

Temurin, for her part, nods to Otgar as the two groups meet. Otgar snaps, and the four Kharsaqs lay their felt out between the two women.

Sarangarel puts her hands on her hips. "You're younger than I thought you'd be."

"The lands north of the Wall don't make much sense," Otgar says. "Gives me a few extra years, though, and I can't argue that. You know the terms?"

"I beat you in a wrestling match, and you grant us our freedom," is the girl's answer. She glances at Otgar's stiff leg, then away, as if to pretend nothing were amiss. Hiding that wicked smirk is easier said than done. "A foolish offer to make when you've got all those people behind you. Unless they're paper tigers?"

"They aren't," Otgar says. She takes off her deel, baring her chest in the process. Already there is a chill to the air—the sun will soon be setting. Goose pimples make her hair stand on end. "We just aren't interested in spilling Qorin blood."

Sarangarel doesn't undo her deel—she merely stands and watches as Otgar stretches. "There is no progress without violence," she says. "You and your people abandoned us; what else were we to do? Qorin survive. If we have to take food out of someone else's mouth to do it—who cares?"

"The Sky does," Otgar says. "I swear, wasn't there anyone around to raise you right? We've got a whole new god, Sarangarel, and she's always watching."

It is only then, when Otgar steps onto the felt, that Sarangarel mimics her. The girl falls into a travesty of a stance. A twinge of regret shoots through Otgar, but only a twinge. "I don't see that god anywhere."

"That's because I'm dealing with you," Otgar says. She slaps her chest. "Now, come."

If this were one of Sakura's stories, it would be grandiose and far reaching—there would be no sweating bodies, only glistening flesh; there would be no gnats, no scrapes, no true struggle anywhere to be seen. And in truth, it is like that in some ways: Sarangarel never stood a chance against the Qorin's best wrestler.

It is over quickly. Sarangarel dives for Otgar's bad leg; Otgar catches her head between her arm and rib cage. Instead of throwing her—what the crowd would want to see—or taking this to the ground—where she could pummel some sense into the girl, as she deserves—Otgar instead shifts her hands. One grabs Sarangarel's chin; the other her forehead.

There is a moment of hesitation, a moment where Otgar asks if this is truly what she wants to do. After all that time spent ruminating over the consequences of murder—is this the thing to do?

But it is as Borma said: this hatred, this anger, is like horserot. It will spread if not stamped out. There is too much to be gained from peace with the Hokkarans, too much to be lost by attacking them. By killing Sarangarel, she shows her meager followers what will happen to them if they continue this line of thought.

And so Dorbentei Otgar twists Sarangarel's head until she feels it *really* crack. The girl slumps over in her arms. Death clings to Otgar's bare skin as she sets her down on the felt, as she gestures for the four Kharsaqs to wrap her up.

"Listen to me," she says, facing Sarangarel's clan. They are young, so young, and Otgar cannot let their lives be stained with blood. She speaks from the very pit of her stomach, her voice echoing out beneath the Eternal Sky. "If any of you get it in your head to attack farms, I'll do the same to you. And you'll be lucky if it's me. Burqila Alshara's going to be back soon, and when she is, she'll show no mercy to anybody stupid enough to destroy her peace. Your ancestors dreamed of a day when they could live without worrying where their next meal came from—I'm not going to sit here and let you ruin it."

From the looks on their faces, from the rattle of their swords, she hasn't won all of them over.

She slaps her chest.

"Put it this way," she says. "I have five thousand here, and five more back by the mountain. The Hokkarans have ten times that *just in the East*. You want regular meals, you hunt here, or you trade with them. Anyone who'd like to say otherwise can come right up to fight me—if you really want to settle this like Qorin."

How do Barsalai and Barsatoq do this sort of thing? Burqila talked like this, too, but at least she didn't have to actually say the words. And this kind of braggadocio was different when it was Burqila who bore the weight of the challenges. It's easy to make Burqila sound intimidating—you hardly have to try.

But who is she to make these threats? Dorbentei Otgar Bayasaaq, daughter of a murdered mother and an unknowing father; Dorbentei Otgar Bayasaaq, with her leg that she can't stand on for more than an hour anymore, with her lost years; Dorbentei Otgar Bayasaaq, niece to a legend, cousin to a god.

Who is she? The voice that spoke just now sounds so little like she imagines herself. Burqila told her more than once: if anything happens to her or Shefali, it will be Otgar who bears the Kharsa's title. Still—she never imagined that day would actually come.

That she'd be here, standing over a body, asking if anyone else wants her to kill them.

She's killed someone today.

It's a fact of Qorin life; it's practically a requirement for a Kharsa.

But there is this awful weight in her stomach all the same, this revulsion coating her skin at having killed one of her own, no matter the circumstances.

Will it ever go away?

Will she ever be Burqila?

The air on the steppes is clear and dry; when it fills her lungs, she feels the prickle of cold her cousin wields like a knife. That blood is in her veins, too. There is something godly even in Dorbentei Otgar.

She stands and she waits for challengers—but they never come. Five hundred Qorin lay down their arms and cross the empty grass. On the other side, they are met with hard stares and distrust—but not with swords, not with the *crack* that has carved itself into Dorbentei's bones.

There will be no war today.

It is late by the time she returns to her ger. Overhead, Grandmother Sky's cloak is more brilliant than ever. If all the Qorin who ever lived cast their kumaq in four directions—even then there would not be so many blotches of white as there are stars. Otgar finds herself trying to spot her cousin's face in the waxing moon, but it is a smooth crescent, without a nose that sticks out like a needle.

Did her cousin see what happened earlier? Will she care, if she did? Since she's left, Otgar has thought of her every day—it's difficult not to with the nightly reminders—but never summoned her. She's confident that if she ever needs Shefali's help, there she will be, but she has not yet been brave enough to ask.

And why should she? The Qorin have everything they need. Life for them is better than it has ever been, even without a god's intervention. There is no reason to call for Shefali, who surely must have better things to attend to than the guilt that coats Dorbentei's guts like spores of unknown fungus.

But she does think of Burqila that way. From how to swing into the saddle to how she strings her bow, she thinks of Burqila and decides whether or not to emulate her.

She thinks of Burqila, too, when one of the Four Kharsaqs says something foolish and there is no one to hear her joke about it. So many people thought of Burqila as aloof, as unfeeling—but this was only because she so rarely spoke. What they did not know was the woman's sense of humor when it came to those who disappointed her. They did not know how vulgar she could be, or how much of her signing was really "Tell them whatever you think is right, I can't be bothered."

None of those things make Burqila a bad leader—but they do make her a different one than people might imagine. The Burqila the clan speaks of in hushed voices as Otgar approaches her ger does not, in truth, exist.

"She would have killed all of them," says one.

And so she might have—but she probably would have scared them shitless beforehand. It's pointless to argue what Burqila might have done when none of this would have happened on her watch.

"This new one, she's soft," says another.

But Otgar killed a woman today, and there is nothing soft in that.

"Why not call down Barsalai? Why not let her deal with it?"

Because the Qorin must solve their own problems, as they always have, or else they will grow roots and die.

Had she been with Burqila, she could have talked to her about this, about the things she'd heard; she could have asked her what to do.

But Burqila is hundreds of li away if she is anywhere, and so Dorbentei must weather this alone.

She walks through the camp to her ger—with a horsehair banner already flying overhead—and tries not to dwell.

Otgar is midway there when she first hears the shouts.

"Come! Come see!"

"She's here!"

"It's her!"

The air somehow feels colder than it did earlier. Otgar takes a deep breath of it, watching as thousands of Qorin flock to the largest of the clan's gers. Already there are some on their bellies outside with their heads under the flaps, already there are twenty packed outside of the door such that no one can get in. The dogs are having a wild time of it—how they bark!

It's enough to make Otgar laugh. Of course her cousin would show up on a day like this. Never when you wanted her, but always, somehow, when you needed her.

"Out of the way, out of the way," she mumbles. They listen—though grudgingly—and so the way to the ger is parted. She steps inside before she can really see what's going on inside; the crowds are too thick to get a good view.

Here are the first things she notices:

It is cold here, truly cold; the tip of her nose numbs the moment she crosses the threshold.

It is dark here, truly dark; and yet in spite of this, she can see good and well the god sitting on a folding chair near the eerie, lightless fire.

It is home here, truly home; on a bench laid out next to her, a pale face in the dark ger, is Minami Sakura. There are shards of glass buried in her shoulder, her foot is covered in blood, her hair is a mess; she is covered in dust and she smells of that accursed swamp in Shiratori—but it is her.

There is no one in the ger save the three of them.

Otgar swallows. She is sure that there are words for this—but she hasn't the slightest idea what they may be.

Thankfully, Sakura does. "You're supposed to tell us to catch our dogs."

"Whole damn crowd caught the dogs for you," Otgar answers—this time, at least, she does not have to think. Sparring with Sakura this way is as natural as blinking.

She stands in the threshold of the red door because she cannot force herself to move forward.

Because if she does—what a foolish idea, that Sakura might smell the death on her.

It is Barsalai who will. Her eyes land on her cousin's, glowing as they are in the dark of the ger. To her surprise, Barsalai is the one that speaks first. "Today was difficult."

Otgar will never get used to hearing that echo in Shefali's voice—not when she spent so many of their earlier years bullying her for sounding like a Hokkaran. How silly she feels to think of that now, how guilty—how close had she come to stamping out Shefali's soft-spoken kindness?

For this is a kindness, bringing Sakura here, and Otgar can't even find the words to thank her.

"Yeah. Today was—"

"It had to be done," says Shefali. She looks into the fire as she speaks, and yet it feels as if she were standing right next to Otgar.

She glances behind. The other Qorin have their faces pressed to the space behind her, stopped as if by a pane of glass. Otgar frowns—but she takes another step into the ger.

"They can't see in," Shefali says. "Or hear. I wanted privacy."

"In a ger? Needlenose, you've been away too long." The joke comes easy—she does not have to think about what happened today if she makes the joke.

Even Barsalai chuckles a little. Sakura does, too, and that eases Otgar's pain more than she'd like to admit. "A little privacy," says Shefali. "I'll stay for dinner."

"Your aaj would strangle you if you didn't," Otgar says. Now that she's taken one step, it's easier to take the next and the next. The spot near Sakura calls her the way their fire calls moths. "What are the two of you doing all the way out here?"

"Dinner, as I said," says Shefali. "I can taste now."

That she cannot taste Ganzorig's stew is a tragedy left unsaid. There will be other things to eat. Otgar takes Sakura's hand. "And you? Aren't you hurt? I can get the sanvaartains to take a look . . ."

"Thank you," says Sakura, though it comes out with more of her Nishikomi drawl than usual. "I'd like that."

"You aren't answering the question," Otgar says. "And you're quiet tonight. Are you sure this is Barsatoq's cousin?"

Sakura presses her lips together and flinches; something in Otgar dies. She scrambles. "I didn't mean— I guess I don't know where you've been—"

"I went back to Nishikomi," Sakura says. "But it wasn't home anymore, so Barsalai offered to take me where I needed to be."

She says it all quickly—but she squeezes Otgar's hand, and leans her head on Otgar's shoulder. If she can smell the death, then she shows no sign of it.

No questions spring to mind, but there are warnings. It is cold here, unspeakably cold; there will be little time to write, and no privacy to speak of; it is a hard life, even with the improvements; she doesn't speak much of the language; she does not know their culture.

But Minami Sakura knows what she wants—and if this is it, well, Otgar is glad to have her.

Barsalai pokes at the fire. Though she is trying to hide it, her fingers are stiff; she has to close them around the stick with her other hand. "I want you to take care of each other," she says. "The Qorin understand what you saw, Sakura-lun, and they will respect you, Otgar. It will be hard—it's better here."

Neither says anything. Before them, the crowd is banging on the solid darkness. Shefali does not stir—not for them. "I ask one thing."

"Name it," says Sakura.

"Come to Fujino on the double eighth."

Otgar and Sakura exchange a look. There can be only one reason they'd be summoned to Fujino on that day.

Shizuka.

Otgar swallows. It takes her too long to think of an answer; Sakura beats her to it again.

"We will," Sakura says. "And I'll try and think of some way to save her. There has to be something. I can't believe that she's—"

Barsalai's response is the thud of an arrow into wood. "She isn't."

"No," says Sakura. "She isn't."

And who is Otgar to argue? She looks up through the hole in center of the ger's ceiling, the moon shining down on her. So long as it hung in the sky, then the Sun would, too.

And so long as there was sun—there would be Shizuka.

"Thank you," Shefali says. A small smile comes across her face then, as she reclines with a quiet groan. "Now—let's eat."

# SOMEDAY

## *Together*

On the double eighth, the Undying Moon visits the Imperial Palace.

It is not the first time she has done this, nor the second, nor the seventh.

In the six months since the Day of Mourning she has missed only twenty-four days of visits—whenever the moon vanishes from the sky, so does the Moon vanish from the palace.

The servants are by now accustomed to the sight of her: her silver hair in its thousand braids; the way she towers over even the Phoenix Guard; her silent, wolfish walk. Rarely do they see her coming—she simply steps out from one shadow or another, fully formed, her silver eye gleaming.

Like a ghost she moves, like a predator. The guards know well enough not to get in her way—not that any of them would dream of antagonizing the Moon. That the palace stands at all is a testament to her might. Ask one thousand soldiers where they were on the Day of Mourning, and you will receive two thousand stories—but the Moon is always the hero.

"I saw her. She had a curved sword, the kind the Qorin use, and she rode by on her white horse and decapitated him."

"I saw her. In her hands was the silver bow she crafted from her own home's soil, and with it she put eight arrows in the back of the Traitor."

"I saw her. She was a twisted thing, halfway between human and beast, and she tore off his head with her own two hands."

So the stories go.

They do not question her as she walks through the halls, as she nods to empty air, as she makes her way ever higher. They do not question her as she approaches the Empress's chambers, and they do not question her as she stops outside of them.

But they do whisper that her limp has gotten worse again, that she is walking as if there are boards on either side of her legs, that she is stiff and old.

"She's going to miss three days next week," says one of the servants—but only after she has passed. He and his colleagues are mopping up the trail of frost that always follows in her wake.

"No," says the eldest among them, a woman named Chihiro. "It's going to be this week. Just look at her."

It is First Bell, as it always is when she visits. The priests are still wandering the halls, making their announcements. A pack of them pass her just before she makes it to the Empress's chambers. As one, they bow.

"Undying Moon, Laughing Fox, Silver-Eye—" begins the priest, but the Moon grunts, and he stops. Haltingly, he continues. "H-Have we offended you?"

How brave of him—he looks up at her, bowed though he may be. Ice crystals refract in the air around her. When she shakes her head, these motes fly through the air.

"Is there anything we can do to assist you?" he says. "Please, only name it. The Empire is forever in your debt, as you well know."

There is a hardness to her regard—a winter that threatens to freeze him where he stands. It is like this every time he sees her. Five years he has trained as priest of the Moon, and five years he has endured the worst of the winter clad only in his foundational garments.

But the Moon's regard is colder than even that.

He does not know if he will ever grow accustomed to it.

"You know already," says the Moon.

He bobs again. "If a Qorin woman on a liver mare arrives at the palace, I am to immediately beseech you."

She nods. The cold in him melts.

"But is there anything else?" he says. "You've visited so often—"

"No," she says.

Away she goes, walking down the halls. He and the others watch her go, wondering how they might have helped her, wondering why it is she is so terse with them.

The Phoenix Guard are the next to glimpse her. She stands before the door to the Empress's chambers and therefore before them.

She does not say a word to them—they simply part. The Moon is mysterious only when she is unfamiliar, and they know precisely why she is here.

"There hasn't been any change," says the younger of them.

There—the icy glance. He swallows and says nothing more as she walks into the Empress's chambers.

The Empress herself does not sleep well. She has not slept well since that day, and who could blame her after what happened? But she is always awake at First Bell, for she knows the Moon is coming. On this night—the twenty-eighth—she is not alone.

There are two others in the room with her. Both women. One is Hokkaran. Dark circles under her eyes speak to her sleeplessness; the hair she once took such pride in is dull and messily piled atop her head. That said, she wears finer robes than the Empress herself: gold-trimmed black, with phoenixes painted in gold foil. She sets aside a scroll as the Moon walks in.

The other is a Qorin, and dark even for that—wide and solid, thick about the middle like a tree. When her eyes fall on the Moon, she stands and takes three limping steps toward her. How grim her countenance!

"There isn't any news," says this woman. "We would have sent for you if there were, you know that."

The Moon says nothing. She removes her bronze war mask and

sets it on the Empress's counter, next to a writing set with which she is all too familiar. The finely dressed woman notices her flinch at the sight—but the finely dressed woman notices everything.

"Aunt," says the Empress, who stands before the threshold to a room farther in. "Our cousin speaks true—there hasn't been any change at all."

And it is then, at the Empress's voice, that the change happens. In the same way a block of ice and puddle contain the same water—so, too, does the Moon contain Barsalai Shefali.

And it is Shefali that they see then. There is no mistaking the way her features soften, the way she seems to shrink, the desperate hope in her green eye. "Let me see her."

"Are you certain?" says the Empress.

Barsalai nods. The finely dressed woman—Minami Sakura—sighs. "Nothing to be done about a romantic, I suppose."

"You know she'll be back," says Barsalai. Her eyes flick between all the others in the room. "All of you do."

No one says anything to argue this—though the Empress, in truth, does not know this. She steps aside with a short bow.

The room is glowing gold, as it is every night, but the breath catches in Barsalai's throat all the same. Anyone may wake early enough on any given day and see the sunrise across the Silver Steppes—that makes the sight no less beautiful.

So it is that she stands in the doorway, lovestruck and speechless, though she has seen this face nearly every day of her life.

Lying in bed—the sheets pulled up to her chin—is Minami Shizuka. She is not sleeping. If she *were* sleeping, she'd be sucking her thumb. Instead, she lies motionless on her back, eyes closed but moving beneath the lids, dreaming of better places than this. She smells of peonies and light, of the sharp tang of metal, of a warm fire and thick blood. Shefali breathes deep of it.

Her wife.

In three steps, she is by the bed. It takes only one more for her to sit at Shizuka's side. How delicately she caresses her wife's face! One finger along the thick scar, another clearing the hair from her brow! Who could watch them dry eyed? For there on Barsalai's face, hope and agony mingle. When she presses her lips to her wife's brow, it is with a tenderness often sought but rarely found.

The Empress cannot bear to watch. "The surgeons say there is nothing wrong with her, but they are not accustomed to dealing with . . . with your sort."

"Gods, Baoyi. You can say the word," says Sakura.

The Empress shows no sign of her discomfort. "Gods, then. The surgeons are not familiar with gods."

"Sanvaartains won't touch her," says Dorbentei Otgar. She leans against the threshold. "You know how superstitious they've always been about the two of you."

Barsalai only partly hears them as she lifts the blanket. Quickly—softly—she searches her wife's body for any trace of her old wounds. They'd healed in the better part of two days—there are no traces left save a thin line of gold at her throat and a starburst of the same on her ribs. And there is, of course, the pit where her heart once was—a cavity filled with gold, flush against the rest of her skin.

Barsalai presses her lips together. She does not cry. Not tonight. She lifts her wife's head onto her lap. Idly she runs her fingers through the hair she has always loved.

"There is the possibility that she may never wake," says the Empress. Her voice is shaky, as if Shizuka's waking is a thing she does not want to confront. "If that is the case—will you continue to visit?"

"Every day," says Shefali without hesitation. "Every day until she does. Eight months, eight years, eight decades, eight centuries."

AND WHO AMONG them can argue with the Moon's rousing proclamation? For each of them know that she is serious, and each of them have their own thoughts upon what that might mean.

But it is Sakura who has a plan of action, and so it is Sakura who elbows her way past the Empress—the Empress!—and sets a large scroll down on the bed next to Shizuka. It takes up most of the bed—and so, too, do the two characters written upon it. "I had an idea earlier."

"She spoke to me about it," says Dorbentei. From her deel, she pulls a skin of kumaq, and this she lays next to the scroll. "I thought it sounded sensible."

"What is it?" says Barsalai. "Please, whatever it is—if it could help—"

"It might," says Sakura. "Baoyi, could you get your great-uncle's inkstone?"

Is it deference, the speed with which the Empress moves—or is it annoyance? Perhaps it is instead shame, or guilt. Whatever the truth of the matter, she does as Sakura has instructed. Moreover, she begins grinding a large batch of ink.

The Moon watches them. She wants to thank her niece, but the words die in her throat. There is a constant note of resentment in Baoyi's scent.

She presses her eyes shut, as if to drive away the image of Kenshiro's body that comes to her—but some things will never really leave you. Her brother. Her only brother. What was he doing in armor? Why did he fight? If he had hid with Baoyi, they might have been able to save him, but . . .

Running a horse to death. Studying for days on end, negligent of his own body.

Kenshiro always had something to prove.

Her poor, idiot brother. Being a god did no less to dull the ache of his absence. She half expected to see him rounding the corner at any given moment with another ridiculous theory. He had never even gotten to see her like this in life.

She'd gone to look for him, of course, when the time came for her to die again. Immersed as she was in the fathomless depths, she could not feel his familiar presence—and the Mother was recalcitrant when pressed. It took until the second visit for her to find him hovering near his inkstone at the bottom of the sea.

He called her a slowpoke.

She made him into a star.

What a difficult thing, to be hated by your own family. When Baoyi returns with the readied ink, Barsalai tries to catch her eye, but the girl will not even look at her.

"What is your plan?" Barsalai says, watching her niece leave the room.

Sakura follows along with Barsalai's gaze. She nods to Dorbentei, who squeezes her cousin's shoulder and tells her that it is not her fault.

But it is.

"It's simple enough. Based on an idle theory I had," says Sakura. "There were two characters written on Yamai's chest when you ate him, you said. They must have been his name—you'd need a true name to kill a god." She opens the kumaq, wrinkling her nose a little at the scent, and drops a little of it into the ink. "I don't think he knew Shizuka's."

"It's a common name," says Barsalai. She is so tired of disappointment.

"But not a common spelling. Hardly anyone throws in Excellence as the second character. He'd know the first, since it's the same as Minami Shiori's, but how many people see the Empress's name with the last stroke included?" Sakura points to the second of the characters and a large line running across it. "This particular character isn't even old; it's fairly new. He might not even have known it. Before it was Excellence it was used as a counter for weights of gold."

Shefali swallows. The woman in her arms seems so small and frail like this. "He was in my head."

"And you can't read this," says Sakura, gesturing at the scroll. Her shoulders slump. "I might be wrong. He might have gotten it from O-Itsuki-lor, but I doubt he would have given it up to a stranger. He might have gotten it from the Toad, and—well. I don't have a good counterargument for that. The Toad was a piece of shit."

Barsalai looks down on Shizuka—on her peaceful expression, on the curve of her lips. With one finger she traces the line across her neck. "What do I have to do?"

"Bless this ink," says Sakura. "Then, we take some of Shizuka's blood—just a drop, don't look at me like that!—and mix that in. Lastly, you paint these characters on her."

"We made them nice and big," says Dorbentei, "so you could follow them more easily."

Calligraphy. If Sakura had told her to bring back a dragon's heart, Barsalai would not have faltered—but her old insecurities find her again. "And if I can't?"

"You will," says Dorbentei. "We'll guide you."

No mocking, no teasing. War has changed her cousin.

Softly, softly, she lays Shizuka back in bed. Blessing the ink takes the barest of thoughts—she dips her finger into it and ice soon blossoms on the surface. Getting Shizuka's blood is more difficult. It is Barsalai herself who does it, bringing her wife's delicate hand to her face. With her sharpened nail, she makes a small cut on the back of Shizuka's hand. This she holds over the ink until that sacred drop of gold mingles with the gray.

Barsalai Shefali has held stars in her hands, has held the Moon's reins, has spent her nights among the heavenly bodies and her days crafting miracles.

But holding the brush is difficult all the same. Her stiff hands are part of it—she must close the fingers of one with the other. Old anxieties nip at her heels like dogs. She could not even read her own wedding oaths—how is she to get something so important, so delicate, right?

But if it is for Shizuka's sake, she would lop the heads off the other gods right this moment.

A brush is nothing.

"First stroke from here to here," says Sakura, pointing with her finger. "Make sure you're imbuing it as you go."

She follows that line, and the next, and the next, breathing cold into the ink with every exhalation. The characters are not perfect—but they are readable, or at least she thinks they might be. Her heart leaps as they take shape, and she hopes, she hopes—

"Last stroke," says Sakura. "Down and to the right."

Hold your breath. Move the brush only when your hands are steady. Do not let them shake. That is what Shizuka told her of calligraphy, and so that is what she does. The last stroke falls into place.

She sets down the brush, cradles Shizuka's head.

"Did it—?"

Dorbentei's words are lost in a shout when the room floods with blinding light. If the sun itself were rising from the gardens, it would not be so bright—but that is because the Sun is rising now from the bed in the center of the room. Light from the characters, light from the eyes that soon fly open, light from the mouth of the wakening god.

To stand in the center of a storm while the winds and rain rage on around you, yet to be untouched by them—that is something like what happens to Barsalai in that moment. The woman in her arms is fire and war and anger. A blaze envelops her, but she feels only the warmth of a campfire, only the warmth of her wife's regard.

For Shizuka has opened her eyes again, and they are trained straight on Shefali's.

How sacred, how sacred, the look that passes between them! Twenty years of dreams and war, twenty years of longing, twenty years of oaths, twenty years of love—communicated without a word. What is joy if not this? What is love if not the way Barsalai holds her wife, the way her grip tightens, the way her mouth opens to speak the silence of their love?

Tears well in the eyes of the Moon. Barsalai Shefali throws her arms around her wife, Minami Shizuka, and rocks her tight. Her hands tangle in Shizuka's hair, her nose is full of Shizuka's scent. When Shizuka's arms wrap around her in turn, Barsalai thinks to herself that all the world could fall away and she would not care.

"Shefali," Shizuka whispers, and it is all Barsalai can do not to howl with emotion at the sound.

"I'm here," she says. "I'm here, Shizuka."

Their hands join, the crescents on their palms meet, and for a moment, all the world does fall away. There is only Shizuka, only the Silver Steppes, only the stars and the endless sky, only the forests and rolling hills. When Shefali's lips find her wife's, it is not simply a kiss but a promise, an oath: this is the world I promise you, this is the world we will share.

When at last they part, when at last their eyes once more meet, it is Shizuka who breaks the silence. "Always?"

"Two pine needles," Shefali says. The word cracks like pottery; she cannot keep her voice steady. Her Shizuka, her Shizuka. Months, she has agonized over her, months she has visited and hoped and dreamed.

And look at her—behold the majesty Shizuka has at last granted herself! The brilliant shroud hovering around her shoulders, radiant as the dawn itself; the crown of bright feathers around her temples; the pure gold of her eyes, with no white to be seen; the fires lapping at her hair. This is the Sun in truth; this is the god. Together, at last: the women they always swore they'd become.

A messenger arrives, but Shefali is too concerned with her wife to pay them any mind, too lost in the well of elation to wonder what might possibly drive a messenger to bother the Empress at such an hour. Shizuka is speaking, and there is nothing, nothing more important in the world.

"Even when the time comes, someday, for us to die?"

"Then someday, together—"

There are years where the paint is too bored to dry, and there are days that build whole empires. The twenty-eighth is closer to the latter, for Dorbentei seizes Shefali around the shoulders before she can finish speaking. "It's her. Burqila. Her liver mare—"

In the years that come, it will be Minami Shizuka, the Phoenix Empress, who is prayed to for decisiveness—but let it be known that

Barsalai Shefali does not hesitate either. Her bones creak and her joints cry out, but she lifts Shizuka all the same.

"Lead," she says to Dorbentei.

It is not a demand she has to make twice. Shizuka throws her arms around Shefali's neck as the two of them race down the halls of the palace—past the priests of the Moon, past the servants scrubbing their trail of ice—to the gates outside. How the servants whisper at the sight of them! The Moon in such a state, carrying . . . Was that the Phoenix in her arms, glowing like a paper lantern, her robes half-open, her hair hanging free as a girl's?

But Shefali does not care what they think and neither does Shizuka. Breathless, the Moon! But to the courtyard she goes, and there at the gates—a woman on a liver mare.

She runs. Her feet slap against the cool stones, leaving ice in her wake, but she runs, and when her mother dismounts, she nearly faints from the joy. Yes—it is Burqila Alshara, returned from the lands beyond the new Wall. There is her deel, there is her mare, there are her two viper green eyes, and there—her arms outspread and ready for the three of them.

How many things does she wish to say to her?

She could tell her of the Qorin, of Dorbentei accepting the position as their new Kharsa, and of the challenges they face with half their population twenty years younger than the other half.

How no one remembers Shefali—but everyone remembers Burqila, and up until now, they have all blamed the Moon for Burqila's disappearance.

She could tell her of the Hokkarans—of Itsuki's last moments, of the assault on the palace and the subsequent efforts to rebuild, of the book Sakura is writing.

She could tell her of Baoyi—of the blue mare she still rides, of her hatred for her aunts, of the long strides she's made toward peace.

She could tell her of Kenshiro—of the boy she so long neglected, of the man who put on a warrior's mask to save his own family, of the son she can finally claim with pride.

But the words die on her tongue. All that leaves her, all that leaves Shizuka:

"Aaj, Aaj, I was so afraid—"

"What were you afraid of?" answers Burqila Alshara. "My daughters have nothing to fear."

And the rest of it—the Qorin, the Hokkarans, Kenshiro, and Baoyi—the rest of it can wait.